CW00665028

HERALD

Book One of Age of the God Eater

Editor: TL Graylock

Cover Art: Eshpur

Cover Design: STK• Kreations

www.robjhayes.co.uk

HERALD

AGE OF THE GOD EATER BOOK 1

THE GOD EATER SAGA

ROB J. HAYES

A NOTE FROM THE AUTHOR

Time for a little info on format. HERALD is book 1 of the Age of the God Eater trilogy, and also the 1st part of the larger God Eater Saga which will consist of 9 books.

The God Eater Saga is a trilogy of trilogies being written and released concurrently. That means I wrote all 3 book 1s at the same time and I'm releasing them together. I've also started writing all 3 book 2s and will be releasing them together as well. I know, it's a strange way to do things, but bear with me.

Writing and releasing the saga this way allows me to weave mysteries, reveals, world building, and character development across the 9 books and across 3000 years of in world history. I felt it was important to do it this way because many of the characters in God Eater are immortals and have been alive a LONG time.

But fear not! Each trilogy is designed to work on its own as well. If you just want to read the main trilogy (AGE OF THE GOD EATER), that's fine, you'll get all the pertinent information you need within those pages. But if you choose to read the full saga (AGE OF THE GOD EATER, ANNALS OF THE GOD EATER, ARCHIVE OF THE GOD EATER), you'll get a much deeper understanding of the world and the story. And there may be some reveals in the past that shine a new light on events in the present.

For ease of understanding when all 3 trilogies take place, here's a handy little summary:

<u>Age of the God Eater</u> (main series)
    Herald (book 1)

<u>Annals of the God Eater</u> (set 1000 years before Herald)
    Deathless (book 1)

<u>Archive of the God Eater</u> (set 3000 years before Herald)
    Demon (book 1)

I know it all sounds a little confusing. Believe me, it was certainly a headache keeping it all straight in my head. But I can assure you it will all make sense in the end.

    THANK YOU for reading, and I do hope you check out all 3 trilogies to get the best understanding of the world.

Rob

PROLOGUE

W hen the Godless Kings sacked Heaven, two hundred angels escaped their wrath. A thousand years later and only ten of the winged divinities remained. King Emrik Hostain was about to make it nine.

Soldiers of the Third Legion died in their dozens as the angel swept through them. A sizzling blade of alabaster light, longer than the tallest of men, trailed lightning in its wake. Men and women threw themselves at the divinity, driven on by a battle lust beyond natural. And Emrik watched the slaughter with grim satisfaction.

His horse whinnied, nostrils flaring at the smell of blood on the wind, and he put a hand on its neck to calm it. Beside Emrik, his Red Weavers worked. Their blood-stained hands plucked at the air, pulling on threads only they could see, eclipsing all fear and doubt within the troops, leaving no room for anything but the call of battle, the lust for the kill. A thousand soldiers, those of the Second and Fourth legions, waited at Emrik's back. Their desire to join the battle was a nervous crackle of energy, and his own blood pulsed in anticipation.

The fires were spreading. Incinerated bodies left behind by the angel's lightning setting the field of barley aflame.

They had been tracking the creature for weeks, following rumours and abstract signs. The Elder Seers had pointed the way, and they were never wrong. Their sight went beyond any mortal vision, dipping into the prescient. Finally, Emrik had caught up with the angel on the cusp of evening in a small farming village. The village would have to be put to the torch, of course. Emrik could not allow the seditions of worship to take hold in his lands, and the farmers had undoubtedly been harbouring the renegade divinity. Never again would he allow his people to worship.

Mortal weapons did little to the angel, just scrapes and grazes which healed almost as quickly as they were dealt, but that wasn't the point. The vanguard were nothing but a sacrifice. The more mortal lives an angel took, the more vulnerable it became.

Two more soldiers of the Third fell, and a brief lull in the fighting allowed the angel time to raise its crackling blade to the sky. A column of searing lightning broke through the blanket of grey clouds. It struck the ground, sending up plumes of dust and fire. Everything the electric light touched burst into flames, and another hundred soldiers died screaming, fires from within ripping from mouths and melting eyeballs in their sockets. Lives given for the cause, and there could be no greater cause than this. Emrik would see to it their families received recompense.

He squinted against the light, a gauntleted hand falling to the pommel of his blade. The angel would not have called down its sigil unless it was weakening. It was finally time for Emrik to join the remnants of the Third in battle.

The last of the lightning struck and faded, the clouds spiralling away from its heavenly source to reveal the crimson sky above. The angel knelt on one knee in the centre of a circle of ash and fire, its lightning-wreathed sword planted in the earth. Soldiers crumbled to charred skeletons, the flesh all burned away to nothing but husks. The divinity's sigil was etched in deep lines all around it. A permanent scar the land could never heal.

Emrik blinked into his hawk sight, his vision now provided by the bird soaring above. From there he could see the sigil clearly, a horseshoe shape with a lightning bolt striking through the centre and feathery wings spread out behind it. Emrik blinked back to his normal sight and let the corner of his mouth tug into a grim smile. Now he knew which divinity he was dealing with.

The Rider, God's own stable master, or at least he had been while the Heavens still stood. It was Mathanial who first showed humans how to break a horse. He had taught them everything they knew about husbandry. Even the horse Emrik sat on was a product of that knowledge. All of it could be traced back to the wisdom of this divinity.

The leather saddle creaked as Emrik leaned forward. "Mathanial. I have waited long to taste your blood."

The angel stood, pulling his blade from the earth and swiping a new trail of lightning through the air in front of him. The remnants of the Third hesitated, their numbers and will both broken. It mattered not, their job was done, their sacrifice made. The angel's immortality shield was broken.

He was beautiful, the Rider, no man or woman could ever deny that. His robe shone white, no spot of ash or blood had touched it, and his feathery wings glistened in the glow of lightning. With charcoal skin, full lips, and eyes translucent as pearls, it was no wonder the villagers had fallen under the angel's sway. They could hardly be blamed. But the blameless died just as readily as the guilty.

A wiser divinity would attempt to flee, stretch his wings and leave Emrik's forces depleted and in disarray. But not Mathanial. The Rider's arrogance and pride were legend, documented in texts from before the Crusade.

The angel pointed his crackling blade towards Emrik and smiled. "Godless King, do you fear to face me yourself?" His voice rang with power and glory, like a perfectly forged bell resonating with the soul.

"I do not fear your kind, divinity," Emrik shouted. "I pity you. And I relish the power I will take from your corpse."

"Come then, Godless!" The angel raised its empty hand to the sky, and a bolt of yellow lightning ripped from the clouds. He caught the bolt, and it resolved into a jagged, crackling spear. The angel took a single step forward and launched the spear with a clap of thunder.

Emrik caught the spear in a gauntleted fist and held it, crackling, just a span from his chest. It possessed a will of its own, a drive attempting to force it onward even grasped in Emrik's hand. Bolts of energy sizzled along the surface of the spear, licking at his skin beneath the armour. The smell of burning hair was strong in Emrik's nostrils, and his skin grew uncomfortably hot around the spear. No mortal hand could have stopped that spear, but the pain convinced Emrik his mortality had not yet forsaken him entirely.

With a growl, Emrik clenched his fist around the haft of the spear, and it shattered in his grasp. A shockwave of light and energy burst out, flattening nearby soldiers of the Fourth and even knocking a few of the Red Weavers from their horses. Emrik sat tall, unfazed. He wiped the fading light and crackling energy from his hand, then reached for his sword. It was time to put an end to Mathanial, the Rider.

"Father, let me," Borik said, already dismounting. "Do me the honour of the kill, and I will make a gift to you of this creature's divinity." Honeyed words, spoken without guile.

Emrik glanced down at his son. Borik was strong. Young and more lithe than brawny, one of many traits he had unfortunately inherited from his mother. Borik, like all Emrik's children, had feasted on more than one divinity in his time. His strength was undeniable. A war waged within Emrik, to protect his son or to believe in his ability. Borik would not be the first of his children to fall to an angel, and Mathanial was strong enough to have survived a thousand years of being hunted. Emrik decided to trust in blood.

"Try not to damage the body too badly, son," Emrik said. "I do not wish to waste any part of his flesh."

Borik drew his sword, a radiant weapon with a blade as black as night save for the bright bloodstains that would never wipe clean. One of the seven Godslayer arms used to end the great tyrant's reign. He saluted to his father and stepped forward to meet the angel. Borik wore no armour, only riding leathers. They would not protect him from the angel's wrath should the fight go badly.

"Let us be at it then, Godless pup," Mathanial said. His sword trailed lightning as it danced in his hands. "I will show you divine purpose."

The surviving soldiers of the Third backed away, forming a ring of steel and flesh around the mortal and angel.

They met with a clash of steel and sparks. Borik was not a short man, but angels often grew larger than any man could hope to measure, and Mathanial over topped Borik by a good head and a half. The divinity was all ebony muscle and fluid grace. The speed of an eagle and the strength of a pack of bears. Yet Borik matched him, dancing away from strikes and replying in kind.

At least for a time.

The difference in skill and stamina soon became clear. Mathanial was divinity, blessed and gifted by the God. He did not tire, and his technique was ever flawless. Emrik grimaced as he watched his son begin to flounder against the angel.

Borik stumbled, caught wrong-footed on a parry, the Rider drove him back, and Borik tripped and fell. Emrik tightened his grip on his sword's pommel and stood in his stirrups. Too late.

The God was never known for mercy, and it was a trait his angels shared. Mathanial raised a hand, and a bolt of lightning struck, forming into a spear in his grip. He drove it down into Borik with a shout of triumph.

Yet Borik was no longer there. His body flickered, and for just a moment Emrik saw two of his son, one impaled upon a spear of lightning and the other on his feet, slipping past the Rider. The impaled Borik faded away like embers blown from a fire.

Borik's Godslayer sword flicked out, and Mathanial screamed as one of his wings fell lifeless to the ashen field. Before the angel could turn, Borik slashed at the divinity's ankle and leapt away. Mathanial half collapsed, his sword flailing, one leg all but useless, and off balance without one of his wings.

"You monster!" Mathanial shouted. "That power was Aranthall's."

Borik circled the angel, keeping his sword up in case of any sudden attack. "Yes, it was," he said lightly. "Tell me, angel, would you like to know how your sister tasted?"

"Savage!" The Rider hissed as he spun about, throwing his spear. Borik slipped around the lightning and darted in. He laid open one of the angel's wrists and stabbed his blade through the other hand. Mathanial's sword dropped from his useless hand even as the lightning spear hit the ground in the far distance. An explosion erupted from the impact, the heat of which Emrik could feel even from such a vast distance. Emrik decided he wanted that power for himself. He would claim the angel's heart.

"Stop," Emrik said before his son could move in to strike the killing blow. Borik backed up, bowing his head, ever obedient. Emrik urged his horse forward and plucked his bow from its place on his saddle. It was a magnificent thing forged from the bones of a pegasus.

"Savage," Mathanial snarled. "Beast. Heathen! Was there no part of the Heaven you did not rape as you sacked it?" His eyes were on the bow. The stables of the pegasi were once the Rider's pride and joy. He had raised each of the flying beasts with his own hands. All dead now. Emrik had not allowed even one of the winged horses to survive.

Emrik took an angel-feathered arrow from his quiver and set it to the string. "Almost all of the divine has a use, angel. Do you know what I will do with you? Your brain will turn children into seers to track down the last of your kind. From your bones, I will forge weapons beyond the power of mortal steel to slay your brothers and sisters. Your wings will make arrows that fly true for miles and never miss. I will feed your tongue to a minstrel, and they will sing songs of my glory that will make men weep. Your blood will extend my son's life a hundred years. The only part of you I cannot use, angel, is your life."

The angel laughed, a sound like a chorus of church bells from the ancient times before the Crusade. Before Emrik tore all the churches to rubble.

"I am Mathanial, the Rider. Herald of the Fourth Age. I die with dignity, Godless King. I only wish I could be there to see you cower and beg when my father visits retribution upon you."

"The God is dead, angel!" Emrik spat. He turned and stood in his saddle, drawing back the bow string. "I was there when Heaven burned. I watched my grandfather take God's head and mount it on my father's spear. I drank the divine blood, and I feasted on God's heart. Do you see your failure? You heralded the Fourth Age. An age in which we humans threw off your shackles, killed God and took divine power for ourselves."

Again the Rider laughed. "How little you know. The Fifth Age is upon us. God cannot die. Humans can die. Even angels can die, but..."

Emrik's arrow took Mathanial in the left eye.

"You're right about that."

The angel slumped over sideways. Dead. One less divinity in the world. Emrik was one step closer to final victory. A thousand years of war, of hunting divinities across the world, was almost at an end.

A cheer went up from the soldiers of the Third and Fourth. Carvers rushed forward quickly, eager to preserve as much of the divinity as they could before any of him spoiled.

Borik licked blood from his blade as he approached. It was uncouth, but at least it was not wasteful. Even a drop of divine blood was worth a fortune. "That was well done, Father," he said. "A lengthy but successful hunt. One more angel dead. Only ten remain, I think."

"Nine."

"They're dying. Your thousand year quest is almost at an end. Soon their divine heresy will be wiped from memory along with the name of the God. We should celebrate." He clapped his hands. "Wine."

"Maybe," Emrik said, eyeing the red glow of the sky behind the clouds. He still remembered when the sky was blue, before the Heavens bled.

Mathanial's words bothered him. The angel claimed the Fifth Age was upon them. But that was only possible if a new Herald had been born. Yet, how could there be a new angel if God was truly dead?

CHAPTER I

What has been lost can be found.
 What has been forgotten can be remembered.
 But what has been killed can never be reborn.

— FUNERAL RITE, FROM THE 3ᴿᴰ SCRIPTURE,
ATONEMENT

Riverden, Helesia.
Year 1058 of The Fourth Age. 1013 years After Heaven Fell

Renira ducked into a crouch and rolled away from the beast's lazy swipe. Her silver-plated battle skirt picked up dust and straw, tarnishing the metal. The lady would be displeased, but those were concerns for later. There was a monster to battle.

The beast was black as the darkest night and large enough to bite a man clean in two. Coarse fur covered its entire body, and its eyes glowed yellow with languid malice. Each paw ended in razor claws that could shred armour and flesh alike, and the ground was littered with the evidence of its deadly prowess. Renira counted three corpses, though some were in more than a few pieces, which made it tough to be sure. None of them had died well.

The Black Beast of Ner had plagued Riverden for years. It stole out at night and raided nearby farms, leaving none alive to tell of its ferocity. Any fools brave enough to confront it at its lair quickly found they were not equal to the task. It was a monster from nightmare, and it had been a burden on the people for too long. For the sake of those lost, Renira had donned her old thrice-blessed armour and, with shield and battle standard in hand, ridden out to face the Beast of Ner.

The monster hissed fire, and Renira raised her shield. She crouched behind it, feeling the searing heat of the flames as they rushed past her in a torrent, her teeth gritted against the effort. When the inferno finally guttered out, Renira emerged unburnt. She stood tall, planted her battle standard in the ground, and let the banner unfurl. A blazing sun with a crescent moon in front. Her family crest, the symbol of house Washer.

"I have no wish to slay you, beast," Renira said confidently. "But no longer can you plague these lands. No longer must the people suffer under your..."

The beast yawned, a mouth full of fangs and blood and rot. Then it sat down, stretched a long back leg over its head, and began licking its arse.

"Well, that pulled all the tension out of the dream."

Renira chewed on her lip and sighed. No longer fighting a terrible beast from legend, she was back in the dilapidated barn. Her silver armour was a plain blue dress long since past its best and used now for the daily chores. Mother would not be pleased she had rolled in the straw and dirt, but it was only one more thing to be washed. Renira's shield and battle standard were gone too; now she held a brush and a large dustpan. The beast, once terrible in her mind, was just a large black cat, still equally vicious but not deadly. Well, not to people anyway. The three rat corpses in pieces nearby were plenty evidence that the cat was still a dangerous monster.

"You could at least try to play the part next time, Igor," Renira said as she went about sweeping rat entrails from the barn floor. The cat meowed and sauntered away as a reply, brushing its tail past her leg as it went. No doubt there would be more corpses to clean up tomorrow, though where Igor kept finding them was a mystery Renira had yet to puzzle out. Perhaps she would have to don the cap of an investigator. There would be clues to uncover, witnesses to question, the truth to shake free. But she had already wasted enough time today, and if she didn't finish her chores, Mother wouldn't let her go see the parade.

Renira finished sweeping the barn clear of corpses and dust, dumping them all in the compost heap as always. Then she collected Yonal Wood's dry washing from the pile and ran it over to his hut near the forest edge. Yonal wasn't there, of course, no doubt in the forest chopping down a tree that had stood watch over Riverden for hundreds of years. But Flora Wood was a kind woman, heavy with her fifth child and barely able to keep track of the other four. She accepted the washing with a smile and told Renira to collect as much firewood as she could carry, then handed over a few carrots out of pure generosity. The people of Ner-on-the-River were a small but close community. They existed just outside of Riverden, living off the land as much as possible and trading favours and good will rather than coin. It was a fine place to live, but not very exciting. Especially as there was no one even close to Renira's age in the little community. All her friends lived within the town limits, and they rarely found time or excuse to visit, except in the summer when the water was warm enough to swim.

The sun was slouching towards mid-morning by the time Renira was done with her chores, and it was a chilly morning at that. The winter months were long and brutal near Riverden, and the water turned icy. Snow and hail were a frequent hazard and made drying the washing so much harder. That was why they had the barn. Mother said it had held horses and other livestock in her grandfather's day, but fortunes turned quickly, and now it only held rats and a fat black cat intent on decorating the place in gore despite Renira's best efforts to keep it clean.

The washing cart was just arriving when Renira made it back to the house. She threw the firewood in the shed, rushed the carrots into the kitchen, changed into a fresh dress of green and brown and dumped her dirty one on the floor. The cart would only stay for a few minutes, just long enough for Poe to offload his cargo, and then it would be back on the way to Riverden, and Renira aimed to be on board for the trip. She couldn't miss the parade. All her friends would be there, and it was her first chance to see royalty in the immortal flesh. It was the event of the year, of the decade even, and Renira would rather dance on a beehive than miss it.

"All done for the day already?" Mother asked. She was busy helping to sort through the cart's washing load. It mostly came from the smithy, but recently a new butcher had opened up shop near the town limits, and they had heard no one could get blood out of aprons quite like Lusa Washer.

"It was an easy day," Renira said. She dug into the piles of washing and helped with the sorting. Bloody aprons one side, ash and grease-smeared shirts on the other. The cycle of washing was an endless one.

Endlessly dull.

"Only three dead rats today, and the washing from this morning isn't dry yet. I stoked the fire a little, and Flora Wood gave us three carrots." There had been four, but Renira had already eaten one.

Her mother straightened up from the washing pile, easing a crick in her back, and wiped her forehead. She was a plump woman but strong, with calloused hands from countless days washing, washing, always washing. Her own dress was faded orange, voluminous and rarely dry, and the morning's work had put a healthy colour in her cheeks. Some of her hair had escaped the braid she wore, and she puffed it out of her face as she looked critically at her daughter.

Like a judge deciding my fate. Guilty! Throw her in the stocks. No fun for Renira.

"I could use your help with this load, Ren. There's a lot come in today and..."

Renira groaned.

Her mother chuckled. "Oh, do you have somewhere else to be today?"

Renira chewed her lip. It was all part of the game, she knew, but if there was even a chance her mother was serious, it would mean another day of washing while everyone in Riverden was celebrating, having fun.

"The parade is today, Mother," Renira said. "No one else is working. All my friends are going, and... Well, the king will be in Riverden!"

Her mother shrugged. "If you've seen our king once, you've seen him a hundred times. He never changes." She exchanged a look with Poe. "I remember the first time I saw him when I was a girl. So strong, and those eyes."

"Mhm," Poe agreed. "I heard he ain't not aged a day in near a thousand years. Old as the age itself, so folk say."

"So folk say," her mother agreed. Her hand went to her chest, rubbing at the necklace beneath her dress. The hidden icon of her faith. No one else ever noticed, but there was no reason anyone else should. It was their secret, daughter and mother.

All just fanciful stories anyway, God and angels and demons. Not like a real flesh and blood immortal king.

"I've never seen the king," Renira said. It was not the first time she had made the argument, but her mother had conveniently forgotten, or at least pretended to. "Please please please. You said I could go if I did the daily chores."

"Hmm. Did I?"

"I'll do extra washing tomorrow."

Poe laughed. "Renegotiating a deal now?"

Her mother nodded. "A foolish mistake, but one I'll be glad to benefit from. An extra load tomorrow in return for the day off today."

It was half a day off at best, but it was also better not to argue and take a chance of the terms becoming even less favourable.

"Go get your warmer coat, Ren." Mother was serious again now, a wary glance towards the eastern sky and the grey clouds hanging above the snow-capped Ruskins. The mountain range to the south and east towered over River-den, and none save the barbaric blood worshippers of Aelegar were fool enough to risk its peaks. "There's a chill in the air, and a frost on its way. It's gonna be a bad one, I can feel it in my teeth."

Renira sped away before her mother could change her mind. She wondered if mothers ever stopped treating their daughters like children, but even at sixteen winters, she was clearly still a child in Mother's eyes. Renira pulled off her light coat and found her warmer winter coat, a padded sheepskin jacket that buttoned closed at the front, though it was missing a button. She dumped her lighter coat on the floor next to her worn dress and rushed back out front before Poe could drive the cart away. She was just in time. The washing was all unloaded, separated into three piles, and Poe was mounting the driver's seat of the cart, reins already in hand.

Her mother pulled Renira aside before she could jump up next to Poe. The delay was frustrating, but she weathered her mother's fussing. Lusa smiled up at her daughter and brushed some stray hairs from her face. Renira might already be taller than her mother, but they had the same long, mousy brown hair that refused to stay in any braid no matter how hard either of them tried.

"Believe it or not, I know what these things are like," her mother said, still smiling. "Keep track of the time, and don't lose your friends. I want you back before it gets dark, and remember you'll need to walk back so it'll take longer."

Renira nodded along impatiently. "I know. I've been to town before, Mother."

"Cheeky. Today will be different. Poe says there's drunkenness in the streets already, before even midday. Here." Mother handed over a small purse, and Renira checked inside to find five bronze ekats. "I know it's not much, but it's been a hard season."

Renira grinned. "It's more than I expected." She clasped the purse to her chest and bowed her head formally, imagining herself entrusted with a great fortune. "I shall spend it wisely, Lady Mother."

Mother shook her head and laughed. "There you go again. I need you to spend one ekat on a loaf of bread. From Tobe Baker, not Firen. Last loaf we got from Firen went mouldy inside of two days. The rest is yours to spend."

"Yes, Mother." Renira made to pull away.

Her mother pulled her back and into an embrace. "Be careful, Ren," she whispered close to Renira's ear. "Say nothing suspicious."

The same order drilled into Renira from birth. "I know, Mother."

"I mean it, Ren. Today of all days, say nothing."

She still talks to me like I'm a child. As if I don't know all the rules already.

Renira gave her a reassuring smile, then climbed up onto the cart next to Poe. It was only a trip into town. There was the parade on, sure, but Renira had been to town hundreds of times. The old driver chuckled and gave the reins a shake, and the mule brayed and started forward.

"A loaf of bread from...?" her mother called as the cart trundled down the drive.

"Tobe not Firen," Renira shouted back without looking.

"Back before...?"

"Before it gets dark," Renira said, waving a hand over her head.

"Have fun!"

CHAPTER 2

I would see built again all which was torn down, made grander than before.
The villages lost will rise into something greater. The people killed will give
their names to a new generation of humans free from the shackles of thrall-
dom. I would unite mankind into a single nation. An empire where human
and angel can live together in peace and prosperity.

— SAINT DIEN HOSTAIN. TALES FROM THE
FIRST AGE

P oe was an amiable enough travelling companion with a host of little
rumours and tall tales about the people who lived in Riverden. Renira
hadn't heard of most of the people he talked about, but she listened all the
same and only stopped the cart driver when his tales started to become too
lurid. It wasn't for nothing that the people of Ner-on-the-River called him an
unrepentant gossip, but then Renira supposed that was a form of gossip as
well. He had been that way ever since his wife passed a few years back, and by
all accounts he now spent most of his nights in one tavern or another,
listening to rumours and introducing a few of his own. Some people called
Poe a dangerous gossipmonger, but Renira thought him harmless enough. He
made some not-so-subtle enquiries as to Renira's father, but that was a tale

he'd have to settle on never knowing. Even Renira herself had no idea. No matter how many times she asked, her mother never answered and always found a way to change the subject. It was Lusa Washer's second best kept secret.

The cart ride to Riverden wasn't too long, and there was little traffic on the road, yet Poe nodded to each passer-by and greeted them by name. Only once they were out of earshot did he turn to Renira and tell her who was sleeping with whom, or which of his neighbours were drunk nine days out of eight. Renira smiled pleasantly to each tale and kept her mouth shut.

No sooner had they reached the town limits, Renira leapt from the cart, heedless of the mud squelching beneath her boots, and waved a quick thank you. She raced away down streets she knew well, past shops and houses and people who laughed at the Washer girl's enthusiasm. It was bordering on midday, and the parade would be starting soon. She wanted to get the loaf of bread from Tobe Baker and then meet up with her friends. Hopefully they'd already have a good position on one of the main thoroughfares in order to see the king and his family in all their radiance. No royalty had ever come to Riverden before, at least not in Renira's lifetime, and she was excited to see their immortal king and his children.

"That'll be two ekats," said Tobe Baker.

Nice try, but I wasn't born in a bucket. "It's one ekat, and you know it, Mister Baker." Renira had selected a nice crusty loaf of brown bread that was barely out of the oven. She dropped it into her little canvas bag and skewered Tobe Baker with her very best frown.

Tobe expelled a weary sigh and scratched a floury hand over his stubble. He was a thickset man with huge hands and a little mouth, and everyone knew he tried to swindle women out of more than they could afford, though he never tried the same trick with men. "Price of flour gone up of late. Cold weather and all that." He shook his head as if sorry for the bad news. "I've had to raise my prices to compensate, I have."

Renira cocked an eyebrow. "If the price of flour has gone up, then maybe you should stop wiping it all over your face." She gave him a grin.

Tobe frowned and pulled his hand away, glancing at it as if just realising it was dusty with flour. "Hmm. Price is still two ekats."

Renira chewed her lip for a moment. *Time to negotiate. I could be an ambassador brokering peace between Helesia and Aelegar.* "The price is one ekat, Mister Baker, or I'll send your next batch of washing back with a cricket in every pocket."

Tobe Baker gasped. "You wouldn't. Drive me mad, all that chirpin'."

Renira grinned. "No, I wouldn't. Just as I would hope you wouldn't over-charge me for a loaf of bread."

Tobe narrowed his eyes at that. "How about two ekats and I'll throw in a fresh baked pastry roll?"

Renira loved haggling. *Not an ambassador, but an exotic merchant from the Ice Islands on the hunt for a good deal.* "What filling?"

"Skyberry preserve from Alfie Pecker," said Tobe. "Freshly delivered this morning so it still has that spicy bite."

"Deal!" Renira handed over two ekats and grabbed the pastry, shoving a corner in her mouth and whisking out of the shop in a twirl of skirts and a victorious laugh.

The pastry was salty and sweet and crispy and long since devoured by the time Renira found her friends. Riverden was a large town with more streets than Renira had names for, but she already had an inkling of where her friends would be. On the eastern edge of the Old Market square was a fountain dedicated to King Emrik Hostain. When the pumps were turned on, three jets of water launched out of the ground to bathe the stone king.

The statue was of a heroic pose, the king atop a mighty horse, a stern and regal glare upon his features and a sword raised and pointing north. When the sky was clear, the water would catch the red light of the sky and make it look as though the king was being bathed in blood. Renira thought it a bit morbid, but it certainly made for quite the spectacle. Of course, the fountain wouldn't be turned on today, but the parade was certain to pass this way.

Renira clambered up over the statue's plaque that read *'Vigilance is the keystone of foundation, preventing insidious decay. Stay strong, stay watchful, stay loyal.'* and pulled herself up onto the statue's base.

"Late as always, Ren," said Aesie. She was the eldest of their little group and liked to think this, along with her higher birth, made her more refined. She was wearing a stunning dress of the latest fashion and the most expensive and impractical fabric. It was a golden ripple that clung to her curves and had sparkling feathers sewn into the shoulders. Judging by Aesie's shivering, it provided no comfort against the encroaching cold.

"Some of us have chores to do, Aesie," Renira said. "We can't all flounce about on sofas and order servants to do all the work." She didn't really mind doing her chores, but it was good to occasionally remind Aesie how most people lived.

"No? Shame that, I do love a good flounce." Aesie pulled a face as though this were all news to her. "Hmm. Maybe next time there's something happening I'll lend you Teft. He's a little slow but very good with his hands."

Elsa giggled. She was the youngest of the four and revelled in the fact. She was also half feral and almost always had dirt smudged on her dress and her face.

"So childish," Aesie said with a sly grin. "When do you turn sixteen, Ren? I want some grownup conversation."

"I've been sixteen for a month now," said Merebeth. She was sitting on the edge of the statue's base, feet dangling, and reading a little book, spectacles perched on her thin nose.

"Sixteen going on sixty," said Aesie. "I want grownup conversation, Beth, not groaning conversation."

Renira giggled at the joke, but Elsa rolled her eyes. "That were awful."

"Was awful, not were awful," Merebeth said without looking up from her book. She had a smile on her long face though.

"Were awful!" Elsa said, sticking out her tongue. Of the four of them, Elsa was the only one who never attended the public school lessons.

"I thought it was funny," Renira said.

Aesie pulled Renira into a hug and then drew back, holding her at arm's length and staring her up and down. "What are you wearing, Ren? Green really is not your colour."

Here we go again. "It was clean."

Aesie glanced down. "You have mud splashed all up the hem."

Renira shrugged. "I said it *was* clean. It's a long way from Ner to Riverden and the roads are muddy."

Aesie was always critical of what Renira wore as though her old clothes and lack of fashionable dresses made her look bad. She never berated Elsa for being dressed in rags or covered in mud though. Renira suffered through it all in good humour, it was just Aesie's way.

"Is that..." Aesie reached out and plucked something from Renira's hair. "Straw?" She dropped it. "You have dirty straw in your hair, Ren."

"Just be glad it's not rat guts."

"Lovely."

Elsa snorted. "You should definitely start wearing rat guts, maybe some bones as well. You'd look just like one of them Aelegar shomans from the mountains."

"Shamans," Merebeth said.

"Bleed you, Beth!" Elsa said.

"Here," Aesie said as she pulled a strip of silver cloth from around her wrist. She plucked another bit of straw from Renira's hair and then used the cloth to tie her messy mane back. "That looks better."

Renira smiled at her. "It's been years since you last gave me a ribbon."

"Has it? I shall have to start again then."

Elsa sniffed and glowered at Aesie. "Why don't you never give me ribbons, Aes?"

Aesie shrugged and turned away. "Because you're probably just use them to wipe your nose."

Renira wouldn't tell anyone, but she'd kept every ribbon Aesie had ever given her. She had a draw full of the little colourful strips back in her room. They were such small gifts, worthless to Aesie, but Renira could never bring herself to throw them away.

Elsa slipped around the stone horse's leg and wrapped her arms around Renira, squeezing her tight for a moment. "Missed you."

Renira squeezed her right back. "Missed you too."

"Good. And don't let miss high and mighty tell you shit. You look good in green, Ren."

Aesie cocked an eyebrow and turned away to stare out over the crowd. She was the glue that held their little group together, and yet they all knew it couldn't last. It wouldn't be long before she had to make a decision about her future, and considering how much money her family had, staying in Riverden was unlikely. There were universities in the capital which would jump at the chance for a large donation and new student, and someone as bright as Aesie could almost certainly get in on her merits alone. When that happened, they would drift apart. Merebeth would lose herself in her father's library, probably buried under a pile of dusty old books. Elsa would find herself a trade and a husband. And Renira would be condemned to nothing but washing clothes every day for the rest of her boring life. It scared Renira. She wanted excitement and adventure, not the mindless monotony of washing clothes until old age made her unable to do anything else.

Thunder rumbled somewhere in the far distance and many people looked up to the red sky. Swathes of grey cloud dulled the crimson, and the wind was blowing hard with more dirty clouds looming on the horizon.

"Oh dear, that's going to dampen things," Aesie said through chattering teeth.

"Bit of rain never hurt no one," Elsa said. "I was once caught in a flood that washed me all the way down The World Vein and almost out to sea, I was. That was the day I learned to swim." She grinned.

Elsa mixed lies and truth so freely it was often difficult to tell the two apart. Of course, Riverden was weeks away from the coast even on horseback, so this lie was all too obvious.

Renira chewed on her lip and glanced towards the clouds in the east. "It's hours away yet," she said, hoping it was true. "The parade will have been and gone by then." She didn't bother to mention it would likely hit just as she was beginning her walk home. The other three all lived within the town. They could be home in minutes as soon as the first drops started to fall.

"Well, it could hurry up," Aesie grumbled. "The parade, I mean, not the rain." She hugged herself and shivered against the cold.

Renira started to remove her coat. "Wear this. My dress looks warmer than yours."

Aesie shook her head violently, dislodging a few blonde strands. "I can't wear that. It's..." She trailed off before pointing out that it was something a poor person would wear, but they all knew what she meant. "Um, sorry Ren."

Renira just smiled and sidled closer. They were perched on the base of the statue, facing the street and looking over the heads of the dense crowd in front of them. Renira shifted next to Aesie and put her arm around her friend. "If you can't wear it, I'll just have to wear it for you," Renira said. Aesie leaned against her, and she did feel cold, shivering in the chill air.

They continued chatting as they waited. Sometimes about the latest book Merebeth had read, or the latest boy Elsa had kissed. Sometimes about Aesie's father and how his trade deals were bringing more commerce into Riverden. Renira never thought she had much to add to the conversations. She could read, but the only book she owned would get her put on trial for heresy. She had never kissed a boy and had little interest in doing so. Most of the boys she knew were dirty, smelly, and far too full of themselves to be worth pressing lips. She knew little about commerce or trade, and none of it would matter anyway unless it brought even more washing to the Washer women's door. The only stories she could tell were the daily count of rat corpses Igor left her, or which shop produced the dirtiest of aprons. *Hardly thrilling topics for anyone.* She found herself only half listening to the conversations, daydreaming instead.

She leaned back and stared up at the king's statue towering above and wondered who had carved it and how. The time they must have spent chiselling out the fine details, getting the pose just right, bringing out the likeness of both man and horse in stone. It was by far the grandest statue Renira had ever seen, but her mother's copy of *The Divine Truth* spoke of a time during the Third Age when the greatest structures, monuments, and wonders of the world had been built.

Renira imagined herself during that time, overseeing a project that would last for millennia. Working alongside divinities to design something that had never been seen before. She would toil shoulder to shoulder with her craftsmen, and in the end they would all stare with pride at the marvel they had worked together to create.

I could be a builder. Just like Saint Dien. The official histories claimed the Saint was a warrior, a conqueror, a uniter. But The Divine Truth had so much more to say about the woman. Saint Dien had laid the foundations of Celesgarde, a city unrivalled in its grandeur. *Or so everyone says. Not that I'll ever see it.*

Aesie shifted, and Renira found herself back on the statue of King Emrik, watching over a street that was no longer empty.

"Here they come," said Merebeth, snapping her book closed and staring towards the west end of the street.

They all stood then, perched on the plinth with the statue, clinging to the stonework and barely reaching the top of the horse's legs. Renira clutched at a poised stone hoof to keep her balance.

The parade was, at its core, a military endeavour. The king and some of his children were out in the lands hunting rogue divinities. At least that was the official statement. The rumours in Riverden told a different story, that there had been no angels for a hundred years and the king was rooting out seditious heretics and touring his kingdom. Every town and city he visited threw a grand parade, and the nobility then threw an even grander ball. Aesie was here for show really. She'd be at the ball with the rest of the rich folk and would probably get a one-on-one meeting with the king. But then none of the others would be with her, and Aesie was ever most comfortable around her friends.

The crowd grew excited as the first soldiers marched into view. Chatter filled the air, and many fingers were pointed. Renira felt it too, the thrill of seeing royal troops, the anticipation of the king himself in their little town. Her stomach gave a nervous flutter, and she shared a grin with her friends.

"Them ones are the soldiers of the Second," said Elsa. Renira glanced her way and gave her an incredulous look. "What? I pay attention to things. See how each of them soldiers has that patch right there on their arm? I hear it indicates which legion they belong to. The crowned hawk is the symbol of the Second."

"How do you know that?" Merebeth asked.

Elsa grinned. "Fabe Fisher told me. It's all very fascinating." Renira doubted Elsa found the symbols of the legions interesting, but it was no secret that she found Fabe Fisher truly fascinating.

The marching soldiers went on for some time, their formation rigid and perfect, each step matched to an echoing beat of a drum. Even the drummers themselves were in perfect order. That, Merebeth said, was the strength of the

Second. They were the king's personal legion, and there was no more disciplined fighting force. Renira asked about the First, but Merebeth pointed out that the First never left Celesgarde. Their job was to defend the greatest city in the world against all threats.

They must think me such an ignorant rube for not knowing any of this.

Aesie grew more and more agitated as the procession wore on, and her excitement was infectious. Before long, all four girls were chattering nervously and standing on tip toes to see further down the street, hoping to be the first to catch sight of someone truly important.

Then the excitement soured for Renira. Unnoticed by most, there were people moving through the crowd. Men and women who wore no uniforms, yet by their purpose of movement and the grim expressions, they were not Riverden locals. They slipped through the press of humanity, and people parted for them, making space without being aware. Truth Seekers, trailing swollen hands through the masses, a single touch all they needed. Nobody seemed to notice. Nobody seemed to care. Only Renira, and only because she had been warned. Her mother knew of the Truth Seekers and how to spot them even when they slipped from the minds of all others. It was a trick she had taught to her daughter early. Don't stare directly at them or you'll lose them in the crowd. Look elsewhere but keep them in the corner of your eye.

Please don't come this way. Shoo! Go chase a whisper.

Renira shrank back against the statue, shifting position to protect herself. All it would take was a touch, the merest brushing of fingers. But the Seekers could not touch everyone. She just needed to stay out of reach.

"I see them," Merebeth said. "I see them. I think..." She was the tallest of the four, and on her toes she could see furthest.

It made sense. The Truth Seekers would move ahead of the king, a brief passing to make certain things were safe for the royals.

"It must be them," Aesie agreed. "See the horses, and that's the royal standard." A banner fluttered in the breeze, the standard bearer marching alone and carrying it with rigid attention. The banner was red with golden trim and depicted a downward pointing sword with a black iron crown hanging from the crossguard, and a pair of white feathery wings behind it. The crest of the Hostain family, the immortal rulers of Helesia.

Renira spared only a glance at the standard and looked back to the crowd. She had lost track of the Truth Seekers on their side of the street, and there were too many people crowded around the statue. Any flailing hand could be one that would bring her and her mother to ruin. She pressed back further against the statue, trying to make herself as small as possible, fully aware it would only make her look guilty yet unable to stop herself. Panic rose in her chest, and her breath caught in her lungs. She glanced about madly, trying desperately to find the Seekers she had lost. She had to avoid them at all costs. *I should run!* It would make her look even more guilty, but Renira could surely out pace anyone still caught in the crowd. And the Seekers couldn't know the streets of Riverden as well as she.

"Ren? You all right?" Elsa was staring at her. Not at the parade, the soldiers, the horses, or the standards. Merebeth and Aesie glanced her way as well.

Renira let out a dramatic breath and clutched to the statue. "Just feeling a little lightheaded suddenly. It's passed, I think." *Stupid. What would they think of me if I ran away for no reason?*

"Come see this." Aesie grabbed Renira's hand and pulled her forward towards the edge of the plinth and the crowd. Renira swept her gaze across the people gathered nearby staring out toward the parade. Faces recognised, turned away, a churning mass of people all shouting and pointing. Surely the Truth Seekers had already passed by now.

"That's Princess Perel," Aesie said. She was pointing with one hand, the other gripping Renira's in a vice. Both their hands were icy cold, and Renira thought they should have brought gloves. Merebeth wore gloves, though she planned for everything.

I have to stop panicking. The Truth Seekers have gone. Just enjoy the parade.

When Renira looked up at the procession, she saw a tall woman striding at the head of a swarthy group who looked more street thug than soldier. The woman wore heavy brown trousers, a bleached bone gambeson, and a leather chest piece that extended all the way down her right arm but left her other arm bare. Her hair was long and dark and braided into three tails, and she wore some form of black paint around her eyes that drew attention to her sharp features. She carried a halberd in the crook of her right arm, the haft longer than she was tall and with a black blade stained red, as though blood dripped along its single edge and three jagged tips. At the woman's side paced a shaggy sabre-toothed wolf so large its shoulders reached her chest. The entire group did not so much march as swagger, and a thrill ran through the crowd at their passing. Even Renira found her breath catching in her throat at the sight of Princess Perel and her Dogs. Word of their savagery spread far and wide, and everyone said it was they who did the king's dirty work.

Renira felt a thrill deep within at seeing the Wolf Princess. *I bet she lives a life full of excitement and adventure. Princess Perel would never wash a dress in her life.* Renira flushed with envy at the thought.

"I heard Perel has killed three angels all by herself," Elsa said with a wide grin.

Aesie scoffed. "Impossible. Everyone knows there are no angels left. The king has already killed them all."

Elsa shook her head. "Then why's he here? Thought this whole thing was about him hunting divinities and such?"

"It's a pretence, Elsa," Aesie said. "A way for him to tour his lands and meet with the important people."

This time, Elsa scoffed. "Prancing about like a cock in the morning. You're just hoping he's looking to finally find a wife for Prince Never Married."

Aesie grinned. "Prince Borik is supposed to be very handsome. And there's always a chance, I suppose."

"Not for you. Anything like his sister, he probably prefers someone with a bit less pomp and a lot more experience."

"That's a polite way of saying gutter trash." Aesie's face dropped the moment the words were out of her mouth. "I'm sorry, Elsa. I didn't mean it."

Elsa crossed her arms and sneered. "You call it like it is," she said bitterly. "I'm gutter trash and you're..."

"Why would you even want to be a prince's wife?" Renira asked, cutting Elsa off before she said something she didn't mean and couldn't take back. "You'll be on your way to a university soon enough. You can study anything you want, Aesie."

Aesie sent an apologetic look Elsa's way and mouthed *sorry*. "You're right, I suppose. It's nothing but a passing fancy really. I doubt any of us will catch his eye."

Elsa shrugged. "I got a couple of things that would catch his eye."

Renira gasped and gave Elsa a playful slap on the arm. "You wouldn't. Not in this weather. You'd catch a cold." In truth, she wasn't so certain Elsa wouldn't no matter what the weather. She was more than a little jealous of her friend's free spirit at times.

"I don't know. Men seem to like it when they're cold." Elsa was showing off now, trying to act experienced to put Aesie in her place.

"Here he is," said Merebeth. "And that's the king, too."

They were riding side by side on grand horses that made them tower over everyone else. Surrounded by soldiers, the most elite of the elite. Royal guard in angel-forged metal armour. King Emrik and his youngest son, Borik, looked like divinities themselves. Borik was youthful and pretty, an easy smile on lips ringed by a neatly trimmed strip of hair that only just touched his chin. He wore no armour, but a rich suit of burgundy that made his dark complexion stand out all the more. He sat as though born astride the horse, one hand on the pommel of his saddle and the other waving to the crowd.

"Have you ever seen a more handsome man?" Aesie asked.

"I prefer them a bit more rugged, but he'd do." Elsa giggled at her own jest.

"What do you think, Ren?" Aesie asked.

Renira had no eyes for the prince. Her gaze was drawn in by King Emrik, as though he had a gravity about him that could not be resisted. Paler than his son, though not by much, the king was tall, a giant almost, and burly with brawn that belied his apparent age. His hair was close-cropped and grey, his beard full and framing a jaw like granite. Like his guard, the king wore black angel-forged armour that only served to make him look even larger. He dominated the air around him, demanding attention. Renira gasped when his pale blue gaze swung her way. *I can't breathe!* Here, she knew, was a man of relevance.

The world turned around King Emrik, and everyone nearby was caught up in his wake. Benevolent ruler and protector to most, relentless enemy and hunter to people like her mother.

Then the weight of his gaze was gone, passed over her without notice, and Renira grew weary, as though the tension of that moment had sucked all the strength from her limbs.

"Of all of us, Ren," said Merebeth, "you are the last one I expected to swoon."

Elsa giggled. "Perhaps she thinks *she* caught his eye? Oh, Princess Renira, take us with you when you go."

"Leave her alone, Elsa," Aesie said.

"What? It's all right for you to call me trash as long as no one touches poor little Ren?"

"Are you well?" Aesie said, ignoring Elsa. "That's twice you've looked on the verge of fainting."

The royal part of the parade was past them now. The imposing sight of King Emrik's broad back looked resplendent with a trailing crimson cape to match the sky. Renira dragged her attention back to Aesie and the others.

"Just a little lightheaded again. Too much excitement probably. Swooning, just like you said, Beth." Something about the sight of the king had unsettled her. An anxious feeling that she didn't like.

He saw me. He saw through me.

The crowd was dispersing now. Some would run off to catch another glimpse of the king further on the parade route, while others would retreat to taverns to talk about the event over too many ales. But the day was still young and the festivities were just beginning.

"Come on," Elsa said, leaping down from the statue. "There's games set up over on Broadlark. Puppet shows, too."

"Will there be food stalls?" Renira asked as she clambered down after Elsa. She turned and held out a hand to help Aesie climb down.

"Are you ever not hungry, Ren?" Aesie asked as she gingerly stepped down.

Renira made a show of considering it, then grinned. "No."

Hand in hand, the four of them squeezed through the dissipating crowd towards Broadlark street. As they went, they argued over which of them had caught the prince's eye. It was fun, but Renira remembered that Truth Seekers were about and kept a wary eye for the tell-tale sign of swollen hands.

CHAPTER 3

Seven were the Godless Kings who took their war to Heaven.

— FROM THE PLAY, THE DAY THE HEAVEN'S BLED

Broadlark street was packed with so many people it reminded Renira of turning over a stone to find a colony of beetles beneath all crawling over each other. The Tri Moon Fayre was known to follow the king about all over Helesia, setting up stalls and plays and games whenever he visited a town, and they had decided to make Broadlark their home in Riverden.

Music echoed out from several makeshift bandstands and there were people dancing in the street, heedless of the dust they were kicking up. A cheer went up from a crowd watching a game where contestants paid an ekat for a chance to throw horseshoes, hooking them around coloured posts.

Renira sniffed the air and her mouth started watering. There were so many food stalls. She saw a whole boar slowly roasting on a spit, fat dripping down and flaring in the fire below. There were strips of duck cooked to a crisp, fish slavered in batter and some sort of red spice. One stall had withered fruit rolled in sugar and speared on sticks like kebabs. She wanted to try everything, but three ekats wouldn't stretch far.

Merebeth sighed loudly. "And we've lost Elsa already." She was tall as a horse and thin as water, wrapped up in a thick woollen dress, matching gloves and a scarf that made her neck look even longer. Nothing ever seemed to excite Mere-beth, but she could talk for hours about books and paper and ink.

"Bloody breath!" Aesie swore. "If she's slunk off to some back alley with a drunkard, I'll..." She sighed. "I don't know, try desperately to talk some sense into her for the hundredth time."

"Good luck with that," Elsa said as she squeezed through the crowd, grin-ning at them all. She was carrying two leather jacks each one brimming with golden mead. She swigged from one and then handed it to Renira and passed the other to Merebeth.

Renira took a sip and winced at the honeyed sweetness, then quickly went back for a bigger gulp.

"Where did you get these?" Aesie asked.

"Try not to sound too accusing, Aes," Elsa said. "Maybe I paid for 'em."

"You don't have any money."

"Broke as a stopped clock," Renira agreed.

Elsa grinned. "All right. I flashed a tit for 'em."

"You didn't!"

"Sure I did. Kid on the stall acted like he ain't seen flesh before. Said take two jacks all for a glimpse."

Renira took another gulp and handed the mead back to Elsa, giving a light bump with her shoulder as she did. "You're terrible. But good work."

Elsa shrugged. "Harmless fun, ain't it. C'mon, Beth, drink up and give the ladyship a sip, I wanna go see the games."

Aesie made a show of staring at the mead with distaste, but after a bit of goading she gave up and swigged down half the jack. They moved off into the crowd, cheering her bravery.

They browsed a few trinket stalls, looking at necklaces and pendants, colourful shawls and exotic masks that had grotesquely pointed chins. Elsa tried to push Aesie into buying one of the hideous masks, saying she'd look better for the prince, but for once Aesie ignored the jibes. Renira spent one of her remaining ekats on a fruit kebab and devoured the withered apple on the end before offering it around. Aesie refused, but Elsa happily snatched two sugared cherries, and even Merebeth picked apart a slice of pear.

They had to push their way through a crowd to see the games, and Renira noticed Aesie keeping a wary hand on her purse. Unlike her own, Aesie's pouch of coins bulged with unspent riches. They watched people try to toss balls into holes Renira swore were too small, duck their heads into water buckets to catch floating prizes with their teeth. There was even a bravery contest where two people put their hands in a marsh viper basket to bet on who it would strike. The owner of the stalls proudly grabbed the snake by the head and squeezed its mouth open to show it was defanged before each contest. It was almost entirely boys and young men surrounding that game.

Eventually they came to a stall boasting targets set a dozen paces back and miniature bows with which to shoot arrows. Elsa near bounced up and down at the opportunity.

"This is the one," she said. "We gotta play. I'm an expert archer, you know. Once won a tournament."

Renira narrowed her eyes. "Where?"

"God's End."

Aesie sighed. "You've never been to God's End, Elsa."

"Have too. Won an archery tournament. They said I was so good at it, they were going to build a statue in my honour."

"Really?" Aesie said haughtily. "I'll look for it next time I visit."

"You do that."

"I will."

Elsa grinned and Aesie smiled with her. "Go on then, Aes. Get your purse out and buy us a shot each."

Aesie sighed. "That would be a poor investment."

"But you're rich."

"And my family got to be rich by not making poor investments."

Merebeth broke the argument by reaching into her own purse and buying them each a try at the game. She was by no means as rich as Aesie, but her father was assistant to the magistrate and so she never hurt for a few ekats to spend.

Elsa went first and despite her claims at being a legendary archer, her arrow barely made it half the distance to the target. Aesie went second and her shot was at least a foot wide. Merebeth made a show of taking off her gloves and rolling up her sleeves. She looked hilarious with the miniature bow clasped between pinched fingers. Her shot hit the outside ring of the target, which wasn't close enough for a prize.

Then it was Renira's turn. She imagined herself a legendary hunter, stalking through the forest on the trail of a monstrous boar with tusks dripping gore. Her job, to slay the beast, to save the travelling merchants it had savaged. She took careful aim, sighting down the arrow, and pulled back the little string, then released. Her arrow took flight and struck the target dead centre. The others gasped, and Renira turned to them with a smug smile.

Renira raised a dramatic hand to the sky. "You stand before a mighty

huntress. Strong as the mountain tall, swift as the river deep, terrible as the fires
of war." She broke into laughter and they all joined in.

"That were luck," Elsa said.

"Was luck," Merebeth corrected.

Elsa rolled her eyes. "Do it again, Ren. I dare you."

Renira shook her head haughtily. "I feel no need to prove my prowess a
second time."

The stall owner handed over a prize of a single white flower with golden
paint around the edges of the petals. It was very pretty. Renira went down on
one knee before Merebeth, heedless of the dirt staining her skirts, and held up
the flower in both hands. "I present my prize to the most beautiful lady in all
the lands."

Aesie laughed. "You are such a mook, Ren."

Merebeth plucked the flower. "I suppose I must accept on her behalf,
whoever she might be." She sniffed at it and smiled. "Thank you, mighty
hunter."

Elsa begged for another shot, but the stall owner shook his head. They
wandered away laughing, and Merebeth tucked the flower safely into her
satchel.

There was still so much to see and not enough time. Renira heard the first
rumble of distant thunder and looked up to see dark, brooding clouds creeping
towards them from the south. She knew the rain would start soon and she really
needed to be home by then, but she was having so much fun with her friends
and didn't want it to end.

Aesie bought them all another drink, chilled wine this time instead of mead
and a cup each to show off her generosity. They stopped by a puppet play that
was obviously more meant for children, but the laughter coming from the audience drew them in. The puppets were wood and felt and had hilariously
enlarged facial features. King Emrik's puppet had a chin as large as the rest of its
head combined and a black crown that kept jauntily slipping down its face, and
there was an angel puppet with a gigantic nose and crossed eyes.

The puppets clashed with raised swords and dramatic noises, all to the coos
of the enrapt children at the front. Then the King Emrik puppet slashed off one
of the angel's wings and red water spurted out, showering the children who all
screamed and laughed in delight.

Renira had seen the story told before in many different forms. It was the last
days of the Crusade, when the seven Godless Kings rode to Heaven to slay the
angels and free humanity from their thralldom. They taught the same story in
schools, ran variations on it in plays, and bards told it in taverns across Helesia.

Of course, Renira's mother told a very different version, read from the heretical books she kept. Her mother's version didn't depict the angels as tyrannical despots, but as glorious winged creatures of light and hope who just wanted to lift humanity up and help them achieve the impossible. Her books told of a God who loved humans and taught compassion. The king's version of the Crusade, taught in school never even mentioned God, just droned on about the evil of the angels.

"This is always my favourite bit," Aesie said, smiling.

The King Emrik puppet danced about on stage, shook his little felt hands in the air, and the great stone gate behind him dimmed and then crumbled to boulders. An angel puppet, this one with a tiny body and wings and a massively enlarged helm for a head, sagged and walked off the stage in a sulky huff.

"Ohhh," Aesie said, laughing. "Doesn't the little puppet look so sad."

"That's not how it happened," Renira said, frowning as the King Emrik puppet danced a lively jig on the field of his victory.

"Hmm?" Aesie asked. "What do you mean?"

Renira suddenly realised what she'd said and startled. She was feeling a little fuzzy headed from the mead and wine and her mouth had gotten away from her. She grinned a little too wide and shook her head. "Puppet show, you know. I much prefer the bard's versions."

Elsa shook her head. "They're not as fun. Bards always focus on glittering swords and heroic horse charges."

"Cavalry charges," Merebeth said. "You should try reading *Seven Kings in Shadow* by Artanial Frost. It's a much more accurate accounting of the Crusade."

Aesie yawned dramatically. "By accurate, she means dry and dull. It spends entire chapters going over troop numbers and formations."

"Accurate according to the king," Renira said before she could stop herself.

"Well, of course," Aesie said. "He was there. Who else would know better?"

Thunder rumbled again, and Renira took the opportunity to stare up at the clouds. They were dark and pregnant and crowding over Riverden now. She chewed on her lip. "I think I should go."

"What? Noooo!" Elsa said. "But I wanna celebrate some more. Stay. Have another drink." She finished with a hopeful grin, offering her half-finished cup of wine.

Renira smiled and shook her head. "I really need to go before the rain starts. Unlike you, I have a long walk home yet, and it's no fun while wet, even with boots on." None of the others had commented on her choice of shoes, but Aesie had definitely noticed. What everyone was wearing was always of such importance to her, and boots with a dress was beyond improper.

Elsa made an unhappy sound. "Aes?"

"Don't look at me. I have a ball to prepare for. I can't spend all day out here with you riffraff." Aesie grinned to soften the insult.

"I might go home too," said Merebeth. "Father doesn't like me out too late, and I have a new book to read. It's about the Shattering, when the Lords Beneath the Ice broke..."

Elsa made a dramatic noise that was at least part growl. "So boring. Please, Ren!"

A hawk cried from somewhere high above, and Renira looked up. The sky was darkening quickly now, already the same rusty brown as the day-old blood of the mice she had to clean up every morning. Grey clouds threaded their way through the red, and to the east a thick blanket threatened more than just rain.

"I'm sorry, Elsa," Renira said. "Don't stay out too late. There's a real storm coming tonight, and you don't want to be caught up in it."

They all shared hugs and Renira promised Aesie she'd visit again soon, then she said her final goodbyes and fled. She felt more than a little guilty leaving Elsa in the lurch but also knew it was probably for the best. With just one of her friends nearby, Elsa would celebrate a little too hard. On her own, she was far more likely to head home early and avoid the late-night revelry, which everyone knew was when things often got out of hand.

Further away from Broadlark street, the crowds lessened, but there were still plenty of people about and the hubbub was making Renira feel uneasy and cramped. It was a rare holiday in Riverden, and though many still worked, there were just as many using the excuse to visit a tavern or celebrate out on the streets, behaviour the town rangers put an end to on any other day.

Renira made a brief detour and stopped at a wool merchant who was just about to close shop. Her mother loved to knit, and, though it was a skill Renira seemed entirely unable to master, she loved trying to learn as it gave her a good excuse to spend time with her mother. She spent her last remaining ekats but counted it a worthy purchase, then turned her feet east and hurried home at a brisk pace. The clouds loomed dark and threatening overhead and low rumbles of thunder echoed over the land, a booming promise of the violence to come.

Renira's feet were aching by the time she reached Ner-on-the-River, and the rain was just starting to loosen itself as she turned down onto the path that led to her house. She pulled her coat a little tighter and quickened her pace, desperate to get home before the mud turned to quagmire.

That's strange. There's washing still out. Three rows of sheets hung from staked out lines in the grassy garden just in front of the house. Her mother would never have left washing out with rain so obviously close. Now it was starting to fall, and there would be only minutes before the laundry was sodden and had to be dried all over again.

Renira rushed over and set about pulling the aprons and towels and shirts from the lines, throwing them over shoulders and in the already full bag she was carrying. By the time she had all the washing down and was under the cover of the porch, the rain was coming down in earnest. The sky lit an angry red with a flash of lightning, only moments later followed by a boom of thunder that shook the rooftops and set shutters rattling.

Renira waited the rumble out, marvelling at how loud it was. *This storm is going to be a big one.*

She struggled with the door and pushed it open, only dropping a few items of laundry. Inside, she quickly dumped them on a dry patch of floor and set about pulling off her boots and coat.

"It's really starting to come down out there, Ma. You shouldn't have left the washing out," Renira called as she laboured. She could feel the heat in her cheeks now she was inside again. It felt good to be home. Away from the press of the revellers and the noise. A knot she hadn't realised was there started loosening in her stomach.

Silence greeted her. No reply from her mother, and nothing but the crackle of a burning log from further inside. The kitchen door stood ajar, and shadows danced on the wooden floor.

"Ma?" Renira called as she finished taking off her boots and picked up the washing, moving it to the table next to the door. It would need hanging again inside, but that could wait a few minutes. "I got the loaf of bread. And I bought something for you."

Still no answer. Renira picked up the bag with the bread and wool in it and made her way to the kitchen. She pushed open the door to find her mother sitting at the kitchen table, an untouched steaming mug in front of her.

"Ma? I bought you some wool for your knitting. It's fine stuff..." Renira froze.

There was someone else in the room with them. A tall man hunched over in front of the kitchen fireplace, shrouded in a dark towel, hands outstretched so he looked to be touching the flames, water dripping from pale, slender fingers. A pang of sudden fear shot through Renira.

"Come in, Ren." Her mother turned to Renira, and there was an odd pained expression on her face.

"Ma?" Renira asked, unsure. She couldn't see the man clearly, but it was no one she recognised. They rarely received visitors and never at such a late time of the day.

Something isn't right here. Does he know? Renira glanced at the pantry. The door was open, but the loose floorboard under which her mother hid their heretical books was still in place.

"Hello, Renira," the man said in a voice like the whispering of a forest. He turned to her and stood, the towel falling from his wings. Renira's gasp was lost in a roaring boom of thunder.

CHAPTER 4

Angel blood is both the easiest part of an angel to harvest and the most universally valuable. A single drop of angel blood can cure illness and disease and extend the imbiber's life by many years. What value would you place on immortality? What value, therefor, can you place on divine blood?

— DEVOURING THE DEVINE BY TERKIS THRANE.
YEAR 47 OF THE FOURTH AGE. 2 YEARS AFTER
HEAVEN FELL.

The music was loud and obnoxious, the ballroom was lavish beyond excess, and the company was sycophantic at best. Emrik stood at the centre of it all, a forgotten flute of spice wine in his hand and a constantly rotating series of aristocratic lickspittles keeping him apprised of their short, pointless lives. They believed what they said and did made a difference to the world, but they were all such small and insignificant flies, their lives embers thrown from a blaze, a brief flare soon snuffed. They could never understand the burden of a truly meaningful existence nor the weight of immortality. The responsibilities he carried.

Borik brought another snivelling shrew of a man to meet his king. He was good with people, was Borik. But then he was also young, barely eighty years to his life, and he had yet to grow weary of the same stories repeated in an endless dreary cycle.

"Father, this is Magistrate Kul." There was a weight behind Borik's grey stare. Imploring Emrik to treat the man with interest if not respect. It was not needed. Emrik had been king for longer than most men could fathom; he knew the intricacies of the political game better than his son ever could. He just bored of it.

Emrik reached out and clasped the man's wrist. An informal greeting, but it usually made men feel important. "Magistrate. A fine city you've built here." Such a lie. Emrik himself had planted the first shovel in Riverden's foundation almost three hundred years ago. Built atop an ancient ruin from the First Age.

"My liege." Magistrate Kul bowed his shiny head, hand still clasped to Emrik's wrist. "I have, uh, but built on what other, more industrious, uh, men started." Perhaps the man was more savvy than he appeared. His words were weighted with humility, and he knew his history. Still a sycophant.

Kul was a short man, barely reaching Emrik's armpit, and pudgy from a life of obvious luxury. His hair was thinning to wispy strands, and an overpowering scent of lavender swarmed around the man like bees to honey.

Emrik held Kul's wrist tight while a Seeker passed behind, slender fingers trailing across the magistrate's back. He shuddered and tried to turn away, but Emrik only tightened his grip. Magistrate Kul winced, and his eyes boggled even at such light pressure. Emrik could crush the man's flesh and bone as though it were parchment, and he made certain the man realised it. The Seeker gave a minute nod and moved away. Emrik released his grip. Magistrate Kul pulled his arm back, cradling it against his body. There was fear in him now. Likely it would only make him grovel more fervently, but Emrik needed to be certain.

The angel was here, in Riverden somewhere. The Elder Seers had seen the signs—and when two of them saw the same thing, it was irrefutable.

Seers were made by feeding the brain of an angel to a child, and it scarred them for whatever meagre lives they could claw out. The Seers were plagued with abstract dreams and visions as often lies as truth. They were unable to escape the dreams, unable to find peace, and most of the children were driven mad within a few years, taking their own lives to end the suffering. Those who survived into their adulthood were the strong ones, the Elder Seers, but even they rarely endured for more than a few tormented decades. Emrik gave them what comfort he could: plush living, decadent food, willing attendants. It was the least he could do for their sacrifice.

"A fine city indeed, Magistrate," Emrik said. "Much larger than the last time I visited. My son speaks highly of the formidable resilience of your people."

"Between the floods and the ice, there is little that can keep the good people of Riverden down," Borik said. He was well into his fourth cup of wine, but it didn't slow him one bit. He was tough stock, Borik, but then so were all Emrik's children. Strong blood showed true, and there was no stronger lineage than the Hostains.

"Well, uh, that is certainly true," Magistrate Kul said with an appreciative nod, still holding his arm close to his chest. "Though we have been suffering from some, uh, bandit raids of late."

That piqued Emrik's interest. "Bandits? In Helesia." He did not permit such miscreants to survive in his kingdom. Laws were set in stone and punishments severe. Heresy of the God stamped out wherever it was found. He would not abide sedition under any guise.

Magistrate Kul nodded. "They come down from the Ruskins to the, uh, south. Blood worshipping savages from Aelegar waylay, uh, merchant caravans, those without sufficient guard to protect themselves."

"And the city rangers?" Emrik asked, his voice like cracked rubble.

The magistrate paled. "Well, uh, of course they are highly trained but only numerous enough to defend the town from attack. We simply do not have the numbers to seek out the bandits where they make camp nor mount an, uh, expedition to destroy them. And, as you know, the savages from Aelegar can be quite, uh, difficult to deal with."

"As I know?" Emrik said slowly.

Kul gulped. "I only mean to say... That is... Your Majesty has had trouble with them in the past."

"We could spare some of the Third to deal with the savages," Borik suggested. "Their numbers are reduced and..."

"We don't have the time," Emrik said. "The angel must be found."

The barbarians of Aelegar had always infested the southern mountains. No matter how many times Emrik led legions to wipe them out, the crazed blood worshippers always returned. His time and Helesia's soldiers were better spent on hunting the remaining divinities.

"Angel?" Magistrate Kul asked.

Emrik narrowed his eyes at the man. "We are here on business, Magistrate. I am hunting for a particular divinity, and my Seers say he is nearby. Could it be he is hiding out with these bandits of yours?"

The magistrate frowned as he considered. Perhaps deciding whether to lie to get what he wanted. "I don't think so, no. There have been no reports of angels. Only men with, uh, savage interest. Barbarians seeking slaves for their gory rituals and such. Foul business, but, uh, no divinity, I'm sure."

"Thank you for your honesty."

Magistrate Kul nodded. "I could make some subtle enquiries on your behalf regarding information on your, uh, divinity?"

Emrik grimaced. "I want no word of this angel spreading, Magistrate."

"No. Of course not. But perhaps I could ask about possible heretical, uh, elements. It can be quite surprising what turns up when, uh, suitable rewards are offered. I daresay it's none of my close acquaintances, but the town is growing and fast. There may be those willing to harbour divinity living nearby."

Emrik nodded. "Subtle enquiries, Magistrate."

Magistrate Kul smiled. "Of course, my liege."

The ball was in full flow, and some people were even dancing. The minstrels were playing some jaunty ditty that increased in tempo every twelve seconds. Emrik had never heard it before. There was a time he knew every song and every step, when he had danced with the most beautiful women in the empire. There was a time he even danced with angels. A thousand years was a long time. So much had changed, and so much hadn't.

He remembered a poem from his youth.

Dance little puppet to the tune of your strings
Cavort prance and tumble, shout cry and sing.
Beware the lure of music, for when it does stop
I'll cut through your strings, and where you stand, you will drop.

Everyone wore a strip of bandage upon the index finger of their left hand. The Offering was a tradition to shed a single drop of blood upon the floor of a host's home and then receive a bandage from the host. A symbol of offering sacrifice and granting protection. Emrik had long ago considered stamping out the tradition, it was cousin to the heretical practice of worshipping blood, after all, but traditions were important. Traditions reinforced principles and authority. Very little controlled a population with such ironclad stasis as tradition.

As always, Emrik could see others waiting nearby, looking for a chance to slip into conversation with the king. He sipped at the glass of wine in his hand and wished such frivolities were not needed. "One more thing, Magistrate. I have need of your icing facilities. We have precious divine material to preserve, and our own stores of ice are running low."

Magistrate Kul blanched. "My liege. We, uh, have no icing facilities in Riverden." The man realised his error. Even the lowest parts of an angel were worth more than the entire town of Riverden. To let them spoil for lack of ice would be something his career could not recover from.

Emrik snorted. "No matter. Ezerel."

The Chief Carver was waiting nearby. He was always close to Emrik, hoping some immortality would rub off on his ancient bones. He sidled up, hunch-backed and clutching a cup of wine in his gnarled hands. Ezerel was all but unique, one of only three people in the entire kingdom who was allowed the life lengthening properties of angel blood despite not being one of Emrik's children, an exception made for two reasons. For a start there had never been a more capable Carver than Ezerel, and even infirm he was a master at preserving every piece of a dead divinity. No one, not even Emrik, knew more about the body of the divine and what it was capable of. And of course, it was impossible to keep the Chief Carver from sampling blood even when strictly denied it. Emrik had long ago decided it was best to allow it rather than deal out punishment.

"My king?" Ezerel's voice was croaky and quiet like the last crackling of dry leaves underfoot. Extreme age did that to a person, and Emrik suspected it was only angel blood that was keeping the Chief Carver alive these days. If he was denied even his meagre drop a month, he would likely perish within days. It was a waste Emrik could not allow.

"Riverden has no icing facilities, Chief Carver," Emrik said without looking at the man.

Ezerel made an appreciative noise in the back of his throat. "A terrible shame. I will set my apprentices to it immediately. Expedited process, of course. It will be hideously expensive, my king."

Emrik nodded. "Magistrate Kul will cover all costs."

"I will? How, uh, expensive are we talking here?"

Ezerel chuckled. "This way, Magistrate." He started to lead the man away.

"Do not forget those enquiries, Magistrate," Emrik said.

Once the two men had left, Borik grabbed a new glass of wine from a passing servant. "You could smile more, Father," he said with a grin of his own.

Emrik ground his teeth in reply. "Have you any idea how many of these bloody things I have been to? A thousand years, a hundred thousand balls, maybe more. Each and every one the same as the last. Every city, town, and backwater village I visit throws a ball in my honour. At the capital, my nobility force me to suffer one a week. Such mindless tedium. The music may change, son, but the steps are all the same. New faces, but the same people no matter how they might be different. Over and over again. Do you not imagine I have seen a thousand Kuls in my lifetime?"

"Yes, well, I find these parties are quite fun when you settle into them. There's dancing and drinking, and pretty young things in tight pants and swaying hips."

Emrik let out a weary sigh. "They are needless excess. Ways for old men to parade their children and young men to impress with their supposed wit. I am neither old nor young. I am timeless."

Borik nodded along to his father's tirade, then shrugged. "Good wine, though. And there are some pretty faces about."

Emrik smiled at that at least. No doubt there were countless young women hoping to catch the prince's eye. They had a better chance with Perel's wolf.

The ball orbited around Emrik, and people flocked to him just to be able to say they had spoken to the king. Borik stayed nearby, except when it was diplomatic for him to dance with a young woman. He did so with enthusiasm, and perhaps no others could see how feigned it was. Emrik smiled and nodded to the conversations, and whenever he added his own opinion, it quickly became law. None would argue with the king. None would presume greater wisdom than an immortal.

It grated on his nerves. There was a time when Emrik had enjoyed gatherings such as this. Before the Crusade, he had been a social animal, dancing with the women and drinking the men into a stupor. Arguing philosophy with sister, and challenging angels to games of skill all knew he could never win. His father had despaired of making him a man worthy of rule, or worthy of a blade, eventually dismissing him as a pretentious fop. Even his grandfather had despaired over Emrik's indulgent demeanour for a time. So long ago. And Emrik was the only one left, despite their immortality. There was no one left who truly understood the Heresy of the God nor why his religion was so dangerous. Only Emrik, the last of the Godless Kings. A final, lonely sentinel standing guard against the truest evil the world had ever known.

"This is the path you set me on, Grandfather," Emrik whispered to himself. "Did you ever imagine I would be forced to walk it alone?"

"My liege?" A new sycophant had appeared to shower Emrik in praise. A tall man in an impeccable brown suit that seemed to shift along with the light in the ball room. A young woman was perched by his side, her arm resting on his. A daughter then, and a young one at that. They were all young these days, even the wrinkled crones.

Emrik nodded at the man by way of response. He tried a smile but fancied it came out as more of a grimace. It wasn't his fault, after all. Emrik didn't want to be here. There was a divinity nearby, he could feel it. More than anything he wanted to be out there, hunting the angel and damn the storm raining down on their heads.

The man continued his introduction, emboldened despite the lukewarm response. "My name is Alyn Fur, I run the local clothing workshops here in

Riverden, and also a branch in New Gurrund and a recent construction in Vael." A monopoly on the clothing trade in any city, even one as small as Riverden, was a healthy way to make untold profit. New clothing was always needed by rich and poor alike. "This is my daughter, Aesie." The girl curtsied. "I was hoping we might secure an introduction to the prince."

Emrik scoffed at that. "Foolish little harpy. Go. Try your insignificant charms on him. See how far they get you."

There were tears after that, and Emrik had to admit he should have handled it better. Frustration had got the best of him, and he would make no more excuses for Borik that night. The cloth merchant apologised as though it were all his fault rather than Emrik's. Emrik suffered through the apology and didn't bother to correct the man. It would soon be forgotten by the crushing wheel of history. Only the truly relevant acts mattered in the grand scheme of things, and even those faded eventually. So many of the details of the Crusade had been forgotten, and there was no more relevant event in all history.

After a few more fools had offered their welcome and thanks, Emrik blinked into his hawk sight. The bird saw nothing but worked wood above and pouring rain, lit occasionally by a flash of lightning. It was no doubt holed up somewhere warm and dry to wait out the storm. A barn or belfry. One more frustration for both bird and man alike. When he blinked back into his own sight, he found Borik approaching.

"I hear you made a young lady cry in my name, father," Borik said with frown. "Bad form."

"It was not my intention." The words were bitter in Emrik's mouth. "I was too blunt." He waved it away. "It will soon be forgotten. The weak always forget their failings and rely too heavily on their successes. The strong learn from every failure and make pains not to repeat them."

Borik nodded. "Indeed. That sounds like Ertide."

"Your great grandfather was a wise man, even if everyone did think him too severe." Emrik didn't need to add that Ertide Hostain was also an inspiring leader and a military genius. He would have to have been. After all, it was Ertide who had started the Crusade against Heaven. And it was Ertide who had grown too weary and made Emrik finish what he had started.

"Much like someone else I know." Borik was grinning. It made him look feckless.

"Base flattery is unworthy of you, son. Why is Magistrate Kul cowering behind you?"

Borik stepped aside to reveal the magistrate. "Well you made the girl cry and he's a little afraid you'll bring him to tears next. So he brought the information to me instead."

"I... I wouldn't say scared. I just wasn't sure it would be, uh, worth the king's time. Best to bring it to the prince instead to evaluate the auth..."

"Enough," Emrik snapped, heedless of the shocked faces that turned his way. "Speak your bloody piece?"

Borik glanced back at the magistrate, but the man seemed shocked into silence. "A young girl has come forward with information, Father. Sedition, she suspects." Borik said.

"And you are only telling me this now?" Emrik asked.

Some of the confidence fell from Borik. "Well, it was only moments ago I learned myself."

"Spare me your frivolity. What are the details? Was the angel mentioned?"

Borik swallowed and then coughed. He stood a little straighter, the soldier in him coming to the fore, reporting as he had been trained. "No divinity was mentioned as such," he said in a low voice so as not to be overheard. "But then none was asked about. The girl in question has come forward of her own volition with suspicion of seditious activity in a nearby community."

Emrik ground his teeth. Patience was never one of his virtues. "Has it been confirmed?"

Borik gave a short nod. "A Seeker's touch. At the very least, the girl believes it to be true."

Emrik considered this, picking at the skin around one of his thumbnails. "Where?"

Magistrate Kul stepped forward. "A small village on the border, Ner. The locals call it Ner-on-the-River. Some farmers and woodsmen mostly, all poor as the dirt they muck in. There's never been any, uh, signs of sedition from that way before."

Emrik looked at the man, and he stepped back under the force of that glare. "What do you know about signs of sedition, Magistrate?"

"Uh... Nothing, really."

Emrik turned back to his son. "Find your sister. Tell her to fetch her Dogs."

"Now?"

"Now!"

Borik ground his teeth together for a moment, so like his father in many ways. "But the ball, and the storm. It would be wiser to wait it out."

"I did not ask for your advice, *son*." Emrik weighted his words. "Find your sister. We leave now. Damn the ball and damn the storm!" He slammed his wine flute down on the nearby table so hard the stem snapped, spilling dark orange wine all over the wood. It did not matter. Emrik was on the trail of the angel again. He could feel it. The Builder might have escaped him once, but he would not get so lucky a second time. Emrik would find the Herald and stop him before the new age could be rung in.

CHAPTER 5

The First Age was an era of darkness. Humanity was a broken people, hiding in caves and forests. Demons roamed the world with savage impunity and made thralls of any they could capture. There was no belief. There was no faith. There was only fear and pain.

— THE DIVINE TRUTH, AUTHOR UNKNOWN

*A*ngels are real. They're real!

Renira's hand was over her mouth, a finger pinned between her teeth, and her eyes were wide as Flora Wood's ample arse. Her mother had told her of angels from an early age, read to her from *The Divine Truth*, *Rook's Compendium*, and *The Seventeen Holy Scriptures*. From before Renira could read, she was taught the foundations of belief in God and the subtle worship. Always they kept her mother's beliefs hidden from others. But Renira had remained sceptical that any angels had survived. And all the teachers in town preached King Emrik's claim that the angels were evil oppressors and that he was hunting them down to free humanity once and for all. But now... Now there was an angel standing right in front of her.

In my home. In my kitchen. Drinking from my favourite mug.

"Hello?" Renira mumbled past the finger in her mouth. The bag slipped from her grasp, hitting the ground with a thump that startled her.

Mother was at Renira's side in a moment, firm hands on her shoulders, guiding her toward the chair she had recently vacated. Renira allowed herself to be pushed down and found her mother's warmth lingered on it. She was shaking, eyes still locked on the angel and the blackened ruin of his wings. They were meant to be feathery, weren't they? Not blackened bone without a feather in sight.

He was tall, this angel, not quite a giant, and Renira had seen taller men, though not many. His skin was pale as ivory and his shoulder-length hair dark as ink. Not old nor young, but more as though time simply had no meaning within his features. He frowned at her—and Renira felt guilt rising within, as though she had done something terribly wrong. She tried to look away but couldn't tear her eyes from the man's wings.

"Drink this," Mother said as she pushed a steaming cup into Renira's hands. Without thinking, Renira lifted it to her lips and sipped. It was hot tea, sharp with some sort of liqueur though Renira could not tell of what sort. She had never known her mother to drink before, certainly not at home.

"You're an angel." Renira cursed her own foolishness. Of course he was an angel. He knew he was an angel. Why couldn't she think of anything smart to say?

The angel sighed and sent a weighted glance towards her mother. "Is she dim?"

"Of course not! She's in shock, is all," her mother said. "She's never seen one of you before."

Renira flicked her gaze between her mother and Armstar. "You're an angel."

The angel sighed. "Must we keep establishing that? My name is Armstar, the Builder. Some call me the Unburnt." Renira's glanced to his blackened wings, charred bone and not a single feather. She quickly dragged her attention away, too frightened to ask the obvious question.

Lightning flashed again outside, and the following rumble of thunder made the cupboards rattle.

"And you are Renira Washer," the angel continued in a slow voice as though she were a startled dog. "Daughter of Lusa Washer."

"You know my name."

The angel sighed again.

Her mother placed steadying hands on Renira's shoulders and gave them a squeeze. "He's a friend, Ren. An old friend. Come to us in a time of need."

An old friend. Mother is friends with angels? Renira turned and gazed up at her mother as if seeing her for the first time. She never really talked about her past, and Renira had never thought to ask. She was her mother, had always been her mother. It seemed selfish now she was confronted by it, but what her mother had been before and whom she had known had never seemed important.

Armstar plucked the towel from the floor and set about dabbing his chest dry. He was leaner than Renira had pictured an angel, not burly but lanky. His fingers were slender and delicate, and his ruined wings twitched occasionally of their own accord, causing him obvious discomfort every time. He wore a rough linen shirt and old, stained leather trousers. An amulet in the shape of a blazing sun hung about his neck, and the long over cloak that was dumped over his chair had two slits up the back to accommodate his wings. He didn't look like an immortal oppressor bent on enslaving mankind, and Renira couldn't imagine her mother being friends with a despot.

Renira struggled to think of something to say. Anything really, just to stop herself from gawking like a mute bumpkin. "Blessed be the reborn," she said with a bow of her head. An ancient prayer from the Second Age, it fell from Renira's lips almost by accident. She'd always hated all those prayers and blessings.

Armstar touched one hand to his head, and the other to his heart. "Blessed be the reborn. You've taught her well, Lusa."

Her mother plucked the fallen bag from the floor and set to digging through it. She ignored the balls of wool and fished the loaf of bread from the bottom, then wrapped it in oiled paper. "Where and when I could. She's still young, and worship is dangerous even in the safety of a person's own home. She knows the basics. Some history and lore. The prayers and the tenets. But nothing of... what we did. Only the basics." Mother picked a waterproofed leather sack from the floor, the one reserved for important laundry delivery regardless of weather, and placed it on the table. It was bulging, yet she somehow managed to fit the loaf of bread inside. She was always so much better at packing than Renira.

Renira was still struggling to find her voice, in awe of the divinity sitting in her kitchen, and bemused by her mother's actions. "What's happening?" she asked.

Mother looked at her, a grave expression full of some hidden meaning. "Go and change your clothes, Ren. Trousers and a shirt. Your warmest winter ones. I've laid them out on your bed already."

"What? Why?" It was far from warm, even with the hearth burning away, but she wasn't cold enough to need to change.

"Then go into my room and find my long waterproof coat, the one that almost reaches the floor, my sheepskin gloves, and my wide hat, the one to keep the rain off."

"Mother..."

Her mother shook her head at Renira to stop any complaint. "Take the cup and make sure you drink it all. I've a few words to have with Armstar. When you're ready, come back and I'll explain... everything."

The angel watched silently. *Not even a divinity can stand in the way of Mother when she takes charge.* In something of a daze, Renira stood, the cup still in her hands, and made her way from the kitchen. The door closed behind her, and for a few moments there was nothing but silence from within. Renira climbed the stairs to her room, sipping from the steaming cup. Her old pile of clothes was gone, folded and tidied away by her mother, and her warmest winter clothing was laid out on her bed. The storm outside battered against her window, rattling the shutters and spraying the old, cracked glass with rain.

As she was getting changed into her warm, sturdy clothing, she heard shouting. Her mother's voice was raised and almost frantic, the sound travelling through the floorboards. There was no reverence in that tone, no awe for the angel.

"This is it, Lusa. The moment that we've been waiting for." That was the angel's voice, loud and commanding.

"I left for a reason, Star," her mother's voice cracked on the words.

Renira she couldn't hear what was said next. She took another sip of the tea and then lay down and pressed her ear to the floor, straining to listen.

Who is my mother? A small washer woman from a community not even large enough to call itself a village, and yet there she was shouting down an angel like he was just another woodcutter rather than an immortal child of God. There was so much Renira obviously didn't know.

"I'm sorry," the angel shouted. "But it has to be now. He's coming."

Thunder shook the house and drowned out her mother's reply.

"Will you tell her?" her mother said, her voice falling as though all the strength had run out of her.

Renira didn't hear the angel's reply. She stood and hurried into her mother's room and rummaged through her wardrobe to find her long coat and hat. It was her travelling coat; one she hadn't worn for as long as Renira could remember. Mother liked to call it a relic from her younger years before she settled down with a daughter. It was recently waxed and well looked after, but there were scars on the leather. Renira had always thought them innocent, scuffs from vaulting a fence, a scrape from bumping into a protruding nail maybe.

But she looked at the coat and its history in a new light and couldn't help but imagine her mother wearing it on some sort of adventure. Perhaps she was more than the washer woman she appeared. Maybe she had fought monsters alongside angels, a warrior like Saint Dien from the old stories in *Rook's Compendium*. The possibilities seemed endless and exciting, and Renira grinned as she considered them.

Renira crept back to the kitchen door, ears straining to hear anything coming from the other side. The shouting had finished, but the soft murmur of voices still sounded within.

"Did you plan it from the start?" Her mother's voice had a sad edge to it. "Was any of it real?"

The angel's voice was hollow. "How can you of all people ask me that? I burned for you, Lusa. You are my..." He fell silent.

Renira pushed the door open slowly, newly dressed and carrying her mother's travelling gear. The angel turned away towards the fire as soon as he saw her.

"Where are we going, Mother?" Renira asked as the door creaked open.

There was a fresh mug of tea on the table, clutched in her mother's trembling hands, and a small plate of dried meat and vegetables. Mother pushed the plate in front of the empty seat and patted the chair. "Sit, Ren. Eat. There's a lot to talk about and..." She trailed off, defeat in the set of her shoulders.

Why do they both look like they lost the argument?

"And not much time," Armstar finished.

Renira slid into the waiting chair and ignored the food. "Is God really dead?" It was a question that she'd always wondered about. Her mother said it was true, but the plays and the school lessons never even mentioned God.

Armstar sighed and turned away from the fire. "Yes. The Godless Kings killed him. You likely know them as Ertide, his son Rikkan, and his grandson King Emrik."

Renira glanced at her mother, but her eyes were closed, a single tear rolling down her cheek. "Eat the food, Ren. You haven't much time."

Never one to pass up a meal, Renira plucked the fork from the table and speared a few slices of undercooked carrot.

Again, her mother shared a look with the angel before Armstar continued. "I'm being hunted, Renira. I'm sure you know that King Emrik hates my kind." There was a bitter edge to his voice, and his gaze was flat and hard. "He has sworn an oath to kill every angel. That is why your mother and you, and many others, must worship in secret. Even a single word of your devotion could see punishment brought down upon you."

Renira nodded, gnawing at a mouthful of dried sausage that tasted of pepper and garlic. It was good fare, far better than they usually ate. *Mother must have pulled all the good stuff out the pantry to find this.* Thunder shook the house again, and the sound of rain pelting against the roof became louder, more oppressive. The storm was growing worse outside, and her mother did not look dressed for it, even if she did put her long coat and hat on.

Armstar winced and shifted position again. His wings looked depressing things, hunched up against his back, black and scorched and trembling. How much worse it must be for him, to see a part of himself so ruined. She had always pictured angels as great, majestic folk with glorious feathery wings, just like her mother had described them.

"He is close," Armstar said. "And so damned relentless. The Godless King knows I'm near and will stop at nothing to have me. To carve up my body and to steal the power in my flesh."

Renira sensed the angel had stopped short, that there was more he left unsaid. She shoved some more uncooked vegetables into her mouth and chewed without enthusiasm. The thought of someone carving up an angel for food was not helping her. It made her feel sick.

"I cannot fight him. I'm no warrior. I'm a builder. And I'm... I find myself in need of help."

Renira almost choked on a chunk of carrot. Another peal of thunder covered her surprise. "Our help?" She glanced at her mother, again wondering what adventures she might have been through in her youth that an angel would be coming to her for help.

Again that shared look between Mother and Armstar. *I'm missing something important.*

"You might have noticed, Renira. I am not at my best." There did seem to be a frailty to the angel that went further than his burned wings. "I need to reach the Cracked Mountains." He sighed. "And damned quickly."

Renira looked to her mother and forced down a half chewed lump of potato. "That's through the Whistle Wood and past Hel's Wall. You'd have to take the western road and stay close to the tree line. Nobody goes into the deep forest." She thought about Yonal Wood's instructions on traversing the woodland. "It's two weeks through the forest at least. And then back again. I'll look after the business as best I can, but I would rather go with you."

A sad smile broke out on her mother's face, and she shook her head, new tears pulling free. Renira had never seen words fail her mother before, but she seemed completely at a loss.

Armstar waited out another peal of thunder before he spoke again. "I need a guide, Renira. Not skirting the forest, but right through the centre. The quickest route to the other side."

Renira shook her head. "You can't. No one goes through the centre. No one." She looked to her mother. "Yonal and Yonash Wood even don't go more than a day in. They say the sun doesn't pierce the canopy, and you can hear things moving deeper in. Things that step too heavily to be human. Maevis Fair lost a husband from them three years back, though she says it was the best thing that ever happened to her."

Her mother was shaking her head. "Just a bear." She didn't sound convinced, let alone convincing.

"Be brave," Armstar said, looking at her.

She did feel brave. Renira made up her mind, her mother didn't know the forest half so well as she did. "I'll go."

Her mother stopped holding back and burst into great sobbing tears. Renira scooted the chair a little closer and placed an arm around her, holding her tight. "I know the forest well enough, and Yonal Wood taught me the basics of navigating under the canopy. I'll take you, your, um, divine, uh, grace. Angel."

The angel rolled his eyes, he did not look amused.

Mother was still sobbing. Renira wasn't sure how to handle it. Her mother had always been a rock upon which she could steady herself. Strong enough for the both of them. Now she suddenly looked older, as though extra years had worked their way into her body while Renira was looking at the angel. Renira found tears of her own stinging her eyes, blurring her sight. She pulled her mother close and hugged her tight.

"I'll go, Ma. You stay and look after the business. There's no monsters. Just a few bears, like you say, and I'll have an angel by my side. A Heaven-sent angel! I'll take the long way back, round the forest edge to be safe." She wiped her own tears on her mother's shoulder. "You won't even know I'm gone. Maybe you'll enjoy the quiet." It was the wrong thing to say. Renira knew it was wrong even as the words left her mouth. Her mother shook from the force of the sobs breaking free.

Armstar rose to his feet, his long cloak in hand. "Lusa." Mother froze at the sound of her name on Armstar's lips.

"Don't you dare do that to me, Armstar." Mother's voice was a shock of cold anger.

"It will help. You'll feel..."

"No! You do not get to manipulate my heart that way." Her mother shook Renira free and shot to her feet. Her hands were balled into fists and planted on the table, and her gaze was tearful but steady. She shook her head. "Not me, Star."

Armstar bowed his head a little and stepped away from the fireplace. "I'm sorry." Another flash of lightning cast the room in stark shadows, faded in an instant. Renira felt the thunder that followed through her feet. The angel turned to her and grimaced. "We've no time to waste."

"In the middle of the storm?" Renira asked, incredulous. "You're madder than a bag of cats. Only fools go out in a storm like this." *And I'm not ready to go. I need time to prepare and to say a proper goodbye to Mother.*

Armstar nodded as he walked past them towards the kitchen doorway. "Which is why we're going now. Every minute I can gain on my pursuer gives us greater hope of breaking free. You don't know how important this is, Renira. How vital it is we escape." She felt there was something more to his words, something he wasn't saying, but found no time to puzzle out any hidden meaning.

"We go out in this storm because the Godless King will not." Armstar strode into the hallway and pulled open the door leading into the night. Cold air rushed in, and Renira felt a shiver pass through her. Outside was nothing but darkness and rain and the chaos of a storm no sane person would risk. Armstar waited at the edge of that darkness, framed in the doorway and the maelstrom beyond. A flash of lightning made Renira forget, just for a moment, that the angel's wings were ruined.

In the ensuing crash of thunder, her mother set about pulling her big coat on around Renira's arms. The coat had almost trailed on the floor when Mother last wore it, but on Renira it only came to the top of her calves. Renira stared at her mother while she busied herself pulling the coat in and buttoning it up, then she tucked Renira's braid of hair in and pulled the collar up to protect her neck. Renira felt a little cumbersome truth be told, but that was far from her biggest concern. She was trying to keep a brave face, but something seemed so wrong about the situation. New tears welled in her eyes and she tried to stop them, tried to be strong.

"Everything is happening too fast." Renira's voice was quiet and small, barely more than a whisper.

Mother's lip quivered, and she stood on her toes in order to kiss her daughter's head. When she spoke, her voice broke on the words. "That's how all adventures begin. Never any warning."

Adventure? Is that what this is?

They stared at each other over another flash of lightning and the following peal of thunder. It seemed there was so much left unsaid. Worst of all, Renira couldn't help but feel they were both refusing to say goodbye.

I'm just being foolish. I'll only be gone a few weeks. She'd be back before either of them knew it and no doubt wishing for another adventure to come her way. But they had never been apart for more than a couple of days before. Not once. The thought of waking up and not hearing her mother humming as she prepared breakfast was a fear Renira couldn't face.

"Lusa." Armstar's voice broke the moment, and Mother stared past Renira, jaw clenched and a fierce look on her face.

"Give us a bloody moment, Star."

Be strong. It's time to be strong. It will only be a couple of weeks, and it will be exciting. She could do this. She *could* do this. Renira drew in a deep, steadying breath and turned to go. One of them had to make the first move, but Mother pulled her back into a tight embrace, clutching at her with desperation. When finally they separated, the tears were gone from her mother's eyes, replaced by a firm determination.

"Here," Mother said. She reached behind her neck and fumbled at the clasp there, then drew her amulet from around her neck. It was a crescent-shaped symbol of the Bone Moon and made of solid metal, no longer than a thumb length, and every bit of its surface was inscribed with runes Renira had never been able to understand.

Renira shook her head. "That's your icon of faith."

Mother smiled and reached up behind Renira's head, fixing the clasp and then tucking the amulet down under Renira's shirt. "And yours too."

Renira clutched at the amulet through her layers of clothing and nodded. Her mother scooped up her old waterproof hat, a flat topped, wide-brimmed thing made of the same leather as the coat. She placed it on Renira's head and smiled. "You look just like I did so long ago." The backpack was heavy, and Mother held it up while Renira slotted her arms through the straps. When she let go, Renira stumbled under the weight of it.

Renira chewed her lip. "I..."

"Listen to Armstar," her mother said. "Do as he says, but don't forget that you know the forest better than he does."

Renira nodded mutely as thunder crashed around them. She wanted to say something. Needed to say something. "Igor sometimes hides rats in the rainwater bucket." It was the only thing that came to mind. *Stupid.* Her mother knew how to do her chores better than Renira did.

"Lusa. Now." Armstar's voice held a note of iron in it now.

Mother ignored the angel. "Eat sparingly. There's enough in there for at least a week, but you'll need more. Travel by day, if you can. The dark is always more dangerous. Follow your heart, Ren. Do what's right." She held up a hand and extended her little finger. "Courage and hope."

Renira raised her own hand, wrapped her little finger around her mother's like they had done so many times before. "Courage and hope." Renira found herself trembling. She didn't want to say goodbye, wasn't sure how to say it. "I love you."

Her mother lurched forwards and held her daughter in an awkward embrace once more. "I love you too, Ren." When they pulled apart, Renira noticed her mother was chewing her lip.

"It's time to go, Renira," Armstar said, stepping out in the deluge beyond the doorway. He took a few steps and disappeared into the darkness and rain.

Renira backed towards the doorway, each step seeming harder to take, her legs more tired. Each step seeming more final than the last. There were no more words. At least none that could make a difference. Mother just nodded, one hand on the table in the hall to steady her. Renira nodded back, clutched at the amulet nestled against her breast, and turned away from her mother and her home. She stepped out into the pouring rain and the darkness of the storm and found the cloaked, hooded angel waiting for her.

CHAPTER 6

The First Age is a lie. There were no monsters but those we made of ourselves. We were free. Until the angels came.

— ERTIDE HOSTAIN ON THE FIRST AGE. YEAR 212 OF THE FOURTH AGE, 167 YEARS AFTER HEAVEN FELL

Driving rain painted the world in indistinct lines of grey, lit by flashes of dazzling lightning. The thunder shook the ground with such might that they had been forced to leave the horses behind and make the journey to the village of Ner on foot. It made the going tough, especially in such oppressive darkness, but Emrik persevered. Even in his weighty waterproof coat he found he was soaked, and his boots sank into the mud almost up to his ankle. It wouldn't stop him. Couldn't stop him. He powered through it, each step tougher than the last, as though the world itself was resisting his progress. Emrik was used to such resistance, he expected it. Let it fight him. He would break the world to his will.

Borik did not fare so well. Too much of his mother in him. Emrik had loved Quel, for a time, but she was a weak woman. Beautiful, smart, passionate, with a head for arguments like few Emrik had ever known. She could twist his words into knots so he would find himself arguing her point instead of his own. Such fire in her, at least at the start. But she had drowned that fire in drink and smoke and a hundred other pleasures of the flesh and even had the gall to blame Emrik for it, accusing him of smothering her then abandoning her. In the end, she was one more gravestone who did not understand the responsibility he carried. At least she had given him a son before she wasted away, even if the boy did take after her.

Borik was rangy, with plenty of stamina but little in the way of raw strength. The sucking mud drained that strength with every step, and it was only Borik's breathless exertion stopping him from complaining. Emrik knew his son; the man did not suffer indignity well.

Perel's Dogs fared even worse. They did not have a drop of divine power in them. Thugs and soldiers too outlandish to follow normal military structure. Their worth lay not in strength of arms or purpose, but in savagery and devotion to their mistress. Some trailed behind, foolishly attempting to wade through the mud rather than walk it, others overexerted themselves by trying to keep pace with Emrik. Likely they would collapse before they reached their destination. They would be left behind. Emrik would never slow his pace for the frailty of others.

Perel walked along the surface of the ankle-high mud as though it were as solid as stone. The power of the angel Ooliver pumped through her veins, one of many, and no mud or water or snow would slow her progress. Perel wore no waterproof clothing, and the rain had long since soaked her through, but if she felt the weight or cold, she did not show it. A true hunter, a warrior, a powerhouse of a woman. Emrik had nothing but the deepest respect for his daughter, but he knew her limitations better than she did. Perel was not suited to rule. She would never sit in council or negotiate. Diplomacy might as well be a foreign word. After all, there was a reason her Dogs followed Perel with a fanatical zeal.

Through the pouring rain, Emrik saw Perel stop up ahead. Hair plastered to her skull and wind whipping at her gambeson, she turned to Emrik. Her eyes were the eyes of her wolf, a dirty yellow with an odd glow and tiny pupils. Emrik envied her that. His hawk could not fly in such weather, and he felt stranded without that second sight from up high, guiding him whenever he needed it. Perel blinked, and her wolf's eyes were gone, replaced with her own dark blues. She grinned, wide and feral.

"Buildings just ahead," she shouted over the din of the storm and the water pouring down her face.

Emrik nodded once and continued, not slowing his pace through the mud for even a moment. He trusted Perel to guide them to their quarry. All he need do was follow his daughter. When it came to the hunt, all he ever needed to do was follow Perel.

There was no sign that they were entering the village of Ner. One moment they were slogging through mud, the rain making a mockery of the landscape ahead of them. Then a flash of lightning showed the squat forms of buildings, details hidden by the darkness and downpour. The ground underfoot became firmer, crushed stone beneath the mud making the going a little easier.

Perel came loping back across the surface of the mud. She had to wait for thunder to rumble itself to exhaustion, and even then she had to shout over the driving rain. "The magistrate said it would be an old farmhouse and barn?"

Emrik nodded, still leaning into the wind and forcing out every step, ignoring the rain pelting him in the face.

"Tesh has found it. This way." Perel turned into the wind once more and moved away faster than Emrik could manage. He glanced back once to see Borik close behind. His son's hands were in his coat pockets, and he had the water-proofed leather pulled tight around him as he struggled against the wind and mud. He looked miserable. Miserable but determined. Behind Borik, the lumbering shapes of Perel's Dogs laboured along. Emrik quickened his pace.

The wolf waited by a dilapidated fence that had probably once been there to stop cattle roaming. It stood with teeth bared, eyes fixed on the farmhouse ahead. Wood and stone, a solid construction built to stand the test of blazing summers, bitter winters, and vicious storms. The windows were shuttered tight against the howling wind, but light showed from within one room on the ground floor. A flash of lightning lit the building in silhouette.

The barn door had been left unlatched and was banging in the wind, providing an irritating beat. Emrik caught up to Perel and her wolf and drew himself up to his full height, standing tall against the buffeting storm. The wind and rain broke around him. There he waited for the Dogs to catch up. No matter the angel, it was wise to throw expendable lives against them first.

Borik reached them, huddling small and miserable. "That banging is irritating," he shouted.

"Leave it," Emrik's reply came moments before a flash of lightning, and he waited out the thunder. "If it stops now, the angel will know we're out here. We cannot allow him a chance to escape."

The Dogs arrived slowly, wading through sucking mud. Even the toughest of the thugs looked miserable drenched by rain and exhausted from fighting the storm. They perked up upon seeing their mistress though. Just the sight of Perel made them stand straighter, put new energy into tired limbs. Emrik ground his teeth at the delay, eyes fixed on the farmhouse ahead, rain slapping at his face.

Most of the Dogs made it, though one could barely stand, and another was lost
to the storm. Perhaps they would find the man once it cleared, sodden and lost.
Perhaps not. It didn't matter. They had enough to draw out the angel within.

"What if he's not here?" Borik shouted. He was close enough that he was
using his father as a wind break. Emrik didn't bother to answer the question. If
the divinity was not here, they would continue to track him, hunt him down no
matter how far he ran, no matter where he tried to hide. Emrik would find the
Herald of the Fifth Age and kill him long before he could fulfil his purpose.

Emrik spat rainwater from between his lips. "Send them in."

Perel was leaning against her halberd. Her smile was bright even in the
gloom. She let out a sharp whistle, calling her Dogs to heel, and barked out
quick orders. Thugs and criminals they might be, but the Dogs knew their work
well. They spread out, circling the farmhouse, surrounding it. They were
nothing but dark stains against a darker backdrop, edging closer to the house
with knives and ill attitude drawn and ready.

Emrik moved closer, feet crunching against the crushed stone of the
pathway leading up to the house. He did not like the idea of facing an angel,
even one of the Third Age, without armour, but it would have been dangerous
to wear in such a storm. His right hand found the Godslayer sword at his waist,
wrapped around the leather-bound hilt that fit his hand as snugly as an old
glove. The Forgemistress had only made seven Godslayer arms, and they carried
three of them to their business tonight. Borik, too, wielded a Godslayer sword,
and Perel's halberd was similarly blessed. There was nothing to fear. Even the
Archangel himself would fall before their combined might.

The Dogs were in position, twelve men and women surrounding the farmhouse, ready to move at their mistress' command. Another flash of lightning
revealed their dark forms hiding by windows, crouched in front of the door.
Quiet work. Brutal work. Dirty work. This was what the Dogs were about. The
thunder struck, a deafening cacophony that echoed around the field and
rebounded off the mountain. Over the top of that din, Perel unleashed a sharp
whistle. The command to attack. As one, the Dogs pounced. Doors were
thrown open, shutters ripped from their windows, and bodies leapt through
into the farmhouse. As the rumble of thunder died down, Emrik heard shouts
as the Dogs barked at each other. A scream tore through the night; a woman's
voice shrill with terror.

Emrik's grip tightened on the hilt of the Godslayer sword, and he waited for
the angel to show itself. Hooded storm lanterns flickered to light inside and
travelled from window to window as the house was searched by the Dogs. One
of the thugs dragged a woman out of the front door. She was of middling years,

plump and short and wearing a loose night shift. The scream was hers, the fear plain on her face. Perel's Dog pulled her from the house into the storm and pushed her down in front of Emrik. She sprawled in the mud, crying out in pain as her knees and hands hit the crushed rock of the pathway. She was crying strangled sobs of terror.

"Bitch were in the kitchen," the Dog shouted.

"Why?" Borik asked.

The Dog shrugged. "Drinkin' tea, by the looks of it."

Borik shook his head. "Why did you bring her out? We could be doing this inside. A cup of tea sounds positively wonderful. Don't you think, Father?"

In the dim light spilling from the farmhouse, the woman clutched muddied and bloodied hands to her chest, staining her sodden shift red and brown. She was still sobbing but tried to rise to her feet. The Dog put a rough hand to her shoulder and forced the woman back to her knees. She cried out in pain again. The other Dogs were still searching the house, the noise of their ransacking loud and damning in its destruction.

"Mercy, lord," the woman said in a pitiful voice. "Have mercy."

"You are Lusa Washer?" Emrik shouted.

The woman was shivering from the cold, kneeling on the crushed stone and clutching bleeding hands to her chest. She nodded once.

"It looks mostly dry inside," Borik said. "Perhaps even warm by the fire."

"Hush," Emrik said.

"Father..."

"I said quiet, Borik."

Perel chuckled. "You could always go hide in the barn, brother. Maybe find a nice hay bale to have a nap on."

"Both of you. Enough." Emrik usually tolerated his children's playful bickering, but there was too much at stake.

"Where is the angel, washer woman?" Emrik shouted, taking a step toward her.

She shook her head wildly. "There are no angels, Your Majesty. You killed them all, everyone says so."

"You know who I am then?" A flash of lightning lit up the trembling woman, and the thunder stole her reply. "Say again!" Emrik roared once the thunder had died down.

"Everyone knows who you are, Your Majesty. The town held a parade in your honour." Her eyes were locked on the ground between them, and she was cringing like a dog expecting a beating. Yet there was something in her voice, a note of defiance maybe. Emrik cursed the weather. It might have covered their approach, but it also slowed them, and none of his Truth Seekers had been able to make the trip. They were fragile people, a curse of the painful process of their creation, and none could stand the noise of the thunder or the violence of the storm.

Borik stepped close enough to be heard over the storm without shouting. "The informant was a friend of the daughter, Father. Perel's Dogs do not appear to be finding any daughter in the house, unless she is superbly hidden."

Emrik waited out another peal of thunder. "Where is your daughter?"

The washer woman paused before answering, not long but a hesitation all the same. It gave away the lie before it dripped from her lips. "In the town, Your Majesty. She went to the parade, to see you. She didn't come back. Caught in the storm, I think. She has friends who will give her a roof for the night."

Perel cackled. "Fewer friends than she thinks." The woman did not startle at Perel's words but remained silent, huddling there on the stone.

"You are accused of sedition and heresy," Emrik shouted.

The woman shook her head violently at the words. "Accused by who?"

"Does it matter?"

"We're innocent, Your Majesty," the woman screamed, eyes still on the ground. "Mercy, please. The Heretic God is dead. You killed him. All his angels, too. You killed them all, Your Majesty. Everyone knows. Everyone says it."

Again Borik leaned in close. "She's right, Father. We have no proof. And she certainly sounds innocent." His merciful streak was another failing Emrik blamed on his mother's blood.

"Are you a Truth Seeker now, son?" A flash of lightning and Borik looked away, unable to hold his father's gaze. "Can you tell a lie just by the sound of it?"

Borik stepped back and shook his head.

One of the Dogs stepped up to the doorway of the farmhouse, something clutched to his chest. He looked up at the rain pouring down and then set his shoulders and ran towards his mistress. Perel took the item from him and inspected it. It appeared to be a book, large and with a hard leather back. Its spine was bent and scored from use, and the leather had the wear of many years and many travels. The pages were starting to yellow, and the rain and wind quickly set to ruining them. Perel glanced through a few pages, then snapped the book shut and threw it at the woman. The book caught the wind and hit the ground before her, sliding to a halt in the mud. The woman glanced at it, and a pained expression crossed her face.

"The Divine Lie," Perel shouted.

A heretical text, though its written title was *The Divine Truth*. It detailed the first three Ages, the Redemption, the Age of Wisdom, and the Golden Age.

It was seditious trash, a waste of good paper, designed to teach people to worship a lying God and shackle them to that falsity and bind themselves by the arbitrary rules contained within. Faith was a disease, and books like *The Divine Truth* were how it spread.

"Tell me again how you are innocent, washer woman," Emrik roared. The raging wind flipped open the leather cover of the book, and the pages started fluttering in the gale, the rain soaking into the vellum. No matter how many copies of that bloody book Emrik destroyed, there always seemed to be more. One more seditious construct of lies he swore he would purge from the world.

A change settled over the woman. She still trembled from the icy rain and clutched her hands tight to her chest, but finally she looked up and met Emrik's stare across the gloom. There was defiance in her eyes. The righteous indignation of the misled, of the foolish who believed the charismatic dogma pressed upon them. How many such sheep had Emrik seen before? How many had died at his sword or because of the laws set by his pen? Could he really blame them? A question he had asked himself many times. Not least of all because he had been in their position once. He had once believed. Worshipped. Been fooled. No more. Never again.

"I am innocent, Godless King. A pity you cannot say the same." The woman's voice rang loud over the storm, all traces of the trembling subservience gone and replaced by her zeal. A flash of lightning ripped through the air, striking the ground nearby. Thunder boomed across the sky, shaking the farmhouse and the very ground beneath them. "He loved you, Godless King."

"Quiet!" Emrik roared.

"The God loves you still! More's the pity," the woman spat.

Emrik squatted down before her, his long coat trailing in the muck. The Dog behind the woman tightened his grip on her shoulders, and she winced at the pain. Emrik stared into her mad eyes. "Your God is dead. I was there. He is beyond love."

The woman nodded. "Dead. Yes. Killed and consumed by you and your bloody family." She met his eyes again, and the smile that spread across her face had no joy in it. "But for how long? The Fifth Age is coming, Godless King. He will be reborn, and you will pay for all your sins! He loves you still, but that love will not protect you. It will not stay his judgement."

Emrik stood suddenly. The weight of realisation settled upon him. This woman. This heretic had not intended to give anything away, but she had assumed Emrik knew more than he did, and in her vicious attempt to wound him, she had given him something new. "So, the God is still dead," Emrik said, pleased. "That is the purpose of the Herald. The purpose of the Fifth Age. To give the God rebirth."

The heretic glared savagery up at Emrik as her mistake dawned upon her. "What do you believe will happen, heretic? The God will be reborn and usher in a new age of peace? A second Golden Age? Do you believe in his lies so ardently that you cannot see the truth when it is upon you? We were slaves. I freed us. All of us. And you would welcome the chains around your neck once more?"

She had nothing to say to that. They never did. In the face of reason, of truth, zealots clung to their faith like a shield. It would not protect them nor her. Not against Emrik. Whatever she believed was irrelevant. Emrik would stop the Herald. He would not allow a Fifth Age to resurrect what he had fought so hard to bury. He would not allow humanity to be enslaved ever again.

"Where is the angel?" Emrik roared, his voice rising above the rumbling thunder echoing in the distance. The heretic said nothing, her jaw clamping shut, staring hatred at Emrik despite the rain pouring down her face. "Tell me, or I will find your daughter and her end will not be swift."

A brief spasm of pain and fear passed across the woman's face, gone in an instant, replaced by that same righteous determination. "Blessed be the reborn."

Emrik growled in frustration. Zealots and fanatics, there was only one way to deal with them. He turned to his children. "Pull back your Dogs."

Perel whistled sharply twice.

"We could try to find the girl," Borik suggested. "Her friend will no doubt help given sufficient... encouragement."

Emrik shook his head. It would take too long. A fruitless endeavour. The girl had obviously been sent away and would likely know nothing. The heretic might break if sufficient pressure were applied, but by then it would be too late. And he had never liked torture; it was the tool of a weak and unjust cause, using pain to convert rather than reason. No, they were losing precious time, and every moment they waited here doing nothing, the divinity pulled further away. He had been here, Emrik was certain of it, and recently. They were maybe only hours behind, but with no clue to the direction. Damn, if only the storm would break. He needed his hawk, his eyes in the sky.

Emrik turned to Perel, his gaze so fierce she looked shocked. "Find me some tracks."

"In this?" Lightning flashed again as if to emphasise Perel's point. "We're better waiting until morning, Father. With just a little light, my Dogs will find them, storm or not."

"Now, Perel. Call in her pack. As many as you need. Find me a trail to follow!"

Perel wiped a hand over her forehead, pressing back the sodden hair that was flailing in her face. Then she nodded and turned to Tesh. Some sort of communication passed between woman and wolf, something no one else was privy to. Another power claimed from an angel, though Emrik could not remember which. So many of their names were lost now. Not enough. It would never be enough until none remembered their existence. Tesh threw her head back and howled into the storm, then sprang past them all and away into the darkness.

Perel turned to her father with a grave look and nodded. "They'll all come. We'll find you those tracks, Father." She lowered her gaze. "No matter the cost." There was something Emrik was missing there. He placed a hand on his daughter's shoulder, and she took a moment's comfort from it.

Emrik turned to the heretic. She stared at him in open defiance, her sedition plain for all to see. It could not be allowed. Emrik raised his right hand to the storm, and a bolt of yellow lightning ripped free of the clouds and struck him. It formed into a sizzling spear of yellow, crackling energy clasped firmly in his grip. Where the rain touched the spear, it evaporated into hissing steam.

The heretic's eyes went wide, and she tried to surge back to her feet only to be pushed back down once more. "Mathanial!" she cried.

Emrik held the sizzling spear. Its form was in flux, energy struggling to free itself from the shape it had been forced into. "The Rider is dead," Emrik shouted. "His power is mine. One by one your champions fall. And yet still you cling to your baseless belief that they are superior."

The heretic shook her head wildly. "You're a monster!" she screamed. The fight went out of her then. Her shoulders sagged, and she buried her head in bloodied hands.

"No. You worship monsters, heretic. *I* slay them!" Emrik raised his spear and launched it at the farmhouse. The wall exploded inward and fires ignited immediately, flames quickly rising to consume. The heretic was still sobbing into her hands even as her home started to burn.

Borik was the first to broach the question. "What do we do with her?"

Emrik had no compassion for those who spread sedition. "What do we do with all heretics?"

By the time the storm broke and the first rays of a crimson morning pierced through the clouds, the farmhouse was a charred shell. Rain and fire had fought each other to a stalemate, but the flames had claimed the greater victory. The heretic woman hung from the crossbeam of the barn door. Her face purple and lifeless, her toes just a hand width from the floor. It was a sign of how close all practitioners of sedition were to redemption. After all, humanity could be saved. All it had to do was forsake its faith in the God once and for all.

A wolf returned even as the smoke was still drifting up out of the farmhouse. It was not Tesh. It limped, unwilling to put any weight on one of its front paws. Perel ran to the wolf immediately and placed her arms around it. The beast mewled and collapsed over sideways into the mud, panting, its tongue lolling. There were tears in Perel's eyes as she spoke to the wolf. The beast was injured, perhaps even dying, and still it had gone out into the storm to help search.

"We found the trail," Perel said with a sniff. "They fled north to the forest."

Emrik ground his teeth. "They?"

Perel nodded. "The angel was not alone."

CHAPTER 7

The forest is a bountiful trove for those who know how to reap it. Barkbane flowers only grow in the wounds of trees that have been scratched by wild animals. When ground into a paste, the petals can be a powerful stimulant. A little can bring a person to full consciousness and keep them that way for hours. A lot can tax a man's heart until it ruptures within their chest. Both are useful applications.

— OF STEM AND PETAL BY LUCI YOLK

They had made it to the forest, though the going had been far from easy. The rain made everything a soggy chore, and the wind buffeted them again and again. More than once, Renira found herself knocked to her knees and struggling to get back up. Each time, Armstar was there, wrenching her back to her feet with divine strength. She was grateful for the assistance, though he could certainly have been gentler about it. The mud was another issue and made the walk to the Whistle Wood take far longer than it should. It was ankle deep sludge that sucked at Renira's boots and then refused to let her pull free. Every step was an act of perseverance and raw strength she was certain she didn't actually possess. No words were spoken, and none were needed. Renira knew she should be ruminating on the decision she had just made, the act of leaving home so suddenly in the company of an angel. Now she thought about it, it seemed like madness. *What was I thinking?* The angel had told her to be brave and, in that moment, the prospect had seemed like her chance for adventure. Now she was committed, her word given. She could not go back. Renira trudged on with silent determination.

It was a blessed relief when they finally reached the tree line. The forest seemed to spring up out of nowhere, a dark smudge on the horizon resolving into fat trunks and branches bristling with emerald needles. On the western side, the forest was sheltered from most of the icy wind coming off the mountains, and the trees there were different, but they had obviously veered east a little, and here they would find needles and little else. At least for now. Yonal Wood said the trees changed the deeper into the forest you went, growing closer together and taller, crowding out the sun and giving a home to creatures far more dangerous than the bears most people claimed lived in the deep woods. Renira had always taken it as idle fancy, stories told to scare her and fuel her imagination. But everyone said the deep forest was dangerous. Bertha Trout, who lived closest, claimed she heard strange noises at night sometimes, though Bertha Trout also claimed rocks spoke to her.

Renira tried her best to find her bearings, but with the darkness so thick and the storm still lashing them, there was little she could do. As long as they kept pushing forwards, they should move roughly north, and with just a bit of light she could hopefully find the woodcutter's marks. They were spread out through the forest with bearings and warnings both.

Renira looked back towards Ner-on-the-River. Towards home and her mother. She couldn't see anything, of course, not in the tumult of the storm. Even when the lightning flashed, she could not see past the pouring rain. Still, she imagined her mother sitting alone in their house, a cup of steaming tea in hand, staring north and bidding them a safe journey. That thought comforted her. That she had a home to go back to. Renira stared south, hands in pockets and huddled against the cold, and hoped her mother would be well in her absence. It would be some time before they saw each other again. Mother would have to fetch the firewood herself, clean the barn of dead mice. What would Igor the Voracious do without Renira around? The thought of the black rat-slaying monster choked Renira, and she fought back the tears.

Armstar laid a hand on her shoulder, his mouth a thin line and his eyes impatient. "Be strong," he said. "Your exhaustion is a fleeting thing. Push on."

The weight of exhaustion lifted like a smothering blanket thrown off and Renira found the strength to press on. They struck out into the woods, picking their way between trees in what meagre light was left to them.

Under the canopy, the storm did not seem so bad. Rain still poured down, the water dripping down in much fatter droplets. Wind gusted through the forest, stirring up branches and occasionally bombarding them with loose needles. Renira barely noticed the lightning anymore, but the thunder still shook them with its booming shouts. She settled into a dogged march, one foot in front of the other over and over again. No thoughts penetrated the fuzzy cloud that settled in her mind. There was nothing except the dragging beat of her footsteps upon the soggy needles underneath.

It came as a complete surprise when Renira found herself on her knees. She collapsed sideways, falling upon the forest floor, and found Armstar looking back in annoyance. His skin was pale, almost waxen, and his ruined wings twitched as rain washed over the blackened bones. Renira opened her mouth to say something, but the words never came, and everything went dark.

Renira woke to tired eyes, a fuzzy head, and an aching stomach. When she moved, she decided that stiff limbs needed adding to that list. She found herself propped up against a tree trunk, her pack on the ground beside her and her hat pulled down a little over her head, so the rain ran off it. Armstar was nearby, kneeling in a clear patch of the forest, his back straight and eyes closed.

An odd anxiety reached up from within. Renira really had left home with this angel. She'd said goodbye to her mother and struck out in the middle of a raging storm. It seemed like madness now she thought about it more clearly. Only a fool would have left in such a hurry. Although, now she thought about it, her mother had laid out Renira's winter clothes. *Did she want me to go? Why would she send me away with someone I don't even know? An angel I've never met. And who is my mother that she claims friendship with angels?* The torrent of thoughts only made the anxiety worse, and Renira found she could no longer take the silence.

"Are you asleep?" Renira said around a mouth that tasted of day-old egg. She could barely even remember their flight from home last night. Everything was a blur of rain and gloom and exhaustion. There was light now though, crimson morning light streaming in through slight gaps in the canopy. The rain had stopped as well, the storm having passed in the night.

The angel sighed and turned to Renira. In the light of a crisp morning, he looked more frail than he had in the dark. His face was handsome but gaunt, and his skin had a yellowish tint. His hair was dark, but there were streaks of lifeless grey running through it. Renira had always pictured angels as towering pillars of strength in its most perfect form with shining wings of white feathers. Those were the stories her mother used to tell from *Rook's Compendium*. Stories of great deeds and battles against demons, of adventures and daring escapades. Her prior relationship with Armstar now put all those stories in a different light, and Renira had to wonder if they were all true. Had her mother been a party to all of them? The Battle of Red Keep. The Last Stand of the Faithful at Mournhold. The Flight of the Chosen.

Mother can't have been there. They all took place so long ago. But she did know this angel, said they were old friends.

"No. I wasn't sleeping. That was meditation. A quieting of the mind and extension of the senses."

"Oh," Renira said and yawned. "It looked a lot like sleeping."

Armstar ground his jaw and then stood with some effort. He looked like a young man yet moved like an elder, as though all his joints ached and each step was an effort. "Eat something, girl. Your mother packed food, and we don't have time to waste. We need to leave now."

"I'm fine," Renira lied. She opened the flap of her pack and rummaged around until she found the loaf of bread and something wrapped in oilskin. A quick sniff told her it was bacon cooked to a crisp just the way she liked it. She drew out a couple of rashers and broke off a handful of bread. "That storm was crazy. How long were we walking last night?"

"Hours. Most of the night." Armstar cocked his head as though listening for something far away.

Renira bit into the bread and chewed. It was an excellent loaf with seeds mixed into the flour to give it extra texture. The thought struck her suddenly; this was the last loaf of Tobe Baker's that she would eat for some time. Once it was gone, it was gone. Renira chewed a little slower, savouring the taste. Many things were behind her now, for a while at least. How long before she'd next hear her mother's voice or smell freshly laundered clothing? The subtle affection of Igor as he wound his way through her legs while she tried to sweep up the messes he left, and the scratches he left in her hands if she ever tried to stroke him. The bickering of her friends. Aesie's sharp wit and Elsa's boundless enthusiasm. The kindness of the Wood family, helping with extra firewood and food despite their ever-increasing brood of squabbling children. Renira would miss them all. She wondered if they would miss her. Perhaps they would wonder where she had gone, that dreamy Washer girl who was always too busy staring at the horizon to settle down and help her mother properly.

"Time to go. Get up," Armstar said.

Renira shook herself out of her reverie and wiped her eyes. She took a sip from her water skin and then a bite of bread and another of bacon. The tastes mixed well in her mouth. "Don't you need to eat?" she asked around the mouthful.

Armstar sent an impatient glance her way. "Not often, but yes." His wings twitched and he winced. "Are you done dawdling?"

Renira found getting up a struggle. It had been a cold night, and her limbs had stiffened. But she didn't want the angel to see that. He would see her as strong and capable, not some distracted dreamer who was a burden to her mother. This was her first adventure, and she had to appear ready for it. Maybe not a warrior, she had no weapon and wouldn't know how to use it if she did. An explorer, then. Intrepid and brave and setting out to discover unknown lands and buried treasures. Renira took another bite of bread and finished off the rasher of bacon and then stared up at the sky for a few moments while she chewed. She wracked her brain, desperately trying to remember Yonal Wood's lessons about forest navigation. Things would be easier if she could find a marker, but until then...

"Renira?" Armstar's voice was sharp as broken glass.

The air was so still now the storm had passed. People liked to talk about the calm before the storm, but often the calm after the storm was more pronounced. One of Yonal's lessons came rushing back to her. She had only been six winters old, and had taken to following Yonal into the forest. His eldest child was still too young at the time, barely a single winter and still attached to her mother. Renira had never known her own father, and Yonal was so kind and strong. He had wisdom to spare when it came to the forest, had known it better than he knew his own house. No doubt he thought it funny to have a silly little girl following him about, but he had shared some of his wisdom, and Renira had listened.

What was it he said? In her head, her voice took on a terrible, overly deep tone that was barely reminiscent of Yonal Wood's voice. *After the rains, look to the sky. You won't see the sun, but find the way the light reflects off the raindrops held in the canopy. If you find them to the east, the sun is to the west. To the north, and the sun is to the south. That one is most important. If ever you find yourself lost in the forest, head south. South is the way out.*

"Renira!" Armstar's voice was urgent.

"Shh! I'm thinking. When did the sun rise?" Renira asked.

"No more than an hour ago. I know you must be tired but..."

"This way." Renira shoved the last of the bread in her mouth, struggled her pack onto her back, and set off with the sun shining on the droplets to her left.

They were heading as north as she could manage, and she was leading just like an intrepid explorer should.

Armstar followed and even strode ahead. Despite his frail appearance and the obvious pain from his wings, he was taller than Renira and had much longer legs. Not to mention the divine strength of an angel. He set a hard pace, and Renira struggled to keep up, quickly finding herself warm despite the chill in the air. Mother had been right about winter; it was setting in fast. The stillness of the air following the storm didn't help, and Renira found her breath misting in front of her as she laboured onward. Her pack soon became an oppressive thing, determined to drag her down. The band of her hat grew soaked with sweat, but she resisted taking it off. Fat drops of water still fell from above and needles with them.

Renira's thoughts turned inward again to everything and everyone she was leaving behind. Her hand went to her chest, gripping the crescent Bone Moon amulet hidden beneath her layers as she thought of her mother. It was foolish, she was out on an adventure with an angel—maybe not the type of angel she expected, but an angel nonetheless. It was everything she had ever dreamed of, and yet her thoughts kept returning home.

"How do you know my mother?" Renira asked between breaths, desperate to stop her mind dwelling on everything she was leaving behind. *I'm on an adventure. Time to look forward, not back.*

Armstar glanced over his shoulder at her, and the movement shifted his wings so one clipped a nearby tree. He cried out in pain and staggered.

Renira winced. "Sorry. Do they hurt? Your wings, I mean."

"More than you will ever know." Armstar straightened up with a groan. There was a sheen of sweat on his forehead, and Renira found it strange to think that an angel would sweat. "The king is close," Armstar said. "We should hurry."

Renira followed quickly, catching up to the angel so she was walking alongside him. Her hand clutched at the amulet. "So how do you know my mother?"

Armstar let out a pained chuckle. "I met her on a battlefield. She was probably no older than you are now. The Battle of Lost Hope is what the historians call it. Human historians, those sanctioned by the Godless King. We call it something quite different."

That answer begged even more questions, chief among them what her mother might have been doing on a battlefield. Could it have been possible her mother was a warrior, wielding a sword or spear in the name of God? It was said when the Godless Kings rallied their Crusade against heaven, there were humans who sided with the angels instead. But that was a thousand years ago, and her mother was no more than forty winters at best. But Armstar had said she was at the Battle of Lost Hope, and Renira remembered that name, though nothing else about it. *Aesie would know. She always paid attention in history class.*

"What was the battle about?" Renira asked. "Why was my mother there? Was she a warrior? Did you fight together? Why didn't she tell me?"

Armstar shot Renira another baleful glare. His posture sagged, and he reached out, bracing himself against a nearby tree and hissing in pain. He was limping, Renira noticed, favouring his right leg heavily.

"She didn't fight," Armstar said. "Your mother hated fighting. She just wanted to help people." The angel shook his head and sighed. Renira opened her mouth to ask more, but Armstar pointed a long, delicate finger. "What is that mark?"

The angel was pointing to a tree whose bark appeared to have been scraped in a particular way. Three symbols: one was a straight line pointing vertically, easily mistaken for a natural scar in the tree. One was a triangle with the points missing. And the third was three diagonal lines with a fourth bisecting them.

"Finally! They're woodsman's marks," Renira said. She rushed over to the tree and knelt in front of it, digging at the earth below with both hands. She scraped needles and dirt and insects away, heedless of the grime getting under her nails.

"What are you doing?" Armstar asked.

"The first mark is a heading for north. If we stand by the tree and look along the line, we should see another tree with a similar mark, that will give us an accurate bearing for north. The second means there is a cache of supplies buried here." She kept digging until her fingers scraped against something metal. It took Renira a few minutes to excavate, but eventually she pulled a small metal tin from the ground—about the length of her forearm and half again as wide. The lid was rusted shut, and no amount of pulling would free it.

Armstar knelt and wrenched the lid open. "Divine strength," he offered by way of explanation.

Renira frowned at that. "Must be nice. I thought you said you were a builder not a warrior."

"Strength of arm is useful for more than just swinging a sword," Armstar said, turning away. "And I'm *The* Builder. Not a builder. The distinction is important."

"To who?" Renira asked. He glared at her, and she looked away quickly. "Sorry."

Renira rummaged through the box. It was mostly food, dried meats and desiccated fruits, wrapped in oiled parchment to make them last as long as possible. This was an old cache, and much of the food had gone to rot despite the steps to preserve it, but a few of the strips of meat were still edible. Renira discarded the rotting foods and took the old meat, replacing them with a couple of her newer fare. There were eight flamers, little sticks that would burst into brief but hot fire when snapped in two. Useful for starting campfires, but little else. Renira took six of those and returned two. She had nothing to give in return.

"Why not take everything?" Armstar asked when he noticed Renira putting things back.

"What if someone else comes this way in need?" Renira said. "These caches don't stock themselves. They're here in case of emergency. The rules are simple. If you take, give back what you can."

The angel shook his head at that while Renira went through the rest of the box's contents. There was not much more they would find useful, and Renira added to the trove a spare pair of gloves her mother had packed. She replaced the box and piled dirt upon it, burying it back where she had found it.

"What does the third mark mean?" Armstar asked once Renira had finished replacing the box. He was studying the tree intently. Three diagonal lines and fourth bisecting them.

Renira frowned. "I don't know. It's a warning, but Yonal never taught me what those mean. He just said if I ever saw one, I should bloody well run."

They spent no more time puzzling over the meaning of that third mark, and neither did they heed it. Renira found the second bearing marker, and they set off on a new heading. True north, deeper into the forest.

CHAPTER 8

Honours only value is in keeping weak men in line by making them believe themselves strong.

— ERTIDE HOSTAIN

The storm passed in the early hours of the morning, and it took the rain with it. In its wake came stillness and clear red skies the colour of apples. There was no one else left who remembered the sky the way it used to be, only Emrik and his brother, Arandon. They alone remembered the endless blue. Everyone else was born and raised under a sky the colour of the blood that drained from the God's corpse.

Emrik still remembered when they had returned to the capital city of Celesgarde a thousand years ago, leaving the Heavens a smoking ruin. He'd looked to his grandfather, Ertide, for an explanation why the sky had changed colour, but the old man had none. He didn't even seem to notice. Now Emrik wondered if the sky would change again if the God was reborn. Then he caught himself in his reverie and chased it away with a growl. The God would *not* be reborn. Emrik would die before he allowed the Herald to succeed. He'd tear down all the kingdoms of men, everything he had built, before letting God take control again.

A bitter cold had seeped into the world with the passing of the storm, and it turned their breath to frost. The ground was already starting to freeze, water-logged earth creating puddles of ice everywhere. The forest loomed up in front of them to the north and stretched as far as the eye could see both to the east and west. Emrik blinked into his hawk's sight and saw the world from up high, soaring through the sky. The forest was mammoth even with such a vantage, an endless blanket of greens and browns and everything in between. What secrets took shelter beneath the dense canopy? Despite his attempts to stamp them out, monsters still lived in the world. Many of them had escaped the sacking of Heaven, others had simply been let loose when the God was slain. They hid now in the dark places, in the deep places, where humanity feared to tread.

Emrik's foot smashed through a layer of ice and sank into a freezing puddle. He stumbled and blinked away his hawk sight, cursing as he pulled a sodden boot from the cold muck. High above, his hawk gave an answering cry. The animal did not like having its vision shackled to Emrik's body for too long. It distressed the bird to be bound to the earth, and Emrik felt that distress far more keenly than he felt any of his own. Animals did not know how to temper their feelings nor overcome them. It was a weakness in beasts. Emrik detested that he had to share in even a portion of that weakness, but he and the hawk were bound to each other by sight and by blood and by the angel's eyes they had eaten. Besides, he could put up with a little of a beast's weakness for the vantage of a bird's sight. Power often came with a compromise.

Borik trailed behind Emrik, his coat pulled close against the cold and his face a picture of distaste. Behind him, stalked Perel's Dogs. Ahead, at the forest edge, Perel waited. She was squatting on her haunches, poking the frozen mud.

"They came this way," Perel said. She stood and walked over to the nearest tree, then trailed a hand over the rough bark. Perel didn't seem to feel the cold. "The angel and a young girl."

"A girl?" Emrik asked, running a hand over his chin and pulling at his beard. "The heretic's daughter?"

Perel didn't answer. She turned to her father, blinked, and her eyes were replaced by the green-yellow gaze of her wolf. There was nothing human in that stare. Perel's body was still hers, but it was the wolf looking out at Emrik.

"There's something wrong with this forest," Perel said. The wolf's eyes flicked from Emrik, to Borik, to the Dogs, and back to Emrik. A knowing gaze, far too intelligent for a beast. "The scents are..."

A howl split the morning peace, drifting out from between the trees and the gloom within. The wolf's eyes started darting about frantically. Perel blinked. Her cold blue eyes returned, and she winced at some private pain.

"The pack won't go in," she said. As if to make her point, five wolves emerged from the forest, slinking out from between trees. They were big beasts with grey fur and sabre-toothed fangs. Kane wolves were renowned for being untrainable, defiant, and savage, but Perel had not only broken the pack to her will, she had bonded to the pack mother. Kane wolves were also known to be fearless, and yet they were racing away from the forest with their tales between their legs, yipping and barking at each other. Only the biggest of the animals, Tesh, remained.

"Oh dear. That's not an encouraging sign," Borik said between blowing air into his cupped hands.

The Dogs began to murmur.

"The pack never runs."

"What could scare a wolf?"

"We should follow them."

Tesh padded up to Perel. Her muzzle was level with Perel's chest. The animal dipped her head and raised it under Perel's free hand. "There is a scent in the forest," Perel said, absently scratching behind the wolf's ear. "Everywhere. It's confusing the pack, and they won't go in there blinded of their senses."

"Their eyes still work," Emrik said, annoyed at the frivolous nature of beasts. "Their ears still work."

"Wolves track by scent, Father." Perel shook her head, as if struggling with her next words. "They're scared of whatever's in there."

"So much for the legendary reputation of Kane wolves," Borik said with a chuckle. "Tell me, sister, do they also jump at shadows?"

Perel rolled her eyes, and the wolf rumbled a low growl. "They also have a reputation for being intelligent, brother. Smart enough to know not to go in there blind. But feel free to prove you're braver than my wolves."

Emrik stopped listening to his children bicker and turned his attention west to where Riverden was a dark smudge on the horizon. His army waited beyond that smudge. Three legions, close to one and a half thousand soldiers. Perhaps closer to one thousand after their recent encounter with the Rider. Any journey through the forest would be slow and a logistical nightmare. But they couldn't be left in Riverden; the town was too small to support so many troops for long, and stationary soldiers caused problems wherever they went.

Emrik found he was picking at his thumbnail as he deliberated. He'd already pierced the skin, and blood was pooling in the nail bed. It was a nasty habit he had picked up centuries ago and couldn't seem to quit.

"Into the forest," Emrik said, interrupting whatever argument the two were spitting at each other. "Both of you."

The wolf glanced into the gloom and growled. Perel just grinned. "I'll find them for you, Father."

"Hah!" Borik said. "I'll wager I find them first."

"And how would you find them, brother? Unless you come across some impressionable young huntsman to seduce into tracking for you."

Borik grinned at that. "I wasn't planning to, but now you mention it, that does sound fun. Besides, you're just jealous I have better luck with the impressionable young men than you do."

Perel hissed out a laugh. "I'll stick to my wolves, thanks."

"Yes, we've all heard that about you."

"You two are my best hunters," Emrik said. He placed a hand on each of his children's shoulders and nodded to them. "I rely upon you both. You can do what no one else can. You find the hidden, track the lost, chase down the hunted. In you runs the blood of kings, the dynasty of saints, and the fires of heroes. Find this angel for me. Hound him through the forest." Both of his children were grinning at his words.

"What about you, Father?" asked Borik. There was an energy in the air now, both Borik and Perel eager to make a hunt of the divinity. Even the wolf felt it; its earlier fear forgotten, it now bared its teeth at the forest and dragged great claws along the frozen dirt.

Emrik ground his teeth together. "I have to return to Riverden. There are orders to give, both there and to your brother in Celesgarde. I'll bring the Second and the Fourth legions north past the western edge of the forest. It will take time, but I will meet you before Hel's Wall."

"We don't have a Carver with us," Perel said. "And I wouldn't trust my Dogs near a drop of divine blood."

Emrik shook his head. "I don't care. I want the Herald dead. If you catch the angel, kill him. Eat what you can, bury the rest." It was a bounty to be given such freedom with the body. A single pint of angel blood could extend their lives a hundred years.

"I reserve the heart," Borik said with a grin.

Perel scoffed. "You can't. Whoever kills the angel gets the heart."

"Oh, sister, you're so slow. That's what I said."

Emrik drew in a deep breath of cold air and let it out slowly. It misted in front of his face, and the moisture clung to his beard. He blinked to his hawk's sight. The bird was over the deep forest, gliding on the warmer currents of air, searching the canopy of trees below. Something moved, something large enough to shake the trees, then it was gone. He blinked back to his normal sight and saw Perel's Dogs slinking into the forest, moving between the trees with determined intent. The wolf had gone ahead of them. The rest of her pack might be too scared, but Perel's sight-bonded beast was no longer entirely mortal like her children. She was a titan among wolves.

"Be careful," Emrik said before Perel and Borik vanished into the trees. "Both of you. There is something in the deep forest."

Perel nodded and for once even Borik did not think to joke about the warning. He knew his father well enough to know that a warning so grave was not given idly.

"Ten feathers," Borik said as he turned back to the forest. "I wager ten angel feathers. I will find the Herald before you." Perel's reply was swallowed up by the trees.

Emrik turned west and started the long walk back to Riverden. His children were strong, he reminded himself. Skilled in tracking and in combat, and each with divine powers lending them strength. Still, he knew all too well that there were monsters in the world that made even angels look weak as a newborn kitten. He hoped he would see his children again. Far too many had already died.

It was midmorning by the time Emrik made it back to Riverden. He set a brutal pace, but he was not slowed by the weakness of others. His clothes were sodden, with rain and sweat both, and his feet ached from the forced march through frozen terrain. He chose to go straight through the city, rather than skirt it. It would save him time, and the sooner he could get back to his camp, the sooner he could contact Celesgarde. Arik needed to know what was happening if he was to defend the capital.

The whispers soon started.

"The king is wandering the streets of Riverden."

"He has no guard."

"Looks like he was out in the storm."

After the foolish parade the day before, half the people in the city recognised him. He did not fear these people. He doubted there would be any attackers within the city limits, but if there were, then let them come.

Magistrate Kul soon arrived on horseback, surrounded by twenty of his house guard. They cleared their way through the rabble and formed up around Emrik as he surged on through the cobbled streets.

"My liege, are you, uh, well?" the magistrate asked in a nasally voice. "I saw you leave the ball last night and..."

"I'm quite well, Magistrate," Emrik growled.

"And the rest of your entourage? You son and daughter?"

There was a horse without a rider in the throng of guards, and the magistrate had yet to offer it. But what good was being king if you couldn't ignore formality and take what you needed? Emrik sped his pace and leapt up onto the saddle of the horse. The beast whinnied and turned, but he quickly brought it under control with a pull on the reins and a stern word. Animals knew their masters well; it was all in the attitude.

"Keep up if you wish," Emrik said. He put his heels to the horse, galloping away down the street with the magistrate and his guard in pursuit.

At the outskirts of his army camp, the men and women of the Second legion greeted their king with the proper respect. The magistrate and his guard were brought to a halt by the threat of sharpened spears, but Emrik bounded from the saddle and forged his way into the centre of the camp on foot. Not far behind, the magistrate laboured to keep up, now he was removed from his horse and his guard. Emrik ignored the man's attempts at conversation.

His personal tent was large but austere, with only what Emrik needed and no luxuries. Out here, away from their barracks, his soldiers lived sparsely, and so did he. It was good for the soul, and in truth he detested the pampering he was subjected to at home in the palace of Celesgarde. There was a time he had lived for such frivolities, but it was many centuries ago. Before they discovered the God's heresy. Before the Crusade.

Four royal guard and a messenger boy waited outside the tent. "Bring the commanders of all three legions here immediately. And summon the Sighted," Emrik said.

The messenger boy nodded quickly, some noble brat by the cut of his uniform and the charging bull insignia on his breast. "Which one, sir?"

"Celesgarde," Emrik said. He was picking at his thumbnail again and forced himself to stop. "I need to speak to my son."

The messenger boy hurried away.

Emrik ducked through the flap into the close air of his tent. His royal guard stopped the magistrate from following, but Emrik signalled them to relent. The soft little man followed him in, wringing his hands in anxious tension. He had not even the wit to project his strength rather than weakness. He stopped just inside the tent and pulled a little leather pouch, decorated with silver trim, from his pocket. He retrieved a needle from the pouch and pricked his left index finger, wincing at the pain. The magistrate squeezed out a single drop of blood and then set to sucking at his finger. Even now, the man clung to his traditions, shedding a drop of blood at his host's threshold.

A trunk of clothing sat at the far side of the tent, an amour stand next to it wearing Emrik's God-Forged plate, and a bedroll and a wash basin the other side. There was a single chair pushed underneath a small table, and upon that table sat papers and a stoppered inkwell. There was nothing else. Emrik needed nothing else. He crossed to the washbasin and immediately began peeling off his sodden jerkin and then his trousers. The magistrate stammered an apology and turned away, as if the sight of a male body was somehow offensive to him. Or more likely he was merely embarrassed by his own pudgy frame. Soft flesh and a weak body, and yet the man had already put in a request for five drops of angel blood. A decade of life and good health. A fortune in crimson. He would get none. Emrik despised the man's weakness.

Stripped down to his undergarments, Emrik picked the wet cloth from the washbasin and began wiping himself down. Despite his age, his body had remained strong, fortified by divine blood. But that didn't mean there weren't injuries. He healed fast, but there was a limit to what could be restored. Scars that would not fade. Wounds given to him by the God that niggled him still. He winced as he wiped down the tight flesh on his abdomen where the God's spear had pierced him. The memory of that spear scorching his insides, lifting him up, his blood dripping down onto the glowing white stones of Heaven's great amphitheatre while God grinned at him. Emrik had almost died that day. He should have died.

"My liege?" asked the magistrate.

Emrik shook his head to clear away the memories. They came strongly these days, ambushing him when he least expected it, and sometimes so vivid it was as if he were reliving them. Emrik took it as a sign, his memories returned to fuel his ambition, to drive him onward. To stop the heresy from ever happening again. He dropped the cloth in the washbasin and grabbed the little towel, patting himself dry.

"What is it?" Emrik's voice was a growl that would have terrified a bear.

The magistrate cleared his throat. "I assume the information, uh, given to you last night was accurate. The young lady came forward of her own accord. She was promised a, uh, reward."

"Of course." And Emrik had no doubt Magistrate Kul wished for his own reward for finding the girl. "She will have it."

"She is here, my liege," the magistrate continued. "Should I send her in?"

"Not yet." Emrik opened the trunk and pulled out fresh clothing, comfortable riding leathers suited for long journeys astride a horse. They would be moving quickly before sundown. He was pulling on his boots when Commanders Barrt of the Second, Hunen of the Third, and Lorel of the Fourth arrived.

They each spared only a moment to pull out their needles and shed a drop of blood upon the threshold.

Barrt was a tall man, rakishly thin and with a bushy moustache oiled to a fault. He commanded the Second with a harsh discipline that set him at odds with his peers. Emrik respected that about him, that and his lack of compromise. Hunen of the Third was a different man all together. He was shorter than most, and his uniform was always ruffled. He treated his position with somewhat less starch and a lot more gruff leniency. The Third were not the most disciplined of soldiers, but they were almost fanatical in their enthusiasm. Lorel, however, was a woman who seemed to take the best aspects of both of her fellow commanders. She was tall and had the cold air of discipline about her but treated her troops with support and strict regime. The Fourth were the tightest band of soldiers in Helesia, and under Commander Lorel, they had won glory in dozens of encounters with rogue divinities and the barbarians from Aelegar.

Emrik's commanders saluted him and he returned the respect. "The angel has fled into the nearby forest," he said. "He has help. A guide, we think, and Perel's wolves cannot track through the trees."

"Odd noises are known to come out of the Whistle Wood at night," Magistrate Kul added with a pompous flair, as though his scant information was paramount to the hunt.

"Whistling, by any chance?" Commander Hunen said with a grin.

Magistrate Kul smiled coldly. "Not quite. And despite the rumours, the woodsmen don't seem to fear the fringes."

"Are we to give chase, my liege?" asked Barrt.

"Through a forest?" asked Hunen. "You're as mad as your moustache, pippa." A slang term for friend, though often used as a veiled insult.

"My soldiers could do it, Hunen," Barrt said in a stony voice. "But then my soldiers know how to stand in a straight line."

Hunen ran a hand along his bald head and looked up at Barrt. "It's probably from all those sticks you insist on shoving up their arses." They set to glaring at each other.

"Enough," Emrik growled, and both men quickly fell silent. They might squabble like children, but they knew to listen when their king spoke. Trained as well as any beast. "Commander Hunen is right. The forest is too dense for our main force. Perel and her Dogs are hunting the angel through the trees. We will ride west and circumvent the forest, hoping to cut them off north before the Cracked Mountains."

"We don't have the horses to mount all of our troops," said Lorel. "Unless we leave some behind." Astute, Emrik noted. Already anticipating his orders.

"Correct." Emrik laced up his final boot and stood, grasping his hands behind his back. He was taller than all three of his commanders. His sister Merian had often joked that there had to be giant in the Hostain line somewhere. "The Third will donate their remaining horses to the Second, and we will take auxiliary mounts from Riverden's stock." Emrik turned his gaze on the magistrate. "You will facilitate this at once."

"We... uh..." Magistrate Kul stammered. "We don't have horses to spare, my liege."

"And yet you will spare them, Magistrate. You will be compensated." He let the promise of reward remain unspecified. The man would eat his own toes for a chance at some angel blood.

"Oh. Well, of course, my liege."

Commander Hunen could hold his tongue no longer, it seemed. "You mean to have us wait here while you continue the hunt, my liege?" he asked.

Emrik shook his head. "No. I mean you to march east, twenty days to the Shadow Fort."

"The border with Aelegar? Those blood worshipping fools have been quiet for two decades. My liege, we will follow you on foot. Do not send us away. We did everything we could against the Rider. A third of my men died to bring down his bloody immortality shield."

"You did. And I am grateful. But the Third's part in this hunt is done. I need you to march to the Shadow Fort, replenish your ranks, and then make north for Celesgarde."

Hunen paused, his mouth hanging open. "The capital?"

"Yes." Emrik took a step forward and laid a hand on Hunen's shoulder, gripping it tightly and pinning him with an intense stare. "I need you to reinforce the First and protect the capital. Protect our home, Commander. Nothing is more important."

All the bluster vanished from Hunen, replaced by a look like awe. His eyes even welled up a little. He saluted more crisply than he had in years. "Yes, my liege."

Emrik nodded once. "Go. All of you. Strike the camp, and make ready to ride while we still have light left to us. Magistrate Kul, find the girl and bring her here once I am done with the Sighted."

The commanders and the magistrate funnelled out of the tent, and then a man of middling years entered, led by a woman in a white dress, padded against the chill. The man wore plain brown robes of sturdy design and made his way forward with tiny shuffling steps. Neither of them gave a blood offering at the threshold, but the Sighted and their aides were beyond the need to follow such tradition. Emrik pulled out the chair before the desk, and the woman led the man to it. He sat and felt about the desk for the paper and inkwell. His hair was grey and his beard trimmed, though not by his own hands. The Sighted, maligned though they were, were afforded high positions of comfort in the kingdom. The woman was his attendant, in all things. She was always by his side, tending to his needs before her own. For though the man was here, his sight was not. His eyes darted about, seeing everything, but it was another man who looked out through those eyes.

An oddity of humanity and the consumption of angels. If a person and a beast shared an angel's eyes, the person could switch to the animal's sight at will, and for that time they would exchange their vision. But if two humans shared an angel's eyes, their vision was forever swapped. The Sighted sitting at Emrik's desk had swapped his vision as a child with another. His sight was back at Celesgarde, where Emrik's son, Arik, ruled as protector and steward. The Sighted did not have an easy life, always seeing through their counterpart's eyes, but they were invaluable. Through them, Emrik could communicate over immense distances. Celesgarde was a hard twenty days' ride from Riverden, with fresh horses needed along the way, and yet he could communicate with Arik with a mere moment's notice.

"We're ready," croaked the Sighted man. His hands were on the paper and the quill, but the hazel eyes of his counterpart were staring at Emrik.

"Tell my son we are on the trail of a new Herald." As Emrik spoke, the Sighted man scribbled upon the paper. His counterpart's eyes turned to read the words.

After a few moments, the Sighted man spoke. "The steward asks how that is possible."

Emrik found himself picking at his thumbnail again. Fresh blood pooled there. "Tell my son I don't know. But it is paramount that this new Herald be stopped before they can ring in a new age." He paused for a moment. He hated the idea of others, not his own children, knowing the whole truth. The Sighted man and his aide could most likely be trusted, but trust never came easily to Emrik. In the end, his son needed to know, and the Sighted was the only way of telling him. "I believe if a new age is rung in, the God will be reborn."

The scratching of the quill continued as the Sighted relayed the information. Again, there was a pause as the Sighted in Celesgarde transcribed Arik's reply. "The stewards asks what do you need from me, Father?" said the Sighted man.

Emrik felt his heart swell with pride at that. Another might have argued against the impossibility or tried to console Emrik, but not Arik. He was simply ready to do whatever was needed without question. Emrik's eldest living son had always been his most dependable. "Tell my son to protect the city. We hunt the angel, but in case they escape, they must not get into Celesgarde. A new age can be rung in from nowhere else. I'm sending you the Third to reinforce your numbers."

Again, the wait while the messages were relayed back and forth. "The steward says It will be done, Father." No minced words from Arik. His confidence showed without them.

Emrik paused a moment but decided to add more. "Arik, protect the bell at all costs."

The Sighted scribbled the words down, then waited. A few moments later, he struck a diagonal line across the page, signifying the conversation was done. The attendant helped the Sighted up, and they both bowed to Emrik before heading out through the tent flap. Emrik snatched up the piece of paper and crumpled it into a ball. He knew Arik would have the paper at Celesgarde destroyed.

The tent flap was pulled open once again, and Magistrate Kul entered, a young girl at his side. She was pretty, despite having mud on the hem of her dress and a smudge on her cheek. Willing to betray her friend for a reward. In most situations, Emrik would detest such treason, but where seditious elements were involved, they often had to rely upon the selfishness of everyday citizens. She stared at him with wide eyes before curtseying and quickly plucking the needle from the nearby table, spilling a drop of blood at the threshold. She didn't carry her own offerance needle yet, an indication that her father had not yet deemed her of marital age. The shedding of blood was a tradition children were excused from, but she had participated freely. Emrik found that interesting.

"You're here for your reward," Emrik said, staring down at the girl.

She nodded just once.

"Riches." Emrik shrugged. "Money can buy many things, but it cannot extend your life. Only blood may do that. The blood of a divinity. That is a true reward."

Magistrate Kul licked his lips, but the girl frowned.

"What do I have to do?" the girl asked. Smart, then. Able to see she had to earn it, though not wise enough to see it was a reward that would never come.

"The angel fled into the forest with someone at his side. We believe it's the washer woman's child."

The girl flushed red and looked away, an internal struggle. She had already lost. Already betrayed her friend once, she would do so again. "Renira. Ren."

Emrik smiled. "Renira. You know her?"

The girl nodded, her eyes locked on the dusty floor of the tent. "Better than anyone."

"Good," Emrik said. "Do you know how to ride?"

"A horse?" the girl asked. "Of course."

"Magistrate Kul. This young woman will need a horse as well. She's coming with us."

CHAPTER 9

Demons come in many forms. Some may be almost human in size and nature and even disposition. There are smaller breeds akin to hounds or boar. And yet others are truly monstrous. All demons share one characteristic: they prey upon humanity.

— POT'S *TREATISE ON DEMONOLOGY*, 1ST EDITION. FOREWORD.

Three days into the Whistle Wood and the forest changed, subtle at first, but the changes grew more pronounced by the day. The trees grew taller and broader, and the canopy became so dense that no glimpse of the sky could be seen. The days were so shrouded in gloom they seemed like nights, and the nights were a haunted time of utter darkness, malicious whispers and threatening roars. Renira woke many times on that third night, convinced there were monsters right beside her. She imagined terrible things slithering through the dark or creeping about on spindly legs, beady eyes full of malice. There were times she detested having such an active imagination. Armstar would not allow a fire, and Renira huddled in her winter clothing and shivered miserable against the cold.

Adventures were meant to be exciting and fun; all the stories said so. Samir

Hafhammer never shivered in the cold when he marched to slay the Den Mothers. Helena Hostain wasn't told *no fire* when she stood against the Shattering and threw the Lords Under the Ice back to their watery depths. So far, Renira's adventure had been nothing like the stories. Cold and damp and with only a distant, bitter angel as company. She silently cried herself to sleep that third night, wishing she had never left.

On the fourth morning, they rose as soon as the scant light would allow. The ground beneath them was crisp and frozen, and the occasional fat drop of water made its way through the canopy and crashed upon their heads. There were no more woodsman's marks so far into the forest, no more caches of supplies. Their food was dwindling, and Renira knew it was her fault. Mother had said she had packed enough to last a week maybe, but Renira ate whenever her stomach rumbled at her, which had always been more often than most people. She should have been smarter and rationed her food. The only compensation there was that Armstar ate little, claiming angels' bodies worked quite differently to a human's.

The angel spoke little, breaking his silence mostly just to berate her for moving too slowly or needing to rest, or maybe just breathing. He avoided most of her questions, and when he did answer it was with vague, snappish replies.

One of Renira's favourite stories as a child was of Hekta Brine, a man also known as the Shadow Knight. He was mute ever since a demon stole his voice as a child. Hekta was one of the first humans to take up arms with Saint Dien and fight against the demons, always searching for the monster who had stolen his voice. He never left the Saint's side, through the Liberation Wars, the Saint's quest to the Catacombs of Black Fyre—Renira particularly enjoyed those stories as they were filled with adventure and ancient relics of unspeakable power—and even her final victory at the Redemption. The Shadow Knight was always at Saint Dien's side, strong, dependable, silent even after he slew the demon and reclaimed his voice. Renira had always thought that silent presence would be a stoic support to the young saint, but now she was starting to wonder if the quiet ever grated on Saint Dien like it did her. Probably not, but then Renira's patience was never exactly saintly.

High above them, much of the canopy was shrouded in white webbing. When Renira squinted, she could see thousands upon thousands of tiny black dots moving amid the webbing. Spider colonies, Yonal Wood had once warned her, were more dangerous than any big predator. Avoid the webbing at all costs, and suck on Bak leaves to fortify the body against the venom. Renira had no Bak leaves and decided she would much prefer just not to be bitten. The thought of so many little spiders above her, filling the forest canopy, drove her to distraction. She imagined them abseiling down on thin strands, landing silently and unknown on her hat, crawling into her hair, burrowing down to find the soft flesh beneath. The thought made her itch, certain she could already feel the little monsters crawling over her skin, all legs and fangs and fat bodies. She shivered, pulled her coat close, and glanced up.

The trees had wounds in places, great rents in the bark that looked like a bear had raked its claws down the wood. But the marks were often too high up for a bear to reach. Some of the wounds seemed old, the tree already healing, but others dripped sticky sap and were clearly fresh. Some also had strange yellow flowers growing from the gashed bark. Renira could not see the spiders having made such scars, as small as they were. Her mind wandered, and she began to imagine a much larger spider, many times the size of a man, with eight spindly legs each ending with a sharpened point. A brood mother for the scuttling mass above them.

"Talk to me," Renira said suddenly, her voice betraying the panic that had crept in. She was breathing hard and not from the meandering pace they set.

Armstar's ruined wings twitched, and his shoulders sagged a little, then he slowed his pace until they were walking alongside each other. "Fine. Tell me what you know of the ages."

"That's not talking to me," Renira said, chewing on her lip. "That's me talking to you." *And the last thing I want right now is to give a sermon.*

Armstar shrugged. "Suit yourself." The angel fell silent, hard stare glaring into the gloom as though he could frighten it away.

"Please talk to me," Renira said. "I need to distract myself from..." She nodded upwards.

Armstar glanced at her briefly and nodded. "Me too."

Renira shook her head. "But you're an angel! You can't be scared of spiders."

Armstar was silent for a few moments and hunched in on himself. "It's all the legs. And the way they scuttle. And those thick, hairy bodies, and... It doesn't matter anyway. I'm not exactly at the peak of my divinity right now. My immortality shield is broken, my wings are a wreck, and I took a wound to the thigh a while back that doesn't seem to be healing quite right." His limp had been getting worse. "I'm afraid I'm quite a poor representation of God's children. So how about *you* talk to *me*. I saw the book your mother packed in your bag. A holy text. *The Rite of the Divine*, if I'm not mistaken."

Renira nodded, pulling her bag off her shoulders and thrusting her hand inside until her questing fingers found the unyielding cover of the book. It took up a lot of space in her pack, space that could have been given over to more food, but Mother had always been a devout believer, even when her daughter thought it all fancy. And it had seemed like romantic nonsense. God and angels and divine power, the Heavens, a blue sky, peace, and open worship of moral principles. Renira was well known to lose herself in daydreams, but Mother's faith had always seemed more fantasy than anything she could imagine. And the teachers at school taught a very different truth, one that made more sense than her mother's faith. Yet angels were real. Renira was walking alongside one, sharing meals with a child of the God. He seemed grumpy but not evil like King Emrik's history claimed.

I still wish Mother had packed more food instead of the bloody book..

"What about the First Age?" Armstar asked. "Tell me what you know. Convince me there is some of your mother in you."

Renira sighed and swung her pack back onto her shoulders, trying to dredge up the memories of her mother reading from the book, if for no other reason than to make the angel eat his words.

"The First Age was the Age of... um, Redemption, I think?" Renira said. She looked at Armstar, but his face was impassive. "When demons roamed the world and kept humanity enslaved as thralls." That much she remembered. It had always sounded equal parts exciting and terrifying. There were stories in the book of the horrible acts the demons had committed and how humanity lacked the heroes to stand up and lead them to freedom. It was a time of great suffering for the people. But the school taught a different truth, never mentioning demons, only that angels came to enslave mankind.

Renira shook her head. She didn't think Armstar would enjoy hearing the king's version of the First Age. He wanted the one from the book. "We had no cities, no towns, only small tribes. Uh, we lived on the move? I think Mother said we were nomadic people back then, always hunted. The demons used us to mine the earth, to find metal for their weapons. Or as food when it was scarce. She said it was a dark time, without hope."

Armstar shook his head and sighed. "Not without hope. Never that. But demons did roam the world back then, keeping humanity in thralldom. Before God realised the potential of humanity and decided all you needed was a push in the right direction and warriors to help you fight for your freedom. Do you know who heralded in the First Age?"

"The Archangel?" Renira asked with a smile. She could not remember his name. In truth, the study of the Rite of the Divine had often bored her, and she spent much of the time she should have been reading it staring out of the window and dreaming of adventure or playing with her friends.

"Either your mother was a poor teacher or you're a slow learner," Armstar said and there was no humour to his voice. "His name is Orphus, the Sword of

Heaven. He was the first of my kind, the oldest of us all and a warrior without equal. Though he doesn't do much fighting anymore. Leaves that to the rest of us these days. It's his plan we're following now. All of this is his damned plan."

Armstar cleared his throat and continued in a more lecturing voice, "He called the angels to war and led Heaven's army against the demons that enslaved humanity. He freed you all. So you could turn on us when it suited you best." She was certain that wasn't how the book or her mother had put it, and it definitely wasn't how the teachers at school said it happened, but then Armstar seemed to have a unique outlook.

"Thanks for the lecture," she murmured too quietly for him to hear. He glared at her all the same, and she wondered if angels had super hearing.

I can't decide if it's all people he doesn't like or just me.

Renira heard a sound like wood slapped against stone, followed by a clicking. It echoed through the forest, seeming to come from everywhere all at once. She looked up to see the little black spiders frantic on their webs, swarming towards the trees. Armstar didn't seem to notice and continued his lecture.

"For a hundred years the forces of Heaven fought against the demons," the angel said, a bitter edge to his voice. "The battles were not evenly matched, but the demons held the advantage of numbers, and many of my brothers and sisters fell once their immortality shields were broken. Even those of us who were made to kill must suffer the consequences of our actions." He looked at Renira, his muddy eyes cold and distant. "But even numbers couldn't save the demons when your people finally rose up and joined the war. Heroes of virtue saw the light of God, the strength his morality offered. They took up arms and convinced others to join them. Dien Hostain was the first. The Saint. The first of humanity's heroes." He sneered. "And the first monster from which all our troubles spawned. If only Orphus had just tore her head off at the start."

Renira was barely listening to the angel. "Do you hear that noise?"

"Yes," Armstar said. "And I'm trying hard to ignore it. It was when an angel was killed trying to free an enslaved camp of humans that Saint Dien took up the hammer. Humans and angels working together for the first time. Dien forged an army with the help of Orphus. They stole the demons' own weapons from them and were trained by the Archangel himself."

"Armstar, stop," Renira gripped the angel's arm and pulled him to a halt. Underneath his dirtied cloak and shirt, she found his arm surprisingly thin. "What is that noise?" It did not seem to be growing any louder, but neither had it stopped. The clicking was a regular beat, and there was a sound beneath it too, an animalistic growl from far away.

The angel glanced deeper into the forest, the way they had come. There was fear in his eyes, a wild panic like a rabbit after hearing a hawk's cry.

"The demons were driven back by the combined forces of humanity and Heaven working together. They were forced underground, into the dark, into places where humanity doesn't tread. And the darkness and isolation is where they remain." He was insistent on telling the story, his eyes intense and locked on Renira.

Renira's breath steamed in front of her, and the sounds of the forest seemed quieter than before, as though all life and warmth were fleeing from the noise behind them.

The dark places where humanity doesn't tread...

"Are you saying..." She stopped and lowered her voice to a whisper. "Are you saying there's a demon in this forest?"

"I don't know," Armstar whispered, punctuating each word. "I've never seen one."

"What?" *What sort of angel is he?* He wasn't a warrior, had never seen a demon, was scared of spiders, and disliked people. Apart from his ruined wings, she was starting to wonder if he was really an angel at all.

"Did your mother teach you nothing?" Armstar hissed. "I was born in the Third Age. By then, all the demons were gone. I told you, Renira, I'm the Builder. That's what I do. It's what I was made for."

There was clearly something in the forest, something only found where the trees grew so dense they blocked out the sun. Something that gouged deep wounds into the bark, and something at least as large as a bear.

Whatever it is, I don't think it's hunting us to make friends or show us the way out. Demons hide in the dark places.

Renira found she was crouching, as though trying to make herself appear small, and Armstar had sunk down with her. His wings twitched and huddled close together at his back. She glanced upward to the webbing, but she could no longer see any spiders moving amongst it.

Renira gripped her mother's amulet beneath her coat. A connection that chased away the paralysing fear. Her mother's indomitable strength and unwavering faith. "I think we should move," she whispered. "Quickly."

They set off again, moving much faster than before. Old branches snapped underfoot, needles scuffed and kicked aside, panicked breath, and the rustle of clothing. They sacrificed stealth for speed and hoped it would be enough to keep them ahead of the thing in the forest. The noises followed them, clicking and scraping and something bashing against the trees.

Images swirled through Renira's mind as they fled, of horns and great teeth, rancid breath and fur crawling with spiders. As the noise of the thing chasing them grew louder, Renira found she was no longer paying attention to where they were going. Both she and Armstar ran through the forest, slipping past great trees without even a thought for the scarred bark.

Armstar slid to a sudden stop amidst the needle strewn floor. He reached out with his hand and grabbed hold of Renira, pulling her to a halt. Renira doubled over, dropping to her knees and drawing in deep, quick breaths, her lungs burning and vision spinning.

"An insidious intelligence remains in demonkind. They are hunters. Always hunters," said the angel.

Renira looked up from her knees to see a forest floor cleared of needles ahead of them. A blank patch of brown earth, veined with green moss, easily two dozen feet across in each direction. Attached to some of the trees were strange-looking cocoons, grey-green in colour.

"It herded us here," Armstar said, squinting back into the gloom the way they had come. If anything, the noises were quieter now.

Renira glanced upward. There was no webbing above them, and the trees were almost bare of needles as well. The crimson light of a cold, sunny morning streamed down upon the nest. One of the cocoons pulsed. They were made from the needles of the trees and appeared to be fused together with sticky, grey mucus. There were three of them. One was sagging, more grey than green, and a rancid yellow fluid was leaking from the base into the earth below. Renira turned away, coughing and gagging as the smell hit her. Only Igor's slain mice, many days old, had ever smelled so awful. The second cocoon pulsed like a beating heart, and as Renira drew close, she felt heat from it. Closer still and she could hear sounds coming from within like hundreds of little slithering voices all crying out at once.

"We have to go," Armstar said. "Now!" He crossed the gap between them and took hold of Renira's arm, turned her to face him.

"Wait!" She twisted free of his grip and ran back to the cocoons. She heard something, a low mumble like a soft voice whispering. "Do you hear that?"

Armstar was staring at something above her, his gaze hard. "I hear nothing." He shook his head wildly. "I see nothing. Move, Renira."

The cocoon before her pulsed again, and Renira reached out and poked it with her finger. It was rough and sticky to the touch. When she pulled back again, thin lines of mucus stretched between the cocoon and her finger. Another mumbled noise so much like someone begging for help. She turned to find Armstar shaking his head.

Slowly, Renira looked up. A man was pinned to the tree above her, the same yellow-green mucus of the cocoons had solidified around his chest, keeping him there. His eyes were open, roving, panicked. His lips twitched, but only a mumble escaped.

Run. Run run run run run!

Renira ignored her careening thoughts and swung her pack in front of her, already rummaging through it. Her hand brushed against the book and the food her mother had packed for her. She pushed aside tightly wrapped bundles of clothing and the flamers she had looted from the woodsman's cache. There, buried right at the bottom of the pack, was a little knife. It was far more suited to cutting cheese than needles and mucus, but it was all she had for the job, and so it would have to do.

"We have to help him," she said. "Cut him down."

Armstar started forward again and grabbed Renira by the arm, pulling her away just as the cocoon split open. A foul stench like rotten eggs and unwashed feet filled the air, and Renira gagged and held her sleeve over her face. Dozens of spindly little creatures, each the size of Renira's hand, scurried up out of the cocoon. They almost looked like spiders but dark green, with long tails. They raced up the tree, climbing over each other in a frantic chase until they reached the man pinned there. The little monsters crawled beneath his clothes, and the man started convulsing. His eyes went wide. Blood soaked through his rags, dripped down to the cocoon below as more of the monsters crawled out of it. Most climbed straight up, seeking out their trapped food, though others spilled over the side of the cocoon and crawled through the needles and twigs, seeking other prey.

A scream tore through the forest, full of pain. Renira turned, searching for the source, but the noise echoed through the trees, confusing her.

Armstar stamped on one of the little monsters that crawled too close, squashing it into bloody pulp. Then he dragged on Renira's arm and pulled her away.

"Stop gawking, Renira! We have to go."

"But the scream," Renira said. "There's someone else out here, Armstar."

"And they don't matter."

Renira stared at him, incredulous. Angels were supposed to be champions of mankind, saviours, not cowards only caring for their own skin.

The angel grit his teeth. "Whoever they are, they're already dead. No sense in us joining them."

The pinned man attached to the tree stopped twitching. One of his legs dropped free in a gout of blood. The limb hit the forest floor, and little crawling monsters burrowed out from the flesh.

Renira stared at Armstar a moment longer, then nodded. Who was she to help? There was a demon in the forest and unless it wanted its knickers washing, she was useless. "Which way?" she asked.

They were turned around, lost. The crashing seemed to be coming from everywhere, echoing through the trees.

"North," Armstar said. "Which way is north?"

Renira panicked, turning in a circle. Then she thought to look up. The canopy was sparse here, the morning sun streaming through from the east. It gave her a bearing and she pointed north. "That way."

The thunderous crashing stopped, but there was something else echoing through the trees. Stumbling footsteps, laboured breathing, coming closer. A boy stumbled out from between the trees into the clearing. His skin was dark as night, and he wore a motley collection of rags. Long matted black hair was plastered to his face with sweat, and he was cradling one bloody arm against his chest. He looked young, maybe only twelve or thirteen winters to his name.

The boy staggered to a stop and glanced up at them, his breathing ragged and eyes unfocused. He collapsed to his knees. "Run!" he said, then fell sideways.

CHAPTER 10

The fourth and most important pillar of faith is sacrifice.

— FROM THE 2ND SCRIPTURE, THE PILLARS OF
FAITH

A tree creaked, the sound of a giant straining to remain upright against something titanic. Renira stared into the gloomy forest but saw nothing. The boy's eyes were frantic, his breath coming in short gasps, but he only twitched on the ground. He had a puncture wound in his shoulder, the same arm he had been cradling against his chest, but it was barely bleeding.

We're being hunted. We have to run. "Come on!" Renira rushed to the boy, stamping on one of the little monsters as she went, and tried pulling him to his feet, but he flopped away from her as though boneless. She tried again, this time gripping under his shoulders and trying to lift him with her own strength. He whined in either pain or frustration. "Just stand up, will you!"

Armstar pushed Renira out of the way and lifted the boy to sitting. He was short and all skin and bones. His head rolled around on his neck; his chin pressed against his chest. "Aaaarnt oooove," the boy said, his words slurring from lips that struggled to form them.

The angel shook his head at Renira. "He's paralysed. We leave him and run."

"Weren't you just telling me a story about how the first humans revolted against the demons? And how it took an angel sacrificing themselves for humanity. Isn't that the virtue your God wished to show us? The very principles of his faith?"

The words of her mother's book came back to her suddenly. "Sacrifice, not for oneself, but for another, is the highest form of worship." Renira didn't really believe the words, had never believed in any of it. They were nothing but idle fancy and stories of adventure. But she was scared, terror bubbling up from within, and she was barely holding it back. Those words, words her mother had spoken to her time and again, gave her the courage she needed to persist.

Armstar growled and sneered. "Perhaps there *is* some of Lusa in you, after all."

Armstar grabbed hold of the boy, wrenched him away from her, and slung him over his shoulder. The boy's flailing arm smacked against one of Armstar's wings, and the angel hissed in pain, then turned and ran from the clearing. "Come on!"

Another tree creaked nearby, and a new smell wafted into the nest. It was musty and stale, like a body gone too long unwashed. Renira glanced back and saw movement. Something huge stalking through the trees, a single claw wrapped around a tree trunk, gouging a rent the bark, then it was gone.

Run, you idiot! With a strangled cry, Renira turned and followed Armstar with as much speed as her tired legs would allow.

Even injured and carrying the burden of the boy, Armstar outpaced Renira. She dodged around trees and leapt over bulging roots, her flight fuelled by blind panic. Behind her, the demon crashed through the trees. There were no thumping footsteps hitting the ground, only the clicking and scraping of claws on wood, the creaking of trees straining against the immense weight.

A shadow dove through the canopy overhead, shaking the trees and showering Renira with needles. Her mother's hat pulled free and fell behind, and for just a moment she slowed, desperate to retrieve it. *It's just a hat. Not worth dying over. Run!*

Armstar was too far ahead, almost lost to Renira's sight as he charged through the trees, limping with each step and carrying the flailing boy on his shoulders. The shadow overhead moved again, leaping forward, shaking the trunks between Renira and the angel.

"Look out!" Renira screamed, her voice rasping on desperate breaths. But her warning came too late, and a tail as thick as her waist, green with scales and tipped with stinger like a scorpion, swung down from above and crashed against the angel. Armstar and the boy both went sprawling amidst the forest floor. Neither got back up. Renira saw glinting yellow eyes turn her way from the forest canopy, and she threw herself to the side, crashing against a tree to arrest her momentum.

Her breath came in short, shallow gasps, and Renira clapped a hand over her mouth, trying to smother the sound. She pulled her knees up close to her chest and made herself as small as possible, even pulling her backpack off her shoulders and hugging it to her chest. She had never been so terrified.

She could think of nothing to do but curl up and hide. Always in her dreams she had faced off against monsters, taller and stronger, armed with shining weapons and protected by impenetrable steel, skilled with many years of weapons training. But those were just stupid dreams. This was real life, and the demon was not just a little black cat with a bad attitude. She had neither weapons nor the training to use them. The closest thing she'd had to a weapon was a cheese knife. Her armour was winter clothing and a waterproof coat. *I'm useless. A scared little girl dreaming of adventure. Helpless and afraid and about to die.* It was her first time more than a day away from home, and she was going to die. Renira prayed then, silently, as she had seen her mother do so many times before.

But the God was dead, and no one answered her prayers.

A tree creaked, and Renira glanced left. High above, she saw a long, bony reptilian leg ending in a hooked claw as large as her arm. The claw dug into the bark of the tree, wrapping around it, and another leg moved slowly into view. The monster didn't touch the ground, it moved through the trees, using multiple trunks to support its immense weight. Renira edged slowly around the tree, away from the beast, just as the tip of a fanged snout moved into view. Claws scraped bark as it crept through the trees, searching for her.

A dozen paces away, the boy lay among the needles. His eyes were open, staring at her, but he couldn't move. He blinked once and his eyes darted upwards just as a long claw wrapped itself around the tree at Renira's back. She stifled a squeak of terror, hand clasped over her mouth. Staring upwards, Renira watched the claw dig into the wood of the tree, showering her in shards of bark. The demon had found her. There was nowhere left to run, no one to save her. She was going to die, paralysed and pinned to a tree while little demons hatched and devoured her.

The tree gave a shudder at her back, and she whimpered, clamping her hand so firmly over her mouth she couldn't breathe, squeezing her eyes shut. It didn't help. She bit down on her finger to stop from screaming and tasted blood.

Renira opened her eyes again to find the world blurry from tears. The boy still lay prostrate, his eyes wide. Only a little beyond the boy, Armstar shifted. The angel had taken a hit from the creature's tail, but even that wasn't enough to put him down for good. He dragged his knees up underneath him, clutching a hand to his side. His tunic was stained red.

The tree at her back creaked again, and Renira heard a swishing noise as the creature's massive tail whipped out in front of her. The hooked barb on the end of the tail was milky white and glistened with venom. Renira pushed back further against the tree and hugged her pack tight. The claw above her scraped along the tree trunk, carving a deep gouge into the wood. The clicking noise started again, the creature's teeth chattering against each other as it searched for her.

Searching for me, but it can't find me. It was so close it should be able to smell her.

Armstar crawled over to the boy and scooped him up into his arms. He stood, leaned against a nearby tree and nodded toward Renira. The angel was slouching and wincing as his wings twitched against the bark. The red stain at his side grew larger, and the angel's skin was pale as sun-bleached bone. Renira waved at him, trying to tell him to run, but Armstar just shook his head and glanced up at the beast still clinging to the trees above her.

The chattering of teeth grew louder, and the tree at her back shook again. The claw above her twisted into the bark, and another claw grasped a trunk nearby. Renira looked to her right as the tip of the monster's snout poked past the tree just above her head. She couldn't stop herself from shaking, nor the tears from streaming down her face. A high-pitched whine wheezed from between her teeth with each shallow breath.

It knows I'm here. Hiding will get me nowhere but dead. This was not how her dreams ever ended. In those fancies she had always been a hero. Saving the day no matter the cost.

Renira wiped tears from her eyes and waved again at Armstar, trying to shoo him away. Then she reached into her pack, drew out an apple and threw it the other way, underneath the demon's reptilian snout. The apple hit the forest floor, and the creature's head whipped about. Renira pushed off against the tree at her back and launched into a sprint, clutching her pack to her chest and fleeing in blind panic. She knew she had no chance of getting away, but hoped her distraction would be enough for Armstar to take the boy and run. She would buy their lives with her own.

Claws scraped against wood, and trees shook from the force as the demon crashed through the canopy, chasing her. Renira slid to a stop and turned, determined to face her death rather than let it take her in the back. The demon was a dark green blur of six bony limbs, crawling through the forest canopy, its tail hanging down below it. Six glowing yellow eyes staring at her from the darkness. The demon's tail swung forward and stabbed her in the chest, driving her down into the dirt and needles.

Pain burst to life all over Renira's body. Her ribs were agony, and she struggled to draw in even the barest of breaths. The creature's tail had hit her backpack and knocked her down, the barbed end stopped by her mother's holy book. But still the demon pressed down upon her, crushing her, the strength in its tail far too great for Renira to fight against. She gasped and flailed, trying desperately to bat away the tail, but it had her pinned on her back. The trees to both sides of Renira shook as clawed limbs wrapped around the trunks, and the monster drew closer. It loomed above, filling her sight. A wide body, six arms and a tail, like some grotesque, reptilian hand splayed out to climb through the forest canopy. Its head was brutish, its snout short, and its mouth filled with row upon row of serrated fangs. Glowing yellow eyes peered down at Renira from both sides of the creature's snout as it lowered itself to devour her.

Renira desperately dug through her backpack, but she could not shift the book, nor the tail that pressed down upon her. Her hands closed around the flamer sticks, each as long as her hand and no thicker than a finger. The demon dipped its head so close Renira could smell its fetid breath. Pale strands of saliva dripped down onto her face, running up her nose and making her gag. The mouth opened wide enough to engulf her head.

Renira gripped two of the flamers as hard as she could and snapped them in half. Her pack erupted into roaring flames. The heat was intense and burned her hands, but Renira drew them out of the pack, screaming as she thrust both ends of the flamers upwards into the eyes of the monster as it lunged down at her.

The demon roared and drew back. The trees shook as it lurched away, trying to free itself from the burning flamer sticks lodged in its eyes. Its tail whipped up and away, slinging Renira's burning pack into the gloom of the forest. Renira lay there for moments that seemed to last for eternity, breathing hard and fast, willing her body to move. Her hands stung from the flamers, and her ribs felt like someone had stamped on her chest. The forest shook as the demon rampaged, crashing between trees and shrieking in agony.

I did it! I defeated a demon.

Armstar lurched into view. The angel didn't bother to ask Renira if she was all right, he reached down, grabbed her arm, and hauled her to her feet. He was carrying the boy again, whose dark eyes stared at her from a face slack with paralysis.

"Stupid girl. Run!" Armstar said, and they both did. This time Renira ran faster than the angel, and the wound in his side bled more with every faltering step.

CHAPTER 11

Sometimes bravery is naught but desperation wearing a fine mask. But true courage lies in the hearts of all men if they have but the opportunity to look for it.

— SAINT DIEN HOSTAIN, FROM ROOK'S
COMPENDIUM

Renira ran. She lost herself in the panic of that mad flight. Trees passed in a blur of brown and green and needles crushed underfoot. Her lungs burned, her laboured breath puffed out in white mist. Sweat and tears and a trickle of blood from a cut on her forehead cooled against her skin, turning icy despite the exertion.

The demon was still behind her. She almost couldn't believe it was real. A demon, just like in the old stories battling angels. Renira had hurt it, wounded it. But not killed it. With every step she imagined it had recovered, found their trail, and was chasing once more. An enraged demon straight out of her nightmare, swinging through the forest canopy, hunting them down. If she slowed for even a moment, it would catch them.

Armstar's cry made Renira jump, and she turned to see the angel had fallen and the boy spilled from his grip. Then something hard hit Renira, spinning her about and knocking her down to roll in the needles. Her ribs stabbed sharp agony in her chest, and her arm and leg joined them. Renira rolled onto her arse and scooted away from this new attack. But there was nothing there, just a tree she hadn't seen. Renira curled into a tight ball, hugged herself and listened to her rapid breathing, trying to make herself still and quiet and small enough that the entire forest would somehow forget that she was there.

Armstar groaned, writhing on the forest floor, one hand pressed to his side, his ruined wings twitching. Still Renira didn't move, couldn't move. The terror bubbled deep down, but there was a horrible numbness settling upon her. As though even moving seemed like such great effort. It would be so much easier to simply fall asleep.

"Stop it!" Her own voice startled her. She hadn't intended to speak, but the thought had loosened her tongue and demanded to be heard. Thoughts were harder to deny once they were spoken, even if no one else was around to hear them. "Stop cowering. Get up and help."

Armstar moaned, gathered his knees beneath him. He toppled sideways and let out a shout of pain as his wings hit the ground. Well, that settled things. She had a friend in pain and had to help. As she struggled back to her feet, she considered the idea that Armstar was not so much a friend as a grumpy burden she had to escort through the forest.

Mother counts him as a friend, and so shall I.

"How bad is the wound?" Renira asked as she braced and helped Armstar up against a tree. His shirt was stained red on his left side, blood soaked into the cloth halfway down his leg.

"Bad enough," the angel said through gritted teeth. "The poison is worse. I can feel it, slowing me down, making it hard to move." Armstar met Renira's eyes for a moment. "You have to go. Run. Get to Hel's Wall."

"Not without you," Renira said as she looked around for anything to help staunch the wound.

Armstar shoved her away, but he lacked the strength he'd had earlier. He was breathing heavily. "I'm not important, Renira. Go north. Find Los Hold. Our acolytes will meet you. Tell them who you are and what happened here."

"Uh huh," Renira grunted. She found she was clutching her mother's amulet underneath her coat, so tightly it hurt her hand. "What about your divine constitution? Mother always said angels were tough." Having someone else to focus on, to be concerned about, helped. She couldn't just retreat into a numb oblivion when there were others who needed her.

"My immortality shield is broken."

Renira pulled at Armstar's tunic around the wound until she could see the torn flesh beneath. Ivory skin stained red and made angry by the injury. It was deep and gaping but didn't seem to be bleeding as much as she would expect such a wound to. She had seen animals wounded before, when her mother was called upon to help them; cows from the nearby farmlands sometimes impaled themselves on broken fences or gashed open their flesh in their bovine conflicts. The wounds always seemed to bleed a lot, but the beasts usually survived with a bit of tending.

"I don't know much about healing," Renira admitted. "Mother used to use a needle and thread whenever I got hurt or on the animals farmer Hay keeps, but I barely remember how..." They were surrounded by needles of a sort, and the thread her mother had most often used was horsehair.

"I don't matter, Renira," Armstar said again. "You have to go."

"And I'm not leaving without you," Renira said it matter-of-factly, the way her mother used to speak to her as a child when she was being wilful and foolish. "We had this argument about the boy when there was a demon looming over us, and you lost it then. Don't make me have it again." She could still just about hear the monster in the distance. Its anguished cries had ceased, but the forest still shook far away with its rampage. It could return at any moment, angry and determined for revenge.

Armstar groaned in pain, but at least he stopped trying to push her away. "How are your hands?"

Renira glanced down. "Um, they're fine," she said, a little surprised. Smudged with ash from the flamers, but otherwise unharmed. She was certain she must have burned herself, but had no mark or scorch to show.

Renira rummaged around the forest floor until she found a couple of sturdy, sharp needles, then used one to bore a hole in the base of the other. Then she plucked a strand of her own hair from her head. It was long and ruddy brown, and she threaded it through the hole in the needle and tied it off. Then she looked at Armstar's wound once more.

"Will this work?" Renira asked.

The angel's chuckle was so brittle it snapped as it left his lips. "I don't know. I'm a builder, not a healer. I saw your mother sew flesh once. She was firm and not gentle." He winced. "And it looked like it hurt. I'll heal given time. But without my immortality shield, I'm vulnerable." That was the third time he'd mentioned an immortality shield, and Renira still had no idea what he meant. A shield was metal or wood, surely, something that could be held up to protect you from danger.

Renira pulled open Armstar's robes a little further so the skin was properly exposed. White as milk, but red around the wound. There was not a blemish on him. Renira, on the other hand, was covered in little freckles. They dotted her arms and legs, and she even had a spread of them over her nose and cheeks. The sight of the open wound made her stomach turn, and she could smell the blood. There was something foul in there as well, yellow and wrong. The venom. But her pack was lost, burned up and thrown into the depths of the forest, and with it had gone all her food and water. She had nothing to cleanse the wound.

Well, he'll just have to pray his angelic constitution is stronger than demon venom.

"Here I go," Renira said, as much to herself as to Armstar. She imagined herself a healer, just like her mother. A bag full of ointments and salves, a patient depending on her skill.

Kneeling by the angel's side, she grimaced as she touched the wound and pushed both sides of the ragged flesh together. Blood and yellow poison oozed out and ran over her hand, making the flesh slippery. She had to reposition three times before she got a good grip and could taste bitter bile in the back of her throat. She set the little needle to the angel's flesh and pushed hard. Armstar hissed in pain as the needle pierced his skin, and Renira thrust it through the other side of the wound, then pulled the hair through.

"How you humans suffer through such pain and rudimentary healing is a wonder to me," Armstar said through gritted teeth.

"Perhaps we're tougher than you think. Not all of us can be blessed with an immortality shield. What is that anyway?" Renira asked, hoping to distract them both. She set the needle to flesh again and pushed hard, wincing at the pain she was causing.

Armstar gasped. "All angels have an immortality shield," he said as Renira pulled the hair through again. "It protects us, heals us. Makes us stronger. It's power derived from our father."

"But you don't have one?" Renira was finding the sewing bloody work and kept having to reposition her hand to stop the flesh slipping away from her. She worked in a daze, concentrating on Armstar's words.

"I do. But it's broken." Armstar's voice hissed between gritted teeth. "There are rules, laid down by God. We were never meant to kill humans. If an angel takes too many lives, our immortality shield shatters, leaving us vulnerable." Armstar's delicate hands curled into fists, and he gripped the frozen earth beneath him.

Renira paused, the needle just poking into his flesh. "So, you've killed a lot of people?" *Maybe the king was right and he is a despot?*

Armstar fell silent, and in that silence Renira heard a bird call. The sounds of the forest returning. She hoped that meant the demon was far away from them now. Renira pushed the needle through flesh once again, and the angel hissed in pain before continuing.

"Our shields used to recover. Repair themselves the same way a body heals, I suppose. But not since the Godless Kings killed my father. Now, once they're broken, they are gone. It's been hard adjusting to life being so... damned vulnerable." He grimaced.

Renira smiled at the angel. "All children learn how fragile they are at some point." She'd meant it in jest, but the angel glared at her and shook his head. Renira pushed the needle through his flesh for a final time. She pulled the hair tight, closing the wound, then tied it off and leaned down to bite the excess hair away. "Will it heal now?"

Armstar closed his eyes and nodded. "Eventually."

"You have some other wounds." A long gash down his forearm was bleeding into his robes, and he had half a dozen scratches around his face.

"Minor things."

Renira peered at his injured arm. It probably wasn't deep enough to sew, but it could do with a bandage. Only they didn't have any spare. She pulled the silver ribbon Aesie had given her from her hair and wrapped it twice around Armstar's wounded arm before tying it in a tight knot. It would have to do.

"Can you walk?" She stood and held out a hand to the angel. She was beyond weary, and her legs and arms felt heavy, but she couldn't give up yet. One of them had to keep pushing forward, and she doubted the angel was going to be much help.

And I suppose I did promise to get him through the forest. He could have mentioned the bloody demon beforehand though.

Armstar clutched Renira's hand, and she pulled him to his feet, leaning against the strain of his weight. Once upright, he swayed and staggered a few steps before catching himself on a tree and leaning there, breathing heavily. "I think I can walk. But I can feel the poison inside."

That didn't sound good. "Can you fight it?"

Again, the angel chuckled. "My shield may be broken, but I'm still more than human. I'll manage." He sounded relentless rather than confident.

Renira nodded and put her little needle in a pocket, then walked over to the boy. He was still and quiet, his breathing so shallow she might have mistaken him for dead if not for his roving eyes so dark yet full of fear. "Can you..." She was about to ask Armstar if he could carry the boy, but the angel was barely staggering upright himself, lurching between trees as he moved onward.

He was not a large boy, shorter than her and skinny as a weed. He also stank worse than a midden heap. His wounds, those she could see, were shallow things, but no doubt the poison had gotten to him. Renira sighed in frustration, but there was nothing else for it. She couldn't leave him behind. She knelt and struggled to get the boy up onto her back, hoping she didn't wound him further in the process. Eventually she got his arms over her shoulders and supported his legs as she stood.

"Just... like carrying... a pig," she said, remembering hauling farmer Hay's hogs about for him a winter back. "Though hopefully... you won't piss... down my back. I mean it!"

The boy mumbled something in her ear.

As she stumbled after Armstar, she quickly realised she had underestimated how much the boy weighed and admitted to herself she had no idea if she was equal to the task.

I could always drop him. Leave him to the demons or the beasts of the forest. But that wouldn't be heroic at all. Mother would never leave anyone behind.

"Is my mother a hero?" Renira called ahead.

Armstar did not reply.

The boy mumbled something with a mouth that barely worked. To Renira's ears it either sounded like *thank you* or *I'll kill you*. She truly hoped it was the former.

Somewhere in the distance, the demon roared.

CHAPTER 12

The alchemical properties of Humblebuck, Titroot, and Carrionshade are well documented cure-alls. That is to say, anyone who takes them is likely to evacuate every drop of water in their body, along with any toxins. Proper distillation and dilution is essential.

— KEMRA PON, *ALCHEMY BY ANY MEANS*

Borik considered the forest a horribly depressing place. Between the gloom and the spiders scuttling through the webbing above, the detritus that seemed to crawl with insects and the noise of some giant beast crashing through the trees like a drunk through a busy tavern. Forests were quite simply not for him. He preferred the hustle and bustle of a city, where leads could be drummed up with a few well-placed questions and some even more well-placed coins. With just a single drop of angel blood, he could buy the services of an army of spies. No one escaped him in a city. But here in the forest, he couldn't tell a track from a trap or a trail from an ant's nest. He'd already come across a couple of the latter, and they swarmed with the little beasts. Thousands of them all scrambling over each other, little legs flailing and... he shivered. Just thinking about it made his skin crawl.

He slipped between the trees and cursed the poor light. His vision was better than most, but there was nothing his eyes could do against overwhelming darkness. Other than brief glimmers of the bronze Bone Moon escaping through the canopy of needles above, the only light was from the fires up ahead. He envied Perel her wolf sight and her sense of smell, but he would have neither of those things. There was no animal he felt comfortable enough bonding with over a course of angel eyes. But that was all right. She had her advantages, and he had his—it was just unfortunate that his advantages tended to be rather disadvantageous when surrounded by trees and wild animals and so much bloody dirt.

Borik passed another tree, trailing a hand along its rough bark, and the full scope of the conflict came into view. He leaned his back against the tree and clapped his hands together slowly. "Quite the battle, sister. I'm sorry I missed it." Torches burned everywhere, some in the hands of Perel's Dogs, and others discarded and sizzling on the forest floor. At least four of the Dogs were down, and three of those didn't appear to be moving. The creature, which Borik decided looked like someone had crossed a sloth with a spider with a crocodile, with no sense for aesthetic, lay oozing on the ground. Blood and something fouler stunk up the air, and the mucus leaking from the creature's mouth appeared to be bubbling.

A much smaller version of the monster scuttled across the ground towards him, and Borik aimed a kick at it, flinging it away. It landed on one of the downed Dogs and quickly burrowed into the man's clothing. He didn't move and Borik had the feeling he probably wouldn't ever again.

"Are you following us, brother?" Perel asked as she put a booted foot on the creature's collar bone and wrenched her Godslayer halberd out of its neck with a spray of steaming gore. The monster was immense, with a span that easily reached twenty metres, claw to claw. Its brutish face was a mess of fresh wounds, burns by the looks of them, and it had something small lodged in one ruined eye.

"I was following a trail," Borik said. "I was hoping it was the angel's, but alas it appears to be yours. I think we can all agree I'm a little out of my element here."

Perel grinned as she wiped the blade of her halberd on a cloth and then tossed the cloth on the slain beast. "Too much wilderness and not enough drunken debauchery?"

Borik pushed away from the tree and skirted around the body of a fallen Dog. "You should try the debauchery sometime, sister. It might loosen you up."

He'd always found it a little strange that his sister had no interest in men or women, and it was ever fun to poke around the issue to make her bristle.

"I'll leave the tedium to you." She quickly turned her attention to her wolf. "Tesh, leave it!" The wolf was sniffing around the tail of the monster, creeping closer toward the barbed stinger on the end. The wolf stopped and growled at the tail. Borik left his sister's side and approached the wolf.

"Easy there, Tesh. You know me." Borik held up a hand for the wolf to sniff, then moved past the beast and crouched down by the tail. It was almost five meters long and thick with muscle. Borik would have expected it to be prehensile, but it appeared to be muscled in a way that meant it would hang down below the creature, capable of delivering a crushing blow of force to prey on the ground. Blood coated the stinger, evidence it had seen recent use, and the venom glinted yellow in the flickering torch light.

"Sound off," Perel shouted. "Who's wounded?"

The Dogs began barking. Eight of them claimed they were unscathed, two complained about minor injuries, and at least one only managed to mumble by way of reply. Perel stalked among her wounded, checking on their wounds. Borik tried his best to ignore the wolf staring over his shoulder and set to the tail with his belt knife. The scales were tough, but once he had sawed through them, the muscle parted easily enough. Tesh growled as Borik separated the stinger from the tail.

"What are you doing?" Perel asked.

"Alchemy, sister. It's the basis of everything we know about preservation, poison, and curatives. And you'd be amazed how often it starts with cutting open a beasty's gooey bits."

With a few more slices, he found what he was looking for, a fleshy sack coloured purple and bulging with viscous fluid. A venom sack. Borik pulled a glass vial from his satchel and took the stopper off, draining the preservation alcohol. Then he made a small incision into the sack and let some of the fetid yellow ooze drip into the vial. The stench was like rotten egg having a competition with human waste to see which could smell worse.

"Alchemy? That why you're carrying around blood vials?" Perel asked, nodding toward the glass vial in Borik's hand.

He waited until the vial was three quarters full, then pulled it away quickly, careful not to spill any venom on his skin. Then he stoppered the vial and held it up to the light from the torch in his sister's hand. "Well, Father said we could take what we wanted from the angel," Borik said. "I thought I'd drink my fill and take a few sips for later as well. Besides, you know how much a vial of angel blood is worth."

Perel shrugged in reply. Borik sometimes forgot his sister had no real concept of money or trade value. She lived in a world of wilderness and wolves. Money was a construct of civilisation, and she wanted no part in anything that it had to offer. Borik wagered his sister wouldn't even bother talking to another human if not for a desire to see their father's will be done.

"A lot," Borik said. "I could buy half a city with just one vial." It was a slight overstatement, but nothing made a point quite like hyperbole.

Again, Perel shrugged. "Why would you want to?"

Borik sighed. "It was more a figure of speech in order to show... You know, it doesn't matter." Perel was grinning at him. "Angel blood is worth a lot!"

"And illegal to sell. By Father's own laws."

They stared at each other for a few seconds and Borik set his jaw. He wouldn't let his sister intimidate him. Or at least he wouldn't let her realise that she did.

Perel turned away from the dead beast and nodded toward where one of her Dogs lay on the forest floor, not moving. "Can you help him?"

Borik approached the unfortunate man. He was still as a frozen pond, laid out on his back and not moving anything save for eyes full of pleading. He had a wound in his leg, or at least what remained of a wound, the flesh around it was melted and sizzling.

"I cleaned it as best I could," Perel said. "Then I closed the wound with a hot dagger." Blisters had already formed around the wound, and there was yellow pus seeping from the melted flesh. The smell of it, combined with the general odour of the man, was overpowering, and Borik wrinkled his nose against the stench.

"You're the wild one, sister," Borik said. "Looks like venom to me. Paralysis."

"True. But I've never seen a beast like this before. You know about poisons and alchemy and all that. What can help him?"

The man's eyes flicked from Perel to Borik and back again. His mouth twitched. "Hhhhhhhhp eeeeeeeeee."

Borik took a step back, away from the stench of the man. "You could try a cure-all, something to flush his system of the toxins, but there's no guarantee this isn't permanent."

Panic entered the man's eyes at the word permanent.

"Could you make one?" Perel asked. "A cure-all?"

Borik grimaced. "Maybe. I might be able to scrounge together some likely ingredients here, but it would take hours. Maybe longer. There would be water to boil, bark to dissolve... Honestly, it's a lot of hassle."

They both knew they didn't have hours to waste. Not with the hunt still hot in Perel's veins. Not with their quarry close. The Dog looked scared. A big man, scarred and clearly no stranger to a fight, yet here he was entirely helpless. There was something a little appealing about that.

Perel drew in a deep breath and raised her voice. "Is anyone willing to carry Arst?"

A silence drifted through the gathered Dogs. A few of them sniffed and had the sense to look away, others just stared on with hungry eyes. This was what happened when men and women were selected from the very worst society had to offer. They were little better than demons.

Perel nodded, though it was clearly more to herself. "Sorry about this, Arst." She hefted her halberd from her shoulder, gripped the haft in both hands and brought it down hard. The blade bit through flesh and bone and the frozen earth beneath. Arst's head rolled clear of his neck. A couple of the nearby Dogs laughed like jackals. Borik looked away in distaste.

Perel wiped her blade clean on Arst's dirty tunic and stepped clear of the pooling blood soaking into the earth. "Anyone else too injured to go on?" she asked. The other two wounded Dogs struggled to their feet. Neither of them, it appeared, had been struck by the tail of the beast. Within moments, some of the scurvier Dogs moved forward, and Arst was quickly stripped of his belongings, everything down to his small clothes.

Tesh approached her mistress and licked at Perel's hand where some blood had splattered. Borik watched it and shook his head. "It's a wonder to me that the Dogs are so willing to scavenge their own dead, yet even the wolf has respect enough to leave the man in peace."

Perel glanced over her shoulder and rolled her eyes at Borik. "My wolves have honour. The Dogs serve their purpose better without it."

"Well, yes, there's a poetry in that, I suppose."

Perel crouched down, staring hard at a patch of dirt that had been brushed clear of needles. Her wolf joined her, sniffed at the dirt and then let out a lingering whine. "We're moving," Perel said suddenly, her voice pitched to carry. "If any of you can't keep up, you'll be left behind." She turned to Borik. "Don't follow me, brother."

Borik held up his hands and flashed Perel his most disarming smile, the one he knew would raise her hackles. "I wouldn't dream of it, sister."

"Good. That angel is mine!" Perel stalked away, disappearing quickly into the gloom so that all Borik could see of her was a bobbing torch. The Dogs followed, slipping in between trees and hurrying to keep up. Tesh remained for a few moments longer, yellow-green eyes boring into Borik. She gave a low growl, then turned and bounded after her mistress.

Borik found himself alone amongst the trees, with only a dead Dog and a dead monster for company. He was hard pressed to decide which one smelled worse. He waited a few minutes, until he was sure his sister and her pack were gone, then left the dead to their open graves and set his feet on a different path. He didn't need to follow Perel. Borik knew exactly where the angel was going, and he would get there first.

CHAPTER 13

Knowledge can be such a heavy burden to bear, especially when weighed down by the need for action.

— ERTIDE HOSTAIN. YEAR 43 OF THE FOURTH
AGE. 2 YEARS BEFORE HEAVEN FELL

"I can't go on," Renira said as her legs gave up beneath her. She collapsed, and the boy spilled from her shoulders to slump bonelessly on the detritus. She was exhausted, tired, hungry. All she wanted was to close her eyes and...

"Renira!" Armstar shook her awake. She startled and opened her eyes to see the same dark forest canopy as before. A part of her had hoped the angel would have let her sleep until morning. She tried to fend him off with flailing hands and closed her eyes to sleep again. "No, Renira. I can't let you sleep."

Go away.

When she opened her eyes again, the angel's face filled her view. His skin was so pale, like fresh cow's milk straight from the teat. His eyes were...

"Stupid girl, wake up!" Armstar said as he pulled her into a sitting position.

Renira suddenly found herself wide awake. She was still exhausted, but the weariness no longer pulled at her eyelids,

"What did you do to me?" she asked.

Armstar grimaced and stepped away. "Get up!" he growled. "We have to keep moving. We have to get out of this damned forest."

"I can't." Renira's voice sounded small and pathetic to her own ears. "I'm so tired." Her limbs felt like dead wood.

I just need a minute to rest.

"Up!" Armstar grabbed Renira's arm and wrenched her to her feet with surprising ease. He kept a hand under her arm to steady her. "Which way is north?"

Renira tried her best to focus, swaying on her feet. He might have forced her into wakefulness somehow, but the edges of her vision were fuzzy. She squinted up to the forest canopy to see webbing shining in the shards of azure moonlight that snuck through the trees. That meant the Caped Moon was up. Without woodsmen's marks or clear sight of the sky, how could she possibly find north? All the trees here were growing on a slant, as though the ground weren't level, but they were not on a hill. Something her mother had once told her came back to her slowly.

Mother had always liked to keep plants, flowers for the house and herbs for the garden. They grew some vegetables as well, and a couple of apple trees sat near the southern fence, but her mother always preferred things with colour, the more vibrant the better. Flowers needed remarkably little to grow, just soil, water, and light. If they had to, they would go in search of that light, leaning towards it. Here, in the deep forest, the trees clamoured together, competing for the light, always trying to outgrow their neighbours. Some leaned one way, and others leaned a different way, but there was one direction none of the nearby trees leaned.

Renira pointed. "That way."

"You're certain?" Armstar said sceptically.

Renira shook her head groggily. "No. But it's my best guess. At worst, it's not the way we came, so at least we're running away from the demon. Yay."

"Let's go then," Armstar said and set off. He seemed stronger than before, his feet surer and his back straighter. Renira had no idea how long they had been walking since their encounter with the demon, but she had to admit she was impressed by his divine constitution. She wished her own was so strong.

Renira stumbled over to the boy. He was exactly where she had left him, paralysed except for his eyes. A dead weight to carry, bearing her down, slowing her, making her legs burn with every step. Just the thought of trying to get the boy onto her back again made Renira want to give up. She simply couldn't face carrying him anymore. She had not the strength left. It would be so much easier just to leave him. It's not like he could argue or even beg for them not to leave him. All he would be able to do was watch them walk away, knowing that he was going to die.

Sounds horrible. A lonely, horrid way to die.

Armstar stopped only a dozen paces away when he realised Renira hadn't followed him. He stood there and watched while she deliberated over the boy. "Saving him has nearly killed us once already. He's a burden. Why do you insist on bringing him with us?"

"Why do you insist on trying to make me leave him behind?" Renira paced around the boy, looking for a long stick. "You could offer to carry him for a bit."

Armstar snorted.

"I thought you'd say that. *I'm a super strong angel. Divine strength. More than human. Thank you for saving my life, Renira, let me help you carry the boy.*"

Armstar glared at her.

Renira said nothing. It had been a terrible impression of him, but she refused to apologise.

"You've already saved his life," Armstar said. "The creature is behind us. If the venom is temporary, he will recover soon and can find his own damned way out of the forest. If it's permanent, there's nothing you can do for him here or anywhere we might take him."

"Well done. That's a very logical way to reason away leaving a young boy to die." The angel couldn't seem to see the difference between what was right and what was wrong, but it wasn't her place to teach him. She had to save the boy. It was the right thing to do. It was what her mother would do.

Armstar was not at all like the stories from the books nor the ones her mother used to tell. This angel seemed callous, caring only for himself. And he was wasting time that could be better spent helping her.

She scooped up a branch from the floor. It was almost as long as she was tall, thick enough that it wouldn't snap under a bit of pressure, and green enough to bend rather than break. "Find me another stick as long as this one," Renira said.

"Why would I—"

"Just shut up and do it. It costs you nothing." She set about stripping the branch of all the little offshoots, wrenching them first one way then the other to weaken them, then snapping them off as close to the main branch as possible. As she worked, it dawned on her she'd just told an angel to shut up.

Standing up to authority. Elsa would be proud of me.

When Renira was done, she had a long stick riddled with knobbly knuckles and still green from life. Armstar dumped a similar branch by her side, and she ordered him to strip it while she slipped her coat from her shoulders and tied the left side of it to the stick, slipping it through the button holes and sleeves. She then took the second stick from Armstar and tied the right side of her coat to that. In no time at all, there was a makeshift stretcher that would hopefully be strong enough to carry a small, skinny, paralysed boy. She rolled the boy onto her coat, knelt at the front of the stretcher, and lifted. It was not easy, and the weight of the boy still felt like an anvil dragging her down, but the stretcher held. Still, she wished the angel would stop being such a stubborn arse and help. Farmer Hay kept a recalcitrant donkey that tried to bite everyone who went near its head, and kick anyone who dared go near its backside, and even it had a sunnier disposition than Armstar.

"Lead the way, Grumpy," Renira said with a forced grin. Armstar set off, and she trailed after him, ignoring the biting cold that seemed to find its way through her winter clothing.

"My name is Renira Washer," she said over her shoulder as she walked, panting at the effort. "I don't know yours, and you can't talk, so I'm going to keep calling you *boy*. If that's alright with you, stay silent. Good. That bundle of grump up ahead is Armstar. See his wings? He's an angel. A real angel. Bet you never thought you'd see one. To tell you the truth, he's a little disappointing. You'll learn that soon enough."

Armstar set a gruelling pace. No more did he stumble between trees, barely able to keep his legs beneath him. Renira envied his vigour. She talked to the boy when she could find the breath, sometimes asking him questions she knew he couldn't answer, sometimes just telling him about Riverden and her friends, or her mother. Even paralysed he was the best company she'd had in days.

As night turned to day, the sounds of the forest awoke. Birds cried and insects chirped, and other, larger animals brought the forest to life with lingering cries and hoots that echoed between the trees. Renira looked up to see sunlight through the leaves above, and the spider webs that had coated the branches were nowhere to be seen. They had passed out of the deep forest. If their course was still true, and they were headed north, they might leave the trees behind them in day or two at the most. That meant she was almost half way through her first real adventure, and it had only nearly cost her life. Always in her dreams, they had been exciting, but the peril had been a distant thing. They were dreams, she knew she'd survive them. The danger of a real adventure, it turned out, was not a distant thing at all. It was close and heart pounding and far more terrifying than exciting.

But I fought a demon. And I won. She was already pondering how she might recount the story to Aesie and the others though she knew they'd never believe her.

Armstar paced ahead of her, his limp almost gone and his back straight. If not for the blood staining his shirt and trousers, she almost wouldn't believe he had ever been injured.

"Look for any suspicious marks on trees," Renira said. "All my food went up with my pack." She didn't bother pointing out that without a woodsman's cache, she might not make it to the edge of the forest. She had no idea how long a person could last without food, but her stomach was already beginning to ache from the hunger. Stabbing pains that near doubled her over. The thirst was even worse and every swallow felt like gravel tearing at her throat.

Armstar grunted but said nothing. He didn't even glance back at her.

"And feel free to take a turn pulling the stretcher," Renira called after him, a sullen tone creeping into her voice.

"Oh no," the angel said without turning. "You're so determined to save him. I carried that boy long enough, and he almost got me killed for the effort. He is your burden to bear." A sly tone crept into his voice. "Of course, if you find it so tiring, you could always just let him go. Leave him here."

Renira glanced back over her shoulder at the boy. His gaze met hers, and he rolled his eyes. Renira had to stifle a laugh.

"Don't worry," she said quietly. "I'm not going to leave you. No matter what, I'll get you to safety. Somehow. I'll get us both to safety. I might leave him behind though." Of course the boy said nothing, only stared at her through dark eyes.

"You don't like humans much, do you?" Renira said, turning her attention back to the path ahead. The last thing she wanted was to run into another tree. Or another demon.

"Your people have hunted mine almost to extinction," Armstar said, his hands balled into fists at his side.

"Not all of us," Renira said lightly. "I didn't even believe you existed until a few days ago."

The angel snorted so loudly it startled a nearby bird into flight. "Ignorance and innocence do not make up for dutiful compliance."

"What?"

Armstar sighed. "When the First Godless King started killing and eating angels, your people clamoured to support him, eager to win a chance to feast on our flesh and blood. We spent centuries and countless lives freeing you from the yoke of the demons. We taught you language, letters and numbers, philosophy and art. We taught you to build wonders that could stand the test of a thousand years. *I* taught your people to build. *I* taught the Godless Kings to build. And you turned on us. The moment you realised what powers our blood held and how you could steal it, you turned on us. Not just the Godless Kings. Not just a city. Not in tens, not even in your hundreds. As an entire people. You killed us. Hunted us. Ate us."

"My mother didn't," she said in a quiet voice. A weak argument. She felt the amulet nestled against her skin under her tunic and itched to squeeze it. But she couldn't spare a hand, so she chewed her lip instead.

"No. Some of you stayed loyal, I suppose," Armstar admitted grudgingly. "But just as a son should not be blamed for the father's sins, nor should the son be praised for the father's virtues." The angel glanced over his shoulder at Renira. "I see a lot of her in you. Perhaps one day you too will earn my respect. But I doubt it. Your mother was special."

"Was?"

"Though I doubt I will ever see her again now. Especially not if you do not pick up the pace." He quickened his footstep.

"It's not fair..." Renira said between breaths as she hurried on, "for you to blame me. I didn't do any of those things. You say it's not fair to blame a son for the father's sins, but that's exactly what you're doing. Blaming humanity for something someone did a thousand years ago. It isn't fair."

"Life isn't fair." Armstar glanced back at her through the ruined, charred bones of his wings. "Have you ever done anything to try to stop them? These humans who still hunt my kind, kill us for our blood?"

"I didn't even think you were real until a few days ago. And I'm only sixteen winters old, what should I have done?" She was tiring fast moving so quickly, and the sweat and rough bark of the sticks was chafing her palms.

"And in another two winters what will you have done?" Despite the quickened pace, Armstar didn't appear to be labouring at all. "After I make it to the Cracked Mountains, will you help me further? Or flee back to your mother? I'll wager you go running back to your life of comfort. Comfort earned off the back of my murdered brothers and sisters."

"Comfort?" Renira gasped in a breath. She couldn't keep up the pace and slowed, her footsteps dragging. "We barely make enough to live. The house is falling apart, and my mother spends all day, every day, washing other people's clothes. We're one step above begging on the bloody streets and you call that comfort?"

Armstar slowed and glanced back at her, a sneer on his lips. "Are you being hunted?"

"Right now. Yes." *Because of you!* It wasn't fair of him to attack her so when she was putting herself in danger for his benefit.

"The Godless King won't stop," Armstar said. "He has sworn to end angelkind, to wipe all trace of the God from this world. To destroy my people. He does not quit. Once he begins something, he sees it through. There are fewer than ten of us left, and every time one of us dies, I feel it.

"So yes. You may live in near poverty, but I call that comfort. I live in constant pain and fear. I am hunted. And if ever I am caught, I will be cut up and served as a feast to the Godless King and his children for the power in my flesh." Armstar slowed to a stop then and turned to Renira, his eyes hard and damning.

"Ignorance may have excused you until now, but you no longer have that luxury. Thanks to your incessant questions, you are now burdened with the knowledge of my plight." There was a mocking tone in the angel's voice. "So, make your choice, Renira Washer. When the mountains are in sight, will you run back to your mother and your easy life? Forget about me and the monsters who hunt my kind? Or will you choose to do something to help me and to help the world? *That* is the choice your mother once made, and *that* is why I respect her and not the rest of your cursed kind." He jutted his chin toward something over Renira's shoulder, and she turned to see markings carved into a nearby tree. Another bearing and another buried cache. Renira's stomach gave a growl at the hopeful thought of food.

"We'll rest here a few hours," said Armstar. "Eat and sleep. Regain what strength you can." Somewhere in the distance a wolf's howl drifted through the forest. "Our flight is not yet over."

CHAPTER 14

Hel's Wall cannot be a natural formation. It is too sheer and too uniform. Yet, the angels have never been humble, and not one of them claims responsibility for its creation, not even the insufferable Builder. This leads me to wonder who created the wall? Who could have raised such a formation from the earth? And why?

— ARANDON HOSTAIN. YEAR 35 OF THE FOURTH
AGE. 10 YEARS BEFORE HEAVEN FELL

When the trees started thinning out, Renira knew they were nearing the edge of the forest. Crimson light streamed in from above, the brilliance of a new day chasing away the chill of a cold night. Without her coat, the cold seeped into Renira's clothing and turned her sweat icy against her skin. The boy shivered. She wasn't sure if that was a good sign or not, but his eyes were closed and his breathing slow. Renira hoped he was merely asleep. Armstar had said little all day and night and settled into a brooding pace that left Renira struggling to keep up. Still, the angel did not offer to help pull the stretcher. By the time the mountains peeked into view through the last of the trees, Renira was certain it was her defiance, as much as her desire to save the boy's life, that kept her blistered hands clasped around the wooden sticks.

A wolf howled. It was becoming a regular noise, and it sounded closer than before. Apparently, it wasn't enough they were being chased by a Godless King and a six-limbed tree demon, now they were being hounded by wolves as well. Every time the howl wailed through the forest, Armstar's wings twitched, and he redoubled his pace.

Renira had a decision to make, and she was fast running out of time to make it. *Do I turn around? Go back home to Mother and put an end to my adventure? Or follow in her footsteps and go on with Armstar and... what? Fight against the king? I'm no warrior. I'm not even a healer like Mother. I'm not anything.*

The Cracked Mountains erupted from the ground in the far distance like a bear's teeth. Snow-capped peaks dominated the horizon. Mother had once told Renira that at the southern base of the mountains were sheer cliffs that served as a border of sorts. They were known as Hel's Wall, and the cliffs stretched on for a hundred miles and had thousands of cracks running through them, large and small. Some of those cracks dead ended or got so tight they'd make a miser's purse strings horny, others doubled back on themselves or looped into another entrance. There were only a handful of passages that led through the cliffs to the mountains beyond, and it was impossible to determine which without prior knowledge.

Armstar stopped at one of the last trees as the forest ended, a delicate hand upon the bark, his eyes locked on the clear red sky. There was barely a cloud to be seen. A few birds soared high above, mostly hawks or such. Renira trudged past the angel, her feet dragging from the exhaustion. They were a mass of pain on top of agony, and she dared not take her shoes off to check them for the fear she had now more blister than foot.

"Get back here, fool," the angel dashed forward and grabbed Renira by the shoulders, pulling her back to the tree line. She should have been angry, but she simply didn't have the energy and collapsed down next to the last tree and hung her head. Sweat dripped from her forehead onto the earth below, and the chill quickly crept in and made her shiver.

The wolf howled once again. Renira sighed at the noise. "Go chase a rabbit, will you? Leave us be."

"Hurry up," Armstar said under his breath. The left side of his tunic had gone stiff with dried blood, but he claimed the wound was healing well, and Renira could believe it considering the ease with which he moved.

The boy remained silent, laid out on the stretcher, but his eyes roved the sky, following the gliding passage of a bird, barely more than a black mark against the bloody red.

"Why are we waiting?" Renira asked. "The cliffs are right there. Or are they further away than I think?" Her vision swam as the smoky numbness of sleep picked apart her consciousness like strands of jerky.

She slapped herself hard on the cheek. The sting of it brought her back awake, and she fumbled in her tunic pocket, then pulled out a little strip of salted meat she had taken from the last woodsman's cache. She shoved it in her mouth and chewed. They had no water, her mouth tasted foul, and her head pounded from dehydration. She wished so badly that it would rain again, despite knowing that with her coat used as a stretcher, the rain would soak her through, and she'd likely freeze to death. It seemed all her options ended in some form of death. A morbid part of her imagination began wondering what it would be like to freeze, or die of dehydration, or starve, or be eaten by wolves. She decided if she died here she would rise again as a ghost and haunt Armstar.

"We can't break from the tree cover while the sky is so clear," Armstar said. "Our hunters might already be at the forest edge, just waiting for us to show ourselves. And I don't like the look of those birds."

Renira groaned in frustration. "What's wrong with the birds? Is it the wings? You don't like that their wings are nicer than yours?"

The angel glared at Renira.

"Sorry. That was mean."

He turned his gaze back to the sky. "The Godless King has a hawk. He can see through its eyes."

"Really? How?"

"Because they ate the eyes of an angel."

The salted meat in Renira's mouth suddenly tasted vile. "That's horrible. I'm sorry I asked."

Armstar snorted. "Did you think I was joking when I said your kind eat mine? How do you think the Godless King and his children have lived so long? Centuries, more, even. They steal time from us by drinking our blood. Make themselves stronger by eating our flesh. Feed our brains to children to make Seers. They..."

"Enough," Renira said, hating the weary defeat in her voice. She swallowed the bit of meat she was chewing and pocketed the rest of the strip, her appetite having fled. She had never wondered where the Godless King got his immortality from. He was a constant. As sure as the sun would rise and water was wet, the king would live on and rule Helesia. He was revered. Worshipped almost as a god himself. Now it seemed a lie. If Armstar was to be believed, everything the Godless King had was stolen from angels.

The wolf howled again. Armstar turned to stare into the depths of the forest. There was something different in the sound this time, something far more insistent. "It has our trail," the angel said. "Come on." He turned back to the mountains. "Hurry up, Andari."

"Who?"

"My sister," Armstar said, again glancing to the sky.

"Another angel?" Renira asked. She wondered if another angel was coming to meet them? Perhaps one with glorious, feathery wings like in the stories. And hopefully one with a sunnier disposition who didn't mind a turn pulling the bloody stretcher.

Armstar ignored her question. "The cliffs are not far, but also not close enough."

"We can make it," Renira said. She squinted north, and the horizon seemed to shimmer and move under her scrutiny. *I can push on. I'll show him I'm not as weak as he thinks.*

"We?" Armstar said slyly. "Have you made a decision?"

Renira lowered her eyes. What would Mother think if she did not return? Would she give up her daughter for dead? Or maybe pack up her life and set out into the forest to search for her wayward child?

There was another thing to consider as well. Could Renira just go back to her old life, even after everything she had been told? King Emrik was hunting angels, devouring them. Barely any remained. And the God... Mother had always preached about the faith of God, how it had shaped humanity and made them more than beasts. But Armstar himself admitted the God was dead. Surely that meant there was no point in fighting against King Emrik. He had already won, and all the angels could do now was run and hide. If Renira went with Armstar now, that was all she could ever look forward to. A life of running and hiding from an immortal king determined to see them all stamped out of existence.

And was the king and his truth even wrong? Her mother might claim God had shaped humanity for the better, but the king's truth insisted the God's angels enslaved humanity. Which was the truth?

The wolf howled again, and there was glee in the sound. They had no more time left. High above, a hawk's piercing cry seemed to answer the wolf. Renira glanced up to see a bird circling above, little more than a dark spot against the red sky. White clouds were gathering in the far distance, above the cliffs, obscuring the mountains beyond.

"Finally," Armstar said. "I never doubted you, Andari, but it's about damned time."

Renira squinted. The clouds looked far too white and were moving too fast, eating up the mountain. As she watched, they gobbled up the cliffs and turned the entire horizon to cotton.

"Time to choose, Renira Washer," Armstar said, glaring at her. "Go back to your mother and your life and be another dutiful citizen of a tyrant king. Or come with me. Help save my people. Choose now."

Renira drew in a deep a breath and gripped her mother's amulet hard in a shaking hand. There was no choice at all. She was being chased by wolves, and they clearly had her scent. If she returned home, all she would be doing was bringing her hunters home with her. It didn't matter if the angels or the king were in the right. She had to keep going, for her mother's sake.

I'm sorry, Ma. I'll come back, when I can. I promise. Please be proud of me. She hoped her silent prayer would somehow reach her mother.

Renira shuffled over and knelt in front of the stretcher, gripping the sticks in blistered hands. "I'll help however I can."

The angel smiled at her. "Good. You're the only one who can."

"What?"

"Move fast!" Armstar said and set off at a jog that had Renira hurrying to catch up and hoping the jostling stretcher didn't shake loose the boy.

A barren, rocky plain stretched out in front of them, and white swirling clouds of madness raced to meet them. Renira's lungs burned, there were glass shards in her boots, and her palms felt scraped to the bone. Armstar raced ahead towards the oncoming cloud. It was a blanket of white that obscured all vision. A freak snowstorm rolling off the mountains and moving at a pace beyond natural. And they were heading into it. Renira wanted to stop, to turn away from the storm, but Armstar ran on, and she had no choice but to follow.

Moments stretched into minutes. Renira's run faltered into a stumble as she passed her limits, and only her own momentum and the sight of the angel's back kept her moving at all. The wolf howled again, clearer now. Renira risked a glance over her shoulder and saw dark shapes emerging from the tree line. The wolf barked and leapt into a loping run.

Renira screamed in alarm as her foot clipped a rock, and she went head over heels, crashing down and bashing her elbows, knees, and hip. New pain burst to life all over, but she didn't have time consider it. The boy had rolled free of the stretcher and was lying face down amongst the rocks, bleeding from a new cut on his head. Renira rushed to his side and desperately began rolling him back onto the stretcher. She'd borne him too far to let him die now. A savage bark warned her the wolf was getting closer. She glanced up, and the beast was near enough for her to see the malice in its eyes.

"Get down!" Armstar shouted. Renira crouched down in front of the stretcher, shielding the boy with her body. The angel slid to a halt behind Renira and pointed a hand towards the wolf. "Fear!" The word hissed through his teeth.

The wolf stumbled and yelped. Its legs gave up, and it crashed down only a dozen loping paces away. It scrambled in the dust for a few moments, then let out a panicked yip and turned, charging away with its tail tucked between its legs.

Renira laughed, a manic sound full of relief. But when she turned to thank Armstar, she saw the snowstorm over his shoulder, and the relief turned to dread.

"Stay down!" Armstar shouted over the noise of the oncoming storm. He pulled Renira close, his body shielding her from the storm, and Renira dragged the stretcher behind her.

The storm hit and everything went white. Even shielded by Armstar's body, the snow whipped around and blew into Renira's face, all but blinding her. She was already cold, shivering from the chill in the air, but the storm sapped her body heat, and she had to clench her teeth to stop them from chattering.

Armstar leaned close, his face pressed against hers so she felt his breath on her cheek. "We have to move," he shouted. "The storm won't stop them. We have to reach Hel's Wall."

Renira tried to force her body to move, but the stiffness had set in quick, and the cold was sapping her will along with her warmth. With the snow coating the ground so quickly, it would be an easy thing to lie down and go to sleep. It looked so soft, like a cold pillow. She always liked her pillows cold, constantly shifting them underneath her head to find the coolest side.

"Renira!" Armstar shouted. She could barely see him, just a vague darkness in front of her, already coated in snow. "Hold on to me, and I'll guide us."

Renira shook her head and shouted against the fury of the storm, "I can't let go of the stretcher!"

Armstar didn't respond. Renira wondered what he was considering. He could grab her and pull her away, and it was unlikely she'd ever find the stretcher again, or would he use that strange power he had to command people and make her leave the boy behind. She couldn't allow the boy to freeze to death in the storm, paralysed and cold and alone. She gripped the sticks even tighter, grateful that the cold was numbing the pain.

"Give me one of the sticks," the angel shouted into the maelstrom. His body shifted, and the full force of the storm smacked against Renira, knocking her onto her arse. She let go of the right stick and clutched the left as tightly as she could, using her other hand to grip the amulet against her chest. The connection to her mother gave her strength enough to force her way back to her feet and lean into the storm.

A hand settled on Renira's shoulder, and some of the weight of the stretcher was taken from her. She couldn't see Armstar. Couldn't see anything but a swirling white vortex.

"Strength," the angel said, and Renira felt some of the exhaustion drain away. "Now walk!"

Renira lurched forward a step and then another, letting the angel guide the way. She closed her eyes against the storm, and her world became darkness and cold and dragging feet step after gruelling step.

Renira lost track of time. One foot after another, trudging on towards eternity. Her feet no longer hurt. They were too numb for that now. The shivering stopped, replaced by a raw feeling that spread throughout her entire body. She leaned into the icy wind and let it batter her. One hand on the stretcher, the other clasped around her mother's amulet. She could feel neither of them anymore. She felt nothing except the weary determination to keep on going. She stumbled, her feet going out beneath her, and her knees hit the ground. The snow cushioned the impact, but there were sharp stones beneath, and the sting of them cutting into flesh somehow made it through the numbness. Armstar pulled Renira back to her feet, wrenching her shoulder so hard it almost came out the socket. The pain was good. It helped focus her. Renira opened her eyes to the swirling white chaos.

I will not die here. I won't. Not to wolves or snow or demons or kings. I will beat them all and survive.

Snow coated her hair and face, freezing against her skin. It caked her clothing, layer upon layer of white. She tried to shake it off but only caused herself to stumble again and almost fall. Something dark rose up before her, stretching upwards until its shape was lost in the twisting nether of the storm. Renira realised the wind had died down a little, and the snow seemed lighter here.

"Almost there," Armstar shouted over the tumult. The thought of being almost anywhere helped, and Renira put the last of her strength into one final push.

The dark shape ahead formed into solid stone, and then she was up against it. She turned and placed her back against the rock, dropping the stretcher and clutching both hands before her face. The rime caked to them was stained red from blood. Everything here had only a light coating of snow, and much of that was melting away.

Armstar dragged the stretcher closer and Renira panicked when she saw the mound of snow piled atop it. She collapsed to her knees and quickly began scooping the ice away, desperately trying to find the boy buried beneath. If he was still there at all. Her questing hands found something, but they were too numb to tell what. She pushed the snow away until the boy's dark skin showed. It looked unhealthily pale, and his lips were purple. He didn't shiver, and his eyes were closed. Renira could not tell if he was breathing. It seemed so cruel that she might have rescued him from a demon and carried him out of the forest, only to have him freeze to death in a freak blizzard. The very same blizzard that had saved their lives. *I'm not dying here, and you're not either.* Renira grabbed the boy and pulled him close. Her mind moved slowly, but she knew they needed to stay warm, and sharing body heat seemed the best way to warm the boy up.

Armstar crouched by Renira's side and tried to peel her hands from the boy. "We can't stay here," the angel shouted over the storm. "We have to find the passage through the cliffs. You must follow me. Leave the boy. I'm sorry, Renira, but he's dead."

Renira stared into the dark face and brushed away some of the ice that clung to his eyes. His purple lips quivered just a little. Renira thought back to her mother, trying to remember what she had said about checking for signs of life. On their way home from Maed Turner's fields, they had found a dog collapsed just by the riverside. The poor creature looked dead, but her mother wouldn't leave it until she was certain. Renira assumed if it held true for animals, it would for people also. She moved her face close to the boy and placed her ear next to his mouth. Over the storm, it was impossible to hear if he was breathing or not. She pulled open the boy's eyelids and stared down into his eyes. They were dark, almost black, but the pupils dilated in the dizzying light of the blizzard.

Renira looked up at the angel. "He's alive!" she shouted. She tried to smile, but her face was too numb.

Armstar reached down and grabbed the boy by his tunic, then pulled him up close and into his arms, so he was carrying the boy like a babe. "Follow close behind me," Armstar shouted and set off along the cliff. Renira couldn't tell which direction they were moving and didn't care. Her legs dragged beneath her, a bone-deep ache resonating throughout her body with every step. She took the pain as a positive sign. She dragged the sticks free from the stretcher as she stumbled on, then slipped her arms back through the coat sleeves.

So close to the cliff, the snow barely reached them. The storm was blowing out from the mountains and towards the forest, and though the currents of the wind whipped the snow about, most of it was carried onward away from the cliffs. They passed dozens of cracks in the stone, some small and others large. Many had rivers of snow melt gushing out. It froze again not far from the cliffs and turned the footing treacherous with ice. Renira stumbled, her hands and knees bloody with the price of steadying herself, but she kept getting back up.

One moment Armstar was there, and the next he wasn't. Renira turned around, panic suddenly rising in her chest. She backtracked, running a hand along the cliff face until she found the crevice. Water rushed out from within, and Renira just caught sight of Armstar's ruined wings, hunched close together on his back, as he turned a corner and vanished from sight again. She stepped through the running water, her feet slipping on the ice underneath, and forged onward, hurrying to catch up with the angel.

"Stay close to me, Renira," the angel shouted, his words barely reaching her.

The crack was so thin Renira would struggle to turn around. Armstar had no chance with his ruined wings and carrying the boy. If she lost him now, she might never find him again.

Down in the crevice, the storm seemed a distant thing. Icy water rained upon Renira, but it was mostly just noise and the cold stream beneath her feet.

She turned right after Armstar, and before her all she could see was rock. She struggled onward, fighting against the little river's course and the voice in her head telling her she was already lost. Another turning to the left this time. Renira thought she heard a sound and followed. Onward she went and still saw no sign of the angel. She called out his name, screamed it, and her own voice echoed back at her. If Armstar replied, the sound was swallowed by the blizzard above and the rushing water below. It was gushing past her ankles now, making her feet feel large and unwieldy. She called out again and again, until her voice was raw, and received no reply.

Renira sloshed through the icy river as it climbed up to her calves. Panic sped her breath and drove her onward. She trailed a bloody hand on each wall of the crack, making sure she didn't miss any turnings. With no sight of Armstar, she took passages at random, reacting on nothing but instinct even though she knew it was a fool's game. She was well and truly lost. The water climbed higher as more of the snow melted down through the cracks in the cliff. Above, she could see nothing but rock and a swirling grey-white mass that blocked out even the deep red of the sky.

When the water reached her hips, Renira stopped holding back and let the tears come. They coursed down her cheeks unchecked, but she forced herself onward. She took a left turn and waded on. The water level was shallower here, only up to her thighs. It was a poor chance, but the only hope she had. Renira took the next right when she noticed the current lessened there as well, dictating her course not at random, but by the lower water levels. Soon the water was barely more than a trickle leaking down the walls of the crevice, and when

Renira looked up she could see the familiar blood red of the sky. It gave her hope.

Shivering and numb and stumbling along, using the walls of the crevice as support, it came as a shock to Renira when a warm hand reached out in front of her and grabbed her by the shoulder. The crevice ended in a sheer edge, and before her stood a figure glowing with a warm light. A woman, tall and radiant and beautiful beyond belief. She had wings of dazzling white, only the tips of her feathers turning to a smoky red. Her sandy skin glowed with life and inner fire, and her hair was like spun gold. She pulled Renira forward out of the crevice and wrapped her in a thick blanket that engulfed her.

Renira collapsed into the woman's arms and felt her mind drifting again. She saw a wide basin carved out of the cliff, with many buildings on different levels also carved into the rock itself. The angel held her tight and radiated a warmth that seeped into Renira's limbs, making them tingle uncomfortably, then scream with spiky pain.

"Welcome to Los Hold, Renira Washer," the angel said in a husky voice. "I thought we had lost you." She was so warm, so comforting. *Just like being hugged by Mother.*

Armstar's pale, delicate face loomed over Renira. His hair was plastered to his head, and he had a hard set to his mouth. "We might yet. Stupid girl, I told you to stay close."

The woman shook her head, tousled golden hair rippling. "She's safe now. I'll warm and heal her."

Armstar snorted. "None of us are safe, Eleseth. I've seen who chases us." He reached out a hand and placed cold fingers on Renira's forehead. She tried to pull away from that touch, but the woman held her firmly, swaddled in a blanket like a babe. Armstar said, "Sleep." And Renira faded away.

CHAPTER 15

My mother moved mountains. She slew demons, united a broken humanity into a people with a singular will. And yet, for all her accomplishments, she was brought low by the same stalker that hunts us all. Time. But angelkind is beyond such a wearisome predator. They are deathless, immortal. Think what humanity could accomplish were we to claim that power for ourselves. Imagine what my mother could have accomplished were she just afforded more time.

— PERSONAL DIARY OF HELENA HOSTAIN, FIRST QUEEN OF THE HOLY SANT DIEN EMPIRE. THE SECOND AGE

Renira was home. Warm and comfortable in her own bed. She woke but didn't bother to open her eyes. Instead she rolled about in her covers, wrapping herself tighter into the paradise of soft sheets, and shuffled her head until she found a cooler spot on the pillow. A contented sigh escaped her lips, and the hardships of her recent adventure seemed a lifetime away.

Perhaps it had all been a dream. There had been a bitter angel with ruined wings and a damning prejudice against humanity. A demon of the forest, lurking high in the trees. And a paralysed boy with skin the colour of charcoal and eyes darker still. An unnatural blizzard that appeared in an instant and raged like none she had ever heard of. And a woman who glowed with divine power. It was exactly the sort of dream Renira always lost herself in. An adventure just like the stories. The terror and pain and hardship seemed so far away now. She curled up tight in the warm blankets and let herself drift off back to sleep.

Someone sat on the edge of her bed. Renira could always tell when Mother sat on the bed by the way the mattress shifted. It meant Renira had overslept and was late in starting her daily chores. But sometimes, if she was quiet enough and feigned still being asleep, her mother would just watch her for a while, maybe brush some strands of hair from her face, and then eventually leave without waking her. Renira hoped it was one of those times. Even with her eyes closed, she could feel the weight on them, the tiredness. An exhaustion that went deep down to her bones. And pain. Her hands and feet hurt, a dull ache that throbbed, the discomfort worming its way past the dulled edges of oblivion and forcing her awake.

"Renira," said a woman. It was not her mother.

She feared to open her eyes to what she might see. As long as she was curled up in bed, cocooned in soft blankets, she could pretend she was back at home. Safe.

"Renira," said the woman again. Her voice was soft and husky. "I need you to wake up now. We need your help."

There was no denying it anymore, no matter how much she might want to. Renira groaned. She cracked open a single eye to see an angel sitting on the edge of the bed. It was the woman from before, the one who glowed. She was taller than anyone Renira had ever seen and bigger too, as though a human had been somehow scaled upwards. Her skin was so tanned it was almost brown, and her golden hair fell in effortless curls around her face. She wore a plain brown tunic and trousers to match, drab clothing when compared to her splendour. Her wings sat bunched up behind her back, soft white feathers turning to rusty red at the tips trailing on the bedding. She was beautiful. Too beautiful. Her eyes soft and golden as a sunset, her nose sharp as a knife and her chin round. She was so perfect she was almost painful to look at.

They were in a small room with only a bed, a washbasin, and a wicker chest with Renira's battered winter clothing resting on top. A single door led elsewhere, and a window was shuttered against the chill of approaching winter. The only light in the room came from a lantern hanging by the doorway, and the angel's natural glow like an aura of pleasant warmth. Renira reluctantly opened her second eye and grumpily admitted to herself that she was awake.

"Do you remember where you are?" the woman asked, her voice soothing.

Renira tried to stifle a yawn and failed. It turned into a full body stretch. She realised she was wearing only a white shift under the blankets and quickly pulled them up around her. The room was not cold, but she felt self-conscious.

"You're an angel." A stupid thing to say, Renira knew, but she was feeling a bit awestruck, and her traitorous mouth said the first thing that came to mind.

The woman smiled. "My name is Eleseth."

The name sounded familiar, and Renira tried to recall where she had heard it before. It had come from her mother's lips. Something read to Renira from the book. She gasped. "You're the Light Bearer. You heralded in the Second Age."

The angel's smile turned sad, a subtle lilting, and Renira felt a pang for its loss. "I did, yes. Long ago."

"How old are you? Wait, that's probably very rude to ask. Sorry." She needed to get control of her mouth before it made her seem an idiot.

Eleseth laughed. "Old enough to realise when time is precious. You have questions, and I will answer as many of them as I can, but right now we need your help. The boy you brought with you is awake." Eleseth sighed. "And demanding to speak to you."

"Thank the God he survived," Renira said. Her hand went to the amulet still hanging around her neck, her mother's icon of faith.

Eleseth frowned. "The God had nothing to do with it, Renira. You did." She shrugged. "And I suppose I did as well. Luckily for you both, my father gave me the power to heal. Now get dressed. The sooner we deal with him, the sooner I can find you some food. You must be starving."

As if to answer the angel, Renira's stomach gave a low gurgle that extended into an embarrassing growl. She was confronted by an ancient angel, probably the most beautiful... anything she had ever seen, and her stomach was making noises better suited to a starving alley cat.

Renira waited until the angel had left the room, then slipped out of bed and rushed to her clothing on the wicker chest. It had been washed and repaired, and though it would never look like new, Renira was glad that the angels had not given her something different to wear. She'd always hated the idea of robes. Her mother's coat was hanging on the back of the door, and Renira slipped her arms into the sleeves once she was dressed. Her hands and feet were still sore, but they had been bound in cloth bandages, and when Renira peeked underneath she could see the wounds were well on their way to recovering. New skin growing over old blisters. Eleseth said she had the power to heal, and there was proof of it.

When Renira stepped out of the room, it was into a crisp night bearing the prickling chill of winter. She thrust her bandaged hands into the pockets of her mother's coat and pulled it a little closer. Eleseth waited nearby, sitting on a stone bench and staring up into the sky. If the angel felt the cold with just a tunic and trousers to protect her, she did not show it. The stars were bright, tiny candle flames amidst the black, and the Caped Moon was out, its top half glowing a fierce blue, the bottom half shrouded in darkness. There were no clouds above, but outside of the basin limits Renira could see the swirling maelstrom of the blizzard still raged. The odd dancing snowflake drifted down into the sanctuary, but other than that it remained untouched by the fury of such a violent storm.

"How?" Renira asked, awestruck.

Eleseth glanced at her. "Divine power. My sister, Andari, conjured the storm, and she controls it. There's only so long it can last though, and it will soon blow itself out. But the snow should confuse your hunters for a time. Do you know where you are?"

Renira had only a vague memory of squeezing through the cracks in the cliff, trailing a hand over the rocky walls, shivering from the cold, and wading through snow melt. The glowing angel waiting for her at the end had seemed a vision. A saviour of warmth and light. "You called it Los Hold."

Eleseth stood and held out a hand. It engulfed Renira's, and walking alongside the angel she realised how much bigger the woman was than a human. Renira barely reached up to her armpit, and she was considered quite tall for a girl of her age, though Merebeth was still the taller.

"It's a sanctuary for angels," Eleseth said. "And for those who risk following the God's faith. It is, perhaps, the only safe place left to us. The Godless King would tear it down to the bedrock if he had the chance, so we have taken great pains to hide it from him." There was a note of sadness in her voice. "Come. I need to take you to the boy. He's... quite irate." Renira took heart at that. If he was irate, then he was alive, awake, and no longer paralysed. It meant she had saved him.

Los Hold sat in a basin that could not be a natural formation. Sheer cliffs rose hundreds of meters all around it, and there were crevices in all of them. Many of the buildings appeared to be carved directly from the rock. There were a few towards the edges that were grand structures with carvings in a language Renira didn't recognise and statues standing guard outside. There were plenty of people, all humans as far as Renira could tell. They seemed unconcerned by the blizzard raging all around the hidden city, and they greeted Eleseth warmly.

As they walked, Renira found herself gawking up at a statue standing at the head of a long stone bridge. It stood almost twice as tall as her and was of an angel encased in bronzed armour, carrying a spear that shone even in the darkness, and with wings of gold and brown. A beautiful work of art and just as she had always imagined an angel should be. Renira jumped when the statue turned its head to watch her pass.

Eleseth laughed. "That's just my brother, Mihiriel. He likes to stand guard outside the Temple of Lore and spook our newer acolytes."

"Must you ruin all my fun, Eleseth?" the angel said in a deep, sonorous voice. "I've not seen this little one before."

"This is..."

"Renira Washer," Renira said as she gazed up at the bronzed angel. His armour was so flawless and complete no part of the body showed except for his eyes, glowing green through slits in his pointed helm. His wings were hunched up high on his back and reminded Renira of a hawk, and his armour was decorated in flowing whorls that made her think of the wind.

Mihiriel's armour rattled as he knelt on one knee before her so they were eye level. Still she could not see into the dark depths of his helm. "So this is Lusa's daughter? She's a bit small."

Renira frowned at that. "I'm a perfectly normal size for a human, thank you. Taller than my mother, at least."

"Really?" Mihiriel said. "It must just be the shadow she cast that made her seem a giant." His emerald gaze flicked to Eleseth. "I like her. She has Lusa's fire."

More angels talking about my mother as if they were friends. Who are you, Ma?

"I have a question for you, Renira, daughter of Lusa," Mihiriel said in a jovial tone. "Each time I rise I fall again. You can set your clock by my ascension. And yet I am forever changing. What am I?"

"A riddle?" Renira asked. She loved riddles. Merebeth was always finding new ones and though Elsa and Aesie had no head and no time for them, Renira often obsessed over puzzling them out.

"Think on it," Mihiriel said, standing.

"I will. And one for you. I have legs but cannot walk, a back but cannot bend. I accept all, but only one at a time. What am I?"

"Ha!" Mihiriel clapped his gauntleted hands together so firmly the noise boomed around them. "You are a chair!"

Renira smiled and nodded to him. "Too easy?"

Mihiriel shook his head quickly and spoke excitedly. "Not at all. No one has ever offered me a riddle back before. I love it! Do you have any others?"

Renira scratched her head, trying to remember some more. "I'll have to think about it."

"Do so, please. I do love a challenge."

"Come along, Renira," Eleseth said.

"Think about it, little Washer," Mihiriel said. "What am I?"

Renira hurried after Eleseth but stared back at the other angel. Mihiriel unfurled his wings and gave them a powerful beat, stirring the dust beneath him. Renira gasped and couldn't keep the grin from spreading across her face. Here was an angel just like the stories her mother told, a radiant giant of a man. Mihiriel boomed out a laugh and strode away.

"I'll have to introduce you to Orphus later," Eleseth said. "If you think Mihiriel looks like a statue, just wait until you see our eldest brother. I swear I've seen him go entire days without so much as a twitch."

Eleseth led Renira on through the sanctuary. It was divided into tiers, with many buildings existing entirely on raised levels extending from the cliff faces. Wooden rope bridges connected the different tiers in some places, and in others they stood entirely apart, raised and unreachable. At least unreachable by anyone without wings.

Acolytes, as Eleseth called them, moved about the sanctuary. They were human, those who had dedicated their lives to the faith of the God and to the service of his angels. Some of them wore robes, others work clothes. Many were at task, tending small gardens or carving wood, tanning leather or smithing. Others appeared in quiet contemplation. Some few even carried books, and Renira recognised one of those as the same book her mother used to read from. *The Divine Truth*. A heretical text, according to the king and his laws. Despite the number of acolytes, though, the sanctuary still seemed empty. It was large enough to house ten times the number Renira saw.

They came to a long, low building carved from the rock. Armstar waited outside, standing with his arms crossed and a sour expression. He wore new robes of deep brown, no longer caked with dried blood. Eleseth towered over her brother angel like she did Renira and made them both look like children.

"Finally awake then?" Armstar said with a mocking smile. "I thought you were going to sleep through the last of the age."

"Armstar." There was a warning in Eleseth's tone.

"What? She's stronger than she looks, sister." Armstar nodded once to Renira. "She deserves to know the truth."

"That's up to Orphus to decide," Eleseth said. "Is the boy still in there?"

Armstar nodded. "Rude little shit. You should have just let me put him back to sleep."

Eleseth sighed, the feathers of her wings ruffling with annoyance. "We can't keep him asleep indefinitely."

"Of course we can. It's called death."

All humour fled Eleseth, and her glow seemed to darken somewhat, sapping the colour from the world around her. "That's enough, Armstar." She turned to Renira and smiled kindly. "The boy is in our infirmary. He's mostly recovered and quite... animated. He refuses to even tell us his name but demands to see you. Could you speak to him? Calm him down."

"Of course. I'll do what I can," she said, hoping she sounded more confident than she felt.

"He's armed," Armstar said. "A surgeon's knife he stole from the human healers."

Eleseth shook her head. "Why were the knives even out? I did the healing myself."

Armstar shrugged, his ruined wings twitching. "Humans like knives. And putting them in things."

"I'll go in first," Eleseth said. "Give me a few moments, then escort Renira in."

Eleseth ducked through the doorway, her wings crowding together on her back to allow her through, and then Renira found herself alone with Armstar again. She smiled at him.

"We made it," she said, feeling some of the tension drain away. They had been travelling together for days now and had faced down a demon together. Renira thought that gave them some kind of bond. Despite his surly attitude, given all they had been through, it was hard not to view the ruined angel as a friend.

"Barely," Armstar said with a snort. "We almost lost you in the cliffs. I told you to stay close."

Renira felt frustration creeping in again. Why was talking to Armstar so difficult? "I tried, but you moved too fast. Not all of us have divine power running through our veins."

The angel smiled at her then, an odd, knowing smile. "Perhaps you're just not as hardy as you think you are."

Renira just couldn't figure him out. One moment he was praising her for being stronger than others realised, and the next he was calling her weak.

"Hardy enough to fend off a demon while you had a lie down."

A boyish scream erupted from the infirmary.

"That would be our signal," Armstar said. "After you."

Renira pushed open the door and walked into a cloying gloom. The

windows in the building were mere slits and provided very little light. Most of
the illumination seemed to be coming from Eleseth's glow. It was a long
building but not wide, and a dozen little cots were lined up either side,
stretching out towards the far end. There was room next to each bed for a table
and a chair, and little else. The building had an oppressive feeling to it and a
sharp smell that made her nose itch, much like some of her mother's harshest
cleaning fluids. Eleseth stood in the centre of the building, her head almost
touching the roof and her glowing wings crouched close together. Her back was
to Renira, and the gentle cadence of her words drifted through the hall.

Renira hurried forward, with Armstar close behind. Just beyond Eleseth,
crouched upon one of the beds like an animal ready to dart for freedom, was the
boy. His skin was dark, though newly washed, and he was entirely naked, apparently unashamed by the fact, and held out a small silver knife toward the angel
as though it might protect him. A pile of clothing, ripped and shredded, sat on
the floor by the bed.

"Renira!" The boy's eyes lit up when he saw her, and he grinned wildly,
though he didn't drop the knife. He bounced up and down on the bed, and
Renira turned away from the nakedness. "Tell them to back away." His voice
held an accent she didn't know, and he seemed to twist the end of each word
into a guttural growl.

Eleseth crossed her arms and glanced down at Renira. "We mean him no
harm, but he will not listen."

The boy spat onto the bed. "Never met an angel that didn't mean me harm."

"Have you met many angels?" Renira asked.

The boy grimaced and looked sideways as though suddenly uncomfortable.
"Tell them to back away."

Armstar sighed. "Enough of this." He stepped forward, ignoring the knife,
and extended a hand toward the boy. "Calm."

The boy's snarling face went slack and all the coiled tension in his body
seemed to fade away. He suddenly looked like he couldn't remember what he
was doing there. Armstar rushed forward and plucked the knife from the boy's
hand.

"There were better ways to do that, brother," said Eleseth.

"There were worse ways. Now at least he might stop snarling for a few
moments while Renira talks some damned sense into him."

The boy crouched on the bed, an expression on his face half confusion and
half serenity. Renira stepped forward and perched next to him. "What's your
name?" she asked. She had saved him, this odd boy, and she didn't even know
his name nor where he had come from.

"Sun," the boy said. He looked at Renira for a moment, then collapsed down onto the bed next to her, his legs folding beneath him. Now she thought about it, he was perhaps not so much younger than her. *Elsa always said boys were slower to grow up than girls, yet they do so all in spurts.* He was all skin and bone, but the sparse hair on his upper lip was evidence he was no longer truly a child. Renira guessed the boy at thirteen or fourteen winters.

She held out a hand to him then. "I suppose it's time we were properly introduced. Hello, Sun. My name is Renira, but you can call me Ren."

The boy wrinkled his nose and looked down at the offered hand as though he wasn't sure what to do. After a few moments, he held out his own hand. Renira clasped it and smiled at him.

"Ren," the boy said.

Renira nodded. "Only my friends get to call me that."

"Friend? Huh. What about them?" the boy asked, jutting his chin towards where the two angels waited.

"Hmm. They can still call me Renira for now. But I think they will be friends eventually. I hope so."

"Where are your parents?" Eleseth asked.

Sun's expression darkened, and he frowned at the angel. "Don't have none."

"Everyone has parents."

"I don't!" Sun looked back to Renira, and there was something like panic in the way his eyes darted about. Renira remembered the man pinned to the tree in the forest, the demons erupting from the cocoon and devouring him. *No wonder he doesn't want to talk about them.* Some pains needed time to come to terms with.

"I only have a mother," Renira said. "So, I guess we're not all that different." She knew all too well the way people talked about a child without a parent. They never said it to her face, but she often heard people call her a bastard.

"How did you end up in the forest?" Eleseth asked.

Sun didn't answer her. He was staring at Renira, frowning in concentration. "Sun?" Renira said. "Why were you in the forest?"

He shrugged, dark eyes darting about and not meeting her gaze. "Gotta be somewhere. Forest seemed a good place. Lots of food. Shelter from rain."

"And demons?" Renira asked.

Sun shook his head. "Don't know what that means."

"A thrilling discovery," Armstar said. "Now Ren here has calmed the savage beast, am I free to leave, sister?"

Sun leapt up and sprang from the bed to stand between Renira and

Armstar. "Only her friends call her Ren!" His hands curled into fists as though he were about to swing a punch at the angel.

"It's all right, Sun," Renira stood and placed a hand on the boy's shoulder. He flinched away from the touch, and she let go quickly. There was something so strange and brittle about the boy. She looked to Eleseth. "Earlier you mentioned something about food? I'm starving."

"Not without me!" Sun said quickly.

"You should rest," Eleseth said. "You've had quite the ordeal and..."

His dark eyes locked onto Renira, full of panic. "You saved me. You wouldn't let him kill me." He thrust out a finger toward Armstar, and the angel just shook his head. "Don't let 'em hurt me. Please, friend."

"He won't," Renira said. "Tell him you won't hurt him, Armstar."

Armstar crossed his arms and said nothing.

"I... I swear to protect you right back." The boy went down on one knee in front of Renira and bowed his head.

"What?" Renira squeaked. She looked to the angels for help, but Eleseth seemed bemused, and Armstar only rolled his eyes. "I really don't need..."

"Where you go, I go," Sun said. "I'll protect you with my life. That's what friends do, right? I swear it."

"I don't think..."

"It's an oath!" Sun shouted. "I swear it." He looked up at Renira, and there was panic on his face. Then Sun placed the base of his thumb in his mouth and bit down hard enough to draw blood. Renira gasped and reached out to stop him, but the boy stumbled away from her. He was breathing heavily, blood on his lips and streaming down his hand. "I swear it by spilled blood!" he shouted, holding up his thumb and letting the blood drip onto the infirmary floor. "When my people swear by blood, it's binding. I can't take it back." There were tears in his dark eyes and he nodded at her frantically. "We're friends. Friends protect each other."

"Uh..." Renira had no idea what to do or say. Eleseth had asked her to calm the boy down, and now he was more animated than ever and had apparently just sworn a blood oath to protect her.

"A blood oath sounds like a serious thing," Eleseth said. The angel took a step forward and held out a soft hand to Sun. "A practice from Ashvold, if I'm not mistaken. May I see your hand?"

Sun looked to Renira, and she nodded at him quickly. He then held his hand out to Eleseth and flinched when she took it in her own.

"You bit quite deep, young man," the angel said. She placed her other hand on top of Sun's, and a soft glow lit up the boy's skin. He tried to pull away, but she held him with ease. When the glow faded and Eleseth released Sun's hand, the wound was all but gone, leaving only marred skin and blood as evidence it had ever been there.

"Now then. Names have been swapped and blood oaths sworn," Eleseth continued. "I think food is a good idea for everyone. But first, we need to find you some more clothes. You appear to have destroyed the last lot we gave you."

Sun glanced down at the heap of shredded rags at the foot of the bed and shrugged. "Want my clothes back." He was cradling his newly healed hand against his chest.

Armstar snorted. "They disintegrated when we took them off you." He caught a glance from Eleseth and sighed. "Fine. I shall find some more clothes for the boy."

The angels escorted them to a large building that was one of the few to be made from wood. There was no sign outside, but it looked just like the tavern back in Ner-on-the-River. Renira smiled as she remembered peering in through the windows of The Swallow's Tail, watching folk drink and swap stories, sometimes listen to a traveling bard. She'd always wanted to go in, but even at sixteen her mother had said she wasn't to enter. Of course, that hadn't stopped her from visiting the odd tavern with her friends in town.

The doors of the inn were large enough for Eleseth to pass through without ducking, and inside there were two hearths burning away, lending an impressive and welcome warmth to the place. There were no stairs and no second floor, although the building was certainly tall enough to accommodate that; Renira could see all the way to the roof, and there were two windows there, allowing the growing light of the crimson morning to shine in.

The room was mostly empty save for a few acolytes eating their morning meal. Kind words were exchanged with Eleseth, and the acolytes greeted Armstar also, though he turned away from them and said nothing. With his wings nothing but burnt husks, blackened bone, he seemed an outcast of sorts among his kind. He was smaller too, almost as though he was as much human as angel. That seemed a strange thought to Renira, and she wondered if Armstar had been more imposing before the destruction of his wings. How might he have looked when her mother had met him? What colour his wings would have been? It was difficult to imagine them as anything other than a dreary grey, but she supposed he might have been as magnificent as Eleseth once.

Eleseth bid them sit down at a table, and Renira quickly found Sun at her side. He was wearing a new set of robes that were clearly ill fitting, and the boy kept complaining about how it itched and felt both too tight and too loose in all the wrong places, but Eleseth calmed him by promising they would find him something more to his liking once they had eaten.

Renira felt crowded. Not just by Sun, but by the angels. Their interest in her was an odd thing that made her feel both special and awkward. She was used to spending much of her days alone, tending to her chores or with her head in the clouds, as her mother liked to say. Having so many people so close all the time, with all their attention fixed upon her, made her nervous. She was worried she might say the wrong thing or possibly eat incorrectly and look foolish in front of the angels. She shifted along the wooden bench, putting some distance between herself and Sun, but the boy scooted along next to her, so close they were almost touching.

Eleseth went to talk to the acolyte in the kitchen, and Sun bombarded Renira with a steady stream of questions. Where was she from? What was it like? How many friends did she have? Were they all her age? Did her mother let her out alone? How did one wash clothes? Could she swim? Renira did her best to answer the boy, but his enthusiasm was tiring. Armstar sat across from them, and Renira could see his jaw tightening each time Sun spoke.

"How did you end up in the forest?" Sun asked.

Renira sighed. "I appreciate the enthusiastic scrutiny, Sun, but what about you? Eleseth said you were from Ashvold?"

The boy fell silent, his gaze dropping to the table and his fingers scratching at the wood.

"A harsh place to live," Armstar said.

"Where is it?" Renira asked. She'd heard the name back in Riverden when she had time for the public lessons, but she had never really paid attention. While Aesie and Merebeth studied with enthusiasm, Renira had daydreamed of adventure and excitement, or sometimes just skipped lessons entirely to spend time with Elsa.

Sun remained silent.

"Far to the east," Armstar said.

Renira sighed at the vague answer. "How far?"

"East of here you can see the Cracked Mountains," said Armstar. "Further east, through the mountain passes, and you'll come to Dien."

Renira nodded. "Named for Dien Hostain, the Saint."

"Well at least you can learn. Yes, named for the Saint. Back then there were no kingdoms. It wasn't until the end of the First Age, when the demons had been driven into the darkness, that God ordered the founding of the Sant Dien Empire. A holy kingdom dedicated to peace, worship, and learning." Armstar scoffed. "Of course Dien Hostain never got to see it, she was long dead by then. It was first ruled by her daughter, Helena."

Geography had never been something she'd really thought about before, and history always seemed largely boring, but then the tutors at Riverden only taught the history of King Emrik's reign, nothing before. There were chapters in *The Divine Truth* dedicated to the Saint, and even more in *Rook's Compendium*. She liked the latter more as those stories were exciting and full of tales of adventure. *The Divine Truth* was always so dry and boring.

"So the God ordered the creation of the Sant Dien Empire?" Renira said. "But not Helesia?"

Armstar nodded. "Helesia didn't exist until the end of Ertide Hostain's Crusade. Until God was dead. Ertide split the kingdom in two. Dien on the east side of the Cracked Mountains, and Helesia on the west side. I'm surprised Lusa never told you any of this."

In truth it surprised her too. There seemed so much her mother hadn't told her.

"Dien is as bad as Helesia," Armstar continued. "It's ruled by Emrik's brother, Arandon. That bastard has dozens of immortals under his command, each with divine strength stolen from my brothers and sisters." There was real anger in the angel's voice. "But the winters are less severe, so I suppose there's that."

"And Ashvold?" Renira asked.

"Further east still, past the Derrian Morass, and you'll find Ashvold. It's mostly desert and volcanoes, arid land and monsters preying on those foolish enough to step out of the cities."

Sun didn't argue.

"I assume you came over the mountain passes to the south though?" Armstar continued. "It's a far more dangerous road, but quicker and without any need to pass through Dien."

"Where?" Renira asked.

"There's a series of mountain passes that start south of Riverden," Armstar said. "Up in the Ruskins. They skirt the Aelegar border and lead all the way to Ashvold. But to make it through those passes you'd need to get past the Black Lake or the fort of Rorash. Karna's forces hold that fort, the last I heard, and they don't let anyone through."

Armstar waited for an answer, but Sun stayed silent, staring at the table in front of him, digging at the wood with a fingernail.

"Who's Karna?" Renira asked. Her world seemed to be expanding far too quickly, and she was struggling to take it all in. She had known Helesia wasn't the only kingdom, of course, but she'd never really considered it before. Other places, other kingdoms, had never really mattered. For all her wishing for adventure, she had truly expected to spend her whole life in Riverden buried under piles of washing.

Armstar glared at her, and Renira looked to Sun. The boy was silent.

"Well? Who's Karna?" Renira repeated.

"She's our sister," Eleseth said as she placed a bowl in front of Sun, and another before Renira. "The Forgemistress of Ashvold." The two angels shared a look as Eleseth sat down across from Renira. "We don't like to talk about Karna, I'm afraid. It's a touchy subject."

"Why?" Renira asked.

Eleseth smiled. "Another time. Eat."

Renira's stomach made a noise like a stretched-out toad, and she felt her cheeks flush red. But no amount of embarrassment was about to stop her from laying waste to the meal in front of her. It was thick porridge with chunks of dried fruit floating within its congealed mass, and Renira devoured it. She looked up from the bowl just long enough to see Sun shovelling his own porridge into his mouth. He was already asking for a second bowl by the time Renira finished her own. It shouldn't have come as a surprise really. The boy was still young and growing, and he had been paralysed for at least two days. He was likely beyond ravenous.

Armstar watched her, a wistful look on his face that made Renira uncomfortable. She wiped at her mouth, sure she must have some porridge on her face somewhere, but Armstar dropped his gaze.

"Your mother sat here once, wearing that same coat." He shook his head. "There *is* a lot of her in you. I just don't know whether that's a good thing or not."

Renira wasn't sure what to make of the angel's words. He had been nothing but complimentary of her mother until now. "What do you mean?" she asked, pushing the last spoonful of porridge about at the bottom of her bowl.

Eleseth returned with two more bowls, and Sun immediately set about spooning his down. Renira stared at Armstar over the table. "Why would it be a bad thing that I'm like my mother?"

"It wouldn't," Eleseth said. "It isn't. Is it, brother?"

They're hiding something. Something about Mother.

Armstar grit his teeth and shook his head. When he looked up, his eyes were dark. "Eat your damned porridge."

Renira dropped her spoon in the empty bowl and stood up. Sun gathered his own bowl into his arms and redoubled his effort at cleaning it, as though the sudden movement were an attempt to steal his food.

"What aren't you telling me?" Renira demanded.

"A great many things," Armstar said, sending a sidelong look at Eleseth.

"Why?" Renira asked, finding her voice rising with the question. Perhaps it was the fatigue still threatening to drag her down to sleep or the sudden food in her belly after so long of going hungry, but she found herself frustrated. Annoyed by the angels' secrecy. And missing her mother.

"Why do you think you're entitled to answers?" Armstar snapped.

"Brother!" Eleseth hissed.

"Fine! How about this? Because unlike your mother, we can't trust you yet. That's as good an excuse as any."

Renira clutched at the amulet under her clothing. "Well, she isn't here. My mother chose to stay home and make sure there was a home for me to come back to. She didn't guide you through the forest nor fight a demon to keep you safe."

"Nor would she have picked up a burden that nearly got us all killed," Armstar said, nodding once toward Sun. The boy clutched at his half-finished bowl of porridge.

Renira felt tears stinging her eyes and wiped them away, refusing to let them fall. "My mother would never have let someone die when there was something, anything she could do to save them. Perhaps you didn't know her as well as you think."

Armstar stood suddenly, his ruined wings twitching. He loomed over her, his face twisted in rage. Then he snorted. "You tell her the truth, sister. Or don't. My part in this is done. It should have been done seventeen years ago. I have my own work to return to." He stepped over the bench and made for the door, disappearing into the wintry morning outside.

Renira remained standing, unsure what Armstar meant. What any of it meant. She looked to Eleseth to find the angel watching her, compassion making her face soft and welcoming. "I'm sorry about that, Renira. My brother can be quite... emotional where Lusa is concerned."

"What did he mean by tell me the truth?" Renira asked.

Eleseth frowned and waited a moment before answering. "It's not my place to say. Just as it was not Armstar's place. This is all Orphus' plan. He'll send for you soon, and..."

Renira shook her head and stepped over her bench, heading toward the door. Sun scooped up the final bowl of porridge and made to follow her, but Renira held up her hand. "I need to be alone, Sun."

The boy stopped, clutching a bowl in his arms and a spoon hanging in his mouth. He glanced about nervously. Renira knew she shouldn't be so brusque with him, he hadn't earned it, but at that moment she just couldn't find it in herself to care. She reached the door and pushed it open, shivering as the cold air hit her. The sky was a deep crimson, and above the cliffs all around the storm still raged. Armstar was only a few paces away, leaning against the side of the inn and watching her. Renira wanted to shout at him, but she couldn't think of anything to say and doubted it would do any good, so instead she stuck her tongue out at him and turned away. She had no idea where she was going, but anywhere was better than near him.

"You can't leave," Armstar called after her.

"I know!" Renira shouted and kept walking.

"Stop acting like a child."

Renira stopped and balled her hands into fists. She wanted to scream in frustration. Instead, she took a deep breath, unclenched her hands, and walked away.

With the blizzard still raging, there was no way she could make it out of Los Hold. And even if she could, she had nowhere to go. As long as the wolves were on her trail, she couldn't return home, couldn't bring them to her mother's door. Like it or not, and she was tilting largely towards not, she was stuck with the angels for now.

CHAPTER 16

The people of the Exodus believed there is something primal and evil about the Blood Moon, the Beast. They claimed it inspires within humanity a savagery, lunacy, and blood lust. Such trite foolishness. It is a moon, no more and no less, and can be tracked with proper equipment.

— KRYSTLE GREYSON, HEAD HISTORIAN OF
STONELORE UNIVERSITY FROM 298-334 OF THE
THIRD AGE. *HISTORICAL RELIGIONS OF PRIMITIVE
HUMANITY*, 2ND EDITION

With nowhere to go, Renira took to wandering the streets and bridges of Los Hold. She needed time alone, to collect her thoughts and calm down. Getting angry with Armstar hadn't helped any of them, but he was just so bloody frustrating. One moment saying she deserved the truth, and the next hiding it from her. There was more to his relationship with her mother than he was letting on, and just the mention of Lusa Washer seemed to make him angry.

She felt guilty for leaving Sun. The boy had attached himself to her, sworn himself to protect her. Renira knew she should be flattered, but it was all just too surreal. *A week ago I was complaining about chores and now I have a boy from Ashvold swearing blood oaths to protect me.* She felt like she had abandoned him with the angels, and his distrust of them was clear for all to see. Perhaps it was just a natural enmity.

Her mother had always told her angels were good and decent, defenders of just causes. Yet the public lessons in Riverden preached the opposite, claiming angels were evil and King Emrik was there to protect them from that evil. But there seemed more to it. Sun acted like he had met angels before and said they had meant him harm. She wondered if he meant Armstar's attitude back in the forest. He had been callous towards Sun, telling Renira to leave him time and again, but in the end he *had* helped save the boy. Her mind ran itself in circles.

Renira passed over a bridge from one plateau to another. She was on the lowest level of the basin and stopped upon the bridge to peer over the side into the crack below. There was nothing but darkness down there, a yawning black accompanied by a noise like a river rushing so fast it was close to breaking its banks. She imagined demons hiding underground, just like they had in the forest, clawing their way through rock. Traversing the underground rivers. She closed her eyes, and she could see them. Squat things with bulbous bodies and long, spindly legs. No eyes, but ears like a bat and tongues like a snake, always flicking out to taste the air. They would wait down in the utter dark and climb up in a flurry of limbs to snatch an unsuspecting person, dragging them down and feasting on their body.

Renira shuddered and moved along, wanting to be gone from the bridge and the monsters her imagination conjured. Always before, when she had dreamed of demons, she imagined herself battling them. Dressed in silver armour that shone with righteousness and armed with a spear called Hope. That fantasy seemed so far away now. Ever since her brush with the forest monster, it seemed foolish to think of herself as some heroic figure. After all, demons were real, as real as angels, and Renira was no warrior.

She walked on through the city and through the morning. People were about their daily business, steadfastly ignoring the blizzard and the threat of danger. Renira nodded to those she passed, greeting them warmly, though most ignored her. She saw no other angels in the city. Armstar had told her there were only a handful of them of left in the world. Hunted almost to extinction by the Godless King.

Renira stopped when she came across an elderly woman hanging up washing. The woman had hung lines between two large, stone houses and had three baskets of damp clothing at her feet. She had grey hair, a face as wrinkled as her washing, and wore a broad, gummy smile as she hummed a tune to herself and pinned washing to one of the lines. A wave of nostalgia broke over Renira, and she had to wipe away tears. She missed her home, and she missed her mother, and just seeing the washer woman at work made her chest ache.

"Can I help you, lass?" the old woman said in a voice thick with an accent. She didn't stop hanging up her load of washing, but beamed a kindly smile.

Renira realised she must have been gawking and shook her head, already turning away before thinking better of it. She looked back at the old woman and smiled. "Actually, would you mind if I helped you?"

The old woman stopped, a patchy old tunic in her hands and an eyebrow cocked. "Oh, you must be new. You want to help me hang up the washing?"

Renira shrugged. "Yes, please. If you'll allow it." She realised it was probably an odd request, but it was something she knew how to do. Something mundane she had been doing her whole life and didn't even need to think about.

The old woman waved at the washing line and laughed. "Madness, but be my guest. Reckon I should know your name before I put you to work though, hmm?"

"Renira Washer."

"Ahh." The old woman dropped the tunic into the basket at her feet and ambled over to a nearby stool, lowering herself onto it with a groan. "Well, suppose that makes a bit more sense now, don't it? My name is Flower. I guess you're looking for a bit of the familiar, eh? Feeling a little lost, are we?"

Renira picked up the tunic and flapped it once, releasing a light spray of water drops. "I suppose so. Everything seems to have changed quite quickly. Too quickly. I saw you hanging up the washing, and it reminded me of my mother. Sounds stupid, doesn't it?" She turned the tunic upside down and pinned it to the line with two little wooden pegs.

"Ah, not at all. Left her behind, did you?" Flower asked, watching Renira with a shrewd smile. "I left my husband behind. Twenty-four years we'd been together, but he wouldn't see the truth. Couldn't bring himself to believe even after an angel came knocking at our very door. Hail was his name. Too scared of the cost of believing in anything but the Mistress." Renira wondered if she was talking about Karna. Flower had an accent so similar to Sun's, and Armstar had said his sister ruled over Ashvold as the Forgemistress.

"So, you just left him?" Renira asked, not meaning it to sound like an accusation. She picked an apron out of the basket and shook it briefly.

Flower shrugged. "Weren't quite like that, lass. We both sat down and decided it together. He couldn't bring himself to believe, and I couldn't keep pretending I didn't. I'd always known the God was real. No matter what the Mistress might say or what the laws claim is right and true. No matter what Hail himself said. I always knew the God was real."

"How?" Renira asked as she pinned the apron to the washing line and reached into the wicker basket again. Her mother had always believed as well, but no matter how hard she tried she had never managed to pass the belief on to Renira.

"I saw him."

"What?" Renira said, pausing with a faded green tunic in hand. "How? He's dead."

Flower chuckled. "Aye, well so is my mother, but I still see her too. Every time I look in the mirror. Every time I look at my daughters or their little uns. Just 'cos someone is gone, don't mean they're not still there. I've seen God, always have. Seen him in the faces of my loved ones. Seen him in the way fish swim in a pond. The way the clouds dance together just so. When the angel came... When Andari came knocking at my door, it weren't to ask for help nor to convince me the Mistress was wrong. She came because she saw me in need.

"My youngest, Ash, weren't well. One of the wulfkin had gotten hold of him late one hunt night. Flaming thing left him alive. They ain't supposed to do that. So Ash were badly hurt and the healers wouldn't do nothing about it. Wouldn't even touch my poor boy."

"Why not?"

"Custom. Tradition." Flower shook her head and spat on the rocky ground. "Stupid flaming law. In Ashvold, no folk'll touch a person been savaged by wulfkin, on account of it being Karna's will. Well, that's a load of dog shit right there, is what that is. The Mistress might release the beasts each Blood Moon and call them back home before daybreak, but who they attack is about as much her will as the rain falling is mine. All I really cared about was that my boy, my youngest, was hurt, and nobody was willing to lift a hand to help him."

It seemed a terrible place that no one would help an injured boy in need, but Armstar had said Ashvold was a harsh land full of monsters.

"Then Andari knocked on my door one night—she stood there looking a true vision, she did. Wings the colour of autumn sunset, and such compassion you wouldn't believe. She told me she knew a place where a person's belief weren't shackled to who was in charge, and she had a sister who would heal my Ash for nothing but the happiness his being whole would bring.

"Those socks won't hang themselves, you know," Flower said with a smile and a nod. Renira realised she had been stood with an odd sock in each hand, listening to the old woman's story rather than hanging out the washing. She could almost see her mother shaking her head and chiding her for getting distracted yet again.

"So, you brought your son here? Just on the word of an angel that someone would heal him?" Renira asked.

"I brought him here on faith, lass," Flower said. "Him and my daughters too, and burn whatever Karna and her wulfkin might try to do about it."

Wulfkin sounded ferocious. Wolves were common enough in Helesia, though Yonal Wood said they didn't like the forest near Riverden. Renira wondered if wulfkin were more like the monster that had chased her into the cliffs. It had been far too big to be a normal wolf.

"I'd always known the God was real," Flower continued, "had seen him in everything I did, everything others did. Well, one of his own children knocked on my door and said my son could be saved, and I knew it then for my faith being answered. Why else would Andari have been passing at just the right time? And why else would she have taken an interest in me and my son? It certainly weren't because they were in desperate need of someone to wash old Horry's aprons, and no one else in the whole world could do it."

Renira chuckled at that. She quite liked the idea of the angels going out in search of just the right person to wash a few aprons. She imagined that might be how they had found her mother. But no. Armstar had said he had met her on a battlefield. She couldn't imagine her mother anywhere near fighting.

"The God might be dead," Flower said. "I've certainly heard it said enough times. But that don't mean he ain't still here."

Renira plucked a pair of trousers from the basket and shook a spray of water loose. "And Andari was right? Eleseth healed your son?"

"Ahh." Flower grinned. "You must have already met our Light Bearer. Aye, she healed my Ash and no payment asked. And though I told Hail I'd come back once our boy was healed, I decided to stay instead. It weren't a surprise when Ash and my daughters decided to stay as well. Ashvold is a hard place to live, and life here is easy enough. And trust me when I tell you seeing our angels take to the sky is a sight that never gets old, even as you might."

When reading her mother's old book, Renira had always imagined angels in flight as a thing of wonder. Dozens of them, hundreds even, taking to the sky on myriad wings, swooping down to do battle with demons. She hoped to see it one day.

"But here I've been telling you my old tale and not asked for yours. Flaming rude of me, that is," Flower said with a smile. "Because word has it, you arrived in the middle of a blizzard, and with Armstar no less. I know for a certainty that old lemon don't go recruiting acolytes. So, what brings you here, lass?"

Renira pushed an empty basket of washing aside and pulled across a full one. The alley between the buildings was already thick with washing hung between five different lines, but there was a nice breeze blowing down it that would help to dry the clothing even in the chill of winter.

"Armstar needed a guide," Renira said as she hung up another tunic. "I think he'd have preferred my mother really, but someone had to stay and look after the house and the business. She's the believer, not me. I just read what she told me to and recited the bits I had to. I never prayed, not really. Not meaning it. My mother prayed every day. Made sacrifices here and there. A coin flipped into a well. A perfectly good apple added to the fire to burn. I never understood it." It had always seemed wasteful to Renira.

Flower chuckled. "Because you don't have faith. Told you, I did, the God might be dead, but he's not gone. He watches us all, sees everything we do. Those offerings your mother made were her way of saying thank you to everything the God has given us. Be it a coin in a well, an apple in a fire, or husband left to diddle himself for a change. What matters is the sacrifice, something you needed, that parting with was painful or made life harder. That's how we show our devotion. That's how we repay the God for everything he's given and done for us."

Renira wasn't sure she agreed with Flower. She had never really discussed with her mother what her belief in the God meant to her nor how it might impact upon Renira. But she had seen her mother make sacrifices time and again. Sacrifices of things they needed or things they could have used. Sacrifices of time spent in prayer to a dead God, time that could be better spent in a thousand different ways.

Renira believed in God. She hadn't before, not really, but confronted with angels, she didn't think she had a choice anymore. Angels were real, so the God had to also be real. But belief wasn't enough. Her mother had faith. Renira didn't. She wasn't even sure what it meant.

Flower stood from her stool with a groan and audible pop as her old knees remembered how to work. She wore a kindly smile as she walked over and placed a wrinkled hand on Renira's arm. Another tunic was held forgotten in her hands as Renira struggled to come to terms with what the old woman's belief meant to her.

"It'll come to you, lass," Flower said. "Just like it came to me. And it obviously came to your mother."

"What?"

"You don't see it?" Flower smiled, full of compassion. "An angel came to your door in need. One of God's children. He asked for help, and your mother sent you. You're her offering, lass. Something she needed, more than anything, and yet give you up, she did. *That* is faith." Flower took the tunic from Renira's hands and reached up, pinning it to the washing line.

Renira shook her head, refusing to even consider it. Her mother might have made sacrifices in the past, but she loved Renira. She would never sacrifice her own daughter. "But she didn't send me away. I volunteered to go. To guide Armstar through the forest, so my mother could look after our home."

"Ah, maybe I was wrong then," Flower said in a voice that made it seem unlikely. "Maybe you weren't your mother's offering to prove her faith." She flashed a wrinkled grin at Renira. "Maybe she was yours."

Renira finished helping Flower hang up her washing, then fled as soon as was polite. The old woman's beliefs worried her. But more than that, the possibility that her mother's beliefs might align with Flower's. Renira didn't like the idea of God demanding sacrifices of his followers. Her mother had always taught her that the God was benevolent, but how could that be if one of the true tenets of his faith was sacrificing that which you held most dear? Even more disturbing was that Renira's actions might be taken as a form of offering. She had gone with Armstar instead of her mother out of kindness, not any sort of payment to God.

She found herself wandering the alleys of Los Hold once more, with no destination in mind and no more clarity to her thoughts than before. The only thing she could say for certain was that she missed home, and she missed her mother. And she knew she couldn't go back. Not while they were being hunted. She swore to herself the next time she saw her mother they would sit down and discuss her faith. Renira needed to know what it meant to her mother beyond the prayers she spoke every day.

I had years to talk to her about faith, yet it never seemed important before, and now I can't think of anything else.

Her eyes were on the road ahead of her, staring at the cracks in the rock beneath her feet. She almost bumped into Eleseth. The radiant angel was standing, staring up at a statue so worn by time most of its features had eroded to smooth stone. It appeared to be of a woman wearing plated armour. She might have been holding a spear or a sword once, but most of it had crumbled away. Words were etched into the stone at the base of the statue and they looked deep and fresh as though they had recently been re-chiselled.

In justice, find purpose. In strife, find conviction. In victory, find peace.

"This one isn't going to come alive, is it?" Renira asked with a somewhat forced smile.

Eleseth chuckled. "No. Most certainly not. This is a statue of the Saint. Or I suppose it was, once. Now it's just a vaguely saint-shaped lump of stone. I come here to think sometimes. She was a wise woman, Saint Dien."

"It sounds like you respected her," Renira said. "Wait! Did you know the Saint? But she's... thousands of years old."

Eleseth glanced at Renira, a shocked expression on her face. "She's three thousand years dead, Renira. Do I look so old?"

"Uhh..."

"Please don't answer that. I didn't know her. Saint Dien died before I was created."

"Created?" Renira chewed her lip at the word. "How? If God is your father, does that mean you have a mother, too?"

Eleseth shook her head. "No. Regardless, I've been looking for you."

"That's fortuitous. I could do with something to distract me," Renira admitted. "Please save me from myself."

"Well, I've quite the distraction for you. I thought I'd take you to meet my brother, Orphus. He's..."

"The Archangel." *Finally! I might get some answers.*

Orphus was the Archangel, the first angel. The Herald of the First Age, and a warrior without peer. Her mother had always called him compassionate and strong, reading from the passages about his virtues, but Renira had preferred reading about the battles and imagining what they must have looked like. How glorious and heroic a figure the Sword of Heaven must have been. She felt a thrill pass through her at the idea of meeting him, and it did wonders at chasing away the melancholy that had settled over her like a wet blanket.

Eleseth led Renira through the city of Los Hold, back towards the bridge where she had met Mihiriel. The angel was still there, standing guard on the bridge. Sun was there too, pacing in front of the statuesque angel, occasionally pulling a face to get Mihiriel to react. Sun was losing the battle. A little further on, Armstar perched on the bridge wall, his legs over the side, staring down into the watery abyss below. Renira realised, with a shock, that they were waiting for her.

"Ren!" Sun shouted when he spotted her.

"Boo!" Mihiriel lurched forward, lifting his arms. Sun let out a shriek and fell over, hitting the ground and scrambling away.

"Stupid angel!" Sun shouted. "That wasn't funny."

Mihiriel laughed, a deep rumble from inside his helmet, and straightened up again. "I disagree. Hello again, little Washer."

"Still a perfectly normal size, thank you," Renira said.

"If you say so."

Sun leapt to his feet and almost bowled Renira over as he wrapped his spindly arms around her. Renira squeaked in alarm, but Sun just squeezed her and let go. He was full of wild energy. "I thought you had gone. Broken Wings said you hadn't, but he's an angel, and they lie, so I couldn't trust him. This place is huge, far too big to search alone. You can't leave me, though. We're friends."

Renira weathered the storm of words with a bemused smile, then assured Sun she had just needed some time to herself. He was an odd boy, full of energy and anger towards the angels, yet he didn't seem surprised by them at all. Armstar glanced at her, a look of disapproval on his face, though for what reason Renira could not decide.

What does it matter? I don't care what he thinks.

"I thought you were going," she accused the broken angel. "*My part in this is done.*"

He glared at her. "I can't leave until I've spoken to my brother."

Renira turned away from him. She felt strangely betrayed that he had asked her to help, then was running away and leaving her. She knew it shouldn't matter, but it did. She cared about his opinion despite herself.

Across the bridge lay a giant structure built directly into the cliff edge and standing apart from the rest of Los Hold. Eleseth called it the Temple of Lore, and the only way to reach it was by the stone bridge, which was wide enough for a cart to cross and easily fifty meters long. At the far end, carved stone statues of angels stood either side of a great wooden door, their drawn swords crossing to form the archway. It was the first door Renira had seen that truly seemed built for angelkind, dwarfing even Eleseth. They crossed the bridge together, and Sun stayed close, tugging at his robe all the while as he tried to position himself between her and any potential danger. It was sweet in a way, that such a young boy thought he could protect her or that she needed protection in a sanctuary full of angels and those who worshipped them.

Armstar laid a hand on Renira's shoulder and made her slow her pace until Eleseth was a fair distance ahead. She turned to him with a scowl, but he wasn't looking at her. "Don't allow the Archangel to intimidate you. You deserve answers."

"What does that mean?" Renira asked, frustrated.

"Just... Damn it. Here." He threw a bit of cloth at her and turned, striding away.

Renira growled. He was so confusing. Why wouldn't he give her a straight answer? She looked down at the cloth he had thrown at her. It was the silver ribbon Aesie had given her before the parade. She'd tied it around his wounded arm back in the forest. It looked like Armstar had taken the time to wash it, but it was still discoloured in places by his blood. Renira gripped it tight in her fist, still not understanding, then thrust it into her pocket and followed.

The double wooden doors seemed heavy, bound by iron strips and on hinges that squealed in protest, shattering the calm serenity of Los Hold. Yet Eleseth pushed them open with ease, her divine strength making short work of it. They scraped against the cold, grey stone floor beyond and came to a booming rest. The air, though chilly outside, was somehow colder within the temple, and Renira saw her breath steaming as she entered. A dozen pillars sat in rows of six on each side of the door, and each pillar was ringed with candles, secured there by metal bands. Wooden cases sat at the base of each pillar, and they each contained books. At the far end of the temple's main hall, five steps led up to an ornate throne carved from stone with feathery decals, empty but for a large leather-bound tome. The hall seemed so desolate, more mausoleum than temple. In the gloomy edges, beyond the pillars, Renira saw doorways leading off into other chambers, and some of those were lit by flickering lights from within.

"He'll be in his library," Armstar said with a scowl. "He rarely leaves it these days. Just sits in there, reading and sending me out to find new books for him."

"We all have our passions and our failures, brother. I think, with what you have been through, you would be more compassionate," Eleseth said.

"You don't know a damned thing about what I have been through," Armstar said and strode away towards one of the doorways that led from the main hall. Renira had always thought the angels would be united in purpose, but Armstar and Eleseth seemed always at odds with one another. *Is there anyone Armstar doesn't hate?*

Light shone from within the corridor, a warm flickering orange that threw impossible shadows out through the doorway. Sun gripped her hand. He was silent now, frowning. He was scared, and Renira found she couldn't blame him. She felt the same herself. Eleseth had promised Orphus would have answers to her questions, and she had a lot of questions. "Would you like to wait outside, Sun? Nobody will blame you."

The boy shook his head. "I'll protect you, Ren," he said and let go of her hand, rushing ahead to walk in front of her.

He's such an odd boy.

The corridor led to a large chamber lit with four lanterns, each burning away on its own little table. All four walls of the room were lined with book-shelves that reached from floor to a ceiling easily eight meters high. Five long tables took up much of the room, each one strewn with books in various states of organisation, some stacked three or four tomes high. A worn rug, the colours long since faded to grey, lay upon the floor, and there was a musty smell in the room, like dust gone far too long without reprisal.

A giant figure stood in the far corner of the room. Encased head to toe in golden armour, with wings of glittering silver. Orphus, the Archangel, the Sword of Heaven, Herald of the First Age. He was holding a large tome in his gauntleted hands, yet the book appeared tiny in his grasp. As Renira watched, the Archangel carefully took a single page and turned it over, then laid a small fluffy tassel down the centre of the book and closed it with care approaching reverence. He placed the book on the nearby bookshelf, slotting it in between two others, then finally turned to look at his company. His eyes were blue, shining like sapphires catching the first rays of sunlight from within the utter darkness of his helm. Renira could see nothing else of his features, only golden armour decorated with ornate sword designs, silver wings, and glowing blue eyes.

"Brother. My final chore for you is done." Armstar's voice carried a note of derision. He walked over to a nearby stool, tossed the book upon it to the floor, and sat, his ruined wings twitching. "I am done."

"This is Renira Washer," Eleseth said. "And her companion. Introduce yourself, boy."

Sun was still half hiding behind Renira and he shrank even further back as Orphus' gaze turned his way. "My name is Sun."

"Interesting," Orphus said, his voice deep and distant like thunder over the mountains.

"I thought you'd be a warrior, not a scholar," Renira said.

The Archangel stared at her for a few moments. He could be smiling or frowning within the depths of his armour. He was easily as tall as Mihiriel, perhaps even larger, and his armour was bulky. The urge to turn and run washed over Renira. She glanced at Armstar and found him watching, and his words came back to her. He had said not to let Orphus intimidate her. *Is this is all some sort of test? What do they want with me?* Surely it all had to do with her mother. She decided she would not fail their test, whatever it might be, and stood her ground, staring up into the Archangel's helm, locking gazes with his blazing sapphire eyes.

"I was created to kill," Orphus said eventually. "But I have long since discovered a passion for learning. There is something about books that makes apparent the fragility of wisdom. Wise words are urgent, unburdened by the need to sound prolific. The meaning is far more important than the delivery. But written wisdom can be structured, designed to stick with the mind. It contains within it the possibility of existing long beyond the lives of those it touches."

He reached down and tapped at one of the books strewn upon the nearby table. "Yet, for all the wisdom I might take from this book, an errant flame, a blot of ink, or an unexpected shower can prove the frailty of its context. Even worse, a sinister mind could alter the words within and pass off folly as reason, fiction as fact.

"Books, I have long since learned, can enslave or liberate a person as surely can a sword. But often, with a book, the subject won't know the difference."

Renira wondered at his words. It was close to the 'truth' the teachers taught in school, Emrik Hostain's truth. That the angels came and enslaved humanity with faith in the God, and they did it with books. The same ones her mother kept and read from every night.

Orphus took two strides and went down onto one knee in front of Renira. She still had to look up to meet his gaze. Despite Armstar's warning, Renira found herself more than a little intimidated. He was just so big.

"I have waited so long to meet you, Renira Washer," Orphus said, his voice a deep rumble.

"Uh... thank you?" Renira said. "But why?"

Orphus turned his blue gaze on Armstar. "What have you told her?"

Armstar shrugged. "Nothing. Or as close to it as I could. She knows God is dead, but I wasn't sure how much *you* wanted her to know." He glanced at Renira. "If my opinion is worth a damn, I think you should tell her everything."

"Tell me what?" Renira asked, frustrated.

"I was hoping to ease her into the truth," Orphus said. "It would be less of a shock."

Armstar chuckled. "She doesn't need easing into it, brother. She's Lusa's daughter. Just tell her."

"I'm well aware of your fondness for Lusa. But not all secrets should be given away freely, and we have to be sure before..."

"Stop talking over me. Tell me what?" Renira raised her voice over the arguing angels. She was sick of waiting patiently for *them* to decide she was ready.

Orphus swung his sparkling blue gaze back toward Renira. She felt Sun's hand in her own once again, close by but hiding behind her. Oddly, it gave her strength, reminded her that she wasn't alone.

"My father is dead," Orphus said. "Slain by the Godless Kings a thousand years ago. But he left us a way to bring him back, to resurrect him. At the birth of the Fifth Age, God will be reborn."

A sick ache wormed its way through her stomach, though she couldn't say why. "What does this have to do with my mother?"

"The new age can only be rung in by the Herald, Renira," said Orphus.

"Aren't you the Herald?" she asked. "And Eleseth?"

"It doesn't work that way. There are rules, laid down by God himself so that an age cannot be rung in accidentally or with ill intent. I was the Herald of the First Age and Eleseth of the Second Age. We cannot ring in the Fifth Age."

Renira clutched at her mother's amulet beneath her tunic. The sick pain in her stomach was making her feel lightheaded, and the library and the Archangel suddenly seemed far away, as though she were looking at them down a tunnel. "So Armstar is the Herald?"

Orphus shook his head. "Armstar was born too early. The Herald must have lived only in the current age." He fell silent for a moment, his gaze flicked up to Eleseth and then back to Renira. "It's you. We've spent a long time looking for you. So long we thought your mother might have hidden you too well. We thought we would never find you.

"You, Renira Washer, are the Herald of the Fifth Age."

CHAPTER 17

How can we provide an accurate accounting of historical events when faced with such censorship? We live in the Fourth Age, which only stands to reason that there were three prior ages. We know this to be true. And yet, we cannot teach them nor even discuss them. For it is impossible to talk about the first three ages without also talking about God.

— RANSIK FAIRNEVER, DEAN OF BRIGHTHAVEN
UNIVERSITY FROM 712-749 OF THE FOURTH AGE.
YEAR 749 OF THE FOURTH AGE

Borik slogged through knee-deep snow that didn't seem inclined to melt regardless of the storm having finally blown itself out. It didn't surprise him really. Winter had been threatening for a while now, and the freak blizzard seemed to have given it all the push it needed. The sun likely wouldn't thaw the snow until spring rolled around, and the winters in Helesia were always longer than in Dien or Ashvold. For now, though, it was powdery and white and clung to clothing, soaking it through. Borik tried to pull his coat closer, but it did nothing. He had dressed for rain, not snow. With each step, his feet sank down into the icy mush, and it rushed in to fill the void, clinging to his britches. Misery was ever belligerent company.

He had lost sight of Perel and her Dogs when the storm front hit them all. If they were wise, they would have retreated to the forest and waited out the blizzard in the shelter of the trees. But Borik doubted it. It was not that his sister wasn't wise, but that she was so damned driven that even the worst of the elements would do no more than slow her down. He had to find the angels before her.

Father's hawk was nowhere to be seen, and Borik was glad of that at least. He hated being watched from the sky, unable to do anything but hide from its view. No doubt the bird had returned to its master when the storm hit and was waiting for clearer skies.

Borik moved along the cliff face and stared into one of the cracks. It was piled high with snow that would easily reach his chest, and the walls were slick with ice. He had to brush much of the icy mush away from the right-hand side of the crevice opening to find the mark. It took him a couple of minutes, but he finally saw it, frozen over with ice. A short gouge in the rock that could easily be mistaken as the rigours of time and weather. It was the tenth crevice he'd checked, but finally he had found the right one.

It was hard going, wading through so much snow, and Borik regularly had to grip hold of the walls of the crevice to help pull himself through. At each turn he had to stop and clear some of the piled snow away to check his direction. He found himself shivering and wished again that the angel could have gone to ground somewhere in a nice big city, with fewer freak snowstorms and more taverns. They hadn't been back to Celesgarde for almost a full year, and that meant there would be plenty of new boys in the local skin houses. Just the thought of it helped to warm Borik. All he had to do first was somehow convince his father to give up the chase and head back to the capital. Impossible was not a word that Emrik Hostain liked, but Borik had to admit it suited his father quite well.

"Hold!" shouted a male voice from above. Borik stopped and held up his hands, craning his neck to find the owner of the voice. A short, ugly man with a black beard thick with frost and long dark hair tied in a tail. He was standing on a head-high ledge Borik hadn't even known was there, brandishing a long spear that could easily be stabbed down into any trespassers. A scuff of feet from the other side of the crevice warned of a second guard. This one was young and bald save for a scattering of brown fuzz on his lips and carried a bow with an arrow already nocked. They were clearly fools, wiser men would have poked him full of holes already.

Borik turned slowly to face the man with the spear, his hands still held up in front of him. "Peace. I'm a friend."

The spear point didn't waver as the man stared at him down the length of it. "I ain't got no friends dress fancy as you, pippa."

Borik smiled at the man. "You might if you attended more balls."

The man with the spear sneered. "I'm never invited."

"Perhaps if you let your hair down and smiled more."

The man with the spear was silent, but Borik heard the second guard drawing the bowstring. It appeared the time for idle banter was at an end.

"All right," Borik said. "I really am a friend. I'm here to see Orphus."

The man with the spear shook his head. "Don't know no one by that name."

Borik felt his jovial mood fade away. It was much to do with the cold and the snow melting its way into his boots. "How about you stop insulting *my* intelligence, and I'll start assuming *you* have some. Take me to see the Archangel now!"

The man with the spear frowned, then glanced toward the other man. "What do you think, Clef?"

Borik reached for the knife sheathed at his hip and flung it at Clef in one motion. Already turning around the spear thrust, he let the point slide past him, grabbed hold of the wooden shaft, and snapped it. He dropped the half meter of spear he was holding and raised his hands once more. The man now holding half a spear gawked in shock, and Clef found himself holding a bow with a severed string. Both men were still very much alive, but disarmed, and Borik had not even had to draw his sword. He smiled at them both in turn. "The Archangel. Now. Lead the way."

The rocky cliffs of Hel's Wall were, unknown to most, full of hidden tunnels and passageways. They threaded through the crevices and cracks higher up so most would never even know they were there. The young man with the impotent bow, Clef, led Borik through the maze of passages, occasionally leaping over large gaps and moving ever north-east. The silence grated on his nerves. It was strange, but he welcomed the silence whenever he was alone, yet silence around others always felt so unnatural, and Borik itched with the need to fill the void with noise.

"Do you know the story of Hel's Wall?" Borik asked as they ducked through a rocky tunnel.

Clef grunted, which seemed about as much as the man ever said. The hairy fellow with the half spear was a bit more talkative though. "It's a natural formation."

"Is it, though?" Borik asked, spreading his hands. "A wonder, certainly, but it's far too cleanly cut to not be built."

They jumped across a crevice, one after another. "How's that?"

"Well, you see, my family have quite detailed maps and records dating all the way back to the Second Age. That's a few thousand years, in case you were wondering. Maps and books fall apart when they're that old, so we hire scribes to make new copies of them every century or so." Borik waved a dismissive hand in the air. "We have a lot of records, but it keeps miscreant scholars in a job, I suppose. I mean, what else would they do? Write poetry about breasts or cocks, I imagine."

Clef chuckled. They had to shuffle along a ledge to reach the next tunnel.

"But my point is, Hel's Wall wasn't here in the First Age. You might be thinking it was built in the Third Age, as most of our wonders were. Nothing like the Golden Age to nudge folk into building useless things everywhere. But no. Hel's Wall appeared sometime in the Second Age, the third century, I believe."

"Fascinating," the hairy fellow said in a flat voice.

"Isn't it? Too uniform to be natural, yet too big to be built by human or angel hands. Really makes you wonder how it got here. And why? A wall this big, basically framing the Cracked Mountains. Passing strange." He grinned over his shoulder at the hairy fellow but received only a glare in return.

"God made it," said Clef from up front. He turned sharply and was gone, vanishing down a tunnel Borik hadn't even seen.

"Well, you're half right. But the big man didn't build it. He pulled it straight up from the earth. You see it's..." Borik trailed off as he turned the corner, and Los Hold appeared as if from nowhere. A city built out of the very rock itself. A huge basin hidden in amongst the cliffs. The sight of it took his breath away.

The ground level of Los Hold was a series of plateaus with stone bridges connecting them. The gaps below led down into darkness and the roar of rushing water.

"And so did he break the damn and unleash the waters of the World Vein," Borik quoted from a book he should not have read. "Washing away the last taint of the demons and leaving them with no haven to shelter."

"That's from the fourth scripture," Clef said, wide eyed.

"A pretty lie, isn't it? With a kernel of truth, as all the best lies do."

There were three tiers to the sanctuary, three levels of rock carved deeper and deeper into the surrounding cliff face. The buildings were squat, ugly things for the most part, though some were much grander.

An impressively large angel stood at one end of a long stone bridge. Borik was ever surprised by the sheer size of the angels from the First Age. They were bloated things, over large and over muscled, and every single one was encased in armour that they never seemed to remove. They were almost living statues of bronze and silver and gold. Well...until they were dead, and their armour was torn away to reveal flesh and blood underneath. Borik wondered how many angels were hiding in Los Hold? How much life could their blood buy for a mortal man? That was one thing he had to admit about angels from the First Age; their bodies were huge, swollen things, but they had more blood to bleed than the later, smaller angels.

Green eyes blazed out from the dark recesses of the bronze helmet as the angel's head turned to watch him pass. Borik wondered which angel it was. There were few from the First Age left alive, but his knowledge of them was not nearly as complete as his father's.

The angel moved, reached out and placed a gauntleted hand on Borik's shoulder. The pressure was not painful, but it was also a touch too great to be considered gentle. He kept his hands very still as the angel bent down to stare at him.

"Godless Prince," the angel said. "What is always coming, but never arrives?"

Borik stared into the dark helmet, pinned by the green eyes. "Uhh. What?"

The angel laughed, let go of his shoulder, and straightened. His wings gave an impressive flap, buffeting Borik as he settled back into place guarding the bridge. "Think on it. I'll want an answer before you leave."

"I detest riddles," Borik said with a shake of his head. "Why don't you just tell me the answer now and we'll both agree you're very clever."

"Think on it."

Borik groaned and followed Clef across the stone bridge, then stopped before two grand oak doors with statues of angels either side. "Now we wait," said the bowman.

"Can't I just go in?" Borik asked. He didn't really have to time to waste. Perel was coming.

Clef laughed and rubbed at the patchy hair on his chin. "You see those doors? Humans can't open them. Only the blessed divinities can."

"Blessed divinities?" Borik shook his head at such a simple notion.

"Gifted by the God himself," Clef said and lifted a hand to his chest, then bowed his head in prayer or salute or something—all a bit pointless really given their God was quite dead. "Blessed be the reborn."

Borik laughed. "The God is dead, Clef. My father killed him."

Clef shook his head. "He cannot die. He is eternal."

Borik decided he should smooth over the situation before it turned into a theological argument. "Fair enough. I'm sorry about your bow, hope you have spare string somewhere."

Borik approached the doors and placed a hand on either one. Then he planted his feet and pushed. Clef wasn't wrong about the doors. They were heavy as sin, with hinges that squealed like a pig who knew it would soon be bacon. Borik hated to admit it, but he struggled to push them open, his strength stolen from the divine not up to the task. He coughed, embarrassed, then edged across to push on a single door and thrust his shoulder against it. He was red faced and sweating by the time the door was open enough for him to slip through. He envied the angels in many ways, not least because none of them ever seemed to sweat.

Borik had interrupted something important. He could always tell by the pregnant silence that said he was not welcome. Still, he'd walked in on far worse things than a secret meeting between angels before. He honestly found it somewhat shocking what some people paid to get up to in the seedier skin houses.

A young woman, dressed in a winter coat, tears in her eyes, pushed past Borik and fled the temple. A young boy with dark skin and a savage glare followed her. That left just three angels in the temple hall, one with wings ruined by fire, a woman who glowed with a soft light, and at the far end, standing in front of a throne, stood the Archangel himself.

"Orphus," Borik said with cheer. He spread out his hands and approached.

The woman stepped forward to meet him, and her soft glow turned to a raging blaze that seemed to pour from her skin. "You dare bring that weapon here?"

Borik stopped his advance. Confronted by a furious angel from the Second Age, he found himself a little intimidated. "It's just a sword."

"That *sword* was used to kill our father." The woman took another step forward and glowing white wings spread out behind her. She dwarfed Borik, and he shrank back from her brilliance. His hand itched towards the sword in question. "You dare to bring a Godslayer arm into a temple of the God?"

"Enough, Eleseth," Orphus said. He turned and began climbing the stairs up to his throne. "Take Armstar, and go after the Herald. Convince her."

Borik held his tongue while the woman and the man with the burned wings passed him towards the door. He recognised them both now. Eleseth, the Light Bearer, and Armstar, the Builder. His father had known them both well once upon a time, but any friendship there had turned to hatred many centuries ago. As soon as the other two angels were beyond the door, Borik turned back to Orphus.

"Herald?" he asked. "Were you talking about the girl? A human? How is that possible?"

Orphus relaxed into the throne with a clink as his armour settled into place. "What do you want, Godless Prince?"

Borik winced at the name. "That's not really fair, considering I'm helping you. Even more so when I tell you the unfortunate news. The Rider is dead."

"Mathanial," the name whispered past a choked breath, and Orphus hung his head with grief. Borik, too, had lost brothers before. Most of them to the blades of one divinity or another. Their families had been at war for longer than anyone but the immortals remembered. He gave the Archangel a few moments with his grief.

"And what role did you play in my brother's demise?"

Borik shifted from foot to foot. "I, uh um, had a hand in it, I suppose." Sometimes the best way to lie was to tell the truth.

Orphus' helm raised again, and his eyes seemed to blaze a cold, deadly blue. "You killed my brother?"

"I had no choice, Orphus," Borik said hastily. "You needed someone on the inside. Someone who has my father's ear. That's me. But your brother..."

Orphus let out a sound halfway between a growl and the snorting of a bull about to charge.

Borik hurried on. "But Mathanial was too proud to run. He chose to stand and fight my father. If my father orders me to kill an angel who won't run away, and I refuse... How long before he starts questioning my loyalty? You know what he'd do if he found out I was helping you. I'd be dead. And you'd no longer have someone on the inside, keeping you ahead of my father's bloody genocide. I had no choice!"

"And how much of my brother's blood did you drink?" Orphus growled.

Borik shrugged, shifting to his other foot again. "Why let spilled immortality go to waste?"

Orphus shot to his feet and shouted, "Because it is sacrilege!"

Borik took a step back, and his hand fell to the Godslayer sword sheathed at his hip before he could think better of it. Slowly, he took the hand away from the sword hilt and held it up empty. He was no fool. He knew, even with one of the Godslayer arms, he was no match for the Archangel.

"And did you also eat his heart?" Orphus asked quietly as he sat back down on the throne.

"No. My father claimed that power for himself."

"Claimed," Orphus snarled. "Stolen."

Borik sighed. They were getting side-tracked, and the Rider's death was far beside the point. "Listen to me, Orphus. I'm here to help you, not spit insults or discuss the morality of what I must do to keep suspicion from separating my head from my neck. You need to leave. Pack up your things and get the Herald out of here."

The Archangel said nothing, but his gleaming blue eyes seemed to narrow behind his golden helm.

"My sister is coming. That storm has slowed her down, but she has the scent, and nothing but death will stop her." Borik paused, letting it sink in. Even Orphus had good reason to fear Perel. "And my father is not far behind. He brings at least two of the Five Legions with him." Borik shook his head. "You can't fight this, Orphus. Not even here. You must flee."

CHAPTER 18

R enira was still trying to figure it all out when the sun went down. She'd found a bench on one of the second-tier platforms, overlooking the entire sanctuary. She watched the peacefulness of it all as people went about their lives. When the last rays of the waning sun dropped over the cliff tops, everyone in Los Hold stopped. Some got down on their knees, and others simply bowed their heads, but all of them spent a few minutes in silent prayer. Even the angels, few though they were, took those moments of peace to pay respect to their fallen God.

Her mother had always prayed at night, to the moons rather than the sun. It was a preference, she said, and each person was free to worship and declare their faith in their own way. Mother had always preferred the Bone Moon, the Matron. It started each cycle a slim crescent and grew larger and larger with each passing day, swelling with pregnancy before finally giving birth to a new star and then growing slight once more. To her, it had always symbolised fertility and parenthood.

Renira gripped the amulet under her clothing and grew sad at the memory. Already, the sound of her mother's voice had faded, and she could no longer remember it. She couldn't tell the angels, especially not now, but she wanted to go home. She wanted to see her mother, be a child again. Protected and safe from the wider world and all its troubles. A silly little washer girl with her head in the clouds.

It's too much! How can I be the Herald? She'd never been responsible for anything before. Her chores each day, maybe. She'd tried to keep a plant in her bedroom once but had forgotten to water it and it withered. She'd thought it dead until her mother took it and nursed it back to health. She couldn't be responsible for the life of God and of all angelkind. It was too much and she didn't want it, not the responsibility nor the weight of expectation.

Eleseth and Armstar came and went. One whispered platitudes at her, promises that she was not alone and they would protect her. The other told her to grow up and accept that life had changed and that she needed to change with it. Renira listened to all their words and said nothing. Armstar called it sulking, but she liked to think it was brooding. After all they had told her, everything they laid at her feet, they expected her to just get on with it. Maybe that's how it was with angels, the children of the God; purpose and destiny walked hand in hand with life and devotion. Well, Renira wasn't an angel, she was human, and until just a few hours ago her fate had involved nothing but washing clothes and watching the world go by.

Eventually both angels left, claiming other business and that time was short. They had told her so much—that she was important, the only one who could ring the Bell of Ages and bring the God back into the world. They had told her they would protect her and that she was safe so long as the Godless King did not suspect *she* was the Herald. She was not alone. But they had not told her how she was meant to accomplish such a task. Ringing a bell sounded easy enough, but if the bell was nearby, Renira had not seen it. Given the frenzied promises of safety the angels were making, Renira suspected the bell was quite a distance away and far from easy to reach.

Sun didn't leave her side. He paced back and forth behind the bench, clearly chafing at Renira's silence and unable to understand. He could not see that the weight of responsibility was crushing her. He did not see the silent tears that rolled down her cheeks as she considered the full impact of the Archangel's claim. She was no longer just some girl from Riverden. Renira Washer, daughter of Lusa Washer. A girl with her head in the clouds and her feet always just off the path. No. She was none of those things now. She was now the Herald of the Fifth Age. Chosen by the God. Although

Renira was a little fuzzy how the God could choose her for anything given he was dead.

A man sat down on the bench next to Renira and joined her in staring out over Los Hold. He was tall and trim, with a soft face and short dark hair and an attractive scattering of stubble on his chin and cheeks. He wore a tailored black suit designed for rugged travel, and it had obviously seen its fair share of just that but looked no less smart for it. A sword sat at his hip, and the man had to readjust the scabbard to get comfortable, yet he sat with a straight back rather than at ease. Behind them, Sun growled like a wolf, but the man ignored the boy, and Sun soon relented. Renira turned back to her contemplation of the sanctuary yet couldn't help but glance at the man again. He looked familiar. She was certain she had seen him before.

He's very handsome. Exactly the type Aesie and Elsa would've argued over. Renira wished one of her friends was here with her. They might not be able to help, but at least she wouldn't feel so alone.

"It's peaceful here," the man said. His voice was barely a whisper, as though anything louder might shatter the tranquillity. "For now." His gaze was locked on the sanctuary and those going about their daily lives within, and he did not so much as glance at Renira.

"It's nice to get away," he continued. "From all the expectation hanging over me."

Renira stared at him and frowned. His sentiment echoed her own so strongly she wondered how he knew. He must have known who she was, there were other benches, but he had chosen to sit next to her.

"My father is a driven man. Purpose and power personified. The definition of manifest destiny." The man stopped and laughed to himself. "He expects all his children to be the same. No. Not expects. Demands. Requires. But with a man who is so... strong and wilful, how can anyone, how can *I* hope to live up to that sort of legend? It's..." He paused, as if considering his next word carefully or maybe searching for the courage to admit the truth. "It's impossible."

The man turned to her then and smiled. He had sparkling grey eyes that seemed to catch the light from nearby hanging lanterns and demand Renira stare into them. "So, you're the Herald?"

Renira's memory lurched into motion, and suddenly she knew why the man looked so familiar. She had seen him before. The day of the parade in Riverden. All her friends had been staring at him, but she had barely spared him a glance, her attention fixed on the father. Renira panicked and edged away along the bench. She considered calling out for help, but none of the angels were close enough to hear anything but a scream, and even then, they would be far too late. Sun noticed her fear and crept forward, teeth bared and ready to pounce.

"You have to ask yourself," the prince continued. "How is that possible? Quite the conundrum."

Renira reached the edge of the bench and considered getting up and running, but the man looked so relaxed, even straight-backed. He looked at peace. Surely if he meant her harm he wouldn't just be sitting there talking to her?

"What do you mean?" she asked.

The prince turned a smile her way. "Orphus, Eleseth, Edaine, Mathanial. Four Heralds. What do they all have in common?"

"They're angels," Renira said without hesitation.

The prince glanced over his shoulder to where Sun crouched. "I mean neither her, nor you, nor anyone any harm, boy. But if you do insist on attacking me..." He paused and grinned. "I'll spank you so hard your arse will outshine the moon."

Sun took a step back, his eyes flicking to Renira. She nodded, and he backed off a few more steps. He wouldn't be able to help her here, and she didn't want him getting hurt trying. She didn't want anyone getting hurt because of her.

"Where were we?" the prince asked. "Yes, that's right. The other Heralds are all angels. Are you an angel then?"

"Do I look like I have wings?"

He leaned back a little, looking her up and down. "No. It really makes you wonder then. How is it possible?" The prince sighed and then turned his smile her way again and held out a hand. "I'm Borik."

"Renira." She slowly reached out and clasped the prince's hand. *Aesie would spit out a tooth for a chance to meet the prince and here he is holding my hand. She'll never believe me.*

Sun sniffed loudly to get their attention. "I get to call her Ren."

The prince raised an eyebrow and let go of Renira's hand. "My friends call me Ren," she said.

"One day then, maybe," said the prince. "Hopefully." He turned back to stare out over Los Hold. "You probably think me a monster. But I am not my father. Orphus would not allow me here if I were. Oh, in case you were wondering, he does know I'm here."

"Why are you here?" Renira asked. She still wasn't certain what the prince wanted. If Aesie's rumours were true, the prince was almost eighty winters old yet looked no more than twenty. That meant he drank angel blood, and yet the angels allowed him amongst them. There was so much, far too much, that

Renira simply didn't understand. About the world, about her place in it, and about the conflict that was even now taking place.

"I'm here to help Orphus. To help you, I suppose. So please think of me as an ally." The prince sighed again and leaned forward. "I want to see God reborn as much as any of them. And I will do everything I can to help you achieve it." He laughed. "Maybe I am as driven as my father, just in the opposite direction. A counterpoint. The other side of the same coin."

"Why?" Renira asked. "Why do you want to see the God reborn?" It was a selfish question, she realised. She was looking for her own reason as much as wanting to know the prince's. The angels might have told her she was the Herald of a new age, but they hadn't given her a reason to care. Why should she risk her life for a God that had been dead so long nobody even remembered his name? Her mother might have always believed and worshipped, but to Renira they had just been stories, and worship had never been anything but another chore.

The prince fell silent, staring out into the sanctuary and rubbing the stubble on his chin. He drew in a deep breath and let it out slowly, deep in thought. "I suppose saying 'It's the right thing to do' is a bit too dull." He smiled bitterly.

"My father is not a kind man. He hunts angels purely for the power of their flesh. He burns entire villages for harbouring divinities. He is violent and ruthless. And he is immortal. And far too strong for me to stand against." The prince glanced at Renira and then quickly looked away. "I know it's selfish, but I'm not strong enough to depose my father. No one is. Except the God. I suppose that makes me a terrible person. I want to see the God reborn, to see my father brought down."

Renira saw the prince was trembling and edged a little closer on the bench. Close enough she could put her own hand on top of his where it clutched at the fabric of his trousers.

"I don't think you're terrible," she said. "I think sometimes terrible things need to be done, and it takes someone courageous to stand up and do them, even if they believe it will damn them." She was comforting a prince! *The prince!* Touching his hand and offering what little warmth and compassion she could.

Oh, Aesie, if you could see me now.

The prince sniffed. "That's very wise. Perhaps you really are the Herald. Sometimes it takes someone courageous to stand up." He met her gaze and smiled.

Renira sighed. "I see what you've done there."

The prince shrugged. "You looked a little conflicted. And as I said, I'm an ally, here to help."

"Thank you."

Sun growled again from behind them. The young boy had stopped pacing and was staring down the steps that led up to their plateau. Armstar was marching up those steps in a hurry, fury on his face and his wings twitching.

"Oh dear, it appears your chaperon has arrived," the prince said. He gave her hand a quick squeeze, then stood up and stepped away from the bench.

"What are you doing, Godless?" Armstar asked as he reached the plateau and advanced upon them.

"Oh, you know," the prince said lightly. "Just corrupting the Herald with my evil ways."

Renira giggled and looked away at the stern glare from Armstar. The angel stepped close to the prince, and they exchanged harsh whispers, but Renira did not hear what was said. When they were done, the prince held up his hands and stepped away.

"You've seen what's coming with your own eyes, angel," the prince said loudly as he reached the top of the steps. "My sister will be here soon, and we should all be gone by the time she arrives. I know I will be."

"What did he say to you?" Armstar asked once the prince was out of sight.

"I assume he's another human you don't like?" Renira was feeling a little testy. The prince had been kind and forthright. He hadn't asked anything of her, only sat and talked, and most of that was answering *her* questions. The angels, on the other hand, seemed so suspicious, desperate to keep their secrets. They expected her to help them for no other reason than they needed it, with no thought as to what she might want or need. And Armstar was the worst of the bunch. He said they should tell her the truth and then blatantly withheld things. It was maddening. *He* was maddening.

"Orphus might trust him," Armstar continued. "We may even need him. But that man is a son of the Godless King. He cannot be trusted!"

Renira stood and walked past Armstar even as the angel sat down on the bench next to her. Sun rushed to follow her. "But you can be trusted?" she asked. "You brought me here under false pretences. You never needed a guide. You knew I was the Herald, even back at my house, but you didn't tell me. Why?"

"I wanted the choice for you to come here to be yours," Armstar said. He didn't stand up to follow her but leaned forward and stared down at the basin floor below. "If I had told you then, you would have felt obligated. I wanted to see what kind of person you were. To see how much of your mother there is in you."

Always with how much like my mother I am. Like he doesn't even see me as a person, just an echo of her.

A thought occurred to Renira. One she needed to know the answer to and there seemed no better time to ask it. "Did my mother know I'm the Herald??"

Armstar paused a moment before answering. "Does it matter?"

"No," she said bitterly. "It doesn't matter. Whatever you said, I wouldn't be able to believe it anyway." She turned on her heel and rushed down the steps as fast as was safe, Sun hot on her heels and asking if she was all right. She didn't want to look like she was fleeing Armstar, but she just had to be away from him.

CHAPTER 19

Pacifism is an ideal the weak cannot afford and the strong will never consider.

— ERTIDE HOSTAIN

Renira woke to a familiar haunting howl. She cowered in her bed, wrapped up in the covers, while the sound echoed around Los Hold. She wanted it to be nothing but a nightmare so she could close her eyes and drift off back to sleep. She was still so very tired. It would be nice to pretend it was nothing, but Renira knew that howl. It had chased her ever since she fled her house with Armstar. A constant threat of sharp fangs behind them, pushing them ever onward. She had seen the beast too. Far too big to be a normal wolf, with sabre fangs and cruel, gleaming eyes. It was a nightmare, but no dream. The wolf had found them. It had found her!

Renira flung the covers away and rolled out of bed, her shift fluttering. Her winter clothing was strewn over the floor where she had left it before climbing into bed earlier. She started pulling on the small clothes and then the trousers and stumbled against the doorway. It swung open into the chill night air. The moon was high and almost full, bathing them all in soft red light. The Blood

Moon. There was barely a cloud in the sky, the aftermath of the storm having left everything calm. She shivered against the cold and struggled to pull her blouse over her head.

Sun sat beside the door, huddled in a stolen blanket, shivering and staring up at Renira with wide, dark eyes. "You heard it?" the boy asked.

Renira nodded. She didn't bother tucking in her blouse and wrestled with her tunic. "They've found us. We have to warn the others."

Sun struggled out of his blankets and stood there shivering. He was still dressed in ill-fitting robes but had managed to procure a short spear from somewhere. It was only as tall as he was and tipped with a rusted point. He held it as though he had no idea how to use it.

"We should go," Sun said. "Ash fall on the angels. We don't need them."

Renira shook her head as she pulled on her mother's winter coat and started toward the nearest building. "It's not about angels and humans, Sun. Nobody deserves to die here." Especially as the attackers were here for the Herald. They were here for her. Every death in Los Hold would be on Renira's shoulders.

She banged on the door of the first building they came across, not waiting for a response. "Get up. We're under attack!" Then she moved to the next building. Before long, both Renira and Sun were hammering on every door they could find and shouting the warning. Some people were angry at being awoken, and others were armed and ready to face danger. The smell of smoke drifted through the lowest level of Los Hold, and a scream split the night air, followed closely by another. Renira raced through the clustered buildings, banging on doors. She had to save as many people as she could.

More screams joined the night and other sounds too. A wolf's howl, a man's braying laughter, metal clashing against metal. Down in the lowest tier of buildings, Renira couldn't see what was happening in the rest of the sanctuary. Her world became flashes of faces, fists pounding wood, screaming for people to get up and run.

She turned a corner to find a dishevelled man wearing stained travel clothes and a gap-toothed sneer. He held a sword dripping gore, and Renira saw at least one body behind him. She slid to a halt and began to back away, but it was already too late. The man had seen her, and there was a hungry glint in his eyes.

"Get away from her!" Sun rushed past Renira, his spear point levelled at the man. The thug laughed and parried the spear, then backhanded Sun so hard the boy crashed against the side of a nearby stone hut and collapsed down to the ground.

The man laughed again and glanced at Renira. "You just wait right there, girly." He turned back to Sun and advanced on the boy, who groaned and struggled to get back up.

Fear threatened to paralyse Renira. Fear of death, of what the man might do to her. But the fear of what he might do to Sun was even greater. Renira ducked, snatched the dropped spear from the ground, and ran to Sun. She stood over him, spear held across her body in both hands, and faced the dishevelled man. Always, in her dreams she had held her spear with confidence, twirling it about and stabbing at monsters with lightning thrusts. Now she held it in trembling hands. She might not know how to use the weapon, but she would try her best. *If I am the Herald then it is my job to protect everyone.*

Again, the man laughed. "Put down that spear, and I'll make it quick."

"I don't want to hurt you!" Renira shouted. "Turn around and leave."

Sun groaned and used the wall to pull himself back to his feet.

"Slow and painful it is." The man reached for her and Renira swung the spear in both hands like a club. He caught the haft and laughed, raising his sword.

The man's laughing sneer turned down, and a look of horror passed over his face. He took a step backward, dropped his sword, and collapsed to his knees. There he sat, rocking back and forth and mumbling something to himself over and over.

"Give me the spear," Sun said. There was blood running down the boy's face from a cut above his hair line, and he swayed on his feet.

"No!" Renira said firmly. "Nobody else needs to die."

"Such naivety," said Armstar as strode toward them and stooped to pick up the dishevelled man's fallen sword. He straightened up and thrust the sword down into the cowering man's back. Renira heard the cry of pain and the gurgling death throes, and turned away from the grisly spectacle. Armstar left the man there, doubled over and dead with his own sword run through his back.

"You didn't have to kill him," Renira said. "You'd already done... whatever it is you do to people." She knew he was a bad man, there was no doubting that, and he'd done things worthy of punishment, but death shouldn't have been it.

"Don't be such a damned fool, Renira," the angel snapped. "You have your mother's idealistic ignorance. Not everyone can be saved or spared. You think you can bargain with these people, beg them for mercy? You can't. There was already blood on his blade. Bodies behind him. He would have killed you and everyone in Los Hold and nothing you could have said would have stopped him.

"Some people are evil. The only justice that will change that is the grave. The sooner you accept that as fact, the better for us all."

"He was still a person, with friends and family, maybe children. He shouldn't have had to die." She was staring down at the body, bent over his own sword, blood leaking out onto the stone. She felt sick.

"We don't have time for this," Armstar said. "Come on." He reached out and grabbed Renira by the hand, striding away and pulling her with him.

"We have to warn everyone. We have to save them," Renira shouted as Armstar dragged her toward the Temple of Lore. Sun ran alongside them, the spear back in his hands.

"By now everyone already knows," Armstar said as he changed direction and pulled Renira along behind him. "Nothing to do but run."

The acrid smell of smoke was stronger now, and Renira could hear the crackle of a fire nearby. The wolf howled again, closer now, and new screams went up in the lull that followed. Renira managed to pull her hand free from Armstar's grip, and he turned to face her, hand outstretched. She knew then he was about to use his power on her. "I can't save them," Renira admitted. "But you can. You're an angel. You can fight."

Armstar shook his head and his jaw clenched. "What do you think my brothers and sisters are doing? Fighting and probably dying. My job is to get you to safety, Renira. *You* are what is important here. Everything else can burn. Everyone else can die. But not you!" His wings twitched as another howl split the night.

A clammy hand gripped hold of Renira's, and she glanced down to see Sun staring up at her, a firm look on his face. "Broken Wings is right, Ren." Blood was still trickling down the boy's face from his head wound, and his bottom lip was starting to swell. One more thing Renira was responsible for. She let out a resigned sigh, nodded, and allowed Armstar to lead them through Los Hold. Sun did not let go of her hand. It didn't make any sense. All this pain and violence and death just for her.

They raced between burning buildings through rubble strewn alleys. Some of the people of Los Hold were trying to pack up their belongings, others fleeing for their lives. Some stopped and bowed to Armstar as they passed, but the angel ignored them all. Twice Renira caught sight of their attackers. Dirty men and women wearing dark clothing, cruel smiles made manic in the light of the Blood Moon. One of them gave chase, until a nearby acolyte leapt from a doorway to tackle the woman. They went down in a tangle of limbs, and the screams of the acolyte followed Renira into the night. The man hadn't even been armed. He had sacrificed himself so she and Armstar and Sun might escape. She would never even know his name.

Armstar slowed to a halt before the bridge to the Temple of Lore, and Renira saw a flash of fur and fangs and claws beyond him. The giant wolf sat before the near side of the bridge, licking blood from its paws. There was a body of a young woman at its feet, ripped apart, insides spilling over the stone. Renira turned from the grisly spectacle and fought against a wave of guilt and despair that threatened to crush her. Tears welled in her eyes, and she wiped them away with her free hand. Sun stepped in front of her, his little spear held at the ready.

"Run back to your mistress, beast," Armstar hissed and raised a hand in front of him.

"That won't work a second time, angel." A woman's voice, so harsh it seemed no different to the wolf's howl.

Renira spun around to find the owner of the voice. A tall woman with long hair braided into three tails and leather armour that did not cover her left arm, and carried a bloodied halberd with a black blade. Renira had seen the woman before, at the parade in Riverden. Another of the Godless King's children. She had thought the princess looked so strong and powerful at the parade, had envied that strength and confidence. Now it was something to fear. Borik had warned them his sister was coming, and even he had seemed scared by the prospect.

"Fear!" Armstar shouted, his hand still outstretched toward the wolf. The beast lowered its head a little, bared its teeth, and growled.

They were trapped. A giant wolf on one side, the Godless King's daughter on the other. "Don't you listen, angel?" the princess said in a harsh voice. "Fool us once. Tsk. Never again. Tesh is no normal wolf. She has tasted angel flesh and drunk more divine blood than I could exsanguinate from five of you."

Armstar pushed past Renira and raised a hand toward the princess. "Sleep!" he shouted.

The princess yawned dramatically and then laughed and started forward, twirling her halberd in her hands. "What was that supposed to do? Should I just lie down? Have a nap?"

Renira checked the beast to find it padding closer to them. Sun faced it, the tip of his spear wavering.

Armstar shielded her with his body. "You are a monster, Perel."

The princess paused and placed a hand against her chest. "I'm flattered you know my name." She took another step, her halberd drawing patterns in the air as she spun it. The staining on the blade was mesmerising. "Give me the Herald.

Where is he? I know it's not you, Builder. Tell me where I can find this new Herald, and I'll let you go."

"No, you won't," Armstar said. "You're too much like your father."

The princess stopped her advance and brought the pommel of her halberd down on the ground with such force it cracked the stone. She sketched a bow from the waist. "Another compliment, such flattery. Thank you, Builder. And of course, you're right." She stood up to her full height again. "So, tell me where I can find the Herald, and I'll let those two go." She jutted her chin at Renira and Sun. "I don't give a bloody shit about your pet humans."

Armstar took a step forward and spread his ruined wings out to their full span. They were nothing but charred bones where no feathers would ever grow, but it was an impressive sight still. "You just missed him, Perel. He's flying north to Celesgarde even as we speak."

The princess seemed to consider this for a moment, sucking at the inside of her cheek. Then she laughed and shook her head. "I'm going to eat your heart, Builder. Tesh, kill the humans!"

Princess and wolf advanced together. Armstar, even with no weapon moved to confront the princess. Sun closed his eyes, screamed, and charged the wolf. And Renira waited between them, helpless. Useless.

A second angel smashed down to the ground between Sun and the wolf. A giant in bronze armour, carrying a spear of shining silver. Mihiriel.

The wolf yelped and leapt to the right, barely avoiding the spear thrust. It threw itself at the angel. Fangs and armour met in a wrenching squeal. Then Mihiriel dropped his spear, punched the wolf in the head, and grabbed it by the scruff of its neck. It thrashed and flailed in his grip, but the angel was too big and strong for it to escape. He tossed the beast away toward the edge of the bridge, and its hind legs went over the drop. The beast scrabbled to save itself, yowling in fear. Mihiriel scooped up his spear and leapt up into the air with a beat of his gold-brown wings. He passed over Renira's head, and landed on her other side just in time to block a halberd thrust from the princess that would have skewered Armstar.

The princess staggered away to collect herself and crouched with her halberd held in one hand to the side. She snarled at Mihiriel. "Another one to taste. Your immortality shield won't save you from me, First Age." She dashed in and slashed upward with her halberd. Mihiriel turned the strike aside with his spear, then thrust. The princess twisted away from the strike and brought her halberd back down in a slash. The angel threw himself out of the way, rolling, his armour clattering against the stone.

"Get them out of here, brother," Mihiriel roared as he attacked. Renira felt a cold hand grip hold of hers, and Armstar started pulling her away from the fight. The ringing clash of metal on metal followed them as they sprinted across the bridge. The giant wolf, still struggling to pull itself up over the edge, snapped at them as they went, but they were too far from it.

Renira was breathing hard by the time they reached the great doors to the Temple of Lore. Armstar placed both his hands against a single door and leaned into it. Where Eleseth had opened the door with ease, Armstar struggled against its weight. Renira threw herself against the door and pushed, staring back across the bridge as the wolf finally found some purchase. The door started to grind open on squealing hinges, and Sun darted through the gap into the gloom beyond.

"There's no one here," Sun said, his voice was high with panic and echoed in the space beyond him.

The wolf scrabbled its way onto the bridge, shook itself, and then fixed its eyes on Renira.

"Go!" Armstar said, grabbing Renira's arm and all but throwing her through the little gap between the doors. She caught a glimpse of the wolf, bounding into a sprint toward them. Armstar followed her through, his ruined wings bashing against the edges of the doors and bringing a scream of pain from him. Then he was through and slammed his shoulder against the door. Sun was already there, pushing as hard as his boyish strength could allow. Renira joined them, and the door began to squeal shut.

The wolf crashed against the other side of the wood with a jarring thud that arrested its momentum. The beast couldn't fit through the gap between the doors, but it was a frenzy of snarling motion on the other side. Claws scrabbled at the wood, and a dark muzzle thrust through the gap a little, snapping and barking at them.

"Push!" Armstar bellowed, and all three of them put everything they had into it. The door squealed again as it began to inch closed despite the wolf battering it from the other side. Again and again the beast threw itself at the door, but finally it swung closed. Armstar reached up and drew across a thick metal bolt from the other door, locking them.

Sweat dribbled down Renira's face. She leaned against the door, despite the sound of the wolf trying to tunnel its way through the wood. Panic and terror had robbed her sight, and she was staring into nothing. Thinking nothing. Sun knelt beside her, panting from the exertion. He backed away from the door and snatched his little spear from the stone floor.

"That ain't a normal wolf," the boy said. "Not even wulfkin grow that big." Renira glanced at him to find his dark eyes wide. He was trembling. Renira looked at her own hands to find she was also trembling and clutching her mother's amulet so tight it hurt.

"No," Armstar said. His ruined wings were twitching. "It's not normal. I can't fight it."

"You don't need to," the Archangel's voice was like the beat of a faraway drum. Renira blinked away the fog of her panic and found Orphus striding into the hall from one of the side rooms. He mounted the steps to his throne, turned and slouched into its stone embrace. He was resplendent in his golden suit of armour and had another book grasped in his gauntleted hand. A giant sword, easily as long as Renira was tall, made of silver and gold and etched with runes, rested against his throne. His blue eyes seemed to pierce the gloom like two shining beacons.

"I have a new task for you, brother," Orphus said. "Get the Herald out of here."

Armstar started forward, leaving Renira and Sun behind. "My part in this was supposed to be over. Haven't I..." He glanced back at Renira for just a moment. "Haven't I already given your cause enough?"

"It is your cause also."

Armstar staggered as he reached the bottom of the steps. "Let me return to my tower, brother. I know how this ends and I do not wish to see it."

Orphus stood and rushed down the steps, caught Armstar even as the ruined angel fell. Renira watched from a dozen steps away as the Archangel clutched Armstar and lowered his head to the other man's ear. He whispered something then and Armstar went rigid. When they separated again, both turned to look at Renira.

Armstar nodded his head wearily. He drew in a ragged breath and it broke free as a sob. "I'll take her," he said.

"I will hold Perel and her wolf at bay," Orphus said. "Give you the time to escape."

"There's no slowing Perel down, brother. There's no hiding from her."

The Archangel sat down on the first step of his throne. "Which is why I will stop her here." Renira would have expected the Herald of the First Age, an age of violence, to relish the idea of a fight, but Orphus sounded weary, sad almost.

"You'll kill her?" Armstar asked.

"No."

Armstar shook his head. "You have to! You're the only one who can. Mihiriel is out there right now, Orphus."

Orphus let out a great sigh. "Go. Get the Herald to safety. Use the hidden tunnel to the top of the cliffs and head north to the Cracked Mountains. I had

an outpost set up halfway up the Fangs. It's hidden from both land and sky."
He gave Armstar a gentle push that sent the smaller angle staggering backwards.

Armstar recovered and snarled at his brother. "There is no where we can
hide, brother. You want me to take Renira, fine. But unless you kill Perel, she
will find us."

"Go!" The Archangel's voice was iron.

Armstar stood facing his brother for a few moments, then growled in
annoyance and backed up a step before turning to his right. "Come with me,
Renira."

Renira watched Armstar head for one of the doors that led off from the
main hall of the temple. Sun followed him, but she did not. She turned back to
the Archangel to find the cold blue eyes regarding her.

"People are dying out there. Your people. Not just angels, but humans.
Your acolytes. They're here because of you. To help you and protect you. And
they're dying because of me. If you can stop this attack. If you can save them.
Why don't you? Why hide in here when you could do something? You're the
Archangel. The Sword of Heaven. Born for battle. So get out there and
fight!"

Orphus sighed, his breath misting out of the dark recesses of his helmet.
"You don't know what you ask. You cannot know the things I have seen and
done, little Herald. I have lived longer than any other creature alive. Rivers of
crimson, carved flesh, smoking pyres; I lived and fought through the First Age
and through the Godless Kings' Crusade." The Archangel raised a gauntleted
hand in front of him and stared at it. Renira realised he, too, was trembling. "I
have killed more than any other creature in history. I will not kill again. A soul
can bear only so much before it breaks."

Renira thought she understood him a little then. It was not that he didn't
want to help his people, but that in order to save them, he knew he would have
to kill others. She didn't want anyone to die, not the people of Los Hold, nor
even the attackers. She didn't want there to be a reason for anyone to have to
die. Her mother had always told her that human life, all human life, was sacred,
and that no one had the right to hurt another. Renira had believed it. She still
believed it. *Don't I?* But what happened when others didn't agree? What choice
did the peaceful have when others came for them with violence? Someone had
to stand up and fight back.

"Renira," Armstar shouted. "Come on!"

The Archangel was clearly in pain, and Renira could think of no words to
help him. She stepped forward and grasped his trembling gauntlet. He was so
massive her hands barely wrapped around a finger each. She stood there,

holding his hand and staring up into his helm through teary vision. Then the Archangel nodded, and the blue of his eyes softened a little.

"I hope one day you can forgive us, Herald. Now go," Orphus said, pulling his hand back and wrapping it around the hilt of his sword. "I will hold our enemies here for as long as I can."

Renira fled after Armstar. They left Orphus there alone in the grand hall of the temple. A solitary warrior in gold plate, with silver wings and a sword that matched. A warrior who would not kill pitted against a monster who would do anything to taste his flesh.

CHAPTER 20

By fire, by ice, by knife in the dark, by drowning, poison, or age.
Thrown from a cliff, a fall down the stairs, mauled by a bear for days.

— 101 DEATHS

The thrill of combat sang in Perel's ears, and she lost herself in the rhythm. She ducked underneath the arc of the angel's spear, then leapt back, pivoting her halberd around her body so the blade whipped about. The angel stumbled backwards away from the blade. He darted back in with a lightning thrust of his spear. Perel frantically slapped the attack away to stop from being skewered.

She grinned, licked her lips, and paced back and forth in the lull. The angel backed up a step, placing himself between Perel and the bridge, and settled into a ready crouch. That was his plan then, why he was fighting so defensively, he meant to delay her. The Builder really must know where to find the Herald.

Perel darted in again, feinted to her left, spun right and sliced her halberd round in a shimmering arc. The angel blocked it on the haft of his spear, grunting with the effort, then brought the tip of his spear down before she could recover. He trapped both their weapons to the ground, stepped into the space, and punched Perel in the face. The world spun around her, and Perel landed in a heap of dust and rubble and pain. She flipped up off her back onto her feet and leapt away just as the tip of the angel's spear buried itself in the rock where she had landed.

First Age angels were always strong and fast, the best warriors the world had ever seen. And their flesh always tasted the sweetest. Perel's mouth was wet with the thought of tearing out the angel's heart and biting into its fleshy warmth.

The angel didn't let up, advancing again and again, thrusting spear jabs at Perel that forced her to back up. She spun her halberd about her body, blocking and searching for an opening. The angel gave none. So she decided to make her own. She leapt into the next thrust, the tip of the spear so close it scored her leather armour and sent a stinging pain along her ribs. She elbowed the haft of the spear aside and swung the butt of her halberd inside the angel's guard. It crashed into his shoulder and sent him careening away into a nearby building. The wall collapsed under the huge angel's weight, and the entire building came crashing down on top of him. Perel watched, panting and wincing against the wound on her ribs. It would heal in minutes, but they would be painful minutes.

Tesh was at the far end of the bridge, scrabbling against the closed door. Perel gave a sharp whistle, and the wolf stopped and turned. The collapsed building exploded outward in a rain of rubble and rock and dust. The First Age angel roared amongst it, his bronze armour dented by her strike and dulled by the dust, but still shining. He took to the air and hung there for a few moments, wings beating, bloodied spear tip pointed down towards Perel.

"Die, Wolf Princess!" the angel shouted and swooped down toward her. She flung herself to the side, narrowly dodging the spear tip. The angel hit her like a rockslide. He punched her in the gut, then brought his spear down in one hand into the meat of her thigh.

Perel screamed in pain, and her leg collapsed beneath her. She tried to scrabble away, but the angel held the spear haft, and the point was buried in her leg. He twisted the spear, and waves of agony washed through her. The angel reached a bronze-gauntleted hand toward her neck. Perel dropped her halberd, drew on the divine power of the angel Daruin, and punched a thunderous fist into the angel's spear haft. The metal shattered under the strike, and the angel stumbled back, clutching at his broken spear.

Perel lurched back to her feet and darted inside the angel's reach. She punched him twice in the gut, each strike releasing a wave of force that sounded like a thunderclap echoing throughout the basin. The angel coughed blood into Perel's face, staggered backward, and collapsed onto one knee. He raised shaking hands to his helmet and coughed more blood into his gauntlets. Perel licked her lips, tasting the angel's life. Spicy like a fiery spirit.

The angel coughed and sputtered. His armour was dented and cracked from the force of Perel's blows, and one of his wings was broken from the shockwave. She couldn't deliver many punches like that before her own arms shattered from the strain.

Tesh reached the end of the bridge and let out a hungry growl as she stalked the injured angel. Perel reached down and gripped hold of the spear head still lodged in her leg. She pulled it out, screaming at the pain, and then tossed it away to skitter across the ground and over the edge of the plateau. It rang as it bounced against the edge, falling into the darkness below them all.

"Show me your power, First Age," Perel said breathlessly. She stepped closer to the angel, ignoring the pain in her leg and the blood running from the wound. It would close soon enough when she feasted on the angel's flesh. "Show me so I can see whether your heart is worth eating, or if I should just feed it to one of my Dogs. Show me!" She wanted to test this monster. She needed to test herself. How else could she claim to be worthy of her father's legacy?

The angel struggled back to his feet. A section of his breastplate fell away to reveal ragged, bleeding muscle beneath. The sight of it made Perel hungry. Her heart raced, and blood rushed in her ears.

"You'll die here, Wolf Princess," the angel said, his voice wet and no longer boasting the same booming confidence. He pulled a hand away from his wound and raised it to the sky. It began to glow. Softly at first, a yellow luminescence that quickly grew brighter and brighter until Perel could no longer look at it. She closed her eyes against the glare, but it was like a sun held in the palm of the angel's hand, and the light burned at her eyes even screwed shut.

A fist slammed into Perel's face, and she collapsed onto one knee. Another hit her, then another, each one hard enough to kill a normal human. Perel flailed out with her hands, useless and unable to defend herself without her sight. Another punch hit her in the chest, and she felt a rib crack. She fell back, yowling in pain. Her face was already swelling, tightening, and her chest was on fire. Still, she could not force her eyelids open against the blinding light.

A howl ripped through the night, followed by a snarl. Metal screamed as fangs scraped against it. The angel roared in pain. The light went out.

Perel forced her eyes open to see a blur of movement. A grey blob latched onto a bronze smudge. The angel punched Tesh as she thrashed about, her jaws locked around his arm. But the wolf was outmatched. Perel struggled back to her feet, lurched forward, and delivered her final hammer-punch to Mihiriel's neck. Half blind, it was a sloppy strike that shattered the angel's gorget and two of Perel's fingers. Mihiriel staggered back, struggling to breathe and still trying to fight off the wolf attached to his arm. Perel leapt at him and sank her teeth deep into his jugular. She bit down and tasted coppery blood rushing into her mouth. Perel gulped down as much blood as she could, feeling the surge of life that always came from drinking of the divine. The angel gurgled, his strength failing. Perel bit down even harder and pulled away, tearing the angel's throat out and swallowing down the flesh.

Mihiriel staggered back a step. Blood pulsed from his neck and ran down his throat, washing his battered armour. A waste of blood, maybe, but the sight got Perel hot, and she found herself dizzy with lust. The angel reached up with a single hand, then collapsed sideways to the ground. Dead.

Perel threw her head back and howled. Tesh joined in. Then, with the sound of their howls still echoing around them, both princess and wolf fell upon the body. They tore off armour and bit down on flesh, lapped blood from where it pooled. A divine feast. And while Tesh went for the juiciest part of any body, the guts, Perel tore open the angel's chest and buried her teeth into Mihiriel's heart.

CHAPTER 21

There is no cure for faith but that a sword may bring.

— EMRIK HOSTAIN

Years ago, a bard had come to Ner-on-the-River and set up in the Swallow's Tail. Renira had crept into the kitchen to listen to him tell his stories, and she remembered one about a young man who lived in the walls of a castle, sneaking about and only coming out at night via hidden passages that always seemed to be behind bookcases. She thought it a fantastically unbelievable tale at the time, but here she was racing up a hidden passage that Armstar had wrenched aside a bookcase to reveal.

The angel was a dark shadow climbing ahead, carrying a hooded lantern, their only light. He set a gruelling pace, and Renira chased behind him, struggling to remember a time when she wasn't running after Armstar. Sun was behind, one hand clutching his little spear, the other sweaty in Renira's own grip. The boy was clearly terrified, but then Renira couldn't blame him. She, too, was scared. But Sun had charged the monstrous wolf, putting his body in the way.

Many years ago, she had been determined to help her mother with the washing, but she'd been so small. Too little to reach the lines and peg the washing out to dry. Her mother had seemed so tall and strong and indomitable back then. She'd knelt in front of her daughter and plucked an apron from the basket of wet clothes, taken it in both hands, and said: *Even the smallest person can wring the biggest change*. Renira had giggled and leapt on the task, wringing out every bit of washing before her mother could hang it up.

The passage wound up through the cliff, carved from the rock itself, and in the swaying light of the lantern, Renira caught sight of mineral seams and fissures bisecting the stairway. She tripped on a stair and almost went down, grazing a hand as she thrust it against the nearby wall. Her legs burned with the effort, and sweat already soaked her smoky clothes.

Did you know, Mother? Did you know I'm the Herald and hide it from me?

Light streamed in from above as Armstar threw open a trapdoor. The angel stepped clear and stretched out his ruined wings, wincing with the pain of having them hunched for so long. Renira followed him into the red moonlight and felt her spirits lift a little with the sight of the sky. Somewhere, high above, a hawk let out a shrill cry that made her shiver.

"We're on the top of the cliffs," Sun said.

They were standing on an almost flat plain of rock that stretched on in all directions for what seemed like miles. Cracks ran through the rock, separating the cliff into thousands of plateaus. Despite the recent blizzard, there was little in the way of snow, but beyond them, towards the forest, everything was covered in a blanket of white. To Renira's left was Los Hold. The basin was a huge depression in the cliff, obvious now she was above it. She crept closer to the edge and stared down at the sanctuary city of the angels and their acolytes. It was burning.

The buildings themselves were carved from rock, but the contents were clearly not. Fires raged around the sanctuary, and ash and embers and black smoke drifted up into the winter sky. There were screams, too, people fighting and dying in their homes. All because of Renira. She had come to Los Hold and brought death and devastation with her. And others were paying the price.

"We have to go, Renira," Armstar said as he closed the trapdoor and doused the lantern.

Below, people ran through the alleys. Some ran from fires, others fled their attackers. A man and a woman, little more than dark shapes so far below, were clutching each other as they sprinted down an alleyway away from a chasing soldier. They couldn't see the ambush waiting for them, but Renira could. She willed them to turn, to break off down an alley or into a building. A silent watcher hoping things would play out differently but already knowing they wouldn't. Another attacker stepped out in front of the fleeing couple. Renira watched as the man was cut down first before he even realised it was an ambush. Her breath caught in her throat as the attacker chasing the couple caught up with the woman and thrust his sword through her belly. Renira's eyes roved across the scene of carnage playing out beneath her. Part of her hoped to see the washer woman, Flower, escaping through one of the cracks. Another part of her dreaded she might see her cut down, her age slowing her and making it impossible to escape.

Was this King Emrik's truth? Slaughtering innocent people in the hundreds just because they chose to believe differently, because they lived with angels. Renira knew that was the law, the Godless King's law, but now she was looking down at the consequences writ full, and it was all just so unfair. The people of Los Hold didn't need to die. Not for their beliefs and not for her.

She spotted the bridge that led to the Temple of Lore. Even from a distance, Renira could see that Mihiriel was down. The giant angel was a blood splatter on the ground, the wolf and princess both tearing at him.

Mihiriel who had seemed so strong and full of power. Who liked to stand still as stone and startle new acolytes when they least expected it. He had lived for over three thousands years. Gone. Dead and devoured. Renira staggered back from the cliff edge and sobbed, bile rising into her throat. "You were the tide," she said through tears streaming down her face. The answer to his riddle. Now he'd never get to share another. "All because of me."

"We don't have time for this self-pity, Renira," Armstar said. She shot him a baleful glare.

"You didn't kill them," Sun said, his face a picture of boyhood earnestness. He didn't understand. He was too young. Too innocent. *He* wasn't the Herald.

Renira shook her head and sniffed back a tear. "I didn't save them either."

"You tried," Sun said seriously. "That's more than Broken Wings did. More than Golden Throne did."

Renira wiped her eyes again. They were sore from the tears. "Smart and brave. You should be the Herald, not me." She faked a smile for him, placed a hand on Sun's head and ruffled his hair. The boy grinned and dodged away, then laughed and stared at the ground, the smile swiftly slipping from his face.

"We run then?" Renira asked Armstar.

He nodded. "The only thing we can do for now."

The hawk cried again, and Renira spotted a small, dark shape pass across the red light of the moon. A moment later and a burning glow streaked upward out of the basin. Eleseth climbed higher into the sky with powerful beats of her radiant white wings. She held a flaming whip in her hands and darted about in the sky, swooping and lunging after something Renira couldn't see.

"That's it," Armstar said. "Time to go while Eleseth catches the bird."

"The hawk?" Sun asked.

Armstar let out a bitter laugh. "That thing is no more hawk than the creature below is a wolf. It's bound to the Godless King. What it sees, so too can he. We cannot escape while it tracks us, so Eleseth has committed to breaking it. And now we must run before others find us."

"What about the prince?" Renira asked.

"If anyone is safe down there, it's him," Armstar said. "Both sides believe him an ally. Now shut up and run." Without any further discussion, Armstar turned and started north towards the dark, hulking shapes of the Cracked Mountains.

Renira didn't follow. Weariness and sorrow weighed down heavily upon her. If Armstar was right then this would happen time and time again. Nowhere they ran would be safe from Perel and the Godless King. *What other choice do I have?*

"Do we follow?" Sun asked. The boy had thrown his lot in with Renira, and she could already see there would be no separating him. He would live and die at her side, and that made her as responsible for his life as she was her own. And, she realised, as responsible as she was for the life of the God himself.

Whether Renira liked it or not, their best chance of surviving was with the angels. She nodded at Sun, and the boy nodded back at her. "Let's go," she said.

CHAPTER 22

Angels of the First Age were created by God to be warriors. Typically they are much larger than a human both in height and brawn. They wear armour which appears to be a part of them, dents, scrapes, and blemishes heal as would skin. Their blood is the most vibrant of all the ages of angels, but one should be wary of the heady euphoria that accompanies consumption.

— TERKIS THRANE, CHIEF CARVER TO KING
ERTIDE HOSTAIN. YEAR 57 OF THE FOURTH AGE.
12 YEARS AFTER HEAVEN FELL

Perel set one hand to each of the great, oak doors and pushed. They creaked, groaned, and held. Behind her, Tesh paced back and forth, snarling through a muzzle covered in angel blood. They had fed well on the corpse of Mihiriel, tearing his carcass open and feasting on the divinity's flesh. His power now coursed through them both. Somewhere high above, Father's hawk cried, and a glowing streak of light flew upward out of the basin. Another angel, but that one was out of Perel's reach. Besides, the Builder had fled into the temple, and so that was where Perel was going.

She stamped a foot hard enough that the stone shattered, and dug her feet in. She bunched her shoulders, placed her hands on the doors, and pushed.

Again, the doors groaned, creaked, squealed. Something cracked on the other side and crashed to the ground. The doors swung open under Perel's brute strength. She bellowed a roar of triumph as she stepped into the temple. Tesh slunk in behind her, head low and teeth bared.

The temple was gloomy, lit only by a few candles fixed to the pillars that stretched its length. Perel reached over her shoulder and pulled her Godslayer halberd from its holster on her back. There, at the far end of the hall, ensconced upon a throne, sat another angel, one even she recognised. Orphus, the Archangel. The Sword of Heaven. A divinity who had escaped her father's grasp time and time again. The thought of being the one to bring the Archangel's heart before her father put a new, savage grin on Perel's lips. Not to mention that she would be the first to taste the blood of the oldest angel. A delicacy no other had ever known.

"My brother is dead then?" the Archangel asked from his throne. He held a tome in one hand, and a giant sword rested across his lap.

Perel licked her lips. She didn't need to answer; her face was covered in the angel's blood. A crimson, divine mask. A laugh burst free of her, and it turned wild, echoing around the empty hall.

"You First Age angels always taste the sweetest," she said as she swaggered on. "Like spiced mead." She still had a bit of angel flesh stuck between her teeth and worked her tongue at it, trying to push it free.

The Archangel stood, sword held in his right hand. A large satchel hung at his hip, its leather strap across his armoured chest. He placed the book he was holding inside and secured the clasp. Then he started down the steps, his pace quickening as he moved to meet Perel's advance. Tesh stalked in the shadows, slipping between the pillars and biding her time.

Perel struck, sliding to a halt and thrusting out with her halberd. Orphus brushed the strike aside and waded forward, wings tucked tight behind his back. He slashed his sword down in grand, overhead blows. Perel brought her halberd up and blocked the Archangel's strikes, but he was relentless, too fast for her to counter, and so strong she was beaten back step by step.

"Is this what you are? What you have become?" the Archangel shouted as his blows rang out against Perel's faltering defence. She threw herself to her right, trying to slip away to recover and launch her own offensive, but he was on her in a moment. A battering blow sent Perel's halberd spinning away to skitter across the floor. Orphus kicked an armoured boot into her chest. She felt a second rib crack from the force and was thrown backward through a nearby pillar. The stone shattered around her, the pillar crumbling, and Perel came to a rolling rest amid a piled of dusty debris. She coughed and struggled to get her hands beneath her before rising unsteadily to her feet. Already the Archangel advanced upon her.

"I was there!" Orphus roared. He slashed at Perel, the reach of his blade even longer than her halberd. She limped away, putting another pillar in between them. Confidence fled, leaving only panic in its wake. How had she so sorely misjudged his strength?

"I was there when your ancestors revolted against their oppressors. I trained the Saint to fight. Gave her the tools she needed to strike back at the demons."

With the pillar between them, Perel couldn't see the Archangel. His sword slashed out, cutting through the pillar as though it were butter. Again, she staggered away, scooping up her fallen halberd and holding it defensively. She could feel Mihiriel's blood working within her, healing her broken rib and pulverised flesh. She just needed to delay a little longer until she was strong again.

"I fought alongside Dien and helped her pull your people from the thralldom of demons. I stood back to back with Helena at the Shattering when she led the charge against the Lords Under the Ice. I was there! The Hostains were noble. Leaders who used their strength to lift up those around them." Orphus stretched out his wings and buffeted Perel with a blast of air. He leapt forward and brought his sword down in a blinding slice. Perel turned the blow aside with her halberd. Orphus' hand shot out, the back of his gauntlet crunching against Perel's face. She hit the door hard enough that the wood splintered and burst apart, the stone around the hinges shattered, and the door fell to the floor with a boom. Again, Perel struggled to her feet, wincing against the pain and the blood running into her eyes. Her breath rasped past her lips, and her ribs felt like knifes gutting her from the inside. She couldn't hope to fight this thing. He was beyond human, beyond angel. Orphus was a true monster and she realised now she never stood a chance. She had to run.

The Archangel glowed gold in the gloom of the temple. His armour shone with power and light. His sword crackled with blinding energy. His eyes were blazing blue embers buried in the pitch-black recesses of his helm. "Your ancestors made humanity what it always could have been. Made you more than the beasts you cowered with." The Archangel advanced again, more slowly this time. "Now look at what you have become. Look at yourself, Perel Hostain. You are a beast once more, no better than the wolf you have corrupted alongside you."

Tesh snarled at the Archangel, pacing in the shadows. Perel sent a frantic wave at her wolf, trying to stop her from interfering. She knew the strength of the Archangel now—Tesh would be torn apart as easily as ripping paper. Perel would rather die a thousand deaths than let that happen.

She levered herself back to her feet, using her halberd as a crutch, and staggered backward as the Archangel advanced upon her. She had been foolish and brash, attacking without any plan. A creature as powerful as this required more than brute strength to best it. She was out in the open now with the night sky above and the bridge at her back. Below, a yawning chasm with a sound like rushing water. The Archangel advanced, eyes aflame.

"It began with your great grandfather, this descent. This regression," Orphus said. He passed the doors, one still ajar, the other flat on the ground.

Tesh snarled again, approaching the Archangel from behind but keeping her distance. Orphus turned and sliced his sword in an upward arc. A blinding wave of light erupted from the blade, splitting both the stone floor and the fallen door in two. Tesh yelped and leapt to the side, barely avoiding being cut in two by the wave of light.

Perel leapt on the distraction and staggered forward, twisting and slicing with her halberd. Orphus caught the halberd by the haft in one gold-gauntleted hand. He wrenched it from her and threw the Godslayer halberd away.

Perel fell backwards, beaten. The Archangel advanced on her once more. She was sweating fear, frantically trying to think of a way to save herself. Orphus kicked her back to the ground and placed a golden boot on her chest, pressing down as he leaned forward, his immense weight buckling her already fractured ribs.

"I knew your father before his fall," Orphus said in a quiet voice. He flipped the grip on his sword and held it above Perel, the tip of the blade hovering just above her face. She flailed at his boot, but it was too big and he too strong. A pitiful, animal whine escaped her throat, and she couldn't stop it. "I showed him mercy once, when I shouldn't have. Remind him of that."

The Archangel hefted his sword upward and threw it into the sky. It shot up and out of sight, a flashing trail of white. Lightning rippled along all the edges of the Archangel's armour, arcing gold and white. With a flash, the divinity vanished, leaving only a fading imprint of his outline written in sparkling light. Perel lay back on the stone floor amid the debris and stared up at the Blood Moon. Panic had scattered her thoughts, and she was struggling to comprehend what had just happened. Tesh limped into view and settled down beside her. Her wolf began licking Mihiriel's blood from her face.

Perel groaned in agony. They had survived the Archangel's wrath, by the virtue of his mercy. The thought was bitter and made her throat tighten with rage. Next time, she promised herself. Next time she would be prepared, and Orphus would find no mercy at *her* hands.

CHAPTER 23

B orik forced his way through a snow-clogged crevice that was rapidly shrinking with every step. He had to admit to himself that he was lost. In his flight from Los Hold, he had not paid sufficient attention to the navigational marks the locals used, and now he was turned around and up to his waist in powdery snow that had soaked him through and chilled him to the bone all at once. He'd have cursed his sister for being so good a tracker if he wasn't far too impressed by that very same ability.

The crevice grew thinner still, and Borik had to turn sideways to scrape his way along. His coat was stained and scratched and torn, and he'd need a whole new set of winter clothing once this adventure was done. Maybe something with a different cut, broader at the shoulders and a deep blue rather than black. Change was good, and it never hurt to ape his father's style a little to remind everyone of his immortal royalty.

"You know what? Screw the winter clothing. I deserve a whole new wardrobe after this ordeal."

He rounded a corner in the crevice and was emboldened by the sight of an open plain shrouded in snow and a green haze of trees in the far distance. The end of the cliffs. He pushed onward, wading through snow and getting more and more worried by how tight the crevice was getting. His questing hand found open air and the breeze that came with it right about the time that his chest got stuck and arrested any attempt at reaching the freedom his hand enjoyed.

"Crap. Bloody shitty crap!" Borik cursed and let out a weary sigh. He briefly considered backing up a few steps and trying his sword against the stone to widen the way, but it was a Godslayer blade, beyond priceless. While it *could* chip through stone, it deserved better treatment.

"Well, what have we 'ere?" said a man as he stepped into view at the end of the crevice. He was wearing a patchwork of hide armours, had skin the colour of coffee, and Borik could smell the stale sweat on him from half a dozen paces away. "Fleein' right into the trap, is it, little mouse?"

"Idiot!" Borik said with a sigh. "I'm the prince."

"Oh," the Dog's face fell when he realised he wasn't going to get to kill Borik and loot his corpse. "What you doing 'ere?"

Borik grimaced at the man. "Following my sister. Getting lost in the cliffs. Becoming one with nature. You know how it goes. Help me out!"

The Dog stared at Borik for a few moments. A grin split his cracked lips. "What's it worth?"

This was a language Borik knew well. Where some men might threaten, he preferred to coerce and haggle. "A drop of blood," he said with a disarming smile.

"Angel blood?" the Dog's eyes lit up with greed.

"No, ferret blood. Of course angel blood, you dullard."

The Dog grinned. "I want a pint."

Borik laughed. He couldn't help himself. "A pint? Idiot. Only my father has access to so much, and you can be bloody sure he wouldn't let you have any. Do you have any idea how much a single drop of angel blood is worth?"

The Dog frowned. "A lot?"

Trapped in a crevice and haggling with a simpleton, Borik wanted to

scream. "A single drop will add ten years to your life." It was a slight overstatement, but a poor man's lack of education was ever a fortune to a rich man. "It
also will cure disease and illness..."

"And make me strong as the princess?" the Dog asked.

Borik sighed again. "No. Angel blood doesn't do that. It extends life and
assures good health. Angel flesh makes a man stronger, and my sister has been
feeding on... Shit! It doesn't matter. Ten years onto your life and good health, or
that same drop of blood could buy you a whole mansion in Celesgarde. You
could live like a lord. Order some servants around, get your boots licked, have a
bloody bath."

"All right," the Dog said, greed in his eyes again. "Hand it over."

Borik ground his teeth at the man's stupidity. "I don't have it on me. But
I'm a bloody prince of Helesia, so trust me when I tell you I pay my debts."

The Dog sniffed and nodded. "Good enough." He gripped hold of Borik's
free hand and placed a boot against the cliff side, then pulled. Borik pushed
with his feet and breathed out, sucking in his chest. He scraped along, the rock
cutting through his clothing and grazing his skin, and then he popped free and
landed on the Dog in a foul smelling tangle. He was, without a doubt, the most
disgusting man Borik had ever straddled, although there was a pirate in Vael a
few decades back who might give him a challenge for that title.

Borik rolled off the man and onto his feet, then dusted himself off and
pulled his ragged coat a little closer against the wind. Morning was on its way,
and the sky was beginning to lighten, but the Blood Moon still shone down
upon them for now. In that muted red light, Borik could see the forest so far
away, across the snowy plain. He wondered when his father would arrive. He
also wondered how he might play the new information about the Herald.

The Dog was staring at him. "What?" Borik asked.

"I'm meant to be patrolling the cliffs. Making sure no one else escapes this
way." The Dog sniffed against the cold and grimaced. "It's right boring, it is. You
wanna help?"

A huge sword of gold and silver, crackling with energy, fell from the sky and
embedded itself in snow and rock not ten paces from them. A few moments
later and lightning burst from the sword and formed the outline of a giant man
in armour. Then, in a flash that had spots dancing in Borik's eyes, the Archangel
appeared, his hand wrapped around the hilt of the sword, his silvery wings
unfurled and majestic.

"Crap," Borik said with a sigh. He drew the dagger from his belt and thrust
it up to the hilt into the Dog's neck, then twisted and ripped the blade free in a
spray of gore that stained the snow red. The Dog fumbled at his neck for a

moment, eyes boggling, then collapsed forward into the powdery snow, his body spasming out its last embers of life.

"Was that necessary?" Orphus asked as he stood from his crouch. His breath misted in front of the dark recesses of his helmet, and his glowing blue eyes were damning chips of ice. He released his sword and left it buried in the ground.

Borik shrugged. "Well, I couldn't exactly have him telling people an angel appeared in front of us and instead of attacking you, we had a pleasant chat. So yes, quite necessary."

"Pleasant? My sanctuary burns. My acolytes are scattered or dead. Your sister killed the eldest of my brothers and ate his heart. Nothing about this day is pleasant, Godless Prince."

"Well, I suppose when you put it like that..." Talking with Orphus had indeed never been pleasant. Between the Archangel and Borik's father, he was starting to suspect that all true immortals possessed little but such bitter moods. "What about the Herald? Did she escape?"

"Yes," Orphus said. He crossed his arms over his broad chest. Despite the sacking of Los Hold, his armour still gleamed a bright gold. "Armstar has taken her north to our outpost in the mountains."

Borik ground his teeth at that. "My sister will follow. You're just putting another of your sanctuaries in harm's way."

The Archangel snorted, and the breath puffed out as mist in front of him. "Not for a few days. Even soaked in my brother's blood it will take time for her to heal."

That the Archangel might have hurt Perel was no small concern. Borik was working for the angels, it was true, but he wished no harm to come to any of his family, especially not Perel. His older sister was a prickly bitch, savage and lacking grace, but she was also fun and passionate and never judged Borik. She was, he admitted, his second favourite sibling. He fought the urge to ask about her, knowing it would only anger the Archangel further.

"So, what happens now? You take the Herald to Celesgarde?"

The Archangel looked to the brightening sky. "No. There are rules to be observed, and she isn't ready. I will return to isolation where I can harm no one else. Armstar and Eleseth will escort the Herald."

"How much should I tell my father?"

The Archangel shifted his gaze back to Borik. "All of it. As much as you dare."

Borik laughed at that. "So, I should stop shy of admitting to sedition and heresy then?"

The angel was silent.

"This is a test, isn't it?" Borik asked. "To determine my loyalty."

"No. We trust you. You have had time and opportunity to betray us to your father, and yet you help us. But we have not forgotten your sins. You owe your life to the blood of my kind. Your abilities were stolen from my siblings when you ate their hearts. We have not forgotten, and we will not forgive. You are helping us, and we appreciate it, but there is no glittering reward at the end of this for you. Only redemption for your transgressions."

Borik shrugged and smiled. "Did you ever think, Archangel, oh glorious Sword of Heaven, that redemption might be the glittering reward I have been after all along?"

The angel snorted. "Not even for a moment." He opened the satchel hanging at his waist and pulled a large tome out, then tossed it to Borik.

Borik caught the book awkwardly, amazed at its weight. It had wooden covers, engraved with divine heraldry, and it was as big as Borik's forearm. "What's this?"

"A book," Orphus said, dumping the satchel on the snowy ground. "Read it. Learn the truth. Pay special note to the section on the Heralds. Perhaps you can use it to convince your father to return to Celesgarde." The angel reached down and gripped the hilt of his sword, wrenching it from the rock and snow.

"Wait. You want my father to return to Celesgarde?" Borik said. "That's where the bell is. If he returns to the capital, he'll fortify the city. An army of angels wouldn't get in."

Cold blue eyes regarded Borik from the depths of the angel's helm. He flipped his grip on his sword and then threw it up into the sky. "The Herald is not ready. We need your father to return to Celesgarde rather than chase her. Make it happen."

Lightning crackled around the edges of the Archangel's armour and wings, and in a flash of light, he was gone.

Borik sat down on the rapidly cooling body of the Dog and opened the tome, resting it on his knees. Perhaps the Archangel thought Borik's job easy. If so, he was a fool. All Borik had to do was the impossible: convince his father to give up the hunt and return to Celesgarde as if there wasn't a new Herald running about Helesia. And the only thing Orphus had given Borik to help with his impossible task was a book that, rather than convince his father to return home, would only serve to make him believe his son guilty of heresy and sedition.

Borik sighed. "The things we do for immortality," he said to the dead.

CHAPTER 24

On wings of vengeance and blood set ablaze, freedom for all mankind!

— THE EXEMPLAR'S CRY

A rmstar slowed to a stop at the cliff edge, and Renira collapsed next to him. She gasped for air and let the fire in her legs turn to a dull ache. The air was so frigid, she knew she'd stiffen rapidly unless she stretched, but she couldn't find the energy to get back to her feet. Sun was lagging, stumbling as much as running, and eventually collapsed next to Renira. He was shivering again, and she put an arm around his shoulders and pulled him close. Armstar leaned over the edge of the cliff face, looking for a way down to the foot of the mountains below.

A whoosh of air warned Renira that they had company, and she turned to see Eleseth swoop in on glowing wings. The angel beat her wings once to slow her speed and hit the ground running. She slowed to a stop next to Renira and Sun and knelt in front of them. Her wings enfolded them both, cutting out the chill bite of the wind, and glowed with the warmth of a roaring hearth. Sun stopped shivering, and Renira felt new energy in her tired limbs.

The Herald of the Second Age, the Age of Wisdom, Eleseth was also known as the Light Bearer. The book claimed she had worked tirelessly during the Second Age to heal the wounds of humanity. Not just the physical wounds, but those that couldn't be seen and were passed on through the generations. The wounds of history and of abuse. Now here she was, using her power once more to heal.

"The bird?" Armstar asked.

"I chased it off," Eleseth said. She stood and shook her wings, then hunched them up high on her back. The biting wind rushed back in to nip at Renira's exposed skin.

Sun pushed Renira's arm away and stood in his ill-fitting robes. "I still don't trust her," he whispered. *What happened to you to make you so distrustful of angels?* Armstar might be callous and bitter, but Eleseth had never been anything but kind and a comfort. She seemed to care about them and their needs, where Armstar clearly cared only for himself.

Eleseth smiled and dropped a small bundle of clothes at Sun's feet. "Change into these. They'll be warmer than that robe and more suited to the mountain trail."

Sun snatched up the bundle of clothes and eyed Eleseth suspiciously, but she had already turned away to consult with Armstar.

They're still hiding things from me. Yet she had no choice but to follow them. They needed her, and she needed them. Sun poked Renira in the ribs and then moved further away from the angels. Renira followed.

He was clearly chewing over a question and working up the courage to ask it. "Are you really this Herald thing?" the boy asked.

"I don't know. I guess so. They certainly seem to think I am." Renira wasn't at all certain. A washer woman's daughter from a little town near the border of Helesia and Aelegar. How could *she* be chosen by the God to ring in the new age? She looked down at her hands. If they had made her the Herald, she certainly didn't feel any different for it. Did that mean she had always been the Herald and never known? "It's a big responsibility. I don't think I want it."

Sun pulled a sour face as he wrestled with the britches Eleseth had given him. He was a gangly boy, a tangle of limbs and dark skin. He reminded Renira of Fabe Fisher back home. All the other boys his age in Riverden had long since started growing into their bodies, but Fabe remained whip thin and bony. Elsa said it made him look regal, but Renira always thought it made him look awkward. Sun had that same awkward look about him, caught somewhere between boy and young man, still growing.

"But you don't have a choice?" Sun asked.

Renira chewed her lip. "It doesn't seem like it. I always dreamed of adventure, but I just expected it to be..." Renira thought back over her daydreams of fighting monsters and rescuing princes for the price of a kiss. Daring heroics and always saving the day just like in the bard's tales and the stories in *Rook's Compendium*. No one ever died in her dreams. She always managed to save them. "I think I expected it to be less frightening."

Sun paused pulling his new tunic over his head, and his dark eyes went distant. "The wolf?"

"Did you see the size of its teeth?" Renira asked in a hushed voice. "They were longer than my hands!"

"But I protected you," Sun said. He finished pulling on the tunic. It was slightly too large for his skinny body and hung awkwardly.

"You did," Renira nodded. She leaned in and kissed Sun on the cheek. Then she straightened her back and put on her most formal voice. "Your debt to me is paid, Sun. Thank you. I'm sure Armstar can point you to the nearest town, and you'll be much safer away from me."

"Ha!" Sun shouted. It drew the attention of the two angels, but they quickly went back to their own conversation. "I'm not done protecting you yet. You need me, Ren." He pointed a thumb at his chest. "That Godless King and his wolf princess won't stop chasing you, so I won't stop protecting you. I swore an oath." He shook his head. "Can't go back on blood oaths. I won't let Glowy or Broken Wings chase me away."

Renira chuckled. Sun's blind optimism was oddly invigorating, despite the dire situation. "They have names, you know?"

Sun nodded. "I do. But they call me *boy*. My name isn't boy."

A thought occurred to Renira. If she wasn't going to be able to send Sun away, she might at least make his presence official. "No, it isn't," she agreed. "It's Exemplar Sun."

Sun frowned. "Exemplar?" his harsh accent made a ruin of the word.

"Exemplar," Renira said. "They were an order of humans formed by Saint Dien. Great warriors and leaders and allies to the angels. Examples of what humanity could be at its best. They fought against the demons in the First Age and against the Lords Under the Ice in the Second Age. I used to read all the stories about them. Great heroes fighting for good."

The stories of the Exemplars in *Rook's Compendium* were always some of the most exciting. Exemplar Yolk's last stand where she stood over the body of Queen Helena against the Drowned Hordes and even fought one of the Lords Under the Ice. Samir's flight across the Big Horns, hounded by demons every step of the way but carrying vital information, the location of the Den Mothers. The Shadow Knight and his quest to recover his voice only to realise the benefits of silence. Even Karta's betrayal, a story of profound tragedy. The stories of the Exemplars were so often of humans and angels fighting side by side against dark forces determined to destroy the world. Renira glanced at Armstar and Eleseth. She wondered if those people, the ones from the stories, thought they were being heroic? Or were they just trying to survive? Fighting against forces they barely understood.

"Exemplar," Sun repeated. "I like it."

"So do I. And if I'm the new Herald, I guess I can make it official." She made her voice deep and formal again. "Exemplar Sun, first guard of Herald Renira."

Sun grinned and stood rigid as if to attention. He really wasn't so much shorter than her when he stopped slouching. He held his left hand against his chest. "I, um, swear…"

"No more blood oaths."

Sun smiled and shook his head. "I swear to protect you, Herald Renira. With my life. I won't leave you. So please don't send me away."

An idea occurred to Renira. She raised her hand into a fist and extended her little finger. Sun stared at her confused.

"Copy me."

Sun raised his hand and extended his little finger. Renira wrapped her finger around his.

"Courage and hope, Exemplar Sun."

Sun grinned. "Courage and hope."

It was fun, even if only for a moment, though Renira couldn't help but feel they were just children playing at roles they didn't really fit. Roles meant for true heroes.

"An Exemplar should wear armour, not rags." Sun pulled on the winter coat Eleseth had brought him and kicked the old robe.

His new clothes were plain brown trousers and a wool tunic that would help to keep him warm in the cold weather. And perhaps most importantly, they weren't riddled with holes. Renira wished her own clothes were as unworn, but the flight through the forest and cliffs had been hard, and though the holes had been patched, her clothes would never look new again. She shouldn't care, they were only clothes, but they were also a link to home. They were the clothes her mother had made for her, painstakingly sewn together from hand-me-downs and scraps of cloth, sheep skin she scrounged from Farmer Hay. Renira shook her head at her foolishness. *Stop being so melancholic. They're just clothes.*

She approached the edge of the cliff. The sun was starting to rise from the east, a shining brilliance that she had to squint against. There seemed no easy way down, and she didn't relish the idea of climbing. As a girl from Riverden, swimming had been an early lesson for her. Every child growing up in the town learned to swim early and well, and in large part because swimming in the river was a favourite pastime for the young. Climbing, however, had never been something Renira had opportunity to learn. It looked a long way down to the ground. Far enough that she would expect broken legs should she fall. Her vision swam, and Renira took a hurried step back away from the cliff edge. *Nope. That fall would definitely kill me.* She really didn't like heights, now she thought about it.

"How far is this outpost in the mountains?" Renira asked.

The angels broke off their discussion. Eleseth looked far from happy and shook her head. "Orphus gave this task to you, brother. Her safety is your responsibility."

Armstar smiled grimly. "It always was." He stepped around Eleseth and stared north toward where the mountains were smallest. "We're not going to the outpost, and we're not stepping foot on the Cracked Mountains."

Renira frowned. "But Orphus said..."

"I don't care what he said. The Fangs are too dangerous even for us. Orphus underestimates the monsters that haunt the Cracked Mountains. And the outpost is just another trap waiting to happen. We need to lose our hunters, and we're not going to do that out here in the wilderness. Perel is too good a tracker. We're going north, around the base of the mountains, to the city of New Gurrund. We'll lose her there, then make our way to Celesgarde."

Sun finished belting his tunic around his waist and joined them. He'd slung his overlarge robe over his shoulders to function as a makeshift cloak. It looked comical but would help keep him warm as winter secured its grasp on the land.

Renira shook her head. If they couldn't lose the wolf princess in the middle of nowhere, what hope did they have of losing her in a city? "But how will we lose her in New Gurrund? You two aren't exactly inconspicuous." In truth they stood out like a broken nose. At times, Renira found herself staring at Eleseth and struggled to tear her eyes away from the woman.

Eleseth smiled, her skin radiant in the morning light. "You might be surprised." She shook out her wings and then draped them around her arms and over her shoulders. The white feathers turned grey, and as Renira watched the pattern shifted until she was certain she was looking at a plain grey cloak. Her glow diminished and rather than a glorious angel, Eleseth looked drab.

She had heard of animals camouflaging themselves in the forest, but never anything like that. Renira approached the angel and reached out a hand, touching the cloak. It looked like wool but felt like feathers. She stroked Eleseth's wings and marvelled at how soft they were.

"Huh. Well that takes care of that, I suppose," she said. "But you're still too... um... please don't be insulted. You're too big. I don't know how things are in New Gurrund, but in Riverden a woman big as you would be all Poe talked about and he'd tell everyone." She'd heard of folk from Aelegar who grew to be giants, but they rarely ventured into Riverden. Whispers of raids and banditry always followed them, and they were usually chased out with stones and insults. She'd even seen a barbarian from Aelegar in the stocks once, his face swollen and bloody and covered in the shit folk had been slinging at him. They were never treated kindly.

Eleseth shrugged, her wings taking form again and spreading out to their full span. "There are some folk who grow almost as large as I, and with a sunny disposition many will overlook my size. It is the best I can offer. It will have to do."

Renira frowned, unconvinced, but Eleseth smiled. "We'll make it work," the angel said. "This is not the first time I've had to hide myself among you."

Renira turned her attention to Armstar. "What about you? Your wings..."

"I'll manage," the angel said with a grimace. His wings were blackened bones, broken in places, and she had seen him move them only sparingly. She doubted he could make his wings look like a cloak, though maybe a shawl made from bones. "Besides, your misgivings don't matter. It's my choice, and I've made it. We're going to New Gurrund. It's either that or we walk into the mountains and find ourselves at the mercy of hunters even more savage than Perel and her wolf. Trust me, no one comes out of the Fangs the same. They are haunted by the old world."

Renira had a feeling she knew what he meant. "Demons hide in the darkness where humans fear to tread."

Armstar gave her a measuring stare, then shook his head. "There are worse things than demons."

Sun stepped in front of Renira and bounced the butt of his little spear on the stone. Armstar raised an eyebrow at him. "What does that mean?"

"I am Exemplar Sun, Herald Renira's first guard. I'll protect her no matter where we go," Sun said, trying and failing to make his voice deeper.

"Of course you are," Armstar sneered at the boy. "Can the Exemplar climb?"

Sun nodded. "My mother taught me to climb when I was three."

Renira placed a hand on Sun's shoulder. "I thought you didn't have any parents, Sun."

The boy's eyes went wide, and he stared at the rocky cliff beneath his feet. He said nothing. He was hiding something, maybe because it was too painful, but Renira thought she should know. Needed to know. If Sun was to be her Exemplar, she needed to know who he was and where he had come from. And why he had attached himself to her so firmly. She trusted him. He had risked his life to save hers, after all, but now she thought about it, she knew nothing about the boy.

"The man above the cocoon," Renira said hesitantly. "Back in the Whistle Woods, in the demon's lair. Was that... Was he your father?"

Sun's eyes darted about as though searching for something on the rocky ground. His hands balled into fists, and then he sagged, nodding. Renira couldn't imagine what it must have been like to see your own father devoured by demons. She lurched forward and wrapped her arms around Sun, pulling the boy into an embrace. He didn't cry, but he trembled as she held him. She felt oddly guilty for not saving his parents. But no. It had been too late for them.

"Why were you in the forest?" Eleseth asked.

Sun pulled away from Renira. He didn't meet her eyes, keeping his gaze on the ground. "We were running away. You don't know what Ashvold is like. To you Helesians, wulfkin are just stories. But they're not. They're real. Half wolf, half man. Monsters released every Blood Moon to hunt us." It sounded a nightmarish place. A land of volcanoes and fire and monsters, but Armstar had said it was ruled over by an angel. "And they're not even the worst of it..."

Armstar rolled his eyes. "I know better than you what kind of place Ashvold is, boy. And we don't have time for this." He leaned forward and snatched the spear from Sun's hands. The boy complained, but Armstar threw the spear over the side of the cliff. "Call it motivation. You want your spear back. Climb. Eleseth, help the Herald." Armstar lowered himself to his knees and shuffled over the edge of the cliff face.

Renira stared over the edge of the cliff again and felt her vision swim and her stomach lurch. Eleseth stepped close, and Renira backed away from the cliff edge. "I think... um..." Renira swallowed, finding her mouth suddenly dry. "I don't think I like heights very much."

Eleseth leaned down and scooped Renira up into her arms, heedless of the squeak of alarm Renira let loose.

"Close your eyes," Eleseth said, then stepped over the edge of the cliff. Renira's panicked cry caught in her throat, and she buried her face in Eleseth's chest. She could feel the wind rushing past her, whistling in her ears, as Eleseth glided down to the ground on outstretched wings. They landed in a patch of loose snow, and Renira scrambled out of the angel's arms and onto solid ground once more. Her eyes were wide and wild, and her heart was racing, blood thundering in her ears.

Armstar and Sun were climbing down the cliff face, but they were going so slowly, crawling like lethargic spiders. Renira trembled as she stared up at them and wondered how they were moving at all. Just the thought of clinging to the cliff side, so high up, made her freeze. She was breathing too quickly, unable to focus. The edges of her vision were blurring. The pain in her hand from gripping her mother's amulet so tight was the only anchor she could find to the world.

"You can't just do that!" Renira snapped. She fell to her knees in the snow, hands digging through the cold to touch the earth below.

"It's all right to be scared of heights," Eleseth said. Her voice was calming, soft and husky.

"I'm not!" Renira said, though a part of her realised it must be true. "I never have been before." She was calming a little now, her breath slowing. "Though, I suppose I've never really been up that high before. I'm sorry. I didn't mean to snap." Everything was happening far too fast, and being scooped up and carried like a little girl without warning was a step too far.

"I see." Eleseth turned and started north. "Walk with me, Renira."

Renira glanced back up to where Armstar and Sun were crawling down the cliff face. The thought of it made her vision swim all over again, and she tore her gaze away. Her feet seemed unstable beneath her, as though the ground were spongy and shifting, but Renira knew that was a lie. She needed a distraction. On shaky legs, she hurried to catch up with Eleseth.

"Not all fears present themselves with honesty," the angel said.

"Huh?" Renira couldn't find the focus to puzzle out the meaning of her words.

Eleseth frowned. "A lot has changed for you in such a short time. Perhaps too much. I wonder if your fear of heights is maybe a fear of change, struggling to make itself heard over the clamour of... well, everything that has happened." Eleseth placed a gentle hand on her shoulder. "It's all right to be afraid, Renira. I am. I've been afraid for a very long time."

"Why me?" The question had been rattling around in Renira's head ever since she had been told she was the new Herald. It seemed even more important now that the people of Los Hold had died because of her. Every time she thought about all those lost lives, the guilt of it threatened to overwhelm her. There had to be a reason, a purpose for it all.

Eleseth walked in silence for a while, golden eyes locked on the horizon. "It's a simple question with a complex answer. I suppose the easiest answer is because you are the right person for the job. Although it might be more accurate to say you're the only person for the job."

As far as answers went, it was a poor one that only begged more questions. But that was something she was coming to expect from the angels. *For once I wish just one of them would give me a straight answer.* "It's all to do with my mother, isn't it? How did you know her?"

Eleseth waited before answering, and the silence told Renira she would learn nothing new today. Herald or not, the angels were hiding the truth from her. "Armstar brought Lusa to Los Hold. It was a long time ago, at least for a human. Fifty years, I think." She had to be mistaken. Mother wasn't that old.

"But Armstar won't tell me why," Renira said. "He says he respected her because she chose to help him, to help all of you, but... He's not telling me everything, and..." She clutched at her mother's amulet, desperately trying to feel a connection there. "Why am I the Herald?"

Eleseth stopped and knelt in front of her. "Nobody chose you, Renira. Not your mother, not Armstar, not Orphus, and not even the God. You simply *are* the Herald."

If that's true then why can't someone else just *be the Herald?*

"It is a big responsibility, I know" Eleseth continued. "More so for you than any since I rang in the Second Age. It is on your shoulders to set the world right. And it's a weight you must carry alone. But that does not mean you have to walk alone. I'll be here right beside you, all the way. Armstar, too, and I guess the boy won't be separated from you either. I will protect you, Renira." She opened her mouth as if to say more, then closed it again.

Renira didn't understand. She didn't understand any of it. It all seemed so surreal, like it was happening to someone else. "Is there a bell?" she asked. If Eleseth wasn't willing to tell her why she was the Herald, the least she could do is tell her how she was supposed to ring in an age. "An actual bell I have to ring? It's not a, um, what did Aesie call them? A metaphor or something?"

"Yes," Eleseth said with a laugh. "A real bell. In Celesgarde. It's quite magnificent."

Renira shook her head, her mind a whirl with more questions than answers. Armstar was the first down the cliff, and he ignored Sun, still clinging to the rock, and hurried toward Eleseth and Renira. His wings were twitching as he strode past them. "We have no time to waste. Hurry."

"I'm waiting for Sun," Renira said firmly.

"The boy will catch up."

"Well, I'm still bloody waiting for him."

Armstar's wings twitched again, but he said nothing as he continued to forge ahead.

Eleseth settled her wings around her like a cloak and stood next to Renira, watching Sun make his slow descent down the cliff face. "He's an interesting boy," the angel said softly.

"He has a name. It's Sun," Renira said testily. "And he's my friend."

CHAPTER 25

Mercy is the mark of the fool.

— ERTIDE HOSTAIN

I t was a glorious day; one Emrik would soon allow the historians to write about.

He strode through the ruined streets of Los Hold in crimson daylight. His black plate armour clinked with every step. Forged in the blood of angels and infused with the crushed bones of the God himself, the armour was nigh on indestructible and as light as a summer shawl. It both protected him and enhanced his already divine strength. God-forged armour, and the only set in existence. There was, perhaps, no more valuable item in all of humanity's history.

They had been looking for this hidden sanctuary for decades. A place where rogue divinities sheltered and spread the filth of their faith to new acolytes, corrupting humanity to their lies even a thousand years after the death of their God. Now it burned. One less place for the angels to hide. The Herald had led them here, and yet he had escaped again.

Smoking wreckage told the story of Perel and her Dogs. Brutality had its uses, and the destruction and murder here would serve to warn others of the consequences of harbouring angels. His soldiers, men and women of the Fourth, swarmed about him. Every building was checked. Survivors were taken, to be questioned and tried for their heresy, and seditious artefacts were fuel to the fires.

Bodies littered the streets, mostly the acolytes of Los Hold, but many of Perel's Dogs had met their end as well. They were human, after all, not strengthened by divine blood. The Dogs served their purpose well, but when faced with the wrath of angels, they stood little chance. Even the weakest divinity, a Third Age angel, would be more than a match for a mere human. Crows and other carrion birds crowded the rooftops, cawing out their impatience at having to wait to dine on the feast laid before them.

Emrik had watched much of the sacking of Los Hold from the eyes of his hawk, but when Eleseth had taken to the skies, he had no choice but to let the bird make its escape lest her fires consume it and rob Emrik of his valuable second sight. Once, so long ago, he had counted the Light Bearer as a friend. He'd even hoped for more than just friendship from her. No more. He had long since stamped out that weakness in himself.

He found Perel near the temple, close to the carcass of a First Age angel. She had blood on her face and struggled to stand when he drew near. She was hurt and badly, wincing with every movement and using her halberd for support. Her wolf lay nearby, its legs twitching in sleep plagued with dreams.

"How severe are your injuries?" Emrik asked urgently, desperate to know she was all right. He held out a gauntleted hand.

"Father, I... I failed you. I'm sorry."

Emrik went down on one knee before her, the plates of his armour sliding against each other. He placed a hand on her arm for support. "How badly are you hurt, Perel?"

She stared up at him, eyes shining, and sniffed back the tears. "I've had worse." She was shaking from the agony of broken bones, already healing but more painful for it.

"Good." Emrik sighed in relief. "Good. You should have waited for me."

The smile dropped from Perel's face, and she lowered her eyes. "Sorry, Father. I wanted to make you proud. I... I misjudged the strength of the Archangel."

Emrik gave her a knowing smile. "As did I, once. It's an easy mistake to make. He is so much stronger than all his siblings."

"He said..." She trailed off.

"Speak plainly, daughter."

"He said he showed you mercy once."

Emrik ground his teeth together and pulled his hand away from Perel. He turned towards the body of the First Age angel. "I was younger, brash like you. I did not yet have the strength to back up my arrogance. Orphus and I fought, and he defeated me." Emrik grimaced as he reminisced. "He should have killed me that day. But mercy is a weakness, and his mercy led to the sacking of Heaven and the death of his God. A fitting lesson for one so arrogant as he."

"He told me to tell you something, Father." Perel sounded hesitant. "He said he wouldn't show you mercy again."

Emrik snorted. "Orphus does not have the courage to face me again. He knows how much angel flesh I have fed on, how many of his kind's hearts I have eaten. He knows I devoured his precious God. How much stronger I have become. Let him come before me, and I will prove to him once and for all how much a weakness his mercy is."

To think they had been friends once. Orphus had been the one to teach Emrik the sword, and for many years he had called the angel 'master'. But that friendship had always been a lie, just as everything the God taught was a lie.

Emrik knelt by the body of the First Age angel. The carcass had been torn open, fed upon, its blood and flesh spread wide on the stone floor of the basin. The armour, even dinted and cracked open, could be salvaged. Angel armour was almost as valuable as the flesh it protected, stronger than any steel humanity could forge. But the body was too far gone to be of any use. Without proper preservation, the flesh and blood of angels spoiled quickly and became not only useless, but poisonous to all beasts, man included. Any who fed on it now would become warped monstrosities.

"Mihiriel," Emrik said as he stared down at the carcass. "The Spear Tip." He, too, had once trained Emrik in the martial forms. The greatest spearman to have ever lived, with the exception of Emrik's own father. "Now Orphus is alone. The last of the angels from the First Age."

Emrik looked up into the sky. "Do you feel it, Sword of Heaven? Do you feel the noose closing around your neck? The blood of your kind draining away? I will find you, as I have found all the others. I will be your end. To the dirt, fall. To the worms, feed. To history, vanish."

Emrik looked back at his daughter. "Mihiriel's heart?"

Perel smiled through her pain, still leaning on her halberd. She raised her right hand, and it began to glow, softly at first but growing brighter by the second. She shook her hand, and the glow faded. "I don't have full control over it yet. And I have no idea what it can actually do."

"More than you realise. I saw Mihiriel blind an entire army with that power during the Crusade. His brothers and sisters swooped down from the sky and tore our forces apart. They could do nothing but blindly await death." He shook his head sadly.

"Also, I'll never need a lantern again," Perel said and laughed. Emrik joined in. Brief moments of humour were good and all too rare for one as old as Emrik.

"I *am* proud of you, daughter"

Perel shook her head and slumped. "But I failed. I let the Archangel win, the Herald escape. I... I lost."

"No. You slew a terrible enemy today. My faith in you is rewarded time and time again."

Perel was grinning from the compliment and struggled to stand a little straighter. "I'm sorry I couldn't capture the Herald for you, Father."

Emrik shook his head and rested a gauntleted hand on Perel's shoulder. "You rooted out one of their last hiding places and sent the Herald scurrying for new shelter. We'll find him. Have you seen your brother?"

"Not since the forest," Perel said. "He was following me. He'll be around somewhere. Borik always turns up after the fighting is done."

Emrik turned his attention to the temple at the far end of the bridge. It had a grand entrance with statues of angels either side and huge wooden doors, though one of those had been torn from its hinges and split in two. Soldiers had looped rope around one of the statues and were busy heaving, pulling the stone angel down. The fabled Temple of Lore. A trove of seditious texts and a breeding ground for heresy. One of angelkind's most revered shrines. An entire temple built to the God's lies.

Emrik motioned to Commander Lorel, waiting nearby with a back so straight she'd make a spear jealous. "Burn it, Commander. Make certain no scrap of paper survives the conflagration." Some would argue that much could be learned from the books housed within those walls. But he had sat at the feet of the God and listened to divine lies for too long. He had been taken in, duped by the so-called trust the God had put in him by telling Emrik his true name. Another lie. There was no trust there. By some trickery or power the God had wrought, those who knew God's name could never share it. Emrik had tried, but even a thousand years after his death, the God's divine laws held. Any time Emrik tried to share his name, the words died in his throat, his hands wrote gibberish. It became just one more reason to kill the last of the angels. If the God's name could not be shared, then he would see it forgotten.

As soldiers with torches rushed forward to set fire to everything in the temple, Emrik turned away and led Perel toward a nearby building that had barely been touched by the fires her Dogs had spread. The wolf yawned, stretched, and followed. Limping along, as injured as her mistress.

They passed another statue, smaller than those of the angels, its features worn by aeons. Already there were soldiers climbing it, looping rope around the statue's shoulders.

"Leave this one," Emrik ordered. "Let it stand. The last surviving monument of this den of lies."

"Who is it?" Perel asked as she peered up at the statue. "In justice, find purpose. In strife, find conviction. In victory, find peace."

Emrik reached out and laid a gauntleted hand on the foot of the statue. "Saint Dien Hostain." Though the God had corrupted her image, the legacy she had left was undeniable. The Saint had united mankind; forestfolk, riverfolk, Ice Walkers, and Ashmen, even the savages from the mountains. Not even Emrik's grandfather, Ertide, had managed such a feat. She remained a powerful symbol, the uniter, the founder of the Hostain dynasty.

Emrik continued on to the untouched hovel and opened the door, holding it wide for Perel and her wolf to pass through, then followed them in, ducking to fit through the door frame. He let the door swing closed behind him and found they were in a sparsely decorated home. Drops of blood stained the stone beneath his feet, proof that even these heretics had followed the tradition of offering blood to their host. It was a way to tell the history of a place, and as with all histories, it was written in crimson.

A kitchen separated a bedroom from a study that housed a desk and a small fireplace. A canvas sack of oats sat on one of the kitchen tops, knocked over so much of its contents had spilled onto the floor. The wolf sniffed at the oats and moved on, curling up next to the hearth where an empty pot smoked above the flames. The wolf began licking its paws and keening at the pain of a snapped claw.

Emrik moved into the study and pulled out a chair for Perel. She lowered herself into it with a wince. Then he moved to the other side of the desk and sat down on the chair there. It groaned under the weight of king and armour. Emrik pulled off both gauntlets and dropped them on the table with a *thunk*, then started looking through the desk draws for paper and quill.

"I could send for Ezerel," he offered. "More angel blood might speed your recovery." If he could spare his daughter even a moment of pain, he would, no matter the cost.

Perel obviously did not miss the generosity of the offer. Even a single pint of angel blood was worth more than all the gold in Celesgarde, and most people could never even dream of such a fortune. All Emrik's children were fed it early in their lives, a constant supply of divine blood that would grant them a form of immortality. It was not true immortality, of course, they would eventually age, though far more slowly than normal. Unlike Emrik, who had tasted the blood and flesh of the God himself. He was truly immortal, and the last of his kind now his father was gone and his grandfather dead.

"I don't think I could stomach any more, Father," Perel said. "I gorged on as much of Mihiriel as I could. Maybe too much." She shifted uncomfortably in her chair and looked embarrassed. "I'm feeling quite bloated, truth be told." The wolf gave an agreeing whine.

The door opened, and Borik sauntered in along with a chilling breeze. Commander Lorel followed him in and shut the door behind her, taking up position in the kitchen. Borik stooped to scratch the wolf behind its ears and solicited a rumbling groan, then turned to Emrik with a grin.

"Father," he said with a bow of his head, then turned to Perel. "Sister. Have you been trying to apply makeup again? You got a little red on your face. Actually, sort of all over your face. It suits you."

Perel smiled, white teeth amid a face stained red. "Too bad you were hiding in the shadows again, Brother. I got an entire angel all to myself, and he was delicious."

Borik hunted around for another chair, but there weren't any. He dumped a heavy pack on the floor and leaned against the nearby wall. "You killed an angel? By yourself?"

"Mihiriel, of the First Age," Emrik said, unable to keep the pride from his voice.

Borik let out a sharp whistle that made the wolf's ears twitch. "That's impressive," he said. "Well done, Sister. Still, looks like he gave as good as he got. Well... almost."

Perel grimaced and shook her head. "This wasn't Mihiriel. The Archangel was here as well. He... He beat me."

"And yet he left you alive?" Borik asked. "Odd."

Emrik found paper and charcoal in the bottom draw of the desk and pulled them out. "The Archangel took a vow to never kill again," he said as he laid the paper on the desk and scraped the charcoal to a point with a fingernail.

"He did?" Borik asked. "When? And why?"

Emrik began scraping the charcoal over the sheet of paper, an image that had once been painted a hundred times, so long ago now that none but he even remembered it.

"After the sacking of Heaven. While the gates burned and the God lay dead, his head on your grandfather's spear. We had eaten as much of him as we could, but there is only so much even three grown men can stomach. And the others were all dead." He rubbed at his chin. "Such a battle it was."

"Seven were the Godless Kings who took their war to Heaven," Borik said.

Emrik nodded. "Seven of us entered. Only three of us lived, and I barely." He shifted in his armour, feeling the God's spear burning his insides all over again. "Still, we were brimming with power and radiating our newfound immortality."

He sketched the outline of three men on the paper, sometimes with the point of the charcoal, and sometimes smudging with a calloused thumb. It had been so long since he'd indulged the artistic urges. He'd almost forgotten how much he loved to draw, so consumed he was with his hunt.

"The Archangel took no part in the battle of Heaven's halls. He stayed here and fought to secure the gate from this side. It was an attempt to cut off our reinforcements, leaving the seven of us to face the God alone. His faith was ever misplaced. Even so, where his God failed and fell to our blades, the Archangel succeeded. He led ten of his strongest siblings, all angels born in the First Age, to battle. They held Heaven's Gate against the bulk of our armies here in Helesia."

Emrik continued to scratch at the page and more details took shape. Three men, all heavily armoured. Two with swords and one with a spear, a large head embedded on the tip. Light shone behind them, rendering them in brilliant silhouette.

"When we exited those gates, we found a slaughter. Fifty thousand soldiers held Heaven's Gate; the greatest force amassed since the Shattering in the Second Age. Immortals as well as mere humans. Back then, your great grandfather fed angel flesh and blood to many of his most loyal warriors." A battlefield strewn with bodies took shape at the bottom of the paper. "Fifty thousand and only a handful of them survived. Fifty thousand slain by just eleven."

A winged man began to take shape on the page as Emrik scratched away. "Of the eleven angels who attacked our forces, only one survived. Orphus himself. We found him standing atop a pile of bodies, his armour dripping gore and wings stained red. He knew his God was dead, had realised it the moment the sky turned to blood, but he fought on regardless. Slaughtering thousands in his rage."

The angel on the page was huge, a monster in armour, his sword crackling with power. With nothing but charcoal to work with, Emrik could not capture the terrifying blue fire in the Archangel's eyes, but he remembered it. The rage and horror and pain in Orphus' stare was burned into him so indelibly even a thousand years had not dulled its edges.

Emrik steeled himself for the next part of the story and felt the bitter grief even a thousand years after the fact. "He was holding my sister's head when we stepped through the gate. I will never forget the dreadful sound it made as he threw it on the ground before us. Nor the vacant stare of eyes still wide with terror before he tore her head from her body."

Emrik wiped tears from his eyes before conquering his pain and adding the head of his twin sister, Merian, to the picture he was drawing. They had been thick as thieves once, and she had gotten him into so much trouble when they were children. She had loved horses, and the smile she wore whenever she rode one was of a joy Emrik had never grasped for himself. She had wanted to be the first human to ride a pegasus. Now no one else would ever get the chance. After her murder, Emrik had slaughtered every one of the flying horses.

"I wanted to kill him." Hot rage bubbled inside Emrik's chest, and his scribbling became frantic as he pencilled in more of the details. "I wanted to tear his chest open and sink my teeth into his heart. But your grandfather held me back. Maybe it was seeing Merian's head or the God's flesh still in his stomach, but the taste for violence had gone from my father. It was something he never felt again. I think the absence of it was what broke him eventually. Even your great grandfather refused the fight. He held me back while your grandfather plucked the God's head from his spear and threw it to the Archangel. A bloody trade. Head for head. Hers for his."

Emrik paused, his sketching done, his hand trembling from the anger. It was far from the greatest work of art he had ever created, but it was accurate. A rendition in shadows and light, everything except the faces, left blank on the page. He had always been awful with faces. He turned the paper around and pushed it across the desk so his children could see it better.

"Orphus said to us: 'Your Crusade is done. You have taken from the world all that is good, and there is nothing left for angelkind but to fade away into memory and myth.' Then he swore, before the dead eyes of his God and my sister, that he would never again take a life. Not angel, nor human, nor animal. He asked that we let him and the last of his people disappear." Emrik ground the charcoal into the desk, crushing it to black stain and flaking shards. "Then he fled, and Heaven's Gate closed behind us." Emrik fell silent, the tale told, his feelings still bitter over the taste of it. He wished he could hear his sister laugh one more time.

"Who broke the agreement?" Borik asked. He fidgeted and pushed the pack at his feet a little further behind his legs.

Emrik pinned his son with a sharp stare. "What agreement?"

"He would never kill again, and you would let the angels fade into memory?"

Emrik gripped the desk so hard wood began to splinter beneath his fingers. "I never made such an agreement. Your great grandfather and grandfather thought it done. They thought they could let the angels disappear, but I knew better. I knew they would continue to spread their heresy. Knew there could be no compromise and the task would never be complete until all of them were dead and eaten. Only then could their God's lies fade away, not into memory, but into nothing. Like weeds in a garden, if we do not pull them out by the root, they will surely grow again.

"That is why we *must* find this new Herald and kill him before he can ring the Bell of Ages, or all of it starts again."

Anger warred with weariness inside. Emrik was not sure he had it in him to fight another Crusade. The first one had cost him far too much. So many of those he loved had died trying to free humanity from the yoke that God had fastened around their necks. Besides, it had taken all seven of the Godless Kings to slay the God, and only three of them had survived the battle. With his grand-father dead, and his father gone, Emrik was now the only Godless King left in the world. His brother, Arandon liked to think himself one, but he was weak and a coward. Back then, he hid behind the walls of Celesgarde when the Crusade reached its climax, just as he was hiding behind the walls of Everheim even now.

Perel shifted in her seat and winced. "I almost had the Builder, but... He can't be the Herald. He's a ruined creature. His wings won't even heal. He's one of the Fallen, Father. Surely that means he can't be the Herald?"

Emrik released his grip on the table and then brought his fist down on it, a large chunk of the desk snapping away to shower his armour in splinters. "It doesn't matter who the Herald is," he said. His anger had gotten the better of him once again, but he could feel it turning from hot to cold. Hot anger was a weakness, but cold anger was a tool with unimaginable power. "We kill them all. Every last angel must die, and then what does it matter who this new Herald was?" Emrik noticed his thumb was bloody, though he couldn't remember picking at the nail bed.

Borik frowned and glanced at Perel, then back to Emrik. "Even Karna? Father, she rules over Ashvold. An entire kingdom worshipping her as though she's the new god. We'd need an army far larger than any we have now, and even then, we'd first have to march through Dien to get to her. I doubt Uncle will allow enemy soldiers in his lands, even if they are yours."

"Especially if they're yours," Perel added. "Uncle Arandon doesn't like you much, Father."

"That's because he's a weak fool," Emrik said. Arandon had always been a thorn in Emrik's side, made worse by their grandfather's decision to split the kingdom in two and give half to a coward who had no idea how to govern it. Still, Dien had a lot of land, many cities, and an army twice the size of Helesia's, if the latest reports were to be believed.

"We can't get any sizeable force to Ashvold without going through Dien," Borik said. "And Uncle will never allow it. What if we drew back, Father? Instead of hunting further and further afield, draining our resources, we could pull back to Celesgarde and fortify."

Perel snorted. "You just want to go back to the city where you can be pampered by pretty boys."

Borik shrugged. "I've told you, sister, I prefer rugged boys. But that really isn't the point. We don't know who the Herald is, but we do know their goal. The Bell of Ages. As long as we protect that, they can't win."

Emrik didn't like the idea of leaving the hunt. It had been his focus for almost a hundred years, hunting down divinities and stamping out their sedition. It was almost complete. He was *so* close. Fewer than ten angels remained, and they were running out of places to hide. Even the firmest of believers in the God's faith only practised in the dark. But it was proving difficult to root out the heresy completely. The smaller their numbers, the more insidious they became.

Perel shifted in her seat again, frowning. "Are we... This is going to sound stupid. Are we certain the Herald is an angel?"

Emrik considered his daughter. She seemed nervous, as though the question might be beyond her bounds. "Tell me your reasoning."

"Near the temple, I had the Builder," Perel said. "I had him! Almost. He was with two humans, a young girl and a younger boy."

"The girl from Riverden?" Emrik asked.

"I assume so. Mihiriel saved the Builder from my halberd and then told him to get the humans to safety. I keep asking myself, why was he so concerned for the humans? For those humans? He let the others burn. Their entire sanctuary sacked, but those two humans were important somehow."

Again, Borik glanced down at the pack at his feet.

"Something to add, Son?" Emrik asked.

Borik met his father's gaze with a look of panic and then nodded. "I found something. But... Here." He leaned down and snatched the pack from the floor, then opened it and drew a large tome from inside and dropped it on the desk with a *thump*.

Emrik stared at the book. He recognised many of the emblems scrawled upon its surface. Angelic sigils, runes, divine heresy. "Why do you have this book?" Emrik spat the question.

"Because it might be useful, Father." Borik leaned over the desk and reached for the book, but Emrik grabbed his son's hand and twisted, forcing him off balance.

"It is heresy," Emrik snarled. He stood, almost overturning the desk. Borik had no choice but to move with his father, his hand still twisted in his grip. "I have spent a dozen lifetimes hunting down these books and burning them. Do you know why?"

Borik winced and whined at the pain. "Because of sedition, Father."

"The worst type of sedition." He let go of Borik's wrist and shoved the boy back against the wall. "The angels may have named the Second Age one of enlighten-ment, but it is a lie. Everything they spread is lies. The Second Age was about indoc-trination. The strongest of humanity was already gone, and all that was left were the meek, those most willing to serve. Then the God tightened his hold with words. The angels of the Second Age, glowing and resplendent, designed to look like beau-tiful saviours. They came, and they brought books." Emrik slammed a fist down on the tome, and the desk groaned under the force. "And then they taught us to read those books. Our very language comes from these seditious texts. We learned to read by reading *them*. And we were forced to read them every day, to memorise the lies held within, to recite them to others. The angels of the Second Age came to indoctrinate us to their God's faith, and then taught us to convert each other.

"Daily reading, daily worship, all to fuel the God's ego and strengthen his grip over us. Generation upon generation enslaved by the winged monsters and these damned books!" Emrik advanced on his son again and gripped him by his tunic even as he cowered against the wall. "So, tell me, son, why have you brought this thing to me instead of burning it as the law, *my* law, states?"

Despite his fear, Borik did not back down, and Emrik had to respect him for that. "Because it could be useful, Father," he repeated and flinched, expecting a blow that would never come. Emrik was not one to beat his children, but that didn't mean he wouldn't punish them for their crimes. "All knowledge is useful. Knowledge is power. You taught me that. And that book contains knowledge we can use."

"That book is like all the others. It contains lies! The promise of knowledge and power, health and happiness, prosperity and freedom from sin. The promises they offer are the trap they used to ensnare us. They are the chains they used to bind us to their will."

Again, Borik stood up to his father. "You think I don't know that? I am not some simple rube who can be tricked with lies of happiness and promises of false power. I am a Hostain. I am your son. Emrik Hostain's son! I know the book is shrouded in lies, Father. But it also contains truth. They couldn't have enslaved us so entirely without it. The best lies are also the truth. The lie is in the delivery and the context, not in the information. There is a section dedicated to the Heralds in that book. Think of the advantage it will give us if we can decipher the truth from it."

"You've read it?" Emrik asked, his voice gone cold. Already he was considering the possibilities. He had never had to kill one of his children before, he wasn't even sure he could, but then none of them had ever been seduced by heresy before.

"Bits of it," Borik admitted. "I only found it this morning. Father, let me go and just look."

Emrik kept hold of his son's tunic. Borik struggled for a moment, then subsided and held up his hands.

"Father, I am not so easily seduced by a few lies scribbled on a page. And you, better than anyone, are immune to any seditious whispering. It cannot hurt to look. If you believe it all false, fine. But what if there is something in there that will help us? Perel posed a question. What if the Herald is not an angel? If that's possible, we need to know!"

Emrik weighed up the evidence. Borik made a good point, though he was treading dangerously close to sedition. Emrik had a spent centuries burning religious texts and breaking icons of faith. If the people of Helesia knew he had looked at an angelic tome, even for the purposes of crushing the divine under his boot more thoroughly, it could open the door to revolt. He glanced at Commander Lorel. Of all his commanders, she was the most trustworthy. Near fanatical in her faith to her king. But none save his own flesh and blood could truly be trusted. Ertide had taught him that, and it was a lesson he learned at great cost.

"Commander," Emrik said. "Find the girl we brought with us from Riverden. Bring her to me, and wait outside until I summon you."

Commander Lorel saluted and made a quick exit. Emrik let go of Borik and gestured toward the desk. "Show me."

Borik straightened his tunic and stepped around his father. Perel watched him all the way, silent and wary. Borik opened the book and flicked quickly through the pages to a section near the middle. Emrik approached warily, as though his mere proximity to the book was dangerous.

As Borik leafed through ancient yellowed pages that crinkled with his touch, Emrik saw references to Heaven's Gate. His grandfather had been the one to open that gate back at the time of the Crusade. The only human ever to force Heaven's Gate open. How he did it was a secret he had taken to his grave. There were pages, too, on the halls of Heaven, including a bestiary on all the monsters the God had kept there. Most of those were dead, killed either during the sacking of Heaven or hunted down during the years that followed. But many were still free. Monsters roaming the world at will ever since their master was slain.

Finally, Borik found the section about the Heralds. Their names and purpose, the Four Ages and what they meant to both humankind and angel. There, Emrik spotted the lies written full. The heresy of the First Age hidden behind false rhetoric, and stories of divine glory. The saviour of humankind: God. Emrik knew the truth though. He was a charlatan. Yet the pages were beautifully crafted, the prose possessing a lyrical quality that seduced the mind and begged to be read aloud. The depictions, too, for there were many, were both pleasing and inspiring to the eye. But nothing about the images was true. History written by those who survived it, and no one survived history quite like immortals.

"Here," Borik said, pointing to a paragraph in the middle of a page about the Bell of Ages. "There are rules that must be observed. Rules set down by the God himself so that no age could ever be rung in by accident, or with malicious intent."

Emrik read the first line aloud. "Only those who carry the *Spark of the Divine* may ring in an age. Only one of God's children."

"What about immortals?" Perel asked. "Surely I've eaten enough angel flesh to carry at least a spark." She used her new power to make her hand glow for a moment to make her point.

Emrik shook his head. "Your uncle tried it the moment he heard about the death of the God. Arandon played no part in the sacking of Heaven, nor the battle for Heaven's Gate. He hid behind the walls of Celesgarde, claiming it was humanity's last bastion if things should go wrong. When the sky turned red, he knew victory was ours. He ran to the top of the Overlook and struck the bell again and again. First with a hammer, then with his own hands. The bell will not ring for an immortal, only for an angel. The God made it that way. He dragged the Overlook from the earth and forged an indestructible bell at its peak. All to fuel his own vapid ego."

Borik pointed at another passage on the yellowed pages. "And here. None born in a previous age will make the bell toll."

Emrik frowned and took a step back. The book was lying. It had to be. "There are no angels of the current age left. I have killed them all. I have read the Annals of the Fourth Age, as written by the angel Innertian herself. She was not named the Historian for nothing. Her records were meticulous and immaculate. So, too, did I memorise the Wall of Records in Heaven's Library before I tore it down with my own hands. Every angel the God created during the Fourth Age is dead."

"I don't doubt you, Father," Borik said quickly. "But unless the Rider was lying, a new Herald is here."

"Can angels breed?" Perel asked. Emrik turned to his daughter, and she shrugged. "I mean, we know they have the parts. A woman eats an angel testicle, and she'll get pregnant just by sniffing at a man." She laughed at the old joke.

"No," Emrik said with a shake of his head. "Some tried near the beginning of the Crusade. The God could not create angels as fast as we were slaughtering them. No pairing ever resulted in a child."

"With each other," Borik added. He had a mind like his mother, always working at angles, never seeing the world as straight forward as it was. "What about with a human?"

Again, Emrik shook his head. "Angels have lain with humans many times over the ages. There was a time in the Third Age when sex with an angel was the pinnacle of worship. It never led to a child though." He paused as the truth dawned on him. "Unless..."

"The Builder," Borik said.

Emrik nodded. "Armstar, a fallen angel. More human than angel now."

"No wonder he risked coming out of hiding to go to Riverden. He had to find his daughter," Borik said with a smile. "I told you this book would help, Father."

Emrik turned a harsh stare on Borik, whose smile faltered in an instant. "Is there anything else about the Herald?"

Borik turned back to the book, flipping the page and reading through the next. "There are a few vague references to a pilgrimage and how it must be done on foot."

Emrik growled in frustration. "That could mean anything. Pilgrimages were common once." He'd made his own back when he was young. A foolish boy on a foolish quest. He'd walked from Heaven's Gate to the Overlook and stopped in every tavern and every willing wench along the way. His was a wasted life until his grandfather had opened his eyes.

"Anything else?" Emrik asked.

Borik kept reading the page and then flipped over to the next. "Maybe. I'd have to..."

"Burn it!"

"But Father..."

"I told you to burn it."

Borik held his father's gaze for a moment short of defiance, then slammed the book closed and lifted it. He skirted around the desk and dropped it in the fire. The ancient pages started to crinkle immediately, and before long the whole book was ablaze.

Borik sighed and turned back to his father. "We know who the Herald is. This girl from Riverden. The Washer girl. We know where she is going. Celesgarde. We should pull our forces back and fortify. Time is on our side, not hers. She's mortal, we're not."

Emrik hated to admit it, but Borik was right. They were close, it was true, but they had no idea where the Herald had fled to. An angel was easy to track, their passage could not go unnoticed, but a human could disappear with ease.

"I can still track them," Perel said, struggling to get up from her chair. "I just need a day to recover. Urgh. Maybe two."

Emrik blinked into his hawk's sight, but the bird had flown back to the forest and was sitting in a tree, preening while a gentle breeze stirred the needles. The Light Bearer had singed the hawk's feathers. It would be days before the bird was willing to fly again. He blinked back to his own sight and watched the religious tome burn in the fireplace.

"Borik is right," he said eventually. "We hold all the advantages. I will take the Second and Fourth back to Celesgarde and personally oversee the fortifying of the Overlook. Borik will accompany me."

"And me?" Perel asked.

"Rest up here as long as you need," Emrik said, though he knew Perel would be gone long before she fully healed. "I do not intend to give up the chase but to spread my net closely. I'll send scouts north to New Gurrund and south to the fort at Breakhold."

Emrik smiled and turned away from the fire to look at his daughter. A savage woman, with as much wolf in her as human. Her mother had been the same way, a wild woman who refused the stink of cities and instead lived in and of the forests. Emrik had only known her a week, and yet together they had made something perfect.

"Harry them, Perel. If you can find their trail, pursue it with all the speed you can muster, and give them no rest."

Perel grinned. "My Dogs won't be able to keep up."

"Then leave them behind. You're more than match enough for the Builder. You killed Mihiriel, the Spear Tip, one of the strongest of the First Age. All by yourself."

"Tesh helped," Perel said, glancing to where her wolf rested by the kitchen fire.

"You are one and same, Daughter." The wolf looked up that and stared at Emrik with yellow eyes that seemed to swirl in the firelight.

Perel nodded. "We'll find them. I'll kill the angels and bring you the Herald's head."

Emrik crossed into the kitchen and opened the door to Los Hold. Cold air found the cracks in his armour that no blade ever could. The angelic sanctuary burned. Anything Perel's Dogs hadn't destroyed, the soldiers of the Fourth were setting to the torch. Commander Lorel waited outside, the young girl from Riverden shivering at her side. Emrik opened the door wide and gestured for the girl to enter.

"Come in," he said with a warm smile. "I think it's time we have a chat, young lady. Tell us everything you know about this Washer girl friend of yours."

CHAPTER 26

There was a time before the Exodus when humanity knew the secrets of metal and rock and fire. So much of that knowledge was lost as were so many of our ships and too many of our people. When we made it to our new home, we were decimated, scattered, starving, and sick with disease. We were a dying people on the edge of extinction. Yet even then we did not look to any higher power to save us. Only when the demons found us did we finally begin to pray. But we prayed to the wrong saviour. We looked to the sky, to the wings of armoured warriors. We should have looked to the sea, to the scales and eyes of the deep.

— LORE KEEPER GRUND OF THE SALLOWBACK
TRIBE. YEAR 5 OF THE SECOND AGE. 6 YEARS
BEFORE THE SHATTERING

I t had been a tiring few days of sullen walking. Armstar said little, and when he did speak, it was to chastise them for moving too slowly. Eleseth was more genial but also wary. She was happy to talk, but rarely said much on the topics that most interested Renira, namely, information about the Heralds and how she had unwittingly become one. Though it was strangely humbling that Eleseth, the Light Bearer, a two thousand year old angel straight out of legend, took the time to heal their feet each night with her divine power. Unfortunately, her power could do nothing for the bone-weary exhaustion that settled into Renira.

Her feet dragged with every step, and her legs felt like they were made from wood, not flesh. Her stomach had moved from constant growling to sharp twinges of pain as though she were being stabbed from the inside. She loved food so much it was torture to suffer such starvation.

Sun fared little better, but he talked all the time, saying nothing of consequence and only to Renira. He told her the Cracked Mountains had been one mountain until a terrible monster took a bite out of it and split it into many. Another time he claimed one of the birds circling overhead was a lizardhawk and was actually a scaly beast pretending at being a bird. Each 'fact' he presented as utter truth, though they all sounded like fancy to Renira. Sometimes he began stories he had heard only to forget how they ended. One of Yonal Wood's boys was much the same way, and Renira had found it charming in small doses, but she'd be lying if she said there weren't times she simply wished Sun would shut up for a while. It was not like the easy camaraderie with her friends back home, built from many years and countless little adventures shared. Sun was trying too hard, almost as though he had never before had a friend.

Early on the third morning out of Los Hold, the city started to rise around them like water swelling from flooded ground. The sun was bright, the air chill, and Renira spotted a grimy haze on the horizon. As they trudged ever closer, it resolved into a city that looked like a crown with smaller buildings on the outskirts, rising quickly to loftier buildings further toward the centre. And above it all hung thousands of trailing wisps of black smoke that congealed into a dark cloud looming over the horizon like the shadow of death. New Gurrund was a sprawling, dirty metropolis the likes of which Renira had never even dreamed of. She found herself fascinated by it.

To their left, Hel's Wall opened, a huge gap where the rock had been dug away to allow passage to the city. At first Renira thought it must be a natural break in the line of cliffs that nearly surrounded the Cracked Mountains, but Armstar shook his head.

"Datomir's Gap was one of the first projects I ever worked on. I was so young and naïve, a decade old maybe. God had given me such knowledge, and the will to use it, but I had not the wisdom to manifest the things I saw in my head."

The angel smiled wistfully as he stared at the gap and for the first time since Renira had met him, he looked young. "I worked with humans, Gresoran and his son Goran. We built a team together, masons from across Dien—this was before the Sant Dien Empire was split in two—and went to work. First from the top chiselling out rock and stone, then later from the bottom. I had to invent an entirely new method of scaffolding to secure waste disposal to the cliff side.

"We worked day after day, year after year, hammering, chiselling, picking. Sometimes the rock was so weak it crumbled at a mere touch and other times it was stronger than any steel we could forge picks from. I had to beg Karna to let us use Heaven's Forge to make stronger tools."

He sighed and shook his head. "Gresoran never saw the finished gap. He died two years before we completed construction, but Goran and I continued. I thought we should name it after the old man, but King Datomir's arrogance would have none of it.

"As soon as we were finished with the gap, I laid the foundations for New Gurrund. I wanted it to be a paradise, but of course you humans turned it into an unlanced boil on the land." He shook his head. "I was still learning. It was all learning for me as much as the generations of builders who worked with me. We moved from project to project. I saw my best workers grow into men, find lovers, start families. I taught their sons and their daughters and their children after that. But I never lost sight of my great project."

He grimaced. "Too late, did Father allow me to begin. At the end of the age."

Eleseth placed a comforting hand on Armstar's shoulder, but he shrugged her away.

"Did he know?" Armstar asked. "Did our father allow me to start, already knowing he would order Mathanial to steal away my resources, my people?"

Eleseth shrugged. "I don't know."

"He gave me everything. And then snatched it away. He still does." Armstar glanced back at Renira and there were tears in his eyes. He quickly sped his pace away from them.

She wished he had kept talking. He spoke about architecture with such passion that Renira herself felt enthused. She had imagined herself as an architect once or twice in her life and wondered what it must be like to see a construct from imagination brought into physical manifestation.

She paid particular attention to the buildings in New Gurrund after that, hoping to find some insights into Armstar's mind in the structures he claimed to have designed. She wanted to understand what made him the way he was, to see what passions drove him. *Why do I even care what he thinks? He's never been anything but mean spirited and cruel.* Yet, she found his opinion mattered. His opinion of her mattered. He had loved her mother in some way, that much was obvious. Armstar had respected Lusa Washer, and Renira wanted him to respect her, too.

Renira clutched at her mother's amulet as they passed into the outskirts of New Gurrund. Many of the city's people had dirt-smudged faces and wore bleary expressions as they walked in a line from the mountains. Miners who had been working through the night. Another team, somewhat fresher, though with no brighter an attitude, trudged toward the mine shaft at the base of the mountain. They all looked so worn down, so weary. Back in Riverden, the people went about their days with enthusiasm, idly chatting and greeting friends warmly. But in New Gurrund, there was barely a word spoken, and those that were seemed in anger rather than friendship.

Cart loads of black rock were pushed toward the city, and these were guarded by men and women in armour, all wearing the emblem of the Hostain family. A circular badge with a sword pointing down, a black iron crown hanging jauntily from its cross guard, and a pair of white wings behind it. Compared to the miners, the guards looked well fed and well rested. Some carried spears, others flatbows. They drove the carts onward, each one dragged by a scrawny mule with dull eyes. Such misery was heart-breaking, and Renira felt it keenly.

Armstar dropped back a few paces, and Renira realised she had stopped and was staring at the sight of so many beaten down miners. "You can't help them. Not here and not now."

Sun glared at the angel from Renira's other side. "We could do something, if Ren wants to." But it was foolishness. There was nothing Renira could do, and she knew it. There was nothing any of them could do. It was not so simple as rescuing the miners or even handing out coin or food, not that they had either. These people were beaten down by their lives, their jobs, their existence. Nothing could save them but for a change in the way the very world worked.

"We are doing something, boy," Armstar whispered. "The best way for you to help them, Renira, is to ring in the new age. The Godless King has driven this land too far into the darkness. Only the God can set things right now."

"How do you know I want to help them?" Renira asked.

Armstar chuckled bitterly at that. "I can feel emotion. Yours. Theirs. Pain and fear hang over this city far darker than that cloud. It is a dull, seething ache. But your pain is sharp. I feel it like a thorn digging into my side, irritating me."

Renira glared at the angel. "I'm sorry my compassion irritates you so." They were harsh words, but she was feeling raw. Her hunger and exhaustion and pain and guilt made the world feel a brutal place. She started forward, leaving the angel to catch up to her for once.

They continued deeper toward the heart of New Gurrund, and the slums occupied by the poorest of the miners eventually gave way to a more affluent neighbourhood full of industry. Armstar led the way. His wings were crouched tight on his back, and he had thrown a threadbare old cloak over them. It gave him the appearance of a hunchback and drew a few stares from those nearby, but not nearly so many eyes as were focused on Eleseth. It was not obvious she was an angel with her wings draped over her shoulders, somehow mimicking the appearance of a cloak, but Renira doubted many had ever seen a woman so tall before, nor one so beautiful. Even with her glow dimmed, she was still gorgeous, and both men and women gawked at her. They were not passing without notice.

The ringing of hammers on anvils was a persistent percussion behind the general cacophony of New Gurrund that drowned out individual sounds. Renira followed along behind Armstar and Eleseth in a daze, staying close so as not to lose them in the crowds. She could smell the delicious scent of freshly baked bread somewhere, mixing with the tang of heated metal. Her stomach growled again at the thought of food, and she looked about for the bakery. She had no money and nothing to trade, but surely they would take pity on a starving girl and boy.

In Riverden, Tobe and Firen Baker had always tried to haggle the prices up, but if ever Renira and her mother were short of money, they would be given bread as a kindness. And any loafs left at the end of the day were given away rather than allowed to go stale and waste. A community of people all looking out for one another even during the hardest of times. But as Renira glanced about, she saw New Gurrund was not that sort of place. Beggars littered the streets, hungry eyes watching those who passed. Some were cripples with missing limbs; others were children who looked too young and weak to work the mines. Guard patrols were frequent, and the men and women in uniform carried spears and clubs and wore harsh, uncaring looks. Dark eyes watched from the shadows cast by the low morning sun; alleyways filled with promised menace. New Gurrund was a dirty, dangerous city.

"This place reminds me of home," Sun said. He was smiling, despite the growling of his stomach.

"Ashvold?" Renira asked. Sun seemed willing to talk endlessly on almost any subject but always fell silent when asked about his past or parents.

"Bresh," he said, though Renira had never heard of it. "It's the biggest city in Ashvold. Far larger than this, I think, and full of people. And sand. Full of people and sand. I used to chase cats through the alleys. Hard to catch though. Rats are easier to catch."

"I used to have a cat," she said, trying to distract them both a little. "A big black monster. The scourge of mice all over our home, and at least three or four others as well, I think. I had to clean up his kills every day. He left bits of them all over the barn." It was a dirty job she had always hated. Strange that now she was free of it, she missed it a little.

"He sounds ferocious," Sun said. "I like him."

"He was. I called him Igor the Terrible or Voracious. Or Cantankerous. It really depended on the day and his mood. But that wasn't really his name. Mother named him Snowdrop."

Sun pulled a face. "That's a terrible name for a cat. Igor the Terrible, I like that better." He slapped a free hand against his chest. "Sun, the Awful. First Exemplar of the Herald..."

"Quiet!" Armstar snapped, half turning to glare at Sun. Sun stuck his tongue out at the angel.

Armstar turned into an alleyway and a few grimy children scurried away like bats from the sun. It was a cut-through and led out onto a different street. New Gurrund was arranged in a large circular shape with the major streets like spokes on a wheel, and all roads led to the centre where the largest buildings stood. "I built this city to be a jewel," Armstar said as he forged ahead, increasing his pace so Renira and Sun had to catch up to him. "And they have hidden its brilliance by covering it in shit. There is no more apt a metaphor for everything humanity touches."

"Riverden wasn't so bad," Renira said as she stepped over a pile of manure in the middle of the street and then dodged around a man carrying four buckets of water attached to a plank of wood across his shoulders. "The people were kind and the streets clean." She had to defend her home. It was nothing like this city, and even comparing the two was an insult.

Armstar snorted. "And your mother should have been at the centre of it. But because she had no formal training, the laws written by idiotic city officials forbade her from practising medicine. On animals as well as humans. I've never met a more capable surgeon, and yet she had to wash clothes for a living. A menial task without reward."

"Or end," Renira said. Mother had never appeared to mind the endless washing, but Renira couldn't deny it had seemed like a punishment from God. But despite the laws that forbade her from medicine, the farmers of Ner-on-the-River and others nearby always came to her when their beasts were injured or sick. She never took money from them and never refused them her aid. "Why is she in Riverden then?" Renira asked. "Why wasn't she at Los Hold with you?"

"Because of you." There was a bitterness to his voice he didn't bother to hide. "She thought it was safer for you to live in the arse end of Helesia than be anywhere the Godless King might find you."

They had moved away from the ringing of hammers hitting anvils and into a district that seemed populated by homes. The buildings here were multiple stories tall, and many had people sitting outside the doors, playing games or simply drinking their morning away. The alleys between buildings had washing lines strung up across them and towels and tunics hung there, obscuring the view of the windows higher up. With the amount of smoke and grime in the air, Renira doubted it was the perfect place to dry the washing, but people ever made do with what they had.

Armstar halted in front of a large building of stone painted in flaking yellow. A woman lounged about just outside the door, sitting on the dusty floor with her eyes closed and an empty cup held loosely in one hand. Armstar hammered on the door and glanced about at the people passing nearby.

"What's the name?" the woman slurred without so much as cracking open an eye. Eleseth knelt and whispered something in the woman's ear, and when the angel stood she was holding a key.

In contrast to the dilapidated front, Renira found a pristine hall inside, well-lit by the sun streaming in through windows on the floor above. The walls were painted white and were clean of dust or mould, and the floor was so tidy she felt guilty for the mud, and worse, she was tracking inside. Eleseth shook her wings free of their cloak mimicry and leaned over to each side, stretching her wings up as high as she could. She gave a pleasant moan and sigh.

Sun followed Renira in and stood next to her, both having little idea of what to do with themselves. Armstar was the last inside and closed the door with a bang, then whipped the cloak off his ruined wings. They twitched and shuddered, and he winced from the pain of having them free once more.

A handsome young man poked his head out from the stairs leading up to the next floor. He had dark hair even longer than Renira's and a scattering of stubble on his cheeks and dimpled chin. He grinned when he spotted Eleseth, and Renira found herself smiling.

"We didn't expect to see you again so soon, Armstar." The young man threw himself over the banister and landed halfway down the stairs. He wore a leather tunic and trousers and had a couple of daggers sheathed on either side of his hip. "And with guests this time."

"We're on the run, Dussor," Armstar said.

"When are you not?" Dussor skipped down the last few stairs and stopped in front of Renira. He bowed from the waist and winked at her as he stood back up. He held out his hand. "Dussor, my lady, at your service."

Renira gave him her hand without thinking and smiled back. "Renira, my lord, at yours."

"You know, I do think... yes, that's the first time anyone has ever called me lord." Dussor grinned and lowered his head to kiss Renira's hand.

Sun whipped his little spear around and Dussor let go Renira's hand and took a step back, holding up his hands in surrender. "Looks like you have a protector."

"It's only a bit of play, Sun," Renira said.

Sun narrowed his eyes. "I don't like him."

"You don't like anyone."

Dussor, still holding up his hands dramatically, edged around Sun. "So, Builder, why are you back so soon?"

"Los Hold is gone."

The smile fell from Dussor's face. "Gone? What do you mean gone?"

Armstar ignored the question and started down the hall to a room at the far end. "Show these two to a room, then bring Kerrel in from outside and find Gemp." He walked through the door and out of sight.

"Gone?" Dussor repeated, though Armstar was obviously out of earshot. "You're just not gonna explain that? No?"

Eleseth nodded gravely and took one of Dussor's hands, pressing it between her own. "We'll explain. Could you find rooms for Renira and the boy? Some food and water for them as well please."

"Food!" Renira said quickly. She felt like she hadn't eaten in weeks. "Yes, please. Whatever you have, anything really, just, um, lots of it?" Her stomach growled as if to make her point.

Dussor smiled again, though he sent a worried look at Eleseth. "Renira and the boy, was it?"

"My name is Sun," he said with a glare.

"And a ferocious name it is. Brings to mind giant balls of light for some reason. Follow me. I'll show you to the spare rooms and then be back with some food." He turned and leapt up the first two steps.

Sun rushed ahead. "I'll go first. Make sure it's not a trap." Renira smiled wearily and let her Exemplar precede her. He was desperately trying to make himself useful wherever he could. It was a sentiment Renira could understand; she hated feeling useless.

"Try to get some sleep, Renira," Eleseth said. "We won't be staying in New Gurrund for long, and when we move, it will be quickly."

Renira followed Dussor and Sun up the first flight of stairs and then turned and followed them up another flight. She'd never been in a house so tall before, even Aesie's mansion back in Riverden only had two floors, but without sight of the ground below her, the fear of such lofty heights seemed a distant thing. Dussor opened a door on the second floor and waved at Sun. "For the young master spearman."

Sun just stared at the young man.

"All right then," Dussor moved to the next door across and opened that one too. "And for the dashing lady."

Sun pushed past Renira and slipped into the room, he looked about for a few seconds and then poked his head out of the door. "It looks safe."

Renira suppressed a sigh and walked into the room. It was small and sparse, with a cot, a chest of drawers, and a table with mirror and washbasin. Renira immediately pulled her winter coat from her shoulders and dropped it on the floor by the cot, happy to not be weighed down by it for a while. Sun had stayed inside the doorway, blocking it as best he could, and Dussor was leaning against the door frame, staring at her frankly and grinning.

"Food?" Renira prompted impatiently. "Lots of it."

The attention of a handsome young man had never been too high on Renira's list of priorities, and with her stomach rumbling every few seconds, it was even lower down than usual. She felt guilty for asking, but the twisting knife in her gut was a far worse pain.

"Your wish is my command," Dussor said and bowed again. He turned to go but stopped and winked at Sun. "Keep her safe, master spearman."

Sun dragged his thumb across his cheek in a deliberate manner that seemed like it indicated some sort of insult. "Go get our food," he said.

Dussor left with a laugh.

Renira waited until the sound of the man walking down the stairs had faded. "You don't have to be so rude to him."

She collapsed onto the bed with a grateful sigh. Her boots needed pulling off, but now she was horizontal, it seemed like such hard work to sit up again. She heard a thump and opened her eyes to see Sun had sunk down against the wall next to the door. His spear rolled into the centre of the room, and the boy breathed deeply, clearly already asleep.

With a groan of effort, Renira rolled out of bed and onto her feet. She stumbled across to Sun and bent down. He somehow managed to weigh even more than he had back at the forest, but Renira scooped the boy up into her arms and carried him over to the bed. She lay him down there and pulled the blanket up over him, then sat down at the foot of the bed and closed her eyes.

CHAPTER 27

The Sanguine Forge lies at the heart of New Gurrund. It is one of only two forges in all the kingdoms and beyond that is capable of smelting angelic armour and weaponry and as such is the only forge accessible to human hands of crafting angel-forged plate.

The cost of keeping the forge running is frankly ludicrous. More coal is consumed in New Gurrund per day than in the rest of Helesia combined per year. The miners required to dig the coal from the Cracked Mountains number in the thousands and suffer regular injuries and maladies of the lung and heart. In addition, there is the danger that coal seams are sometimes followed too deep and breach into the subterranean caverns. We are rarely able to close those breached mines quickly enough before the madness spreads and entire work details must sometimes be put down.

It is therefore my recommendation that the Sanguine Forge be shut down and allowed to cool and a trade deal with Ashvold pursued instead. The Everforge in Ashvold is directly by the fires of Mount Sunder, and so there is no need to mine coal.

— SUMMARY ECONOMIC REPORT, INSPECTOR
BRINE. YEAR 957 OF THE FOURTH AGE, 912 YEARS
AFTER HEAVEN FELL.

R enira dreamed of two giant wolves slobbering with rage as they chased her through frozen tundra. She was wearing nothing, and though she knew she was cold, the chill didn't quite reach her. There were people all around her, walking with her, but they were all just pale shadows. High above, the sky was bizarrely blue, the colour of a river lily, and both the searing sun and Blood Moon watched her run.

She woke to find she had fallen sideways at some point and now lay at the foot of the bed, shivering from the cold that had seeped into her body. Her neck ached, and she was so stiff it hurt to stretch out her legs and arms, but there was a smell in the room that was far more urgent than her pains. Food!

Sun was still in the cot, snoring softly, the blanket thrown wild and his limbs strewn about in awkward angles so he looked like he'd been fighting off demons in his sleep. Renira pulled the blanket back up over his chest and turned to find the food.

Dim golden light from the Bone Moon shone in through the only window in the room and provided little in the way of illumination, but it was enough to see two large plates on the nearby table. The washbasin was full and had been moved to the floor along with the little mirror, and Renira spotted a couple of towels folded nearby as well. She ignored them all and fell upon the plates of food like a starving bear. The bread was brown crusty and long past its best, but Renira tore into it with her teeth and followed it with a bite of the dried herby sausage on the plate and then a small wedge of sharp cheese. Flavours filled her mouth, and she didn't bother taking the time to relish them, but swallowed the food down as quickly as possible and then reached for more. The only thing to drink was weak brown ale. It all tasted sublime.

Sun sniffed and opened his eyes, yawned and blinked the cobwebs away. He stared up at Renira and smiled. "I dreamt of monsters. We were fighting them together."

"Did we win?"

The boy frowned, and Renira could guess his answer.

"I think we won. Look, there's food," she said. She reached out a hand and pulled Sun upright and to his feet, then ushered him to the table. He collapsed down into the seat with all the grace of a falling cow, then started shovelling food into his mouth and chewing lethargically. Renira left him to it and crossed to the single window. It opened out into a slim alleyway with nothing to see but the next building along and a sliver of the street. She watched for a while, seeing flashes of people passing. It was full night, but the streets looked busy enough.

Renira moved to the door and placed her ear against it. She could hear nothing from the house beyond. She couldn't decide if that was a good or bad thing. Perhaps everyone had gone to bed for the night. Even angels needed to sleep. Prudence suggested her wisest choice was to crawl back into bed and doze the night away. With a mostly full stomach and a good night's sleep, she imagined she would wake refreshed in the morning, ready for another day of running away from everyone and everything chasing her. Unfortunately, prudence had never been one of Renira's qualities. She reached out cautiously for the door handle and tried to turn it. It was locked.

Outrage made her suddenly hot. They had locked her in. Confined her like some unruly child or a prisoner. She had committed no crimes, had done nothing wrong. They might think they were protecting her, but there was a difference between protection and imprisonment. How dare they lock her in? She was struggling, fighting for their cause, wasn't she?

"Ren, are you all right?" Sun said around a mouthful of bread. "You're pacing."

Renira stopped. She didn't like being locked up. Her mother had done it once, back when Renira was young and had been throwing a tantrum over which dress she would wear. It had seemed so important at the time, but then everything seemed like life and death to a child.

"They've locked us in," she said churlishly as she crossed to the window.

"Why?" Sun asked as he reached for the flagon of ale.

"Because they think I need protecting." She couldn't keep the anger from her voice.

"That's why I'm here," Sun said. "You don't need a locked door." He jumped up from the chair and grabbed his little spear from the floor. "I'll protect you."

Renira ground her teeth. "I don't need you to protect me either, Sun."

The boy's face dropped, and he frowned.

"I don't need you to protect me, Sun," Renira repeated more softly this time. "I just need you to be my friend."

"Then what do I do?" He twisted his hands around the spear.

"Friend things. You have had friends before?"

Sun was silent for a few moments, staring at her, then he shook his head. "My mother wouldn't let me out and the servants wouldn't talk to me. Too scared."

"She sounded like quite the tyrant."

Sun snorted and nodded. "She is. I hate her. I wish she was dead."

He was still struggling to come to terms with his parent's death. "Well, I'm your friend, Sun. And you're mine. And friends help each other."

"Help?"

Renira nodded. "You know how to climb."

"Of course I do. It's easy."

Renira threw open the window and shivered as the cold air rushed in around her. She stuck her head outside and looked towards the street. It was lit by hanging lanterns and the pale golden bronze light streaming off the Bone Moon, but little else. Some people passed by on foot, and Renira could still just about hear the ringing of metal on metal in the distance. New Gurrund, it seemed, was a city that never slept.

"What are we doing?" Sun asked. He had his spear in one hand, and a strip of dried sausage in the other.

Renira turned to the boy with a grin. "We're escaping." She knew it was a foolish thing to do. Reckless and impulsive. But they had locked her in, and she was not going to just sit back and accept it.

"Yes!" Sun ran toward the window and looked down to the ground two stories below. "It's about time we ditched those angels."

Renira chuckled. "We're coming back, Sun. We're just... going out to explore the city."

The boy shrugged, stuck his dried sausage in his mouth, dropped his little spear out of the window, and then clambered over the ledge and started climbing down the side of the building. Renira watched him scuttle down to the ground. He made it look so easy, and he was down in the alley in mere moments, waving for Renira to join him.

I can do this. It's only a short climb. She imagined herself a daring thief in the night. Hooded and with a billowing cloak as she scaled buildings, leapt over rooftops, and stole from the rich. A thief of the people like Davin Drake from all the bard tales.

She swung a leg over the sill and straddled it for a moment before pulling her other leg up and over. Renira sat there for a few moments, staring down at the ground, the young boy waving excitedly at her. The world wouldn't sit still, it kept shifting and swimming. Renira clutched hold of the sill so tight her fingers hurt.

So slowly it seemed to take an eternity, she manoeuvred herself about until she was facing back into the room and hung onto the sill with both arms. Her heartbeat raced in her ears, and she could feel sweat running down her face despite the cold air. Her coat was still in the room, lying on the floor in a heap. She should go back and get it, to keep her warm against the winter cold. But Renira knew if she clambered back into the room, she wouldn't have the courage to climb out again. It was now or never, and damn the coat!

Eleseth's words came back to her. *Not all fears present themselves honestly.*

Well, maybe the angel was right, and the best way to overcome her fear of being the Herald was to overcome her fear of heights.

Renira lowered herself bit by bit until her arms were straight, her fingers digging into the sill and the only thing keeping her from falling to her death. Her feet swung in free air, and she found nothing to step on. How had Sun managed it so easily? There were no footholds to brace against. Nothing but empty drop. Her heart hammered fit to burst. Her arms trembled from the effort of holding on.

"Ren, stop thrashing about," Sun said. "There's a little hole in the stone near your right foot. A bit further to the right."

Renira quested out with her right foot, swinging it back and forth until her boots caught on something. She wedged her toes into the hold and froze there.

"Good," Sun continued. "Now reach down with your left hand and find the little knob of stone sticking out. Grab it hard with your fingertips."

Renira had to force herself to let go of the sill with her left hand and felt panic surge through her until she had the knob clenched between white fingers.

"How close am I to the ground?" Renira hissed.

"Uh... Real close. Now let go with your right hand and step down to the next sill."

Renira looked down. It seemed like the ground was miles away, Sun waving up at her from an impossible distance. Her vision swam, her fingers slipped, and then she was falling.

No time to scream, only a squeak of wild alarm escaped her lips. She landed half on top of Sun as he moved to catch her, and half on her arse, bashing her elbow so hard on the ground it buzzed with tingling pain.

"Shit shit shit shit shit. Bloody shit!" Renira snapped, furious at herself and trying to rub the pain from her elbow.

Sun managed to pull himself out from underneath and stared at her with wide eyes.

"What?" she asked testily. "You think that's bad, you've never heard Elsa get angry. She once told Eyan Wellcock he was a mouldy bloody arsetick feeding off so much shit he was full of it." She laughed as she remembered the bemused look on the boy's face as Elsa berated him. The laughter helped dull the pain.

She allowed Sun to help pull her back to her feet, dusted herself off, and then hugged herself tight against the cold. When she looked back up at the window, it seemed such a long way. Renira shook the fear away and moved to the end of the alley. She looked left and right but saw no sign of either Dussor or the woman who had been guarding the doorway.

"You're terrible at climbing," Sun said as he crowded her at the end of the alley.

Renira cocked an eyebrow at the boy. "Well, you're terrible at running."

"Am not."

Renira grinned. "Prove it!" She turned and sprinted out into the road, heading further into the heart of the city with Sun close on her heels.

They were both laughing and out of breath by the time Renira slowed to a stop at the side of the road next to a lively sounding tavern. She declared herself the victor. Sun had kept up well enough, but with legs shorter than her own, he stood no chance of catching her. It felt good to do something foolish and for no reason but fun. Ever since she had met Armstar, her life had been nothing but gloomy with a side of peril, and Renira felt diminished because of it. She had no time to daydream of battling monsters when fighting actual monsters. And the actual monsters were far more deadly and far less fun to fight.

"I almost had you," Sun said, struggling for air and grinning. "I had to dodge around that horse."

"All I'm hearing are excuses," Renira said. Sun had kept hold of his little spear, but now Renira looked, it seemed more like a stick. The metal point had long since snapped off, and the end was barely even sharpened. If Sun was to be her Exemplar, they'd need to get him a proper spear at some point.

Even late at night, the streets of New Gurrund had people moving to and fro. Noise spilled out of the tavern with a sign outside naming it The Blind Pig. Most of the clamour was formless, but Renira heard men and women laughing from within. A couple of guards with truncheons on their hips stood outside. They were both hulking men and eyed Renira and Sun for a few moments, then disregarded them with some comment about children being worth less than the mud they stood on. Renira took the hint and decided it was time to move away from the tavern before their choice was taken from them.

The main street they were on ran straight into the centre of New Gurrund. Armstar claimed he had built the city, and it definitely had an ordered feel to it. The further in they moved, the taller the buildings grew, and before long they were crowded in on both sides by houses that reached for the sky. They all had a similar style to them with sloping roofs and ornate guttering.

"Where are we going?" Sun asked as they wandered.

"I don't know. Elsa used to say the best way to learn a city is to get lost in it. But I'm far from certain she had the experience to back the claim up."

"Who's Elsa?"

"A friend from Riverden. You'd like her. She's half feral like you."

"I'm not half feral. I'm fully feral!" Sun growled dramatically, and Renira had to laugh at the stupid face he pulled.

"Like a wulfkin?" she asked. She still didn't know what a wulfkin was, but they sounded dangerous.

Sun's smile dropped and he sulked. "I'm not a monster."

"Sorry."

"I'm *not* a monster!"

"All right. I'm sorry, Sun. Do you hear that?" she asked. There was a lot of noise coming from the next street over, shouting and laughing, raised voices competing with each other. Light spilled up over the buildings so bright it made the smoky air glow like embers in a fire. "Let's check it out."

Before Sun could argue, Renira strode towards the nearest alleyway and straight into it, using the cut-through to cross streets. The alley was dark and close and smelled like sewage. A rat scurried away from their passing. And then they were through.

A bustling market spread out before them with shops lining the open square and stalls aplenty set up everywhere there was space. Despite the time of night, it was as busy a market as Renira had ever seen with people walking between the stalls, vendors shouting out prices, competing with each other, trying to attract attention. Renira smelled something cooking, a spicy, meaty aroma that set her mouth watering.

"What is this place?" she said, full of wonder.

A man leaning against the wall beside her shifted at her words. "New to the city, I guess?"

"We are."

He grinned and stepped away from the wall. He was a tall man with pale skin smudged with dirt around his pitted cheeks. He wore dirty leathers and a dagger glinted at his belt. "This is the fabled Night Market of New Gurrund. We sell everything and anything here, and people flock from all over Helesia to visit. You, uh, from the south?"

Renira nodded. "How did you know? I'm from Riverden."

"Ahhh." The man smiled wider and extended a hand. Renira took it, and he gave her hand a gentle shake. He did not let go. "I have family from Riverden. Wonderful people. Wonderful place. So kind. So giving. Would you like me to show you around? I'd be happy to be your guide."

Sun stepped in front of Renira and poked the man with his stick until he let go of Renira's hand. "We don't need a guide," he snarled.

"An Ashman? Or should I say Ash boy?" The man smiled again and this time it looked oddly predatory. "Strange company you keep, miss Riverden."

"Let's go, Ren," Sun said, pushing Renira along but not taking his eyes from the man.

"Ren, is it?" the man said as they retreated towards the Night Market. "Nice to meet you, Ren. I hope we see each other again."

They stepped into the first aisle of stalls and were quickly absorbed by the noise and clamour. "I didn't like the way he was holding your hand," Sun said, a deep frown on his youthful face.

"Neither did I," Renira said. She glanced back but couldn't see the man anymore. "Thank you for saving me again, Exemplar."

Sun brightened at that. "It's my duty," he said quite pompously.

Renira laughed and turned her attention to the stalls. They were so busy it was difficult to move without brushing past people. To her right, she saw a squat man selling plucked birds with pimply white flesh and separately the feathers with colours ranging from dark brown to vibrant green to white as snow. The man was bellowing out prices in a voice that bellied his small stature. To her left, a young girl stood on a stool behind a brightly coloured stall that had clay pots lined up all along it. The girl was younger than Sun, with dark skin and a green kerchief wrapped around her mouth and nose. She was laughing with a customer while popping open lids on the clay pots, using a large spoon to scoop out spices, then laying them out on squares of cloth and deftly tying the squares into pouches.

Someone bumped into Renira from behind, and she moved on, Sun staying so close he was almost clinging to her. She passed stalls selling cooked lizards. Renira had never eaten lizard before and couldn't imagine the scaly beasts tasted pleasant, yet the smells wafting out from that stall were enough she was sorely tempted to try. Another stall had figurines the vendor, an old man with gnarled hands and wooden teeth, claimed were carved from angel bone. The likenesses of the figures were so detailed, and the man pointed to some and rolled off names Renira recognised from stories. There was Hectar Howl, the man who died thrice. And beside him was Rikkan Hostain, one of the seven Godless Kings and the finest spearman to ever live. And of course there were no fewer than six figurines of the Saint and dozens of King Emrik. Renira grinned and chatted with the figurine vendor for a while, but another customer soon shoved her along to take her place.

Sun kept close, but he rarely so much as glanced at any of the stalls. He kept his eyes on the crowd, holding his spear as threateningly as he could whenever someone came too close. He did pause at a shop at one of the edges of the square and stare longingly through the window. The shop sold weapons from swords to axes to bows to spears. Many were stacked in barrels, while others were hung on racks on the walls. A burly guard with a sword buckled at his belt stood sentry at the door, and he soon growled at them both to move along.

"Some good quality steel in there," Sun said, glancing back over his shoulder at the shop as they shuffled along down a new aisle of stalls.

"You could tell through the window?" Renira asked.

Sun nodded. "My mother is a smith. Tried to teach me, but I always found it boring."

Renira frowned but she didn't press him over it. She was having fun for a change, and so was Sun, and the last thing she wanted was to ruin that by prying into secrets he didn't want to share.

They stopped at a stall selling books, and Renira ran her hands over some of the covers. She had never been much for reading, her mother had always made it seem a chore, but Merebeth and Aesie both loved to read. She wished she could buy a book and take it back to her friends. The look on Merebeth's face when Renira presented them with a book from another city would be well worth the price.

"Look, a jewellery stall," Renira said and dragged Sun along.

The stall was a drab setup compared to most that seemed to draw the eye by draping colourful cloths over every surface. This one had a large table with a faded brown towel over it. An old woman with a face as wrinkled as a tousled blanket sat behind the stall, calmly threading a needle through an old pair of socks. She looked up and smiled as Renira approached. The table was strewn with all sorts of jewellery from rings to amulets, bracelets and earrings. Some were wooden, some metal, and others were made from bone or ivory.

"They're so pretty," Renira said as she bent down and looked closely at a ring that was made from three interwoven bands of wood, each one a slightly unique shade.

"Mmm," Sun grunted, not even looking. He was staring across the way at another stall selling cooked sausages.

"My mother never let me wear jewellery," Renira said conversationally as she browsed. "Some of my friends wore rings or bracelets and what not. I was always a bit jealous." She picked up a wooden earring that was three coloured circles intersecting in the middle and forming a new pattern. It reminded Renira of a flower, the way the petals curled up and brushed against each other.

"Are your ears pierced?" the old woman asked. She looked up from her sewing, but her hands didn't stop moving, deftly working. She had a kind smile and pale blue eyes.

Renira shook her head.

"I can do it for you here if you'd like to buy the earring." The old woman reached under the table and pulled out a glass jar filled with clear liquid. There were a dozen little metal needles lying at the bottom of the jar.

"Does it hurt?" Renira asked.

The old woman chuckled. "Oh yes. Ask your friend."

"Your ears are pieced, Sun?"

Sun turned and looked at Renira with wide eyes, then frowned at the woman. He nodded sullenly. "Everyone in Ashvold has their ears pierced," he said. He tapped the helix of his left ear. "We wear earrings with our names on our left ear, and our mother's names on our right." He shrugged. "I lost mine."

"You lost them?" Renira asked. "Both of them."

He stared down at the cobbled ground. "I don't know if it hurts. Had it done before I was old enough to remember."

Renira chewed her lip. She did want to do it. Partly because she had never been allowed before, and partly because she'd always thought earrings were pretty, and the wooden one with the circles especially so. But it was pointless dreaming. She put the earring back on the table. "I don't have any money," she admitted.

"Oh," the old woman's smile vanished, and her eyes narrowed as if she suddenly expected Renira to steal the earring and run off.

Behind Renira, a man cleared his throat. "Sounds like you need a loan."

Renira spun on her heel, ready to grab Sun and run, only to find Dussor standing there. The acolyte had saddle bags thrown over one shoulder and a satchel hanging at his hip. He grinned at her. "Fancy meeting you here, my lady." He glanced at Sun and nodded. "Master spearman."

Sun thumped the butt of his stick on the cobbles.

"Are you following us?" Renira accused.

Dussor held up one hand in surrender. "Hardly. I didn't even expect you'd leave your room."

Renira crossed her arms as she stared at him. "Because you locked us in?"

"Precisely." He leaned to the side and looked at the old woman. "It's not as bad as it sounds."

The old lady shrugged; her eyes still narrowed. "Not my business."

"So what are you doing here?" Renira said. She was feeling both embarrassed at being caught and angry for feeling embarrassed. *Dussor was the one who locked me in the room; he should be embarrassed.*

"Picking up supplies," Dussor said, patting the saddlebags on his shoulder. "We've a long journey ahead of us apparently."

Renira narrowed her eyes at him. "A convenient story."

"The truth often is."

She glared at him, and he smiled back.

"Fine," Renira said eventually, aware they were blocking up the aisle and people were glaring at them as they shuffled past. "That does make sense. You still locked me in the room."

"I did. Little did I expect you would break out. Let me make it up to you. How much for the earring?"

The old woman behind the stall perked up at that. "Five ekats for the earring and another two for the piercing."

Dussor blew out his lips and reached into his saddlebags. "I really hope this makes things even between us."

Renira stepped in front of him before he could pull out his purse. She wasn't about to let him pay full price, not when there was haggling to be done. "Seven ekats is outrageous," she said as confidently as she could muster. This wasn't like buying bread from the Bakers nor driving up the price of washing loads. She had no idea what an earring was worth, but she knew everyone always charged a little extra.

The old woman finally put down her sewing and leaned forward. "That earring is a masterpiece, carved by Blind Jak Hooper himself. And it's only five ekats."

"And the piercing," Renira reminded her.

"That's paying for a service." The old woman grinned, and Renira knew the game was joined.

"I suppose if the carver is blind, it explains why he only made one earring. They're supposed to come in pairs. We'll give you two ekats, one for the earring and another for the piercing."

"Bah," the old woman waved a wrinkly hand in the air. "That's just insulting. And don't think I don't know he can't pay. Saw him willing to fork out the full seven."

"Uhhh," Dussor said, stepping forward.

"Stay out of this," Renira told him and then turned back to the old woman. "He's a fool not yet figured out he's born."

Dussor stepped back and stood next to Sun. The boy shrugged and went back to staring at the sausage stall.

"I passed a metal vendor selling a lovely silver bracelet for just six ekats," Renira said. "I can go get that and save myself the money and the pain. Nicer work, too. Very intricate."

"Pfft. That'll be Vhonan Reese. His wares might look silver, but they're painted wood and no mistake. You buy that bracelet you'll be washing green off your wrist for days. Six ekats. Four for the earring and two for the piercing."

Renira smiled. The biggest mistake of any negotiation was being the first to alter the terms. "Two for the earring, don't try to deny it's also painted wood. And one for the piercing, any fool can stab a needle into flesh and I've got two standing just behind me."

"You might be surprised about that, girl," said the old woman, but she was still smiling. "Four for the earring. One for the piercing. Best I can do."

That was the woman's second mistake. Whenever a haggler said *best I can do*, it always meant they could concede just a little more. But sometimes it was better to quit before the best terms were struck, so both parties walked away happy they had made a good deal.

"Done," Renira said and grinned. "Now you can pay her. Five ekats please, Dussor."

Dussor shook his head as he reached into his saddlebags and retrieved five bronze ekats from his purse. "All that for two coins," he said as he stacked them on the table.

"So speaks a man whose never had to count out a living," said the woman.

Renira nodded. "Born on a summer's day, he was."

Dussor held up a hand in surrender again. "I'll give you another ekat if you make it really hurt." He winked at the old woman.

She chuckled. "Oh, the pain comes free. Round here, girl. Sit on this stool and hold still. And don't say I didn't warn you."

A few minutes later and Renira was strolling along behind Dussor, desperately trying not to rub at her ear. The old woman had pierced her needle right through the lobe and it throbbed like a bee sting. But she had her very first earring and a new story to tell her friends when she finally made it back home. *If I make it back home.* The maudlin thought popped into her head unbidden, and she willed it away. She was determined to have fun tonight and not dwell on the impossible quest the angels had laid at her feet.

"Is it still bleeding?" she asked Sun as they waited while Dussor spoke to a merchant selling all manner of coats.

"A little bit. It looks pretty though."

"Thank you. Did you really lose your earrings?"

Sun looked away not meeting her gaze. He bobbed his head, then shrugged. "You can lose things on purpose as well as by accident."

"Want to talk about it?"

He shook his head, and Renira decided she wouldn't press the issue until he was ready. Sun was running from something, hiding from something. She understood that now.

Dussor reached an agreement with the merchant, handed over some coins, and then started away. "One more stop and then we're done for the night, my lady," he said over his shoulder as he walked. "I think you'll enjoy this one, master spearman."

Dussor led them back to the weapon shop. The guard standing outside eyed them all suspiciously, but Dussor walked straight in without a word, and both Sun and Renira followed.

"You can't very well be my lady's protector if you don't have a weapon worthy of the task," Dussor said as he perused a barrel bristling with short spears.

"You don't have to keep calling me that," Renira said.

Dussor glanced at her and winked. "I don't, it's true. But I quite like calling you my lady, my lady."

Renira shook her head and turned away before letting herself smile. She quite liked it, too.

"Here," Dussor said, plucking a spear from the barrel. "Drop your stick and give this a twirl." He tossed the spear to Sun.

Sun snatched the spear out of the air and swung it about like a club in both hands. Renira had to take a step back to stop being hit. She saw the shop owner flinch, expecting the worst.

"Ho hoo," Dussor said. "You might need some lessons. Best ask Gemp to teach you. The old man has forgotten more about soldiering than an entire legion could ever know, which is fitting because he's also older than an entire legion."

He paid the shop owner for the spear, and they strolled out of the shop newly armed. Sun was near vibrating with excitement and had to be told to stop playing with the weapon since they were still in a crowded market.

As they were leaving the market, Renira looked up to the Bone Moon shining golden light down upon them. Her mother had chosen the Bone Moon as her icon of faith, and for that reason it always had a special meaning for Renira as well.

She gasped. Crouching atop one of the three-storey shops, staring down at her was a demon! It held a human shape, but there was nothing human about it. The creature was a grey haze, but its mouth was all darkness, the savaged remains of a cat hanging from jagged black teeth. Its eyes were two burning coals, boring into her.

The little monster screeched, a piercing noise that hurt Renira's ears and cut through the hubbub of the market. It turned and dashed away out of sight. A thick tail swished out behind the creature as it disappeared.

A dangerous atmosphere settled over the market as shoppers rushed away, some in the middle of deals. Vendors started packing away their wares and shop doors were closed and bolted. A rack thin soldier stormed into view. She was wearing a ruffled uniform and pointed to some of the shop guards who were milling about.

"Form up," the woman shouted. "Did anyone see it? We need to know which one it was if we're to kill it."

Renira pointed the way the little demon had gone. "It went that way, over the rooftops."

The soldier approached, sparing Dussor a scrutinising glance, but focusing on Renira. "You saw it? What did it look like?"

"Uh, almost human?" Renira said.

Sun nodded. "With a tail." Renira breathed a sigh of relief that Sun had seen the thing too.

"What colour was it?" the woman asked impatiently.

"Grey," Renira said. "I think."

"It's the Grey," the woman shouted. "We need ceramic knives, nothing else will hurt it." She turned to Dussor. "Get the children home and stay inside. The little monsters sometimes follow those who have seen them, and the Grey has killed children before. It has a taste for young flesh." She turned to go.

"It's a demon?" Renira asked, pushing down her anger at being called a child.

The woman glanced back at her and frowned. "A what? There's seven of the little beasts. Well, six now. There used to be seven. A bloody plague on this city, killing animals and causing mischief mostly, but sometimes they do worse things. The Grey is one of the most violent, though not the most. If you see the Red, just run. And scream for help. It doesn't like crowds but will happily attack a lone child." She turned away again and strode toward the gathering group of guards.

Dussor grabbed Renira by the wrist and tugged her on, striding down an alleyway with purpose.

Armstar had said that demons came in many forms and that they had all been driven into the dark places where humanity no longer tread. But Renira had imagined them all to be monstrous like the forest demon. That thing, the Grey, looked almost like a child, and it was roaming the streets of a city, not hiding in the dark places. But it had to be a demon. How else could it have been so strange?

They walked in silence, and Renira kept scanning the rooftops, her eyes peeled for those two burning coals of the Grey's eyes. The woman had said the demon sometimes followed those who had seen it, and suddenly every shadow looked like a demon hunting her.

CHAPTER 28

The stench of the city caught in the back of Perel's throat and left a foul taste there. New Gurrund was a festering shit stain of a settlement, a blight on the landscape. A foul tumour nestled at the bottom of the titanic Cracked Mountains, worming poisonous tendrils into the earth, gutting the range from the inside.

The sun was up yet provided little heat, and the cold of winter had set in, turning the world around the city white with frost and a thin blanket of snow.

It was just five days since Los Hold had fallen and her defeat at the

Archangel's hands. Her wounds were not fully healed. Her ribs hurt, and her left leg sent jagged knives through her flesh with every step, making her limp. Her one consolation was that Tesh had fully recovered and was energetic as a pup, new divine strength running through her veins.

The trail had gone cold the closer they got to New Gurrund. Too much foot traffic obscuring the signs of their passing. Too many people and their smells, not to mention the stench of the city itself. Even from half a day away, it was all either Perel or Tesh could scent, and the closer they got, the worse it stank. Like an annoying itch she couldn't seem to find or a headache that just wouldn't shift. Perel hated cities, and New Gurrund was the worst of all. She cursed the Herald and the angels for heading north out of Los Hold instead of south toward Breakhold. It smelled of fish all year round, and half the city was floating on the lake, but even that was preferable to the smog of New Gurrund.

People stared as they passed, no doubt confused by the sight of an armed woman alone but for the company of a kane wolf. Or maybe just because Tesh was far larger than any other wolf that had ever lived. Older and larger.

Perel had found Tesh as a pup. She had been only seven years old at the time, learning to ride with her mother out in the forest. They had come across a single wolf pup, abandoned by its pack and barely able to stand. She had been a mewling little thing with an injured back leg wrapped in some sort of huntsman's wire. Perel was too young to have tasted even her first drop of angel blood, but she knew what it could do. Her education was part of the deal her father had struck with her mother. Perel was raised by her mother, but she was taught the truth about the world, about the God, and about her family.

Perel's heart had broken at the sight of the wolf pup and its plaintive cries. She'd been a sickly child herself, always suffering from one malady or another. It was either fluid in her lungs making her cough, or spiking fevers that had her trapped in waking nightmares, or odd fits that left her legs paralysed for days. Her mother had no idea what was wrong with her, but tried every remedy she knew. They all failed.

Perel had begged her mother to rescue the wolf pup, but she refused, saying it was nature's way of carving the weak from the strong. It was as if she couldn't see she was saying the same of her own daughter. Perel had snuck out that night and rescued the pup. She spent hours laboriously untangling the wire around its legs and suffered countless nips and bites. Even after all her work, it was clear the pup would never walk again, her legs were too mangled, bones broken and flesh torn.

She'd expected her mother to be furious when she learned Perel had disobeyed her. But instead, she smiled with such pride. Perel then begged her mother to take them to her father, knowing he, if no one else, could save the wolf pup. The pride had vanished then, replaced by a sadness Perel hadn't been able to understand at the time. She did now, though. She knew now what her mother had grasped back then: their time together was at an end.

Even at seven years old Perel understood that the Godless King was not a kind man, and that she was begging for something worth more than most people could imagine. But he had listened to her, and then made his offer. Perhaps Perel should have thought about it, about the consequences, but a child so young rarely thinks past the moment. She agreed without question, so eager to see the pup saved. And her mother had wept.

The deal was simple. The wolf pup was saved. The carver's set its broken bones and a single drop of angel blood sped its healing past the impossible, and a single drop was given to Perel as well. All her maladies vanished. No more fevers or fits. She was cured, healthy and free of pain for the first time in her life. She was so grateful, but she hadn't understood the price. The act of willingly drinking divine blood had bound her to her father as surely as the name they shared.

It started an addiction that she could never free herself of—even if she wanted to. No other taste could ever compare to eating angelic flesh and drinking divine blood. No other goal in life would ever be as important as chasing the immortality offered by taking it from angels. But that wasn't the real payment for the life of the wolf pup.

As soon as it was certain the pup would walk again without issue, her father had made them share an angel's eyes. Tesh gulped it down without hesitation, but Perel struggled. Eyes are far larger than one sees on the surface, and she was just seven years old. She could never forget the feeling of it bursting and crunching inside her mouth. It took everything she had not to vomit. And with the sharing of those eyes, Perel and Tesh were linked, bound together through sight and something far deeper. They were bound together through love and devotion. Wolf and girl; closer than friends, closer than sisters, closer than lovers. They were more like one creature with two bodies.

Perel's life with her mother was over. She saw the woman again but rarely, and it was always painful. Her mother seemed to age so quickly, or maybe Perel had aged slowly. Time passed differently for immortals.

Perel had moved to Celesgarde with her father and many siblings. She trained with weapons, day after day, year after year. She practised using her bond with Tesh and, with the depth of that bond, discovered some abilities even her father had not known were possible. The sharing of the eyes had not just linked them by sight; Perel could also share Tesh's sense of smell. She was fed angel blood, a few drops a year, she and Tesh both.

Immortality skewed her perspective. Each day seemed less important when you know they will never run out. Her mother grew old, even as Perel stayed young. Eventually Perel went one day, and the cabin in the woods was empty. Her bond with Tesh told her it had been that way for a long time, years at least. Time had passed, and it had taken her mother with it, but it had forgotten Perel and Tesh. Like all the Hostain family, time no longer had meaning to them.

Almost two hundred years now, Perel and Tesh had been together. She had seen her wolf raise pups of her own, time and time again. They had fought together, feasted together, hunted together. Even without shared language, no bond had ever been deeper.

Perel shook herself out of her reverie. The people of New Gurrund talked in harsh whispers. These were the slums, where the poorest citizens toiled their lives away. Miners and breeders, useful for nothing else. Perel glanced at them as they stared at her and wondered how many years the eldest of them could claim. Miners rarely lived for long. Thirty years maybe. A blink of the eye when compared to an immortal. Of course, so small a span was suitable for a life that meant nothing.

"Beast."

"Savage."

"Monster."

Perel did not need her wolf's hearing for the insults to reach her. She had her own powers now, taken from the angels she had killed. Her senses were sharper and more subtle than any human who had ever lived. Even striding past a gathering crowd, she could pick out the individuals and their words. But she ignored them.

Her father had told her long ago the mundane people of the world wouldn't understand her and Tesh. They couldn't. But they didn't need to. They were not immortals. They didn't matter. He was right. What did the ignorant opinion of some poor miner, at best only years away from the grave, matter? His blood was weak, his words nothing but mindless offal, and his thoughts fleeting. The mundane led such simple lives. Once Perel and Tesh were out of sight, the miners would go back to complaining about the sky, or the weather, or the mines that both gave them work and killed them all at once.

"Go back to the forest, beasts!" Perel did not need to turn to know it was the man with a crooked nose and few remaining teeth who hissed the words.

A rock sailed through the air, and Tesh leapt sideways, avoiding it. Her hackles raised, and she growled, teeth bared in warning. Perel was less lenient.

She stepped to the side and pivoted her halberd around her body then upward in a swift arc that split the air and severed the man's arm at the elbow. He collapsed to the stony ground, the shock at seeing a bloody stump where his arm should be blocking out the pain for a few moments. Then the screaming started. He would be throwing no more rocks this day, or any other. She doubted he would live long at all. The wound was clean, the halberd a Godslayer weapon that could cut through stone, but he would get it dirty and infected. He would no doubt be dead within days. A fitting punishment for ignorance and poor choice.

Perel flicked the blood clear of the halberd's blade and continued into the city. No words were needed, and she was certain no others would try to harm her wolf. It didn't stop the stares or the whispers, but Perel could live with those. More importantly, she could allow others to live with them.

The first guards to stop her did so at distance, with spears and flatbows. Ten of them, all armoured in breastplates bearing her own family crest. Could it really be they had never heard of the Wolf Princess? She smiled dangerously but made no aggressive moves. It would take a lucky shot from a flatbow to kill her, or Tesh, but that did not mean it was impossible. Besides, she knew from experience that arrows hurt no matter where they struck.

"My name is Perel Hostain," she said loudly. "You may have heard of my father, what with him being the king and all."

Some of the soldiers shared looks, and then an older man stepped forward. He'd once had dark hair, but it was turning to grey, and the lines about his eyes told of a hard life and battles seen. There was a look soldiers got when they'd been in one too many wars. Haunted. Immortals never succumbed to such foolishness. Maybe because they knew the true value of life was far smaller than most people realised.

"I remember you, my lady," slurred the ageing soldier. He saluted with a closed fist against his breastplate. He had a burn scar on the side of his face that tugged at his lips. "I used to be in the Third. I was there at Rorash when the walls fell." He smiled, but that haunted look stayed in his eyes.

Rorash had been a bloody mess. A mountain fortress straddling the southern pass in the Ruskins, it nestled on the very edge of Helesia's border and guarded the most direct route from Ashvold, the only route that didn't lead through the kingdom of Dien. Forty years ago, Perel had been at Rorash by chance, a fruitless hunt of the Light Bearer. Karna had attacked, unleashing her army on the fortress. With them had marched the legendary Amaranthine, Karna's own force of immortals, humans she fed from her own divine flesh and blood. It was an overwhelming show of power, and the legion guarding the fort had been all but wiped out. Perel held the gate alone while the soldiers who survived the initial assault escaped, but when the Forgemistress herself joined the battle, even Perel had to flee with her tail between her legs. She hated to admit it, but she was no match for Karna's strength, for the power of an angel who devoured other angels. Ashvold had held the fort of Rorash ever since, a gateway into Helesia if Karna should ever want it.

Perel gave the old soldier a respectful nod. The men and women of the Third had fought hard and deserved that much at least.

"Disperse," Perel said.

The soldier frowned. "My lady?"

Perel sighed and started forward, Tesh matching her pace. "I assume you have no idea of the whereabouts of two angels and their human companions?"

The soldier shook his head. "New Gurrund has a few monsters, but no angels, my lady."

"Then take your soldiers and go. Leave me be, because the people I need to speak to will not come close while you are here."

The old soldier walked alongside her for a few paces. "You mean the Silver Hands, my lady? They're dangerous folk. Your father has ordered them stamped out."

"And have they been?" Perel asked.

"No."

"Good. You're dismissed." Perel quickened her pace and left the man behind.

The city of New Gurrund rose up around her like a pestilent boil. As if the stench of the place wasn't bad enough from a distance, it became worse further in. It burned the back of Perel's throat and made her eyes itch. How a smell could make her eyes itch was as mysterious as it was unwelcome. The city was covered in the smog of industry. Forges working every hour of the day, smelting iron into steel and forging weapons and armour. But as much as she hated the place, she knew its true purpose. The centre of the city was a smith unlike any other, with forges built to withstand temperatures that would melt even Heaven's Gate. Here, in New Gurrund, was one of only two forges in the world that could melt down the armour of First Age angels. A forge where angel-forged weapons and armour could be made. Perel didn't understand the full process of making angel-forged armour, but she didn't need to. Her father understood it. Here was where his armour had been made, forged from the bones of the God himself.

Walking the streets without purpose would get Perel nowhere. Neither she nor Tesh could track anything in such a metropolis. She hated to admit it, but in a city like New Gurrund, Borik would have been the better choice to track the Herald. His ways and means had nothing to do with looking for signs and trails and everything to do with greasing palms, making deals, and whispering promises in the right ears. Perel didn't have his people skills, but she needed to emulate his methods as much as she could. She ducked into a nearby tavern with a sign outside that read *Black Lung*. Tesh followed. The common room was almost abandoned so early in the day, but there were some cloaked figures in the far corner where the shadows were deepest. The owner was shaking his head even as Perel pricked her finger with her own needle and shed a drop of blood offering on the floor.

"You can't bring that monster in here!" he said in a quivering voice.

Tesh stared at the man while Perel picked a table and sat. The wolf then joined her, shoving chairs aside and never taking her eyes from the owner, even when she sat down on her haunches and rested her great head on the table with a weary, toothy yawn.

Perel rested her halberd across the table and leaned back in her chair, stretching happily. Her leathers creaked. They'd need oiling soon or they'd crack. Perel damn near lived in her armour, but proper maintenance was essential.

"Two ales," she called to the owner. "And food. Something warm for me. Meat for Tesh here. Raw if you have it." Tesh barked like a puppy.

"We don't..." The owner blustered and paced behind the bar. "It's an animal!"

Perel finished stretching and pinned the man with a cold stare. "And yet her manners are better than yours. Ale and food, or I'll cut your throat and let her eat you."

The threat worked, and the man soon approached with two mugs of ale. Tesh growled as he came close. He placed the mugs on the edge of the table and almost tripped over a chair as he fled. Perel laughed and pulled one mug close and pushed the other toward Tesh. The wolf lapped at the ale, spilling as much on the table as getting in her mouth. Perel raised her own mug to her lips and drank deeply. It had a taste somewhere between roasted chestnuts and mud, but it quenched her thirst well enough.

Food was slow in coming but worth the wait. The bowl of hot stew had strips of pork and cubed vegetables floating in it. It had a spiced taste, almost like cinnamon. Tesh received a slab of beef, cold for many days and raw. The owner delivered it on a plate, but Tesh quickly threw it on the floor and set about devouring it, holding it in her paws and sawing off chunks with her rear teeth.

Perel was just finishing her stew when a man in a miner's smock entered the tavern. He had thin strands of greasy hair combed over his head and a nose that looked to have been broken many times. He waved to the owner for an ale and edged past Tesh, then sat at the table behind Perel.

"Out back," the miner said quietly. Perel turned to find him intent on his mug of ale. She wondered if this was how Borik lived his life? In whispered fragments and one-sided conversations? It sounded exhausting. She much preferred the direct route.

She picked up her halberd and left a single silver rund on the table. It was probably paying far over the odds, but she didn't care. Money was only useful if you spent it, and the meal had been generous portions at least. Tesh knocked over a couple more chairs on her way out. They weren't really in her way, but a wild flick of her tail sent them scattering. Most animals were beyond vindictiveness, it was a human trait, after all, but there was as much human in Tesh as there was wolf in Perel.

The street outside was as busy as the inn had been empty. Perel skirted the outside of the tavern until she found an alley. A woman and a boy waited in the gloomy depths, trying to hide their faces in the shadows, but Perel's wolf sight picked them out. The woman was middle-aged with tired eyes and black hair that reeked of boot polish. The boy had a sallow complexion that spoke of malnourishment, and he kept fiddling with something in his coat pocket. Perel nodded back toward the street, and Tesh bounded away.

The woman spotted Perel as soon as she stepped foot into the alley. She held up a finger to her lips and watched as Perel approached. The boy watched the other direction and startled as Tesh appeared there, stalking down the alley toward them. Woman and boy were now trapped between a giant wolf and an immortal. The boy looked fit to panic, his fear showing clearly on his gaunt face, but the woman only smiled through teeth made yellow by corn die. All this was for show.

"Hear you're looking for us," the woman whispered. Perel could smell her breath from half a dozen paces away. Like milk left out in the sun.

"You're with the Silver Hands?" Perel asked. She stopped within striking distance, and Tesh crouched ready to pounce from the other side.

The woman held up her hands and smiled again. "I'm just an errand girl. You want to speak to Digger. And it happens he's willing to listen. He's been expecting you ever since the mayor sent that request last year."

Perel hid her ignorance and took a menacing step toward the woman and, just as she looked set to cower, stepped aside. "Lead the way. But if this smells like a trap at any point, I'll feed you to the wolf." Tesh growled in response, her yellow eyes gleaming in the gloomy alleyway.

The woman and the boy hurried off. Perel waited a moment as Tesh padded up to her. The wolf yawned expansively and nudged Perel with her head.

"The sooner we find the Herald, the sooner we can get out of this shit hole." She scratched Tesh on the head.

Tesh shucked Perel's hand away and caught it in her teeth, holding it for just a moment, the pressure painful but not enough to break the skin. Then she let go and leapt forwards, panting and tongue lolling. Eating Mihiriel had her acting like a pup again and it made Perel happy to see it.

They moved east towards the edge of the city where the miners were thickest. Here there were carts on metal tracks being pushed to and from mines deeper into the mountains. Men and women covered in dirt and wearing the faces of the downtrodden. The woman veered off into an old mine shaft off the side of the road. It was all but boarded up with only a sliver of an entrance. Tesh growled at it. The wolf wouldn't fit through the gap without widening it, and Perel doubted the Silver Hands would be pleased with that.

"Stay here. Guard the entrance," Perel said. She noticed the boy standing close by, watching and listening. "And if you think anything has happened to me, break through this flimsy barrier and savage everyone you can find." She grinned at the boy, and he somehow managed to look pale even under the dirt and grime. Tesh set to pacing outside the mineshaft as Perel and the boy squeezed their way in.

Dark rock and loaded flatbows greeted Perel. The gloom held no secrets from her sight, and she could see four men a dozen paces into the shaft, each one armed and with their fingers on the triggers. The woman leaned against the nearby wall, and the boy stepped past Perel, positioning himself between her and the bowmen.

"I'll take your weapon please," said the woman. "Just as a precaution. You'll get it back."

Perel hesitated. "You know what this is? A Godslayer blade. If you steal it, my father would bring these mountains down on your head to get it back."

The woman edged forward and placed a grimy hand on the haft of the halberd. "Just a precaution. You'll get it back. We've no wish to anger the king more than we already do." Perel held her gaze for a few more moments, then let go of her halberd.

"So where is this Digger?" she asked.

"Right here," said the boy. All trace of fear had fled him, and he stood a little straighter than before, but he was still a boy and looked no more than twelve years old. Now Perel looked closer, something about him seemed off. His eyes and attitude were far older than his face.

"You're the leader of the Silver Hands?" Perel asked, grinning.

Digger shrugged. "In New Gurrund. For almost sixty years now."

"Immortal then?" Perel said. "I'm sure my father would be very interested to know where you got so much angel blood."

The boy laughed. "Your father knows full well there's a black market for angel parts. He's just never been able to find it. And he never will."

"I found you."

Digger shook his head, greasy hair flopping in front of his eyes so he had to wipe it back. "We found you."

Perel sniffed. The boy smelled of dirt and sweat, but the men behind him, those armed with flatbows, stank of fear. "Your people were watching even before I entered the city?"

Digger kicked at a stone, sending it careening off the tunnel wall. "Of course. We watch everyone. I have to know who is coming to and from my city, if I am to keep the peace." He smiled. "Which is how I know you were not the first. Your father sent scouts ahead of you. They arrived through the pass just a day ago. Five soldiers and a young girl who does not look like she belongs here. New Gurrund ain't the type of place for the dainty." Again, that smile, cruel and mocking. The boy was an immortal for certain, one not bound to the Hostain name. By law, Perel should kill him right there.

"They have nothing to do with me," Perel said.

"Oh." The boy's smile turned sweet as rotting meat. "Perhaps you're more interested in a couple of angels and their human companions?"

"They're here?" Perel asked. She knew it. They were close. She could almost taste them.

Digger singled out another stone and kicked it further into the darkness of the mineshaft. "Maybe some people matching the description arrived two days ago. But they didn't make quite the stir you did. No severed limbs."

"Where are they?" Perel asked, her voice a low growl. Outside, she heard Tesh rumble in response.

"Information is the most valuable commodity I own," Digger said. "Even more so than angel blood. I rarely give it away for free."

Perel hated playing games, especially when her opponent thought they held the advantage. She closed the gap between them in a moment and wrapped a hand around the boy's neck, lifting him off the ground with ease. She squeezed. Not too tight, not enough to crush his larynx or snap his neck, but enough that his eyes bulged. Even so, Digger didn't panic. The men behind him with flat-bows started to, but Perel held the boy up as a shield between them.

"Where are they?" Perel growled again. Claws scraped down the wooden blockade behind her as Tesh tested the strength of the barrier.

The boy wheezed, struggling to draw breath past Perel's grip. He stared at her, one eye covered by his greasy flop of hair, the other gleaming in the dim light. "Kill me and you'll never find them," he croaked.

Perel looked past the boy at the men with their bows. "Sure I will. I doubt everyone in your organisation has your resolve."

Digger croaked out a laugh. "They don't know. I don't know."

Perel felt hot anger burst to life inside her chest, and Tesh started scrabbling more insistently on the wooden barricade. These stupid bloody games. "Then what good are you?" Perel hissed, her grip around the boy's neck tightening.

"He can find out," the woman said. The boy nodded urgently, no longer able to speak past Perel's grip. "We have people following the angels, but only Digger knows how to summon them. Kill him and you lose your chance. Our people will go to ground, and you'll never see any of us again. This is your only chance. *He* is your only chance. Let him go."

Perel considered for a few more moments, then dropped Digger to the ground with a thud. One of the bowmen pulled the trigger on his flatbow. Perel lurched to the side, grabbed hold of the bolt as it passed her, twirled around, then sent it flying back to its origin. The bolt hammered home into the man's neck. He staggered back, clutching at the wound, the blood already pouring down his tunic.

"Stop!" Digger screamed, surging back to his feet and putting himself between the bowmen and Perel. One of the other men had already dropped his bow and was desperately trying to staunch the bleeding of his comrade, but it was pointless. The other four bowmen looked even more nervous than before, gripping their flatbows in shaking hands. These were thieves and thugs, not soldiers. Perel doubted they had ever even met a real immortal, only the boy. He had the long life, but clearly none of the strength that came from eating divine flesh. "Stop!" Digger said again, holding up his hands. The men obeyed him without question.

"Bash is dead," said the man tending to his wounded friend.

Perel smiled. "That's what happens when someone tries to kill me. So don't do it again." The scrabbling at her back grew more intense, and Tesh ripped one of the wooden boards away in her teeth, widening the entrance. "She'll be through soon," Perel continued, thumbing behind her and wincing dramatically. "And she takes threats to my life even less graciously than I do. So, talk fast."

Digger nodded. His calm self-assurance was gone now, replaced by an urgent fear. "I don't know where the angels are, but I have people watching them. That's how we operate. I can find out. It'll just take a little time."

"So, get started," Perel said as Tesh ripped away another wooden board. One of the bowmen moved, changing his aim to the tunnel entrance.

"I wouldn't do that," Perel said. "Keep it trained on me. She takes threats to my life quite seriously, but I take threats to her life as finality."

"Uh..." the bowman stuttered.

Perel sighed. "I will bloody kill you if you point that thing at my wolf."

Digger threw up a hand to stop the bowman. "I told you. I don't give out information for free. I want one."

"One what?"

"One of the angels." There was real greed on the boy's face now. It was disgusting on one who looked so young. "We might know where they are, but we couldn't kill them ourselves, even if we had a dozen of your Godslayer weapons."

"There are only seven," Perel said.

"Seven, a dozen, a hundred," Digger continued. "Even the lowliest of angels would tear through my people. We're spies and thieves, not soldiers. But you're going to kill them. And I want one." He smiled, his eyes feverish. "As much of one as you leave intact."

Perel shook her head. The boy was overstepping his boundaries. "My father would never agree. He wrote the laws, and they state all divine bodies belong to him."

"So what? Your father ain't here, and I'm not doing business with him. My deal is with you."

Perel considered even as Tesh ripped free another wooden board and shoved most of her huge head through the gap, snarling and snapping. One of the bowmen panicked, turned, and ran. Her father would never agree to such a deal, even if it did mean catching the Herald. Angel corpses belonged to him, the power they contained his to mete out, at least in Helesia. Only Hostain family members, those bound by blood, were allowed to feast on an angel's heart and claim its true power for their own. Even his own wives were never given angel blood or flesh. But the boy was right, Emrik Hostain wasn't there. And he never had to know how much Perel had given up. A single angel, one of two, didn't seem too great a sacrifice in order to bring her father the Herald's head. Besides, once the Herald was dead, she would have no further need of

Digger or his Silver Hands. Father would be doubly pleased with the head of the Herald and of a rogue immortal.

"You get the Builder," Perel said.

"The one with burned wings..." Digger said as if he was weighing up the deal. He would say yes. Even if Perel cut the Builder in half and only gave Digger his legs, it would still be a deal worth taking. "A small reward, but acceptable."

"And no heart," Perel said.

Digger's expression soured. "I want the heart."

Perel shook her head slowly.

Digger didn't look pleased. "Deal."

"And the deal is off unless the humans are with them," Perel added. "A boy and a girl."

CHAPTER 29

The first pillar is Worship, to praise the God for all he has given, and all has done. He is the one and the all, the father and the saviour.

The second pillar is Prosperity, to succeed and to grow, to flourish even when times are hard. The gifts he has given must not be squandered.

The third pillar is Glory, to gather renown and spread the word to all reaches. His power and generosity must be sung to one and all, and all must love him.

The fourth pillar is Sacrifice, to give all you are and all you have is to prove his love is returned.

These are the pillars of faith, upon which God rises, and humanity will rise with him.

R enira was busy braiding her own hair when the door burst open and slammed against the wall. The wrinkled old soldier, Gemp, stood there, a grimace on his gnarled face and half a carrot in his mouth.

"We're leaving. Now!" Gemp barked. He turned away before Renira could ask any questions.

She shook her hair free from the half-finished braid and instead tied it into a tail with the blood-stained silver ribbon Aesie had given her, then she scooped up her coat from the floor and then followed Gemp out of the room and down the stairs.

"What's going on?"

"I don't know," Gemp growled around his carrot. "They don't tell me nothing. I just follow orders. They say we're leaving. We're leaving." He flashed Renira a knowing grin over his shoulder. "Easier not to ask questions."

For two days they had been locked up in the acolyte's house, and Armstar had forbid any but Dussor, Kerrel, or Gemp from leaving. The boredom had almost been more than she could take, but Renira had found a book to read to distract her. It was a copy of *The Rite of the Divine*, much like the one that had saved her life during the demon attack in the forest. It was a dry text full of prayers and passages detailing the God's glory, a struggle to concentrate on, and Renira often found her mind wandering instead of decrypting the words on the page. When not reading, she spent her time staring out the window, but now and then she was certain she saw a little grey shape darting over the rooftops. Renira couldn't shake the feeling of burning red eyes watching her.

Downstairs, the angels and their acolytes were in frantic motion as they shoved supplies into packs. Armstar and Kerrel were in the study, standing over a little table and staring at a map. Armstar pointed, and the woman shook her head. Kerrel was tall and strong with skin as dark as Sun's and a scar that ran from the base of her hairline, through her left eye and lips, to the bottom of her chin. Renira had no idea how the woman had come by the scar, nor how someone could survive earning such a wound. Kerrel seemed to be the leader of the little group of acolytes, though Renira had not spoken to her much. They seemed a close group, secretive by nature, and only Dussor was amiable enough to spend time chatting. Gemp seemed to communicate mostly through grunts and withered chuckles. Renira glanced around for Dussor, hoping to catch sight of the handsome young man, but he was nowhere to be seen.

"Are you sure you want to do this?" Kerrel asked. Her eyes were bright and her features fierce, her posture tense as though ready to spring into action in an instant. She reminded Renira of Igor, full of feline power and grace. "We don't know what's down there."

"I know," Armstar said.

Kerrel shook her head again. "It's closed off for a reason, whatever that is." She glanced over at Renira and frowned. "Can we really risk—"

"Rumours," Armstar said. "It's closed off because of where it leads. The rumours are there to deter anyone from investigating. It's safe... mostly." He didn't sound certain.

"Right. Like Kutvekar is just rumours?" Kerrel asked with a savage shake of her head. "I've been to that cursed city and seen…"

Armstar frowned at Renira as he closed the study door, shutting her out. She really wanted to know what Kerrel had seen in Kutvekar. And where it was. She edged closed and pressed her ear against the door, straining to hear through the wood.

"Catch," Dussor said. Renira turned just in time to raise her hands and catch the large backpack flying her way. It was heavy, and the impact knocked her off balance and onto her arse. "Ooops. Sorry about that."

Dussor stopped beside her and extended a hand. At least he was gentleman enough to pick her up after knocking her down. Renira took it, warm and calloused in her smaller hand, and he pulled her to her feet.

"What's in this thing?" Renira asked as she hauled the backpack up after her.

"Oh, you know, bit of food, a bed roll, an anvil in case any emergency blacksmithing needs crop up, and the weight and expectation of a thousand years of angelic hope." He finished with a grin.

"Ah, no wonder it's so light."

"Would the dainty lady like me to carry her things?"

She shot him a venomous glare. She still wasn't sure how to deal with Dussor. *Elsa never had a problem talking to boys. What would she do? Probably throw herself at him lips first. At the very least she'd brag.*

Renira wriggled a little to get the pack comfortable on her shoulders. "This is nothing. I once carried a horse from Farmer Hays' stable all the way to the market."

Dussor blinked at her, a slow smile spreading across his stubbled cheeks. "A horse?"

"All right, you've caught me in the lie. It was two horses. One on each shoulder."

They stared at each other for a few moments. Dussor's face twitched. Renira felt her own mimicking him. Then they both burst into laughter together.

"I'm here," Sun said as he staggered down the stairs rubbing his eyes. "What did I miss? What's funny?"

Dussor shook his head, still grinning at Renira. "One on each shoulder?"

"Like parrots."

The young man turned, still chuckling, and strode towards the kitchen. "We're gonna have to teach you to lie better, my lady."

"What did I miss?" Sun asked again around a yawn.

Renira shook her head at him. "You were asleep again?" It seemed every time she had gone to see Sun over the last two days, she'd found him snoring softly or thrashing wildly, and always tangled in bed sheets. She envied him that. Sleep seemed to come difficultly for her now, and it was often plagued with nightmares.

Sun shrugged. "Nothing else to do." He held his spear in one hand and stopped next to Renira, leaning heavily on it.

"This one is yours, Exemplar," Dussor said with a grin as he reappeared from the kitchen holding another pack. Dussor dumped the pack at Sun's feet and then pulled a winter coat out of it. It was thick leather and lined with wool, similar to Renira's own but without the stains and scars. "It's going to be cold where we're headed. I thought you might like to keep warm."

Sun grinned and quickly snatched the coat and pulled it on over his arms. It fit him well, though was a bit long, and made him look older somehow. Room to grow into, as her mother liked to say. It would certainly be better than the ill-fitting robe he had been using as a cloak. He started buttoning up the coat, despite the warmth of the building.

"Still don't trust him?" Renira asked Sun in a quiet voice.

Sun shrugged, but he had a smile on his face. "He's all right, I suppose." It seemed the way to the boy's heart was through gifts, first a spear and now a coat.

"I thought we were staying in New Gurrund a while?" Renira asked Dussor as he busied about dragging another two packs from the kitchen.

The stairs creaked as Eleseth made her way down them, her wings folded over her shoulders as a cloak. "Good morning, Renira," she said. "A woman with a giant wolf as a companion was spotted entering the city. She made quite the scene."

They'd found her again!

"The Wolf Princess," Renira said, an icy finger of fear souring her stomach.

Eleseth nodded. "We can't stay here with Perel close by. We'll leave as soon as possible. Armstar has a plan." The angel did not sound confident.

Sun twirled his spear about, the point scraping against the wooden walls. "Let her come. Now I have a proper weapon, I'll kill that wolf for you, Ren."

Renira smiled. In truth, she'd rather never even see the wolf or the princess again. They scared her, and it was more than just the danger they posed. The wolf princess seemed more demon than the monster they had faced in the forest. A far cry from the woman Renira looked up to back during the Riverden parade. No. Now she knew Perel was close, Renira agreed with Eleseth, the sooner they were gone from New Gurrund, the better. The last thing she wanted was the people of the city caught up in the hunt. They didn't deserve to suffer on Renira's behalf. There was enough suffering in the city already.

The study door swung open and whoever had won the argument, neither angel nor acolyte seemed happy about it. Armstar grimaced as he stalked through the house, gathering things into his own pack. He couldn't wear a backpack like the rest of them, not with his ruined wings, but had a large satchel hanging by his hip. He threw his patchy old cloak over his back again, making his wings look like a deformed hump, and affected a stoop. It was a simple yet effective ruse.

The sky was overcast, its deep rouge making the clouds look like roiling mud. The sun was above them somewhere, but Renira couldn't see it past the smog. Their breath misted, and the icy chill crept inside her coat. Kerrel and Dussor went ahead, hurrying away down the busy streets. She pulled her coat close, clutched her mother's amulet in one hand, and watched them go. She hoped they'd make it safely. She liked Dussor, he treated her like a person rather than a burden.

Their flight did not go unnoticed. Five people, including a hunchback and a giant of a woman, moving through the city with speed and purpose was bound to draw attention. Armstar took turns seemingly at random and chose alleys to cut through on more than one occasion. They passed shops and homes, guild halls and markets, and forges. New Gurrund had a wealth of forges scattered all over it, and each one seemed to be in constant use, the fires never going out and the anvils rarely silent.

"Ren?" A woman's voice and one she recognised, though it wasn't possible.

Renira slowed to a halt. Standing in front of a large tavern, holding the reins of a sleek black horse, was Aesie. Renira had to blink to make sure she wasn't imagining it.

"Keep moving, Renira," Eleseth said. She had been bringing up the rear of their little group.

"What are you doing here, Ren?" Aesie asked, a broad smile on her pretty face. She was wearing a brown riding skirt and a warm winter coat that was as white as snow. Both looked as though they had never seen harsh conditions. She was also wearing sturdy riding boots that went up to her calves and wool gloves that matched her coat. It was an outfit designed to be as fashionable as it was functional, and it suited Aesie from her booted toes to the purple ribbon in her apricot hair. Renira had missed her friend's effortless grace and beauty.

Renira laughed and quickly crossed the few steps between her and her friend. She threw her arms around Aesie, and the girl squeaked in mock alarm before hugging her back, their embrace made awkward by the pack on Renira's back. "You have no idea how good it is to see you, Aesie," she said.

Aesie laughed and squeezed her tight for a moment before letting go. She was grinning wildly, and her face was flushed. Her hair was tousled as though just back from a ride, and her breath steamed between them. "What are you doing here, Ren?" Aesie asked again. She glanced over Renira's shoulder at her companions and frowned.

Renira shrugged, a jovial mood overtaking her. "Oh, you know. Excitement and adventure. I fought a demon."

"You did not," Aesie said and pulled a sceptical face. She held it for a few seconds, and then both were laughing. "Really, I can't believe you're here of all places."

"Me either. To be honest—"

"Renira," Armstar's voice cut through the mirth like scissors through silk. "We don't have time for this. Come along!"

Aesie glanced over Renira's shoulder again. "Who's the hunchback? And all the others?" She swung her gaze back to Renira and gasped. "Ren, have you joined a circus?"

Renira snorted out a laugh, and Aesie giggled. "No. Well, maybe. It's an adventure. I'm off seeing the world."

Sun stepped up beside Renira. He stared at Aesie suspiciously, spear gripped in both hands.

"It's all right, Sun," Renira said with a warm smile. "This is Aesie, my friend from Riverden."

Armstar grabbed hold of Renira's hand and started to pull her away. Renira tried to resist, but weakened or not, the angel was still far too strong for her to stop. "Armstar, let go."

"We don't have time for this, Renira," he said, pulling her back out into the street.

"I know! Just give me a moment." Renira wrenched her hand free and stood up to Armstar, holding his gaze as best she could. They could afford a moment for her to speak to her friend, and if they rushed away now, it would only look more suspicious.

They stood there, in the middle of the street, staring at each other while people passed them by on both sides. Aesie broke the silence, interjecting herself once more. "What's going on, Ren?" she asked, all good humour gone. "I have some soldiers accompanying me. Should I fetch them?"

Armstar's gaze snapped to Aesie, and he raised a hand. "Forget..."

Renira quickly stepped sideways, putting herself between them. She scowled at Armstar. "Don't you dare."

When Renira turned back to Aesie, she had to force a smile. "Why do you have soldiers with you?"

"They're an escort," Aesie said, still frowning at Armstar. "I met the prince at the ball back in Riverden, you know the one after the parade? We were joking about it and all, but it really happened. I met the prince!" She grinned wide and truly did seem happy. "He really is so handsome. And charming. Told me I was pretty as spring thaw, which is... I guess pretty?"

Renira shrugged. "Wet and cold, usually."

"Hmm. Well, I took it as a good sign. Next thing I know, my father decided we had got on so well together I should come and meet him here in New Gurrund to get on even better." She looked back to Renira and winked. "Well, I'm officially here to look in on the new factory and make sure its production quotas are... you don't care about any of that. But really I'm here to spend some more time with the prince in the hopes that... you know." She grinned again.

"Borik is here?" Renira asked.

Aesie frowned. "Prince Borik, you mean. And no." She let out a dramatic sigh. "It turns out the whole trip was a waste. The factory is running just fine, and the prince moved on to the capital. But my father has arranged for some of the king's soldiers to escort me to Celesgarde from here. Apparently, I'm to either marry a prince or attend a university, and damn whatever I think about either option." She gave a sly smile. "I'm thinking I might do both."

Eleseth stepped close and placed a hand on Renira's shoulder. She leaned in and whispered in Renira's ear. "Armstar is right about this. We need to go. Now."

Renira nodded and turned back to Aesie. "I'm sorry. I have to go. We'll catch up back in Riverden. Soon." She turned and started after Armstar.

"Wait," Aesie said, hurrying after them, her voice rising. "What's going on, Ren?"

Renira stopped again and turned. She waited for a few people to cross in front of her, then rushed in and gave Aesie another hug. "I'm so glad you're getting to go to a university in the capital. I'll see you again soon. Everything's fine. I'm going to have such a tale to tell you, you'll think it's all one of Elsa's lies." She turned and fled after the others, ignoring her friend calling after her.

The rest of their flight through the city passed by as a blur to Renira. She hated leaving Aesie like that, with no explanation of what she was really doing in New Gurrund or where she was going, but there was nothing else for it. It was dangerous enough that Aesie had even seen Renira, especially with Perel so close on their trail. She could only hope her friend would move on to Celesgarde and forget she had even seen her.

Maybe, once everything was over and the new age had been rung in, she could find Aesie again, and they could swap their stories properly. The idea of sitting down with her best friend and chatting over a mug of tea set a fierce longing alive in Renira. They had so much catching up to do. Renira had only been gone a couple of weeks, but so much had happened. And she wanted to ask how Merebeth and Elsa were doing, and if Aesie had heard from her mother, and how the meeting with Borik had really gone. She'd even tell her friend about her own meeting with the prince. A part of her wished Aesie were with her, keeping her company on her adventure. She remembered dreams like that from the past, the two of them seeing the world, battling monsters, and getting into trouble. Childish dreams. No. After the new age was rung in, they could meet again. They were both headed to the same place eventually anyway. The new age could only be rung in with the Bell of Ages, and that hung at the top of the Overlook deep within the city of Celesgarde.

Armstar led them on a meandering route that took them hours to traverse. They circumvented the centre of the city, where the grand forges of New Gurrund belched out smoke, and arrived at the northern edge. It was a far different place to the southern reaches. Here in the north, New Gurrund seemed an empty place, more a ghost town than thriving city of commerce and industry. Many of the buildings grew large and ornate and looked more newly constructed than those around them.

Gemp grumbled as they went, chewing on a strip of dried beef. "Northern mines are all but closed down. Too many rumours of monsters this way. Rich folk took to buying up whole streets and building bloody mansions. Rest of the place is near dead. A right waste."

"Monsters?" Sun asked. "Or demons."

"There are no demons in the mines," Armstar said as he turned down another alleyway to cut through onto a different street.

"There's bloody well something down in those old mines," Gemp said. "Not that you'd tell me about it. Soldier's lot, that is. Follow the light, live in the dark."

"Does the Grey live down in the mines?" Renira asked.

Gemp gave her an appraising look. "Aye. Now what do you know about that?"

"Nothing really. We saw the Grey and it... Well, it was grey. It almost looked human. The soldiers said it could only be harmed by, uh..."

Gemp grunted. "Clay cuts the Grey, or so they say." He chuckled. "Some folk say they're a plague on the city, but I've never heard of them doing any real harm. I know some people say they take children, but no one ever has a child been taken. That makes me think it's all just shit. The little demons do exist though. I watched the townsfolk torture the Blue when they caught it."

The idea of it made Renira uneasy. She didn't know if the creatures were demons or not, but the Grey looked almost human. Almost like a child. "What did they do to it?"

Gemp pulled a face as though the meat he was chewing tasted off. "Folk strung it up near the Sanguine Forge. They didn't know how to kill it. Each of the little demons can only be hurt by one thing, or so they say. They tried a whole lot of different stuff." He shook his head sadly. "Turns out just about anything can hurt them. They tried burning it, and the thing screamed. Didn't die though. They tried cutting it with iron, ceramics, glass. It screamed like it hurt, but still it didn't die. Wasn't until they tried bashing its head in with a rock that they put it down for good."

"That's horrible," Renira said. She knew heretics were executed all over Helesia. Anyone who was found with seditious materials or harbouring a divinity, or anyone interrogated by a Truth Seeker and found guilty, they were executed by law. She had even seen the aftermath in Riverden where the local laws were death by hanging, but to think of people torturing a creature, even one suspected of being a demon, in public was terrible.

"Aye, it was. Almost as terrible as the cheering. You ever seen an execution? No? Well, I seen bloody plenty. Nasty shit. Folk cheer it like it's the best bloody show they ever seen."

Renira felt sick to her stomach. "And they had no proof it had actually done anything wrong?"

Gemp shrugged. "Far as I know it's all rumour. Nobody ever come forward saying they lost a child to one of the little demons. Someone said one took their dog once, but I guess that was enough."

"Enough to condemn a creature to torture and death?" Renira asked.

"Don't take much, girl. Don't take much at all."

"It doesn't matter," Armstar said. "I already told you, there's nothing down in the mines. No demons. No monsters. Just... trust me."

Dussor and Kerrel were waiting for them at the city outskirts. The sun was starting to dip below the eastern horizon when Renira saw them waving. They were standing outside a large stone building apart from all others nearby. It was built of rough grey stone and had small, barred windows. To Renira, it looked much like the gaol from back in Riverden, only smaller and without any guards sitting outside. She had once seen a man languishing in that gaol, his hands gripping hold of the bars of his cell window, face pressed against the metal. She never knew what that man had done, only that he was there one day and gone the next. A body hanging from the Riverden gallows. It had seemed such a waste of a man's life, but when Merebeth had asked what else should be done with someone who unrepentantly breaks the law, Renira had no answers. She found she rarely had answers, only questions and so many of them.

"It's about time," Kerrel said. She wore a severe look that tugged on the scar bisecting her face. A half empty bottle of whiskey dangled from a hand that trembled.

"Dirty works done," Dussor said, he was fiddling with a ring on little finger, twisting it around and around, and he wouldn't meet Renira's eyes.

Armstar ignored them both. He stepped up to the building, pulled the door open, and moved inside without a word. Eleseth, still bringing up the rear, bowed her head to both Kerrel and Dussor. "Thank you for waiting. And for your sacrifice."

"Tell me it's worth it," Kerrel said, staring at Eleseth like she was the last rays of light on the final day. "Tell me this is what we've been working for all these years. That the result will be worth the cost. Worth every drop of blood spilled." It was an intense thing to say, and the pleading look on Kerrel's face only made it seem more grave. Renira glanced down to see a splash of red staining the stone beneath their feet. It looked like someone had thrown water across it, trying to wash away the evidence, but some violence had happened here and recently.

Eleseth nodded and placed a large hand on Kerrel's shoulder. "This is it. The Herald will bring salvation to us all. God will forgive you. I promise."

There were tears in Kerrel's eyes. "For everything?"

"For everything."

Kerrel let out a ragged breath and stared at Renira then. Renira didn't like the look in the woman's eyes, full of feverish hope like a drowning woman seeing dry land. "Thank you," she said, her voice breaking on the words. "Thank you!"

"Uhh..."

Kerrel rushed forward and sank down onto one knee. She grabbed one of Renira's hand and held it between her own. They were scarred hands, spotted with red stains. "Blessed be the reborn," Kerrel said. "Let his light fill me and shine from me. I am but a vessel for his will. Forgive me."

"Um..." Renira looked around for help. Eleseth caught her gaze and gave her a nod. "You're forgiven?"

A ragged sob burst from Kerrel's lips, and she trembled with it, still clutching at Renira's hands. Eventually the scarred woman let go and stood, wiping her eyes. She took a deep breath and then sighed it out. There was no tremble in her now. No question or indecision. Whatever conflict she had been suffering, it was gone, leaving only resolve. "Let's move," the acolyte said in a firm voice.

Renira chewed her lip. The whole thing made her uncomfortable. She did not like being treated like some messianic figure. She was not the Saint nor an angel. She still wasn't sure she wanted to be the Herald. She had no right to forgive anyone for anything they had done. And yet, two simple words seemed to provide Kerrel with such comfort. Even if they were a lie, even if she had no right to speak them, surely it was worth it to give that comfort to another? It had cost her nothing but given Kerrel so much. But then why did it make her feel so uncomfortable?

"I still think it's madness going down there," Gemp said, chewing on something again.

"Good job nobody asked you, old man," Dussor said.

Gemp nodded. "True enough. They never do."

"Are there really demons?" Sun asked. "Like the one in the forest?" He clutched his spear tight and suddenly seemed small. The fading light caught in his eyes and put an unnatural glint in their darkness.

"It's a mine, Sun. That demon from the forest wouldn't fit down there," Renira said a bit too sharply. The encounter with Kerrel had left her feeling awkward and snappish.

"There's no demons," Dussor said with a smile. "Only darkness and rock." He stopped smiling, and his face went grave. "And the ghosts of all the miners who didn't get out in time."

"Ghosts?" Renira squeaked. Elsa used to tell ghost stories all the time. The Maiden of White Water. The Seven Deaths of Fairweather Yhom. She seemed to have no end of the gruesome tales, and Renira always felt her skin tingling and eyes beginning to well up every time she was told one. She hated ghost stories.

"Dussor," Eleseth said as she strode past them.

Dussor grinned. "Sorry, my lady. There are no ghosts." He waited for Eleseth to enter the building, then turned back to Renira, nodded, and mouthed the word. *Ghosts.*

Renira was no longer certain if she was more scared of the wolf princess chasing them or the abandoned mine they were about to step foot into. She clutched her mother's amulet with one hand and found Sun gripping hold of her other. It was warm and clammy, but the contact gave her strength.

There wasn't much to see inside the building. One half of it was set up as a watch post, with a table and chairs, a small stove for boiling water, and a cot with ruffled blankets. It was abandoned, but Renira spotted blood stains on the table and the stone floor beneath. She didn't say anything but had a feeling there would be bodies hidden somewhere nearby. It seemed both the angels and their acolytes were willing to kill for their cause. For her cause, when she thought about it. She supposed that meant the blood was another thing on her conscience. She hoped their end had been quick at least, but even that was scant comfort. How many people had to die for her now she was the Herald? How many more people might die once the God was reborn?

The other half of the building was locked behind iron bars. A gaol cell, the only occupant a wooden trapdoor with chains crossed over it, the links secured to the stone beneath.

"Keys?" Armstar asked.

Kerrel shook her head. "Didn't have any on them. The governor probably keeps them."

"Eleseth. Do it."

Eleseth strode to the bars and gripped the door in both hands. She wrenched it hard, and both the hinges and lock gave way easily, the door coming free in her hands. She leaned it against the bars, then stepped inside the cell and reached out for the chains holding the trapdoor in place. The links bent and tore apart under her strength.

Sun leaned in close to Renira. "Why isn't Broken Wings that strong?"

Renira shrugged. "He said it was something to do with his immortality shield being broken."

"Eh?"

Dussor cleared his throat, and Renira glanced to her other side to find him standing close. "It's best not to ask," he said. "Armstar can be quite grumpy, though I'm sure you haven't noticed."

Renira shook her head. "Cheery as a sunflower in summer usually."

Eleseth finished tearing the chains away and then snapped the lock holding the trapdoor in place. Whatever was down there, the people of New Gurrund had gone to a lot of trouble to keep it locked away. Eleseth pulled open the trapdoor, and a plume of dust came with it. An earthy smell filled the building, stale air and something musty.

"Everyone climb down quickly," Armstar said. "Close the door and leave as little trace as we can."

Gemp grumbled. "The last time I'll say it, Armstar. Are you sure about this? Not many folk remember these old mines, but those that do say they're a maze. Some say the passageways change as you walk 'em. And there's things down there just waiting to come across lost fools." He finished by reaching into a pouch on his belt, pulling something out and shoving it into his mouth to start chewing.

"I built this city, and I dug these mines with my own hands. There's nothing mystical about them, just darkness and rumour. And believe me, we will be the most dangerous things down there. We need to make sure we lose Perel, and down there she will never find us."

"Where do they lead?" Renira asked. "We're not just descending into mines to hide, are we? I don't fancy being trapped underground. You're leading us somewhere. So, what's down there?"

"Art. The greatest work of art ever created. Or at least it should have been. Now shut up and move!"

It didn't seem like much of an answer to Renira, but it was certainly the only one Armstar planned on giving her. He tucked his wings in tight and leapt down into the mineshaft, followed quickly by Eleseth. Kerrel turned around and slid feet first into the hole, then started climbing down a ladder. Then it was Renira's turn. She peered into the darkness. It seemed a fair way down, but she could see faint light far below. She turned around and gingerly began sliding her feet into the hole, pausing while she found the first rung of the ladder.

Sun was standing close by, staring at her. "You can do it, Ren. Far easier than climbing out the window."

The reminder of that night and the fall did nothing to bolster her spirits. She kept imagining the Grey down in the dark with burning coals for eyes, waiting for her. She clutched to each rung so hard her hands hurt, but climbing down a ladder in the dark was not nearly as bad as down the outside of a building. For a start, she couldn't see the ground below her, and for some reason that made things better. It was a shock when her foot found solid rock rather than another ladder rung. Renira backed away into the arms of Eleseth. The angel held her for a few moments and warmth flowed out of her, surrounding Renira in a soothing glow, so motherly and tender.

Sun was the next one down, grinning even as his feet touched the rock. "It's too easy with a ladder," he beamed with pride over how quickly he had made the climb. Renira shook her head and tried to summon the energy to pull herself free of Eleseth. There was something so calming and reassuring about the angel, her embrace was both comforting and protective. It made Renira want to close her eyes and fall asleep in Eleseth's arms.

Dussor and finally Gemp made the climb down, and their little group was ready. Armstar pulled a lantern out of his pack and brought a flame to the wick. "We have at least a day's walk ahead of us before we reach the breach. I don't intend for us to stop."

He set off at a brisk pace and left them to follow.

They were in a rough-hewn mineshaft, just tall enough for Eleseth to walk without a stoop and wide enough for three of them to walk abreast. Every dozen steps or so a rotting wooden prop, two vertical beams and a cross beam, was nailed into the shaft to help keep the tunnel stable. Renira noticed a few picks left strewn around the floor, the metal rusting.

"What happened here that they were in such a rush as to leave their tools behind?" she asked as they made their way through the tunnel. Sun was at her side, his spear held tightly in his hands.

"Who says they left the tools behind?" Dussor said as he slotted in between Renira and Sun. "Maybe the things down here took the bodies but had no use for the tools."

He glanced down at Renira, a grave look on his face. "You hear stories. Pale hands in the dark scratching at walls, fingernails torn bloody. People locked down in the darkness so long they lose themselves, eat each other, eat themselves, gnawing away at their own arms just for a scrap of meat." He snapped his teeth together dramatically.

"You're not funny, Dussor," Renira said. She felt like she could feel eyes watching her from the darkness, making her skin itch.

"Who's trying to be funny? It's a warning. There are things down in the darkness, my lady. Terrible things. Things with sharp teeth and no eyes. Things that tear flesh and devour..."

"Shut up!" Renira gave him a shove and hurried forward to walk next to Eleseth.

They came across a junction at which the tunnel split three ways. Armstar didn't even hesitate as he turned down the left tunnel. They all followed without question.

"What's down here, Eleseth?" Renira asked. "Why won't Armstar tell us?"

The angel sighed. "I don't know. I assume he has his reasons for keeping it secret. Whatever those might be."

"You don't know?" It seemed incredulous that the angels might be keeping secrets from each other.

"He won't tell me either. Orphus said to follow him and to trust him. I'm managing one of those things."

"You don't trust him?" Renira asked, her voice a whisper that seemed to echo throughout the tunnel.

"I find it hard to trust one of the Fallen. He's no longer... bound to our father." Eleseth shook her head. "But I believe he's still loyal."

Renira frowned. She had heard Armstar called many things, the Builder, the Unburnt, Broken Wings, but she'd never heard anyone call him Fallen before. "What does that mean? Fallen? Is it because of his wings?"

"No," Eleseth said wistfully. "It's the other way around. A fallen angel is one of us who has committed a great sin. Broken a rule the God laid down for us. There are only two Fallen. Armstar and Karna." Sun made a noise almost like a whimper.

"Karna is the Forgemistress?" Renira said. "You said she rules Ashvold. Do you know her, Sun?"

The boy shook his head savagely. "Why would I know her?"

"Karna is my sister," Eleseth said with a weary sigh. "Probably a truer sister than any other. Karna was... is an angel of the Second Age. For a long time she was a friend. We spread the word of God together and taught humanity to read and write and how to forge tools with runes that would enhance their purpose. Then she betrayed us. Betrayed our father."

That was something the books never mentioned. They said all of God's children loved him without reservation. "How?"

"Karna sided with the enemy. When Ertide Hostain started his Crusade, he had no weapons to fight us. His tactic was to attack angels with numbers, to throw lives at us until we had killed too many and our immortality shields broke. Only then were we vulnerable enough to murder. Karna changed all of that. In secret she forged seven weapons, the Godslayer arms, and gave them to our enemy. She gave them the weapons they needed to kill the God. She did it without us knowing, otherwise our father would have stopped her."

Why would an angel turn against God? What could make one of his own children help kill him?

"Why did she betray God?" Renira asked.

"I don't know," Eleseth said sadly. "I asked her once, years after Ertide's Crusade was ended. She didn't answer, just tried to kill me. I miss her, the way she used to be before..."

"You know why she did it," Armstar said from up front. "Karna desires power as much as the Godless King. That's why she learned from them." He glanced over his shoulder. "We might both be Fallen, but Karna and I are nothing alike. She devours other angels."

"What?" Renira said.

"Keep moving, Herald," Kerrel said, gently pushing Renira in the back.

Armstar forged ahead until his lantern was a lone spot of light in the darkness. Eleseth's glow dimmed until it was barely visible. She settled into a maudlin mood and looked unwilling to say more.

"It's true," Sun said from beside Renira. "Karna eats other angels. And worse things. She feeds people her own blood. I've seen it. Everyone in the palace sees it."

Renira frowned as she tried to take it all in. "You lived in the palace, Sun?"

The boy nodded. "I'm..." He fell silent but looked like he wanted to say more. "People disappear in the palace. We weren't supposed to talk about it. Just... That's why we escaped."

"What do you mean people disappeared?"

Sun's hands clenched around his spear, and he stared at the ground. "Angels aren't the only things Karna eats."

Renira wished she could ferret out all of Sun's story, but every time she thought she was getting close, he clammed up.

They continued in silence for a while as Renira considered the implications. She wasn't certain which, if any, of her protectors she should now trust. Armstar was a grumpy, heartless bastard. In fact Renira had only met one man pricklier to deal with, and Brut had good reason; the old veteran had lost both his legs to a rampaging bull and lived on the charity of the people of Riverden. But Armstar had been with Renira from the beginning of this adventure, and her mother had trusted him enough to send her only daughter off with him. Yet Eleseth seemed so kind and gentle. She had saved Sun's life.

There was too much at stake, too much she didn't yet understand. And it felt like everyone was lying to her, keeping things from her. *One way or another, it's time to start digging some truths out of them all.*

CHAPTER 30

Exemplar Karta's betrayal is what we term a confluence point. A moment in history when one person makes a decision so profound it alters the very fabric of society and causes a shift. The Exemplars were humanity's greatest heroes, and yet, Karta tried to bring down everything Saint Dien had tried to build. Exemplar Karta caused the Shattering.

— HIDDEN HISTORIES: THE SECOND AGE BY
RENNIFER SONG, CHIEF HISTORIAN AT EVERHEIM
UNIVERSITY

A few hours into the march and Renira found her feet scuffing the rocky ground. Her legs ached, and her mind drifted. The rock around them glistened wetly in the swaying light of the lanterns, and she wondered if there was water nearby, some underground river or cavern filled with cool, still water that had never seen sunlight. It was oddly romantic to think of a giant lake underground sitting undiscovered and untouched. They could be explorers, the first humans to see the lake. Renira would name it Lake Solitude, and it would forever sit on maps with the name she had given it.

"We need to stop," Kerrel said.

"No," Armstar was up ahead and didn't even glance over his shoulder. "There's no time."

Kerrel stopped regardless and gazed at Renira, a look of reverence on her face. "The day will soon pass, and I haven't prayed."

"God will understand," Armstar said.

Gemp and Dussor stopped alongside Kerrel, and even Eleseth halted. Sun was at the rear, barely paying attention and yawned loudly, looking up at the others only when he realised everyone had stopped.

"I'm hungry," he said.

Renira's stomach gave an answering rumble of agreement. "I wouldn't mind something to eat."

"Perhaps a short break," Eleseth said. "Give our Herald some time to rest."

Armstar finally stopped. He glanced back at them all, wings twitching. "Fine."

Kerrel took a step toward Renira. "Will you join us, Herald?"

"What?" Renira blurted. She didn't like the way Kerrel looked at her, eyes all wide and that warm half smile. It was the way a freezing woman might stare at a fire, knowing it was her salvation.

"Will you join us in prayer?" Kerrel held out a hand.

"I... uh..." She had done this thousands of times with her mother. Every day before bed, they had prayed together to the God. But it had always been ritual, just something she did with her mother, never something she believed. And the moment she had left with Armstar, as soon as her mother wasn't there to enforce it, she had stopped.

Kerrel's face went stony. "Will you join us in prayer to the God, Herald?"

Sun hustled in front of Renira, holding his spear across his body. "Back off. If Ren doesn't want to, she doesn't have to."

All eyes were on Renira now. Kerrel starting to look suspicious. Gemp calculating, Dussor confused. Armstar had a sly smile on his face, and Eleseth looked concerned.

"It's all right, Sun," Renira said. She put a hand on his shoulder and gently moved him aside. "Of course I'll pray with you."

Kerrel beamed, the scar on her face making the smile awkward, but the reverence returned. Renira caught Armstar shake his head and sneer as he turned away, clearly disappointed.

Why is he disappointed in me? Isn't this what he wants?

"Which way is north?" Kerrel asked. "Builder, which way?"

Armstar sighed and flung out an arm, pointing. Somehow he could tell even deep underground with no sun or moons to guide him.

"Here, Herald," Kerrel said, taking Renira's arm and pulling her along. "Beside me. We'll pray together. For salvation and... for forgiveness." There was something urgent about it, something desperate. Earlier, Kerrel had asked God to forgive her, asked Renira to forgive her. Now here it was again. Renira wondered what the woman had done that she was so desperate to be forgiven for.

She knelt beside Kerrel, facing a rough stone wall that glistened black with damp. Gemp and Dussor knelt behind them, Gemp grumbling about his knees and Dussor showing off by standing and then kneeling a few times as if trying to find the right spot. Then each of the acolytes took out their icons of faith. Renira knew all this, had seen it with her mother and had been through it every day. Everyone who worshipped had their own icon.

Gemp, for once not chewing on anything, pulled out a ragged cloth doll from an inside jacket pocket; it was a rabbit, Renira thought, worn and faded and many times stitched together. One eye was a button, the other was missing. Whatever its significance, the old man handled it with a tenderness she would not have thought him capable of. He brushed aside some dust from the rocky floor, then placed a small brown scarf there, and eventually rested the doll on the square of cloth. Finally, he bent his head to it, whispered words spilling from his lips.

Dussor reached into his bag and retrieved a small book no bigger than his hand. When he opened it, the pages were all blank. He flipped through to the middle and there, pressed between the pages was a flower with purple petals and a long green stem. He raised the book to his face and drew in a deep breath through his nose, then closed the book again and held it sandwiched between his hands.

Kerrel drew a dagger from her boot. Her hands trembled a little as she held it, the blade reversed so it was pointed at her chest. Renira saw spots on the blade, and as she peered closer, she realised they were blood and rust. The blade had obviously not been cleaned in a long time, perhaps since it had been used.

"Forgive me," the lead acolyte mumbled.

Renira tore her eyes from the bloodstained blade, feeling awkward as though she had intruded on something deeply personal. She found Kerrel staring at her again, eyes full of pleading. She didn't know what to do, hated being put in such a situation. But if she could ease the woman's conscience even a little with no more than a few words, then surely they were worth speaking. That was what her mother would do. Kindness for kindness' sake.

Renira nodded at Kerrel. "Forgiveness," she said. Then she reached inside her blouse and pulled out her mother's Bone Moon amulet. It was not her icon, she didn't have one, but it was more important to Renira than that. It was her connection to her mother, no matter how far apart they might be.

Renira didn't pray. While the acolytes mumbled their words and begged the God for wisdom and the strength to go on and offered up their sacrifices, Renira only stared at the amulet in her hand and silently asked her mother if she was doing the right thing. She got no answer.

The prayers only lasted a few minutes, and then Gemp and Dussor stood and salted rations were handed out. Renira knelt with Kerrel a while longer while the scarred woman stared in silence at the rock wall before her.

Wondering why your prayers go unanswered? Renira couldn't understand it. No one alive had ever seen or heard the God, yet still these acolytes believed and prayed and hoped he would speak to them from beyond the grave.

"What's the significance of the dagger?" Renira asked.

Kerrel startled and fumbled the dagger. It clattered to the stone, and she quickly scooped it up and thrust it back into its boot sheath. "Sorry, Herald. I was lost in my own thoughts for a moment."

"You can call me Renira."

Kerrel gazed at her, a smile tugging on her scar. "Thank you, Herald."

"Please call me Renira."

Kerrel kept staring at her and shook her head.

Renira fought the urge to roll her eyes. "The dagger?"

"Oh," Kerrel frowned, and her hand strayed to her boot, stroking the sheath. "I... I..."

"You don't have to tell me."

"I do!" Kerrel said quickly. She shuffled around to face Renira and grabbed her hands, holding them tightly in her own. That disturbing look of reverence was in her eyes again, and Renira wished she hadn't asked.

When she spoke, it was with a feverish urgency. "I grew up in Dien. A city called Alderist. It's... Ah, tell it like it is. It's a shit hole. A lot like New Gurrund. Not the smog or forges, but lots of trade and the gangs. Half the city is built into the mountain, hewn right from the rock, and the other half is a sprawling shanty. There's no rangers there, and the gangs rule everything. Their word is law as much as the king's.

"I used to live in the mountainside, dreamed about living out in the light. My da was a Cutter. That's, uh..." She trailed off, took a deep breath. "Cutters kill people for money."

"That's horrible," Renira said. She knew criminals and bandits existed, had seen some in stocks back in Riverden, but they had always seemed like such a distant story.

Kerrel's face crumpled in pain, and she nodded. "It is, aye. Horrible."

"Sorry," Renira said, giving her hands a squeeze. "I didn't mean to insult your father. Was he kind? To you, I mean?"

Kerrel nodded and smiled. She was not so old as Renira had first thought. Older than her, for certain, but still young despite her scars. "From what I remember, he was wonderful. Kind and loving. He used to bring me cakes every day.

"One day he, uh... he killed the wrong person. Was paid to kill a merchant but got it wrong, I think. Killed some noble brat. Gangs made an example of him so the king wouldn't come down on them. My ma tried to stop it. They killed her, too."

Renira gave her hands another squeeze.

"The gangs in Alderist take orphans in and train them up to work for them. They trained me to be a Cutter just like my da."

"Oh..." Renira to pulled her hands away. She'd never met a criminal before, especially not a murderer. Kerrel gasped and clutched her hands together. She stared at the ground hard.

"I was good at it. I'm sorry, Herald, but I was so bloody good at it. Killed a lot of people with that very dagger. Then I fell foul of the same crime my da did. Killed the wrong man. I met the bastard who killed my da, head of one of the gangs. I don't think he knew who I was, but I knew him. I remembered him! He welcomed me in with open arms, and I stuck my dagger in his neck. Ain't sorry for that. So much else, everything else, but not that.

"Had to run after. Alderist wasn't safe. Shit! None of Dien was safe, so I came to Helesia. I still remember every face. All of them. My kills. My..."

"Your victims?" Renira asked. She didn't mean it to sound so cold and accusatory.

Kerrel winced as though Renira had stabbed her and nodded slowly.

Renira wondered if this was a consequence of the God being dead? Kerrel had moved, run away, but she hadn't moved on. She was stuck, praying to the dead, begging for forgiveness for the same old crimes day after day. She was stuck. Would God's rebirth finally allow her to move on?

Does she deserve to? She's a murderer. Renira offering her forgiveness suddenly took on a new meaning. *Would I have said the words to offer her comfort if I had known? Would Mother have offered her comfort knowing she was a murderer?* Kerrel certainly seemed repentant, begging for forgiveness, but was that enough?

They started moving again, Armstar setting a gruelling pace. Renira found herself walking beside him. Armstar was sullen as an autumn sun and grumpy as a drunk wasp, but there was something oddly comforting about him. Perhaps because he was her mother's friend. She felt a kinship to him.

"You look lost," Armstar said quietly.

Renira sighed. "Well, we are underground, and I have no idea where we're going. I am the very definition of lost."

The angel's mouth twitched into a smile, but it was gone quickly. "I know the way, and that was a deflection."

Renira chewed on the question. It was probably a stupid question to ask an angel. "How do they believe so strongly in someone they've never seen? They know by your own admittance that God is dead, yet they pray to him every day. Ask him for forgiveness, offer up their sacrifices. Where does that faith in an absent father come from?"

"Absent father..." Armstar sighed, and for a moment he looked truly broken. He opened his mouth to say something, then closed it, and the vulnerability vanished.

"The thing about faith is that it doesn't need reason or purpose. Or proof. It just is. If you can believe in God without him showing himself, that's faith."

"What if I can't believe without that proof?"

"Then maybe you already have your answer. It's just not the one you were hoping for." He glanced at her then and smiled. He seemed less the bitter grump and more kind and fatherly. Renira wondered if this was the side of him her mother saw?

"That doesn't sound like something an angel would say. Aren't you supposed to be all *Believe in God. He is mighty and benevolent*?"

Armstar shrugged. "I'd rather you make up your own mind. Even if in doing so you condemn us all."

Renira snorted out a laugh, but when she looked at Armstar, his face was deadly serious. "No pressure then?"

Aesie scratched a little mark into the supporting beam. The stone she was using scraped away old, rotting wood and revealed a lighter colour beneath. It wasn't much of a trail, but she hoped it would be enough for someone to follow. One mark on the supporting beams each time the tunnel split and the group picked their new direction.

Renira and her odd troupe were almost out of sight again, the light from their lanterns nothing but a spot of yellow in the distance. If Aesie lost them now, she could wander the tunnels for the rest of her life and never find the way out. And it wouldn't be a very long life given that she had no supplies and no light save for the softly glowing earring in her hand.

It had been a gift many years ago from her father, to make her stand out even in the dark. A pair of metal earrings of birds in flight, they absorbed light during the day, and glowed a little during the night, or in this case, the dark. It wasn't much of a light to guide her through the tunnels and the glow would fade soon, but for now it was just enough to stop her tripping over rocks or running into tunnel walls. She hurried after the bobbing light in the distance, moving as quietly as possible but closing the distance so she didn't lose them. She could hear voices drifting down the length of the tunnel, but they were indistinct sounds.

Aesie knew she should have waited for the king's soldiers to return and tell them what she had seen, which way the Herald had gone, but that would never be enough to earn the reward. It was likely too much time would have been lost, and they would have escaped. So, she had set out on her own, following Renira and keeping her distance so she wasn't spotted.

It was a skill she had learned to follow her father around, both in their estate and out in Riverden. Aesie had gotten quite good at trailing a person and just as good at sneaking into her father's study and picking the locks on his drawers to read his private correspondence. That was how she knew the truth. Her father was dying of lung rot. A slow disease, it took many years to kill a person, and her father had already had it for quite a few according to his physician's letters. There was no cure. Well, there was no cure any doctor could offer, and even with all the money and business they owned, they couldn't afford one drop of the only thing that could save Aesie's father. One drop. And yet King Emrik was offering more than that. Dangling the reward of divine blood in front of Aesie, and all she had to do to earn it was betray her closest friend. It sounded like such an easy price to pay, but it wasn't. It was the toughest decision Aesie had ever made.

Renira would understand eventually, and it was for her own good really. These people she had fallen in with were heretics, and Aesie would turn them in and rescue her friend. They might even go on to Celesgarde together afterwards. She had already secured a spot at the Arkenhold University, and with a few coins in the right place, or a good word from the king even, she was certain she could get Renira in as well. Yes, it was for the best. Renira might not agree at first but... It was for the best.

Ahead, the group stopped for a moment, the bobbing yellow light shining around dark figures standing still. They were crowded around something, talking, their words lost to Aesie. She heard a scrabbling noise behind her and turned, holding up her earring. For a moment, she thought she saw two dots of burning red further back in the darkness of the tunnel, but they were gone so quickly she dismissed them as fancy or the lingering spots of light upon her eyes. Any scrabbling was probably just rats. An old mine shaft like this was likely infested with the little vermin. That thought sent a shiver down her spine. Rats were nasty little creatures, scurrying about in the dark and stealing food from people. Merebeth had once said they were really quite clean, as far as beasts went, but they certainly didn't look it. Besides, most people said they carried all sorts of diseases and ailments, so Beth had to be wrong regardless of how improbable that seemed.

When Aesie turned back to Renira's odd group, they were moving again. She hurried forward, following the light at another split in the tunnel and making a new mark on the next supporting beam. She passed where the group had stopped and glanced down to see bloody brown rags in a pile, old bones strewn about nearby. It looked an awful lot like a baby's swaddle, but Aesie didn't have the courage to look any closer. Renira's little group moved faster now, their pace quickened. Aesie hurried after them once more.

Such an odd troupe, a hunchback, a giant barbarian from Aelegar, a woman with more scar than face. Not to mention the little boy playing at being a solider, and the old man who looked like he had two feet in the grave yet was still desperately clinging to life. But Aesie supposed heretics came in all shapes and sizes. It was just a shame Renira had fallen in with them. It was probably her mother's doing. Everyone knew Lusa Washer was a bad influence, shirking the laws whenever it suited her.

"Well, what have we here?" said a man. A hand landed on Aesie's shoulder. Fear pulsed through her, a terror so sudden it purged all thought.

She spun, dislodged the hand from her shoulder, and punched the young man in the face. He accepted it with a grunt but little else and then surged forward. A hand wrapped around Aesie's neck, and she was shoved up against the rocky wall of the tunnel. Sharp edges dug into her back, softened by her winter coat. She struggled against the man's grip, punching him again and again.

"Stop it!" the man said, warding off her attacks with his free hand while still gripping hold of her neck with his other. "Stop bloody hitting me, woman."

Renira heard a commotion behind them. Raised voices and a grunt of pain, a woman squeaking in alarm. She turned to see Dussor was gone. A short way behind them, barely visible in the dark, two figures struggled up against the wall of the tunnel. Kerrel was the first to react, drawing her sword and stalking towards the conflict, her lantern raised. Renira followed quickly with Sun running at her side.

"Stop hitting me, you feral bitch!" Dussor snapped. He had someone pinned up against the tunnel wall with one hand while the other was desperately protecting his face from a flurry of punches. By the split lip, at least one of those punches had connected. The woman Dussor had pinned stopped her attacks when Kerrel arrived with her sword drawn.

When Renira got close, a wave of weary guilt washed over her. "Get off her!" Renira shouted. She slipped in front of Kerrel and then put both hands on Dussor's chest and pushed. Dussor let go of Aesie's neck and backed off a couple of paces. He wiped blood away from his lip and glared.

Renira turned on her friend. "Aesie. What are you doing?"

More light flooded the tunnel around them as the others arrived. There was panic in Aesie's eyes, and she glanced around at all the faces staring at her. She was breathing heavily, and tears streaked down her cheeks.

"The bitch was following us," Dussor said. He spat bloody spittle onto the ground.

"She's Renira's friend," Eleseth said.

"Why was she following us?" Armstar sounded angry.

"Enough!" Renira said and turned on the others, putting herself between them. "Leave her alone. Go stand over there, and let me handle this." She pointed down the tunnel, the way they had been heading. They weren't helping matters, and they were more likely to get answers out of Aesie if she wasn't terrified.

Kerrel shrugged and turned away, sheathing her sword. Gemp, chewing on something that looked like a green stick poking out of his mouth, went with her and the two of them started talking in whispers. Dussor grumbled and backed up to stand against the far side of the tunnel, but he kept his eyes trained on Aesie. Eleseth joined Kerrel and Gemp. Neither Sun nor Armstar moved at all. Sun had his spear held ready, and Armstar placed his lantern on the ground and folded his arms. He motioned toward Aesie. "Deal with it, then."

Renira held Armstar's hostile stare for a moment, then turned back to Aesie. There were more important things than the angel throwing yet another tantrum. "Why are you following us?"

A look of panic crossed her friend's face again, eyes darting between them. She blinked away tears and stared at the ground. She was still panting, and her hands were balled into fists, clutching at her skirts, but she sniffed, and when she looked up again there was some clarity in her gaze. "To rescue you."

"Rescue me?" Renira said, suppressing a manic giggle that threatened to burst from her lips. "From what?"

Aesie glanced around those still gathered nearby. "From them. Ha—haven't you been kidnapped?"

Armstar groaned and turned away, leaving the lantern on the rocky floor.

"Don't mind him," Renira said. "A winter's bite is cheerier than Armstar."

Aesie shook her head. "You haven't been kidnapped?"

Why did everyone think she needed protecting? The angels, Sun, now even Aesie. And what was worse was that they were right. She did need protecting. She just didn't want to need it. In her dreams, she had always been the protector, fighting to save those who couldn't save themselves.

"Of course not. What made you think I've been kidnapped?"

"Them!" Aesie said, waving a hand around. "They're all a bit... I mean..." She paused, and then the words just rushed out of her. "You've never left Riverden before, and now here you are in New Gurrund with an odd bunch of vagabonds I've never even met. And they don't exactly look... nice. This one grabbed me by the neck. He grabbed me by the neck! I'd expect this sort of thing from Elsa, but not you, Ren. Who are they all? How do you know them? What are you doing here?"

Renira considered how much it was safe to tell Aesie and quickly realised the answer was nothing, or as close to nothing as she could get away with. The more her friend knew about angels and Heralds and the God, the more danger Aesie would find herself in. She needed to go back, follow her father's wishes all the way to the capital and the universities. Live a life free of the peril Renira was neck deep in.

"They're my mother's friends. And I'm helping them. That's all I can say, Aesie. You need to head back to New Gurrund. It's not safe here. Armstar, can we send someone back with Aesie?"

"No. We can't spare anyone. She got here alone; she can find her way back on her own."

Renira ground her teeth. Armstar couldn't be so callous that he would be truly be willing to leave a young woman alone down in the mine without any light. *Don't be stupid, he's definitely that callous.* He cared little for anything but his quest.

"We can't just leave her here!"

Armstar sent her a withering look over his shoulder. "Yes. We can." He walked back to them and plucked the lantern from the floor. "We're moving on. Keep up."

"Bring her along, Renira," said Eleseth. "Right now, that's safest for all of us. We'll figure out what to do with her later." The angel turned and followed the light of the lanterns.

"Is the hunchback really in charge?" Aesie asked quietly.

Renira took Aesie's hand and pulled her along. The last thing any of them wanted was to be left without the light of the lanterns. Sun walked on the other side of Aesie and kept glancing at her. Dussor paced behind them, dabbing a cloth against his split lip, and Renira could feel his eyes on her back.

They chatted and swapped stories as they walked, each of them taking it in turn to lurch into another league of their journey, neither one telling it in order. When Renira told Aesie of her arrival in New Gurrund and sneaking out to the Night Market, Aesie gasped. She pulled Renira to a stop and grinned as she stared.

"Well, it's about time you started wearing some jewellery, but why did you pick something so drab? It's always browns and whites with you. So dull. And wood. Wooden jewellery now. Absolutely no sense of fashion."

Renira smiled. She knew some people, including Elsa, found Aesie's relentless worship of fashion to be exhausting, but Renira had always liked it. Through Aesie, she got to see such beautiful things, even if she knew she'd never own anything so grand.

"I didn't exactly have much money, Aesie. Or any. Actually Dussor paid for it."

Aesie snorted. "That just makes it even worse, Ren. You can't go around accepting jewellery from any rude stranger you meet. Here." She reached out quickly and undid the clasp, slipping the point out of Renira's ear. She gasped quietly, it was still a little sore.

"Sorry," Aesie said. She pocketed Renira's wooden earring and reached into a pouch at her belt and pulled out a small silver bird with a blue gemstone set in its eye. A soft haze of light shone from the earring. Aesie grinned. "We'll match!" She turned her head to show she was wearing an identical earring.

"Aesie. It's far too expensive."

Aesie waved away the comment. "Tsk, hush. This is why you need me, Ren. It's only money, and I have plenty."

Renira knew she meant it well, but the comment still hurt a little. Money had never come between them. They both always knew Aesie was rich and Renira was one day ahead of destitution, but when they were together it never seemed important. Aesie was generous, always giving away things she said she didn't need or were out of fashion. It pained Renira she could never give anything back.

"And now..." Aesie squinted as she gently poked the silver earring through Renira's ear. "If we're ever lost in the dark, we'll be able to find each other." All done, she pulled back, grinning in the soft glow of her own earring.

Renira touched her new earring and suddenly wished she had a mirror so she could see it. Tears welled in her eyes, and she hugged Aesie fiercely. After that, everything felt almost normal again for a time. If Renira tried to block out the fact they were trudging through an abandoned mineshaft that may or may not be filled with child-eating demons, that she was the Herald and the only one capable of bringing the God back to life, and that she was being chased not only by the Godless King but also his wolf princess, she could almost pretend that it was just another day of talking about everything and nothing with Aesie. For a short time, all the danger and fear seemed further away.

But it wasn't just another day, and no matter how hard she pretended, Renira knew nothing was normal. Her life would never be normal again, and she mourned the loss of it. She didn't know if she was doing the right thing. Bringing the God back to life was certainly what her mother wanted, it was what the angels wanted, but Renira didn't know if *she* truly wanted it. All she knew was that she didn't have a choice. The Godless King wouldn't stop chasing her. That scared Renira more than she ever thought possible.

CHAPTER 31

"We're here," Armstar announced. Though *here* appeared to be a dead end. In the lantern light, Renira saw nothing but boulders and rubble. A collapsed tunnel. Armstar had led them to a collapsed tunnel at the far depths of a mine. She started to consider the possibility that the angel was quite mad. *Actually, that would make a lot of sense.*

As Armstar placed his lantern on the ground, Renira dumped her pack and slumped down against one of the walls of the tunnel. She was exhausted again from so much walking. Time had lost all meaning down in the darkness, and she couldn't tell if they had been walking for hours or days. In the grand scheme of things, it probably didn't matter, but right now it was the grand scheme that didn't matter to Renira. Her feet hurt and she was tired and they were lost in a mine!

"Ohhh, my feet hurt. They hurt so much," Aesie whined as she sank to her knees, her dusty riding skirts billowing out around her.

"Just your feet?" Renira asked. "My thighs feel I've been wearing sandpaper."

"Well, if we're making it a competition, my back is aching like a stubbed toe."

"You're not even carrying a pack. If you had my shoulders you'd think you'd been pulling old Poe's cart like his poor mule."

Aesie stretched her neck to the side. "If I had your shoulders, I wouldn't be surprised if someone hitched me to a cart."

Renira mock gasped.

"What?" Aesie asked. "Too harsh?"

"Little bit."

"Sorry." She reached out and patted Renira's knee. "You have lovely shoulders. Definitely not too broad or anything."

Sun collapsed next to Renira. His head lolled and rested against her shoulder, and he was snoring softly in mere moments.

Armstar and Eleseth began clearing the tunnel, using divine strength to shift boulders that no human would be able to. Kerrel crouched down and stared back the way they had come, her dark skin and clothes making her almost invisible beyond the lantern light. Gemp leaned against the far tunnel wall and closed his eyes, sleeping while standing up, though even asleep he still appeared to be chewing on something.

"He's staring at me again," Aesie whispered, glancing up at Dussor and then away. She wasn't wrong.

Dussor paced. Much of his good humour was gone since Aesie was found following them, and he kept glaring at her. Renira was somewhat used to it. All the boys back in Riverden stared at Aesie, often many of the men as well. Elsa had always hated that, the effortless way Aesie's beauty drew the attention of others, but Renira had found it oddly liberating. She often felt invisible around her closest friend, and that gave her a strange sort of freedom. But Dussor's attention was different. Renira had actually quite liked being the centre of his attention. For a time it had made her feel special; not in the same way as being the Herald, but in a more normal way.

"Maybe he likes you," Renira whispered, trying to lighten the mood and not sound bitter about it.

"I think the problem is he doesn't like me," Aesie said. She looked up and met Dussor's stare. "I'm sorry for hitting you. I didn't realise you were so fragile."

Dussor snorted and turned on his heel, continuing to pace up and down the tunnel. It was almost funny. Before, he seemed to have an irrepressibly good mood, but all it took was a couple of punches from a young woman and he was sulking worse than Armstar.

"How do you know him anyway?" Aesie asked. "Is he another one of your mother's friends?"

"I guess so," Renira said, though she really wasn't so sure. She knew nothing about her mother's life as an acolyte nor whom she might have called a friend.

"I don't mean to sound harsh, Ren. But why you? Why are you here instead of your mother?"

"I can be useful," Renira said defensively. "I saved Armstar's life back in the forest." She still had the little needle she had used to sew his wound closed, nestled away in her coat pocket. She wasn't really sure why she kept it. Maybe it was out of nostalgia for the life she had saved. It made her proud whenever she touched it and remembered that she had saved a life.

"But you can't fight. Unless you were secretly taking lessons from old Fumper all these years."

Old Fumper was the head of the Riverden guard and well known to be less than useless in a fight unless being stabbed were a sought-after skill. Legend had it he had been stabbed in every major conflict Helesia had seen in the past fifty years and was somehow still alive and allowed near sharp objects.

"And," Aesie continued, leaning forward and lowering her voice, "you don't really believe in all this angels and Heralds stuff, do you? I mean, I know your mother did, but I thought you were smarter than that."

"I didn't. But it's become quite difficult to deny. You know angels are real, Aesie?"

"Sure," Aesie said flippantly. "I mean they were, once, I guess. But they were evil. Spreading sedition and..." She trailed off, aware that Armstar had ceased digging and was staring at her. "They're not really angels, Ren. He's just a humpback and she's a freakish giant. Probably one of those Aelegar savages. But angels? The king killed them all. The God was never anything more than a mad dictator."

Eleseth was staring now, and even Gemp had opened his eyes to direct a hostile gaze toward Aesie. Still her friend forged on. "They were never divine, just immortal creatures who used humanity for their own ends."

Renira sighed. *This is not going to end well.*

Aesie was repeating the lies the Godless King spread, the lessons forced upon everyone as children. Renira had sat through the same lessons Aesie had, but even then they had sounded like lies. Her mother made her attend the lessons but warned her not to listen, and each night they had spent time reading through *The Rite of the Divine*, learning the other *truth*.

Armstar snorted and shook his head, then turned back to the collapsed tunnel and hefted another boulder. For a moment Renira thought he might throw it at Aesie, but he sent it sailing over their heads into the waiting darkness. Aesie gawked at the feat of strength.

"She'll learn soon enough," said Eleseth as she, too, returned to shifting the blocked passageway.

Aesie leaned in close, her skirts rumpling. "Surely you don't really believe, Ren?"

Renira gave her friend a weary smile. "I really don't know what to believe anymore, Aesie. I've seen things. Demons, angels, a princess eating the corpse of a man, an angel. He *was* an angel. I had spoken to just hours earlier. Eleseth can fly! I flew with her. Sort of. It was more a gliding, and she carried me really.

"I know King Emrik outlawed all worship of the God, even talking about him like this is enough to have me thrown in gaol or worse. Why would he have set those laws if the God never existed? It's all a big contradiction. But the God was real. The Godless Kings killed him, but he existed."

Aesie blew a few strands of hair away from her face. "Well of course he did. He was a tyrant, and the Godless Kings overthrew the tyrant and freed us all. You'd know that if you ever paid any attention in the lessons. It's all the more reason to do as the king says. If he can kill the God, he can definitely kill a couple of foolish girls from Riverden." She was missing the point.

"But they say the God can be resurrected," Renira said. "If the Herald rings in the new age."

"So? What if it is all true? All that about Heralds and ages and resurrection, blah. Why would anyone want to bring the God back? King Emrik already saved us from him once."

Renira hadn't even thought that Aesie might be opposed to the very idea of the quest. But then she hadn't seen the destruction of Los Hold. She hadn't seen the peaceful way they lived and the carnage wrought in the name of the Godless King. She bought into the lies King Emrik had spread. *How many others believe the lies? Does anyone but a handful of the faithful even want to be saved?*

Dussor was glaring at Aesie again, his pacing stopped. "You really don't get it. Just bleating along like a good little sheep. Everything you've been taught about the God and your immortal king has been lies. The God was our saviour and will be again. Your king is the bloody dictator."

Aesie struggled back to her feet and faced the acolyte. "That's one way of looking at things. *Your* way." She had never been able to back down from a fight, even when on the wrong side of it. But this was different. This wasn't a few foolish children back in Riverden. This was life or death, and Aesie didn't realise what danger she was in.

Dussor clenched his fists. "My way? It's *the* way. It's the truth!"

"According to you," Aesie said calmly. "I've heard a different *truth* from someone else. You say you're right and they're wrong, they say the opposite. Which am I to believe?"

Gemp grunted. "Maybe believe the side being murdered for their beliefs, rather than the side doing the murdering?"

"I..." Aesie trailed off, her argument dying in her throat. "I'm sorry. I didn't mean... I'm just trying to understand." She looked to Renira for support. But Renira didn't have any to give. She, too, was still trying to understand it all.

Most of the people of Helesia grew up believing King Emrik. He said the God was never anything more than a ruler of immortals, the angels were oppressors, and that humanity had revolted and thrown off the shackles of false faith. He outlawed all worship of the God, even talking about him was a crime that carried a terrible and final punishment. His *truth* was spread far and wide throughout his cities and villages. The God's faith was hidden away in the dark and secret. It was dying out, only the remaining angels and the most devout acolytes keeping any spark of the God's faith alive.

"We're almost through," Armstar said as he dropped a rock the size of Renira's head on the ground.

The air seemed to change a little. It tasted fresher in the lungs and cooled Renira's skin. She had barely even noticed how close and muggy the tunnel had gotten until the wave of fresh air washed over her. As Eleseth and Armstar cleared away more of the rubble, the air grew colder still, and underneath the sound of shifting rock and rubble, Renira swore she could hear the rushing of water echoing from far away.

She shook Sun awake gently and pushed the boy away from her shoulder, ignoring the patch of drool he'd left there. She eased herself off the ground and pulled her coat closer around her. It was cooling off quickly now fresher air was wafting into the tunnel. She edged along the wall closer to the two angels still clearing away debris, hoping to catch a glimpse of what lay beyond. The tunnel seemed to end, and Renira saw nothing but darkness swallowing up the lantern light. There was a sound of rushing water and something else that could have been singing, though that couldn't be right. Certainly no one else mentioned the melody. Armstar and Eleseth finished clearing away the boulders and shared a look.

"This tunnel didn't collapse," Kerrel said, looking up at the tunnel ceiling. "And there's a cavern out there. Where did the blockage come from?"

"I put it here," Armstar said. "To stop curious fools from finding this place. And it isn't a cavern." He stepped out past the end of the tunnel onto a ledge of rock surrounded by nothing but darkness. "Eleseth, show them."

They all moved forward on to the rocky ledge to stare out into the darkness, and Eleseth moved beyond them. "Stand back a bit," she warned.

Eleseth's cloak rippled as she unfurled her wings in one glorious beat. They began to glow as bright as any hearth fire Renira had ever seen, so bright she had to squint. Aesie gasped and stepped backward, but Renira took a step forward. The light from Eleseth's wings reflected off hundreds of polished surfaces hidden around the great cavern, but even so it only illuminated a small section of it. It was enough. They stood at the raised edge of a gigantic cavern hundreds of meters tall and spreading out far into the darkness, and in the centre of the cavern was a massive spire built from cut stone. It stretched all the way from the cavern floor to the roof, and Renira struggled to comprehend the size of it.

"Welcome to Star Reach," Armstar said sadly. "Or what's left of it."

"You're an angel!" Aesie's voice was a squeak of alarm.

Renira turned to find her friend sitting on her arse in a tangle of skirts, staring at Eleseth with eyes wide as dinner plates. Renira went to Aesie's side, and her friend just pointed at Eleseth. "She's an angel." Finally she was starting to believe.

"Ignorant and slow. A dangerous combination." Armstar pulled the cloak from over his shoulders, revealing his own ruined wings.

Aesie shifted her gaze between Eleseth and Armstar. She was trembling when she finally turned to Renira. "They're real."

Renira nodded. Maybe now Aesie would realise Renira had been telling the truth about her adventure. "Demons too. I think it's all real, Aesie. Everything the king has been telling us is a lie. This is real. They are real. Not evil. Not despots. Just... a dying people, hunted for their blood."

Dussor scoffed. "Told you."

Sun stepped back and crouched next to Renira, leaning on his spear. "There's something down here, Ren. I don't like it. I can hear it calling me."

"Ignore it," said Armstar. "Nobody who follows that call ever returns."

"I hear it too," Renira said. In truth she had no wish to find out what it was, she was just thankful someone else could hear it. It meant she wasn't going mad. She had one arm around Aesie's shoulders and put the other on Sun's knee, offering what scant comfort she could. "What is it?"

Armstar didn't answer her.

"Is there a way down?" Gemp asked. He was the closest one to the ledge and was leaning over the abyss, staring down at the drop. How he could stand it, Renira didn't know. Just thinking about the height made her feel uneasy. Eleseth could fly down, but the others would surely have to climb. This time she would do it as well. Whatever it took. She'd show Aesie and Sun and the angels that she didn't need protecting *all* the time.

"There are steps," Armstar said. Renira breathed a sigh of relief. No matter how much she filled herself with bravado, in truth she had no idea how she'd have managed a climb. She'd struggled with the bloody ladder.

Gemp edged even closer to the edge, his foot scraping the stones. "You sure? I don't see them."

Armstar laughed. "Because you're looking."

Gemp let out a startled gasp. "God's breath! You're bloody right. Where did they come from?"

It was time to go, and no amount of waiting around was going to make it any easier. Renira pulled Aesie to her feet. Her friend was still gawping at the angels, her hand at her mouth.

"They're real," she said again. Renira was proud she had taken the revelation better. Well, a little better at least.

"You thought I was lying?" Dussor said with a scowl. "You thought all of us were lying?"

"I thought..." Aesie stopped and shook her head, blinking rapidly as she collected herself. "King Emrik said..."

"The Godless King is the bloody liar."

Renira left the two of them to their argument and crept close to the ledge. She ducked under Eleseth's raised wings and leaned forward. The sight of the drop so close stopped her in her tracks.

"There are steps all the way down," Eleseth said. She smiled in that way she had that made Renira feel safe and loved all at once. "But I can carry you again if you would prefer."

Renira glanced over her shoulder. Aesie and Dussor were still arguing, and it looked quite heated. Dussor was waving his arms about, and Aesie had hers crossed and her jaw clenched in her intractable way. Renira knew it well, Aesie would argue ice was hot and fires were cuddly when she got like that. Sun was staring between the two, as if trying to follow the discussion. It was just like her best friend to waltz in and steal the attention. Renira had never minded before, but this was *her* adventure, and Dussor was... charming and handsome, and he had been focused on her. She didn't like feeling so jealous.

"We'll drop her off at the next village we come to," Eleseth said, following Renira's gaze. "She doesn't belong here, Renira. She's not one of us."

Renira glanced at Eleseth. The angel might be right, but a part of her wanted Aesie along. She wanted her best friend by her side. Someone to talk to about the responsibility at her feet. Aesie was argumentative and hated being told she was wrong, but she was also supportive and brave. She had always stood up for Renira, even when they were still children. But Eleseth was right. It was best for them all if they sent Aesie on her way as soon as possible.

"I'll take the stairs," Renira said. She was tired of needing protecting, of being a burden to the angels. It seemed facing her fear of heights was the least she could do to start remedying that.

"Are you sure?"

Renira looked up at the angel and nodded firmly.

"Good. Take it slowly."

Gemp and Armstar and Kerrel were already on their way down, and Renira almost changed her mind when she looked at them. If she looked at the people, she could see them moving down steps that shifted between grey and translucent rock. But the moment Renira tried to focus on the steps, they vanished before her eyes, and the others looked as though they were standing on nothing. The same was true of the closest step to her. She knew it was there. She could see it out of the corner of her eye, but as soon as she looked at it, it vanished. She couldn't shake the foolish feeling that it would disappear the moment she set a foot upon it, sending her to fall to the churning water below.

Renira edged her foot forward gingerly until her toes were over the edge of the drop. She dangled her foot for a few moments before it connected with the step. It held when she put weight upon it. Renira slid her other foot over the edge and placed it, too, on the first step. Then she stood up straight and tried to ignore her pounding heart. *Easy as breathing. And everyone always says the first step is the hardest.*

It was a painfully long process, sliding her foot to the edge of each step and then over the drop and down to the next, each time expecting the step to disappear out from under her. Sun gave her encouragement from the ledge, and Renira didn't have the heart to tell him it was more annoying than useful.

The others were already down and exploring the floor of the cavern when Renira made the mistake of looking down. The steps vanished from her eyes and suddenly she was standing on nothing, staring down at rushing black water far below. Her vision swam, twisting this way and that, and Renira squeaked in alarm. How was she not falling? She knew she should look away to conjure the steps back out of nowhere, but she was fixated on the drop below and panicking, unable to move.

Sun shouted something. Eleseth's voice joined the boy's, but still Renira couldn't make out any words. The world lurched. She thought she was standing still, but with her vision swimming, she couldn't tell. She stumbled, one foot catching on the other, and sat down, but the stairs were gone. Renira felt the drop take her, her hip bouncing off stone, and then she *was* falling. She screamed. One second, two, and then she hit the icy black water, and it swallowed her.

CHAPTER 32

An angel's immortality shield is no protection against the elements. They burn, freeze, or drown as surely as any human. We can use this.

— KING ERTIDE HOSTAIN. YEAR 38 OF THE
FOURTH AGE. 7 YEARS BEFORE HEAVEN FELL

E leseth dropped the packs she had been gathering, unfurled her wings, and leapt out into the drop. She beat her wings just once, angling down to the water where Renira had disappeared, then tucked into a dive.

They couldn't lose the girl, not now. If they did, everything they had been working toward for the past three hundred years would die with her. She was their last chance, even Orphus admitted it.

Wind rushed past her, and Eleseth hit the water like an arrow in flight, piercing down into the dark, churning depths.

She could see nothing in the darkness. Her own luminescence barely lit the water no matter how brilliant she shone, and the water distorted what little vision she had. The current carried her along, and Eleseth felt something hard bash against her wings, drawing out a bark of pain that lost her precious air. She swam against the current, angling deeper, knowing that Renira's heavy coat would have dragged her down. The cold enveloped her, sapping at her strength.

Eleseth twisted one way then the other, frantically searching, and knowing that it was useless. The underground river was too deep, too cold, flowing too fast and down into places where no human or angel should ever tread.

A light flickered in the depths. A cold blue glow that shone small in the darkness. She struggled against the burning of her lungs, fighting the need to gasp and knowing it would be her end if she gave in to her body's demands. Eleseth kicked toward the light, her eyes fixed on the blurry pulsing blue. The current sped her along, and something else bashed against her wings. Eleseth ignored it and kicked, pushing closer to the light.

A body floated limp in the dark depths, ragged about by merciless currents. Eleseth reached out and grabbed hold of something, a trailing end of a coat, and pulled Renira in close. She was unconscious, perhaps even gone already. Eleseth gripped the girl and angled for the surface, kicking hard. She unfurled her wings and gave a single beat, speeding her ascent. Her lungs burned, and she could feel her body at its limits as it struggled for air against her will. Then she broke the surface of the water and gasped, hauling Renira up beside her. The girl didn't move or breathe, and they were both still being carried along with the current, away from Armstar's cursed tower in the centre of the cavern.

Again, something bashed Eleseth's wings, causing her to cry out in pain. She spun and reached out with her free hand. Her fingers gouged into smooth rock, cracking the stone. She clung on for her life, holding them both against the freezing black water that tried to wash them away.

"Wake up, Renira," Eleseth shouted. Water splashed into her mouth and set her coughing. "Damn it!"

Eleseth heard Armstar shouting something and sucked in a deep breath to reply. "I have her. She's not breathing," she screamed against the fury of the rushing water. Eleseth looked up to find she was clutching hold of a circular pillar jutting out of the water. At one time it might have served a purpose, but that was long past, and now it was just a crumbling relic of a place everyone but Armstar had forgotten even existed.

She saw a little yellow light in the distance, over the rushing of the water. A lantern. She squinted and saw Armstar standing at the raised lip of the shore-line, staring helplessly toward her, waving a hand in the air. Eleseth shifted Renira up onto one shoulder to free up her other hand and reached up, her fingers digging bloody gouges into the rock. She climbed up out of the water with Renira's small form slumped on her shoulder. It should have been easy, but the cold had sapped so much of her strength that Eleseth struggled. She paused for a moment, gathering her remaining strength. The rock crumbled beneath her fingers.

Eleseth pushed away from the pillar, kicking with her feet and turning in mid-air, she spread her wings wide and beat them hard. She sailed towards the shore, but with her strength all but gone and her wings sodden, she couldn't fly, and it was too far away. Just before she crashed back down into the water, Eleseth threw Renira with both hands into the waiting arms of Armstar. She hit the water again.

Her fingers found solid rock even as her head went under and water enveloped her. Eleseth gripped hard, and the rock cracked and crumbled beneath her strength. The current gripped hold of her. Her strength fled, her numb fingers slipped, and she was dragged down into the drowning dark.

Then there were hands, warm and strong, wrapping around her wrist. She kicked out the last of her strength, and they pulled, and Eleseth broke the surface. She clambered up onto the rocky shore, retched up a mouthful of icy water, and collapsed, her strength entirely spent.

Sun raced down the invisible steps far faster than was safe. The light bouncing around the cavern had faded, and he could barely see a pace ahead of him, but none of that mattered. Ren was in danger! He was moving so fast, and his feet had already missed a few steps, making him stumble. He couldn't stop his head-long flight now even if he wanted to.

The ground came as a surprise, and Sun went down hard, expecting another step. His ankle twisted beneath him, his knees smashed into the stony ground and he rolled, dropping his spear. Ignoring the pain in his ankle and his bloody knee, Sun scrambled back to his feet. He limped over to where Broken Wings waited, the lantern a beacon in the dark.

Sun heard a splash over the sound of rushing water. Broken Wings caught something in his arms and placed it gently on the stone floor. Gemp and Kerrel rushed to the water's edge where a glow was fading fast. As Sun drew closer, he saw Ren lying on the ground, Broken Wings fretting over her, placing his ear close to her face. Glowy struggled out of the water, half pulled by Gemp and Kerrel. The big angel collapsed. Her glow was diminished, and she wasn't moving save for the trembling. Sun felt utterly useless. He had no idea what to do, and Ren still wasn't moving.

"She's not breathing and her skin is ice," Broken Wings said. He fretted about for a few more moments. "Eleseth, what do I do?"

Glowy groaned, still shivering. Her wings were sodden and dull, her normally sandy skin pale as alabaster. Still, she struggled up to her knees and crawled over to Ren. The angel placed a hand on Ren's chest, and some of her glow returned. It was soft, like a candle on its final few flickers before being snuffed out. Ren's chest started to glow as well and she spasmed and vomited up dark water over the rocks.

"Is she all right?" Aesie shouted, still slowly working her way down the steps with Dussor beside her.

"No!" Sun shouted. He turned back to Ren, ignoring any reply. He blamed Aesie for this. Ren had clearly been trying to show off by walking the steps alone.

"She's breathing," Broken Wings said. His face close to Ren's again.

"Why isn't she awake?" Sun asked.

Glowy collapsed again, this time next to Renira, her wings sprawled out like a bird hit by a stone in flight. "I can't... I don't have the strength to warm her." Her teeth chattered, and the words came out slowly. Her eyes rolled back in her head.

"We need to get them inside," Gemp said, nodding toward the great tower in the centre of the cavern. "Out of this breeze and away from the chill coming off the water. We need fire."

Broken Wings stared at Gemp for a few moments and then swung his gaze to the tower. He seemed to be considering, questioning whether it was worth letting them into the tower to save their lives. Sun made the decision for them all. He walked over to Ren and grabbed her under the arms. She was heavier than he had imagined. He started dragging her toward the tower.

Aesie rushed over to Sun. "What can I do?" she asked.

Sun stopped dragging Ren for a moment. "Grab her legs," he said through gritted teeth.

Dussor was a few steps behind Aesie. He dumped the packs he was carrying. "Stand aside," he said tersely and all but shouldered Sun out of the way. He stooped and picked Ren up in his arms as though she weighed nothing and strode away toward the tower. Sun felt a sting to his pride, but he swallowed it down. On any other day, he might have snapped at Dussor for taking charge, but Ren was in trouble, and she mattered more than his wounded pride. Aesie ran after them, chatting away to Ren as though she were awake.

Armstar, Gemp, and Kerrel were up and carrying Glowy between them. "Out of the way, boy," Broken Wings said as they hurried past toward the tower.

Sun found himself alone on the shoreline. The water rushed behind him, and that odd wailing song found the gaps in the tumult, calling to him, demanding he strike out into the darkness and find its source. He was alone again, just like he had been in the forest after the demon had ambushed his kidnappers. He tried to hide it, tried to pretend it was just a bad dream, but he knew the truth. He'd hidden behind a tree and watched as the demon dragged his paralysed kidnappers away. They'd still been alive. He remembered the fear on Flame's face as the demon scooped her up. He'd never seen what had become of them, but he knew. His kidnappers were dead, eaten by demon spawn. And he had done nothing to save them. Could do nothing. Now Ren was dying, and once again he could do nothing.

He watched as the others reached the base of the tower, looking so small against its bulk. They stood around for a few moments, then disappeared, having found a way inside. Sun trudged back to where Glowy had pulled Ren from the river and picked up the lantern. He made his way to the packs Dussor had been carrying and attempted to pick them all up. He settled for wearing one, carrying a second, and dragging the third. He was useless. He couldn't save Ren, couldn't fight the wolf or the princess. He was no Exemplar, just a boy pretending he was a help rather than a hindrance.

Sun trudged onward toward the tower's base in a sulky daze, considering all the things he wasn't. He barely noticed the uneven ground or the little spikes of rock growing out of the floor. The pack he was dragging caught on one, and he heard a rip. The bottom tore out, strewing much of the contents around the rocky ground. He wasn't even a good pack mule.

The skin between his shoulders felt spiky. It was a feeling he knew well, a feeling his mother had warned him never to ignore. He was being watched. Sun looked up, past the invisible steps toward where they had entered the cavern. It was too dark to see anything but a vague shape and twin glowing red dots. The Grey had followed them.

CHAPTER 33

While each angel is both stronger and faster, more resilient than any human, they are also each possessing of numerous unique abilities. Tinere, the Wanderer, for instance was able to camouflage himself so perfectly you could trip over him and swear he was rock, and had feathers stronger than steel. That is why their hearts are so highly prized.

— TERKIS THRANE, CHIEF CARVER TO KING ERTIDE HOSTAIN. YEAR 47 OF THE FOURTH AGE. 2 YEARS AFTER HEAVEN FELL

Perel looked at the building sceptically. In the thick gloom of the early evening it appeared inconspicuous enough, but she smelled blood. A day at most since it had been spilled. She sniffed at the air. The bodies were still nearby. Tesh padded over to a nearby storm drain and scratched at the grated metal.

"That didn't take you long," Digger said, eyeing the wolf. "It took my people almost an hour to find the bodies."

Perel didn't even bother to look at the boy as she sneered at his words. "Your people are idiots."

"They found your angels, didn't they?"

Tesh returned from the storm drain and stepped close to Digger, growling. The wolf was bigger than the boy, yet he showed no fear even when facing down her sabre fangs. Of course he didn't need to *show* it, Perel and Tesh could both smell the sickly sweet terror sweating off him.

Perel smiled. "That remains to be seen. They went in this building and didn't come out?"

Digger nodded. "There's an old mineshaft entrance in there. Your father closed it decades ago. He forbade anyone from stepping foot in that mine." The boy grinned. "I wonder why."

Perel started toward the door to the little stone building.

"Don't forget our deal," Digger called out after her. "You'll bring the body of the Builder back to me."

Perel waved over her shoulder but said nothing. Tesh caught up to her side and growled low in the back of her throat. Perel laughed. "Not yet. We'll kill the little immortal when we come back."

The wolf snapped her jaws, impatient, and Perel buried her free hand in the coarse fur around Tesh's neck. "Why care for immortal flesh, when we'll soon be feasting on divinity?"

Perel kicked the door, and its hinges exploded. The door crashed to the ground, and she was through before it hit the floor, her halberd held at the ready. Tesh followed her in. Silence and stillness greeted them. Tesh padded forward, muzzle to the ground. There was dried blood underneath the table to the left, the tang of it still sharp to Perel's nose. The smell coming from the open trapdoor beyond the bars was stale air. There was a faint odour of sweat as well, then a much sharper and more recent perfume, something with jasmine and rose hips as its base. Tesh brushed through into the open cell and stared down into the trapdoor. Perel blinked into her wolf's sight. A rickety old ladder of rusted metal rungs, solid stone a dozen feet below, footprints scuffed in the dirt.

Perel blinked back to her own sight and started toward the trapdoor. There was something else, she noticed, a mark just in front of the opening. Someone had scratched it there and recently, the gouge in the stone leaving little shavings of rock. Perel grinned. A new trail to follow, and someone was leading them in the right direction.

Broken Wings had found a room with good ventilation, large enough to accommodate them all yet small enough to trap in the heat of the fire. He also directed them to fresh stores of preserved food and clean water and wood that could be chopped to burn. It escaped no one's notice, not even Sun's, that the angel seemed to know his way around the tower intimately. Before long they had a fire going and, under Glowy's instruction, Ren had been stripped of her sodden clothes and wrapped in three separate blankets. They were both huddled in front of the fire as soon as it got going, Ren a small bundle in the arms of the angel. She still hadn't woken, and her face was so pale, her lips blue as ice, Sun wasn't certain she would.

He'd seen people die of cold before, on the streets of Bresh. It was a dangerous prospect living on the streets of any city in Ashvold. There were months where the fires burned low and the land turned cold. Not to mention wulfkin hunts whenever the Blood Moon rose. Sun had run the wulfkin gauntlet once. He'd had no choice. His kidnappers couldn't let him be caught, especially by any servant of Karna. Night to night, city to city, always fleeing. Keeping one step ahead of the wulfkin and knowing that daylight was their only respite. His kidnappers had done so much for him. They'd rescued him from Karna, kept him safe on their flight, taken him from Ashvold in search of safety in Helesia. All that, only to be killed by a forest demon as soon as they thought they were all finally safe.

The fire crackled, and Broken Wings reached into the blaze and shifted the embers, then placed another plank of wood into the flames.

"She called you the Unburnt once," Sun said, shifting his gaze across the fire to stare at Broken Wings. "Back in the forest."

Broken Wings met Sun's gaze without blinking and held his hands above the flames once more. His skin did not burn, though he winced from the heat. "One of many names I am known by."

"What about your wings?" Sun asked.

Broken Wings glared across the fire at him and slid his hand inside his tunic, fingers brushing across the amulet he wore. Renira did the same thing often.

Eleseth shifted a little. Her wings folded around Ren and started to glow. "Armstar's ruined wings have nothing to do with fire," she said. "They are because he's one of the Fallen."

Aesie extended her hands toward the crackling fire. She and Dussor were sitting close, their argument forgotten for now. "I still can't believe angels are real. Sorry, I mean, I guess I can't believe you are real. Well, you must be." She sighed. "I know it's probably a stupid thing to say."

"Then don't say it," Sun muttered.

"It's just... We were told you were all gone. Dead. But here you are and you're..." Aesie shook her head. "Real. Alive."

Eleseth smiled kindly. "Lies are often easier to swallow because they are what you want to hear. Whereas the truth will sometimes ask more of you, to venture beyond comfort. I forgive you for your ignorance."

Kerrel and Gemp were the only ones not crowded around the fire. Kerrel was out scouting the tower, and Gemp leaned against the nearby doorway, chewing on some grain and keeping an eye on the corridor beyond. "I always thought Karna was the only Fallen?" Gemp said.

Broken Wings said nothing, staring into the fire, his ruined wings twitching.

"What sin did you commit?" Sun asked. With the mention of Karna, he found himself intrigued. There were things the people of Ashvold never talked about, and the queen's divinity, or lack thereof, was one of those things.

"Nothing you need to know about, boy," said Broken Wings.

Glowy shook her head and sighed. "Fallen is a title we reserve for angels who have committed the greatest sin. The God knew what angel blood could do both to and for humanity. He recognised, even at the beginning, that it would lead to strife and chaos and disaster. So, he laid down the rules, those all angels are bound to follow. The first of those, the greatest of them, is to never allow a human to drink divine blood. The Fallen are those angels who have willingly given their blood to a human. Armstar's wings are his punishment, along with the utter ruination of his immortality shield." Broken Wings glared at Glowy, and she held his stare. "He is closer to mortal than any angel has ever been."

"My punishment," Broken Wings said, holding his hand in the flames and grimacing. "You don't know a damned thing, sister."

"If it's such a great sin, why didn't your God just decide any angel who shared their blood would die?" Aesie asked.

Dussor frowned at her. "Not our God. The God."

Aesie shook her head. "He's not my God."

"He's everyone's God."

Another shake of her head. "Then by that same logic, King Emrik must also be *your* king, *everyone's* king, which makes you and you and you and all of us heretics."

"That's not..." Dussor growled in frustration. "God overrules Emrik."

"Why?"

"Because he does."

"Hmmm, very convenient."

"The Fallen don't die because the God believes in redemption," Glowy said as Dussor opened his mouth to argue further. "He believes all of us, even the greatest sinners, should have the chance to earn his forgiveness."

"What about Karna?" Sun asked, hoping no one would notice his interest. "She feeds humans her blood every night."

"I am nothing like her," Broken Wings said with venom.

Glowy narrowed her eyes at Sun. "She does. Though I would wager not a lot of people know that."

Sun lowered his own gaze to the flames and cursed himself for revealing how much he knew.

"Karna is Fallen. After the Crusade ended and our father was killed, my sister revealed her betrayal. She and Orphus fought, but he wouldn't harm her. Not even her. Not even after she revealed her hand in the Crusade." Eleseth let out a ragged sigh. "She fled from us and claimed Ashvold as her own. In order to protect her borders, she created her Amaranthine, her own immortals, bound to her by the blood she feeds them. Her blood. But my sister is also something else entirely. She feeds humans her own blood, yes. But she also eats other angels." Glowy shivered, her wings ruffling. "She was always... driven, but I didn't see her lust for power until it was too late. And it is too late. For her."

Sun shifted uncomfortably, feeling as though just talking about Karna might somehow draw her from halfway across the world. "But her wings aren't ruined. She doesn't have any," he said.

Glowy looked at Sun with an odd expression, as though she were looking through him to the truth he hid within. "She cut them off rather than suffer the pain. I'm told it's excruciating."

"It is," Broken Wings said bitterly.

Aesie sighed. "Why don't you just cut them off as well? If it would save you the pain."

Broken Wings snorted. "Because I am an angel. Ruined or not, they are my wings." He shifted his gaze to Glowy. "I am not Karna. I do not allow humans to feed off me to grant power. I did it once to save a life and because..."

"Whose life?" Ren asked, her voice weak and trembling.

Sun was up in an instant and rushed over to stand close by, though he had no idea what he could do. "Are you all right, Ren?" he asked, anxious.

She glanced at him and smiled. She looked half a corpse, cold and pale and weak. Then she turned her attention back to Broken Wings, and the faint smile fell away. "Who did you give your blood to, Armstar?"

Glowy pulled Ren a little closer, she looked so small, like a child wrapped in a parent's embrace. "Rest, Renira. Conserve your strength."

"Who?" Ren repeated, her voice cracking on the word.

Broken Wings dropped his stare to the flames once more. "The only person worthy of it. Your mother."

Ren seemed to deflate at that, as though her need to know was the only thing keeping her back straight. "What happened?" she said. "I was on the steps."

"You fell," Aesie said. "Eleseth dove into the water after you and pulled you out. How do you feel?"

Ren moaned. "Cold. Like ice has seeped into my bones. I'm sorry for causing such a fuss."

"Good," Broken Wings said. He threw another plank of wood onto the fire, then stood and joined Gemp by the door. Sun glared at his back, not that it did any good.

"I carried the packs, Ren," he said.

She smiled up at him. "You're stronger than you look."

He grinned. "It was easy."

Glowy unfurled her wings and stood. She was entirely naked, her own clothes drying with Ren's near the fire, and glorious. Perfect regardless of her enlarged size. Sun found himself staring, enrapt.

Aesie coughed. "It would be polite to look away," she said sharply. But Sun couldn't, he was transfixed by the naked angel.

Ren pulled open the neck of the blanket she was wrapped in, and her eyes went wide. She quickly pulled the blanket close again. "Why am I naked?"

Glowy chuckled as she bent over and plucked her clothes from the ground. "We needed to get you out of your wet clothes to warm you, Renira." She was smiling when she turned back around, and her gaze settled on Sun. He felt heat flush his cheeks but still couldn't look away. "Is this your first time seeing a naked woman, boy?"

Everyone looked at him, and Sun felt himself grow hotter still. He couldn't tear his eyes away from the angel's body, couldn't find his voice to talk. Tears streamed down his cheeks. "Beautiful," the word whispered from his lips unbidden.

"Oh dear," Glowy said. She settled her wings around her and it looked just like she was wearing a faded grey cloak. Sun finally tore his eyes away and sat back down on his arse, wiping away the tears and hoping everyone would stop staring at him. He felt exhausted, yet couldn't say why. Couldn't pin down what he was feeling as though he were a boiling stew, his emotions bubbling to the surface one after another.

"Rude little boy," said Aesie.

"It's not his fault," Glowy said, pulling on her clothes beneath the cover of her wings. I am the Herald of the Age of Wisdom. Father created me to inspire awe within humanity. But, uh, men often confuse that feeling with desire. It's not the first time this has happened."

"Why?" Ren asked, her voice faint and weary. She leaned toward the fire, trembling. "Why did the God make you to inspire awe? Why did he need to?"

"Because the demon war was over," Glowy said. "Humanity no longer needed warriors to help free it from thralldom. Father decided what was needed was scholars and leaders to teach humanity language and numbers, to bring knowledge to the people. We showed you how to form lasting communities, develop land for farming, and domesticate animals. We spread the word of the God, his teachings and his wishes. He wanted so much for humanity. To see you grow and prosper, to become the pillars of the world, holding it up with your strength. It was his greatest desire that one day you would not need him. That you would end the strife between yourselves. And if the demons did somehow return, you would stand against them, united and strong.

"But he also knew there would be resistance, those who would thank him for freeing them but refuse all else he had to offer. Father knew that people would be more willing to accept the knowledge he offered if it came from angels who were not warriors but appeared more than human. So, he made the angels of the Second Age to be radiant. And I, the Herald, to be the most awe-inspiring of us all." Glowy smiled then. "I have since learned to tone it down somewhat. But, well, sometimes I forget myself. And my company. I am sorry, boy. I didn't mean to... confuse you."

Sun glanced at Dussor. The older man said nothing, keeping his gaze on the fire, so Sun decided to mimic him. "I'm sorry, too," he said and glanced at Aesie. "It was rude of me to stare. Sorry."

"Apology accepted," Glowy said. She shook her wings and the cloak vanished, revealing that she was now fully clothed. "You should try to get some sleep, Renira. You all should. We'll be moving again soon."

"We should get moving now," Broken Wings said from the doorway.

"Renira is not yet recovered, brother," said Glowy, iron in her voice. "We will stay here a few hours more."

That seemed the end to the argument, and before long the angels were talking in secret again. Sun shuffled closer to Ren, and she smiled at him, her eyes drooping.

"I was worried," Sun said. He didn't want to be left alone with the angels and the acolytes. Without Ren, he wasn't sure what he would do.

"I'm fine, Sun. Just cold and tired. And embarrassed. I didn't mean to cause such a stupid fuss. I was just trying to... to do something on my own for once."

Sun nodded, trying to hold his tongue. "I saw the Grey," he said. He couldn't hold it in, and only Ren would understand. "It followed us."

Ren's eyes flicked open for a moment, but they soon closed again. "We'll be all right," she murmured. "We're safe."

Her voice trailed off into a soft snore and she was asleep. Sun retrieved his spear and then sat down close to Ren. He wasn't so sure they were safe, but if the Grey did come for them, he would protect her with his life.

CHAPTER 34

Stand strong, stand true
Shining light refrain
A bulwark against the dark.

Shield of humanity
An unbroken heart
The hope that united spark.

Saint Dien. Saint Dien. Saint Dien. They cried
And from out of the darkness she strode.

Where once they fought, they struggled un-united
Now bonded too firm to erode.

— A WILL UNBROKEN

I *almost died again. What is that now, three times or four?* It worried Renira
that she couldn't remember.

She had just wanted to do something by herself, to show the others she didn't need protecting. Instead she had messed up and needed saving again. The cold had seeped into her and wouldn't leave. Even a few hours sleeping by a crackling fire did little to chase away the chill. She'd almost crawled into the flames, so close she felt it licking at her fingers, but frost still ran through her veins. She was back in her mostly-dry winter clothes now and had an extra blanket wrapped around her coat. She shivered, and her teeth chattered.

They set off into the tower. Armstar led through winding corridors and cut through rooms that had once seen purpose but had been abandoned for so long they were filled with nothing but darkness and dust spirits that fled rolling across the floor away from falling feet. The angel claimed that much of the bottom levels of the tower were almost solid rock, with only a few passages through them. They climbed stairs whenever they came to them, always heading upward.

Sun stayed close to her side at all times, his spear in hand and a resolute look on his face. Renira no longer found his presence annoying, she was surprised to realise. The boy was comforting, his presence at her side a constant she could rely on. Aesie and Dussor walked close together, and Renira caught the whisper of harsh words shared between them. Even the proof of angelic existence had not convinced Aesie the Godless King was in the wrong, and Dussor seemed to have taken it upon himself to educate her. Renira wished him good luck with it —Aesie had a stubborn streak that put even the most curmudgeonly of mules to shame.

She felt the bitter pang of jealousy and hated herself for it. Aesie had swanned in and taken the spotlight, as she always did, and despite her brush with death Renira was invisible again. Dussor's jokes and smiles and *'my lady's'* were all gone, he'd not spoken two words to Renira since Aesie had thumped him. And Aesie herself seemed more interested in Dussor than in talking to Renira. So often, Renira had imagined going on an adventure with her best friend, but it was nothing like this.

Some of the rooms they passed through had supplies stored in barrels or boxes that had yet to rot away, and Armstar knew exactly what was kept in each one. More than once, he stopped them for a few moments to go digging through the supplies to replenish their own. Renira was starting to suspect the angel knew the tower well, and that he had led them down there not just to escape the wolf princess, but because he wanted to see it again. It clearly held some special meaning to him. Other rooms held building supplies, mostly planks of wood already cut to certain lengths or blocks of worked stone. Some of the rooms had suffered structural damage. Collapsed roofs or walls, rubble strewn across the floor. Some were even in a state of repair, with wooden supports and ropes used to hold crumbling sections in place. Renira noticed Armstar eyeing them with scrutiny each time they passed, and he rarely looked pleased by what he saw. Renira guessed it was because they looked fit to give way at any moment.

They entered a room filled with paintings. Each one was framed in dark wood and covered with an oiled cloth. Armstar tried to move them quickly along, but Eleseth stopped.

"Where did you find these?" she asked, her voice full of wonder. She pulled the covers off one painting after another, revealing the splendid artwork underneath.

Each of the works of art was a beautifully depicted scene of resplendent angels. Shining lights beating back the darkness. The angels were always in the light, and in the darkness the shapes resembled humans rather than demons.

"I rescued them," Armstar said. He stopped by the far doorway and looked like he wanted to leave, as though he couldn't bear to be around the paintings. "Leave them be. They are not for human eyes. They are my... personal collection now."

"We thought them all destroyed or lost, brother," Eleseth said.

"They were. Too many of them were. I saved what I could. Salvaged some from fires. Not enough." This was not the usual bitterness Renira had come to expect from the angel, it was grief. Pain laid bare. *Typical of him. He grieves for the loss of art but not people.*

Eleseth uncovered another painting, this one of Orphus, Renira recognised his ornate golden armour, pauldrons, greaves, and gauntlets all decorated with designs of swords. He was standing in front of a field of slaughter and carrying a head in one hand. Before him was a pillar of white light and three dark shapes emerging from it.

Eleseth knelt and ran gentle fingers over the painting's frame. "These should be displayed. Not hidden away to decay down here."

"And where would we display them? Everywhere we go, we are hunted and murdered. Los Hold was our largest remaining sanctuary. Destroyed in a single night. And not even by the Godless King's hand, but by that of his feral daughter. If Emrik had been there, none of us would have escaped. He's too strong. Too powerful. Too mad. I preserve what I can down here, in the hope that one day... One day I might be able to display it again without the threat."

"What are they?" Aesie asked.

Armstar sent her a withering look. "Paintings."

Aesie approached one and stared down at it. "I assume you have an adult answer?"

Dussor tried to stifle his laugh and failed. Gemp quickly silenced him with a glare.

"They are all that remains of the greatest gallery ever assembled. By the greatest artist to have put brush to canvas," Armstar said.

Aesie crouched down and looked closer. "The signature says Akkran."

"Yes. She was a true wonder."

"I've never heard of her. My father has a gallery with a number of artists' work, but none with this name."

Renira had known Aesie for over a decade, most of their lives, and she had spent time in her mansion, but she'd hadn't known her father owned a gallery.

Eleseth uncovered another painting, this one of a tower in the process of construction. Renira marvelled at the details and the number of people who appeared to be working in the labour yards at the base.

"There's no reason you would have heard of her," Eleseth said. "Akkran has been dead for almost a thousand years, and this is all that's left of her legacy." She turned to Armstar. "There were five hundred paintings in the gallery, depicting the grandest moments from the First, Second, and Third Ages. And the worst moments in the history of this world. This is but a handful."

"All I could save," Armstar said sadly and shook his head. There were tears in his grey eyes. "So much beauty lost. Even Ertide wasn't cruel enough to burn the gallery down, but Emrik set his will on wiping out all memory of the God. All trace of memory. He is mad, sister."

Eleseth shook her head, true anger on her face for the first time since Renira had met her. It was frightening. "Do not absolve Ertide Hostain of any sin."

"You think I don't know that?" Armstar snapped. "If not for him, none of this would have happened. If not for him, Emrik might have been an artist to rival even Akkran. Instead he is a monster unlike any the world has ever seen. Ertide will find no absolution from me or from anyone else, but he was not the one who tore down my tower!"

"This tower?" Renira asked, pointing at the painting of a tower under construction. "This is what we're standing in?" She imagined what it must have been like while it was still under construction. Hundreds of people working upon it, filling the corridors with noise and activity. How joyous it must have felt to see the tower taking shape, growing brick by brick.

Armstar nodded. "Star Reach. What's left of it after the Godless King brought it crashing down eight hundred years ago."

"You built this place," Renira said, certain now. Before, he had called it the greatest work of art ever attempted.

Armstar looked crestfallen. He crossed over to join her by the painting. "I built cities and temples, theatres and walls, palaces and shrines, everything I was told to by kings and craftsmen. By father. But this was to be my greatest. Armstar the Builder's greatest work, a tower so grand it reached for the stars themselves. I was going to fill it with art. Statues, paintings, song and dance and poetry and classrooms for people to learn, to create. It was to be the greatest gallery ever built, an eternal monument to the beauty of human and angelkind working together. I was a damned fool."

Sun edged into the room, his hands held tight to his chest as though he was afraid to touch the paintings. "Buildings aren't art."

Armstar snorted and sent a scathing glare his way. "A typical human appreciation for art. You think the word only applies to depictions on canvas. It is far more expansive than that. It is the expression of imagination to inspire emotion. Whether it take the form of a painting, or music, or a play, or a building. It is art. And if my tower had been completed it would have inspired such emotion that none who looked upon it would not be awed. Even Emrik understood that once. Perhaps more so than any other."

Eleseth placed a hand on Armstar's shoulder, but he shrugged her off and turned away. "The Third Age was the Golden Age," she said. "A time of culture. Angels, like Armstar, were created more human than before. Not to inspire, but to join with humanity. To create. Some were musicians or scholars or painters or sculptors. All took students. Father wished his children of the Golden Age to teach humanity to express itself without violence, and there is no more poignant form of expression than that of the artist."

Eleseth paused for a moment and looked at her brother. "Armstar was unique among the angels of the Third Age. Not the Herald, but the only builder. He taught humanity how to express itself through the houses they lived in, the places where they worshipped, and the wonders they built."

Armstar snorted. "I built cities and museums, forts and mines. Galleries for displaying others' art. Theatre halls for plays or concerts. I rebuilt the capital around the Bell of Ages. None filled the hole inside of me. I knew I had something else to give.

"It was always there in my mind. I could see it from the moment I stepped from Heaven. It only grew every day every year I worked on other projects. Star Reach, a tower of unmatched height and majesty. Then finally father was done with me, no more orders. I approached the king and Terin Hostain understood the importance of such a structure, of something that would stand above the rest of the world. A monument so colossal it could be seen even from the other kingdoms. A tower so large it could house the population of Celesgarde if needed.

"For a hundred years we mined, and we built. Tens of thousands of people worked with me, all seeing the glory of the project they would help bring to the world. Their names, all of them, are written on the stones of this place. A hundred years, and the foundations of Star Reach were complete. A man-made cavern unlike any other, and the base of the tower that would one day be."

Aesie sighed and shook her head. "Just like a man to erect a tower and call it glorious."

"BE SILENT!" Armstar roared. "You ignorant puddle of sin."

Aesie backed up against the wall, eyes wide and fearful. Dussor stepped in front of her protectively. Armstar deflated then, as though the outburst had sapped the will from him.

Everyone was silent. Renira stepped forward until Armstar looked at her. "What happened?" she asked.

"Mathanial, the Fool, happened," Armstar said it with such spite it shocked Renira.

"The Rider," Eleseth said. "The Herald of the Fourth Age."

Armstar threw up his hands in exasperation and turned away. "The Third Age was not finished, sister. We had so much more to show humanity. So much more to create. But no, Mathanial came along and rang in the Age of Heresy. The arrogant bastard."

Eleseth sighed. "That was not how it was meant to be, Armstar, as well you know. The Fourth Age was meant to be the age of exploration and expansion. It was the Rider's job to take humanity beyond this continent and to colonise the rest of the world. To reclaim what was lost during the Exodus. To spread the word and teachings of the God to others who might have also survived and yet be living in darkness."

"Yes, a pretty line, sister. One I heard from the Rider's own lips a thousand times. It was very well rehearsed."

Eleseth ignored him. "Ships were built in great numbers, huge vessels able to carry settlers and withstand the rigours of prolonged ocean travel. Horses were bred who could ride for days with a human on their back. Humanity spread out in all directions, as was God's will."

Armstar chuckled bitterly at that.

An age of adventure and exploration sounded like fun. That was what their age, this age should have been. Until the Godless Kings corrupted it.

"And all that work towards bringing culture to humanity, all that progress towards them discovering who they truly are was forgotten," Armstar said. "Mathanial stole the resources and manpower from me, from Star Reach.

Construction ground to a halt. I had only my own acolytes to rely upon, and we were barely enough to erect the first level of the tower."

Renira glanced at the painting again. "It looks like you managed more than one level here."

"Yes. Thanks to Emrik." Armstar knelt by the painting. "The Godless King was once a man of faith, if you can believe it. An artist with a rare skill. A poet. He loved nothing so much as to sing and dance and drink the night away with women."

Renira couldn't imagine it. She had only seen the Godless King once from a distance, but he seemed cold, the type of man who sucked the mirth from a room. And everything else she had been told, from the angels and even from Borik, painted the king as a monster, desperate to wipe out angelkind and harvest from them as much power as he could. But of course he couldn't have always been that way. He might be a thousand years old, but he was still human, and Renira firmly believed that everyone had some good in them.

"Even as the Fourth Age was taking hold of the hearts and minds of humanity, Emrik arranged concerts and exhibitions," Armstar continued. "He wrote a play about the First Age and had it made. For a full year it was all the people of Celesgarde could talk about. So, I went to him with hope, and I asked him to help me build Star Reach the way it was meant to be. A work of art greater than any other, built to stand the test of ages and calamity.

"Emrik threw his passion behind this tower. Men, money, resources. He pored over the plans and learned the intricacies faster than any other I had taught. He even suggested changes I had not considered, ways to improve the structural support. For years, construction of the tower raced forward at a pace I had not thought possible. Here!" Armstar pointed at the painting of the tower. "Akkran painted the scene, wanting to capture the full scope of the project before it was complete. This is me. And there, Emrik." Renira peered closer and saw in the fine details at the base of the tower, an angel with brown wings, conferring over a table, a tall man standing next to him.

"Each day was a whirlwind of construction and joy. Each night, a celebration of the work achieved. He made it a celebration. I had never met a man like Emrik before, and rather than him believing in me, I found myself believing in him. He was a friend and a man I would happily have served. He could have asked me to build anything, and I would have without question."

"You loved him?" Renira asked.

Armstar sent a seething glare her way, but it was a fleeting thing. He nodded and stared mournfully at the painting. "I did."

"What happened?" She had to know. This was the man hunting them, hunting her. The Godless King. The man Armstar had just named friend. How could he have changed so drastically and so fast?

Armstar took a deep, shuddering breath. "His grandfather, Ertide Hostain, happened. The first of the Godless Kings. He was seduced by a demon into tasting angel flesh, and he corrupted his entire family in secret. But more than that. He gave Emrik the one thing he had been truly missing all his life. Purpose. Tangible purpose. Emrik was always a driven man, but he struggled to find a focus for that drive. He tried his hand at everything and excelled every time, but nothing provided him with the purpose he desired. To leave a mark upon the world, one that will never be forgotten. Even the tower, my tower. Well, that was the problem, wasn't it? It was my tower. Ertide gave Emrik the purpose he had always wanted. Kill God, and never be forgotten.

"But even that wasn't enough for Emrik. No. That was his grandfather's vision, his father's legacy. He had to tear down all the God had a hand in building. Had to stamp the God's name from the face of the world and hunt down all of us who served him. Because that... that is how Emrik will leave his legacy." Armstar drew in another shuddering breath.

"Is this where you have been all this time, brother?" Eleseth asked. "Almost a thousand years have passed since Ertide's Crusade ended, and I have seen you maybe five times. You've been hiding here, in the crumbling remnants of your tower."

Armstar glowered at Eleseth. "I haven't been hiding. I've been rebuilding. Doing work that would take a thousand men a thousand years, all on my own. I would never have left, but Orphus found me and told me..." Armstar glanced at Renira. "He told me you existed."

Renira frowned in confusion. That meant her mother had fled the angels before she had been born, before they even knew she was pregnant. *Why, Mother? Why did you try so hard to hide me from the angels? She must have known I would be the Herald. But how?* Renira felt like every answer only led to more questions.

"Star Reach is dead, brother," Eleseth said, shaking her head. "Let it rest."

"I can't," Armstar snapped. He glanced around at everyone else in the room. "This tower is my purpose. It is my reason, my sole reason for existing. You don't understand. None of you understand. Restoring Star Reach is the God's will, not just my own. This place is more important than you realise. You just can't hear him."

As if to answer Armstar, a haunting howl echoed through the tower. It seemed to come from everywhere at once and sent a chill running up Renira's spine that made her shiver violently. There was something horrifying familiar about that sound, and by the look on Sun's face, he knew it too. What would it take to stop her?

"It's her!" Sun said, backing away from the nearest doorway. "The wolf princess is here."

Armstar and Eleseth shared a glance, and this time they were obviously in agreement. "We need to go. Now!"

CHAPTER 35

The spy's marks had vanished, but Perel and Tesh no longer needed them. Perel could have followed the perfumed trail even without her wolf's nose. The darkness down in the tunnels was near complete, but such a hindrance no longer bothered Perel at all, not now she had taken the power of Mihiriel. She allowed the power to flow into her hand, and a fierce light burst to life in the centre of her fist. It grew brighter and brighter, chasing away the shadows, burning them with its harsh luminescence. There was no heat, only a shining brilliance that grew in intensity until Tesh was pressed up against the wall, whimpering, and Perel had screwed her eyes shut yet could still see it.

She let go of the power and watched the light fade. It was a powerful tool, one that could be used for great effect in several situations, but it was useless unless she could figure out how to control it. She needed to know how to hold the level of light steady, rather than letting it grow until it was as blinding to her as it was to everyone else. Mihiriel had not seemed to have such a problem, but then it had been *his* power. He had been born with it, instinctively knowing how to use it from the moment of his creation. He'd also had a few thousand years of practice backing him up. But he was dead now. Perel had killed him and taken his power, and it would be a final insult to his existence that she should learn to control it.

Once the light had all but faded, Tesh howled testily and bounded away into the waiting darkness of the tunnel. Perel followed more slowly. Again, she played with the angel's power and used it to bring a light to life in her hand. It was almost like a physical seizing of the power. It felt a little like there was something in her hand, grasped between her fingers. Something cold. Something that throbbed with a fire that didn't burn. She gripped it, her fingers closing around nothing, and the light flared brighter. She relaxed her grip, uncurling her fingers, and watched the light fade. The darkness rushed back in. Perel gripped again, beating back the dark with blinding light. She grinned. The shadows were like starving dogs smelling a fresh kill, too afraid to come close enough and too hungry to leave it alone.

As she walked along after her wolf, Perel played with the light. If she tightened her hand into a fist, the light built quickly, soon becoming too bright to see anything but the searing white. If she uncurled her hand and straightened her fingers, the light faded to nothing almost as quickly. She curled her fingers just enough so it was almost as though she were holding a small ball, and the light began to build slowly. When she straightened her fingers just a little, the light started to fade. There was no holding the power level, but with small movements, curling and uncurling her fingers, she could keep the level of luminescence manageable. It revealed the hewn rock around her, the dull, featureless tunnel.

A laugh built up inside, and Perel let it escape. It felt good to laugh. Usually Perel only found humour in laughing at others, but this was no vindictive braying. It was joy. Joy at her own strength. Some immortals spent years, lifetimes even, mastering the powers they took from angels. Perel had figured out her newest power in just a few days, a few hours when she really thought about it. Only Father was so brilliant. He had a knack for divine power. He understood it in a way others did not. Could not. Some called him a savant, a genius whose talent for wielding the divine was proof of his right to rule. Perel didn't care what those same people said about her; she was just happy she had inherited her father's natural ability to wield the power they seized.

She followed her nose and her connection to Tesh. She could always tell where the wolf was, direction and distance. A connection that went deeper than their linked sight. Deeper than the power to communicate with animals, a power she had taken from another angel. Deeper than even her father knew. He refused to explore the connection to his hawk, it was a tool to further his desires and nothing more. For Perel, it was different. She and Tesh were one. One spirit. One soul. One purpose. They understood each other without the need for cumbersome things like words. It was an instinctual level of understanding.

People mocked her for her bond. Mostly her brothers and sisters, but there were others as well. Never to her face, but Perel's ears were sharp enough to pick up a whisper from a hundred paces, and Tesh's senses were finer still. And also more inscrutable. The wolf could sense attention and intention. They walked through a room, and through Tesh, Perel could tell who was watching them, talking about them behind their hands. Their words were rarely complimentary.

People said she slept with wolves. It was not technically untrue, but the fools did not mean slumber. They could not seem to understand that she had no interest in sex or even human companionship. In the early years when she had been at her father's court, suitors had thrown themselves at her time and time again, first men and then even some women. They didn't love her, didn't understand her, simply wanted the prestige of being attached to a princess. Perel had chased them all away, sometimes with words, other times with claws and teeth. Most often with claws and teeth, if she was being truly honest. Her father hadn't liked that. He rarely forbade her anything, but she was not to bite people. Even if they really deserved it.

Courtiers soon took her lack of interest as insult. It was her fault, something had to be wrong with her because she didn't want them, didn't want anyone. They called her savage and feral. Words meant as insults, and she had taken them as such at first. But after a few decades of bearing those insults, of demanding retribution and never feeling sated even when it was taken, Perel had discovered a new way of dealing with them. She took away their power. People liked to call her savage and feral, so she would be savage and feral. She had turned their insults against them and wore the words as her strength.

Savage? Fierce, violent, brutal. Perel had always tended towards those traits, but now she leaned into them with everything she had. Now, people no longer whispered the word as an insult but as a warning.

Feral? Wild and untamed. Dangerous. Again, Perel took the insult and made it strength. She had become dangerous, unpredictable. She refused to act how others expected and no longer held back anything. She let her passion show, whether it was at her thrill for the hunt or for breaking a man's arm for having the gall to bump into her. That last one had put a very quick, very final end to a ball thrown in her father's honour. He had not thanked her, it was not his way, but neither had he chided her.

The dark and featureless tunnels had caused her mind to wander, and Perel came back with a start. Tesh was waiting just up ahead, a dark grey form standing before an expanding darkness that even the light from Perel's hand couldn't penetrate. A low growl rumbled from Tesh's throat, a warning not to approach too quickly. Perel saw the tunnel ended ahead, opening out into a cavern of some sort.

Perel left the confines of the tunnel and stopped on a ledge of rock that looked out into the cavern. She held her hand aloft and closed her fingers slightly to make the light brighter. Points of light sprang to life in the great cavern as polished mirrors took up the shine. It was huge. A gargantuan hollow in the earth with some sort of pillar in the centre far larger than any structure she had ever seen before save for the Overlook resting in the centre of Celesgarde. Perel heard rushing water, smelled the icy crispness of it. Fresh water, running off the nearby mountains, probably flowing all the way to the World Vein.

Tesh threw back her head and howled. The cavern caught the sound and tossed it back at them over and over, the echo fading slightly with each repetition. Perel glanced at her wolf, and Tesh yipped back at her, tongue lolling.

"I'm glad you find this amusing," Perel said. And she was glad. Happy that after centuries of life, her wolf could still find joy in small things. It was the behaviour of a pup, not a matriarch.

There seemed to be no way down from the ledge, and the base of the tower was a long way away. Perel leaned over the edge and closed her fist a little tighter, letting the light build. The river was below, icy water rushing by. The ground floor of the cavern was a few dozen feet down and easily just as far away. Perel could make the climb down with ease. The swim across would be tough, the water both cold and moving too fast for her to walk over the surface, but again Perel was sure she could manage it. The only problem would be that both the climb and the swim would take time, and the Herald already had a lengthy head start. If only it was still water. The power she had taken from the angel Ooliver allowed her to walk upon still water. Rushing water was something else entirely.

Tesh growled again, her wolf's eyes locked on Perel. It was a warning, without the need for words. The wolf could sense that Perel was considering something foolish.

"Hush!" Perel hissed. "You'll make me nervous."

Perel grinned as she shifted her halberd to her right hand and held it by the middle of the shaft. It was no javelin, but she'd wielded the thing long enough to teach herself how to throw it, and her divine strength made up for a lot.

"Father would be furious if he knew I was about to throw one of the Godslayer arms into a pitch-black cavern," Perel said. She glanced at Tesh, and the wolf stared back at her, unimpressed. Perel whipped her arm forward and threw the halberd. It sailed through the air, swallowed up by the darkness. Perel listened and heard it connect with the ground and skitter along the rock. Tesh sighed.

"It'll be fine," Perel said. The weapon was forged with ground angel bone and bathed in the blood of the God; it would take more than a few bounces along some rock to blunt its edge. In fact, in the century that Perel had wielded it, it had never once needed sharpening.

Perel began backing up. She let Mihiriel's light shine from her hand, bright enough that she could keep the lip of the ledge in sight. Tesh growled again, but Perel ignored her wolf, trusting instead in her own abilities. A dozen paces back and she stopped, crouched down, then launched herself forward into a sprint. She crossed the distance in a heartbeat and leapt out over the edge of the precipice. For a few glorious moments, Perel soared. They could take an angel's power, they could steal their life, but one thing humans could never take from an angel was their wings. Humans could not fly. But in those few moments, Perel felt close at least. Then gravity gripped hold.

Bile rose into her throat as she fell, faster and faster through the darkness. She gripped her right hand into a tight fist and the light flared to life, revealing the water behind her, the rocky ground of the cavern rushing quickly toward her. She bent her knees just as she hit the ground and felt the rock crack beneath her from the impact. She tucked into a roll, and then sprang back to her feet, grinning madly.

"Easy!" she shouted up toward where Tesh sat on the ledge of rock. She heard the wolf's groan echo back to her. Perel held her hand aloft, shining the light toward the tower. In the distance she could see a red glint, her Godslayer halberd. She quickly retrieved it. For all her bravado, it felt good to hold the weapon again. It felt right. The power to kill God, in her hands. When she turned back toward the river and the ledge of rock, Perel saw Tesh walking on thin air. The wolf was halfway between the ledge and the cavern floor, walking as if on steps, but there was nothing beneath her.

Tesh bounded down the rest of the way, and Perel met her at the cavern floor, so close to the rushing water of the icy river the noise of it was a roar.

"Invisible steps," Perel said with a laugh. She poked at the first of the steps with the butt of her halberd. It clanged against the rock, but still Perel could not see the rock, even when looking directly at it. "You cheated."

Tesh nudged her hard enough Perel stumbled. Then the wolf padded forward, nose to the rocky ground, following a scent. Perel followed her wolf to a damp patch of rock near the water's edge. It was far away from the tower. Tesh snuffled around the damp patch and rumbled deep within her chest.

Perel knelt and sniffed. "Blood," she said, glancing up at Tesh. "Human, not divine. Sweat as well." Her senses were not as refined as Tesh's, but through the wolf Perel could smell fear in that sweat.

"Someone was hurt." The wolf watched her through yellow eyes, it was all the confirmation Perel needed. If Tesh could still smell the residual fear on the scent of sweat, it meant they were close. Less than a day behind, maybe only hours.

Perel shifted her halberd to her left hand and continued to flex the fingers of her right, the light she held in her grasp pulsing with each movement. "They went into the tower, Tesh. You can track them faster than I. Go. As quick as you can."

Tesh threw back her head and howled, then bounded away, loping toward the tower, the thrill of the hunt roaring within her. Perel sprinted after her wolf, barely managing to keep up even with her divine speed. The Herald was close. The angels were close. And soon, Perel and Tesh would feed on them all.

CHAPTER 36

Choice is all we ever have. The choice to fight or flee. To give in to hate or to turn the other cheek. The choice to believe and to worship, to be better than heathens and beasts, or to fall to decay and savage ruin. It is in those choices that salvation lies.

— THE FIFTH SCRIPTURE, RESOLVE.

They'd been fleeing for hours. All the corridors and rooms passed by Renira in a dark grey blur. Even with frequent stops to adjust their direction, she was struggling to catch her breath and ready to drop. But they couldn't stop. They had to keep running. The wolf princess had already proven they couldn't hide from her. Their only chance was to run.

Armstar led and moved with typical divine stamina and no thought for the humans lagging behind. Neither Eleseth nor any of the angel's acolytes seemed to suffer too much from the brisk pace. The Herald of the Second Age had already recovered from her swim in the icy cold waters. Renira envied her that. She could still feel the cold deep inside, even as the effort of running made her skin damp with sweat. It was a gruelling flight through the tower. What was worse, Aesie and Sun were both also suffering, and there was simply nothing

Renira could do about it. Her friends had to face their tribulations alone, just as she did.

Armstar pulled them to a halt again, the passage ahead blocked by fallen rubble. It appeared a large section of the wall on this level of the tower had collapsed. They had been seeing signs of attempted repair for a while now. His love for his project was clear, but what was even more clear was that it had turned toxic. He was a man whose wife had died, yet he refused to bury her, trying desperately to keep up the charade of life, and he had been at it for a thousand years.

Renira leaned against the far wall, the one that seemed most stable, and sank down onto her arse. She was breathing heavily and could taste salty sweat on her lips. She stared straight ahead at nothing. Sun bent over before her, hands on his knees, retching from the effort of running for so long.

They had been moving steadily upwards whenever they could, but the stairs were often blocked or even gone entirely. Then Armstar would lead them from one side of the tower to the other in search of a staircase that would allow them to continue their ascent. In many places, the walls were cracked and sagging outward, and only a combination of rigging and well-placed planks of wood were keeping them from collapsing entirely. The truth, though Armstar seemed incapable of admitting it, was that the tower was collapsing. Inch by inch. Level by level. Century by century. The repairs needed were more than one man could handle, even an angel.

You can't re-live the past and call it the future. Sometimes you have to let the past fall to ruin behind you and build the future anew. Why can't Armstar understand that?

Armstar began pulling fallen stones away to clear the passageway. Eleseth dragged him aside, and the two angels whispered at each other urgently. They did that a lot. Harsh whispers, as though it might stop everyone else from realising they were arguing. Squabbling siblings with too much history and anger between them to be friends, held together by their elder brother's will. *Falling apart as surely as this tower.*

Aesie leaned against the same wall as Renira, just a few paces away. She looked exhausted, though unlike Renira, Aesie was obviously doing her best to hide it. Dussor stood close by, smirking and strutting about, showing off that he was still full of energy and ready to go. Gemp caught Renira's eye, and she saw him sigh. A moment later, he strode towards Dussor and took him by the arm, pulling him away further down the corridor. Aesie watched the two men go, then leaned more heavily against the wall. Exhausted, Renira's closest friend looked on the verge of tears, and it broke Renira's heart.

Renira shuffled sideways along the wall until she was sitting just an arm's reach away from Aesie. She struggled for something to say, a way to start the conversation. It was stupid. They'd never had a problem talking before. She'd known Aesie since they were just five winters old, and conversation had always come so easily to them, even when there was nothing to say.

They'd met in a bakery, Tobe's bakery. Renira and her mother had only just arrived in Riverden, and Mother was looking for work after the magistrate had ruled she couldn't practice medicine even on animals because she didn't have a relevant education. Renira hadn't understood at the time. All she'd known was that they had moved into grandfather's old farmhouse and were struggling to even feed themselves. The people of Ner-on-the-River didn't know them, most of them had never even met Lusa, and those who did remember her were ancient. The farmhouse roof leaked, the kitchen hearth was blocked by nesting birds, the sole surviving barn was infested with rats, and both Renira and her mother were starving. The only thing that differentiated them from the beggars on the streets was that they were clean. Mother would never allow them to wear dirty clothes when washing them was so easy.

Tobe Baker had apologised that he had no work to give but had taken some small pity on woman and daughter, offering them an old loaf of bread from the previous day's first batch. It wasn't much, but it was an act of kindness that prompted Mother to repay it the only way she knew how. She offered to wash Tobe Baker's apron for him, which certainly needed a good wash.

Then a well-dressed man had bustled into the bakery. Renira's mother stepped aside at once and pulled her daughter with her. The man had paid neither of them any attention. Men like Aiden Fur didn't usually do their own shopping, but Aesie had insisted she was hungry, and her father had never been able to refuse her anything. Renira and Aesie had locked eyes, and in that moment a lifelong friendship had been born in the way it can only with children. Before Aiden Fur had paid for his daughter's pastry, Renira and Aesie were talking, a whirlwind of words that no adult had any hope of following. They'd been friends ever since, despite the difference in their stations. Never once since had they struggled to find something to say to one another.

Renira remembered something her mother once said. *When a job seems too large or daunting and you can't figure out where to start, just dive right in.* Of course, she had been referring to a mammoth pile of washing at the time, but wisdom was often found hiding at the bottom of a pile of dirty socks.

"Hello," Renira said.

Aesie startled and turned to Renira, an odd look of panic crossing her face. Then it softened, replaced by a welcome smile. "Hello back," she said and sank down against the wall next to Renira. Sun crept closer, using the far wall and his spear for support and staying close enough that he could hear what was said.

An awkward silence fell between them. Renira struggled to think of something else to say. *Why is this suddenly so difficult?* But she knew why. Aesie knew. She knew the dangerous secret Renira had been hiding all her life, that her mother worshipped God.

"You scared me back there, Ren," Aesie said quietly. "I thought you were going to drown, and... I really don't have a reason to be here without you."

Renira reached up with her hand and clutched her mother's moon amulet underneath her coat. She ran her thumb around the raised edges of it. "Why are you here, Aesie?" It sounded more like an accusation than she intended. Maybe it was. She knew Aesie left Riverden from time to time, away with her father on business, sometimes even to Celesgarde, but the chances that it would coincide with Renira's first time of leaving Riverden seemed beyond low. Renira imagined nefarious reasons for the apparent coincidence. A betrayal, her best friend working with her enemy to thwart her heroic quest. She shook her head and cursed her imagination. She hated suspecting her best friend of foul play.

"I told you, I was supposed to meet a prince." Aesie bit her lip, her gaze far away. "I thought it was going to be all fancy dresses and courtship. A few dinners maybe. Then back to Celesgarde for a wedding. I thought..." She sighed. "I thought I was going to marry a prince. I am such a bloody idiot, I actually thought that. I never thought I would be covered in dirt and sweat, huddled in a cold tower underground, running for my life. I suppose that's what happens when you trade a gallant prince for a wolf princess. Oh, I really am foolish, aren't I, Ren?"

"Truth?" Renira asked.

Aesie nodded. "Truth."

"You're pretty bloody foolish. Do you really want to marry a prince?" Borik was handsome enough, she supposed, and charming too. But Renira didn't trust him, and she couldn't quite say why. Everyone else seemed to. Well, not Armstar, but he trusted no one.

Aesie smiled, though there seemed to be little humour in it. "A means to an end. Marrying a prince has some benefits you just can't find anywhere else. Well, apart from marrying the king, I suppose. He's a bit old for me though."

Renira sent her friend a withering look. "He's a bit old for everyone, Aesie." She clutched her mother's amulet a little tighter. "But why are you here? You don't have to be. You really shouldn't have followed me."

"You don't have to be here either, Ren."

"I do." Though now she thought about it, the idea of running away, being free of the angels and the wolf princess and the Godless King. It all seemed quite enticing. It wasn't really her quest anyway, and she wasn't sure it was the right thing to do. The truth was, Renira was going through with it because she knew it was what her mother would want. *Would she? Mother tried to hide me from the angels.*

Aesie shook her head. "Well, I do too. I thought you were in trouble. I thought I'd come and rescue you or something. Like one of your stupid stories, Ren. I'd be the gallant hero and you my damsel in distress."

Renira chuckled. "Riding in on a pegasus? Take my hand and help me up behind you. Oh, mighty hero, take me away and save me from this peril."

Aesie nodded. "Something like that. Though my horse didn't have wings, and I left it behind. Also, the stories never tell how much horses smell. Anyway, it turns out you are in trouble, just not the sort I thought. I..."

Renira glanced at her friend to find tears in her eyes.

"I don't know what to make of all this, Ren. Angels are real. They're real! I guess I always knew they were, that's how the king and his family live such long lives, and there's a whole trade in divine blood and... But angels are real. You know, with wings and all that. Eleseth's a bloody giant."

Renira nodded. "You think she's big, you should see Orphus."

"They get even bigger than her?"

"Much bigger."

"Bloody breath, the world is strange."

Renira bumped her shoulder against Aesie's. "If it helps, it was a shock to me as well. You could have talked to me about it earlier instead of spending so much time arguing with Dussor."

Aesie laughed bitterly. "When? You have a little boy following you about like a second shadow."

Sun looked up at that. "I'm not a little boy."

Aesie shook her head. "No? You are a boy, yes?"

Sun nodded.

"And you are little, yes?"

Sun glared at her.

"So, you're a little boy. Maybe go find a stone to kick or something. Let the adults talk." Aesie dismissed Sun with a wave of her hand and turned her attention back to Renira. "And besides, I'm still trying to come to terms with the fact that angels are real. And I know their names. And they're a thousand years old. And one of them is the Herald. And I'm sorry if I've been spending so much time with Dussor, but he's just about the only thing out of all of this that I actually understand." She was crying now, fat tears rolling down her cheeks, streaking the grime.

"He's not an angel or a prince or anything. He's just a man who seems determined to keep arguing with me, despite that I punched him. I punched him, Ren. I punched someone! I've been on the run with you for all of a day, and I've already resorted to violence like... like... like Elsa. I'm just like Elsa. Flirting with anything in a pair of trousers and punching boys for no reason." She laughed, and it quickly turned to a sob.

Renira shifted around and pulled Aesie into a hug. She felt her own tears stinging her eyes and coursing down her cheeks. The exhaustion she could cope with, the brush with death, the threat of being chased, but seeing her friend break down in tears was too much. Renira had no words to make everything all right, no wisdom that could calm Aesie or make things make sense. So, she just held her tight and cried right along with her. It didn't seem like the sort of thing a hero would do, but then Renira was quickly realising she wasn't a hero. Those were just dreams she had once held. Illusions designed to make a dreary life seem more vibrant.

"I'm not like you, Ren," Aesie said between sobs. "I don't know how to deal with all this. I didn't grow up with it around. I'm not brave, and I don't have your strength."

Renira pulled her friend tighter for a moment, drying her eyes on Aesie's blonde hair. Then her words sank in, and Renira pulled back, letting go. "What do you mean I grew up with it around?"

Aesie stared at her through puffy red eyes still wet with tears. "You know, your mother. Her books and stuff."

Panic gripped hold of Renira. It was cold, even colder than the chill that had crept in since almost drowning, and it coiled around her gut with a gnawing ache. "How did you know about my mother, Aesie?"

Aesie frowned and shook her head. "Um, I've been to your house. We've known each other since we were... I don't know. It feels like forever." She sniffed and wiped her nose on her jacket sleeve, then looked appropriately embarrassed. "She had those books and icons and stuff."

Aesie said it as if it were common knowledge, but the books and icons were proof of faith, could get her mother killed. "Did you tell anyone?" Renira asked, clutching at Aesie's arms. "Did you ever tell anyone what you saw?"

Aesie frowned and shook her head. "No! I'm not stupid, Ren. And I'd never do that to you or her. People can believe whatever they want. Who am I to question it? I just thought... I don't know. What was the point in believing something that wasn't real?"

Renira's pulse raced, and she struggled to catch her breath. The thought that anyone might know her mother's secret, even her best friend, was terrifying. It would take so little to accuse her mother of heresy. She wanted to go home. She had a horrible feeling deep down in her gut, and knew it wouldn't truly go away until she saw her mother again. "Sorry. I just... I don't really know how to deal with all this either."

"Um, I don't know how to deal with it either," Sun said quietly.

"Really?" Renira asked. "You're holding up far better than either of us, Sun. Almost seems like you were born to it."

Sun shrugged. "I'm used to being chased."

"By whom?"

Sun frowned at her. "Bigger boys, wulfkin." He sniffed and turned away, and Renira couldn't help but think he was lying. He had said before his parents were fleeing Ashvold and had even mentioned a palace.

"Sun..." Renira started.

"Get up, children," Eleseth said loudly, taking two steps away from Armstar and turning her back on him. "We're moving on. Back down two levels."

Aesie caught Renira's eye and mouthed the word *children*.

"No, we are not!" insisted Armstar.

"We've been over this, brother. The path is blocked," Eleseth's voice was iron.

"And between us we can shift it. I can rig up another series of netting." He pointed behind him to where a section of the wall was crumbling and held in place only by rope and planks of wood. The rope was weaved into a tight netting, pulled taut and secured further down the wall, close to Sun. "It will be just as quick as backtracking."

Eleseth shook her head. "We can spare neither the time nor the effort, brother. You said there is another way through, two levels down. We head there and continue the ascent."

"No! Orphus put me in charge of bringing the Herald to Celesgarde. I choose our path, sister. Not you!"

Renira sent a look at Aesie. "Mum and dad are fighting again," she whispered, but there was no real humour in it. The two angels disagreed more and more, and Renira couldn't help but feel they would all suffer the consequences.

The angels were standing so close that Eleseth towered over Armstar, but the smaller angel did not back down. "You have lost perspective, brother." Eleseth whipped out her hand and cut through the rope secured to the wall. It went loose and the rigging fell away.

"No!" Armstar cried, but it was too late. The wall let out a rough grating noise and then shifted, the planks of wood tearing loose. Rocks and rubble crashed into the corridor ahead of them, filling the passageway with dust that set them all coughing, human and angel alike.

Armstar's voice cut over the noise of settling stone. "How could you be so stupid?" As if in response, the tower gave a shudder and a groan.

The stony walls undulated like a snake. A noise like a distant landslide echoed dully from somewhere below. Renira clutched hold of Aesie, and her friend held her right back, both clinging to each other as though that might keep them safe if the tower fell apart around them. Sun collapsed to his knees, his spear held in front of him like some sort of ward. A loud crack sounded, and both Armstar and Eleseth staggered backwards just as the floor in front of them fell away, stone crashing against stone. Dussor and Gemp and Kerrel reappeared from the far end of the corridor, weapons drawn and moving at a sprint, but there was nothing they could do. The tower gave another groan, the noise reverberating around them all, and then fell silent.

"Ooops," Eleseth said finally, once some of the dust had settled. The glow of her wings had dulled a little, and she winced as a final rock gave up clinging to its place in the tower and fell down the hole she had inadvertently created.

Armstar glared at the other angel, his hands balled into fists. "The tower is fragile," he said through clenched teeth. "Something a builder would know and a stupid damned philosopher would not."

Eleseth held up her hands. "I'm sorry, brother. I didn't mean to... I know this tower is important to you..."

Armstar shook his head savagely. "Well, now we're definitely taking your path. Assuming the lower levels are still there." He turned away from Eleseth and stalked past Renira. His ruined wings were twitching with annoyance, but there was grief, not anger on his face. Sorrow at the devastation of his dream.

Sun was on his feet first but waited for Renira. Ever the loyal protector. Renira clambered to standing and pulled Aesie up after her. She realised Kerrel was watching her, that same look of awe on her face from before. Renira turned away, unable to take seeing it.

They all moved on without another word, though at a slower pace than before. The partial collapse of the tower made them all want to take their time over the passage, rather than set off another rockslide.

After a while, Renira couldn't take the silence anymore. "So... Dussor?" Renira asked, pitching her voice low so only Aesie would hear.

Aesie shot her a grin. "He's handsome. In a boyish kind of way."

Renira glanced over her shoulder. Dussor noticed her watching him, so she grinned and turned away. "It's hard to tell under all those bruises."

Aesie gave her a playful little shove. "Stop it! I'm embarrassed enough already. I've never hit anyone before." They both glanced over their shoulders in unison.

"What?" Dussor asked, his face going red even in the dim light.

They both turned back. She hated to admit it, but it was quite fun making him squirm. "Are you sure you've never thrown a punch before? You did a good job of roughing him up for it being your first time."

"Stop!" Aesie said again and then broke into a grin. "It was a good punch though, wasn't it? He has a black eye."

They walked in silence for a while, and Renira found she was clutching at her mother's moon amulet. "Thank you," she said quietly.

"Hmm?"

"For coming to rescue me. I might not have actually been in trouble... or at least not the sort of trouble you thought, but you still braved the darkness alone to come and rescue me. My gallant hero. Thank you."

Aesie winced. "No. It's, um, it's nothing you wouldn't have done for me."

She'd never known Aesie to deflect praise before. Rather, she usually sought it out and basked in it. It was odd that her friend would seem so diminished, almost timid. "But I didn't," Renira said, watching Aesie closely. "I just ran off with Armstar, without a thought about you or Elsa or Beth. I hope they're alright. I hope my mother is all right. I said I'd be back in a few days. It's been weeks. She must be worried sick."

Aesie didn't look up from the stone floor. "How did it happen? Why did your mother stay behind?" There was a strange tremor in her voice.

"Someone had to keep the cycle of washing flowing," Renira said with a humourless chuckle. "Armstar turned up in the middle of the storm, you know on the night of the parade? He was hurt and being chased, and he needed help getting through the forest. Or, he said he needed help. I volunteered to guide him through while Mother kept everything going back home. I said I'd be home in a week at most. A little adventure for me."

"You always did want to go on an adventure. Never stopped talking about it."

"I did. I just guess I thought it would be a bit less... dangerous. Less scary. Fewer demons."

Something niggled at Renira then, something that didn't entirely make sense. She tried to puzzle it out as they walked, letting her feet follow along after Aesie, the passageways and rooms passing by her in a hazy blur of grey stone and piled rubble barely held back by rigging and wood. Armstar came to their house to see Renira's mother. He asked for a guide through the forest, but he didn't ask for Renira specifically. He didn't correct her when she said she'd only be a few days. But Armstar knew beforehand that Renira was the Herald. He must have known that he would have to convince her to come rather than Mother, and he must have known she was going to be gone for longer than a few days. She remembered him telling her to be brave before she even made the choice, and in that moment she had felt truly courageous.

He manipulated me from the start, making it seem like it was my choice. That power he has, to flare or dampen emotions, the one Mother forbade him to use on her. He's been using it on me from the moment we met.

Renira looked up. Aesie had pulled ahead a little, and beyond her the others kept going as though nothing was wrong. She opened her mouth to speak and heard a thud from behind followed by a strangled squeal of pain and terror. Renira turned, already knowing and dreading what she would see. Just a dozen paces away, a huge black wolf crouched as though ready to pounce. Dussor was trapped, an arm and his neck already in the beast's jaw, blood dripping from its maw. He flailed at the wolf with his free hand, but it had no effect. Behind the wolf, a figure emerged from the darkness, carrying a halberd and snarling like a wild animal.

The wolf princess had found them.

CHAPTER 37

Morality, as a concept, loses all meaning when confronted by nature and instinct. The wolf does not debate morals as its jaws close around its prey. The deer does not question whether it is right to flee and leave behind the weak. A tree does not refuse to grow in fear of shading out others desperate for light. Instinct, not morality, governs survivability.

— RODRIT HOSTAIN. YEAR 512 OF THE
SECOND AGE

"Herald," the wolf princess snarled. "I've come for your head."

The wolf growled and dragged Dussor back and forth. His eyes were full of fear, staring at Renira, pleading. But there was nothing she could do. There was nothing any of them could do.

"Let him go," Renira said. She wouldn't let Dussor die for her, wouldn't let anyone else die for her. "You can have me. Just let them go."

"Of course," the princess said with a savage smile. "Get rid of that, Tesh."

The wolf bit down, powerful jaws tearing and crushing into soft flesh. Blood spurted as Dussor died. Aesie screamed, and Renira felt the world tunnel before her. The wolf princess couldn't be stopped, couldn't be reasoned with.

She was going to kill them all, and there was nothing Renira could do or say to stop it.

"Run!" Kerrel roared the word as she drew her sword and charged. "FOR THE HERALD."

No one ran. Shock and fear rooted Renira to the spot. She stared at Dussor's body, watched blood pool beneath him, dripping through cracks between the rocks. His eyes were distant, unseeing. He was already gone.

Kerrel sliced her sword down. The wolf princess side-stepped the strike and punched Kerrel in the stomach. Kerrel's sword dropped from limp fingers, clattered to the stone. She bent over, dazed, and gasping for air. The wolf princess slammed Kerrel against the broken, crumbling wall of the corridor, stepped back, and drove the blade of her halberd through Kerrel's stomach and into the rock behind. Kerrel choked, blood gushing from her mouth. She pawed at the halberd with one hand and at the princess' face with her other. Then she went limp, still pinned to the wall. A few chunks of stone cascaded down around her body. One of the sections of rigging had been hit by the blade, and now hung as limp as Kerrel's corpse.

The wolf princess slowly turned her head to stare at Renira. She grinned. A wolf's grin, full of teeth and the promise of death. Behind her, the great wolf finished toying with Dussor's mangled corpse and threw it aside. He crashed against the wall next to Kerrel, dust cascading free and showering them both.

"No," Aesie said. She was beside Renira now, walking forward step by plodding step, eyes wide as a full Blood Moon. "Stop. Please. I didn't want this."

Renira caught her friend by the arm and pulled her to a halt. Aesie turned to look at her, but there was nothing but horror in those eyes. Aesie had never seen such savage violence before. She hadn't been at Los Hold. Hadn't seen what the wolf princess was capable of.

The wolf stepped up beside the princess, a red snarl on its lips, blood still dripping onto the stone. The princess gave her halberd a tug, and Kerrel's body jerked, but the blade was stuck in the wall. A few more stones shook loose though, and the rigging was sagging in places. Renira followed the line of it. It was secured to the wall beyond her, back where Sun was standing.

"Renira," Eleseth shouted. "Get back!" Finally, the angels started moving, but it was too late. Neither of them was a match for the wolf princess, both had admitted as much. But not all fights were decided with the clash of steel, and where even divine strength would surely fail, perhaps the cold crushing oblivion of rock might succeed.

"Sun," Renira shouted, pointing with her free hand even as she still gripped hold of Aesie with the other. "The rope!"

Sun lashed out with his spear, metal sparking against stone, and cut through the rope with one swipe. The rope whipped away, and the rigging sagged. The tower gave another shudder. Renira just had time to see panic on the Perel's face as she struggled with her trapped halberd, then the wall collapsed on top of princess and wolf both.

Rocks, stones, and cut blocks as large as boulders spilled out into the corridor, engulfing the princess and wolf, crushing them. The tower gave another shudder and a groan, and the floor beneath Renira shifted. Then the passageway in front of them, right where the princess had been, fell away into darkness.

Renira turned and ran, dragging Aesie along behind her. The tower lurched and they were all thrown to the floor. Aesie screamed and tugged at Renira. She turned back just as the weight of her friend falling into darkness pulled her half over the edge. Aesie hung from Renira's hand, her legs kicking the air below, tears streaming down her cheeks. Renira held on, gripping Aesie with one hand and clutching to the cut stone block of the floor with the other. Her vision swam from the effort. She wasn't strong enough. She met Aesie's eyes, and Renira felt her heart break. She couldn't take the weight, and if she tried, Aesie would drag her down to oblivion with her. She had no choice but to let go.

"I'm sorry," Renira hissed, meeting her friend's pleading eyes. She loosened her grip just as the stone beneath shifted once more. The floor fell away, and both Renira and Aesie fell with it, swallowed by the darkness.

CHAPTER 38

There is a world under our feet, and we never knew it.

The angels tried to steer me from this exploration with dire warnings of danger. Bah. I believe this simply means they are hiding things. They will not deter Uidoe Field from the greatest discovery of the age.

The caverns and tunnel systems beneath the Sant Dien Empire are so extensive I cannot believe them to be natural formations. They stretch from the Ashlands to the western coast, though many are flooded. More, there are ruins down here of an architectural style I have never encountered before. I believe a civilisation once thrived here, yet they are gone. Just gone.

I have my assistants gathering samples for further study. I will not allow the truth to remain buried.

— - EXCERPT FROM UIDOE FIELD'S FINAL
JOURNAL. DATED 17TH DAY OF BRINK YEAR 892 OF
THE THIRD AGE. JOURNAL FOUND YEAR 929 OF
THE THIRD AGE

Renira awoke to darkness and pain. Everywhere hurt, except the places that were numb, and that, she knew, was probably worse. She was lying flat on something cold and hard, left arm curled beneath her, and her right stretched out in front. Something warm tickled its way down her forehead, ran down her nose, and dripped. She felt fuzzy. Cold. A groan escaped her lips, loud in the peaceful stillness of the dark. She struggled to draw in another breath. Something was on top of her, something heavy with no give to it, crushing her with its weight.

Renira's heart quickened. Fear smothered her. She struggled. Her legs pushed against something hard and unyielding, and her left arm was trapped beneath her so tight she couldn't move it. Only her right arm was free but raised above her head—she could barely move other than to flail about and waggle her fingers. She panicked, kicking out as much as she could with her legs. She moved a little, her left hand scraping across rough stone as her body shifted. Something above her groaned, stone grinding against stone, and dust cascaded down into her face. She held her breath and tightened her throat, but the cough still erupted, and the jerking movement made her chest hurt in such a confined space. She let out a whine that was all fear and frustration and scrabbled about with her right hand, attempting to clear as much rubble away from her head as possible.

Another noise drifted toward her. A sobbing that sounded inhuman down in the dark. *The Grey! Sun said he saw it following us. What will it do if it finds me here, trapped? Or Aesie?*

Aesie! Renira had let her go, dropped her friend, sacrificed her to save herself just moments before the ground made the choice moot. How could she have done that to her best friend? She had to make amends. Aesie had fallen with her. Renira had to find her. *She has to be all right.*

She set to scrabbling more frantically, moving rubble away with her right hand and pushing with her legs while she wriggled her body side to side. Bit by bit she felt herself moving, her own weight crushing her left hand into the rough stone beneath. Her head bumped against stone and brought a wave of dizziness with it, but Renira persisted, tilting her head to the side and squeezing underneath the rock.

She realised then that she had no idea if she was crawling to freedom or deeper into her tomb. Her right hand felt empty space, but there was no guarantee it was a way out. Without light, even if she did crawl out of the rubble, could she ever find her way out? Would she ever see light again? *Stop it! What else am I going to do, lie here trapped underneath rock and wait to die? No! I have to keep moving.*

Whatever happened, however she might find herself trapped, she would struggle to fight her way free. Besides, Aesie was down there as well, as trapped as Renira, perhaps unable to move. Maybe even hurt. *Please be alive, Aesie.*

She wriggled and pushed with renewed vigour, determined to fight her way free of the confining rocky coffin. Sweat poured down her face as Renira struggled, and the rock above and below scraped her head, taking off layers of skin. By the time she'd wriggled out of the stone tomb, Renira was certain every bit of her was scraped raw and bloody. But at least none of her was numb anymore, and she counted that as a harsh victory.

It was pitch black. Usually her eyes took some time to adjust to the darkness of night, but when they did, she had passable night vision. Her mother had always said it was because she had eaten shade snails as a child. That they only came out at night, and by consuming them, Renira had stolen their ability to see in the dark. Renira couldn't remember eating shade snails or any other type of slimy creature, but Mother had insisted it was true, always with a smile on her face. Wherever she was now, there was not even a memory of light.

With a start, she remembered the earring Aesie had given her. It glowed faintly in the dark. Renira raised a hand to her ear and winced at the pain. The earring was dark, dull metal.

What if Aesie is dead and that was the last gift she ever gave me and I've broken it? Renira shook her head at the foolishness of it. She would not believe her friend was dead, and it was only an earring.

She got to her knees gingerly, arms raised above in case she found a sudden ceiling. Her head hurt enough already without adding another bump to her growing list of injuries. She got to her feet and slowly stood up to her full height, then took a deep breath and let it out as a sigh of relief. It turned into a mad cackle and then into tears.

The sobbing started again, a haunting noise that drifted through the still air and seemed to come from all around. Renira froze, her imagination plaguing her with fears. In her mind she saw the source of the sobbing as a small girl, dressed in white, curled up with her back turned away. Then, as Renira drew close, she saw blood staining the white rags. The girl's hands were misshapen, each finger tipped with a long talon. As Renira closed, the young girl stood and turned. Her face was a horror Renira couldn't describe, and her sobs turned to blood-curdling screams.

Renira crouched back down, an unwitting whimper escaping her lips. She knew her imagination was playing tricks on her, but the waking dream had been so terrifying she felt paralysed. "Stop it," Renira said, her voice barely even a whisper.

"Stop it," she said again, louder this time. "Stop it. Stop it. Stop it!" Each time she spoke it was more loudly than before. It was not directed at whoever was sobbing, but at herself, at her own stupid imagination playing tricks on her and freezing her in fear when what she needed to do was act.

"Ren?" said a small voice.

"Aesie? Is that you?" Renira asked in a rush, turning around in a circle though still able to see nothing at all.

"Yes!" Aesie said, voice wavering. "Ren, where are you?"

"It's too dark to see anything. Keep talking. I'll follow your voice."

"I'm sorry, Ren. I'm so sorry."

Renira angled herself toward the sound and took a slow step forward, her hands stretched out before her. "What for?"

"For everything. It's all my fault. Dussor is dead, and it's my fault!"

"What?"

"She followed me. Perel followed *me* into the mines."

Renira stumbled over a rock, kicking it with her big toe. She stopped and bit her lip against the pain, the only thing she could do to stop herself from screaming. When the pain lessened enough to continue, she limped forward, shuffling her feet step by step to prevent another accident.

"It's not your fault, Aesie," Renira said. "It's mine. Everyone is here because of me. The angels, Sun, Dussor, and Kerrel. The wolf princess. You. You're all here because of me. To protect me. Or to kill me. It's not your fault. It's mine."

She saw a soft blue glow, barely more than a haze of light. But in that glow, Aesie was huddled in on herself, hugging her knees drawn up to her chest.

Renira stumbled towards her. "It's me, Aesie." She knelt and quested out with her hands until she found Aesie reaching back. A moment later and they pulled each other close, clinging to what comfort they could offer down in the darkness. Renira's traitorous imagination pictured them found this way in a hundred years, two corpses clinging to each other with nowhere to go.

"You can't blame yourself," Aesie said. Her fingers clutched at Renira's back, holding her tight. "I chose to follow you. It's my own stupid fault I'm here." She sniffed and trembled.

Renira wiped tears away with her left hand and felt the sting of all the cuts and grazes there. "In that same logic, you *can't* blame yourself for the wolf princess being here. She chose to follow us."

Aesie laughed, but it turned into a sob. "That sounds like something Beth would say."

"Merebeth is wise beyond her years."

"It's all those books she reads," Aesie said. "I hope she's all right. Without you, I'm not sure Beth would ever leave her library."

"I'm more worried about Elsa. I swear I sometimes think we're the only ones holding her back from going on a punching spree."

Aesie chuckled. "I'm honestly surprised it's you out here and not her."

"Don't tell her I said it, but she's terrified of leaving Riverden. Elsa likes to pretend she knows about the wider world, but she admitted to me she's scared of leaving. She never liked being alone, not since her da left. Elsa would never have set out on her own. And me, well it wasn't really my choice. I didn't know what I was getting into. I didn't know..." She tried to tell her friend she was the Herald, but the words caught in her throat. For some reason, she didn't want Aesie to think of her as the Herald, destined to ring in a new age. The way Kerrel had looked at her with such reverence. Renira didn't want that, especially not from Aesie. She just wanted Aesie to see her as her friend. Just Ren. The same old cloud-headed girl she'd always been.

"Do you hear singing?" Aesie asked.

Now that Aesie mentioned it, Renira could hear something. A haunting noise drifting through the dark, melodic and wilting. There were no words, or at least none that Renira could understand, but some music had no need for clunky things like words. That was a lesson she had learned from a travelling bard who occasionally stopped at Ner-on-the-River. She never knew the bard's name, but she liked to think she knew his heart. He wore it for all to see every time he plucked at the strings of his lute. Renira could never hear the words he sang, not through the windows or over the hubbub of the tavern occupants, but she always felt the soul and emotion of the music. Down there in the dark, she felt the soul of the music again, and it was sadness. A haunting melody that ebbed and flowed like waves lapping the riverbank.

Renira closed her eyes, resting her head on her friend's shoulder. Weariness rose up to claim her. She hurt everywhere. Bruises, scrapes, and worse. She was cold, the chill having never quite left her after almost drowning. But most of all, she was tired. Tired of running, of being chased. Weary of being in danger. And so tired of being scared.

"Ren?" Aesie asked.

Renira felt herself growing heavy and relaxed into it. The quiet music, so soft and distant, lulled her. Images formed in her mind, the beginnings of dreams that vanished as quickly as they appeared. Everything started to feel fuzzy and numb. Comfortable.

Then Renira was shaking. She didn't like it, wanted it to stop. She grumbled at the shaking, but it persisted relentlessly.

She came to, still surrounded by darkness, unable to see anything. Aesie was shaking Renira by her shoulders and saying something, but it took Renira a few moments to focus on the words.

"Wake up, Ren. There's light. Two of them. There!"

Renira shuffled around sluggishly until she, too, saw the lights. Two of them, just as Aesie had said. Two little red lights in the darkness, like coals burning in the ashen remains of a dead fire. The Grey had found her.

Renira kept the two little lights in sight and manoeuvred around until she was beside Aesie. She kept her friend's left hand clutched in her right, unwilling to let go. If they lost each other now, in the darkness, they might never find each other again. Especially not with a demon down there with them. It was too much to hope that the Grey was as blind down there as they were. Armstar had said the demons had been driven into the dark places where man feared to tread. Of course they would be able to see in those dark places.

She scrabbled around the stone ground with her left hand, searching for a rock she could use as a weapon. She doubted it would be much use against a demon, but it would be better than nothing. She was sick of being frozen in fear, and if she was going to die by the Grey's hands, then she would die fighting just like she did against the demon in the forest.

"What's going on?" Aesie asked. "What is it?"

Renira considered lying, telling her friend that everything would be all right. There seemed little point. It would provide no comfort if the Grey decided to come for them. "They aren't lights," she said. "They're eyes. It's a demon."

Aesie whined.

"The people of New Gurrund called it the Grey. They said it could only be killed by..." Renira tried to remember. "I don't know. Nothing that we have."

They huddled there together, hand in hand, Renira armed only with a small rock. The singing continued. "Are you sure it's a monster?" Aesie asked eventually. "It's not moving. Perhaps it's just lights?"

The Grey blinked, both burning red eyes blinking out of existence for a moment, and Aesie squeaked, clutching more tightly at Renira's hand. "Is it going to kill us?"

A moment ago, Renira would have said yes, but now she was growing less certain. It must have seen them, it was staring right at them, and any demon could tell neither Renira nor Aesie were any threat. They were an easy meal.

I'm done waiting around to be eaten. She drew in a deep breath, struggled to her feet, and stepped forward towards the demon.

Aesie tugged back on her hand. "What are you doing?"

Renira took another step, dragging her friend with her. "It found its way down here. It must know a way out." Each step leant her more confidence. She didn't know if she was doing the right thing, but at least she was doing something.

"But what if your friends can't find us?" Aesie asked.

"We don't even know if they're alive, Aesie." It was a possibility she didn't really want to consider, that the collapsing tower might have taken them all with it. What if by collapsing that wall, Renira had killed Sun and Gemp and Eleseth and Armstar along with the wolf princess? *Stop it! I just have to deal with what I do know and what's in front of me.*

"We can't just sit here and wait for someone else to rescue us. And if that demon is going to kill and eat us, it's going to do it whether we sit here or march toward it. So, we might as well hope it's a friendly demon and ask if it knows a way out."

"Oh," Aesie said. "I didn't realise there were friendly demons as well. When you said monsters, I assumed they were all... you know, flesh-eating beasts."

Renira was quiet at that. She had only two experiences with demons, and one was the forest monster which had definitely been trying to eat them all. Or possibly worse. But her mind was made up, and her course was set, and her feet were following it. Besides, she had a rock in one hand and a friend in the other. Together, they had survived the wolf princess; they could survive whatever the dark threw at them.

They went slowly, clinging to each other for comfort as much as necessity. Each shuffling step seemed to take forever, and each step brought the burning eyes of the Grey a little closer. Then the eyes disappeared, and Renira heard the whisper of clawed hands scrabbling across stone. She tensed, bracing for the attack, and held her little rock out in front of her like the shield she had so often dreamed of using to protect the innocent. The eyes reappeared, further away once again, two little points of burning light, red stars in the night sky.

"Did it just run away?" Aesie asked.

No, that didn't seem quite right. Why would a demon be running from them? "Or is it leading us?" Renira said.

"Leading us where?"

"Its lair?" Renira said with a shrug. Aesie's grip on her hand tightened. "Or maybe the way out? Friendly demon. Just keep hoping it's a friendly monster. You are a friendly demon, right?"

They followed the Grey again, and as soon as they got close enough that Renira was starting to think she could see the fuzzy outline of its face illuminated by the light of its eyes, the little demon disappeared and reappeared further away. They followed it again, still shuffling slowly, making certain of every footfall.

At first Renira thought she was imagining it, but it soon became too obvious to deny; the singing was growing louder. She knew then where the Grey was leading them. It was taking them to the source of the music. Music Armstar had warned them not to listen to. He had said no one who followed it ever came back. And yet that was where they were going.

Not like we have any other choice. One more danger to face down and say 'you shan't take me today'.

The light was shocking when it appeared. The Grey disappeared again, and Renira heard claws on stone to her left. She turned, and there in front of them, no more than a hundred paces away, soft white light spilled out of a doorway in the stone around it. She gave Aesie's hand a little tug and heard her friend gasp.

"Light!" Aesie cried, relief clear in her voice. She tugged free of Renira's grasp and ran for the light. Renira caught sight of the Grey ducking inside the lit room, and then she ran after Aesie. When finally she could see her own feet again, the relief that flooded Renira made her laugh. The light came from a single door, and the rest of the world was still shrouded in darkness. Renira had no idea if they were still in the tower or back in the cavern. Maybe they had fallen even deeper.

Aesie reached the light first, and Renira was shocked at how dishevelled her friend was. She had never seen Aesie appear anything but her best, always fashionable, makeup on special occasions. Even when they were children, Aesie was always careful to present herself as was proper for a girl of her station. Now, she looked like she'd been taking fashion tips from a beggar. Her coat was gone, her dress ripped, her hair a mess, and there was dried blood on her arms, showing through her torn sleeves. She slid to a halt when she reached the doorway and looked inside. Then she gasped and fell away, hand clamped over her mouth.

Renira reached the doorway a few seconds later and felt her own legs almost give way as she saw what was inside. There was an angel inside the room, chained up and singing.

CHAPTER 39

They're coming! Oh God, I'm so sorry. Why didn't I listen?

The ruins are not deserted. This underground world is not empty.

There are only two of us left. We've barricaded the door, collapsed the foyer, but I can hear them. They scream in the dark. Their claws scratch at the rock. We are almost out of light.

God, please save me. They're coming!

— EXCERPT FROM UIDOE FIELD'S FINAL JOURNAL.

FINAL ENTRY

The prison was large and square, with two entrances opposite each other. It was lit not by lanterns or torches, but by white feathers fallen from the angel's wings. Yet his wings were black, dark as a raven. Only once the feathers had fallen did they seem to glow with an intense white light like feathery stars among the night sky. The angel was chained up, his legs secured to the ground, his arms hanging from chains reaching up to the ceiling. There were no manacles. Instead the final links of the chains were driven through flesh and bone. His body seemed to have healed around them, proving his incarceration was not recent. His dark wings were stretched out to the sides, secured to the far walls of the prison by half a dozen metal bolts driven through the bones of each wing.

He looked like an insect specimen at the school back in Riverden, killed and pinned, limbs splayed out for display. Only the angel wasn't dead. He was very much alive. And singing.

Renira crept into the room. Aesie, a step behind, grabbed hold of Renira's hand. They clutched each other for comfort. The angel hadn't seen them yet. He was hanging limp in his chains, his arms and wings pulled back. He was naked, or near enough that the difference didn't matter. A few rogue strips of ragged cloth hung from his emaciated body, dirty grey against the charcoal of his skin. The angel's head was down, drooping, dark hair hanging almost to the ground in matted curls. Now they were closer, Renira could tell the angel was singing in words, but she did not recognise the language. The melody was soft, rising and falling, the tempo speeding and slowing. The sound of his voice was almost mesmerising.

Aesie gave Renira's hand a little tug, pulling her out of her reverie. She pointed with her free hand, and Renira followed it to see the Grey crouched in the far corner of the angel's prison. The little demon was indistinct, a fuzzy grey shimmer more impression than actual shape. Its red eyes glowed fiercely, making it appear malevolent. But it had led them here, out of the dark and into the light. A demon had led them to an angel.

Renira stopped by the feather that had fallen furthest from the chained angel and stared down at it. There were a dozen other fallen feathers, each one glowing just as brightly, shedding more light than any lantern ever could. Renira crouched down and picked the feather up. No matter what else happened here, they would not get trapped in darkness again.

The singing stopped.

"You've arrived," the angel said. He had a voice like old leather, creaky yet somehow comforting. He lifted his head, and Renira caught a glimpse of his face behind the matted curls of hair. He was younger than she had first thought, the face of a boy just starting to become a man. A broad nose, thin lips, and eyes so black they were voids drinking in the light. "The last hope of the dying. And the viper in a wolf's den."

Renira glanced at Aesie quickly and then back to the angel. "Who are you?"

"Moon. My name is Moon. I'm God's Apostle." He looked from Renira to Aesie, then frowned. "Don't tell me they've written me out of history already. You were right, by the way." He twisted in the grip of the chains, staring underneath his wing toward the Grey. "I was certain we were still at least a century too early." He relaxed back into the grip of the chains and looked up at Renira again. "What year is it?"

Renira had no idea how to answer that. She had been taught about years back in school, but that had been some time ago and it was simply not useful for a washer girl to know.

"Year one-thousand-and-fifty-eight of the Fourth Age," Aesie said. Of course she would know. Renira supposed dates were very important to merchants.

The angel grinned. "The Age of Heresy draws to an end. Mathanial must already be dead. Poor Mathanial. He never wanted this for his age. He wanted to see the world, to explore it and discover its secrets." Moon sighed. "Poor, poor Mathanial. I never did like him much, overly fond of horses. Very strange."

Aesie tugged on Renira's hand and frowned at her. Whoever the angel was, there was something off about him. But Renira didn't feel like she was in danger here, and she was certain there was something to be learned from him. She tucked the glowing feather into a pocket on her coat and took another step forward.

"I've never heard of you before, Moon. Are you an angel from the Third Age?" She judged by his size. Eleseth said the angels from the First Age were all giants, and those from the Second Age were not much smaller, but angels from the Third Age were made to appear more human, and Moon looked no taller than Dussor had been.

Moon laughed, a deep chuckle that rattled all his chains. "Third Age? No. I was made before the Ages, Renira Washer." He raised his head and fixed her with his void eyes.

"How do you know my name?" she asked.

"I know a lot of names. Faces. Some are, some were, some never will be. I've been waiting for you. Or, I suppose I've just been waiting." Moon gave the chains attached to his arms a little tug. "I don't really have much of a choice. But I knew you'd come. You always come here."

"What do you mean? How did you know I'd come here?" Renira asked, desperate and afraid to know the answer.

"I already told you, you always come here. You're usually brighter, I think. I have seen it." Moon frowned. "Well, maybe, I've not seen it. I've seen around it."

"He's mad," Aesie said. "My father told me about this. People kept in prison too long go crazy. Something to do with being locked up with only their own thoughts."

"You're half right," said the angel.

Renira wanted answers, and she had too many questions to keep straight. "You brought us here on purpose. After we fell, you got your demon to lead us here."

"Demon? No. No. No demons. Well, maybe me. Am I a demon? Oh, you mean Tamuel?" He twisted about to look under his wing toward the Grey again. "He's no demon. He's... Was forgotten. Trapped down here when Emrik closed the mine. I tried to... Hmm. I guess I tried to play God, create my own angels. I failed. He's a failure. All my children are failures. But then we're all failures, so maybe I didn't fail. I love them all the same."

Renira looked at the Grey. A shifting form, indistinct, like clouds on a rainy day. "I don't understand. You created him?"

"Of course, you don't," the angel said. "Because you don't know. Because I haven't explained it yet... Or have I? How many times have we had this conversation?"

"Pretty sure this is the first," Renira said. Aesie was right, the angel was clearly mad, but she wasn't sure it was because he was chained up. And mad or not, if he was as old as he claimed, then he might have some answers. "What is wrong with you, Moon?"

"Aaah. That." Moon nodded his head and smiled. "My vision is unstuck. One of the God's little gifts, I think. He tried to make me the perfect angel, able to see everything. It didn't work. I was *his* failure. Ah, well... his first failure. One of many." The angel chuckled and it quickly turned into a full raucous laughter. Then he stopped suddenly.

"I see the past how it should be, the future how it could have been, and the present how it will never be. Nothing I see is real. It makes figuring out the truth quite difficult, you know. Of course, I know what happened because I lived it, didn't I? Or was that, too, how it should have been?"

Aesie let out a sigh. "We're not going to get any sense out of him, Ren. Let's just take a couple of feathers and go, use the light to find a way out."

Moon laughed. "Oh, you don't go just yet, Aesie Fur. Your friend has some questions for me, though she won't much like the answers. No matter how I answer them, you never like the answers. But I suppose that's your fault, not mine."

"You know my name as well," Aesie said, her eyes wide and voice trembling.

"Of course. You are usually here, though sometimes you're not. Sometimes you died. In the fall or in the storm. Sometimes in the crib." A nasty grin spread across his face. "Things go better those times." The smile faded. "Up until a point."

Renira felt Aesie's hand tug free of her own and glanced back to find her friend had backed away a step, a deep frown on her face. She couldn't decide what Moon meant by sometimes Aesie died. She couldn't decide what any of his *answers* meant.

"What questions do I ask?" Renira said, turning back to the angel.

Moon swayed back and forth at the end of his chains. "You always ask if you're doing the right thing," he said eventually. "Always."

Renira considered taking Aesie's advice and leaving. With the light from the feathers, they might be able to find their way up and out, or at least back to the others, and it was already quite clear that Moon was mad. But he also might have answers, if she could just ask the right questions. Eleseth and Armstar were hiding things from her, she knew that much. She just couldn't figure out what and why.

"Why are you here?" Renira asked eventually. "Did the Godless King imprison you?"

"Ertide?" Moon said with a laugh. "No. He was my friend."

"Ertide is dead," Aesie said quietly. "His grandson is the king now."

"Emrik is king?" Moon raised his head and sent a piercing stare Renira's way. "Oh dear, you really are in trouble." He started laughing again. "We are all in a lot of trouble."

"Who imprisoned you then?" Renira said.

"God, of course. Well, no, he was already dead. But his two minions, Orphus and Armstar. Are they dead yet? I hope they're dead. Sometimes they're dead, but other times they live forever. Those times are not good for anyone. Better dead."

"You said you are God's Apostle. Why would he imprison you?"

Moon's chains rattled as he settled on his feet. "Who do you think told Ertide what eating angel flesh could do for a human? Me! One of many truths I whispered in his ears. Or were they ever true? Hmm."

Armstar had said it was a demon who seduced Ertide into tasting angel flesh. But Moon didn't look like a demon. He looked like an angel, a child of the God. Renira found herself shaking her head at it all. "You orchestrated the war between humans and heaven? Deliberately?"

"Yes."

"Why?"

Again, Moon fixed Renira with that black stare. "To kill him, of course. To kill God."

"What?" Renira said. "Why would you want to kill God?" she asked, her voice rising. "He made you. He created all the angels."

"No," Moon said solemnly. "No, that's not quite right. *I* made *him*. Or *we* made him. Hmm. He and I made him. Then he made me. Yes. Yes, that makes sense."

Renira was still trying to figure that out when Aesie asked a question.

"What other truths did you whisper to Ertide? How did you make him turn against the God?"

Moon's head snapped toward Aesie, and he looked confused. "You never ask any questions, little viper. Never."

Aesie sucked in a ragged breath. "Well I'm asking one now. I can ask some more, if you like. Why is the sky red? Why is water wet? How is it strawberries taste like summer? And why did Dussor have to die?"

Moon smiled at her, white teeth amidst a dark face. "I told him the truth about the great heresy. I told him of God's great lie. The sky is red because the God is dead. Water is only wet when it flows. Memory is an imperfect encapsulation of sense and nostalgia. And, uh, I have no idea who that is."

"What truth?" Renira asked. "What is the truth about the great heresy?"

"I've already told you." Moon frowned. "Have I? Yes. I've definitely told you that one. It's not my fault you're too stupid to realise it."

Aesie bristled. "I'm not stupid. You're just crazy."

"Be quiet, viper," Moon spat. "I'm here to answer her questions, not yours. You shouldn't even be asking any. Stop changing the past."

Aesie fell silent again, but Renira could see her trembling.

"You're running out of time to ask, little last hope. The other one will be here soon, and you don't want to be here for that. You were still here for it once." The angel shook his head. "The worst of all outcomes. The birth of a new terror."

Renira took a couple of steps forward. "Why did you kill God?" She was close enough that she could see his face clearly now, and she could see the conflict on it. He had youthful features but an old face, and his eyes were two fathomless pits.

"I didn't," Moon said quietly. "I just told Ertide how he could do it. How to steal an angel's power. How to forge weapons that could pierce our shields. No, wait. That was Karna. I definitely told Ertide how to open Heaven's Gate. I gave him the means. What he did with it is not my responsibility."

"You've already admitted you convinced him to turn against God," Renira argued, tired of his fecklessness. "You gave him the means and the motivation. Take responsibility. Stop lying, and tell me why you killed God?"

Moon let out a low chuckle and spoke in a whisper. "*That* is the question you always ask. But I never know why. Why do you want to know, little hope? What makes the why so necessary? Please, help me understand."

Renira ground her teeth together for a moment, then realised she was clutching at her mother's amulet again. An amulet of the moon. The answer came to her. "Because I'm supposed to bring him back. And I want to know if that's the right thing. Is the world better off without God?"

Moon shook his head. "No. No better."

"Then why kill him?"

Moon went limp again, leaning against his chains, his head dangling, face covered by his hair. A single tear dropped to the ground. "For love."

"Love of whom?" Renira asked. "Ertide?" This angel answered each question with a riddle of new questions. She wasn't even certain he was telling the truth about any of it. Maybe he was lying to her, just like everyone else.

A bitter chuckle slithered from Moon's lips. "Yes and no. He was my friend. For the love of the sun, I saw no other way."

"What does that mean? What does any of it bloody mean?"

Moon started and pulled against his chains, then looked sidelong at them, as though surprised and confused to find he was confined so. "You should go, little last hope. You're out of time. Follow the child; he'll lead you to the surface." Moon went limp again, his head hanging.

"I'm not leaving until you actually answer my questions!" Renira snapped.

"Suit yourself. But you never survive if you stay. She's coming, and death rides her. We all fall if you meet." He drew in a deep breath and picked up his song again. Still, Renira could not understand the words, but she knew the emotion now. The song was sadness and grief. A eulogy for the angel's love.

Renira took a step back and found Aesie beside her, a glowing feather in each hand. "He's talking about Perel, isn't he?" she said. "Please tell me we're leaving now."

Renira looked back to the singing angel. God's Apostle. She realised then he must have been the first angel, even older than Orphus. Even older than the ages. How long had he been chained up down here, all alone? Whatever he had done, surely an eternity in prison was too harsh a punishment?

"Do you want us to free you?" Renira asked. She wasn't even sure they could. The chains looked far too sturdy for them to break, but she was willing to try. If he was right and the wolf princess was coming, she would try.

Moon stopped singing again and looked up at her, surprise and gratitude on his face. "No. You aren't the one who frees me, little hope." He lowered his head again and picked up his song where he left off.

Aesie took hold of Renira's hand. "Time to go, Ren. I'm long past sick of this place and him." They skirted the chained angel, making certain to stay out of reach. The Grey was waiting by the far door and slipped out when they drew close.

"You never asked," Moon said just before they left his little prison. "You didn't ask if you were doing the right thing. You always ask. Oh, I see now. Perhaps there is hope, after all. Stop asking others for reasons, little hope. Find them yourself, or they won't mean a damned thing anyway."

They slipped out of the prison and into a winding staircase that led up into the dark. The Grey waited for them a few steps ahead, his form somehow even less distinct in the light of the Apostle's glowing feathers. Behind them, Moon started singing.

CHAPTER 40

Peace by compromise is another form of capitulation. You cannot compromise with evangelical zealotry. There is no give in them; they will eat away at your way of life until one day you realise it is their rules you are living by and your once compromise was just a drawn out surrender.

— ERTIDE HOSTAIN. YEAR 44 OF THE FOURTH
AGE. 1 YEAR BEFORE HEAVEN FELL

Perel and Tesh ran side by side, a blurred collage of green and brown flashing all around them. A forest, the Ruined Veil deep in Dien, one of the last great wildwoods, filled with secrets. Filled with monsters. She blinked into her wolf's sight for a moment, and everything came into sharp focus. Where her own sight could not keep up with such speed, rendering everything in vague impressions, the wolf saw clearly. Every tree, every leaf, every root, every insect desperately trying to crawl out of the way of the woman and wolf. In Tesh's vision, everything was so much clearer. Perel blinked again, seeing through her own eyes once more, and felt an immediate loss. The world was a less vibrant place to humans than it was to a wolf.

Tesh sniffed the air and slowed her pace until she was walking. Perel pulled up beside her wolf, breathing hard. Tesh wasn't even panting. The run hadn't taxed her at all. Perel had been at her limit, sprinting, and for almost an hour now. The wolf could have run like that all day and counted it easy exercise. There was a scent on the balmy summer air, a sharp animal musk. It played on the edges of Perel's sense of smell, but her sight bond to Tesh enhanced all her senses. Even father didn't understand how. That had been a humbling thing to realise, that Emrik Hostain didn't know everything.

Tesh growled softly; she could always sense when Perel's concentration slipped. The wolf was focused, living in the hunt, not plagued by inner musings and a wandering mind. Perel envied her that, along with a great many other things. The wolf knew no mercy, no conscience, no hate. She had no old grudges to settle, no siblings taunting her yet remaining beyond retaliation. The wolf had no expectations to live up to past surviving from day to day. As long as she provided meat for her pack, for her children, she was content. There were times Perel wished she had been born a wolf.

With another soft growl, Tesh padded away, vanishing into the under-growth. Perel considered switching their sights again, just for another moment. It was an oddity, that she could activate the sight bond whenever she chose but the wolf could not. A form of dominance, in a way. A reminder to the wolf that Perel was in charge. Not that she would ever use the bond that way. They were equal in almost all things. Almost.

Perel sniffed the air and started forward, picking her way through the under-growth as quietly as possible, leaving no trace of her passage. The leaf litter crushed beneath her feet with a whisper, spongy and damp from yesterday's rain. A buried twig snapped beneath a footfall, loud as a thunder crack in the quiet. A nearby bird took to the air in a flutter of wings. Perel cursed her human clumsiness and continued, more careful this time.

She stopped behind a hazelthrush bush, its wide leaves obscuring her from the trickling stream beyond. A perfect vantage. Hidden from view, the strong scent of the bush masking her own human stench. A duwn stood by the water's edge. It was a large creature, as tall as Perel and twice as heavy. It had four legs, each ending in a delicate hoof, and two small vestigial wings upon its back. Father claimed they had been able to fly once, that they were the result of a pegasus and a deer breeding. No doubt the Rider's influence upon the world. The pegasi were apparently his crowning achievement. Perel would have liked to see one of the flying horses, but her father had made sure no one ever would.

The duwn looked up for a moment, its long snout twitching as it sniffed the air, ears flicking back and forth. Perel went still, even slowing her breathing, half closing her eyes. The duwn sniffed a few more times, then lowered its head to the ground and began chewing on a small sapling it found there.

Perel knew her wolf was close, but there was no sign of her. She blinked into Tesh's sight and was shocked to find the huge wolf on the other side of the stream, hidden within the undergrowth, waiting. Perel could see herself in her wolf's eyes, picked out clearly even hidden as she was. But her gaze was drawn to the duwn. It looked vibrant, alive. She could feel the blood pulsing through it. Perel felt both their mouths salivating at the thought of biting into its flesh. She blinked back to her own sight and felt the loss of definition again.

Perel had no weapons save her own hands and a boot knife. She could make the kill if need be, divine strength removed any advantage the duwn might have, but Tesh was better suited for the kill. She would savour it more as well. As good as it felt to tear the life from a creature with her own hands, it would mean more to Tesh. To a wolf, such an act was fulfilling its very purpose.

Perel burst out of the bush with all the noise of a rockslide. The duwn bolted in an instant, not even taking the time to look up at Perel. It leapt across the stream, aiming for the bushes on the far side. Tesh exploded out of the undergrowth in a flurry of sabre-teeth and ragged claws, colliding with the duwn and knocking them both to the forest floor. They fought there for a few moments, teeth and claw versus hoof and horn. The duwn, ambushed and wounded, tried to secure its freedom with force. It had the weight advantage over Tesh, but Perel's wolf had eaten angel flesh and had drunk the blood of the divine. She moved faster than any wolf and struck with such terrible force that each blow tore huge rents in the duwn's flesh. Eventually the creature went down, mewling and still trying to get away even though only one of its legs yet worked. It scrabbled on the ground for a time. Tesh moved in and sank her sabre-teeth into the beast's neck, ending its struggle for good and lapping down mouthfuls of hot blood.

They feasted there beside that stream, surrounded by green trees and the sounds of the forest. It felt right. Natural. Peaceful even, despite the cooling body of the duwn at their feet. And when they slept, it was curled up together, content with full bellies and the knowledge that they were safe. That they were queens of the forest.

Perel coughed and tasted blood and rock dust. It wasn't the blood of the duwn, hot and sweet. Nor the blood of an angel, the taste of which had always been beyond any comparison she could level at it. It was her own blood. She coughed again and felt more of it spatter her lips. Something was broken inside, something vital. She opened her eyes to darkness and felt the cold pressing in on her.

When she tried to move, she found she couldn't. Memories of falling tumbled back to her. She was trapped. Crushed by rock, buried underneath a ruined tower. Left to die alone.

Not alone, she realised. Never alone. Not her. Tesh was nearby. Her wolf's presence was a beacon of sharp pain stabbing at her. Tesh wasn't just nearby, she was buried along with Perel. She could hear her wolf whining, a soft, high-pitched keening that made her angry and desperate.

Perel wriggled and squeezed until her hands were beneath her. Her left leg hurt like the bone was on fire. She hoped it was only broken and not crushed, but she had neither the time nor the space to investigate the pain. She pushed with her hands, finding as much purchase as she could with her right leg as well. Nothing moved save for a scattering of rubble and a new wave of dust drifting down and making her cough. She was trapped, a tomb of rock burying her alive.

Tesh whined again.

"No," Perel said, her own voice a whine so close to Tesh's. "No." More firmly this time. "No!" She felt a fire light inside, the heat of it creeping into her voice. "NO!"

Perel drew in a deep breath, settled her hands and braced her feet, and pushed. Her back hit the rock above, unyielding as the mountain. But it was not just her strength she possessed. Perel possessed the strength of angels, the power of the divine. She had consumed dozens of angels, including the strongest, those from the First Age. She would not let a few paltry stones stop her. She would not allow anything to keep her from her wolf.

A scream tore from her mouth, the burning in her arms becoming unbearable, the pressure against her back agony. The rocks shifted. At the end of her breath, the darkness swimming in front of her eyes, Perel felt the rock slide off her back. Finally, she threw the weight aside and stood, gasping in a breath and stumbling as her left leg threatened to collapse. It was broken, but she didn't have time to set it.

Perel closed her right hand into a fist and chased the darkness away with Mihiriel's light. She was in a large chamber that appeared to be carved from rock. There were boxes stacked in one corner and some of them had been dashed open, old relics spilling out. There were statues of white stone in the depiction of angels, books and scrolls, a carving of a lion. One of the walls and most of the ceiling had given way, and everywhere lay the proof of that. Rocks, some huge cut stone, others rounded boulders, were strewn about everywhere. She raised her hand and tightened her fist, but the hole in the ceiling seemed to go on for a long way, like some giant worm had decided to tunnel its way through the tower, carving stone away and leaving only debris behind.

Tesh's whining brought Perel back to the room, and she turned away from the hole above. She clambered over rocks, further into the wreckage of the store-room. It was tough going, dragging her left leg along with her, gritting her teeth against the pain. Against all the pains. She was riddled with too many injuries to bother counting. Tesh was in trouble, and no paltry wound was as important as that. She let her bond guide her, illuminating the way with Mihiriel's light streaming from between her fingers.

Her wolf was buried, and not shallowly. Where a single large stone slab had fallen on Perel, Tesh had been buried beneath many. She was alive though. Through their bond, Perel could feel her wolf below her. The pain Tesh was in tore at her nerves, as did her wolf's terror of hopelessness as she scrabbled feebly at the stone trapping her. Perel could smell the fear. And the blood.

She knelt, taking the weight off her broken leg, and shuffled her fingers beneath the first of the rocks. Her strength was great, but it was not limitless, and she was already tired. Even so, Perel growled as she heaved on the rock, lifting it up bit by bit until she could throw it to the side. Then she bent down again and worked on the next slab of stone trapping her wolf.

It seemed to take an age to shift each rock. More than once, Perel lost her grip and dropped a slab only to hear a frantic whine from below that ripped her heart in two. Tears and sweat and blood mixed together as she shifted rock after rock. And then she reached down, and her hand found fur, coarse and damp with oily fear.

One of Tesh's sabre-teeth was broken, snapped off near the root and leaking dark blood. Her ear was torn and her fur matted with gore. A sharp spike of rock had thrust into her chest and was grating against a rib. Perel edged down into the hollow she had created and sniffed at her wolf. She knew the truth before she was willing to admit to it. Tesh's heartbeat was slow, her breath bubbling in her lungs. She had lost too much blood. Taken too great an injury. Her own feeble attempts at resistance had long since stopped, and she lay still, tongue lolling, yellow eyes fixed on Perel. She smelled like dying prey, full of fear.

"No," Perel whispered, holding her wolf's huge head in her lap. "You can't die. Do you hear me, Tesh? You can't. I don't allow it!" Tesh shifted a little, licked once at Perel's hand, then went still again, breath barely even a whisper.

"I'll dig you out. Then I'll find one of those damned angels and feed them to you, Tesh. Fresh angel. How does that sound? Something worth living for."

Tesh lay there, breath getting shallower. Perel could even feel her dying through her bond. A thought occurred to her then. It was a bond that no one truly understood. A bond that held more power than anyone realised, even her father. Perhaps, through that bond, she could somehow force her wolf to cling to life. Maybe she could give Tesh her own strength to keep going.

It was desperation more than reason that took hold of Perel. She blinked into Tesh's sight and saw herself, kneeling on cold rock, covered in blood and wounded. Crying over her dying wolf. She saw herself, lit only by Mihiriel's pulsing light. Beaten, desperate. Pathetic. She saw herself...

Tesh died.

The wolf's heart stopped. Her body sagged. Her vision froze.

"No," Perel whispered. Grief and horror mixing together. She turned her head left, then right. All she saw was herself, looking pathetic, beaten, ugly and bawling. She tried closing her eyes. It didn't help. She struggled to her feet, tripped and went tumbling down the pile of rocks she'd dug away from Tesh. All the while seeing nothing but herself, trapped in the worst moment of grief she could ever feel.

"No, no, no, no, no..." Perel scrabbled away on hands and knees, tears streaming down her blood streaked cheeks, but no flood of tears could blur the sight that assaulted her. Her wolf was gone. Tesh was gone, and she had taken Perel's sight with her, leaving her forever trapped in the last vision her wolf had ever seen. A constant reminder of Perel's utter failure, of her loss. It was too much. She felt the walls closing in. Blood rushed in her ears. The hole that had opened inside her heart swallowed her. And through it all Perel saw her own frozen face, twisted in a hideous moment of mourning.

Perel screamed. No words. Just emotion. Fury and sadness and fear and rage all mixed into one cry that sounded so much like a howl. She reached up to her face with her hands and fingernails dug into flesh. The pain was a distant thing. The agony of flesh nothing but a drop in the ocean when compared to the open wound of her heart. Perel dragged her hands down, clawing bloody gouges in her face. She carved her own eyes out of her skull.

CHAPTER 41

The demon was massive, half again as tall as a man, and its skin was torn where horns had ripped out through its flesh. It held its blood-forged blade high in the air and screamed out a challenge so loud the mountains shook as though thunder rattled their bones. But the Saint was not cowed. With her Exemplars at her back, she faced the demon and said:
"Not today do I die, monster. Not here do I fall. You. Will. Break!"

— THE LAST LIGHT OF THE EXEMPLARS, *ROOK'S*
COMPENDIUM

It was a relief when Renira finally slipped out between the crack in two rocks and saw the blood red sky overhead. Even half-hidden beneath the canopy of broad-leafed trees, it brought comfort to her. It was not that the sky held some special place in her heart, but more that it was a symbol that they had left the mines and caves and tower behind. Preferably forever.

They had also left Dussor and Kerrel, dead and buried. Renira had not known them well. Kerrel's intensity had bothered her, and she had admitted to being a murderer, but Dussor had been friendly and charming, and she wished she had gotten to know him better. They had died for her, protecting her. The grief over the two they had lost and the four others they might yet lose, finally broke over Renira. Now they were above ground again, she could no longer hold it back. She collapsed onto her knees on the forest floor and sobbed quietly into her grazed hands.

Aesie slipped out of the passage between the rocks next. They had climbed the stairway for what seemed like forever, until their legs burned from the effort, until they were both sweaty and out of breath from the exertion, and both were on the edge of collapse. They were chased by a scream that seemed to grow in intensity as it echoed. Equal parts grief and horror and fury. That had pushed them both on a little harder, burying the exhaustion under a blanket of fear.

"I can't even see it anymore," Aesie said.

Renira glanced back through her tears. The stairwell had exited into a tight passageway between two boulders each as large as a few houses stacked together. Looking back, Renira could no longer see where they had emerged, as though it were somehow hidden from the outside. Part of her was glad; she did not want to go back.

The Grey sat on top of one of the boulders, staring down at her with its burning coal eyes. It looked no less demonic in the light of day, its form fuzzy and indistinct. Staring at the Grey was like staring into a writhing bucket of maggots; it was impossible to keep track of one, and the constantly moving mass soon made Renira feel ill. Ceramic knives, she remembered. The soldier had said only ceramic knives could hurt it. Not that it mattered any more. It never had. The Grey meant them no harm.

"Thank you," Renira said.

The Grey just stared at her.

"That seemed like a far easier and quicker way up," Aesie said as she sat down next to Renira. "Why do you think Armstar led us through the tower instead?"

It seemed obvious to Renira. "He didn't want us to meet the Apostle." She wiped at her eyes with the heel of her hand, and the tears made the grazes there sting anew. "He was willing to risk us climbing through a crumbling tower rather than let us speak to Moon."

"You think Armstar was afraid of what that crazy angel would say? He called you, what was it? The Last Hope of the Dying."

He did call me that. And he called you a viper.

Aesie let out a mewling whine. "I'm tired, Ren. I want to go home."

Renira shook away her frustration and reached out, putting a hand over Aesie's shoulders and pulling her close. Aesie leaned in, wrapped her hands around Renira's waist, and sobbed into her chest. "Dussor is dead," she said.

Renira nodded and swallowed down the lump in her throat. She could be strong for her friend. She could be strong for both of them. "You really liked him?"

Aesie trembled, either a shrug or another sob. "I don't know. He was an arse. He was... normal. He told me about his family. His sister made shoes. His father worked the mines. He loved the night sky and the sound of rain." Aesie sniffed. "He had a favourite spot, halfway up some stupid mountain near the city. He was strangely charming."

"I thought all you did was argue? When did he find time to tell you all of that?" Renira asked. She felt a stupid, selfish twinge of jealousy.

Aesie burst into proper tears, clutching at Renira like a tree in a flood, the only thing stopping her from being washed away by her grief. Renira felt that same grief rising within her again, but she pushed it down. She could remain strong. She tried to search for some words of comfort.

"He was lying," Renira said when Aesie stopped shaking. "When the Apostle called you a viper. He was lying." Aesie let go of Renira and looked up at her, eyes wide and shining. She had gone very stiff, and there was something strange behind her gaze that Renira couldn't place. "They've all been lying to us, to me. Angels, princes, kings. My mother." Renira shook her head. She just needed one person she could trust. She just needed Aesie.

The viper. What if she's lying, too? Renira shook the thought away. She would not distrust her best friend on the mad ravings of a chained up angel.

"So, what is the truth?" Aesie asked.

"I don't know," Renira admitted. The Godless King had spent a thousand years telling his lies, forcing them on the people of Helesia. He said the angels were the monsters and that the God was a despot who sought to control humanity. The common people lied to themselves as well as everyone else, telling each other that angels didn't exist, that perhaps they never existed. The angels' lies were seditious, as much omission of truth as untruths. The Apostle lied, claiming that he had made God, and in return the God had made him.

But the worst betrayal of all was that Renira's mother had lied. To her. All Renira's youth, her mother had read to her from the book, told her stories of resplendent angels doing glorious battle, beating back the demons and saving humanity. But Renira had seen the paintings hidden away in Armstar's tower, and the angels hadn't bothered to hide the truth of them. Renira had seen Orphus standing over a field strewn with the corpses of people, holding a woman's severed head. It did not look like glorious battle to Renira. It looked like bloody slaughter. The book her mother read from said that the God had sent his angels down to save humanity from the demons. But there was no mention of where the demons came from. She was starting to think the whole world had been built upon lies. How long did the truth have to be forgotten before it no longer mattered?

The sun was setting in the west, the light fading from the world, and the red sky was darkening quickly. No Blood Moon tonight; the Beast was hiding. Instead, the Matron was rising; the Bone Moon was a bright bronze beacon above.

Renira looked down at the Apostle's feather. It had lit their way up the stone stairs, but now they were above ground, the feather was black. She dropped it and hoped never to see it again.

"I see lights," Aesie said, but she was not looking to the moon or stars. She was staring out toward the forest, past the trees and massive boulders flecked in green-yellow moss. The flickering glow of torches or lanterns not so far in the distance. Renira couldn't tell how far they had travelled underground, but they had left the city of New Gurrund behind and passed underneath Hel's Wall. They were out beyond it now, in the wilderness. A forest she had no name for, and unless she was mistaken, the lights Aesie had seen belonged to a village.

"Maybe we should investigate?" Renira asked.

Aesie nodded. "They might have an inn." She perked up a little. "I would kill for a..." She stopped, and the smile fell from her face. "I would give anything for a bath and a hot meal. And a hairbrush."

Renira sighed. "We don't have any money. I suppose we could rely on the generosity of strangers?" She caught Aesie staring at her incredulously. "What?"

"I wish I had your optimism, Ren. Generosity of strangers? I think we're better off just paying for what we need." She held up her left hand and wiggled her fingers at Renira. Three of those fingers were adorned with simple metal rings, and two of them were gold. "A woman should never be without some means." She finished with a humourless giggle that seemed out of place in a face so recently ravaged by tears.

They started down the slight hill, picking their way between boulders that looked almost like building blocks. Renira remembered Armstar claiming the Godless King had torn his tower down, and she supposed the stone had been left where it fell. A thousand years and still the forest could not entirely hide the evidence.

"Let's hope it's a village and not some sort of bandit camp," Renira said, feeling far from optimistic. It'd be just her luck to run into a bunch of bandit barbarians down from Aelegar.

"Bandits?" Aesie scoffed. "You've been listening to old Frenlow too much. There are no bandits this far north. Too many soldiers. We're not that far from the capital, maybe a week's ride. Hmm, more like two I think."

"And what would we be riding?"

Aesie shrugged. "We'll throw some reins over that wild optimism of yours."

Renira thought of the Grey and glanced behind them, but the little demon was gone, and she could see no sign of its glowing red eyes. She wondered if it had gone back underground, to see to its father. How could the Apostle, an angel, be father to a demon? So many lies, half-truths, and omissions, it was no wonder Renira couldn't make any sense of her situation. But one thing was for certain. The further she was from Armstar and Eleseth and the longer she spent without them, the less she felt like the Herald of the Fifth Age and the more she felt like a young girl from Riverden caught up in a situation far too imposing and important for her.

They stumbled out of the tree line onto a dirt road with hanging lanterns every few dozen paces leading off into the depths of the forest. Some of the closest lanterns were lit, but most were dark. There was a sign outside the village proper that read Greenlake, and the nearby buildings were stout things built of red wood. There were a few people about, one man carrying a barrel of oil and refilling the nearby lanterns, a few others moving about on business of their own. A couple of cloaked figures on horseback were standing around outside a larger building than most, a third horse by their side without a rider. As Renira and Aesie drew closer, a third person walked out of the building and nodded to their companions, pointing to a stable attached to the main building.

Aesie nudged Renira in the ribs lightly. "An inn, if ever I saw one. Hopefully they have rooms and food and enough water for a bath."

Greenlake seemed aptly named, for the village was built around the shore of a forest lake that gleamed turquoise in the pale moonlight. Most of the buildings had light shining from within shuttered windows, and while the village was clearly not large, it seemed very much alive. The inn had no name and no sign, but the noise and warmth spilling out the windows made it seem welcoming. Renira let Aesie take the lead; after all, she was the one with the rings to trade, and she was also far more knowledgeable about things like this.

The smell was what hit Renira first. It wasn't the faint smell of stale ale or the even the scent of men and women relaxing with a few drinks after a hard day's work. It was the smell of something cooking. Roasted chicken on a few plates gave her all the clues she needed, and Renira's mouth was watering before the first set of eyes had turned their way. Not many took too much interest in the two girls, but those who did had pity in their gazes, and if Renira herself looked half as bruised and battered as Aesie, then she couldn't blame them.

The barkeep was a rotund woman with red cheeks, black hair just starting to grey, and no fewer than three aprons around her waist. She was also one of those with pity in her eyes. "What in the bleeding gateway happened to you two girls?" she asked in an accent so like back home in Riverden Renira felt homesick.

Aesie pulled Renira up to the bar and collapsed onto the nearest stool, before treating the barkeep to a weary smile. "What hasn't happened to us? We fell down a cliff. We were buried alive for a time. Chased by wolves. Saw a demon." She glanced at Renira. "Is that what we're calling it?"

Renira shuffled onto the stool next to Aesie and nodded, not trusting herself to speak.

"You're spinning me a tale," the barkeep said.

"I wish we were," Aesie said without flinching. "I really do."

"What happened to your parents?" the barkeep said.

Aesie shook her head sadly. "We were travelling with some others, but..." She paused and sniffed, then drew in a ragged breath and continued. "The wolves got them. It's just us now." The lie she told was so convincing, even Renira half believed it.

The barkeep wiped her hands on one of her aprons and leaned forward, taking hold of each of their hands. "You poor dears. You must be so scared."

Aesie nodded. "Scared and tired and hungry. Please tell me you have a room available. And food. And baths."

Renira watched the barkeep draw back a little, caught between the desire to offer two young girls safe succour and the possibility that they were perhaps not what they seemed.

"We can pay," Aesie said and slipped a silver ring from her finger. "I lost my purse in the fall, I'm afraid, but this is worth at least five runds." She sniffed again. "At least it was when my father bought it for me."

The barkeep's eyes softened. Money always seemed to do that, as though compassion were something that needed to be bought rather than offered freely. "Oh, you poor little pups. We've plenty of room and food to spare. We don't generally offer baths to customers, but seeing as you two girls are in such a sorry state, I can offer you use of the family bath this once."

"Thank you," Aesie said. "Thank you so much. And could we maybe have a bottle of wine as well?"

"Of course, dearie," the barkeep said. She fished under the bar for a moment and then placed a green glass bottle on the bar along with two clay mugs. "I'll just get some food brought out and whip my useless nusband into filling the bath. Likes to sit on his arse all day and blame his back. As if he knows what a bad back is, done nothing but serve drinks his whole life. Carrying six children to term, now that's what a bad back is like." The woman was still listing off complaints as she walked away and into the kitchen.

They took their wine and slipped into chairs at a nearby table that seemed far too large for just the two of them. There were only eight other people in the tavern now Renira counted, and most looked like locals. The three cloaked travellers entered and found their own table. Two men and a woman, and each of them looked almost as weary as Renira felt.

"Rooms and food and wine and a bath all for a ring?" Renira asked.

Aesie smiled tiredly. "I know. Talk about paying over the odds. We could stay here for a week on the price that ring would fetch. To tell you the truth, I still have my purse strapped to my thigh, but I'm saving the coins for passage."

Renira shrugged.

"To Celesgarde," Aesie said, nodding as if that had been the plan all along. She pulled the cork from the bottle and poured wine into the two cups.

Renira took one of the cups and sipped at it. It tasted of raspberries and had a sharp bite that was somehow both distasteful and pleasantly moreish. She greedily downed the rest of the cup.

"I thought we'd go back to Riverden," she said.

In truth, she hadn't even made the decision to abandon the angels' quest yet. She imagined they were still in the tower, with Sun and Gemp, searching for Renira even now. A part of her wanted to go back to them, to question them for the truth, to demand to know why Armstar held her mother in such high regard despite despising the rest of humanity. All those questions they'd been lying to her about or dancing around half truths. Another part of her felt guilty at leaving Sun in their care; the boy was clearly no fan of angels, and he had lost his family to the forest demon, whether he was willing to admit it or not. He had attached himself to Renira, and abandoning him felt like a betrayal. But the thought of going home again, of seeing her mother again, of sleeping in her own bed, warm and loved and protected, that thought kept playing around in Renira's head. She missed her mother and Elsa and Merebeth, she missed Yonal Wood and his ever-expanding family, she even missed Igor the Terrible and the mice he left her each morning.

Life had seemed so much simpler back home. Renira had her routine and her dreams. She had comfort. Now she had the threat of death and the responsibility and expectation to bring the God back to life. She hadn't asked for that. She certainly didn't want it. But could she turn her back on it?

The barkeep brought their food out and promised them the water was being warmed for a bath and would be ready soon after they had finished eating. Before she left, Renira asked the woman her name and discovered she was called Brunhelm, though most people in Greenlake called her Bru. She thanked Bru and then fell upon the meal like a starving pig. It was roast chicken breast, potatoes, a whole host of coloured vegetables she didn't bother to examine, and thick ham gravy. She and Aesie barely spoke as they devoured the food in a frenzy so unladylike even Elsa would have been aghast.

A shaggy grey dog slunk in from outside and plodded closer, snuffing the air. It sat by Renira's chair and whined until she dropped a morsel of chicken on the floor for it, which it devoured happily. When it looked up again, she saw the beast had golden eyes. A few moments later, Bru spotted the dog and chased it outside with a broom, grumbling about strays all the while.

"I'm not going back to Riverden, Ren," Aesie said as she leaned back in her chair, sipping at a cup of wine. "I'm going on to Celesgarde. My father has holdings there, he bought them last year, and I have an entry permit signed by King Emrik himself. Don't look at me like that. My father sought permission before sending me away after the prince. I'm going to Celesgarde. I am. I'm going to enter the Arkenhold University, and I'm going to learn every bloody thing they're willing to teach me." She frowned and pushed her plate a little. "My father is ill."

Renira had only met Alyn Fur a handful of times despite knowing Aesie forever, yet he had always seemed an indomitable man, full of humour and energy. "How ill?"

"Lung rot."

Renira reached across the table and gave her friend's hands a squeeze. "I'm so sorry, Aesie." Everyone knew there was no cure and that lung rot was a slow and painful death sentence once it took hold. She couldn't imagine watching someone go through it, especially not someone so loved.

Aesie was silent for a moment, then looked up and forced a smile. "I'm going to Celesgarde, and I'm going to find a cure for him. No matter what it takes." She nodded as though that made the wish somehow more attainable. "You should come with me. Why go back to Riverden? I could find you a job in Celesgarde or maybe even get you into the university with me. That would be wonderful, we could be together, study together. A fun adventure, just like you always dreamed."

Renira smiled. It did sound fun. A new place, knowledge to be learned and the company of her closest friend. Then she shook her head. "My mother..."

A shadow passed over Aesie's face. "We'll bring her up as well. It's the capital, Ren. There are plenty of clothes that need washing."

Renira laughed. "It does sound fun."

Aesie drew in a deep breath and sighed it out. "Come with me to Celesgarde and think about it. Then, if you decide you want to go back home, I'll send you back to Riverden. Horse and carriage, the fastest we can find. Please." She lowered her gaze and suddenly looked every bit her young age. "Come with me. I don't want to go alone."

Renira promised to think about it, and Bru came back to tell them the water was ready for their baths. She ordered a patron named Konan, who looked a lot like he was related, to look after the bar, then led Aesie and Renira through the kitchen and into a small bath house. It was cosy, with a gently sloping wooden floor and a drain in the centre of the room. A single wooden bathtub sat near the centre, filled and steaming. Four more buckets of water waited nearby. There was a single table and chair pushed into the far corner and a small mirror sat upon the table. The glowing remains of a fire crackled away in a hearth set against the left-hand wall, and a fifth bucket of water stood on a hot grate over the flames.

"Only got the one tub," said Bru. "So, you'll have to take it in turns. When one of you is done, just pull the cork near the bottom to let the water out, then crack the door and give me a yell. Those buckets are heavy, and I'll come help you fill up a second time." She smiled warmly. "You girls take your time. Room'll be ready when you're done."

They thanked Bru and then set about deciding who should go first in the tub. In the end, Aesie insisted Renira take the first dip as she had been longest without, and the call of the hot bath eroded her will to resist. She undressed, marvelling first at how battered and torn and stained her clothing had gotten and then again when she noticed just how many little injuries she had picked up. She was covered in scrapes, grazes, bruises, and scabs. Arms, legs, chest, belly, head. It seemed no part of her had escaped the ordeal. *I guess there's a point where you hurt all over, and your body just gives up trying to decide where hurts most.*

She took off her mother's amulet last. The crescent-shaped moon had been with her from the start of her adventure and there were spots of dried blood on the silver metal, hidden in the grooves of the runes. Her blood. She scraped a nail along it and the blood flaked away, but the metal beneath had turned black as though her blood had seeped into it, staining it.

Renira clambered into the tub and sank down into the steaming waters, gasping somewhere between pleasure and pain as the water both soothed her aches away and flared all her cuts and scrapes into a harsh resonance. The gasp turned into a contented moan, and then Renira sank down and was blowing bubbles in the water, watching wisps of steam detach themselves from the surface and float up into nothing.

Aesie chatted while Renira soaked, talking of the brilliance of Celesgarde and of all the university would provide for them. A place to learn and a place to belong. Renira found herself caught up in the dream. She imagined a library without end, row upon row, stack upon stack of books. She had never been one for the textbooks like those in school, history had always been too dry for her, and learning the names of so many long dead queens and their children was a chore.

But there would be stories in the library as well, books with daring heroes and thrilling escapades, monsters and villains. The tales of Saint Dien and her six Exemplars. Renira would find those books and spirit them away, dodging a cranky old librarian who deemed them below the reading abilities of the students. Renira would find a secluded alcove, lit only by a single flickering candle, burnt almost to a nub, and she would devour the books and the stories contained within. A fun little dream.

She sighed into the steaming water. And she would know those stories for lies. Real adventures weren't fun or heroic. They were dangerous and terrifying. Monsters couldn't be slain with courage and a quick sword; they could be wounded by trickery and then run from before they could recover. Villains weren't maniacal despots who gave the hero a chance to fight back; they were vicious killers who murdered without hesitation or mercy. Life was not at all like the stories.

Renira lay there in the tub a while longer, the steaming water up to her chin, lapping at her lips. She stared into the shifting reflections and refused to let her imagination dream. Refused to let her mind lie to itself. Then she ducked her head under the surface and scrubbed at her face with her hands and washed as much grime as she could from her hair. By the time Renira stood and clambered out of the tub, the water was grey from muck. She felt guilty that Aesie would have to go second.

They pulled the cork from the tub and let the water drain out, then Aesie called for help from Bru. The burly barkeep sauntered in with a couple of towels in hand as well as a hairbrush. She handed a towel to Renira, who gratefully wrapped herself up in it, and then put the other on the table along with the brush, before plucking a bucket from the floor and rinsing out the bath with some cold water.

"You were muckier than a mud rat," she said as she produced a little cloth and gave the tub a quick wipe. "No matter. My little ones used to get far worse back when they actually were little." She chatted as she placed the cork back in the tub and started hefting the buckets of hot water with the indomitable strength of one used to daily labour.

Renira sank down in the chair and stared into the little mirror on the table. She barely recognised the person staring back at her. She had never been chubby, but there had always been a healthy flesh on her cheeks and neck. That was gone now. She looked worn thin. Hardened. Her eyes had dark rings underneath them, and she counted seven small scratches on her forehead, nose, and chin. Even her freckles were fading. The girl who had left Ner-on-the-River was gone, replaced by a young woman with haunted eyes and a dark frown. She tried a smile in the mirror and it seemed oddly false as if she couldn't remember how to do it. She glanced down at the hairbrush and then back up at the mirror and her tangle of hair.

"There you go, dearie," Bru said over the sound of sloshing water as she poured the final steaming bucket into the tub. "Your room is ready whenever you're finished. We can't claim the comfiest beds in Helesia, but by the looks of you two, you'd sleep on straw and be happy for it as long as it came with a roof over your heads."

"You're not far wrong," Aesie agreed as she began stripping off her tattered dress. "I don't even mind about the roof so much as long as it's warm. I've almost forgotten what it's like to sit still and not shiver."

Bru laughed. "Well, you'll have warmth and a roof over your heads here. Honestly, you girls look like you've been on the arse end of luck for a while now."

"Oh, it's not been so bad," Aesie said as she finished stripping off and stepped into the tub. "I mean, apart from being scared to death every moment and chased by wolves. The cave in wasn't much fun. And I hurt everywhere. Actually, now I think of it, it was quite horrific. I'm glad it's over." She sank down into the tub, keeping her long braid of hair outside so as not to get it wet. Renira envied her that. She wished she'd thought to braid her own hair so tight to keep it from getting too mucky, but she had her mother's hair and it always came loose no matter how tight the braid. Now her hair was a tangled nest of mud, blood, and probably a few bugs trying to make a new home.

"Where are you two girls headed?" Bru asked as she stacked the buckets away. "And where are you from?"

"We're from Riverden," Aesie said. "South of here by a fair way."

"I'll say," Bru agreed. "That's a long way to travel on foot."

Aesie moaned as the hot water worked its magic on her. "I had a horse for some of it. Had to leave it behind in New Gurrund. We're on our way to Celesgarde. We're going to university."

Bru let out an impressed whistle. "Your parents must be... um..." She stopped, obviously trying to think of a polite way to say it.

"Wealthy?" Aesie asked. "Mine are. My father owns a clothing factory and several shops across Helesia. He'd be mortified to see the state of my dress as it is now. He made it himself." She shared the details of her life so readily. The truth of it, yet before she had lied just as easily. Renira watched Aesie in the mirror's reflection.

Bru finished clearing away the buckets and filled another with cold water from a hand pump. She caught Renira's gaze in the mirror and smiled. "Feel free to use the brush, dearie."

"Do you have scissors?" Renira asked.

Bru stopped and crossed the distance between them, then gave Renira's hair a good consideration. "Oh, I don't think we need to go that far. It's in a state and no messing about, but a bit of care and a while with that brush will sort out those tangles."

Renira just stared at Bru through the reflection in the mirror. She felt strangely numb. Raw. Suddenly the weight of her hair was like an anchor, dragging her back down into the depths where she had left those who died protecting her. She needed it gone. She needed to be free.

"Thank you, but I'd rather just cut it off."

"But you've got such nice hair. That brown, like a nice wooden table polished to a shine."

Renira shrugged. "It's just hair. It'll grow back."

Bru frowned over that but disappeared and came back a while later with a large pair of scissors. "You sure about this, dearie? Can't take it back once it's done."

Renira nodded and held up a hand. "I'm sure."

"Oh, away with you," Bru said. "You'll only make a mess if you do it yourself. I've cut the hair of five children in my lifetime, I'm sure I can manage something that'll look respectable. Can't go wandering around the capital looking like you were sheared by a blind spidermonkey."

Renira smiled at that. She lowered her hand and let Bru start snipping at her hair, watching matted brown masses fall to the bath house floor. Bru tutted occasionally, frowned a lot, and picked at least one wriggling little beastie out of Renira's dwindling mane. By the time she was finished, there wasn't a lot of Renira's hair left, no more than a hand-and-a-half length all over. Part of her mourned the loss already, her mother had always seemed so happy when brushing her hair.

I'm being stupid. It's just hair. This way, maybe the Godless King won't recognise me.

Bru fretted. "Well, that's about as good a job as I can do. Shorter than I'd have it myself, but it'll grow back, as you say."

Renira tried out a smile in the mirror. Shorter hair suited the woman staring back at her far more than longer hair. She tilted her head a little, and the smile turned to a frown. She was certain her hair had been darker, a chestnut brown rather than the pine it now seemed. In the mirror, she saw Bru staring, looking far from convinced. Renira struggled to care.

"Thank you," Renira said, trying to sound genuine. "It's good."

"You sure?" Bru asked.

Renira nodded. She knew she should be more appreciative, Bru really had done a good job, but she just couldn't seem to find a way out from under the blanket of numbness that was smothering her.

"Well, all right then," Bru turned away, taking the scissors with her and made for the door. "When you two are done, give me another shout, and I'll lead you up to your room." She stopped next to Renira's pile of clothes and stared down for a moment. "That's an odd-looking amulet."

Renira stood from the table a little too fast, knocking over the chair. She hastened over to her pile of clothes and picked them up in arms still a little damp from the bath.

"A family heirloom," she said. "Given to me by my mother before I left home."

Her mother had never been so stupid as to leave it lying about for anyone to see. *Always keep it hidden*, she had said. *Never give anyone a reason to suspect*. But Aesie had suspected. No. She had known.

"Hmm," Bru said with a shrug. Then the barkeep smiled and walked away.

Renira turned to find Aesie leaning with her arms resting on the sides of the tub. She was staring at Renira with a cocked eyebrow and a grin. "It suits you. Brings out your cheekbones." She pulled her hair free of its braid and ducked her head under the water.

Celesgarde. Not on the heels of the angels, or with some great responsibility to bring about the Fifth Age, but to go to university. To learn and gain the tools to do something with her life. It really was a nice dream.

Renira took her pile of clothes back to the table and stared down into the mirror. She tried out that smile again, but it felt false.

"It was never my battle," she whispered to her reflection. "And I shouldn't have to fight it."

CHAPTER 42

Only in the face of scrutiny can we be honest. Only in the absence of honesty can we be corrupted.

— ARANDON HOSTAIN. YEAR 412 OF THE FOURTH
AGE. 367 YEARS AFTER HEAVEN FELL

The next morning found Renira as groggy as a drunk before payday. She should have slept the night away, comfortable and content. Aesie certainly had. But Renira had lain awake half the night fretting over her decision. She had come up with no good answer, only falling asleep when her tired mind was simply too weary to continue arguing with itself.

She dressed in her old clothes, stained and ripped as they were, yet she had no other choice. Besides, wearing her mother's coat felt right, no matter how battered it might have become. It was the coat she had worn on her adventures, and now it was the coat her daughter was wearing on her own trials.

They made their way down to the common room around mid-morning and Aesie seemed in high spirits. She chattered about all the things they would see and do at Celesgarde and how the Arkenhold University was by far the most prestigious with the most interesting fields of study. She mentioned economic prediction models, cyclical trends based upon historical data, and geographical demands on trade. None of which sounded in the least bit interesting to Renira, but in the face of such rampant enthusiasm, she found it hard not to be caught up in the excitement of it.

Bru brought them a breakfast of scrambled eggs, crusty bread, and some sort of sausage that filled the little wooden plate with grease. It tasted sublime, and Renira wolfed the entire meal down and would have considered stealing Aesie's plate if her friend hadn't ravaged the breakfast with equal fervour.

There were only three others in the common room, the cloaked travellers from the night before. In the light of day streaming in through frosted windows, Renira could see that two of them were wearing the uniforms of soldiers, black with yellow trim. Swords hung from their belts, and both man and woman looked like they had seen a conflict or two. They had hard eyes and a grim set to their mouths and reminded Renira of Gemp. The other man wore no uniform, only brown leather suited to riding and gloves that seemed a size too large for his hands. His hair was slicked back on his head, and he picked at the breakfast daintily, taking time to chop both sausage and bread into small chunks and grimacing with every bite like he was eating fetid mud.

When they were finished eating, Aesie asked Bru about the possibility of hiring a carriage from someone in the village. The barkeep sighed and spread her hands. Apparently, carriages and carts made their way through Greenlake from time to time, dropping off supplies to the general store, but they were far from regular. She recommended asking Tain, the store keep, and gave directions to his little shop.

By day, it was clear that winter had the village of Greenlake in its frigid grasp. The muddy road outside the inn had frozen into miniature mountain ranges complete with little lakes of ice that made a satisfying crunch underfoot. Aesie hugged herself against the chill, her coat long since lost, and Renira was not fairing much better. Her mother's coat had so many little tears in it, the cold breeze blew right through her.

Greenlake was a spread out village with a few dozen buildings all dotted around the lake for which it was named. It was about the same size as Ner-on-the-River with no more than a couple dozen families living there.

"I miss home," Renira said, stopping by the side of the inn. Then the rest of it came out as a flood. "I miss home. I miss Riverden. I miss Igor and his proud way of displaying his kills. Poe and his rumours about everything and everyone. Yonal Wood and his family. I miss Merebeth and Elsa. Even washing, Aesie. Dammit, but I miss washing. But most of all I miss my mother."

Aesie's smile dropped, and she stared at Renira. The corners of her mouth twitched, and she looked as though she had something to say. Then she sighed and stared at the muddy ground.

"I can't do it, Ren," Aesie said with a ragged sigh. "I can't do it alone. I'm not... I don't have your strength. I mean, I know I'm smart, and my tongue is quick, sometimes a little too quick, but I'm not strong like you. You never give up. Even when the rest of us have, when we're too tired to go on, you just keep going." She stepped forward and took Renira's hands. They were cold, icy even.

"You give me too much credit, Aesie," Renira said, shaking her head. "You're the glue that's always held us together. You're pretty and smart and rich. You dress nice and talk like a lady should, and everyone looks to you first for what we should do. I'm just... I'm invisible around you."

Aesie was staring at Renira like she'd grown a tail. "You are such a bloody stump, Ren. You actually think that?"

Renira nodded.

Aesie sighed. "Do you remember how me and you and Beth and Elsa met?"

"I met you in Tobe's bakery."

"You did. Marched right up to me and started talking like we'd been friends for years."

Renira frowned. "You talked back."

"Of course I did. I was what, five winters old? I'd have talked back to a chair if it struck up a lively enough conversation. What about Merebeth? Do you remember meeting her?"

Renira had trouble remembering how they had met. She thought Merebeth and Elsa were always there with them, that they had been Aesie's friends since before Renira had come to Riverden.

Aesie shook her head. "Beth was such an awkward, lonely little thing. She'd turn up to lessons, sit on her own saying nothing, then go home soon as teacher said we were done. Until you ran up to her one day and asked what she was reading. You dragged her over and made her sit with us and kept asking her questions about her books."

"I did?"

"Oh, she talked for absolutely hours about... what was it? Canal construction, I think. Bleed me, but I was bored senseless and yet there you sat, enthralled. Or at the very least making a good show of it. And Elsa. Do you really think I'd be friends with Elsa if not for you, Ren? She's..." Aesie sighed. "She's a bloody street rat. I'd not even have noticed she existed if not for you. You spotted her down an alley, brawling with a couple of boys twice her size, and pulled me and Beth with you to stand up to them."

Renira did remember that. "I thought it was you who stood up for Elsa."

"I was the one who insulted the mouldy toe rags until they buggered off, but you dragged us down that alley, Ren. Not me."

"Elsa was livid."

"She was," Aesie agreed. "She said she didn't need some pampered stick in a dress standing up for her and threatened to kick me in the shins and make me eat mud."

"That does sound a lot like Elsa."

"She only calmed down when you did that stupid thing you do. You just walked up to her and introduced yourself like we were all meant to be there. I don't think she had many friends, and she's been clinging to you ever since. Just like that little boy clings to you."

"Sun?"

"You know he's in love with you, right?"

Renira shot Aesie a frown.

"The truth is Beth doesn't leave her library unless she knows you're coming down from Ner and Elsa... Bloody breath, Ren, me and Elsa would tear strips off each other without you around to stop us. I was never the one holding our little group together. You were. And I was..." Aesie sniffed loudly. "I was terrified you'd actually find yourself an adventure like you kept threatening too. Because... Well, because I didn't have any other friends and I didn't want to be alone."

"You were scared I was going to leave?" Renira asked, incredulous. "I thought you were gonna run off to university and leave me behind to rot in Ner underneath a pile of old washing."

"A right pair we are. I still don't want to be alone, Ren. I need you to come with me. Do you remember the school scavenger hunt a few years ago? We had to look for a white feather, and no one in Riverden had one for sale."

Renira smiled at the memory. "Elsa said she knew a roosting spot where white eagles stayed all year round. Up near the base of the Ruskins." Elsa had said the spot was no more than an hour's walk, but three hours later they all had to admit they were lost. They should have known it was a lie from the start given that the Ruskins were a full two day's hard ride from Riverden.

"We were all so bloody tired," Aesie continued. "Foot sore and cranky. Well, I was cranky." She was. Renira remembered the arguments with Elsa. "But you kept us going. Past when the rest of us wanted to give up. You pulled us along with you. And we found the feather."

Renira smiled. "We found a wood pigeon nest and the feather was more grey than white."

Aesie snorted. "You found us the way home as well." She didn't mention that it had been full dark by the time they got home. The scavenger hunt was long since over, and Aesie's father was in the process of organising a search party for his wayward daughter.

"I don't know if it was your..." Aesie glanced around them and then lowered her voice to a whisper. "Faith. Or maybe just an unshakeable will, but you refused to give up. And you refused to let us give up as well." She let go of Renira's hands and sighed. "I don't have that, Ren. I don't have that strength, that determination. So I need to borrow it from you. Please come with me to Celesgarde. You don't have to stay, but if you decide you want to, I will find a way to make it work, whatever it takes. If not, I'll send you home. But please, please come with me that far at least."

Renira wanted nothing more than to turn south and head home, but Aesie was right. She wasn't one to give up. Not even when the going became tough and not even when those around her had passed their limit. Her mother would still be waiting if she was gone for a few more weeks, and from Celesgarde she could certainly send word that she was alive and well. But it would mean giving up on the angels and their quest. It would mean giving up on her responsibility as the Herald. Didn't she owe it to the angels to see their will through? Wouldn't that be what her mother would really want?

Moon was right. I'm still looking for others to give me reasons.

Renira nodded, more to keep Aesie happy than because she had truly made her decision. Surely she could decide later. She'd be going to Celesgarde either way. Maybe it would even be easier without the angels at her back. Without them, she could sneak up to the bell and ring it and run away before anyone noticed.

There were plenty of people about, some amiably chatting, while others went about their daily work. A group of four woodsmen passed by in front of the inn, a giant draft horse dragging a tree behind it that carved fresh mountains in the mud. Renira assumed they had a lumber mill somewhere nearby, but it was probably hiding behind the other buildings. She watched them pass, and then her eyes were drawn to the lake and the grisly spectacle staked just ten paces in front of it.

"I suppose," Aesie said, "if we can't hire a carriage, we might be able to hire some horses. I don't have enough rings to buy two, but maybe we could convince the owner to accompany us and take them back once we reach Celesgarde? Wait, do you know how to ride, Ren? It doesn't matter, I can teach you. Let's go find this store and see if they have any suggestions." Aesie started off down the road, further into the village. Renira didn't follow.

She crossed the road slowly, angling for the lake and the body staked out in front of it. A woman, short and plump in life, no doubt, but in death she appeared diminished. She was dead, there was no doubt about that, drowned by the looks of it. Her skin was unnaturally pale, her lips blue and iced over, her head lolling. Mousy brown hair hung down in frozen clumps around a bruised face. She wore a simple green dress, an extra skirt for layers, all stained with mud. She was still wearing an old apron scorched from oven heat, as though she hadn't had time to take it off. She was tied by hands, feet, and chest to a large wooden stake. Hung around her neck, and dangling by rope, was a wooden sign with one word written across it in red paint. It said *HERETIC*.

Renira stared at the body, a sour feeling curling its way through her gut. She had known people were executed like this, of course. She had seen similar back in Riverden once or twice, and everyone knew the laws regarding anyone who worshipped the God or harboured a divinity. It just seemed different now. Closer than it had ever been before.

Aesie came back, moving with an urgency, and grabbed hold of Renira's hand. She tried to pull her away from the spectacle, but Renira leaned away from her friend, refusing to be moved.

"How all them bloody angel worshippers should get their dues," said a man. Renira glanced to the side to see he was a giant of a fellow with arms as thick a horse's neck crossed over his barrel chest. He wore simple trousers and a blue shirt stained with sweat. He smiled savagely at the corpse. Renira studied his face for a moment and found nothing but malice in the stubbled chin and deep-set eyes.

"What did she do?" Renira asked quietly.

"Ren!" Aesie hissed, tugging at her hand again.

"Angel worshipper," the man said in a voice as thick as his arms. "Worshipped angels."

"That's it?" Renira asked.

The man glanced at her and narrowed his eyes. "Yeah, that's it. Ain't nothing else needed. You pray to those feathered freaks, you get what's coming." Two others approached, also big men, and one had a wood axe hanging from his belt.

"She lived here?" Renira asked tonelessly.

"Sure."

"For how long?"

The big man shrugged. "All her life. Sesh from down the lake." He pointed to a house across the water.

Renira knew she should stop. She tried to. But she needed to know. "You knew her. How long have you lived here?" Her voice had gone cold, distant. At the same time, something hot and angry bubbled up from inside, chasing away her control.

The big man sniffed loudly. "All my life. You got a problem, girl?"

Renira turned to the man and took a step toward him, her hands balling into fists. He didn't back away. "She lived here all her life," Renira said, her voice an angry rush hissing through clenched teeth. "You have lived here all your life. So, I assume you knew her all your life. Yet you treat her like a stranger, a monster. Did she have family? Do they know what you've done?"

The man sneered down at her. "Her sister painted the bloody sign."

Renira gasped in horror. Sister turned against sister for no reason at all. "On what evidence was she even executed?"

The big man's lip curled into a snarl. "Don't need no evidence on a Seeker's say so."

"A Truth Seeker?" Renira whispered, the reality of the situation suddenly breaking over her. Her anger fled as quickly as it had appeared, drenched in cold terror. Her mother had always warned her about Truth Seekers. They were death to people like her, people with secrets to hide.

Aesie pulled on her hand again. "Ren, let's go." This time Renira didn't resist, but just as she was pulled away, the big man's hand shot out and gripped hold of her other arm.

"You're seeming right knotted on Sesh's behalf, girl," the big man said, his grip like iron. "Odd thing that, for a heretic you don't even know. I'm starting to think we got another one."

One of the big man's friends laid a hand on his shoulder. "Let her go, Ban. She's probably just never seen a body before."

"Shut up," the big man shrugged off his friend's hand. "Go fetch the Seeker. He ain't left yet. Seen his horse in the stable." His friend grumbled something and stalked off toward the inn.

"Let me go!" Renira seethed, tugging at her arm to no avail. The big man was far too strong and had a grip like tree roots. "I was just curious."

Aesie came to her rescue. "Let her go!" she stood on her toes and swung her fist at the man. The punch hit his arm, and he didn't even flinch. Aesie, though, pulled back her hand with a hiss of pain and clutched at it, blowing on it as though that might reduce the pain.

The big man laughed and gave Aesie a shove with his free hand. She careened backward and tripped, landing on her arse in the frozen mud.

"Aesie!" Renira tried to go to her friend's side, but the man's grip just tightened around her arm until she was cringing at the pain of it. "Let me go!" she shouted.

He did, and Renira stumbled, almost losing her footing. She rushed to Aesie's side and knelt there, clutching at her friend. Others were arriving now, lots of them. None of them looked like travellers, so Renira assumed they were villagers, come to see the show.

"What is this, Banyarl?" asked an older man, just as burly but with wrinkled eyes and hair the colour of gritted frost.

"Reckon we caught another one," said the man, Banyarl. "Busy tanning my hide for Sesh. Saying we was wrong doing the king's justice like we did."

"I didn't say that!" Renira shouted. She glanced around the gathered villagers, more arriving by the moment but saw not even one kind face. They penned her and Aesie in on all sides so they couldn't run.

"Oh, what now?" said a nasally voice. The crowd before the inn parted, and the three travellers approached, their rough spun grey cloaks around their shoulders. The villagers bowed their heads respectfully as the traveller not wearing a uniform passed. Renira noticed again that he was wearing heavy gloves that looked too big for him. Her heart sank. Why hadn't she seen the signs just like her mother had taught her?

"We have been accosted and assaulted," Aesie said, rocketing to her feet like she was standing to attention. "That's what. I demand this thug apologise right now!"

The traveller with the gloves stopped just inside the circle of villagers and looked bemused, first at Aesie, then at Banyarl, and finally at Renira. "I'm not sure whether to thank you all or arrest you for saving me from that sloppy gruel of a meal you people call breakfast." He waved a finger around at them as if randomly deciding whose side of the story he should hear first, then pointed at Banyarl. "You, hick, tell me what happened."

Banyarl blinked a couple of times, his mouth hanging open, then repeated the lie he had told the old man. The Truth Seeker raised an eyebrow at Renira.

"I didn't say that!" Renira said. "I just..."

The Seeker took a step forward, and Renira backed away only to bump into one of Banyarl's friends who glared down at her.

"She has an amulet!" Bru shouted from the porch of the inn. "I saw it last night. Looked like it had symbols on it, like one of those, what do you call it? Icons."

Renira stared aghast at the barkeep over the heads of the villagers. Just last night the woman had been friendly, motherly, even. She had chatted with them both while cutting Renira's hair. Now she leapt on the chance to persecute her and had all but sealed Renira's fate.

"Hold them," said the Truth Seeker in his nasal voice. At his command, the two soldiers surged forward around him like a river around a rock. The woman grabbed hold of Aesie, pinning her arms to her side and holding on tight. The man did the same to Renira in such an efficient manner she had no chance to fight back. "Let's see the truth, shall we?"

The Truth Seeker grabbed the leather thong around Renira's neck and pulled it until her mother's amulet was in his hand. He stared at it for a moment, eyes roving over the inscrutable symbols, then tugged it so hard the cord snapped. He threw it to the ground and stamped upon it. "Icon indeed. Heretical filth."

The villagers jeered at her like a pack of starving dogs sniping at a wounded bear. The Truth Seeker held up his hands for quiet and waited until the noise had died down.

"Not definitive proof, but damning, nonetheless. Now let's find out for certain." He pulled off one of his gloves, revealing a hideously large hand stained the colour of coffee. He reached out, almost tenderly, and Renira flinched, trying to pull away, but the soldier behind just held her tighter. The Truth Seeker trailed his hand lightly across her face.

Renira felt nothing. His hand was clammy and the touch unwelcome, but there was no sense of having her thoughts ripped from her head, or any sort of invasion of her mind. She stared into the leering face of the Truth Seeker, and he stared back, his expression slowly turning to confusion.

The Truth Seeker took a step back, and his hand fell to his side. Everyone was silent, waiting on his judgement.

"She's the Herald," he said, a slow smile splitting his lips.

"What does that mean, sir?" the soldier holding Renira asked.

"I'm not sure." The Truth Seeker frowned, stroking at his chin.

Renira felt her heart sink, the full horror of the situation dawning on her. She had survived forest demons, wolf princesses, the razing of Los Hold, and a tower collapse. And now she was undone by a few villagers and their ingrained hatred of the divine.

A clamour rose up as multiple voices shouted to be heard. Some wanted to know what it meant. What was a Herald? Others wanted to know what was to be done? The Seeker himself was forced to admit he had no idea what a Herald was, only that it was most certainly something to do with angels, and the king would want her executed. Renira found herself in a whirl of noise and activity, but she was struck by the look on Aesie's face.

"It's you?" Aesie asked, her face aghast. "You're the Herald?"

Renira felt a tear run down her cheek. "I'm sorry," she said; her gaze locked on Aesie despite the clamour going on around them.

Aesie was shaking her head. "It's all my fault," she said, her voice holding an edge of panic. "I didn't know. Oh shit, Ren. I swear I didn't know she was after *you*."

The tumult continued around them, a raging storm and Renira and Aesie in the calm, quiet centre. She shook her head as realisation dawned, but she didn't want to admit it. "That's how the wolf princess found us. Aesie, you led Perel to us."

"I didn't think it was you," Aesie said, tears in her own eyes now. "I thought it was one of the angels."

Moon was right. I can't trust her. I can't trust anyone.

Renira shook her head and slumped in her captor's arms. The soldier let her go, and she collapsed onto her knees. She was so tired, so weary. Between the animosity of the crowd, people who didn't know her and had no reason to hate her, and the betrayal of her closest friend, Renira simply couldn't find the will to go on. She was done. Broken. Betrayed.

"Quiet!" the Truth Seeker shouted, his voice cracking a little on the words. He waited for the din to die down before clearing his voice and continuing. The soldier who had been holding Renira joined him at his side. "We went through all this yesterday, but I suppose I will have to do it again for the benefit of you backwards peasants." He glanced down at Renira on her knees. "And you, of course. Due process and all that."

The Truth Seeker fell silent for a moment, then cleared his throat again and spoke in a practised voice. A judge delivering his official verdict. "My name is Truth Seeker Polarch, official of His Majesty King Emrik Hostain's divinity judiciary force. I have looked into... um... What's your name?"

Renira stared at the frozen mud beneath her and thought of nothing. Too tired and too numb to care anymore.

"Name, woman. What's your name?"

Renira didn't answer.

The Truth Seeker sighed. "I have looked into this woman's heart and found it swimming in the deepest heresy. She is a harbourer of rogue divinities and a Herald of angels. The sentence for her crimes is death by execution. Now, as per his majesty's laws it is up to the community to decide upon the method of execution. Can I just assume we will be drowning this one as well?"

There was a brief round of muttering, and the older man stepped forward and nodded. "Fetch the bucket and another stake."

"No need for another stake," said the Truth Seeker. "I'll be needing a cart though. You'll be compensated, of course. I have a feeling his majesty the king will want to see this body himself."

"We're still executing her though?" asked the older man.

"Of course, we are," snapped the Truth Seeker. "She's a bloody heretic, man!"

Aesie wailed, pleaded, bargained, and even threatened. Eventually the Truth Seeker grabbed her face and was still for a moment, then he let go and shook his head to the soldier holding her. "She's working for the king. Let her go. She can make her own way from here." Aesie was pushed out of the circle of villagers, and Renira lost sight of her friend. Her betrayer.

The bucket, when it was finally dragged up from the lake in the centre of the village was almost as large as the tub Renira had bathed in the night before. It was low and wide and filled with cold water and bits of broken ice floating on the surface. The big man who had accosted her dragged it in front of Renira, and she stared down into her own terrified reflection. They were really going to kill her. Drown her in icy water. She struggled, thrashed. Useless. Too late to escape. Too weak to fight back.

Strong hands pulled her arms behind her, and rope wrapped around her wrists, binding so tight she gasped in pain. Then the Truth Seeker nodded once, and someone thrust Renira's head down and into the freezing water.

The cold was a shock, and she gasped down a mouthful of water. The coughing hit her immediately, and her blurred vision started going dark. She struggled and thrashed impotently, unable to free herself from the clutches of the person holding her head underwater.

Cold. Wet. Dark.

The hands holding her underwater disappeared, and Renira threw herself backwards out of the bucket, coughing and vomiting up icy water as she landed on the frozen mud and flailed. She blinked the frigid water from her eyes and looked upon a blurry scene of chaos.

The soldier who had been holding her had his sword drawn and was facing the Truth Seeker, who in turn had gone rigid, the point of a spear at his throat. Behind him stood Gemp, snarling through his beard. The villagers of Greenlake looked shocked, many already fleeing, while others stood and watched or reached for belt knives and wood axes.

A shout sounded from above, and then Eleseth hit the soldier like a burning rockslide, crushing him into the frozen ground face first. Her wings and hair were blazing like molten gold, and her impact caused even more of the villagers to turn and flee. She stood up to her full height, wings spread, and picked up the soldier by his broken neck, then tossed him aside like a child's doll.

The second soldier drew her sword and charged at Gemp. The old acolyte pushed the Truth Seeker aside and pulled the haft of his spear in front of him to block the savage cut. The soldier pulled back, preparing to thrust. Sun broke through the crowd of remaining villagers and stabbed his spear into the woman's side. She yelled, but before she could react, Gemp stabbed his own spear into her neck. She died gagging on her own blood and clawing at the spear lodged in her flesh.

Renira lay on her side on the freezing ground watching it all. More people dying because of her. She hadn't chosen it, but they were dying for her, because of her mistakes. If she had just kept her mouth shut and ignored the atrocity, none of this would have happened.

Banyarl, the big villager who had started it all, ran at Eleseth with a large belt knife. The angel saw him coming but did not react. The blade hit her arm, skidded harmlessly across the skin there, and snagged in her robe. She turned toward the man, hair and wings glowing like the sun. He dropped to his knees in front of her. She buffeted him with a wing, knocking him down face first, and then placed a booted foot on the back of his neck.

"Kill them!" screeched the Truth Seeker as he backed away toward the inn. "Protect me! By order of the King."

Through the parting crowd, Renira could see him all too clearly. Both gloves were back on his hands and he was holding one hand to a small, bloody scratch on his neck. Behind him, striding along the road, came Armstar, clutching the wolf princess' halberd in one hand.

"Stop it!" Renira screamed from the floor. "Please don't kill anyone else. Not for me."

Eleseth glanced over her shoulder at Renira, and then took her foot away from Banyarl's neck. The big man immediately scurried away.

"Why not?" Armstar shouted back.

The Truth Seeker turned just in time to see him coming, and Armstar's free hand shot out and grabbed the smaller man by the throat. He dragged him a few paces along the ground and then tossed him into the remaining circle of villagers, those either too scared or too stupid to have run. The Truth Seeker curled up in a ball on the frigid mud and mewled.

Eleseth tore loose the rope binding Renira's hands and helped her stand, draping a glowing wing around her shoulders. Some of the chill started to leave Renira, but she was still shivering, and her lungs felt like they burned with cold.

"Enough people have died for me already," Renira said. "I can't... I don't want anyone else to die."

The two dead soldiers seemed damning enough. The man with his neck broken, his face bloody and half crushed, tossed aside to cool in the mud. The woman with trickles of blood still leaking from the two spear wounds, a look of shock and pain frozen on her face. But it was more than that. Dussor and Kerrel murdered underground, their bodies buried and forgotten under so much stone. The people of Los Hold slaughtered in their homes. Mihiriel, torn open and devoured. Renira didn't want anyone else to die because of her. Even then she realised the futility of it. They wouldn't have let her go willingly and not without a fight.

Why is the world like this?

Armstar stopped before the Truth Seeker sprawled on the ground. "These people?" he asked, pointing with the blade of the halberd, swinging it around at the villagers still nearby. "They were trying to kill you, Renira. Executing you for a supposed crime. A crime they had no proof of. What was it? Knowing an angel?"

Renira pushed free of Eleseth's warm, glowing wing and stepped forward to stand on the other side of the Truth Seeker. She shivered and wrapped her arms about herself.

"It doesn't matter why. They made a mistake. They don't deserve to die for it."

Armstar shook his head. "A mistake implies it was not what they intended. They knew what they were doing. They were murdering you."

"Fine!" Renira hissed, her breath ragged and trembling. "They were murdering me. Me! Well I forgive them. All of them. So, leave them alone!"

Armstar smiled cruelly. "I'll give you that. They can go." His eyes fell to the Truth Seeker at his feet. "But not this one. He has other crimes to answer for. Crimes against angelkind." Armstar stooped down and grabbed the man by his collar, hauling him to his feet and holding him between them.

"I've committed no crimes," the Truth Seeker bawled. "I'm just doing my job. By the king's orders."

Armstar's voice was cold and clear. "Take off your gloves."

The Truth Seeker didn't hesitate, pulling off his gloves and revealing hands that seemed too large for his body and with skin too dark for his complexion.

"Now," Armstar continued. "Tell everyone how you became a Truth Seeker."

Renira glanced around for help from the others. Eleseth looked on, her wings now folded behind her back. Sun held his spear ready toward the villagers, prepared to defend her. Gemp stood by, stony faced and chewing on something. And Aesie leaned against the cart the villagers had brought out, her hand clasped over her mouth.

"I can't," the Truth Seeker whispered. "It's forbidden by the king himself."

Armstar's jaw tightened. "You're more afraid of him than you are of me?

He's days away at least and ignorant of all this. I'm standing here holding your life in my hands."

The Truth Seeker closed his mouth and raised his chin. He was trembling like lake water before a storm.

"So be it," Armstar said. He gripped hold of the man's forehead, leaned in close, and whispered one word. "Terror."

The Truth Seeker dropped to his knees, his eyes large as the Blood Moon and turning almost as red. His trousers turned damp as he pissed himself, and he stared up at Armstar with a slack, quivering jaw.

The angel smiled. "Now, tell everyone how you became a Truth Seeker, and I'll make it stop."

"My hands," the Truth Seeker said, his voice a breathless whisper. "They chopped off my hands and replaced them with an angel's."

Armstar stared at Renira. "An angel died so this worthless shit could hunt down people who hold beliefs that don't fit with the Godless King's lies!" He looked back at the Truth Seeker. "And let's hear just what he has done with this hideous *gift* he has been given." Armstar pointed the halberd at the drowned woman whose body was still staked near the water's edge. "What did she do to earn her death, Seeker?"

"She wouldn't pay," the Truth Seeker said as tears streaked down his face. "They accused her, and she'd done nothing. No heresy. But she wouldn't pay me to declare her innocence."

Armstar leaned a little closer to the Truth Seeker. His ruined wings were trembling with rage. "So, you declared her guilty?"

The Truth Seeker nodded, still trembling. "Yes," his voice was barely even a whisper.

Renira couldn't understand how someone could do such a thing. Just because the woman wouldn't pay this man, probably couldn't pay him, he had her killed. Murdered by her neighbours, people she called friends, her own bloody sister, for less than no reason. For a lie! This woman, Sesh, hadn't just been murdered because she couldn't pay the Truth Seeker, and it wasn't just to make an example out of a supposed heretic. She had been killed to hide the truth, to hide the Truth Seeker's secret, his corruption within a corrupt system. It was all just so wrong!

"He'll do it again," Armstar said. He was looking at Renira, eyes full of cold righteousness. "He is already an abomination, a sin against angelkind. If I let him go, he will do this again. Another village, another woman, another murder. People like him do not stop, Renira. They cannot be reasoned with. So, what would *you* like me to do?"

Renira looked at him aghast. "You want me to pass judgement on him?"

"He just passed judgement on you," Armstar said. "With no proof. No confession. You have proof of his sin, his crime. You have his confession. You have more right to judge him than he you. So what is it to be? Should he live or die?"

"I won't do it," Renira said, wiping tears from her eyes. It was an impossible choice. If he was allowed to go free, the man might do the same again. He probably would. Once the shock and fear had worn off. Once the threat had passed. On the other hand, who was she to judge another person? Any other person. Who had that right?

Armstar stood up straight and whipped the halberd in an upward slash that cut across the Truth Seeker's chest and face. Renira felt drops of blood spatter her and stared on as the man fell backward, already dead. The fallen angel stared at the body for a moment, his gaze cold as the depths of winter.

He spoke in quiet voice so only Renira could hear. "Even your mother understood, sometimes sacrifices have to be made for the greater good. Not everyone can be saved. Not everyone can be redeemed."

Renira shook her head, eyes locked on the dead Seeker. Her mother would never have agreed to murder a man. *Would she?* She had always said all life was sacred. But what if she was wrong? Renira shook her head at it all, and her mother's prayer came back to her. "No soul is lost nor life so vile that God cannot rede—"

"Don't!" Armstar hissed. "Don't you dare spit out words you don't even understand." Armstar strode past her, leaving Renira to stand over the body of a man who had just tried to have her killed.

"The rest of you may go," he said loudly. "But leave the cart."

The shock that had held the villagers in place vanished, and most of them broke and ran. The ones who didn't were quickly dragged away by their friends. They had learned an unpleasant truth today, that they had recently murdered one of their own over nothing but suspicions and a lie. Renira wondered if that harsh reality would leave a lasting lesson. It had for her.

Is Armstar even wrong about this? She didn't know.

Sun ran to her side. His boyish face looked like it had a new edge to it, an older air that hadn't been there before. "Are you all right, Ren?"

Renira looked at her Exemplar. They hadn't been apart for more than a couple of days, but he seemed taller somehow.

"No," she said, tearing up again. She surged forward and wrapped her arms around him. "No, I'm not."

"Get in," Armstar said, waving at the cart. "We need to be gone from here long before they think of sending word to New Gurrund."

Eleseth rested a hand on Renira's shoulder, slowly guiding her and Sun toward to the cart. Aesie was still there, hand over her mouth, fear and guilt mixing together on her face to make her seem a child once again.

"I'm sorry," Aesie said, her voice choked with tears.

"What for?" Armstar asked with narrowed eyes.

Renira shook her head and looked at Armstar. "It doesn't matter." She turned her gaze to Aesie and nodded. "It doesn't matter," she said slowly. Whatever she had done, Renira wasn't about to let Armstar kill Aesie. Especially not before she'd decided what to do about the betrayal.

CHAPTER 43

Sun stared into the twisting flames of the campfire, watching the fire dance as though alive. It reminded him of a time before all this. Before running, before the forest demon had killed his kidnappers. Before meeting Renira. He remembered a time sat at the foot of a great throne, gnawing on bone like a mangy dog, watching people cavort to the ecstasy of flayed flesh and burning feet. When there were whips and smouldering coals, people and flames danced alike. The smell of burning blood as fat drops plummeted onto the coals was a stench that would never leave him.

He wondered how long he could stay hidden, how far he'd need to run. Karna wouldn't come for him herself, but she'd send others to get him. He was beyond the reach of the wulfkin but not beyond the reach of her cursed

Amaranthine. She would never stop sending others to bring him home, and no one was beyond her reach.

"Hey!" Gemp said, resting a gnarled hand on Sun's shoulder. He was chewing on something, the end of a small stick poking out between his lips. "Don't poke the fire with your spear, lad. Good spear deserves to be treated better than that."

Sun hadn't even realised he was doing it, but he pulled his spear back. The waxed wood at the butt had a smudge of ash on it and had darkened slightly due to the flames. Dussor had given him the spear, picked it out specifically for him. Now Dussor was dead. Sometimes it seemed everyone who helped Sun ended up burned, buried, or eaten.

"Can you teach me how to use it?" he asked. "It's a long way to Celesgarde, right? Time enough to train me."

Gemp chuckled and scratched a hand through his mess of grey hair. "Lad, it takes years to learn the spear, not weeks."

"Oh." Sun sighed and settled his eyes back toward the flames.

"But we'll do what we can, eh? Not tonight. We could all use a bit of rest, I reckon. Even the angels look tired. But every other night from now to Celesgarde. Once we stop, I'll spend an hour or two drilling the bad habits out of you." He sounded grumpy, but when Sun looked up, he could see the old man smiling, the stick twisting between his teeth. "Might be by the time you need to use it again, you won't fumble the thrust."

Sun felt his cheeks go hot. "You saw that?"

"Aye, I saw it. But no one else did. Well, maybe the woman we killed. But she's not telling no one."

"We killed?" Sun said, his voice quavering. He'd never killed anyone before. He wasn't sure how he felt about that. He wasn't even sure he felt anything.

Gemp grumbled. "Aah shit. Don't go getting all guilty on me now, lad. You only helped. I did the killing there, and if not for you, I might be the one face down in the mud. Did a good thing."

Sun pulled his arms close. Even sat by the fire, he felt a bit cold suddenly. "I helped."

"Yeah," Gemp said with a smile that was obviously forced even to Sun's eyes.

"I helped kill someone."

He'd seen people die before. People died in Ashvold all the time, and Karna took joy in the murder, though she liked to call it sacrifice. She demanded it. Some were sacrificed to the wulfkin or the twisted mutations she kept locked up in the catacombs, and others still were tortured to death on altars, the why of it was something Sun had never been able to understand. But he had never killed anyone before. He knew he should feel guilty, or remorse... but he didn't.

"Shit," Gemp said and turned away. He stalked off towards where they had left the cart and hitched the horses to the trees.

Sun looked down at his hands. There was no blood on them. How many deaths was he responsible for now? Surely his skin should be stained red, even if no blood had ever touched his hands.

He was still trapped in his dark musings when the log he was sitting on shifted as Renira sat next to him. She seemed changed as well, more maudlin, less sure of herself. The tower had done that to them all. Almost as though they had all left the better parts of themselves underground.

The silence stretched between them like leather over a drum, pulled so taut even the slightest tap sounded thunderous. "I like your hair," Sun said eventually.

Renira chuckled and touched her hair, it was only just longer than Gemp's now, but it seemed to suit her. "Me too," she said. "I haven't had it this short since I was a child."

"It looks lighter as well," Sun said.

"You think so too?" Renira smiled. "I thought it was just me."

"Maybe it will start glowing, like Eleseth's when she gets angry."

"I hope not. I'm far too skinny and pale, I'd look like a candle." She sighed. "Thank you, Sun. You saved us, back in the tower. You didn't hesitate, and that saved us. And then you saved me again in the village. That's three times now."

Sun nodded. "That makes me one up on you."

"How so?"

"You saved me twice. You pulled me out of the forest, even when I couldn't move and Broken Wings was telling you to leave me. And then in the sanctuary, you grabbed my spear and wouldn't let the soldier kill me."

"Perhaps we should stop counting," Renira suggested. "Protecting each other is just what friends do. Doesn't need to be a competition."

Part of him wanted to *whoop* with joy at the praise, but the guilt wouldn't let him. Not guilt over the person he had killed or the people who had died for him. He felt guilt over Renira. It didn't make sense to him.

"I thought I'd killed you," he admitted. The little fear that had been niggling at him ever since his spear sliced through the rope. "I couldn't... You were gone. I thought I'd killed you. I'm supposed to protect you, not kill you. I swore an oath."

"I remember."

"By my own spilled blood I will protect you with my life. I can't break that. I won't be an oathbreaker."

"You didn't!" Renira said. Her hand found his, and she squeezed it hard. "You didn't kill me, Sun. You saved me. Just like an Exemplar is supposed to. Just like a friend should. You saved us all."

"Dussor and Kerrel, though. The wolf princess. I killed them?" Again, he looked down at his hands, certain he should find them covered in blood. Just like *hers* when she fed her Amaranthine.

"No, you didn't. I did. I told you to cut the rope, and we were only ever there because of me. Dussor and Kerrel sacrificed themselves to protect me. And *she* killed them. The wolf princess was after me. None of this is your fault, Sun. It's all mine. I'm the Herald. No one else."

Sun didn't know what to say to that. He squeezed Renira's hand, hoping it would provide the same comfort she gave to him. He felt guilty all over again, this time for the lies he had told. Renira was his friend, the only friend he'd ever had, she deserved the truth.

"They weren't my parents," he said suddenly, before he could realise how bad a decision it really was. "The two who were with me in the forest. The demon got them, but they weren't my parents. They just... kidnapped me." He meant to say rescued, but even now the word still didn't seem quite right.

"Oh." Renira was staring at him, and he couldn't bring himself to meet her eyes. "What happened to your parents?"

Sun opened his mouth, the truth right there just waiting to be told. But then he heard *her* voice in his head, as if carried by the wind from hundreds of miles away.

"You are my Dark Star," Karna whispered in his ear. *"A thing the God decreed could not exist. When the angels hear of you, they will come for us. They will throw everything they have at my walls. And if they get in, they will kill you. They cannot allow you to exist. You are heresy incarnate. And you are mine. Only I can keep you safe."*

"Sun?" Renira squeezed his hand again. "What happened to your parents?"

He shook his head and pulled his hand free of hers. "I never knew 'em," he lied. "Never had any parents, I guess."

"I never met my father, and my mother refused to tell me about him. But I had a father. Just because you don't remember them, doesn't mean you didn't have them. Why were you kidnapped?"

Sun shrugged quickly. He couldn't tell her the truth, not now. He couldn't tell her that he was rescued from the one person in the world even more dangerous than the Godless King. "They never said. Just took me off the streets and said I was theirs. I guess they meant to sell me or something."

"Perhaps they really wanted a child but couldn't have one. Maybe they saw you on the streets and thought they could give you a better life."

Sun nodded. Renira had a way of looking at people and seeing the best in them. He liked that. He hoped that maybe she could see the best in him and he could live up to it, at least in her eyes.

Aesie hovered at the edge of the firelight, not daring to approach any further. Renira knew. Her friend knew the truth, but she hadn't told the angels, and Aesie could think of only one reason why. Armstar had little love for humans, that much was obvious. If he knew the truth, there was no telling what he might do. The wisest thing for Aesie to do was to stay as far away from either of the angels as possible. To stay as far away from everyone as possible. But there was a long way between here and Celesgarde, weeks at least, maybe more depending on the route they took. She couldn't be certain to keep out of reach all that time. What about when she slept? What if one of the angels just brushed her and revealed the truth? She had to know. What if all angels were Truth Seekers just like the dead man back in Greenlake? She couldn't stay here, no matter how much Renira might want her to. Would Renira even want her to?

Armstar also stood apart from all the others. He was out near the cart, staring at something on the ground. As Aesie crept closer, she could see Princess Perel's long weapon in front of him. The angel seemed to be considering it, hands balled to fists at his side. His skeletal wings twitched as Aesie drew close.

"What do you want?" he asked in a voice that dripped hostility.

"I have questions," Aesie said.

Armstar snorted and shook his head. "Go find a library. I'm sure there are some your Godless King has not yet burned down."

Aesie crept a little closer, making sure to stay out of reach. She placed her back against the cart and debated how to go about asking her questions. "Is the spear important?"

Armstar's wings twitched again, and he glanced over his shoulder to pin Aesie with a flat stare. "It's a halberd. One of seven weapons used to slay the God. Yes, it's important. And far more powerful than its previous owner ever realised. Yet if I knew how to destroy it, I would in a heartbeat."

Aesie fumbled at the gold ring on her finger, still trying to figure out the best way to approach the question she really wanted to ask. Abruptly she remembered the time Elsa taught her to swim. Down by the river, during the summer when the waters were low and slow. Everyone else was already in the water, swimming about like fish, splashing each other and giggling with the fun of it. Aesie had been waiting by the water's edge, too scared to take the plunge or admit to her friends that she didn't know how to swim. Then Elsa was there, stripping off her dress. She noticed Aesie hesitating and asked why. Aesie finally admitted the truth. Elsa had said it was easy and the best way to learn was to jump in with both feet and deal with the consequences. It had seemed like foolishness at the time, but Elsa had compounded the lesson by nudging Aesie in the back so hard she went into the river headfirst and fully dressed. The lesson Aesie had taken from that day was not how to swim, but that it was better to jump in feet first rather than wait for someone to push you and take the choice away.

"Is it true?" Aesie asked. "What you made the Truth Seeker say back at that village, is it true? About the hands of an angel."

Armstar turned away from the halberd and took a step closer to Aesie. She wanted to back away, to turn and run, but she knew it would give the truth away. Then they would all know she had something to hide.

"I didn't make him say anything. I made him tell the truth. What he said was the truth. For once in his cursed life."

Aesie took a deep breath and gripped hold of the cart at her back, using its solid weight to keep her legs from quivering. "So, if he was a made a Truth Seeker by having his hands replaced by those of an angel, does that mean all angels are Truth Seekers?"

"Ahhh," Armstar said with a humourless grin. "It doesn't surprise me this question comes from you. Of all the members of our little group, you are undoubtedly the most *human*." He said the final word as though it tasted foul in his mouth, and it was all he could do not to spit it out.

"Yes, we are all Truth Seekers."

Aesie felt her shallow breath catch in her throat.

"And no, we are not all Truth Seekers."

"Um, what?"

Again, that humourless grin. "Humans. You never realise how easy you have it. Can you ride a horse?"

Aesie swallowed hard, her fingers digging into the cart at her back. She glanced left to where the horses were hitched to a tree, their noses to the ground snuffling for any food that could be found.

"Yes," she said quietly.

"Can the Herald?" Armstar asked, taking another step closer, his ruined, skeletal wings twitching.

"Renira? Um, no. I don't think so. I don't think she ever had a chance to learn."

She considered screaming, calling for help. The angels revered Renira as the Herald. Surely, she could get Armstar to tell her the truth without being so menacing. But Aesie had betrayed her, and Renira hadn't spoken so much as a word to her since they left Greenlake. Besides, she didn't really deserve Renira's help, not after all she'd done. And Renira still didn't know the half of it.

"But she could learn?" Armstar asked. "She has the potential to learn, even if she doesn't have the skill right now?"

"Of course," Aesie said. "I could teach her."

Armstar spread his hands wide. "All angels have the potential to be Truth Seekers, or to sight bond animals, or to influence the emotions of those around us. But not all of us have the favour to do it."

"The favour?"

"Of God. Our abilities are not learned through practice and hard work; they are given to us by God's favour." He shrugged. "Or taken away by his removal of favour. Except God is dead. He can no longer grant or remove anything. We are, all of us, stuck the way we were when he died. Unable to improve ourselves. Stagnating in the lack of his brilliance. But you humans don't have that restriction. You can take any power you want from us. Do you know how?"

"I have an idea," Aesie said, hoping she could cut the angel off before his anger built too high.

"By killing us. Eating us." Armstar took another step forward. "Consuming us however you can. Longer life from drinking our blood. Strength from eating our flesh. Sight bonding with animals by eating our eyes. Red Weavers are made by washing their hands in the blood of angels, and Black Weavers by bathing in meal made with our ground up bones. Does any of this seem fair to you?"

Armstar took a final step forward so he was close enough to reach out and touch her. Aesie had nowhere to run to, pinned up against the cart.

"Armstar!" Renira shouted. Her voice held an edge Aesie was not used to hearing from her friend. Like iron refusing to bend.

The angel glanced at Renira, then back to Aesie. Some of the anger seemed to have fled him already, and he narrowed his eyes at her. "No. Not all angels are Truth Seekers. I am not a Truth Seeker. Why? Do you have something to hide?"

Aesie swallowed hard, and her legs finally buckled, dumping her on the mud and decaying leaves.

"Hey!" Renira crossed the last of the distance between them at a jog and gave Armstar a push with both hands. "Leave her alone! She doesn't deserve you trying to frighten her. You have no idea what we went through without you."

Armstar stooped and plucked the halberd from the ground. "How did you get out of there without us? There is no other way up the tower."

Renira shook her head as she stepped in front of Aesie. "Yes, there is. A prison and a stairwell. You know it."

Armstar almost seemed to pale in the moonlight, an impressive feat for someone with such ivory skin. "You should know he lies. It's all he does. That's why he's there."

"Go away, Armstar," Renira said, standing her ground.

The angel grumbled something Aesie didn't hear and paced away into the gloom of the forest, taking the halberd with him. Renira turned to Aesie and extended a hand, pulling her to her feet.

"Thank you," Aesie said. "He can be really scary when he's angry."

Renira nodded. She hadn't let go of Aesie's hand yet and in the dim light there was a gleam to her eyes. "Why was he angry?"

Aesie considered lying, but she'd done enough of that of late. She needed to tell the truth, for her sake more than anyone else's. "Because I asked him if he was a Truth Seeker. If all angels were."

A silence like a stone wall fell between them, and in that quiet Aesie wondered if she had broken their friendship for good. Renira was the forgiving type, always slow to anger, often forgiving before it even arrived, but Aesie couldn't blame her friend for being furious this time. Unwittingly or not, Aesie had betrayed Renira to her most dire of enemies. The moment stretched between them, further and further until Aesie thought she were about to snap along with it, and she couldn't take it a moment longer.

"I'm sorry, Ren."

"You betrayed me!" Renira's voice came out as a hiss. She took a step back from her friend, and the night air filled the space between them. She was trembling and not from the cold.

"I... I did," Aesie said. She was crying again, but Renira couldn't find any tears to join her. She was angry enough to scream though and she did not like finding that rage inside herself.

"Why?" Renira demanded quietly. She balled her hands into fists, her breath tight in her chest. "After everything we've been through, Aesie. Why?"

Aesie shook her head urgently. "I didn't know it was you. I thought it was one of them, the angels. I thought if I led Princess Perel to them, she'd spare you. Free you from this nonsense. And the king offered me a drop of blood. Angel blood to cure my father. I... I didn't know!"

"Now you do," Renira said coldly. "Now you know. You've seen the angels are real. You know I'm the Herald. Do you still think it's nonsense?"

Aesie was silent for a moment, and Renira could see her friend trying to come up with a diplomatic answer. Or maybe another lie. Everyone was lying to her, the angels, the Apostle, her own mother. The one person she had thought she could rely on for the truth was her best friend, but even that was false. It all made her so angry.

"Yes, I do." It was the last thing Renira had expected Aesie to say. "I think it's madness and foolishness and nonsense. But none of that matters. Because you believe it. It matters to you.

"Please don't send me away," Aesie begged. "Don't leave me behind. Let me help. I mean really help. Let me make it up to you. You're my best friend. I don't want to lose you over this. Over a misunderstanding."

"A misunderstanding?" The words came out as a squeak of rage. "You almost got us all killed!"

"I..." Aesie shook her head and stared at the ground. "I don't know what else to call it."

"A betrayal!" Renira hissed, and Aesie cringed as though expecting a strike.

"You're right," Aesie said. She was crying again, unable or unwilling to meet Renira's eyes. "It was. I... I betrayed you, and I'm sorry. I'm sorry. I'm so sorry, Ren."

"You keep saying that, and I... I don't know whether to believe you."

Aesie looked up at that, eyes wide and wet, searching as if desperate for Renira to take it back. But she couldn't. Renira could no more take back the words than Aesie could the betrayal.

She couldn't deal with it right now. The anger inside of her was hot and nasty and she hated how it made her feel, how it made her want to hurt someone. "Get some sleep, Aesie," Renira said, hiding the rage and making her voice flat.

She turned away before her friend could see her turmoil. Aesie had lied to her, betrayed her. But she was still her friend, her best friend. And she hadn't known what she was doing. Surely she deserved a second chance? Renira felt sick to her stomach. She didn't know whether or not to let Aesie remain, but what she did know was that Armstar and Eleseth could not be allowed to learn the truth. If the angels found out, there was no telling what they might do.

Renira made her way back to the campfire. Sun was lying on the ground, nestled up against the log he had been sitting on. Armstar and Gemp were nowhere to be seen, out in the forest, beyond the light of the fire. They had been ambushed enough recently, it was good sense to have a watch set up, and angels were the perfect watchers. They needed so little sleep. Gemp, on the other hand, was the type of man who snatched moments of shut eye wherever he could and functioned on far less sleep than Renira would have thought possible.

Eleseth knelt in front of the fire, her wings couched behind her, the glow all but faded so they seemed pearly white in the light of the fire. She fed another small log to the flames and used a little stick to poke the embers back to life. She was as dirty and dishevelled as the rest of them, despite her divinity. That was what the Godless King had done to the world, to the angels. They had once been lords, living in luxury and leading humanity down paths of faith and culture. Now they were vagrants, refugees on the run, hiding in the shadows and as scared of humanity as humanity was of them.

Renira pulled another small log closer to the fire and sat upon it. It seemed the benefit of stealing a cart from a logging village was that cut logs were the one thing they weren't lacking. Food, on the other hand, was running quite scarce since most of their supplies had been lost to the cave-in at the tower. As if to make her point, Renira's stomach let loose a whining growl.

Eleseth glanced up and smiled. "I can promise you a hearty breakfast," the angel said, her voice like soothing bells in the distance.

"Like you promised to protect me all the way to the bell?" It was such a churlish thing to say. Her anger was making her snap at everyone. "Sorry. That was not kind of me."

"True though." Eleseth shrugged, and the feathers of her wings whispered against each other "You should sleep, Renira. I'll watch over you."

The angel wore a kindly smile, a motherly smile. Renira wondered if that, too, was by design. Eleseth had said she was made by God to inspire awe in humanity, to spread the God's faith. But then, perhaps she was made to project comfort as well. To some she was awe-inspiring, to others she was comforting, and to others still she was captivating. All rolled together into a single angel to ring in an age of faith and learning. A Herald made to reflect the age she was to bring about.

"I have a question," Renira said, swallowing her anger.

"You want to know whether you're doing the right thing," Eleseth said. "You're questioning whether the world needs the God to be reborn or whether we are better off as we are. I can tell you..."

"No," Renira said sharply.

Stop asking others for reasons. Find them yourself, or they won't mean a damned thing anyway.

Her hand wormed its way up to her chest and she clutched for an amulet that wasn't there. The Truth Seeker had torn it from her, and in the chaos of their escape, she had left it in the mud. Lost and forgotten. Her mother's icon of her faith: gone. She shook her head to clear the thoughts away. It was only a stupid necklace, after all.

"I don't need you or anyone else to tell me I'm doing the right thing. I've seen enough of Helesia now to know we need God," Renira said, staring into the flames as they slowly devoured the log. "Even back in Riverden, I saw people punished for believing in something more than an immortal king. They were placed in stocks, their tongues cut out to stop them from spreading heresy, pelted with rocks and left to die. And no one cared. People we had known for years were found guilty of heresy and sentenced to death, and their friends and family cheered the executioner. It's disgusting!

"My mother is so scared of being discovered that she hides her faith from everyone. She has never done anyone any harm. Her faith has never brought misfortune on anyone but herself, yet she is forced to bury it from others in fear of what they would do to her. People she has lived next to, drank with, laughed with, her friends. She lives in constant fear of them, of what they would do to us if they found out.

"And yet, she never stopped believing. She never stopped practising her faith in the shadows. I didn't understand why." Renira's mind was a whirl as she considered all the thoughts she had been damming up for so long.

"I'm still not sure I understand why, but her faith has always been important to her. Helping her through dark times, comforting her when she's sad. It gave her perspective when we lost people and hope even when we had nothing. It gave her so much and asked so little in return. She never tried to preach her faith to others, but it was always there to keep her going.

"Who is the king to decide that's not right? That she should be persecuted for the harmless act of believing in something other than him?"

Sun blinked awake at the sound of her rising voice, rubbed at his eyes, and stared at her. Renira waved her hands through the flames of the camp fire, feeling the heat brush against her skin, a painful mirror to the anger inside.

"We saw it at Los Hold as well. Persecution of people based upon their faith. The people, your acolytes, had no weapons. They should have been left alone, but the wolf princess didn't just kill angels. Her thugs swept through Los Hold and murdered everyone."

Eleseth frowned, a deep sadness settling on her.

"And in Greenlake..." Renira felt her throat tighten at the thought. A cold shiver ran through her, and she struggled to collect herself. "They tried to kill me. Not just the Truth Seeker. A mob of villagers because I had the temerity to ask whether a woman deserved to die for the accusation of faith.

"Well, I know the answer. She didn't deserve to die, even if she had placed her faith in the God instead of the king, yet they murdered her without proof anyway. Then they turned on me." Her throat tightened and strangled any more words before they could form. But she still remembered the barkeep, Bru. She had been so kind the night before, so compassionate as she filled the tub, chatted with them, cut Renira's hair. And then the next day she had levelled an accusation right at Renira for no more than wearing her mother's amulet about her neck. It was all so wrong.

"Ren?" Sun asked. He started shuffling toward her, but Renira shook her head at him. She didn't want comfort right now, she wanted to feel angry. She needed the fire that had lit inside of her.

"This world is broken. The Godless King has shaped it in his image, and it is an image of distrust and violence and hate. It is broken and it is horrible, and *I* can't change it. I don't know how. I'm not strong enough." She swallowed and then drew in a ragged breath. "The world is broken. And I think... I believe only God can fix it."

Renira clenched her fist in the flames as if she could take hold of the fire. "That's my reason. That's how I know I'm doing the right thing."

She looked up to find Eleseth glowing. Her hair and wings the colour of a distant sunrise, shedding more light than the flames of the campfire. And she was smiling, the smile of a proud mother who has seen their child do something they know they never could.

"You're right, Renira," she said, her voice hoarse as though she were holding back her own tears. "The world is broken, and only God can fix it. But you're also wrong. *You* can change the world. Right now, you're the only one who can."

"Are you all right, Ren?" Sun asked. His eyes were bright with worry.

She pulled her hand out of the flames and held out an arm. He shifted toward her, wrapping his arms around her chest and squeezing her tight. She laid her own arm across his shoulders.

"What was it you wanted to ask?" Eleseth said.

Renira swallowed down the lump in her throat and took a steadying breath. "I want you to tell me about the Heralds. Not what they are. But who they were."

Eleseth's smile was full of gratitude. "You want to know who has come before you. How we helped shape the Ages. Then I shall start at the beginning.

"The First Age was an age of war, and so Orphus was made a warrior. You've met him, and he is much as he seems. He wears his heart on his sleeve, as the saying goes, although I suppose vambrace would be more fitting in his case. There is little hidden beneath the surface except for a keen mind. But his is a mind strategic in nature. He was made to think of all situations as conflict, a battle to be fought and won. Forces to be moved around a battlefield. Arguing with him is..." Eleseth sighed out a laugh. "It's intense. A challenge and one he is always more prepared for than you. He thinks steps ahead, not just one or two, but many. A warrior and a strategist."

Eleseth's smile dropped. "I am told he once revelled in battle and bloodshed. I was not alive during the First Age, but I have spoken to my brothers and sisters who were, and they told me of a different man from the one I know. A warrior who coated his armour in the blood of his enemies and was never happier than the moments before a battle. Those points in time where all preparation have been made, and all that is left is the skill and power of those fighting each other. He was made that way, I suppose, though I know a very different man to those stories."

"He was the first angel?" Renira asked.

"Yes."

"The very first?"

Eleseth frowned. "Of course. The only angel made before the Ages began."

Does she not know about Moon?

"What does he look like under his armour?" Sun asked.

"I don't know," Eleseth said with a shake of her head that set her molten hair tumbling. "A First Age angel's armour is a part of them, as much alive as they are, it even changes with them. His armour has always been decorated with swords, but it was only in the past few centuries that books started to take shape as well. I have known Orphus all my life, and I have been alive a long time, but I have never even seen his face. Only when they die and their armour is removed are we able to see the person beneath the armour. I'm not even certain he knows what he looks like underneath."

It seemed odd to Renira. If a Herald is a representation of the age they were bringing about, what did that say about an age rung in by an angel who hid their true appearance?

"Don't underestimate Orphus," Eleseth continued. "He might seem aloof and brooding. Definitely brooding. But he cares more for this world and for humanity than you will ever know. After all, the God made him to free your people from slavery. He knew the Saint, trained her, helped her unite your people. Orphus always wanted the best for humanity even after..." She sighed.

"Ertide, the first Godless King, his betrayal wounded Orphus deeply. Compounded by the fact that he did not see it coming. Yet, Emrik's betrayal was most bitter for Orphus. He had known the boy since birth, we all had, but Orphus trained him just as surely as Edaine nurtured his artistic spirit."

"What about you?" Renira asked. "You're the Herald of the Second Age. Tell me about you."

Eleseth frowned for a moment, then nodded. "The Second Age was the Age of Wisdom. I was made to bring..."

Renira shook her head. "Tell me about you, Eleseth. What did *you* want? What do you want? I know about the Second Age, my mother told me all about it, but I know little about you. Other than you're kind and brave and strong."

"And you glow," said Sun. His head was resting on Renira's shoulder, and there was comfort in the closeness.

"What did I want?" Eleseth opened her mouth to say more, then closed it again, her eyes going distant. Eventually she smiled and pushed another log onto the campfire.

"You have to understand, we were, all of us, made to love God. He is our father and our mother. He is parent, protector, tutor, and guide. He is the source of our strength and the light that shines from us. We were made to love him, yes, but we all would have willingly even had we not been. How could we not love our parent?"

Renira felt Sun stiffen and pull away from her. She glanced to find his eyes locked on the flames, a frown creasing his brow. She wondered if it was because of the mention of parents and a child's love for them? If he had never known his parents, it was likely a sentiment he simply couldn't understand. Renira couldn't imagine having never known or loved her mother, but she'd be lying if she said she hadn't occasionally wished to have known her father. Or at least, know who he was.

"What I wanted was what he wanted for me," Eleseth continued. "To make him proud, and to do it by fulfilling the purpose he had laid out for me. To bring his light to the world. To spread his faith across the Sant Dien Empire. To teach humanity to be more than the demons who had enslaved them for generations.

"What I want now is for humanity to find its way again. You have been lost in the darkness for so long, in an age that should have ended centuries ago, ruled by madmen and fallen angels. And it saddens me that I cannot be the light that guides you all. Not this time. My age has passed. My people are all but gone, hunted to extinction. I find it ironic that angelkind must now rely on humanity, even though it is humanity that has brought the world to the state it is in."

Renira let the silence descend as Eleseth fed the fire again and Sun brooded nearby. She already knew a lot about Edaine, the Herald of the Third Age, and she had no doubt that Armstar would be the better authority on who the man himself was. But there was one Herald she knew almost nothing about. "What about Mathanial?"

Eleseth snapped out of her reverie with a shudder. "The Rider. Mathanial was full of energy. So excited to see the world. Not just the Sant Dien Empire, but everything beyond. There is so much beyond this kingdom that has never been explored. Beyond Dien, beyond Ashvold. Beyond the Primal Mountains to the far east and the Tvean Sea to the west. We've never known what's out there, but something is. After all, you came from the sea originally."

"The Exodus?" Renira said.

Eleseth nodded. "Humanity arrived to this land on dozens of immense boats, fleeing something. Before even the First Age. You came here looking for salvation and found only thralldom at the hands of demons."

Sun poked a log back into the fire with his foot. "What were we fleeing from?"

"I don't know. None of us do. I think that was part of what excited Mathanial so. The unknown. He designed boats that could stand against even the roughest seas and balloons that could lift dozens of men at a time. He bred horses that could ride for days and mules to withstand even the most frigid weather the Primals could throw at you.

"Mathanial sent out expeditions to explore beyond the borders drawn on any maps. None ever returned.

"I think that was his greatest regret, even more so than his age being corrupted by the Godless Kings. He never got the chance to explore for himself, and he never found out what happened to the humans and angels he sent in his stead." She paused, and a smile lit her face. "I fear there may be things more dangerous than any of us beyond the borders God set. Mathanial, more than any other, would have loved to find out.

"He was an arrogant bastard," Eleseth said, her golden eyes glowing in the light of the fire. "The youngest Herald, but he always thought he was in the right. He and Orphus used to fight like you wouldn't believe. It didn't matter what it was over, they would find a way to bring it to a conflict. Mathanial was the only person I've ever seen able to make Orphus lose his temper. And the shouting matches between them... I swear they once screamed at each other so loudly the building came down around them."

Her smile slipped, replaced by a look of grief. "He had something none of us other Heralds ever did, not even Edaine. Mathanial had an unbridled passion. It often manifested as a temper he could barely restrain, but also as a charm no others could match. When he talked, people stopped and listened. He once lectured me for three whole days on the proper way to brush down a horse, and it never even occurred to me to interrupt him."

Sun snorted. "Sounds like a bore."

Eleseth nodded. "Most people would have been. But that was Mathanial's charm. His passion for the things he loved was infectious."

Renira thought she had a better grasp of the angels now. At first, she had thought them cold, long-lived creatures who cared little for humans with such brief spans, but that was because of Armstar and his hostility. Yet even Armstar had revealed something to her down in the tower. He, like all the angels, was a creature of passion, and his passion was artistic expression. He went to extraordinary, even dangerous, lengths to preserve artwork. Not so others might one day look upon it with a security that the Godless King had robbed from them all, and not even so he could look upon it himself down in the dark. He preserved the art for the sake of the art. It existed, and so it deserved to be protected.

Orphus seemed distant, a once shining example now dulled and near lifeless. But Renira thought she saw the truth of that too now. His passion was battle, the thrill of combat, and it was a passion he had denied himself for a thousand years. He continued to deny himself, even now when it would do his people the most good. Renira wondered if it was sorrow of the things he had done that made him hold so tightly to his control, or whether it was fear of what he might do if he ever allowed himself to express his passion once again. An angel born to kill.

And Eleseth. Renira could see the truth of Eleseth so clearly now she knew to look. Her passion was people. Her brothers and sisters, the remnants of angelkind. Even humanity, those who sought to bring an end to everything she held dear. She loved the people of Helesia, human and angel, and wanted to see them all shine as brightly as they could.

"So, all the other Heralds were angels?" Sun asked.

"Of course," Eleseth said. She retrieved her stick and poked at the fire, sending up a small plume of ash and embers.

"Then how is Renira a Herald? Are you an angel?"

Renira smiled at sun, finally feeling a little like herself again. "Sure. I'm just hiding my wings in my other coat."

Sun snorted a laugh. "You'd be a terrible angel."

"Thanks."

"You got scared climbing out a window. You'd never be able to fly."

"There are rules," Eleseth said. "Or I suppose criteria might be a better word. Set down by the God himself. Renira is the only one who meets those criteria. I guess it would be more fitting to say she is not currently the Herald, but instead that she is the only one capable of becoming the Herald."

That was not what Orphus had told her. The Archangel had claimed she was the Herald. He had made it sound like she had a destiny to ring the Bell of Ages and bring about the Fifth Age and the resurrection of the God.

"Every time before," Eleseth continued. "All of the previous Four Ages, an angel has been made specifically for the honour of ringing in the new age. But that isn't possible now. There are no angels who meet the criteria, and with the God dead there can be no new angels. We have spent centuries searching for someone, and we have come to the conclusion that you, Renira, are our last hope."

The Last Hope of the Dying. The Apostle really did know who I am. And what I have to do. And he knew Aesie betrayed me. I wish I could remember what else he said.

"What are the criteria?" Sun asked.

Eleseth placed another log on the fire and poked at the flames. "The Herald must have been born in the current age. This, alone, rules out all the angels who are left. The Godless King has hunted us to extinction, and none of my brothers and sisters of the Fourth Age still live.

"The Herald must possess a spark of the divine. A simple immortal won't do. It must be someone who has more than just devoured an angel. And the Herald must know the true name of the God from God himself."

"Wait. I don't know the name of God," Renira said, a moment of panic surging through her. How could she be the Herald if she didn't meet all the criteria? Was she going to fail before she even tried?

Eleseth smiled. "You will. Before you reach the Overlook and the bell, you will know. It is important to remember, Renira, though the God is dead, he is not gone. I promise you, when the time comes, you will know his name."

"What about the middle one?" Sun asked. "The spark of the divine?" He narrowed his eyes at Renira, but she just shrugged at him.

Eleseth didn't answer right away, she sighed and then turned to stare into the darkness beyond the firelight. When finally she turned back to Renira and Sun, she had a wry smile on her face.

"That isn't my secret to tell. Just know this, Renira. Your mother was very special to us all, but none more so than Armstar."

Renira felt a cold hand close around her heart, stealing her breath and putting a dull ache in her chest. *Is she saying...* Renira chewed on her lip and tried to deny the thought. *Is Eleseth saying Armstar is my father?*

"Lusa gave up a lot to have you, Renira. She tried to hide you both from the Godless King and his agents. And also, from us."

"Why?" Renira asked, unable to hide the urgency in her voice. "Why would she want to hide me from you?"

"She's your mother. She wanted to protect you."

"From you?"

"From what we are asking you to do. I won't try to hide this from you, Renira. Breaking into Celesgarde, storming the Overlook, and ringing the Bell of Ages is as dangerous a task as any you could imagine. The Godless King will be watching, his troops will be ready. And he will kill you rather than let you reach the bell.

"Emrik is committed to wiping all trace of the God from this world and will not balk at the murder of a young girl in order to stop the God from being reborn. You believe the wolf princess was terrifying? She was but a pup compared to the father.

"Your mother took you into hiding because she realised what you could become and knew that we would one day ask you to do this. Her love for you proved stronger than her love of the God.

"But a daughter cannot hide behind her mother's skirts forever, Renira. Lusa knew that, and that is why she also let you go with Armstar."

In the silence that followed, Eleseth placed another couple of logs on the fire. They looked so small in her hands, but each was as large as the one Renira sat on. The angel stood and stretched out her wings for a moment.

"Get some sleep, both of you. We'll be leaving at dawn, and we have a long way to go. From here we head to Celesgarde. It's time. Celesgarde is at least two weeks away, and we'll be pushing hard to get there. The sooner we get you to the Overlook, the better. Before the Godless King can call in even more soldiers." She turned and stalked away into the night, the glow of her wings fading until the darkness swallowed her completely.

Eleseth sat cross-legged upon the frozen forest floor, her fingers buried in the leaf litter. She had suppressed her glow as much as she cared to, but it didn't stop animals from investigating. Insects swarmed toward her, walking across her fingers or buzzing by to land on her shoulders. Birds and bats tweeted and chirruped from up above, staring down through eyes as dark as the Godless King's heart. A few small mammals, stirred out of their hibernation by her proximity, braved to come closer. A couple of rabbits with noses twitching and ears swivelling in case of danger. A dozen mice swarming out of a hole in the ground, drawn close despite the snake that coiled nearby. A doe, young and foolish and insatiably curious of the world. A couple of wolves padded close, drawn not by Eleseth but by the lure of easy prey. They sniffed at Eleseth from a distance, then turned and loped back into the night, unwilling to risk their lives. Something much larger stirred from the depths of the forest, a great hunter that slept not for weeks or months of winter, but for decades. For centuries. It sensed her, not drawn like the less intelligent animals, but woken by her presence nonetheless. A monster of the old world, and one not even an angel of the Second Age wished to draw the attention of.

Eleseth reached out a hand, and the doe stepped closer, its head dipping and rising as it tried to sense any danger the angel might represent. It sniffed at her fingers, then took another step and licked at her hand. Eleseth curled her fingers around the beast's neck and whispered her thanks. Then she gripped hard, snapping the doe's neck. Her glamour broken, the rest of the animals held in her thrall turned and scattered, running back into the dark and slithering into their holes.

Only the doe remained, lifeless and warm. It would feed them all for a day or two at least, assuming they had time to cook it. Assuming the great hunter she had awoken didn't come to investigate. It would be hungry after so long asleep, and she hoped it would be more likely to investigate Greenlake than a few weary travellers. Renira might have begged mercy for the villagers who had tried to murder her, but that didn't mean they deserved it, and Eleseth would not lift a hand to save them.

A rustle of leaves behind warned Eleseth that someone was coming. Someone who lacked the sense and ability to walk quietly. "Hello, brother."

Armstar took another few steps and crouched down next to Eleseth. His wings, the proof of his falling, twitched as the ruined bones draped over the forest floor.

"How much did you tell her?" he asked in a soft voice that lacked its usual bite.

"As much as was safe. No more than she needed to know." She glanced over at Armstar. Her brother had a hand in one of the pockets of his robe and was fiddling with something.

"She met the Apostle beneath Star Reach," Armstar said, his tone like that of a naughty child caught in the act by a parent.

Eleseth felt her calm shatter in an instant. "Moon is alive? What is he doing under Star Reach?"

"Yes, and nothing," Armstar said with a frown. "He's chained up."

"He should be dead!" Eleseth hissed. "The Apostle is too dangerous to keep chained up, Armstar. What if he escapes?"

"Don't insult me, sister," Armstar said with a dismissive wave of his hand. "I am the Builder. I know how to build a prison. Moon is never getting free."

"What is he even doing there?"

"Don't blame me for that. Orphus brought him to me not long after Heaven fell. He's been there ever since, chained up and mad as ever. And singing. Always damned-well singing."

"That's what that noise was," Eleseth said. Now she thought about it, she knew she had recognised it from somewhere. Moon had been one of the greatest musicians the world had ever seen. Half the epics bards still sang today were of his composition. He had also been a friend, a brother, a champion of their cause. Up until the moment he decided not to be and turned humanity against the God and gave up the secrets of angel flesh and blood. He had always been half mad, but no one ever expected he could commit such horrors against his own kind.

"How much did he tell her?" Eleseth asked, suddenly aware that the Apostle could have ruined their plans yet again.

"I don't know. Hopefully not enough to reveal the truth. He speaks in riddles and lies. I know the truth and still can't figure out what he's saying most of the time."

Eleseth shook her head and sighed. She stood and swung the body of the doe up onto her shoulder. "It doesn't matter, I suppose. She'll learn the truth eventually. We must hope she doesn't figure it out before we reach Celesgarde. This is our last chance, brother. Orphus has bet everything and everyone on this. If we fail, if Renira realises the truth, the Godless King wins."

Armstar looked up at his sister and shrugged. "Emrik won a thousand years ago, sister. We all just refuse to accept it."

CHAPTER 44

Not all tools fit every purpose. If I wish to paint a window, I do not use a hammer. To mop the floor, I would not use a chisel. So, too, with people. I send a warrior to fight, a general to lead, and a bureaucrat to govern.

Once I know the strengths of a man, I know which job he is suited for. And once I know the weakness of a man, I know how to break him.

— ERTIDE HOSTAIN

Two weeks after putting the flaming ruins of Los Hold behind him, Emrik arrived at the gates to Celesgarde. It was a settlement like no other, as much a fort as a city and large enough to dwarf all others in Helesia. Founded by Saint Dien in the First Age, then made grander and grander still during the Third Age, much of it erected by the Builder himself, it was designed to be the pinnacle of human civilisation. A city three thousand years old, constructed then reconstructed again and again, each time made larger and more secure.

Buildings of worked stone towered above cobbled streets with seams so small they were almost invisible. A sewage system that connected to every building in the city and diverted the waste far to the west where it flowed into the river Brak that eventually connected to the sea. Entire districts devoted to industry, with wells so deep they tapped into the subterranean world and never ran dry. A palace built for the Hostain dynasty, grand as a burning sunset and as fortified as a turtle's back. And in the centre of the city, towering above everything, the Overlook.

Never before or since had anything so opulent been constructed. It was solid stone, a series of twisting paths each wide enough for five men abreast, wound around the God-made mountain. Two hundred feet above the city, the Overlook extended out over Celesgarde, hanging over the buildings below, casting homes and workshops in shadow like a great sundial. And at its pinnacle, the Bell of Ages hung in its divine shrine.

None of the people below even knew its significance these days. Emrik had carved away all mention of the God or his angels as anything other than tyrants. He had broken murals, torn down statues, and scratched scripture from the rock itself. He only kept the bell because it could not be destroyed. The God had made it at the height of his power and forged it to be truly indestructible. Emrik had never understood why before, yet now it seemed obvious. The God had made the bell as his vessel to be reborn should humanity ever rise against him. The bastard was as wise as he was sinister. A thousand years dead and yet *still* not gone.

The walls around Celesgarde were the only part of the city no angel had a hand in building. They had not been needed during the Third Age. It was the Golden Age, a time of peace and prosperity where humanity could indulge in its artistic side and each and every person could discover who they were and what their existence meant to the world. Like all things of the God's creation, the Third Age was a lie.

People wrote sonnets to the God and his glory, they created frescos to his wonder, and they built temples to his faith. The Third Age was never about humanity discovering itself, it was an age devoted to stroking the God's ego. But the peace had been real, and because of that peace, the Builder had not thought to erect walls around the city of Celesgarde. It was not until the Fourth Age, until Ertide Hostain had discovered the truth and set humanity on the path to freedom, that they began building the walls. Fifty feet high and thirty wide, built of solid stone. Ertide had learned much from the Builder, and he used that knowledge well. They encircled the city, bristled with armaments designed to target anyone or anything attacking from both ground and sky. Even the angels considered them nigh on unbreachable. Celesgarde might have been the Builder's most magnificent creation, but the walls around it were humanity's.

At the beginning of the Crusade, when the angels were winning the war, Celesgarde had proved to be the greatest and last bastion of humankind. Emrik had been there, standing atop the walls and facing down everything the God could throw at them.

Angels had swooped down from the sky, plucking soldiers from the walls or raining fire and worse down upon the defenders. Monsters, some as large as buildings, had thrown themselves at the walls, tearing great gouges out of the stonework. Men and women had died in their hundreds, their thousands, during the Battle of Celesgarde. But the walls held. And after a hundred days, when the siege broke, the angels broke with it.

That siege had been humanity's grand crucible. And after, Ertide Hostain united the survivors and took the Crusade to Heaven. Emrik had lost family in that siege, two uncles, an aunt, a brother, and five cousins. Over half the Hostain legacy reduced to nothing but fading memories and names etched onto the Wall of Remembrance.

So many memories built into the very stone. And none but Emrik remembered any of it. It was ancient history he had all but scoured away in his efforts to finally and utterly destroy the God.

Now, as he passed through the gate into Celesgarde at the head of almost two thousand soldiers, he renewed a vow he had taken long ago. The most important vow he had ever sworn.

"My breath is your end made manifest. My hands are the tools of your demise. I vow to wipe all trace of you from this world," Emrik said as softly as a summer breeze. And then he added something new to it. "I will not allow you to be reborn, even if I have to sacrifice all of humanity to stop it."

Arik waited for them on the other side of the wall. Emrik's eldest living son and the city regent. It had been years since Emrik had seen his son last, he had been out hunting divinities for so long, but Arik looked well. He was a broad man, as stout as Emrik though not quite as tall, and wore both his age and his power well. Even in a tailored suit more fit for ruling than warring, Arik managed to appear threatening. Of course, that had a lot to do with the tower shield strapped to his back and the hand axe hanging from his belt. A menacing weapon with a curved edge and spiked poll in the shape of a charging one-horn. It was one of the seven Godslayer arms. Emrik himself had snatched the axe from the ground, ignoring his brother's severed hand still wrapped around the haft, and buried its blade in the God's gut.

Seven weapons they had used to kill the God, and Emrik had wielded two of them himself, but really it had been his father who had done most of the work. Rikkan Hostain, the Shield of Empire. Skilled enough to challenge the God himself.

As if the disruption of two thousand armed soldiers entering the city wasn't enough for the common folk, the city-side gate entrance was lined by men and women of the watch, holding back the people. Arik alone waited at the end of the tunnel.

"Father, the city is yours," Arik said with a formal bow. When he straightened back up, he was grinning. "It's been far too long."

Emrik swung a leg over his horse and slipped to the ground. He wore riding leathers, his armour in the carriage train behind, so he stepped forward and hugged his son.

"I missed you, boy!" He growled into Aric's shoulder.

Arik's embrace tightened into a crushing, desperate clutch. "And I you, father."

Arik had always been the best of his sons. As stoic as a mountainside, as fair as blind justice, and as strong as angel-forged steel. Emrik gripped his son tightly and lifted him a little, laughing. No sooner had Arik's feet touched down, he repaid the favour, and by the time they separated they were both grinning like children about trouble. It truly had been far too long since he had seen his son.

The whole procession stopped behind them. Two thousand soldiers and all the rest that came with any army on the move. All waiting for king and prince and their reunion. Borik sat astride his horse, leaning on the horn and wearing a sardonic grin.

"Brother," Arik said, tearing his eyes from his father and smiling broadly at Borik. "Get down here and give me a hug, you lackadaisical mook!"

"I wouldn't want to intrude," Borik said, his tone bordering on mocking.

Arik snorted. "Either you get down here, or I'll pull you from your saddle and dangle you by the legs like I did when you were a boy."

Borik clearly knew a serious threat when he heard one and slipped out of his saddle. No sooner was he on the ground than Arik was on him, wrapping him in a hug that could have crushed a bear. When Arik let his brother go, both men were cackling like geese and breathless for it. Emrik smiled at that. There was little greater joy in life than watching his boys at play. It was just a shame that only two of his sons still lived. The maudlin thought chased away his smile and threatened to lead him down a dark path.

Ride, ride into the light
On wings of steel and hearts borne on rage.
Ride, ride into the dark
Gaping nether devourer of stars.
Ride, ride to the grave
Where time has lost and memory all that remains.

Emrik found it strange that he had lost so many sons and their faces, their voices, their essences escaped him now, and yet he could remember the words to a poem he had written as a child as clear as glass.

"Tavern later?" Arik asked after both men had stopped laughing.

Borik slapped his older brother on the back. "You couldn't keep me away. Who have you been drinking with in my absence?"

"My sons," Arik said. "They can put them away, but they don't like to laugh like you do, brother. Too much of Father in them. Too maudlin."

"Hmm?" Emrik grunted, a frown on his face. "If you boys had seen the things I've..."

"Exactly, Father!" Arik laughed. "They inherited all your seriousness and none of my mirth. I'd blame their mother, but she wields her knitting needles with more skill than I my axe."

Borik threw up his hands. "Of course Sephone is still alive. I always thought her far too relentless to die."

"Careful, brother," Arik said. "That's the mother of my children."

"A compliment. It was a compliment. Sephone is as relentless, and beautiful as the turning of seasons. As vibrant as spring, passionate as summer, elegant as autumn. And a frigid bitch to boot."

Arik swung a lazy punch at Borik and he danced away, both men laughing.

They were holding up traffic now, and quite a crowd was gathering to watch. It was always the way. Everywhere Emrik went, people came out to watch him. It was ironic, he thought, for people who lived such short lives, to spend so much of it watching an immortal king. And for a man with so much time, he barely even noticed those with so little.

"He's off again," said Borik as he swung his leg over his horse. Emrik ignored him and made his way back to his own beast.

"What do you suppose Father ponders when he drifts off like that?" Arik asked.

Borik chuckled. "Probably thinking about how the God tasted. A bitter bite, I think, like spicy whiskey."

"No," Arik said, pulling his horse in line next to Borik's. "The God would have a taste unlike anything you could describe. Like the flavour of the first sunrise in spring."

Both boys laughed. And both were wrong. Angel flesh had a wonderful taste, some sweet like wine, others spicy like curry. Some even tasted like succulent roast pork glazed in honey. But the God had not tasted of anything good. His flesh had tasted of ash and bile.

They left both the soldiers of the Second and Fourth and the men and women of the city watch behind them and rode fast enough through the streets of Celesgarde that no crowds could form to watch their king pass. Father hated parades, but Borik loved the attention. There was a thrill to being the centre of so much scrutiny, and there was nowhere in all Helesia where there was more of it going spare. A busy horde of a city, with common folk, soldiers, nobles, merchants, whores, thieves, and even a busy trade in tourism. Celesgarde was more than just the capital city of Helesia, it was the capital city of humankind, and people from all over Dien, Ashvold, Aelegar, and even the Ice Islands made pilgrimages to see it.

Borik had been away far too long. By now there would be new boys in his favourite skin houses, rugged young men who didn't even know his name. Breaking in a new whore was ever a favourite hobby of Borik's. They always had so much to learn and were full of enthusiasm.

When they reached the palace gates, the guards snapped to attention. They knew their regent, of course, but this was something rare. The king was home, and it wouldn't be long before the entire palace was a bustling hive of activity as servants raced to get even the most disused of rooms cleared of dust and polished to a shine. It was ironic really, as father detested the pageantry of it. He'd much prefer a bit of dust in a room to a gaggle of servants trying desperately to make it look all kingly.

They dismounted in the courtyard, and a stable hand raced over to take their horses. Arik thanked the boy by name, but Father didn't even spare him a glance. No sooner were they on their feet, then Emrik was striding away toward the main entrance with a rush like the tide was coming in. Arik, always in the very best shape of his life, kept pace easily, but Borik lagged. He much preferred a saunter to a march and never bothered trying to keep pace with his father when he got like this.

The palace was an elaborate thing, and Borik had not realised how much he had missed its labyrinthine halls until he set foot in them again. It was eight wings of grandeur, built on a scale that boggled the mind. As a child, he had roamed the halls at will, exploring for no other reason than he could, and more than once he had found himself lost and alone.

He knew the rooms had once been filled, and each wing had once had a name and specific branch of the family assigned to it. But that was a long time ago. The Crusade culled the Hostain family irrevocably, and now most of the wings were empty. Arik and his children and their children filled one wing, maybe two now, but few of Emrik's other children had taken the opportunity of their long lives to breed. Borik was of the wrong persuasion to have children, and Perel was more interested in wolves than she was men. Imren had a few children roaming around somewhere, maybe more than a few knowing her proclivities, but they were so elusive Borik couldn't even remember their names. Besides, Imren had never really liked the palace and much preferred to spend her time out in the city and in her own holdings.

Of course, Emrik's children weren't the only Hostains left in the world, but Uncle Arandon ruled Dien, and he and all his progeny shunned Celesgarde just as they shunned Emrik. Whatever love had once existed between Emrik and his brother had long since been lost, and he loathed to talk about it. Both men were a thousand years old and Borik supposed that came with an unhealthy amount of baggage.

The central wing of the palace was by far the largest, with four floors and no fewer than sixty rooms, including a grand hall that regularly held balls and functions in the king's honour, even when he wasn't in attendance. It was important to keep up appearances for the aristocracy, after all. The other seven wings weren't much smaller; each had three floors and forty rooms and connected to the edge of the central wing and to the wings adjacent. All the wings had domed rooftops, and from the high vantage of the Overlook, the palace looked a lot like a giant empty turtle shell with seven smaller shells arrayed around it. And that didn't even touch on the vault and catacombs waiting beneath like a monster trapped in the basement.

Servants spotted the king as soon as he stepped into the palace foyer. Some bowed and offered their thanks that Emrik had returned safely, others rushed off to spread the news of his presence. Arik laughed and admitted he had hustled out to meet them and hadn't bothered to inform the staff of the king's return. *Surprise breeds ingenuity* had always been one of his favourite sayings.

Despite his long absence, father knew exactly where he was going and made straight for his own chambers, ignoring the servants except to demand food and wine. Arik hurried along beside the king, and Borik trailed after them. Always a step or two behind, a slinking shadow of the two titans.

Borik spared a brief thought for Perel, hoping she was all right. As much as they fought and mocked each other, there was no one who was quite so understanding of his oddities. He already missed his savage sister.

Arik increased his pace and got to the king's study ahead of them. He pulled a set of keys from a pocket and slid one into the doorway, unlocking it and pushing it open even as Emrik stepped through. Father paused there, just inside his old study, glancing about. With his memory, he was likely searching for anything that might have changed, tell-tale signs of an intruder. If he found any, they didn't seem to bother him, and Emrik paced around the edges of the study, trailing a hand across bookshelves, cabinets, paintings, and hearth.

Arik followed his father in, and Borik slipped in afterwards. They both watched their father for a few moments, neither willing to break the silence in case it knocked the king out of his reverie. When finally Emrik arrived at his desk, he pulled out the chair and sank down slowly into it. For a few moments he slouched there with his eyes closed, breathing evenly and deeply. When he opened them again, there was cold steel behind his sapphire gaze.

"Report," Emrik said, his voice gone cold as winter. "I want to know everything you have done with our defences."

Arik popped the catch on the leather strap across his chest and caught the giant shield before it hit the floor, then placed it against the wall next to the door. He approached their father's desk and snapped to attention in front of it, just like the soldier son he had always been. Sometimes Borik wondered if his father was disappointed that he wasn't more like Arik, more a soldier and less a rogue. Then again, Emrik Hostain was never one to begrudge his children their own strengths and weaknesses. Sometimes a soldier was needed and that meant Arik, other times a hunter and that meant Perel. And occasionally, the king needed a good spy.

"We've arranged the majority of the city watch around the Overlook, Father," Arik said. "But the number of real soldiers has been limited. For years now, the best have been sent on to the other legions, and the First has been manned by whatever was left. Not a one of them has ever even seen an angel."

He ground his granite jaw for a moment, as though trying to decide whether to say what came next. "To tell the truth, the watch is under-manned and simply not up to the task of defending Celesgarde against a divine assault. I have had to keep a sizeable number of troops in the city itself to keep the peace, while diverting as many as I can to the Overlook.

"Ten soldiers, the best I can manage, guard the shrine, rotating every six hours. I have established ten checkpoints, each with three members, along the paths leading up to the shrine, again rotating every six hours. The walls are guarded, day and night, and the weapons atop the walls are always mounted and manned. It has been as much as we can manage, and most members of the watch have been working double shifts since you gave word to fortify the city. There's no dissension amongst the ranks yet. Yet. The Legions you have brought with you, the Second and Fourth?" Arik asked.

Father picked absentmindedly at his thumb nail. "Almost two thousand men and women. Weary from a forced march, but hardened by years on the hunt. Each of them has seen an angel and seen what the monsters can do. Many are veterans."

"Are they to be incorporated into the watch?" Arik asked.

Father ripped a bit of skin from his thumb as he considered. "No. Combine the Second and Fourth under your direct command, Arik. Absorb the watch into their ranks and bolster the city defences in all areas. The walls should be swarming. Get the engineers to work. I want scorpions constructed on every available rooftop. Triple the gate guard. Troops on every street and quadruple the guard placements at the shrine."

Arik nodded along to each of their father's orders. "For how long are we securing the city so tightly, Father?"

"As long as it takes. We hold all the advantages here. The Herald is human. She must come to us. She has a limited life span, while we are immortal."

Arik's jaw was working again, grinding his teeth against each other so harshly Borik thought he could hear it. "We are, yes, but the troops aren't. And the city can't support it, Father." The words tumbled out of his mouth quickly, as if he needed to get them out before he could think better of it. "We have limited supplies. Certainly not enough to feed two thousand extra troops indefinitely."

"Send word to the rest of the kingdom," Emrik said. "Raise taxes on food produce. Increase our stores."

"That's a lot of traffic, Father. In and out. The gates will be swamped and..."

Emrik gripped the desk and stood, his chair scraping across the wooden floor of his study. "I am aware of the problems, son. What I need from you is solutions. We will hold Celesgarde for as long as it takes. There is nothing more important than protecting the Bell of Ages."

His gaze flicked across to Borik and then back to his eldest son. "This is it. The end. The Archangel's final move. He has revealed his hand by the act of protecting the Herald and shown me how to win. The Herald dies. The angels die. God remains dead. His name forgotten, the last vestiges of his faith crushed beneath the heel of humanity. If the people of Helesia must starve to bring about this victory, then they will starve knowing that their sacrifice buys them freedom.

"Understand this, son," Emrik continued. "This is the most important order given since your great grandfather ordered what was left of humanity to rally forth and lay siege to Heaven. For a second time Celesgarde stands as the greatest beacon of humanity's power, the last bastion against the corrupt divine, with our family at its head. We will not falter just so a few mortal peasants might fill their bellies."

Arik sighed and sagged a little. He nodded. "I'll dispatch the orders via the Sighted at once. New Gurrund, Vael, Riverden, Earnlast, and the Helesian side of Hope are to redirect a third of their food supplies to the capital."

Borik wondered how that would go down in Hope. It sat to the far north, straddling the Helesian-Dien border north of the Cracked Mountains, a city built to guard Heaven's Gate should it ever re-open. Borik had been there a few times in his life and it was a city riddled with corruption, just as he liked it. Not for nothing was the Helesian side of the city referred to as Poor Town, and those on the Dien side looked down on their neighbours.

"No doubt they'll levy the smaller towns and villages in their influence," Arik continued. "That should bolster our stores long enough to sort a more permanent solution."

Borik sniffed loudly from his spot near the doorway and then cleared his throat. "I have a suggestion," he said slowly, certain neither his father nor brother would like what he had to say.

Arik glanced over his shoulder and raised his eyebrows. "Have you been hoarding food again, brother?"

Borik chuckled. "I doubt my old penchant for stealing a few extra pastries at dinnertime would solve your food crisis. And besides, I long since divested myself of that flaw in favour of far more interesting vices. No, I'll leave the logistics and economics of the city's defence to dull minds better suited to it." He sketched a lazy bow.

"My suggestion lies in the specific defence of the Overlook and the shrine itself."

Father's eyes narrowed. "Speak."

Borik pushed away from the wall and stepped up to the desk, standing next to Arik and looking all the smaller for it. "It's all fine and well simply increasing the number of soldiers up there, but there comes a point where all they'll be doing is stepping on each other's toes. What we need, especially at the shrine itself, is quality over quantity. Now we can't spend the rest of our immortal lives up there personally, we have far too many other things to be about. But we could do with people of both power and fortitude guarding such an important prize."

His father already saw where Borik was leading them, and he was staring down at his desk, shaking his head slowly. Arik caught Borik's gaze and shrugged.

"I think it's time," Borik continued, "that we made some more immortals."

"No," Emrik ground out, his cold eyes still fixed on his desk.

"I'm not talking about full immortals like ourselves," Borik said quickly.

"You reserve that privilege and honour for members of our family and rightly so, Father. But maybe it's time to break into the stores of angel flesh Ezerel and his carvers guard, and make ourselves some... I don't know, let's call them Champions. Soldiers of unfailing loyalty who can be trusted with the strength feasting on divine flesh can offer them, with none of the lengthened lifespan that drinking angel blood offers. Strong, yes, but mortal."

Arik frowned at that. "A waste of angel flesh, giving it to people with limited lifespans."

Borik threw up his hands in exasperation, wondering just how much more convincing the two would take. "It's only a waste without purpose." He turned his full attention to their father, where the final decision would be made. "How much of our stores of divinity would you give up to end this war once and for all, Father?"

"*My* stores," Emrik said. "And all of them."

"All of them," Borik echoed. "By creating Champions, we increase our chances of holding the Overlook in case of divine assault. By withholding blood, we remove the threat of immortals not bearing the Hostain name. If need be, we can always kill them once their need is expended. A few meals of angel flesh will make them strong but little threat to any of us, and they do not need to win against a divine assault, but merely hold the Overlook long enough for us to arrive. Hmm? I think it a rather inspired solution, if I do say so myself."

Emrik sat, the chair creaking under his weight. Borik caught Arik's gaze again and gave him a slight nod, the same nod he had shared with his brother countless times in the past. It was a plea to back him up, and Arik sighed when he saw it.

"The only reason Uncle Arandon has held Dien against both us on one side and Ashvold on the other for so long is because of the immortals he keeps," Arik said. "Clearly, Father, they can be useful if their loyalty can be secured. What Borik proposes... It has an inherent safety to it. Make them strong, but make them mortal."

Emrik nodded. "Do it. Bring me a list of candidates and liaise with Commander Loren of the Fourth. Her troops are by far the most disciplined." He leaned back in his chair and pressed fingers to the bridge of his nose.

"Father?" Arik asked.

"I wonder," Emrik said, his voice lilting a little. "If *he* ever needed to sleep? It is a harsh reality, that no matter how strong consumption of the divine can make us, we must still rest like even the most common of peasants."

"I'll have your orders carried out at once, Father," Arik said, saluting like the proper soldier he was. "And have someone bring some food." He turned on his heel and strode from the room, scooping up his shield.

Borik stopped at the doorway briefly to see his father almost asleep on his feet, staggering toward a plush half couch in the corner of the study. He pulled the door closed behind him and found Arik waiting there.

"It's been a long few weeks," Borik said as they paced down the corridor away from Father's study. Already Borik could hear the hustle of the palace in motion. "He's barely slept. But now you're around, he feels he finally has someone to share the load with, I guess." There was a bitterness there that Borik couldn't quite hide no matter how hard he tried. He didn't resent his brother at all for the trust their father placed in him, but that didn't mean he wasn't envious of that faith.

Arik clapped his brother on the shoulder, and Borik stumbled under the force. "I have duties, brother," Arik said. "Father's orders and the running of a city. Go, find yourself a bath and clean up. I suggest shaving that wispy arse fluff you're growing."

Borik rubbed at his chin and cheeks. "I think it looks rather grisly."

Arik raised his eyebrows. "It makes your chin look like a shaved rat. How do you expect to find yourself a nice boy sporting such flaccid whiskers?"

Borik flashed Arik a grin. "The same way I always do, brother. With a few coins."

Arik laughed. "Bathe, brother. Shave. Visit the kitchens and eat something that isn't desiccated meat or stale biscuit. I'll find you once my duties are complete and we'll celebrate your return properly."

"It has been a while since I had a good ale, and the rest," Borik said. He, too, was feeling weary. It was not for lack of sleep, though, but more that keeping secrets was tiring work.

CHAPTER 45

While the king may own land and title, city and district, it is to the common man that the streets belong.

— ARANDON HOSTAIN

A seedier looking rim stain of a tavern, Borik had never seen. The Dripping Bucket, as the faded sign hanging askew proudly proclaimed, was a few hundreds planks of rotting wood hastily nailed together and squashed between more structurally sound stone buildings either side. The more Borik stared at it, the more he thought someone had tried to build a tavern in an alleyway that simply wasn't large enough for the project. No fewer than three drunks decorated the steps leading up to the doorway, and they ranged from mildly conscious to drowning in a puddle of their own vomit and piss. The racket coming from within sounded like four different arguments happening at the same time and each in a separate language, with a baseline squeal of someone torturing a lute to death. One of the windows of the second floor had a woman's spotty back pressed up against it, her skin wiping up and down against the glass. And the stench surrounded the place was rancid enough to chase away flies. He hadn't even set foot in the tavern yet and already Borik loved it.

Inside, the atmosphere was thick as porridge and cloying as perfume. There were a few spots of blood on the floor, but Borik wagered they were from bar fights rather than traditional offerings. The common room was thin and long, stretching back into smoky gloom, lending further credence to the whole place being a makeshift shanty thrown together in an alley. Despite the general odour and pestilent feel of the place, it was buzzing.

Borik squeezed past two burly men who stank of leviathan oil and slipped around a table covered in cards and coins. He wasn't much one for gambling himself, always preferring games rigged in his own favour, but he understood the draw of them.

Arik wasn't hard to find. He was the tallest man in the tavern and the only one dressed in finery rather than rags. He was also perched on a chair, with one foot on a table, a tankard waving around in his hand, as he told the story of Ignar Staggerlite's last stand at Breakhold, a three-hundred-year-old tale with Arik himself as the hero. He had just reached the point of the cavalry charge where he crushed the barbarian warlord's forces against the lake edge and drove them into the deadly monster-infested waters. It was a stirring story of heroic battle and no one told it quite like Arik himself, but Borik had heard it more times than he cared to count. Regardless, he appeared to have the rest of the table enrapt.

"The warlord's axe flew at me," Arik said. "Black as the darkest night and stained by the blood of all those he had murdered. I tried to pull my horse aside, but too late! Severed the poor beast's head at the neck. It crashed down into the shallows and I leapt from the saddle just in time to stop myself from being crushed under its weight.

"I stood there in the frigid waters, shards of ice crashing against my greaves. Bloodied, dazed, enraged by the murder of so many soldiers under my command. And that monster, that evil blood worshipping savage stalked toward me. Dressed in ragged furs, metal sewn into his skin like horns, the scalps of those he had slaughtered hanging from his belt, Ignar Staggerlite raised his sword..."

"And you struck his head from his shoulders with a single mighty blow," Borik said, clapping slowly.

Arik turned and wobbled from his perch on the table. "Hah! Brother, you made it. My brother shortens the legendary duel Ignar and I fought, but yes, that is how it ends."

Arik downed the last of his tankard and raised it to the air. "FIRST!"

All around the tavern, tankards slammed against tables in a drumming beat and men and women chanted, "First!"

Suddenly Borik understood. This wasn't just some seedy tavern popped up out of nowhere, it was a meeting place for soldiers of the First legion, those tasked with protecting Celesgarde and those most loyal to Arik. At least for the night, it was. Judging by the faces of those not joining in the chant, Borik assumed there were some locals far from pleased at the appropriation.

Arik clambered down from the table and collapsed into the rickety chair. "Fetch some more drinks, Sergeant," he said to a bald man with a scarred lip. "The rest of you, enjoy the atmosphere."

The soldiers who had been seated at the table got up and moved away, pushing against the crowd until there was a small pocket of space around the table. Arik pushed one of the other chairs out with his foot and nodded to it.

"What do you think, Brother?" Arik asked.

Borik slipped into the proffered chair. "It's not as bad as the last time I visited. What was that shit hole you took us to called? The Rutting Red, was it? The ceiling thumped so hard from the upstairs festivities, my ale was more dust and lice than booze."

The bald sergeant returned with two tankards and slipped them onto the table, then saluted briefly and stalked away.

"You have them well trained."

Arik grinned as he raised the tankard to his lips. "The First know their business well."

Borik gulped down a mouthful of ale and immediately spit half of it back into the tankard. It tasted like vinegar had gone to war with fish guts. "I take it back, Brother. This place is an atrocity to mankind and by far the worst tavern you've ever taken me to."

Arik slammed his tankard down. "I always aim to outdo myself, little brother. Of course, next time I'll have to find somewhere even worse."

"You may have reached the pinnacle." Something small and furry brushed against Borik's leg and he steadfastly refused to look down to find out what.

Arik roared out a laugh again and then leaned forward, grabbing Borik's neck and pulling him forward until their foreheads touched. "I missed you, little brother. Now tell me everything. How have you been?"

They swapped stories. It had been almost a year since Borik had last been to Celesgarde and a lot had happened. From the angels hunted, to the men bedded, and the niggling fear of a lost sister. They worked their way through three more tankards and while the taste never improved, Borik found he at least got used to the acidic aftertaste. At some point a hopeful bard tried to murder another lute, but was quickly silenced by a barrage of mugs launched his way.

"How is Sephone?" Borik asked after Arik had finished naming his half dozen grandchildren. The question was more a courtesy really. Sephone had never liked Borik, often blaming him for being a bad influence on her husband. Borik, on the other hand, just found he had little time for her, such a dull thing, she was.

Arik went quiet, his face wistful. The sound of the tavern suddenly seemed an intrusive racket.

"Oh shit! Sorry, Brother," Borik said.

Arik shook his head. "She lives," he said quietly enough Borik had to lean forwards. "For now. Time eats away at her, gnawing like termites to a foundation. I think when she goes, she will take the best part of me with her. Or maybe she'll leave the better part behind, the bits of me she improved by sharing her life. Hah! You'll get me as maudlin as Father."

Arik swigged another mouthful and winced at the taste. "What of you, Brother? Still no urge to settle down? Find yourself a nice man and quit your whoring? Or maybe a woman and start a family?"

Borik snorted into his tankard. "Not a chance. Why would I ever want to settle down when the ultimate end can only be abandonment and pain? Don't take this the wrong way, Arik, but I see the way you're mooning over Sephone. Why would I want that for myself? They die, Brother. They all die. I'd much rather continue my whoring than commit to watching someone I love grow old and wither time after time."

Arik waved a drunken hand in the air. "Bah! Even Father doesn't deny himself love. He's had enough wives to grow cold to it, yet his passion still runs hot when the right one presents herself. You can't live forever and refuse the connections to those around you."

Borik swallowed down more of the vile swill. "Of course I can. Look at them all, Arik," he gestured expansively to the room. "Their lives are but brief flickers in the greater flames of, uh, us. One moment they are children, then adults, then gone." He tapped a hand to his chest. "But we endure. Forever. Or close to it. Why would I want the pain of that loss? Why would I submit myself to that agony? Hmm. Why do you?"

Arik's smile was slow and wide. "My life is better for the time I spent with her, little brother. My appreciation is greater for the children I have. My sons. Best thing I ever did."

"Not that bloody duel with Ignar what's his face?" Borik asked.

Arik grunted. "Stories no one but me even remembers anymore. It was... three? Three hundred years ago. Give it another three hundred and I probably won't even remember it. But my children's children's children's children's... Descendants. They will be my legacy, little brother. More than my forgotten deeds, the people I killed, the papers I signed. People, not history, that's what's important."

Borik leaned forward conspiratorially and lowered his voice to be certain no one else would hear. "Tell me something, Arik, do you ever think about what happens after Father wins?" The topic wasn't seditious, but it trod a fine line.

"Eh? After all the angels are dead? Phew! I'm not sure even Father has planned that. Do you think he'll retire? Abdicate and find a nice cabin in the woods and paint daisies for all eternity?" Arik giggled.

Borik couldn't find a smile of his own. "That's not what I mean." He had to pick his words carefully. Treason was a subtle art, after all. "I mean what happens to us when all the angels are dead, hmm? Once all the stores of divine blood run out?" He glanced about, but no others were close enough to hear him. "Father is the only true immortal left. We..." He pointed a finger between himself and Arik a few times. "We are reliant upon angel blood to sustain our lives, and it is a finite resource."

"Oh, Brother," Arik said. He pawed across the table and grabbed Borik's hand, squeezing tightly. "When all this is over and the angels are finally purged from this world. When none even remember there ever was a God, and when his heresy has been bloody well stamped out for good and all. Weeee..." He wagged his own finger between them. "We will grow old and wrinkled and grey and die. All of us will. Only Father will remain."

Borik frowned and shook his head. "But that's just it. Doesn't death frighten you, Brother?"

Arik shrugged and leaned back in his chair, waving his empty tankard in the air for a refill. "You're so young, Borik. We'll live for hundreds of years on the angels we have already consumed. And Father's stores will keep us alive for hundreds more even once the last of the bastards has fallen. Besides, my own inevitability doesn't frighten me, it never has. What frightens meee," he tapped a finger against his chest, "is seeing my boys grow old and die. What frightens me is that I might fall in love again and forget Sephone's face and the sound of her voice." He shook his head wildly. "Immortality is far more frightening than death, Brother, and I face it every day."

"You're drunk," Borik accused.

Arik swigged from his newly refilled tankard. "Bloody right. This shit is strong."

They both laughed and gulped down some more ale. As their tankards slammed down on the table, Arik leaned forward and squinted at Borik. "You're young, little brother. What are you, a century? Don't let the fear of death rule you. You'll live another five hundred years yet, and then... then we'll see if you still don't regret it."

"Regret what?"

Arik frowned and shook his head. "Regret what?"

"That's what I'm saying," Borik said. "You said I won't regret it."

"Did I?" Arik drew in a deep breath and gripped the table hard enough the wood cracked.

"Uh oh!" Borik stood suddenly and grabbed his brother, hauling him out of the chair and towards the exit. They just about made it outside before Arik sprayed vomit all over the street. He never was very good at holding his booze. Borik had to admit that maybe Sephone was right and he was a bad influence on his brother.

"She's gonna kill me," Arik slurred as Borik slipped his brother's arm over his shoulder and steadied himself against the weight. The palace was a long walk away.

"She won't."

"I love her."

Borik smiled as he started, half dragging his big brother as his feet stumbled drunkenly beneath him.

"I know you do."

"Don't... don't let fear stop you... stop you from finding that... for yourself."

Borik carried his brother home with a heavy heart. He had hoped to convince Arik of his cause, but now he knew better. Arik had always been Father's staunchest supporter, believing whole-heartedly in his Crusade to remove all trace of the God from the world, but more than that he had convinced himself it was the right thing to do. It was foolish. A waste of the most precious resource the world had ever known. One did not take a hammer to a lump of coal just because they dislike the colour black. But it was fine. Borik was used to working alone, to keeping his own council above all others. He could manipulate his father all on his own.

There would already be fewer troops on the Overlook, and that would be good for the angels. A few pitiful champions with a mere taste of divinity would be no match for Orphus, and fewer soldiers crowding the path would make dragging the Herald girl up there much easier. The God would be reborn, even if Borik had to defy the rules of the world and ring the bloody bell himself.

CHAPTER 46

We hold here, atop these walls, against this horde. We hold and we fight because we must. Our families are in danger, our friends, our children. Our way of life is under threat. If we fall here, our enemies will never let us crawl free of the chains around our necks. We will forever live in thralldom to the angels and their God. I will not allow it. Stand with me, brothers. Stand by my side, and let us show them that they can bleed!

— ERTIDE HOSTAIN, AT THE BATTLE OF
CELESGARDE. YEAR 42 OF THE FOURTH AGE. 3
YEARS BEFORE HEAVEN FELL

After weeks on the road, sneaking by towns and villages, dodging the sun and travelling almost entirely by night, Celesgarde was finally in sight. The city rose up from the fields around it like a defiant white scar amidst an ocean of green. The snow had not yet reached the capital city of Helesia, yet winter had gathered her clouds into a frothing grey blanket made darkly ominous by the crimson sky above.

Renira had never felt so anxious. Everything they had planned for, everything they had been moving toward since Armstar showed up in her house in the middle of a storm, it all led here. The weight of responsibility had never felt so crushing. Even now, having decided to go through with it, having aligned her will with that of the angels, Renira felt trepidation simmering within. It was not over whether she should go through with it, but more how she could accomplish such a thing. They stood a far better chance of failure than success.

The roads into the city were busy, traffic lining up outside the gate so thick it was visible even from a distance. A throng of humanity all pressed together into a seething mass.

They were so close and yet still felt an age away from their goal. Even from almost half a day's walk away, the Overlook was visible above the walls of Celesgarde. An intimidating structure Armstar had taken great pride in describing more than once in the past few days. A structure risen from the earth around it by the God himself at the dawn of the Second Age. Up at the pinnacle of the Overlook, sat the Bell of Ages. Their goal. Renira's goal.

My destiny, I guess. Though it feels more like a death sentence.

The Godless King had brought all his armies and power to the city of Celesgarde and now held it tight in an iron fist of control. Reaching the bell seemed an impossible task. Yet she was going to attempt it. No. She was going to succeed. She had to succeed.

The roadside inn behind them bustled with morning activity. Renira smelled fresh bread baking in preparation for breakfast. It brought back memories of Riverden, of haggling with the Baker boys and begging for pastries. Memories of holding her mother's hand as a child, staring up at adults in conversation and pretending to understand what was being said. Renira missed it all with an aching pang. Not just her mother—her soft voice, strong hands, and loving eye—but Riverden too. All the people she knew, the easy life she had lived. It all seemed so distant, like a dream or story she had once heard from someone else. Not her own life.

"A lot of soldiers by the gate," Eleseth said. Her wings were grey and draped over her shoulders like a cloak. She still stood a full head and a half taller than even the largest person Renira had ever seen. She leaned against the wall of the stable, watching over distances that turned everything into a dark blur.

Armstar squatted nearby, a ratty old cloak draped over his ruined wings, making him seem a hunchback, a swathe of rags wrapped around Perel's halberd to disguise it as a sturdy quarterstaff. "Emrik will have them checking everyone who enters the city. There's no way in."

"You built the place," Eleseth said. "Are there any other ways in?"

Armstar picked up a fallen blade of straw and ripped it in two. He had been quiet of late, brooding alone as often as joining the others each night. Renira found she missed his company somewhat, though not his anger and spite. She still didn't know the truth, had not managed to work up the courage to ask, but the question rolled around in her mind over and over again. *Is he my father?*

"I didn't build the walls," he said. "There wasn't meant to be any need for them. The city was perfect without them."

Gemp and Sun came trotting out of the inn. The old acolyte was chewing on a strip of dried meat, and Sun was chomping down on an apple. They had been growing close over the last few weeks, the old acolyte teaching the boy how to use a spear with at least some degree of skill. Renira often found Sun copying Gemp, adopting his mannerisms, most notably his habit of always having something to chew upon. She was glad he had found another friend. He'd need the support soon enough.

"Cook says the bread'll be ready soon," Sun said around a mouthful of apple. "Breakfast is two ekats a head." He buried his teeth into the apple and chewed noisily. It was twice as expensive as most places they had eaten of late, but then food was starting to get scarce. The travellers they talked to on the roads said taxes on food had gone up. No one was happy about it, especially with winter rolling in.

"It don't look good," Gemp said quietly.

"Smells good enough," Sun said with a grin. It slipped from his face, and he fell silent when no one else laughed.

"I hear about ten days back," Gemp continued, "the king came through with two whole legions. They're all holed up in the city. Thousands of soldiers. The walls are alive with patrols, and the innkeeper said there's soldiers on every street, though most seem to think they're more like armed thugs. City watch was good at keeping the peace, but these boys are causing more trouble than they're preventing."

So the king was definitely there, in the city, waiting for her. Searching for her. Renira remembered the weight of his gaze from the parade in Riverden, though it seemed so long ago now. Back then she had never imagined that he would be looking for her. She had never imagined that she would be in such direct opposition to everything he stood for and the laws he upheld.

"That doesn't sound like the people of Celesgarde are very happy," Eleseth said thoughtfully.

"Inside the city, no," Gemp said. "Outside, yes. Soldiers at the gate are searching everyone who comes through, thoroughly. Folk are backed up for miles, and the gates get shut at night. There's a few inns here and about, and they're all pleased as a dog licking its own balls. Trade outside the walls has never been higher. There's even markets being set up round and about, merchants and other folk needing to sell their wares but unwilling to wait upon the city watch, nor pay whatever *tolls* they decide to charge on a day."

"How unhappy are the people inside?" Eleseth asked.

Gemp pulled a sour face. "Simmering, but they'll never boil. The king is the king. He could start pulling folk out their homes and cutting their throats for nothing but painting the cobbles red, and people would thank him for using a sharp knife."

"Why do they let him do it?" Renira asked, though she already knew the answer. People didn't rise up against their lords. They hunkered down, complained about things that were out of their control, and lived their lives. It was the easy option, the safe option. She couldn't blame them for it.

"Folk'll let a lord or magistrate do just about whatever they want," Gemp said. "Ingrained obedience. They don't reckon they have the right or the power to fight 'em or change a damned thing. Kings can get away with even more, and Emrik Hostain ain't just *a* king. He's *the* king."

Armstar grunted. "He's a monster, a thief, and a murderer."

"He's immortal," Gemp said. He held up his hands when Armstar looked set to argue. "It don't matter that he stole that immortality from your kind, nor all the strength and power he has. He's immortal, and half the damned kingdom has seen how strong he is.

"It's all fine and well saying people should rise up and throw him down, and some of us are fool enough to heed that cause, but you can't go damning anyone who just shuts up and gets on with their life. You just can't. Most of us only get the one life, and it's too bloody short to be throwing it away on a mad quest."

Armstar glared daggers at Gemp. "If more of your people stood up and refused..."

"It's easy," Gemp said, interrupting Armstar, "to take a stand when you've already lived a thousand years and done everything you wanted in life. Easier still when you've been wronged and want some measure of retribution. Most of the people in that city don't even know that angels still exist. Most of them have never even heard the word God except next to the word tyrant, and not a one of them feels particularly wronged by their immortal king. They just want to live their short lives in peace, and they know the best way to do that is grin and bear a few months of eating shit."

The old acolyte shook his head sadly. "I know what you want, Armstar. You're hoping there's some way we can get folk to rise up and cause enough of a distraction to sneak the Herald up onto the Overlook. It ain't happening, and it ain't fair to expect folk to do it. This ain't a rebellion. It's six bloody fools relying on hope and prayer."

He was right. They were on their own in this. But that was always how it started. In the First Age, when the demons had humanity enslaved and the angels were desperately fighting to free them, the course of the war had only changed when one woman, the Saint, had taken up the arms of a slain angel to help fight against their oppressors. Others had joined, her Exemplars and then others still, lending their aid. They had formed an alliance with the angels, eventually leading to Heaven's victory over the demons. Of course, that one woman who started it all had been Dien Hostain, and it was her descendant Renira now had to take up arms against.

"So, what you're saying is we're on our own?" Armstar asked.

Again, the old acolyte shook his head, but it was Eleseth who answered. "No. We're not on our own. While you've been hiding underground for the past few centuries, we have been establishing a network of believers. People willing to risk everything to keep the word of the God alive. Los Hold was our sanctuary, true, but it was only a monastery to teach people. For generations now, we have been sending acolytes like Gemp out into the world to recruit others. To bring back word of the Godless King's atrocities. And to keep an eye out for the Herald. It was one such acolyte who found Lusa. Without them, we would never have had the chance we do now."

"They'll help," Gemp said solemnly. "Can't ask 'em to fight for you. There's not enough to go toe to toe with a squad of soldiers, let alone three legions. But they'll help how they can. Try to cause some sort of distraction."

Aesie crept out of the inn looking refreshed. She alone had taken the opportunity the previous night to bathe. Renira had joined the others in simply wiping themselves down with wet cloths. She could have joined Aesie, she knew, but the last time she had trusted an innkeeper, she had almost been drowned the morning after for heresy. Besides, things had been odd between them since Greenlake.

Her best friend had betrayed her, and Renira couldn't forget that. Something had broken between them. No matter how much she wanted and tried to trust her friend, suspicion always wormed its way into Renira's head. None of the others knew, Renira still feared what Armstar might do if he learned of Aesie's betrayal, but that just made things worse. She had no one to talk to about it, and the one person she truly wanted to talk about was the person who had betrayed her.

Aesie joined them silently. She had been quiet ever since Greenlake, speaking rarely and never meeting Armstar's gaze, nor drifting close enough for the angel to touch her. She had a new blouse and skirts designed for travel, though not nearly as fashionable as her old pair, and had purchased an old dress for Renira as well. It wasn't as warm as her winter clothes had been, but the dress was in far better repair and made for a better disguise. No one looked twice at Renira when they thought her Aesie's maid. She was back to being invisible. Still, she refused to get rid of her mother's coat. It was the last link she had to her old life.

"Can they help you get into the city?" Armstar asked. "Because any distraction is worthless unless you can get past the soldiers at the gate."

"We could fight our way through," Sun said optimistically. "Two angels, me and Gemp. A few soldiers wouldn't stand a chance."

"We'd never make it to the Overlook," Eleseth said. "The moment we reveal ourselves, soldiers will swarm from all over the city, and the longer we take to reach the bell, the more chance that the Godless King and his children will arrive. They might be on the walls already, just waiting for us to make a foolish move."

"I can get us in," Aesie said with a bright smile that curdled the moment she looked at Armstar. "At least, I can get most of us in. You angels will draw too much attention."

Renira wanted to trust Aesie. She really wanted to trust her. *Is this just a ploy to separate me from the angels?*

Armstar chuckled bitterly. "And just how do you intend to get Renira through the gate?"

"As my handmaid," Aesie said breezily. "I have a travel permit signed by King Emrik himself. I was always supposed to head to Celesgarde after New Gurrund. I can claim Ren is my handmaid, Gemp and Sun are my bodyguards, and that we were set upon by bandits or wolves or something on the road. The soldiers at the gate won't ask too many questions when I present them with this." She pulled the leather-bound travel permit out of her satchel. "But a giant woman and a hunchback will probably pique their interest. You don't exactly blend in. Sorry."

"We would have to find another way into the city," Eleseth said, turning away from the roads and looking toward Armstar.

"You will," Armstar said and pushed to his feet. "I'm not going any further. I never was."

"What?" Renira asked. She didn't know why, by the idea that Armstar was leaving scared her. Perhaps it was because she still had so many unanswered questions, or maybe because he was the only one who had been with her from the start.

"A bit late to be crawling back to you tower," Eleseth said, seeming to loom over Armstar. "I suppose I should have expected it."

"I have somewhere else to be."

"Where?" Eleseth asked in a voice like cracking ice. "There is nowhere more important right now than here."

Armstar shrugged. "There is one place."

"Where?" Eleseth repeated.

Armstar said nothing. Gemp and Sun said nothing. Aesie was silent and looked ready to bolt like a hare with a shadow passing overhead. Renira just shook her head, feeling as if her entire world were collapsing around her, and she was suddenly terrified that it was all too much.

How could she hope to succeed without Armstar? He was grouchy at times, scary at others, and treated all of humanity as if it were nothing more than rat entrails he was forced to clean up each morning, but he was Armstar, the Builder. He cared. Underneath the gruff exterior, he cared more deeply than even he was willing to admit, and Renira knew she would be dead five times over already if not for his protection. And she still didn't know. She had to know... *Are you my father?*

"Orphus gave *you* this task, not me," Eleseth continued, her voice hissing through clenched teeth. "I know my part in his plan, and I am willing to carry it out, but you..."

Armstar met his sister's stare and shook his head. Renira felt something pass between them then, but she was panicking too much to ferret out its meaning.

"I *am* following Orphus' plan, sister," Armstar said slowly and deliberately. He glanced sideways at Renira. "I was never supposed to enter Celesgarde."

"Why didn't he tell me?" Eleseth asked.

Armstar held his sister's stare in silence for a few moments, and eventually the Light Bearer backed down from her younger brother.

"Go then," she said, sounding defeated. "I will finish your task myself."

"I'm not running away," Armstar said. "I'm just not going with you."

Eleseth shook her head. "There seems little difference to me." She strode away.

Armstar clenched his hands into fists a couple of times, then turned and walked the other way, toward the inn.

"How can we do this without the angels?" Sun asked, putting voice to the question that was on all their minds.

Gemp caught Renira's eye and nodded to her. "You're the Herald, Herald. I think that makes it your choice. We go in with your friend's permit, then we do this without divine assistance. I think that'll make it a lot harder, but if that's the path you choose, so be it."

The weight of expectation and responsibility was too much, crushing down as surely as the rock that had trapped her underground. The Apostle's words still rattled around in her head. He had called her *the last hope of the dying*. It was all too much.

Without another word, Renira turned and fled after Armstar.

"Here to beg me to come with you?" Armstar asked. He was sitting on an odd stone construction, open to the sky and blackened by fires that were designed to be lit underneath. It looked as though it had once been used to cook food out the back of the inn but had long since fallen to ruin.

"No," Renira said. She stopped next to Armstar and pushed herself up to sit next to him on the stone structure. "It'll probably be easier without you grumbling every step of the way."

They were facing north. Renira had once asked why the sun never moves in the north, but rises in the east, travels across the south, and sinks below the horizon in the west. Her mother had said it was a wise question and had immediately pulled her holy book from its hiding place. She flipped to a beautifully illustrated page of a pillar of light and hundreds of figures bowing down to show their obeisance before it. Then her mother had said: *What need has the sun to shine from the north, when that is where Heaven lies. And from Heaven's Gate shines forth the glory of God, his splendour unmatched even by the sun.* It had always seemed a simple answer to Renira. Too simple. Now she was starting to wonder if it were somehow true. Did Heaven lie to the north? Was the God so arrogant that he refused to share the sky with even the sun?

"What then?" Armstar asked. "You want to know where I'm going? Why I won't tell Eleseth. She's right, this is our last chance. But if we should..."

"I don't care," Renira said, interrupting him. The arguments between the angels were their own business, and she had long since become weary of worrying about them. "I don't care why you're leaving. I just want to know one thing from you, Armstar." She swallowed hard and steeled herself. She couldn't decide if she were more afraid that he would refuse to answer or that he would answer and she wouldn't like what he had to say.

"Who is my mother to you?"

"Ah," Armstar said and then fell silent. He clutched at something around his neck, something hidden beneath his clothing, and Renira felt another pang of loss for her mother's amulet left back in Greenlake.

"I told you about Emrik's betrayal," Armstar said eventually. "How I thought him a kindred spirit, and how painful it was for me when he arrayed himself against us. We worked so hard on my tower and he betrayed me and brought it crashing to the ground. You might find this hard to believe, but I have had a difficult time making friends with humans ever since." He stopped and glanced at her. Renira gave him a flat stare in return.

"I know," Armstar continued. "For a long time, I didn't even try. I thought you all capable of the same evil. More than capable, I thought you all harbouring the same sinister thoughts.

"I met Lusa on a battlefield, healing the wounded from both sides without care for what armour people were wearing. I had taken no part in the battle, I'm not much good in a fight, but I was there, unable to bring myself to do anything but watch.

"I tried to stop her from healing a legion soldier, I even spread my wings and tried to impress the glory of the divine upon her." He glanced down at Renira and gave her a bitter smile. "They were feathered back then. Not nearly as resplendent as my Eleseth's, but with feathers the colour of the sky lit by the final dying rays of the... you get it. Your mother pushed me away and went right back to trying to save the soldier's life. She cried when she failed, then said a prayer for his soul. A prayer to God. I had not heard anyone utter that prayer in... centuries."

Renira knew her mother's prayer. "No soul is lost, nor life so vile, that God may not redeem," she said, reciting it from memory. "The sun has set on your time, and Heaven waits at the end of the light."

"She was too damned kind for this age. What I found in your mother was a true kindred soul. A lover of art, without even a single violent note in her song. She loved poetry above all else." Armstar smiled, and Renira had never seen a smile so genuine from him. "She kept a little book filled with fragments. Words that had meaning to her beyond the definition. Sentences that flowed together as beautifully as mixing paint. And when I asked why she kept a book of scraps, disjointed particles of what could be such beautiful poetry, she told me: *One day I will use this book to create a poem you will want to preserve.*"

The angel fell silent, and Renira felt she needed to fill that silence. There was something uncomfortable about the way Armstar spoke about her mother. "I never knew she likes poetry. She... never told me, I guess."

Armstar chuckled. "You could fill all the books in all the worlds with things children don't know about their parents."

Renira thought about the question she really wanted to ask, but she feared the answer. What would she do if Armstar was her father? What would it mean? But Eleseth had said Renira contained the divine spark. How else could that be if not from Armstar?

"We were together for a while," Armstar said. "A long time by human standards, though only a moment for an immortal. Lusa already believed in the God, already practised her own form of worship, taught to her by her parents, and to them by their own. She met my brothers and sisters and the acolytes of Los Hold. She even got into an argument with Orphus once. They never told me what it was about, but your mother faced down Orphus and refused to concede. Such fire, she had, but never the type that burns.

"We spent many years visiting villages, recruiting and spreading the word of the God. She dragged me away from my tower. I wanted to hate her a bit for that. I wanted to want to go back... but I also didn't. With Lusa, my dead tower just didn't seem as important." Armstar smiled, his eyes locked on the northern horizon yet somehow even more distant. His hand reached inside his robe and closed about something.

"We even found the vault of the Forgemistress. A treasure trove everyone believed lost, its location known only to Karna herself. We stayed there too long. We took little but learned much and were blind to the wards Karna had placed about the vault, warning her of intruders." His face turned grave. "Lusa and I faced Karna together, and we both paid the price for our audacity."

"What happened?" Renira asked after it seemed the angel would say no more.

"Your mother saved my life. And I saved hers. It cost me my wings."

"Because you gave her your blood?"

Armstar nodded sadly. "The greatest sin an angel can commit. Your mother drank only a few drops of my blood, and my wings erupted into an inferno. Ironic, isn't it? I am the Unburnt. I had never felt the pain of flames before. Now I feel it every day. Half a century on and my wings still feel as though they are burning from the inside." His ruined wings twitched beneath the ragged cloak, a gesture Renira had seen time after time, now revealed with more meaning than she could have imagined.

A thought occurred to Renira. Her mother was an immortal! Maybe not a true immortal like the Godless King, but she had tasted angel blood. It must have extended her life, perhaps by many years. That was why only the elders of Ner-on-the-River remembered Lusa Washer. She had been gone from the village for far longer than a handful of years.

Renira reached out and gripped hold of Armstar's hand. He was trembling, either from the agony of his wings or the pain of his memory. He flinched at her touch but didn't pull away.

"Thank you," she said. "Without your sacrifice, I wouldn't exist." She looked at his wings again. The price of her mother's life. The price of Renira's very existence. When she looked at it like that, Armstar had every right to be grouchy.

Armstar growled and leapt down from the stone oven they were sitting on. He pulled something from his robes and stared at it for a moment, then turned and threw it to Renira. She startled and fumbled the catch, almost dropping it before catching it by the leather thong. It was her mother's amulet, the one she had given Renira on the night she left with Armstar. The one she thought she had lost in Greenlake. Renira clutched the amulet against her chest and felt as though she could feel her mother close by.

"One of a pair," Armstar said. "The only things your mother and I managed to keep from Karna's vault."

Renira opened her hand to stare down at the amulet, but it wasn't her mother's. That amulet had been of a crescent moon, its every surface inscribed with runes she didn't recognise. But the amulet she held now was of the sun, and instead of hundreds of runes, it bore only one, carved in the centre of the dark grey metal. She flipped it over and there was another different rune carved into the reverse.

"What does it mean?" Renira asked.

Armstar shrugged. "I don't know. I'm the Builder, not the Forgemistress. Here." He reached inside his robes again and pulled out another amulet, held it dangling from his fingers. It was the partner, the moon. Her mother's amulet. "I found this one in the mud in Greenlake. You should be more careful."

"Are you..." Renira's throat closed around the words, and she had to swallow before you could speak again. "Armstar, are you my father?"

The look that passed across the angel's face was impossible to read. It could have been pain or grief, or even guilt. All Renira knew for certain was that Armstar was fighting something.

"Here." He threw the amulet he was holding to her, and Renira caught it. When she looked up, all emotion seemed to have drained from Armstar's face, and he looked like a weary statue, rendered artless by the rigours of time.

"Your mother and I can't go with you, Renira. But that doesn't mean we can't protect you. Wear those amulets. Don't lose them, and don't ever take them off." He turned away, facing north and started walking.

"Wait!" Renira shouted and started after him. "Answer me. Are you my father? I want to know. I deserve to know the truth."

Armstar stopped. He faced away from her, silent for a while, his shoulders slumped, and for a moment she thought she might actually drag a straight answer from him. Then he straightened up and glanced at her over his shoulder.

"Grow up!" Armstar snarled. "Open your eyes and see the world how it really is instead of how you wish it could be." Renira staggered back from the venom in his voice.

"You say that, yet you've been manipulating me from the start. Even back home, you told me to be brave, you forced courage on me to make me come with you."

The angel shook his head. "I never once made your decisions for you, Renira. Only gave what you needed to make them for yourself."

"But... but you argued with me constantly. You tried to get me to leave Sun behind in the forest."

"And did you?"

"No. But you didn't help either."

"Choices have consequences. Sometimes you have to face them alone."

"You tried to make me pass judgement on the Seeker back in Greenlake."

Armstar's smile was weary. "And did you?"

She shook her head. "But you killed him anyway."

"That was my choice. My judgement. Not yours. Don't you dare take the guilt for yourself." He sighed. "I was only ever trying to prepare you. Because Lusa never did."

"What do you mean?"

"Eleseth won't say it, she doesn't have the will. So it falls to me. You're going to have choices to make, Renira. And whichever you choose lives will be lost. There are people between you and the Overlook who will stop at nothing to see you fail, and there is no way to save them. So don't try." He turned away from her. "That's where Lusa failed. She never grasped that not everyone can be saved. But that's all right, as long as you make their sacrifices mean something. As long as they die for a reason, a good reason, even if it's not their own... then their deaths won't have been in vain. You can be better than her, but only if you stop trying to be her."

He snatched the halberd from the ground and started walking again, and this time Renira did not stop him. She watched him for a while, until he was no more than a dot on the horizon. She clutched both amulets, one in each hand, and felt utterly abandoned.

Renira found the others in the common room of the inn. They were gathered around a table, close to a corner and as far away from any prying eyes as possible. There was food on the table, four empty plates and two full ones. Fresh bread, still warm from the oven and soft. Scrambled eggs, a couple of rashers of bacon. A red fruit Renira had no name for.

She stopped at the entrance where the offerance needles sat on a small table. *Grow up.* Armstar's words echoed inside her head. She'd gone her entire life without observing the tradition of shedding a drop of blood on the threshold, relying on her age to excuse her. But now it seemed wrong to claim she was still a child. Renira pricked her finger with a needle, wincing at the pain, and squeezed out a single drop of blood to fall upon the tavern floor, staining the boards next to countless others. A history of the inn written in blood. She dropped the needle in the water bowl and sucked on her wounded finger as she threaded her way through the occupied tables of the common room and slumped into one of the waiting chairs. She had no appetite, but the smell of the food in front of her demanded attention even so.

"Armstar?" Gemp asked the question when it seemed no one else would.

"Gone," Renira said as she drank down a mouthful of bitter ale. She picked up a knife and fork and went at the plate of food as though it might be her last meal. She felt tired in a way that had nothing to do with exhaustion. Raw, used up. Confused and alone, even surrounded by her friends.

"Is he coming back?"

Renira shook her head as she shovelled a fork full of scrambled egg into her mouth. She could feel both amulets against her chest now, and they felt strangely heavy, as though they carried the weight of expectation with them. *Stop being so dramatic. Grow up.*

"No sense wasting it then," Gemp said and reached across the table, pulling the spare plate in front of him. Sun stole a rasher of bacon before Gemp could stop him and both man and boy were soon chewing away on Armstar's breakfast.

"We have a decision to make," Eleseth said, her voice lowered to a whisper that was lost in the din of the common room.

Renira washed down some bread with another mouthful of the ale. Why people drank the stuff for breakfast was beyond her, but it seemed that was all they had, so drink it she would.

"You mean *I* have a decision to make," she said. "A decision that affects everyone. Or are you willing to make it for me, Eleseth?"

The silence that descended on their table made the noise in the common room seem a roar. Eleseth, the Light Bearer, an angel thousands of years old, refused to meet Renira's gaze.

It was always going to be my decision. That was one of the things Armstar had been trying to teach her from the beginning, in his own way. She'd thought him manipulating her, using his power to play her emotions, and he had to a degree. But she saw now he'd blanketed her fear or exhaustion to allow her to make decisions unburdened. He'd argued with her, tried to get her to change her mind, but when she made her decisions, he didn't try to alter them, only forced her to deal with the consequences herself instead of running to someone else for help. Armstar had done more to prepare her for this than any of those who had held her hand or protected her or tried to take away her burdens. *He did what a father should, in his own stupid messed up way.*

"That's what I thought," Renira said. She had known they would make the choice hers. She had spent the time watching Armstar walk away thinking about it. Even her mother, were she here, would leave the choice to Renira. She would want her daughter to make her own decisions, find her own way. After all, there was only so much protection a parent could offer a child, and the most important part of that protection was preparing them for a time when they were without it entirely.

Grow up.

"Is there another way into the city?" Renira asked.

All eyes turned to Gemp, and the old acolyte stopped chewing, his mouth full of bread and egg. "I don't know. Been a long time since I was last in Celesgarde, and I never had to sneak in before."

Eleseth shook her head. "I know of no other way to get you into the city."

Renira glanced at Aesie, and her friend smiled back uneasily. "Can you get in alone?" she asked Eleseth.

"I believe so," Eleseth said. "Though not without attention. The walls are designed to defend against the sky. But they are designed to protect against many, not one. I believe I can make it past the weaponry, but once I do all pretence at stealth will be lost."

Grow up. Make the decision. Commit.

She stared at Aesie. It did seem like her friend wanted to make amends, that she was sorry. But she had lied before. She was so very good at lying. A viper. But Renira didn't see any other way. She had to trust her friend one more time.

"Aesie will get us into the city. Then what?"

"You'll need a distraction if you want to make it up the Overlook," Gemp said. "Something that will draw the soldiers away and force people out onto the streets. You'll need chaos."

Sun tried to steal another rasher of bacon while Gemp was distracted, but only succeeded in getting thwacked with a fork. He frowned. "Nothing distracts people quite like fire," he said sullenly.

Gemp nodded at that and pulled his hand away from his plate, letting Sun steal the last rasher. "Fire demands attention. You can't ignore it, or it just gets worse. We could set a number of fires all at once, pull the soldiers in a dozen different directions and get the whole city out on the streets."

"With just the four of us?" Aesie asked sceptically.

"Three of you," Eleseth said. "Renira will need to remain close to the Overlook to take advantage of the distraction, and so I will be able to find her." She looked at Renira then. "You won't make it to the top without me."

Renira felt her heart grow heavy. There was something Eleseth was not saying. Something she was talking around.

Grow up. People are going to die.

Armstar was right. It weighed heavily upon her heart, though she knew it was a necessary evil. People were going to die. A lot of them. Soldiers, citizens, maybe even her friends. *Me.*

People were going to die, and it would all be for her. There was no other way. Resurrecting the God was the only way to fix the world, to fight the king. For that purpose. For that reason, and only that reason, Renira would accept people dying for her. After all, it was the only way she could come to terms with the deaths of all those who were already gone. The people of Los Hold, Dussor and Kerrel, the soldiers at Greenlake. Sacrifices made all for the purpose of Renira fulfilling her destiny. Their deaths had to mean something.

"Two of you," Renira said, looking at Gemp and Sun, before turning her attention to Aesie. "Your job is to get us inside. After that, you're done. Go to your father's holdings and forget about us." She wanted Aesie involved as little as possible. She tried to tell herself it was to protect her friend, but the truth still whispered in the back of her mind. *I can't trust her.*

Aesie opened her mouth to argue, but Sun got there first. "One of you," he said, poking Gemp in the ribs. "Wherever you go, I go, Ren."

"No, not this time." Renira said. It was a decision she had already made, and one she would fight tooth and nail for. None of her friends were coming with her. She would spare Eleseth the fate if she could. "Sun, you can do more good with Gemp than with me."

He opened his mouth again to argue, but she cut him off. "You're one person. A young boy, still learning how to hold a spear. You'll only get in Eleseth's way at the Overlook, and I have no doubt I myself will be doing enough of that. Gemp will need every hand he can get, regardless of age or skill with a spear. The best way you can help me, the best way for you to protect me, is not by my side, but out in the city."

She turned her attention to Aesie. "And you were never meant to be involved in any of this, Aesie. You're risking enough just getting us into the city, and I won't allow you to risk any more. The rest of us have nothing to lose but our lives. You have your family to consider. What will the king do if he finds out you've betrayed him? What will he do to your father and mother? He knows who you are, and I will not allow you to risk your family for this cause. For a goal you don't even believe in."

Aesie's eyes went wide. "I... um..." She glanced around the table. "I hadn't thought about that." She lowered her head and said no more, but Renira could see her friend was scared.

Gemp said he'd need a few days to contact the acolytes inside Celesgarde. He'd been to the capital before but never to meet with other acolytes, yet he knew where to go and what signals to make to draw the right attention. Renira just hoped the acolytes in hiding hadn't been driven underground by the soldiers prowling the streets. She gave him three days and no more. Something about the situation seemed urgent to her, as though Armstar's departure made the need to complete her quest more pressing. It was foolish really; the Fourth Age had already lasted a thousand years, it could last another day or two. And yet it felt to Renira as though any more delays were no more than procrastination, giving time and opportunity to realise the foolishness she was planning and back out.

Three days. Three days and Gemp and Sun, along with as many acolytes as they could muster, would start fires all over Celesgarde. Eleseth would shed her cloaked glamour and soar into the city to meet Renira at the foot of the Overlook. Three days until countless people would die so Renira could make her way to the Bell of Ages. Until she sacrificed everything to ring in the Fifth Age. And she knew it would be a sacrifice, just like the worship God demanded.

Grow up. A part of growing up was to stop hiding from the truth. *All those lives will be my sacrifice. And I'm his.* In order to see his father reborn, Armstar was willing to sacrifice his own daughter.

It was the one thing she would not talk about, not even to Eleseth, and especially not to her friends. Even if she did make it all the way up to the Overlook and rang in the new age, the Godless King would catch her. She knew now why her mother had hidden her from the angels for all those years. Because, succeed or fail, Renira wasn't coming back.

CHAPTER 47

A man can be neither born to the blade nor led to it. It is a calling, one that cries out to man's soul.

— RIKKAN HOSTAIN

Emrik paced along the wall around his city, flanked by both Arik and Borik. Soldiers of the First, Second, and Fourth legions manned the walls, their combined forces still not enough to watch every street in the city. They snapped off crisp salutes as Emrik passed, rather than bow and scrape. He liked that. They should see him as their leader, their king, not some substitute for a dead deity.

The sun was high, bright in the crimson sky, yet there was little heat to it. Winter had Helesia firmly in its grip, and Emrik's breath steamed in front of him. Despite the chill, he was warm in his armour. Padded gambeson underneath God-forged steel plate, painted black as a moonless night. It was the most unique armour the world had ever seen, the only one of its kind, and near impervious. It also got unbearably hot in the sun, even in the depths of winter, and Emrik could feel himself sweating. He hadn't wanted to wear his armour on a tour of the defences, but Arik had insisted, and Emrik admitted that his son knew best in such matters. The soldiers responded well to seeing their king as a warrior, and the armour was grander than any crown could ever be.

"We have no idea if these measures are working or not," Emrik said. He stopped above the gate and stared down at the throng of citizens lining up to be let through into his city. Each one was questioned and searched, but the truth was they had little idea of who they were looking for. A young woman, a younger boy, and a couple of angels. The angels would be easy enough to spot, especially the Builder and his ruined wings, but the Herald herself might as well be invisible. Some hick girl from the arse end of nowhere, she could be anyone.

Borik joined him, turning around to lean his back against one of the parapets and staring up at the red sky. "It could all be for nothing anyway," he said with a smile. "You sent our dear sister after the Herald, and Perel can track a raindrop in an ocean. I'd say the chances are high the Herald is already dead, and the wolves are feeding on her corpse."

There was a thought Emrik had been suppressing, refusing to give voice to, as if that refusal could make it less real somehow. He shook his head slowly and gripped the parapet hard, armoured fingers digging gouges through solid stone. "I think your sister is dead."

Arik stepped up beside Emrik, back straight and arms crossed. He, too, wore his armour. Angel-forged plate almost as tough as Emrik's own but painted red to match the sky. He nodded and bowed his head, joining his father in grief.

"What?" said Borik. "Perel can't die. She doesn't know how."

"It's been more than four weeks, son," Emrik said, his voice soft. Borik and Perel were close, her death would hit him as hard as it did Emrik himself. "If she were alive, she would have made contact. I can only assume that the Herald lives and Perel does not." It served no one to lie to himself or his children about it. The truth was often hard to bear, but shouldering it rather than hiding from it, was what made people strong, and he would never abide weakness.

Borik only shook his head. "You have so little faith, Father." He said it lightly, even knowing how dangerous a word *faith* could be. "She's alive." He sounded like a man clinging to a vain hope of rescue even as the axe was falling. A fragile hope that took reason with it when it shattered.

Emrik wished he, too, could cling to that hope, but he needed his reason intact. Perel was dead. His daughter was dead. And he would grieve for her when there was time. When the Herald had paid for the death with her own.

Emrik turned his back on all the citizens queuing at his gates. Every day the queues grew and grew, and every day people went home without gaining entrance to Celesgarde, or they camped outside, hoping to be first to enter the next day, a blooming shanty town of huts and hovels and dishevelment. He hadn't anticipated the delays to traffic and commerce, and his city and his people were paying for that lack of foresight. Part of him would happily sacrifice them all for his goal, but what use was there stopping the Herald and wiping out the last of the angels, if none of his people were around to benefit from a world truly forever free from the God? Helesia had to go on. Celesgarde had to go on. He needed a better way.

"I need options," Emrik said, staring out toward the towering Overlook. Every day he watched it, waiting for the Herald to make her move. He hated it. It was a mountain built by and in the name of the God, an unbreakable monument to himself. A giant boil in the centre of Emrik's otherwise splendid city.

Neither Arik nor Borik said anything. When Emrik looked at them, they were shocked. They were not used to him asking their opinions so blatantly. Like everyone else, they were used to him leading without question, certain of the path he trod with no room for doubt. They needed to be reminded he was human. Immortal, but still human.

"My father once told me I was born in the wrong age," Emrik said, quietly enough only his sons would hear. "He meant it as an insult, you see. A man like him, a titan, unrivalled in the martial arts. He expected... demanded I be just as proficient. I was his firstborn son; how could I be anything but the perfect product of him and my mother?" He smiled grimly. "Too much of my mother in me. Not enough Hostain.

"I was awful with a sword and even worse with a spear. Every day my father beat me black and blue with training blades, and I never improved. He sent young lads out to spar with me. I think he hoped I would face them with a passion that I could not show against him. He hoped I would beat them, get a taste for the cruelty inherent in victory, and ride that wave of bloodlust to improvement.

"You see, at first, he thought it a matter of motivation, that I simply didn't want to learn how to fight. He was a fool. At that age, I would have done anything to gain his approval. So, I fought the boys he sent against me. And I lost to them. All of them. I became an embarrassment, his embarrassment. He never once stopped to consider that the problem might not be with the student unwilling to learn, but with the teacher unable to comprehend."

There were things Emrik wouldn't say, even to his own children. Not even in whispers. That his father was a stupid man, vain and without subtlety. That he drank too much and cared too little. He was never physically violent outside of their training, not with Emrik or his siblings, and not with their mother, but there was violence that cut more deeply than a beating. Broken bones, bloody noses, and black eyes healed; but the scars left on children by a father's sullen resentment, by the love he withheld and the disappointment he did not hide, were ones they all bore their entire lives. Even now, a thousand years later, Emrik could not deny the pain of his father's disappointment.

"He told me I was born in the wrong age," Emrik continued, his eyes fixed on the Overlook. "And it was perhaps the most subtle thing my father ever said because what he meant was that I was born to the wrong father, and he wanted a different son. A son with the same passion for violence that he had."

Borik huffed out a laugh. "Grandfather sounds like a fool."

Emrik turned to see his youngest son lounging against the parapet, watching the clouds move across the sky like a man without a care in the world. He envied Borik that. That freedom of spirit was a trait Emrik had always nurtured in his son, as surely as it had been stamped out within him by his own father.

"Even fools have their uses, son. Your grandfather, for all his failings, was the greatest warrior humankind had ever seen. Never forget, it was your grandfather who struck the killing blow. Your great grandfather and I helped, the other Godless Kings gave their lives to the battle, we distracted God and dug our own steel into his dying flesh, but it was Rikkan Hostain who will always be remembered as the man who killed God. I, for one, would rather remember him in that moment, than any that came before or after."

Rikkan Hostain had been cold and distant before the Crusade, but afterwards Emrik's father had been less. He was diminished by his achievement rather than emboldened. None but Emrik knew the truth of that.

"And besides," Emrik continued. "He was right about me. I was born in the wrong age. Your great grandfather, Ertide, said the same thing. He called me to the Overlook, and we sat in the shrine, next to the bell. I think he knew then the truth, but he didn't reveal it. He spent years planning his Crusade, decades even.

"Ertide sat me down in the shrine, overlooking the city and asked me what I saw. My father would have said buildings and rain. He saw only the surface of things, cared little for context and meaning. I was young, and I thought that was what grandfather wanted to hear, so that's what I said. *Buildings and rain*. I was used to seeing disappointment on my father's face, but I saw it then on grandfather's, and it was more than I could bear." Emrik still remembered every line and crease and frown. If he had paper and charcoal, he might have scrawled then a likeness of his grandfather. Not a composed piece, but true art, a face captured in the midst of emotion. Except no, he couldn't. Regardless of his skill with paint or pencil, faces were always blank to him on the canvas.

"I told him the truth then, despite the fear that it might get back to my father. I told Ertide that I saw life on a scale no canvas had ever reached before. The city was alive. People on the streets like blood pumping through veins. Each building, each block, the bones that structured it all. The market was the heart, from which all trade flowed, keeping the people circulating. The city lived on its trade, and it all passed through the market.

"The palace was the head, the brain, the mind. That's where the orders come from. The palace controls the city, the place where authority and reason stem from.

"The Overlook... well, I was young and full of vigour. You might imagine how I described that hideous erection."

Borik sniggered, and even Arik broke into a smile.

"When I was done, Grandfather smiled at me and repeated my father's words, that I was born in the wrong age. Then he explained why it was not an insult. Ertide Hostain was a tactician. He belonged in an age of conflict and strife. He was born to win wars, and bereft of any to fight, he eventually started his own. Rikkan Hostain was a warrior without equal. Even the angels of the First Age respected him long before we started taking the power of their divinity. Battleborn, the angels called him. We called him the Shield of Empire. But I had an artist's mind. I was born to create, to bring meaning to a world bereft of it, through expression.

"My father saw it as a weakness. But not Ertide. He recognised my ability to see beneath the surface and taught me the truth. That art can be transposed onto all other pursuits. He made me see that my father was also an artist. That his pursuit of excellence had turned his martial ability into an art form. When I looked at it like that, I saw how my father expressed himself through his grace and brutality in battle. I found a new appreciation for my father and what he could do. After that, I dedicated myself to learning that same form of expression. Not for him. Every time before I had tried to learn to fight, it had been for my father, but now I was learning for myself. I wanted to be able to express myself the same way my father did." Emrik felt a bitter tang at what came next.

"Of course, my grandfather also told me something else, that his son was a terrible tutor without the patience to teach others. So, I approached Orphus. Who better to teach me how to fight than the father of everything humanity knew about combat? I dedicated five years of my life to learning how to fight. I did almost nothing else during that time. I learned how to express myself through the combat, rather than attempting to mimic my father's expression. I mastered it well enough to stand toe to toe with the God in single combat, and I survived. Which is more than can be said for anyone save my father. I was never as good as him. Even with a thousand years, even with the number of angels I have devoured and as strong as I have become, I would still be no match for my father on his worst day.

"I tell you this because there are still things I have never managed to master. Some art forms even now I fail to fully comprehend." Emrik paused. Admitting weakness had never been easy for him, even to those he trusted most.

"I proved myself my father's son when I learned to fight, but I never managed to prove myself my grandfather's blood. The finer points of tactics escape me even now."

He turned around again and spread his hands, motioning to the citizens gathering below. "This is not working. The Herald can slip through our net. Perhaps she already has. Celesgarde cannot house three legions for an indefinite period, and soldiers with nothing to do quickly become a worse problem than that which they are there to solve."

He glanced first at Arik and then turned an apologetic stare at Borik. "At this point, we must assume that Perel has failed and that the Herald is already here. I need options, and I have none. Luckily for me, you, Arik, are more like your great-grandfather than anyone I've ever known. You think inside the box, but you know every corner, nook, and cranny. And you, Borik, are unlike anyone else. You think so far out of the box, I doubt you've ever even seen it."

"Oh, I've seen it, Father," Borik said seriously, then cracked into a grin. "It just looks like a sphere to me."

Arik cleared his throat. "I disagree, Father. I think this is working. The fact that the Herald is still in hiding is proof of that. She may have entered the city, but her angel allies have not. Can not. They'll not sneak past our guard, and any attempt to fly into the city would be met with overwhelming force." He gestured out across the city, where a quarter of the buildings now had war scorpions on mobile housings, all pointed toward the sky. The bolts would do little enough damage to an angel's immortality shield, but a hail of them would make it very difficult to fly.

"However, you are also correct. It isn't sustainable, and the longer it goes on, the more the discipline of our soldiers will slip. What we need is a trap. Something to draw the Herald out of hiding, only to tighten the noose once and for all."

Emrik frowned. "A trap needs bait. We have nothing the Herald wants."

"Of course we do," said Borik. "We have the *only* thing the Herald wants." He pointed a slender finger out towards the centre of the city where the Overlook poised above them all. "It's the only bait which will work, Father. Give the Herald exactly what they want. Access to the Overlook."

"No. I will not allow the Herald to even get within sight of the shrine. All it takes is her to reach the bell, and all this is for nothing. We don't even know what power she might have."

Borik shrugged. "She's human. Any one of us could kill her with a stern glare."

"She's the daughter of an angel," Emrik said. "Who knows what that might mean."

Arik was quiet, staring out towards the Overlook with a thoughtful look on his face. A tactician weighing up the risk and rewards of his next move. "Borik has a point, Father. The Overlook is the bait. But we don't need to give the Herald access to the Overlook, only make it look enticing enough for her to make her move.

"Reduce the number of troops stationed in and around the Overlook. We keep enough hidden along the paths to slow the Herald down should she try to make for the top, and if all else fails, our new Champions are up there waiting. It doesn't matter how strong she might be, all we need to do is slow her down long enough for us to reach her before she rings the bell."

"That's what I just said," Borik complained. "That's my plan."

Arik smiled. "I took your *rough* plan and refined it, little brother. I made it work."

Borik snorted and shook his head. "You just worded it differently and claimed the credit."

"Such is the life of a bureaucrat."

"Such is the life of a younger brother."

Both had a chuckle at that while Emrik considered. He hated the idea of making it easier for the Herald, but some sacrifices had to be made. They had to assume she was already in the city, and they needed to flush her out. Time might be on their side, but discipline was not.

"Do it," Emrik said. "But stay ready, both of you. She is close. I can feel it."

CHAPTER 48

*Little is known about the Shattering, and even less about the Ice Walkers'
Lords Under the Ice. I have requested that the Archangel come and talk to
me about it, as surely he lived through the conflict and is reported to have
fought against these lords the Ice Walkers worship, but alas I receive no reply.*

*What we know is that the Ice Islands were once an expansive plain of ice
that extended far out into the ocean, but when the traitor Exemplar Karta
summoned the Lords Under the Ice they—whatever they were—shattered the
plain into thousands of islands when they and their minions invaded the
fledgling Sant Dien Empire.*

*I fear we may never know the truth, as the Lorekeepers—those heretical
priests of the Lords Under the Ice—were all but wiped out. Those who are left
hide out in the deepest islands on the ice and every expedition we've sent to
them is never heard from again.*

— KRYSTLE GREYSON, HEAD HISTORIAN OF
STONELORE UNIVERSITY FROM 298-334 OF THE
THIRD AGE

R enira walked alongside the line of those waiting to get in to Celesgarde and stared up at the walls. Her stomach had taken up residence in her throat.

The walls were imposing, dark grey stone, pocked with tiny windows just large enough to loose an arrow from, and almost featureless save for time's weathering fingers making mockery of everything humans built; here a stain, there a crumbling brick. That was the difference between things built by angels and those by humans. Everything the angels built stood the test of time, unaffected by age and by weather. Never changing. But anything humans made crumbled and changed, needed rebuilding or replacing. Everything humans made was temporary.

From the ground, it was impossible to see anyone up on the top of the walls, but she had no doubt they swarmed with soldiers. Perhaps even the Godless King himself was up there, watching and waiting for her. She had the urge to turn back, to pull free of the line and run... anywhere else. *Home.*

"Close your mouth, Ren," Aesie said quietly. "Our guard can stare like simpletons." She nodded behind her to where Sun and Gemp followed. "But you're a handmaid to a wealthy merchant. You're here to attend me, not gawp."

"You're good at all this," Renira said to her friend.

"I have to be," Aesie said, keeping her eyes locked on the soldiers at the gate. "Playing with you and Elsa and Beth was fun, but I was just pretending. A child toying at something she could never be. A brief escape from the plans my father had laid out for me." She glanced at Renira, and there was a shadow of guilt in her eyes. "I'm good at this because it's who I really am."

Renira cursed herself a fool for never having seen it before. She knew Aesie was born into money and power, but she had always just been Aesie. The young girl who dressed fancier than the rest of them had ever seen and went home to a mansion every night. They'd known each other since before Renira had even realised that folk could be different, and they had been best friends all that time. But Renira was only now starting to see the real Aesie. She walked with a straight back and a haughty expression. She didn't even glance at all the people they were walking past, those *common peasants* waiting in line to enter the city. They were beneath her notice.

Aesie was bedraggled, for a certainty. Even after a bath at the inn and a fresh dress from a pop-up market stall along the road, her hair was a mess, the braid barely held together by ribbon and hope, and she looked like she'd spent weeks on the road. But there was something about Aesie, in her bearing, the way she walked and even the way she looked at the world around her. It screamed importance, money, power, influence. People on the road, those waiting to get into Celesgarde, didn't argue with her for striding past them. No, they lowered their eyes and bowed their heads. Renira tried to remember if people had always acted that way to Aesie, but her life in Riverden felt like so long ago the memories slipped from her like water through fingers.

This is the truth of her. The young girl I thought I knew... she was the lie.

"Thank you," Aesie said in a whisper, though she was still staring ahead. "For trusting me again."

Renira said nothing. She wanted to. To reassure her friend, to offer a smile and comfort. But she couldn't. *Because I don't trust you.* Trust was odd like that. A lifetime of building and it could be laid to waste in only a moment.

"I don't like this," Sun said as they stopped just a few paces away from the gate. A soldier in black armour, lacquered to a shine, with two golden strikes over his right breast, approached.

"Quiet lad," said Gemp. "Ain't nothing for us to do or like but look the part. As much as we can. Try to look surly."

"I am surly," Sun said.

"Of course you are, lad."

The soldier eyed them suspiciously underneath bushy eyebrows and a mop of dark hair. A sword hung easily from his belt, and he carried a small book and pencil in his hands. Beside them, the line of those waiting to enter the city ground to a halt. If Aesie felt even the slightest guilt at their inconvenience, she didn't show it. Renira held her breath. If Aesie was going to betray her again, now would be the time.

The soldier opened his mouth and drew in a breath. Aesie spoke over him. "Sergeant. I didn't realise the Second were now in charge of common guard duty. Is Commander Barrt well?"

The sergeant closed his mouth, and his bushy eyebrows drew even closer together. He stood a little straighter and nodded. "Yes, ma'am. He is well and good. There's been some talk of a threat to the city, I'm sorry to say. The Second have been, uh, assigned to help protect the capital until His Majesty can assure its safety."

The sergeant's eyes flicked to Renira for a moment, and she smiled at him, hoping to appear as timid as possible. Then he glanced behind them toward Sun and Gemp.

"That would explain why the lands around Celesgarde are in such disarray then, I suppose," Aesie continued, the tone in her voice demanding the sergeant's attention once more.

"D—disarray, ma'am?"

Something changed with Aesie, something Renira couldn't place. The world around her seemed to grow still and quiet. Displeasure flowed from her, and Renira felt the need to bow her head and cower. The sergeant felt it also and lowered his eyes to the little book he was carrying.

"What else would you call it, Sergeant?" Aesie said, her tone short and sharp as a razor. "When wolves and brigands roam the lands you should be protecting. I set out from Riverden with a carriage, three house staff, and five guards, all veterans. Now look. Do you see a carriage? Any horses? All I have left of my staff is my house maid, and she only survived because of the heroism of her husband who now lies dead on the road, his head separated from his body." Aesie turned to Renira and patted her on the arm. "I'm sorry to bring it up, dear."

Renira had no idea how to act. She sucked in a stuttering breath and looked down at the ground, hands at her side and itching to clutch at the amulets around her neck. She had hoped Aesie would slip them through without attention, but instead she was drawing all the attention to them. Another soldier from the gate moved to join the sergeant, and there were mutterings from the folk gathered on the road waiting to enter the city. Some of those were whispered assents about the lands being unsafe, and others sounded like impatient grumbles at the delay.

"This," Aesie continued, waving a dismissive hand at Sun and Gemp, "is all that's left of my guard. An old man who eats so much I can only assume he's riddled with worms, and a boy with less experience on the road than myself."

Sun shifted uncomfortably but said nothing. They all needed to sell the ruse, and that meant people needed to believe that Aesie was in charge and not to be argued with.

Aesie drew in a deep breath and let it out slowly, visibly composing herself. When she spoke, it was quieter and without anger. "I am sorry, Sergeant. I didn't mean to get so worked up. My feet hurt, my back aches, I'm cold, and it's been a long time since I've had anything to eat but indiscernible dried meat. It does not agree with my stomach, you understand."

Gemp chuckled, but quickly fell silent when Aesie fixed him with a stare. She turned that same damning stare on the sergeant next. "I just want to reach my father's holdings and forget this entire ordeal ever even happened." She waved her hands in frustration and then clenched them into fists before letting out another deep breath.

"Sorry, ma'am," the sergeant said. "It's, uh, the, uh, K—king's orders. We're to search and question everyone attempting to enter the city." The other soldier moved to flank him, and two more from the gate were taking notice. Renira felt her gut tighten. They should have waited in line like everyone else.

"I am here, *Sergeant*," Aesie said, her voice tight and hostile, "by invitation *of* the King." She reached into her satchel and pulled out the leather-bound travel permit bearing the king's seal. "Secured at vast expense by my father who, I might add, owns the factories that make your boots. So, you can thank him for your more than serviceable footwear. And, as you can see, we have nothing to search because it was all stolen on the roads that you and your men are supposed to be keeping safe!" Her voice rose with each word until everyone nearby was wincing.

The people waiting on the road were nodding along now, the grumbles becoming louder as more and more of them found their voices and started to agree with the angry aristocrat. The sergeant and his troops didn't fail to notice the growing disquiet.

"Let me, uh, see the permit," the sergeant said. He took it from Aesie and glanced at it for all of two heartbeats. "Seems to be in order, ma'am. Can I just have your name?"

Aesie drew herself up to her full height, which, despite her imposing presence, was slightly shorter than Renira's. "Aesie Fur. My father's holdings are on Rinksweld Row."

"Right you are, ma'am," the sergeant said, scribbling in his little book. He snapped it shut and stood out of the way, bowing a little from the waist and gesturing for them to approach the gate. As soon as Aesie had stepped past him, he turned to the crowd on the road and started hollering for quiet.

Renira followed after Aesie, keeping her eyes to the gravel below their feet. Sun hurried to catch up and Gemp sauntered along last, looking every part the veteran soldier. They were a ragtag band who looked nothing like the escort Aesie had described, and yet she had secured them entrance to the city without being searched or detained.

There were soldiers everywhere. They lined the road leading through the wall, and there was even more waiting for them on the other side. Renira felt her heart racing, breath coming in short, shallow gasps. Even if Eleseth had been with them, they would have been overwhelmed by the sheer number of soldiers in the city. This was only a small part of the place, a tiny part, and Renira could see hundreds of people in the black and gold of the legions. She had no illusion about what they were waiting for. They were waiting for her.

Aesie's arm slipped inside Renira's, and suddenly they were walking along arm in arm. Her friend smiled at her; all trace of the angry noblewoman vanished. She was just Aesie, Renira's friend. The same one who had once delivered Renira a new ribbon for her hair every day for a full month, each one a different colour than the last. Back in Riverden, they had faced down bullies together, pulled Elsa out of fights, spent entire days lying on grassy fields daydreaming about their lives. Even talked about their futures, about whom they might marry and what they might accomplish. Aesie had always mocked her when Renira said she wanted to fight monsters and protect people, but it was only ever in jest. Since then, they had fought monsters. Together. They had faced down wolf princesses, Apostles, Truth Seekers, and mobs of angry villagers. Together. And Aesie had betrayed her. Renira wished, truly wished, they could do the rest of it together as well, but she couldn't forget. She could forgive. She already had. But she couldn't forget.

The soldiers continued to watch them, some paying close attention and others barely bothering to look away from their conversation with their comrades, but it didn't feel quite so scary with Aesie at her side. Despite the loss of trust, she still took comfort from her friend.

They passed through the wall without any trouble and into the city of Celesgarde. Buildings rose up three storeys high all around them, and Renira found herself gawping again.

"Now," Aesie said, and Renira was terribly glad of the distraction. They were clear of the throng of soldiers and into the city proper where men and women ambled after their jobs. "This being my first time in the capital as well, I have a pressing question. Where is Rinksweld Row?"

"Don't matter," said Gemp. "We've got our own business to be about. Lad, you're with me. Renira, good luck." He stepped away, but Sun didn't follow, and Gemp soon turned back with a look like gathering storm clouds.

They were stopped in the middle of the street, a few people passing here and there, soldiers on patrol, greedy merchants watching them from the stalls set up on the sides of the road. Some of those merchants called out their wares, and others called out promises to buy whatever people were selling.

Sun was staring at her, dark eyes always so unfathomable. He didn't quite look the young boy she had rescued from the forest demon anymore. He was taller, grown in just a few weeks, and lean too. They all were, Renira supposed. Weeks of poor food and hard travel. But Sun wore it well. He didn't slouch anymore, and with a straight back, he was almost as tall as her. He carried his spear like he knew how to use it. With Gemp training him, maybe he did. Not a man grown, still not even close, but Renira could now see glimpses of the man he would one day become. If he survived long enough to reach it. Renira readied her arguments again, expecting Sun to give one last go at demanding he should go with her. Instead the boy just lurched forward and wrapped his arms around her.

"Good luck!" Sun said, squeezing her uncomfortably tight. Renira returned the hug. Then Sun pulled away and fixed her with that dark stare once more. "We'll meet here, Ren. Right here. When it's done."

She nodded and hated the lie even before she spoke it. "Right here."

The boy raised his hand and extended his little finger. "Courage and hope."

Renira felt her throat close and couldn't force the words past it, so instead she just nodded and wrapped her little finger around his. Then Sun turned, and he and Gemp cut their way through the merchant stalls, ducking into an alleyway between buildings, and then they were gone.

"Hopelessly in love with you, Ren," Aesie said.

"Shut up, Aesie. It's not like that."

"If you say so," Aesie said with a beaming smile. "Just us girls again. How should we go about finding Rinksweld Row? I suppose we should ask a soldier?"

"I'm not going with you, Aesie," Renira said, bracing herself for an argument.

Aesie only nodded. "I had a terrible feeling you were going to say that. You've got three days. What are you going to do, hang about on the streets like Elsa, digging through trash and flirting with criminals?"

They had been stopped in the road for too long and were starting to attract the attention of nearby soldiers as well as merchants. "I'll make my own way from here," Renira said. "It's time you distanced yourself from this. From me."

Aesie stepped closer. "This isn't Riverden, Ren. The streets here are dangerous. I've heard stories."

Renira shrugged, trying her best to appear nonchalant. "There's plenty of soldiers about."

"Yes. And they're all looking for you."

"I'll be fine, Aesie," Renira said sharply. "All I have to do is survive three days. I am capable of that much."

Aesie snorted but stepped closer and embraced Renira. "Three days is a long time to be alone." She grabbed hold of Renira's hand and passed something to her, clenching her fingers around it. "For food and somewhere to stay. Find a tavern or something. It's more than enough to stay an entire week, let alone three days."

Renira nodded. She didn't need to open her hand to know it was Aesie's last golden ring, and she wouldn't risk showing it to anyone who might be watching. "Come and find me at my father's holdings once this is all done, Ren. Bring Sun and Gemp too, I don't care. Just... come back. Please."

Everyone seemed to think Renira would ring in the new age and then walk away without the slightest consequence. None of them were willing to admit the truth. Renira gave Aesie one last smile, then turned and walked away, heading down the first street she found and desperately willing her tears not to fall.

CHAPTER 49

Pain is no barrier to enlightenment. It is the channel through which we pour ourselves into the mould of rebirth.

— FROM THE 6TH SCRIPTURE, SALVATION

Gemp set a harsh pace that Sun struggled to keep. He moved them down alleyways and across streets, finding gaps between buildings Sun wouldn't have realised were there. The old veteran seemed to know his way through the city as surely as a rabbit in its warren. Now and then, Gemp stopped next to a building and drew a line onto the stonework with a bit of charcoal. He always moved on quickly, before Sun could catch his breath and ask what the symbols meant.

The morning passed to midday, and then midday passed into the afternoon, and the sky began to darken to a moody burgundy, and still Gemp moved them on. They passed by houses and workshops, through small markets and court-yards filled with trees or stone daises. Always dodging around people and horses and carts. So many people.

Sun's feet scuffed the cobbles more and more often as they slogged on, and every time Gemp stopped for a moment, he leaned against a nearby wall, and it was all he could do not to collapse.

They were both sweaty and unkempt. Gemp had a scruffy beard and wild grey hair, and Sun's hair was matted into locks, his own beard little more than wisps of patchy growth on his lip and chin. They looked like vagrants. Armed vagrants. The soldiers patrolling the streets kept wary eyes on them.

Finally, as the last rays of sunlight faded to black, Gemp found what he was looking for. Another alleyway, and another black line of charcoal, and the old veteran let out a grateful sigh.

"It's about time," he said, his voice full of gravel. He walked up the seven steps that led to the doorway of the house and knocked five times.

"What are we doing here, Gemp?" Sun asked, detesting the weariness in his own voice. He was so tired of running. Of spending all day every day moving on. Ever since leaving Ashvold. No. Even before that. Ever since Flame and Branch had rescued him from Karna's palace, he had done nothing but run, escaping one threat after another and always, always being chased.

"Can't do what we need to alone, lad," said Gemp as he scratched at his bearded chin. "We need allies. Lots of them."

The door opened, and a young plump woman with a cleft nose and dark skin. Sun saw her grip tighten on the door and her eyes narrow. "Who are you?" she demanded.

"Hello there," Gemp said. "The name's Gemp, and this here is Sun. We're from New Gurrund, and, um, crap. Look, we're here to buy a, uh, kettle?" He winced.

The woman's eyes flicked past them to look up and down the street, then she smiled widely at them. "We got just the one you're looking for, friend. Why don't you and your boy get in here, and we'll show you what we have for sale." She opened the door and backed away into a hall decorated with a gaudy green and orange rug and lit by a lantern on a small stool.

Gemp muttered a couple of pleasantries as he stepped over the threshold, and Sun followed the old veteran in, entirely bemused. The woman led them down the hall, asking Gemp about their trip from New Gurrund and the state of the roads. Gemp answered with a smile and a laugh. She led them into a kitchen where a pot of something was bubbling away over a fire. It smelled of meat and salt, and Sun found his mouth watering at it. The woman opened a door into a pantry and then pulled back a rug, revealing a wooden trapdoor. The smiles and vain pleasantries were gone now, and she pulled on an iron ring to open the trapdoor, then handed a lantern to Gemp.

"Someone will be down to see you soon enough," the woman said in a hurried voice. "There's water and food and beds down there, and you're free to use them. Now go. Quickly."

Gemp climbed down without another word. Sun ached to ask questions but followed the old man. The woman shut the trapdoor above them, sealing them in the musty smelling cellar, lit only by the flickering lantern in Gemp's hand.

They found the water first, collected in a barrel with the lid just placed on top. Gemp shoved his hands in and scooped up handfuls to his mouth, slurping it down. Then he ambled over to one of the beds, which was really just a pallet on a wooden bench, and collapsed onto it with a groan and a grateful sigh.

"What's going on?" Sun asked, slurping down his own mouthful of water. It washed the dust from his throat and tasted as sweet as any fruit. "Who is she? And what kettle are we buying?" He finished by splashing some of the water on his tired face.

"It's code, lad," Gemp said. He was sat on the pallet with his back against the wall and his eyes closed. "I had to find a house with the right mark on it to let me know it were friendly. Then, asking to buy a kettle is code for saying we're acolytes and we need shelter."

"Code?" Sun asked.

"It's dangerous to talk out loud about being an acolyte. It's dangerous in Helesia to say anything that might make people think you believe in anything but the king. You saw those people back in the forest, the way the villagers were trying to drown the Herald. That was just a village, this is a city, and the seat of the Godless King's power.

"Most people here have an almost fanatical belief in him, and can you blame them? He's been their king for as long as any of them have been alive. They age, he don't. His soldiers patrol the streets. He is the authority, the only authority. And anyone who does believe differently, anyone who is even suspected of being a divine sympathiser or worshipper of God is executed. Suspicion and hearsay have long since done away with trials or proof. Truth Seekers roam the streets with gangs of soldiers, interrogating folk at random. Those found guilty are dragged away and either never seen again or executed publicly for a crime most folk don't even understand."

The old veteran shook his head. He seemed smaller down in the dark cellar, his spear leaning against the wall. Maybe it was just that he seemed larger in the presence of the angels he worshipped.

"The Godless King has an iron grip on this city and on the kingdom, and the only way we acolytes can survive is to be smart about it. That means sneaking around, using codes and covert symbols. It means hiding in cellars and pretending to buy bloody kettles. And it means, as often as not, taking our own lives instead of getting caught."

"Why?" Sun asked. The idea seemed so abhorrent to Sun. No one in Ashvold would even contemplate taking their own life, it was far too wasteful. Better to earn Karna's favour by giving yourself to the wulfkin than leave your family the burden of your body.

"To protect others, lad." Gemp opened his eyes and groaned as he stood. He started searching the shelves and crates. "Truth Seekers can't pry everything out of a person, but anything they can't, a few days of torture surely can. We learned early on that when one person gets took, the rest of the acolytes in the city quickly follow. So now we operate in small groups, not knowing who the others in the city are. We communicate via symbols etched onto walls and are rightfully wary of others.

"It's shit, I know. But it works. Check the trapdoor if you like, but I'd wager we're locked in here. Even now, that lady is checking with her own contacts to find out everything she can about New Gurrund." He found a shelf with boxes on it and a wheel of cheese in one of those boxes. Gemp took the wheel back to his cot, cutting off slices with his boot knife without offering any to Sun.

"In Ashvold, the people worship Karna," Sun said. "She don't give them a choice. The first hour after sunset, everyone stops and faces towards her acropolis. They bow their heads and repeat her prayer for ten minutes. Then, if it's a Blood Moon, the wulfkin are released. It's said those who die are the ones with doubt in their hearts rather than love."

Sun paused and splashed some more water over his face. "But it's a lie. The ones who die are the ones who have nowhere to hide. The wulfkin hunt because that's what they do. And everyone just says those who get caught are sacrificed for the greater good." He found a second cot and sank down cross-legged onto it, resting his spear across his knees.

Gemp grunted and stuck another slice of cheese in his mouth.

"Why do you worship the angels?" Sun asked.

Another grunt. "Ahhck, worship is an odd word," Gemp said eventually. "I believe in the God. I pray to him each night. Mostly hoping he makes things better, I suppose."

The old veteran fell silent, but it wasn't enough of an answer for Sun. They had come all this way, sacrificed so much, for a cause he couldn't really understand. But he felt he should. One way or another, his mother had always intended Sun to be involved in the conflict between humanity and God. She had never told him why or how. But she called him the Darkstar, a thing that shouldn't exist, a weapon against her true enemy. That was why Karna would never stop looking for him, because she believed that Sun was somehow her only hope to fight against God. None of it made any sense to Sun. He didn't want to be a weapon for his mother. When Flame and Branch had taken him, he had gone willingly. Renira might miss her own mother, but Sun had no reason to miss his. She mixed kindness and cruelty, and Sun had enough little scars to remind him of her displeasure.

"But why?" Sun asked, trying to clear his own mind of dark memories. "Why pray? What makes you so sure the God will make things better?"

Gemp glanced at Sun from underneath bushy eyebrows the colour of storm clouds. "I was a soldier once. In the Third Legion, long before you were born." He sliced off a chunk of cheese and stared at it on the blade of his knife. "I saw things. Did things. Can't make up for them. Ain't enough lifetimes even for an immortal to make up for what I did, nor what I ordered others to do in the name of their king. In the name of my king."

The old man shook his head, eyes still fixed on the cheese speared on the end of his knife. "War ain't glorious, lad. No matter what the history books say. No matter what's painted on some shitty canvas, and no matter what young fools like to believe.

"No soldier who's seen battle comes out of it the same. It becomes a part of you, worming its way deep into your heart until you can't see it no more. Until you don't even know it's there or what it's doing. But it is there. A festering wound no surgeon can touch.

"The violence is bad enough. Ordering others to violence, even worse. Worse still is turning a blind eye to the horrors. The moment you see someone doing something so horrific you know you should stop them... but you don't. That's when you know you've lost."

"Lost what?"

"Yourself." Gemp's mouth worked, as if trying to form the next words and failing.

"The people of Helesia revere their king," he said at last. "The soldiers of his legions damn near worship him. We'd seen him fight angels, seen him kill them. We'd seen him feast on their corpses, still cooling there on the battlefield. The men... my men. I think they thought they were honouring him or something. I... I don't know. Bloody idiots, is what they were.

"We were in the mountains, in Aelegar. Came across some town, nothing but a village really. Warriors were all gone, hunting or some such. Nothing left but old men and youths, women too pregnant to hunt. It weren't a battle, just... bloody slaughter. I saw my men... They were eating a woman. She weren't no angel. Just a person in the wrong place at the wrong time, believing the wrong thing. They were laughing about it. Joking about what powers they would take from her flesh. I should have done something.

Should've stopped them or... Ahh, shit! I didn't. I just turned and walked away."

"That's horrible," Sun said. He knew it was the wrong thing to say the moment Gemp's eyes met his. There was pain there, so much it was close to breaking the old man. But Sun had no idea what to say. No one had ever talked to him like this. Karna told him nothing but vague whispers of what he would do for her, and none of the others in the palace were allowed to talk to him. Only Karna's Amaranthine spoke to him, and he couldn't trust anything they ever said. They were tools of his mother's making.

Gemp grunted and shoved a slice of cheese into his mouth. "I ran. That night. Left my armour and weapons, snuck out in the dead of it, and ran. Deserted my post and fled back home. I had a wife, two sons, both younger than you. At least they were back then. Long time ago. I thought I could go back, lose myself in my family and forget everything I'd seen and done. They'd make everything better, take away the pain. I thought I'd be happy with them like I was before."

Gemp sliced off another chunk of cheese and just stared at it. "Don't work that way though. The war followed me home. I brought it home. I couldn't forget. Couldn't forgive myself, even after they did. I was angry, always angry. Started looking for fights, shouting at my wife..." He paused for a moment and shook his head.

"I even threatened my boys with violence. Never hit them, mind. I didn't. Bad as it got, I stopped myself. But it was never enough. The war was in me in a way I didn't understand. And I knew one day I'd take it too far. I could see it happening. I knew one day I'd take that need to fight and give it physical form. So I ran again. Just left them. They were safer that way. Safer away from me.

"Eventually I found the fight I was looking for. Or made it happen. Everywhere I went. Taverns, most often. Drunken brawls and pointless scuffles. Everywhere I went I found someone to fight. Didn't matter who. Didn't always win, but that didn't matter either. Losing felt better than winning. Losing made me feel human again.

"That's how Eleseth found me. Broken nose, bust up ribs, who knows what else." Gemp let out a bitter, humourless chuckle. "I'd started a fight in a roadside inn. I don't even remember why. I lost that one hard. They beat the crap out of me and threw me outside to die by the road. An insignificant end for a life wasted. But I woke to her standing over me, glowing as she does. She put me back together, mended my hurts. Least those on the outside. She got me back on my feet. Then she told me she'd done what she could, but she could only heal my body, and my wounds went deeper than that."

The old man poked at the wheel of cheese with his knife, piercing it with little holes. "I couldn't figure out how she knew, but she did. She saw inside me, I guess. Looked deeper than the wounded flesh and stupid bloody decisions. She saw a person hurting. It's what she does ain't it? She said she couldn't heal what was broken inside, but she knew someone who could." Gemp shrugged. "She weren't wrong."

"The God healed you?" Sun asked sceptically. "Even when dead."

Gemp smiled ruefully. "No, lad. I healed me. With time and care and the courage to face the evils I was punishing myself for. Eleseth helped me see it all. She took me to Los Hold and gave me a place where I could rest and learn to forgive myself. Hard work. Shit, it was hard work. And I'm not saying I never feel guilty no more. There are times when it eats at me. But I learned to live with it, without letting it destroy me."

Sun frowned. "So the God didn't do anything? He didn't heal you. I still don't understand why that would make you believe in him."

Gemp chuckled. "He sent her to me. Eleseth healed my body and gave me a chance to mend what was deeper than the flesh. I never believed she just happened upon me right when I needed her most. The God sent her to me, to give me a chance to heal myself. That's proof enough. Reason enough to believe."

Sun still wasn't convinced. It seemed to him that Gemp was dressing up coincidence as providence.

"The thing is, lad," the old man continued. "You can't ask others to give you a reason. You've gotta find it yourself. I had to break before I found mine. I hope yours comes easier." Gemp gave a final grunt and nodded, then closed his eyes again, the wheel of cheese half eaten in his lap.

Sun watched him for a while. The old man's reasons were his own, and it was clear that even thinking about them still pained him. But he was wrong about Sun. He believed already. He'd grown up knowing that the God was real because his mother never tried to hide the truth. She'd told him from the beginning that the God was real and Sun was one day to be her weapon against him. He already believed because he needed something from God. He needed protection, someone to keep him safe, and not even the Godless King would be able to stand up to Karna when she came for him. Only the God could stop his own fallen angel.

Sun whispered a prayer then, though it was not for himself and not even for the God. He whispered a prayer for Renira, that she would be safe, and that she would reach the Bell of Ages unharmed.

It wasn't long before the trapdoor opened again, and an ancient man clambered down the ladder into the gloom of the cellar. Sun stood and gave Gemp a thump to wake him. The old veteran opened groggy eyes and groaned. No sooner was he awake, he sliced off another chunk of cheese and stuck it in his mouth.

The ancient fellow was all skin and wispy white hair and walked with a cane. He and Gemp spent a long time speaking in harsh whispers. Sun found himself uninvited to the conversation and sat back down on the bed he had claimed, waiting for others to decide his fate. It seemed he was always letting others decide that. Even his escape from Ashvold hadn't really been his own choice. It had been the acts of a group who would do anything to keep every weapon they could out of Karna's hands. Rebels within Ashvold. Perhaps Flame and Branch had been acolytes too. Perhaps that was why they were so determined to get Sun away from his mother.

Eventually the ancient man nodded and banged his cane against the trap-door twice. As soon as he was gone, the trapdoor closed. Gemp limped back to his bed and collapsed into it. There was a meeting set for tomorrow, and it was up to Gemp to convince them all to help their cause. Until then, there was nothing to do but eat and rest. Things didn't sound nearly as easy as Gemp made them out to be, but Sun agreed on one thing. A good night's sleep would do them both the world of good. He hoped Renira was finding the same, wherever she was.

CHAPTER 50

To sight bond an animal is no small thing. It creates a pathway between man and beast and more can be shared than simple sight. But there must also be a level of trust developed, for while man sees through beast's eyes, the beast also watches through the man.

— THE CAUTIONARY TALE OF WILFRID HOSTAIN, THE WILDLING PRINCE

The sun set, sky fading from crimson to onyx, and the streets grew icy. Renira's feet ached. She'd done half a circuit of the Overlook, trying to subtly spy on the paths that led up to the summit. There were four of them and each one twisted around the God-made mountain before joining up and leading to the shrine that sat upon the ledge of rock that hung out over the city. Renira had seen only the two paths leading up so far, but they were both guarded.

Whether or not Sun and Gemp managed to create a distraction, Renira knew she had no chance of reaching the summit without Eleseth's help. She doubted she'd even make it onto the base of the Overlook itself. The soldiers were letting no one through, and anyone who tried was detained and then taken away by men and women who looked suspiciously like Truth Seekers, with gloved hands that rarely seemed in proportion to the rest of the body.

There was no more she could do today, and the traffic on the streets was thinning now night had set in. With so many soldiers about, Renira doubted she had anything to fear from thieves, but she had much more to fear from the soldiers themselves. It was becoming too conspicuous for a young woman to be out alone, staying close to the Overlook. She needed to find shelter, food for her rumbling belly, a safe bed somewhere out of the stabbing cold. Two more days to wait, and she would be of no use to anyone if she was frozen solid in an alley when the time came.

A street sign sat illuminated in the corner of a crossroad, a lantern hanging above the signs. One of the signs pointed away from the Overlook and read *Queen Furluw Street*. Below it hung another sign claiming there was an inn along the street and rooms were available.

Renira turned to follow the directions of the sign and noticed a dappled cat sitting at the sign's base, barely inside the circle of light from the lantern. It watched her as she walked, ignoring all others on the street. There was something odd about its golden eyes. They looked far too human and familiar. She blinked, and the cat was gone, leaving Renira to wonder if it wasn't just her mind playing tricks on her. *Am I really missing Igor that much?*

The inn on Queen Furluw Street turned out to be a grand building standing tall amidst several workshops. Some of those were still operating even now night had fallen, and the smell of industry was strong in the air. The inn was called the *Coachman's Rest*, and the stables outside were far from busy. A sign outside pointed the way to a nearby market. The noise and warmth that spilled out onto the street was a beacon that snared her and reeled her in like a fish on a line.

Inside, the place was spacious and brightly lit by two hearths in the common room alone. A large staircase to Renira's left led up the floors above. An ancient innkeeper stood at the far end behind a bar. Renira counted six wooden kegs behind the man, and he was chatting with a woman wearing riding leathers. Most of the tables in the common room were empty, and one of the hearths had a bard sitting on the flagstone, fiddling with a lute and picking at a plate of food, occasionally throwing a morsel to one of the nearby shaggy-haired dogs who crowded him.

Renira stopped by the entrance and took an offerance needle, pricking her finger and shedding a drop of blood on the floor where it was soon lost amidst countless others long since dried and soaked into the floorboards. Then she made her way to the bar and waited while the innkeeper glanced at her, then made his apologies to the woman in riding leathers.

She was a few fingers shorter than Renira, a woman of middling years with long black hair and skin the colour of burnt sand. She gave Renira an appraising look, then smiled and picked up all four mugs of ale from the bar and joined three other travellers who were gathered around one of the few occupied tables.

"Miss?" the innkeeper asked, and Renira got the feeling it wasn't the first time. "Can I help you?"

Renira shivered and pulled her mother's torn and battered coat a little closer around her, despite the warmth of the inn. She nodded and drew in a deep breath.

"I need a room and food. Three days. No. Two days, I suppose."

The innkeeper narrowed his eyes. "Just two days, is it?"

Renira nodded. "Two nights and two days." *And on the third night I'll be... well, I won't be needing an inn.*

"Well," said the innkeeper, his eyes still narrowed in suspicion. "I hope you don't mind me saying, but I'll be needing payment up front. Room is five ekats a night. It's dear, but the Coachman's Rest has some of the best rooms in the city. Food will be..."

Renira fished the gold ring Aesie had given her out of her pocket and slid it onto the bar between them. The old innkeeper stared at the ring for a long moment, then looked up at Renira.

"We don't serve thieves. Out!" he barked, eyes sharp as flint.

"I didn't steal it," Renira said. "My friend gave it to me."

"Aye, I'm sure," the innkeeper said. He snatched up the ring from the bar and threw it at Renira. "Get out, girl. And take your stolen goods with you. If I see you round here again, I'll hand you over to the city guard and let them deal with ya."

Renira stumbled back away from the bar, clutching the ring to her chest. All eyes were on her now. Everyone in the inn watching her, even the dogs, one with strange azure eyes. She didn't know how Aesie did it, paying with rings like it was the most natural thing in the world.

She turned and fled from the inn into a cold street. It was almost deserted save for a few soldiers on patrol, not paying attention to anything but each other and the steaming mugs in their hands. One of them glanced at her, said something, and they all laughed. Renira turned away from the inn and started walking, keeping her head lowered and making sure not to draw the attention of the patrol. She stopped by the stables and looked inside. A yellow light shone from within, and as she crept closer, she could feel it was warm in there. Horses tended to make any stables warm, her mother had taught her that when she had gone to tend old Masey's mare after it had tripped and sprained an ankle.

A glance about the street assured her the soldiers weren't watching. They were far too engrossed in trying to keep themselves warm. Renira pulled the stable door open a little, glad it didn't squeak on its hinges, and looked inside. She couldn't see anyone, just a long corridor with stalls either side and a room at the far end with table and chairs. A couple of lanterns hung above, bathing the place in enticing yellow light. Only five of the dozen stalls were occupied. She slipped inside the stables and pulled the door closed behind her, then found the nearest empty stall. It had fresh straw on the ground, though that didn't mask the stink of horse and leather.

Aesie might have been able to convince the innkeeper the ring was hers to sell. She'd have used the gold to buy them a room and food and all the good grace they could hope for. Renira supposed that was the benefit of her station. People believed her because she expected them to. Renira decided she would have to emulate that somehow. *Conviction and confidence. I have to stop being so meek.*

She crept into the empty stall and put her back against the wall, sinking down into the corner and pulling her mother's coat as close as she could. It had served her well, that coat, through rain and snow, cave-ins and certain death. It was ripped, torn, faded, and scuffed, but it was still warm. And if Renira closed her eyes and pretended, she imagined she could still smell her mother on the coat. That light scent of lavender and wax soap. *The smell of a washer woman.*

She missed her mother. She missed her home, her little arch nemesis, Igor the Terrible. Renira missed feeling safe and loved and warm. And the sweet thought of those memories of home were only made bitter by the knowledge that she would never see the place nor her mother again. Renira clutched at her amulets and closed her eyes, letting the warmth of the stable carry her off to a fitful sleep.

She dreamed of angels battling with humans, winged monsters flying out of a glowing gate, darkness and light clashing and burning each other away. She dreamed of herself at the centre of it all. And she dreamed of a rat, sitting above her in the rafters of the stable, watching her through human eyes.

CHAPTER 51

Is the concept of faith truly so abhorrent? Do not you have faith that your horse will bear your weight, that water will quench your thirst, that the sun will rise each morning? Faith is but a tool we use to accept the world as it is. Have, then, faith that God still lives, that he loves you. For sure as the sun will rise, he will return to us.

— THE PREACHER

Renira grimaced as she scooped up the last disembowelled rat Igor had left her. Only three of the little *presents* today, yet the cat sat proudly on the rafters, cleaning the entrails from his claws while watching Renira to make sure she didn't come too close. The little monster never let anyone but Mother touch him, and Renira had the scars to prove she had tried. She took the remains out to compost and dumped them there with all the others. It stank like nothing else, but come the spring, it would make good fertiliser for the vegetable garden.

She found her mother setting up the washing line, the first load of clothes ready to hang out even so early in the day. The sun was low, but there wasn't a cloud in sight, and though it promised to be a chilly day, at least it would be a dry one. Mother was humming something, some lively ditty she had picked in the tavern last night. Renira longed for the day when she would be allowed to visit the tavern along with Mother, but she claimed there were some things Renira simply wasn't ready to learn yet. As if she didn't already know it all. She was friends with Elsa; there wasn't a single thing Renira didn't already know about drinking and debauchery.

Renira joined her mother silently, and together they started hanging up that first load of washing. After a while she found herself humming along in time. It was as peaceful and pleasant as Renira could remember. But she had the feeling she was being watched. An itch between her shoulder blades that felt like eyes on her. Renira turned to check, but there was no one there. When she turned back, Mother was gone. The sun had risen, and the day suffered from winter's bite. The house was cold and empty, and the washing they had been hanging up whipped about on the line as the wind gusted at it from all directions, and dark storm clouds gathered above.

She was dreaming. Renira knew it. She was dreaming, and none of it was real. She opened her eyes to the same stable stall she had curled up in the night before. She was chilled to the bone and shivering with it. A dull light spilled in through the open doorway, promising a cloudy day.

"Good morning," said a woman with a husky voice.

Renira startled and tried to get to her feet, but her limbs were still asleep, and she only ended up sprawling in the hay. She scrabbled to the far corner of the stall and stared up at a face she recognised from the inn the night before. The woman who had been at the bar when she had entered. She was short and stout, had glossy black hair and skin the colour of sand, and she spoke with an accent Renira recognised. *She's from Ashvold.* The woman was leaning over the wall of the neighbouring stall, a steaming clay cup in her hands. Renira noticed her nails were black.

"I recognise you," said the woman, smiling broadly. "You're the ring thief from last night."

"I didn't steal it!" Renira said as she got to her feet and edged toward the door of her stall. "I've never stolen anything."

"No?" asked the woman. "I sense a story. I like stories."

It was early morning, if Renira was any judge, and there was no one else in the stables save for the horses. "What are you doing in here?"

The woman shrugged. "I always check on my horse before breakfast. I like to make sure Terin is fed before myself. What are *you* doing here?"

"Sleeping."

"Aye, fitfully by the looks of it."

"Not exactly the most comfortable bed I've ever slept in. You're from Ashvold."

The woman nodded. "How can you be sure?"

"Your accent. I know a boy who speaks just like you do."

"Aye, do you?" She smiled and looked genuinely amused.

Renira judged she was close enough to the door and leapt for it, hitting it with a solid thud. It didn't budge, and she collapsed back into the stall, rubbing at her arm where she thought she'd have a new bruise soon.

The woman chuckled. "That looked painful. I admit, I may have locked the stall. I tell you what, I'll unlock it and let you out if you tell me your story."

Renira made a dive for the gap under the stall door, slithering through to escape. She made it most of the way before a pair of black riding boots stepped in front of her and she looked up to find the woman smiling down at her again.

Renira let out a sigh. "What do you want?"

"Seems to me you have a tale to tell, and I'd like to hear it," the woman said and held out a hand to help Renira up. "It's not often I find a girl sleeping in the stables, and you don't look like you belong on the streets. You know my accent. All very strange." She shrugged. "I'm curious. It's one of my many many failings."

Renira slithered the rest of the way out of the stall and stood on her own, ignoring the woman's hand. She glanced at the stable door again and wondered if she could make it.

"I tell you what. I'll buy you breakfast."

Renira snorted. "I don't think the innkeeper will let me back in."

The woman tsked. "Ah, burn the oily fool. You let me worry about that wet fart. Or you can run, I won't chase you. Far too early for such effort. So, free breakfast and all you need to do is tell me why you're here, all alone, sleeping in a stable. It sounds like a good deal to me."

Renira didn't think the woman meant her any harm, and judging by the curved dagger hanging from her belt she could have done so at any time. Her stomach gave a gurgling rumble, and that made the decision for her. She was starving, and now food was being offered. The very idea of turning it down was out of the question. She nodded her assent, and the woman grinned at her.

"Ah, wonderful! The name's Sky," the woman said, holding out her hand again and smiling broadly. "It's a pleasure to meet you..."

"Ren," Renira said and took the woman's hand.

"Like the bird? Ha! Coincidence is such a baffling thing." She walked away without elaborating.

Renira followed Sky into the common room of the inn. She ignored the table full of offerance needles by the doorway. She had already observed the tradition the night before, and the innkeeper had still thrown her out. Sky ignored it too and made her way to a table already occupied by three men, then waved to the one remaining chair, and retrieved another from a nearby table. Finally, she signalled to the old innkeeper who was standing behind the bar, yawning and paying very little attention.

"Everyone," Sky said. "This is Wren. Wren this is Shadow, Rock, and Little Rock."

"Really? Picking up strays again, Captain?" said the big man.

"Only the interesting ones, Rock," Sky said. "Found her sleeping with the horses."

Shadow was a pale man with a sickly pallor to his skin and long hair that framed his face and looked as though it had never even seen soap. He had a scattering of stubble and a mean look. It was the sort of face Mother had always warned her to stay away from. The man called Rock was a huge fellow who barely fit in the seat he was occupying. Despite his shirt doing little to hide his beefy arms, he was pudgy. He looked a lot like a babe with the body of a giant. Little Rock, on the other hand, was only slightly smaller than Rock and had skin as dark as Sun's and a full beard of curly hair. He smiled at Renira, and the lines around his eyes convinced her he smiled a lot.

"Little Rock?" Renira asked.

The man nodded. "A truly common name in Ashvold, I'll tell ya. The men in my family have been named Rock for three generations, starting with my grand pappy. He was called Rock." The man grinned and winked at her.

"I could probably have figured that out."

"Aye, maybe. But did you know, my da was also named Rock."

Renira sighed and Little Rock burst into laughter.

They didn't look like merchants, and they were a long way from Ashvold. They looked more like mercenaries now she thought about it. Maybe a group of sell swords looking for work in a foreign kingdom, blood on their blades and deeds both heroic and nefarious to their names. Renira smiled at the idea.

"Two Rocks and not a brain between them," Sky said. "It was all very confusing. I decided I needed a way to differentiate between the two, so my orders wouldn't get mixed up. Hence, Rock and Little Rock."

Rock grunted and said nothing, but Little Rock smiled up at his slightly bigger comrade. "A man of few words, but great insight." He laughed at the jest though no one joined in.

"Thought I told you what I'd do if I saw you here again, girl." The innkeeper's face was full of thunder as he ambled over. He was wearing a stained apron and a look that said he had been up all night.

"The girl denies the ring was stolen," Sky said pleasantly, standing to meet the innkeeper and blocking Renira from his view. "And I think you have no proof otherwise. Now, I know this little kingdom of yours doesn't always like to deal with inconsequential thing like proof, but in Ashvold we believe crimes should only be punished if they are real." Sky moved in an odd way as she talked, swaying from side to side, but so subtly it was almost unnoticeable. Renira found the movement mesmerising. The innkeeper stared at Sky, mouth hanging open as though he were trying to catch flies.

"I... uh..." the innkeeper said.

"Quite, and so elegantly put," Sky said, still swaying a little. She placed a hand on the innkeeper's shoulders and turned him away from the table. "I've invited her to share breakfast, a charitable act sort of thing, and I'll need a fifth plate. I know you won't mind. No skimping on the portions now. Off you go, there's a good man." She patted him on the arse to get him moving.

The innkeeper stumbled away in a daze, and Sky returned to the table, slipping into the open chair and leaning back, rocking it onto two legs. "So," she said that same broad, toothy smile. "You have a story to tell me." She reached forward and plucked a blade of straw from Renira's hair. "I do hope it's a good one. Love a good story."

Renira couldn't tell the truth. But she'd a little from watching Aesie, and the trick to a good lie seemed to be to start with a small dose of truth. "I'm from Riverden. It's a town to the south, at the edge of the mountains."

Sky nodded. "Aye, I've heard of it. Close to the Aelegar border, I believe."

"Mmm." Renira nodded and forged ahead with her lie. "I left home to go on an adventure of sorts. At least, that was the plan. There was a merchant, a woman I'd, um, had dealings with was making the trip to Celesgarde to start a life of learning within the universities."

"A merchant looking to study at university? Hmm. Always those money that miraculously have time to spend it on frivolous things like learning."

Renira nodded. "I, uh, don't know which university. She needed a hand-maid, one willing to make the trip with her and look after her on the road. I volunteered, though I don't think my mother wanted me to go. She thought it was dangerous."

"It looks like she was right about that," Sky said. "Your clothes have seen better days, I think. Ran into some trouble, did ya?"

The innkeeper returned with five plates of food and slid them onto the table. Sky murmured a husky thanks, beaming a dazzling smile at the man, then turned her piercing stare back on Renira. She didn't even touch her food. "Continue, please. I'm eager to know how you ended in such a... state."

Renira let out a humourless laugh. "There really isn't much more to tell. I'm a fairly terrible maid apparently. I didn't know half the duties I should have, and those I did perform were not up to the mistress' usual standards. Not a day went by when she didn't berate me or threaten me."

"Sounds quite dull," Sky said, still not touching her food. Rock and Little Rock, however, were demolishing their plates, while Shadow picked at his.

Renira panicked. Sky was being so kind because she wanted a story and Renira was telling a boring lie. She decided to spice it up with a few more hints of the truth. "There were wolves, they chased us. That was, um, fun, I suppose. If you count fun as being terrified for your life."

"Oh, I do," Sky said, smiling again. Little Rock laughed and they shared a glance. "Please, go on. Any other, excitingly dangerous escapades?"

Renira was deep into the lie now and found that it flowed easily. She let her imagination take control and weaved a story of hardship, incompetence, and a villainous noblewoman who bore no resemblance to Aesie whatsoever. Well, maybe a little resemblance. She found it worrying just how easy—and how fun —it was, to make up an entirely new life for herself.

"And what about the boy?" Sky asked.

"Boy?"

Sky speared a sausage on her plate. "Aye, you said you knew a boy with my accent. I'm always eager to hear of my fellow Ashmen."

"Oh, he..." Renira paused. She hadn't mentioned Sun at all during her fake story and it would sound strange now if she added him in. "I met him back in Riverden. Before I left."

"A shame," Sky said as she bit the sausage in half.

Renira shrugged. "That's where my story ends. As soon as we reached her father's estates here in Celesgarde, I was given my leave in no uncertain terms. Good riddance to the bitch."

"And the ring?"

Renira shrugged as nonchalantly as possible. "Payment. For my services between Riverden and here."

Sky tutted. "That's a hefty payment for such a terrible job as you apparently did. Does this reprehensible merchant of yours know how you were paid for your services?"

Renira said nothing. She grinned and tucked into her plate of breakfast. There were fat sausages, mushrooms, and two bread buns that were still just about warm from the oven.

"Well," Sky said. "That was certainly quite a tale. Wouldn't you agree, boys?"

Little Rock laughed. Rock had his eyes closed as if asleep, and Shadow was fiddling with his dark gloves, scratching fingers underneath the fabric.

"And what are your plans now?" Sky asked.

Renira shrugged again, biting into a sausage and suppressing a moan of pleasure at the flavours. She couldn't remember the last time she had eaten so well. Judging by the quality of the food, the Coachman's Rest was clearly no roadside inn, but one that catered to a higher class of clientele. She wondered again just what these four people from Ashvold were doing in Celesgarde. She imagined they were spies, scouting the fortifications, paying off informants inside the city. It was very exciting.

"I guess I'll find work, maybe?" Renira said around a mouthful of sausage. "I can't go back home yet. Not until I've found my adventure."

Sky's smile dropped at that. "Adventures are rarely as exciting as bards make them out to be, Wren." It was a sentiment Renira understood all too well. "As it happens, we are soon to be travelling south. We might even make it as far as your Riverden. Would you like to join us? Perhaps we could deliver you back to your mother safe and sound. We make for quite formidable guards."

The two Rocks both chuckled at that. They looked like soldiers, though Renira saw no weapons or armour other than the belt knife each of them carried.

"What is it you do?" she asked, unable to restrain her curiosity. "From what I hear, Ashvold is a long way away."

The two Rocks fell silent and glanced at Sky.

"We do a lot of things," she said. "Currently we're hunting down a lost possession."

Renira frowned. It was a vague answer at best, but she had no right to question them any further. After all, she had just been lying to them about her own purpose in the city.

"If you're going south," Renira said, "could you take a message to my mother, if you make it as far as Riverden?"

"We're not a messenger service," said Rock in a voice that suited his name.

Sky sent the big man a glare, then turned a smile on Renira. "I can't guarantee we'll make it that far, Wren. But if we do, I'll be happy to carry a message for you. After all, words are weightless, yet their meaning is often heavier than stone."

"Thank you," Renira said hesitantly. Sky had so far shown her nothing but kindness and with no reason to. She knew she should just be thankful, and once she would have been, but now she was suspicious. Nobody helped out of the kindness in their hearts.

"My mother won't be hard to find. There's a little village just east of Riverden called Ner-on-the-River. Or just Ner. It only has twenty buildings to it, and my mother's house is the largest. Her name is Lusa, she's a washer woman by trade."

Sky nodded. "I'm sure that's enough to go on. What would you like me to tell her?"

Renira pushed her final sausage around the plate a little as she thought about what she wanted to say. She knew the message couldn't be long, nor could it give the truth of her purpose away, but she needed her mother to know she was alive.

"Tell her," Renira said and paused for a moment. "I made it to Celesgarde, and I know who I am now. I met my father." There was so much more to say, but there was also nothing else. By the time the message reached her mother, Renira would have either succeeded and brought the God back to life or failed and the Godless king would have secured his final victory. *Either way, I'll be gone.*

"That's an odd message," said Little Rock. Shadow nodded in agreement.

"What would you know about it?" Sky said sharply. "I'll let you critique Wren's message the moment you become a mother or a daughter. Until then, both of you, I suggest you keep quiet on matters you'll never understand."

"Whatever you say, Captain," said Little Rock, holding up his hands. His smile faded quickly.

"I'll try my best to deliver it," Sky said. "Though our route south may not be direct. Perhaps you'll even beat us there."

Renira smiled wistfully. "I doubt it." She fished the ring Aesie had given her out of her pocket and placed it on the table in front of Sky. "Thank you. I have nothing else to pay you for your kindness, so this will have to do."

Sky frowned at that. "This ring is worth a lot more than the price of a messenger, Wren."

"Don't forget breakfast," Renira said with a shrug. "This was a meal worth a fortune in itself."

"Still..."

Renira shook her head at Sky. "I don't need it anymore. At least I know if I've paid you for your time and effort, you'll have a reason to deliver my message."

"Hmm." Sky argued no further and slipped the ring onto her index finger, turning her hand about so it caught the light. In truth, it didn't suit her at all.

They finished their breakfast while Little Rock told a story about Ashvold that made it seem like the happiest place Renira had ever heard of, completely at odds with all Sun and Armstar had told her. He talked about great parties thrown for no reason other than to celebrate existence, and of fine wines, finer foods, and debaucheries that had Renira blushing. She hadn't heard anything so bawdy since the last time Elsa bragged about her exploits. *And at least half of those had been blatant lies.*

She felt better now, more at peace. With the knowledge that her mother would get her message, that she might understand that it was Renira's choice and that she had accepted the consequences, she felt as though she had made the final step she needed to. Now she could go through with her quest with a light heart and the determination of one who had put their affairs in order and made peace with their decision.

It was midmorning by the time Sky announced it was time they got underway, and Renira said her goodbyes to all of them. Shadow scared her, with his dark looks that suggested violence, but both Rock and Little Rock were fun enough that she would miss their laughter. Sky gave Renira a hug before sending her on her way and again promised she would try her best to deliver the message to her mother.

Out on the streets again, Renira looked up at the Overlook. It didn't look nearly as daunting as before. A bird was watching her from the rooftop of the inn. It was a large crow, with mangy feathers on its wings, and it stared at Renira with icy azure eyes.

CHAPTER 52

When Saint Dien formed the Exemplars, she chose the people closest to her,
those she could trust with her life and her heart, with her dreams and with
her failures. At their core was a triad of purpose: To fight. To lead. To Inspire.

— *ROOK'S COMPENDIUM*, 2ND EDITION

Sun was full of restless energy and the need to spend it by the time the young woman opened the trapdoor and ushered them out. There was only one more night to go before it was time. Time for him to cause a distraction. Time for Renira to ring in the new age. He still wasn't entirely certain what that meant, but he was excited to see it. He hoped God would smite Karna, and then he could live a normal life away from her.

The woman never told Sun her name, but she said the acolytes had gathered, and they were all waiting on Gemp to convince them of his plan. The old veteran seemed nervous at that, his hands shaking as he changed into the new clothes the woman had given them. She took both their spears away, claiming they would draw too much attention, and the clothes she had given them were warm winter wear, but not made for travelling or fighting.

By the time they were dressed, Gemp looked like an old man long past being useful to any trade but sitting on his arse and telling younger men how to act. Sun looked an apprentice, used to running errands rather than fighting for his life against forest demons and wolf princesses. He was not pleased by the change, but the woman assured them they would draw far less attention. Gemp accepted it all with distracted grunts, but Sun complained enough for them both.

The woman led them out into the cold, sunny afternoon streets of Celesgarde. People were everywhere, going about their daily duties completely oblivious to what was going to happen. Sun liked that. It made him feel special. Not in the way Karna had called him special, but in a different way. He knew something none of these people did. He knew what was going to happen. He was party to a secret, and nothing made a person feel important quite like a secret.

Soldiers were out in force, large patrols of men and women wearing black armour with gold strikes embossed upon the breast. There was an arrogance to the way the patrols walked as though they owned the streets.

Eventually they came to a large building that smelled to Sun of rotting pig. It was located so near the wall that Sun could see soldiers patrolling atop it, and everywhere in the district were signs of industry. The sounds of hammers hitting anvils rang out, mixing with raised voices to create a cacophony that drove Sun to distraction. People came and went to every building, warehouse, and workshop. Many were bringing supplies, others were buying goods, and some were looking for work.

The woman spoke to a burly man at the doorway for a while and they laughed over some joke she told. Sun wasn't listening, but he assumed they were speaking in some sort of code. He was staring at a statue that thrust up out of the middle of the street. A broad man in heavy plate, his sword held before him, point to the earth. He couldn't read the plaque—Karna had never taught him words, only runes—but he guessed it was a statue of the king. Sun grinned at the statue. This was where the rebellion would truly begin, right under Emrik Hostain's stone nose.

Then they were ushered in, and the smell was worse. Sun had never experienced a tannery before, and he didn't want to ever again. Whatever they were using to the cure the leather smelled like the arse end of a wulfkin.

Once they were inside the tannery, all pretence at normality was abandoned. The woman led them through the workshop quickly, with only nods toward those labouring away with knives, brushes, and buckets. They went down into the cellar, not via a trap door, but a full flight of stairs that led so deep underground, even the din from above sounded far away. It reminded Sun of the dungeons in Karna's palace where they kept the prisoners for sacrifice, and deeper where they kept the corrupted monsters that Karna grew.

They came upon a metal door, and the woman knocked twice, then three more times. After a few moments, the door opened, and Sun and Gemp walked into a room filled with the leaders of the Celesgarde acolytes.

The old man from the night before was there, bent-backed and leaning on his cane, eyes sharp despite his age. Sun counted ten others as well. Some were old and others young, men and women, some wearing work overalls, and others huddled into voluminous winter clothing. Some had skin as dark as his own, and others were as pale as Armstar. The one thing they all had in common, was an air of scepticism.

The woman closed the door behind them and walked past Sun and Gemp, taking the only unoccupied chair. It did not escape Sun's notice that there were only enough chairs for the leaders of the acolytes, and the honour of sitting was not even afforded to Gemp.

"Now what?" Sun asked Gemp. He pitched his voice as a whisper, but it seemed to echo around the near empty cellar, finding the space between loosely stacked crates and barrels and hiding there for a moment before launching back out into the room. The lanterns flickered and cast everyone in sinister glows, and Sun felt his mouth go dry.

"Now, lad," said Gemp, "we try to convince these fine folk to do what's right." He seemed diminished somehow, as though taking his spear and armour away made him smaller and less significant. He no longer looked like a swarthy veteran, but just an old man with the weight of the world bearing down on his wrinkled shoulders.

Sun thrust his hands into his pockets and stared at the gathered acolytes. Their faces ranged from disapproving to downright hostile, and he reckoned they had already made up their minds.

"Any chance I could have your names?" Gemp asked, taking a step forward. The Celesgarde acolytes were all sitting, chairs arranged in a semi-circle facing Gemp. Sun quickly stepped up beside the old veteran, not wanting to be forgotten or left out of the proceedings.

The acolytes introduced themselves, each with a single name of an animal. Gemp smiled and nodded and waited until they were done. "Codes, is it? Well, my name is Gemp, and it's the name I was given by my ma'. This here is Sun, and I reckon even he can see you've all already made up your minds about us and what we're here to ask. But I'm gonna go on and ask it anyway." He glanced down at Sun and shrugged. "Not like we have any other options."

The old man with the bent back, who had introduced himself as Sparrow, narrowed his eyes. "We ain't gathered here to be talked down to by the likes of you. You say you're from the New Gurrund order, and that might be true. We ain't got no way to prove it one way or another, but you knew the right codes to get yourself a meeting, and I suggest you don't go wasting it with petty insults."

Gemp grunted and nodded to the old man's words. "Too right. Too right. My apologies."

"Bah," said Duck, a young woman with freckles on her pale cheeks and unruly black hair. "Stop wasting time with insults and apologies and get on with what you're here to say so we can get back to work. Hard enough to make a living with all these bloody soldiers on the streets, and I'm starting to think that's your fault."

Gemp glanced down at Sun. He had a look on his face like pain and when he finally spoke, he was stuttering. "Well... I, uh, guess that ain't all that far from the truth. I mean, it ain't really our fault... but it's cos of us, I suppose."

"Why are you here?" asked a mountain of a woman called Frog. Her thick arms were crossed, and her eyebrows made her frown a continuous line.

Gemp fidgeted on the spot. Sun had never seen him look so uncomfortable, even in those moments of grief after Dussor and Kerrel had died. "Because it's time. The time. The one we've all been waiting for." He sniffed and shifted again. "This wasn't meant to be me. Eleseth was meant to be here. She's better at convincing folk of things. I think you all know that. Couldn't get her into the city though."

The woman who had put them up the previous night, who had since introduced herself as Bear, cleared her throat. "What time is it, Gemp?"

"Right," Gemp said and shifted on the spot again. Sun realised he was nervous. "It's time, uh, to do your parts. To stop hiding in the shadows and, um, fight for, well... for what you believe in."

Sparrow shook his ancient head. "Fight. No offence, lad, but you look a little past your prime. And I think I have at least ten years on you. My fighting days were done long ago. You're lucky I made it out of bed two days in a row just to talk to you."

"I didn't mean fight fight," Gemp said. He wiped his brow, sweating despite the chilly air in the cellar. "Eleseth was meant to be here. She or Orphus would know what to say. I'm just..."

"Orphus?" asked the mountainous Frog. "You know the Archangel?"

"Of course, I know him. This is his plan. And I'm messing it up." Gemp shook his head and seemed to sag. "I should never have let her go off alone. I was better as a spear at her side, not trying to talk you lot into helping her."

"Her?" asked Duck.

Hawk, a towering man with the muscles of a work horse, stood. "We're done here," he said in a voice so deep it threatened to boom if he spoke in anything but a whisper. "I've got a shipment coming in I need to oversee. Next time only call me in if it's important." He started walking, making for the door, and some of the other acolytes got to their feet as well. All the while Gemp just shook his head and mumbled to himself.

Renira was counting on them. She needed the distraction only they could cause, and without it she was sure to fail. Not just fail, but without a distraction she would probably be captured, maybe even executed. He couldn't let that happen. He stepped in front of Hawk and the big man stopped, staring down at Sun like he was a puddle of horse piss in the road.

"Sit down!" Sun hissed at the huge man, clenching his hands into tight fists.

"Get out of my way, boy," said Hawk,

Sun shook his head. "You said you'd listen to what we have to say. Well you haven't listened to me yet, so sit your arse down and listen."

"Sit back down, Hawk," said Frog, her jowls wobbling with each word. "Let the boy speak, then we can all leave together." Hawk shook his head but returned to his seat and sat with thick arms crossed and a scowl on his face.

"Thank you, lad," Gemp said quietly, for Sun's ears only. "I think I lost them there."

"What's wrong?"

Gemp shrugged. "Not good with crowds, nor being in charge. Not since..."

Sun didn't think he was good at being in charge either, but he'd make a burning good show of it for Renira's sake. He took a step forward, aware that all the acolyte leaders were watching him now.

"You gonna say something then, boy?" asked Sparrow, his gnarled hands curled around his walking stick.

"I don't know much about any of this," Sun said. "I'm not an acolyte like you all. I don't even really know what that means. I guess you all believe in this God Eleseth kept talking about. I don't. Never met him. Only time I ever heard of him before a few weeks back was from my mother, and she hated him. Blamed him for making her the way she is, I suppose."

"Real inspirational," said Hawk with a snort of laughter.

"I'm not meaning to be," said Sun, fixing the big man with a dark stare that he couldn't hold. "The Herald is here. Not the big one in armour, and not Eleseth either. The new Herald. Ren. She's human, like you and me and Gemp."

Some of the acolytes interrupted, asking how it was possible? Others started talking with each other, claiming Sun was lying.

"It's the truth," said Gemp, taking a step forward to stand next to Sun. "I swear on my belief everything the boy says is truth."

"I'm her Exemplar," said Sun. "That means I'm supposed to be by her side, protecting her. But I'm here instead, because the best way I can protect her now is to convince all you to help."

"You're her Exemplar?" asked Hawk with another snort of laughter. "You're a child."

Sun nodded at that. "Maybe. But I don't see adults like you lining up to take the job. You're here mocking me for my age and trying everything you can to get out of helping. Well, I'm the one standing in between Ren and the Godless King, while you adults hide in your cellars and call it belief. I might be young, but that makes me more a man than any of you."

That shut Hawk up. The big man leaned back in his chair and went back to glowering at Sun. A few of the other acolytes started talking to each other in whispers.

"Tomorrow night, Ren is making her move," Sun said. "She and Eleseth. They're going to make their way up to the top of the Overlook and ring in the new age."

The acolytes looked unconvinced.

"They don't know, lad," said Gemp. "They don't know what it means. When the new age begins, the God will be reborn."

The cellar exploded in noise as acolytes began talking loudly to one another or shouting questions at Gemp that Sun couldn't make out. Only the old man, Sparrow, remained silent, leaning on his cane and staring at Sun with furrowed, thoughtful eyes. Hawk was shouting at Frog, asking what the point of their belief was all this time if it was in a dead God. Bear was listening to another of the acolytes, shaking her head vigorously. Everything was noise and anger, as though all of this was a big surprise to them.

Sun felt Gemp lay a hand on his shoulder, and he turned to find the old veteran shaking his head. "They're not gonna help, lad. Look at them. Not a one of them is an actual believer. They play at it because of the danger, because it makes their lives feel more important. They like the secret, the feeling that they belong to something bigger than them. I doubt any of them have even seen an angel before. We're on our own here." He sighed and turned around to leave, shaking his head and seeming older and smaller than before.

Sun was about to follow when he caught Sparrow's gaze. The ancient man was watching him with eyes dark as tar, and there was something else there. A pleading look, like a wounded man who just needs to hear that things will be all right. That he isn't going to die.

"Shut up!" Sun hissed at the acolytes. No one paid him any notice. "SHUT UP!" he roared, his voice cracking with the words. This time, the acolytes fell silent and turned toward him. Some of them looked scared, others angry. Some just looked confused.

He stepped forward and stared at Sparrow. "What is belief to you?"

The old man didn't answer, so Sun turned to the loudest of the acolytes, Hawk. "What is belief to you?"

Hawk grimaced. "I suppose I thought that God is watching. That if I lived my life by his rules. Came here and did my part with the rest of you from time to time. Taught my children to do the same. I guess I thought I'd go to Heaven when I pass. That God would let me in."

Sun shook his head. "God is dead. Heaven's Gate is closed. Not even the angels can get in."

He turned to Bear, ignoring the fear on her face. "What is belief to you?"

Bear looked caught by the question, but she wiped at her eyes and answered. "I like to believe things can be better. That one day we might not be living under the heel of an immortal king who kills anyone who disagrees with him."

Sun smiled savagely. "And how will that change happen? Who will bring it to pass if not you?"

Bear shuffled on the spot. "I suppose I thought the God would. The book teaches he did it before, saved us from the demons. I thought... well, if we need saving again, he'd be here for us."

"God is dead," Sun repeated. "The same immortal king you fear killed him. And he'll remain dead unless we do something about it."

Sun turned to Sparrow again. He wasn't sure why exactly, but the old man had a weight to him. His opinion mattered, not just to the other acolytes, but to Sun as well. "What is belief to you?"

Sparrow shook his head as he looked at Sun through teary eyes. "What is it to you, boy?"

"I don't believe in the God. I know he's real. I've met enough angels to know that's true. But he's dead, and I've never met him. I believe in Renira. The Herald. She saved me. When I was as good as dead, she risked her own life to save mine, even when an angel was telling her not to. She's doing it again now. Risking her life, not for herself, but for everyone else. For you!"

Sun looked at Bear. "Like you, she believes the world can be a better place free of the Godless King. None of us have the strength to depose him, but the God does. That's what she believes. And I believe in her. Ren is risking her life for everyone. For you, for me, for the people out in the streets who don't even know it.

"That's what I believe in. Not the God. I believe in her trying to make the world a better place the only way she knows how."

Gemp cleared his throat. "Aye. The Herald is the only one who can do it, but she needs our help. We need to create a distraction. A little risk on your part, compared to the risk she's taking upon herself."

Sun glanced up at the old veteran, and he seemed more himself again, standing straighter, a new fire in his eyes.

"What guarantee do we have that it will work?" asked Frog. She was one of the few still sitting.

"None," said Gemp. "Renira will do her best to reach the Overlook. Eleseth will help her. The Light Bearer is coming here, to the centre of her greatest enemy's stronghold. But they're certain to fail without our help. We need to cause a distraction the soldiers in the city can't ignore. Pull as many of them away from the Overlook as possible."

Again, the acolytes started talking amongst each other, shouting as often as not. Sun saw Gemp's jaw grinding at the hesitation they were showing. "This is Orphus' plan," the old veteran shouted, adding his own voice to the cacophony. "The Archangel himself gave us this mission."

Sparrow met Sun's gaze again. There was hope there, he thought. The hope that things could change, that even he might see it before his time came, but still the ancient acolyte hesitated. Sun remembered something Karna had once told him. She said that hope could be a good motivator, but fear was always better. And better than both was shame. Sun approached the old man slowly, through the din of people shouting at each other yet saying nothing.

"You called me a boy," Sun said, staring down with a frown at the old man. "What does it say about the world, when a child is willing to risk everything for your cause, yet an old man who's had more than his share of years is too scared to do the same? What does that say about your belief? Your conviction?"

Sparrow looked away, unable to meet the intensity of Sun's stare any longer. Sun realised he was trembling anger, and he saw Sparrow was trembling too, not with anger, but with shame. After a few moments, the old man stood, leaning heavily on his cane to do so. With his bent back, he was no taller than Sun. He lifted his hands and then slammed his cane against the ground three times. Slowly, the rest of the acolytes fell silent.

"Most of you are too young to remember when Orphus last came to Celesgarde," Sparrow said. "Most of you have never even seen an angel. Well I have. The Archangel came, and he made a believer out of me. How could I not put my faith in a being who could create someone of so much strength and purpose? It's been so long I think that belief has waned somewhat. Replaced by awe for the Godless King.

"For too long I've hid in the shadows, saying the words I thought I was meant to. It's become a show and nothing more. We say things we don't believe, teach values we don't hold to." He drew in a deep breath and shook his head sadly. "It's time for that to stop. God is dead. They admitted that themselves. Then it's time we put our faith elsewhere. Restrain them!"

CHAPTER 53

Is it not one of the finest professions for a man to hunt out cures to ailments and infection? A physician's job is to cure ills and extend life. Well, I say mortality is a disease, and we already know the cure. What could be more noble than eternity?

— ERTIDE HOSTAIN

Aesie strode through the palace halls with her eyes locked on the servant's broad back. The woman was a head again taller than Aesie, with a tightly braided bun of dark hair that pulled on her skin and gave her a severe expression. She had seemed suspicious when Aesie told her why she had come to the palace, but servants were trained not to interfere with their masters' affairs. That was something that never changed regardless of where in Helesia one was. Aesie clung to that thought to give her comfort. Familiarity when all around her seemed dangerously new. She could do this. She had to do this.

The palace was a grand thing with halls and rooms to spare. Luxurious carpets padded the stone floor in a trail of red that mimicked the colour of the sky. Aesie ignored it all as best she could. She was going over the conversation in her mind again and again. One wrong step or misplaced word could spell her end. She knew too much, and most of it amounted to heresy, whether she believed it or not. Did she really have a choice whether to believe it or not? Could one deny the truth that was before their eyes simply by choosing not to see it? It seemed a far-fetched delusion to Aesie, to willingly fool one's self into ignorance.

All too soon, it seemed, the servant in front of her stopped and gave her a haughty glance. It was all quite rude, and any other day Aesie would have bristled and given the woman the sharp side of her tongue. She might be a palace servant, a direct employee of the king, but Aesie was above her. Her father's fortune and businesses gave her an aristocratic station that should have seen her treated with respect, not suspicion. On any other day, she would have treated the woman's insult with the severity it deserved, but for the sake of her father, she would weather the insult. Today. Tomorrow was an entirely different situation.

"Wait here," the servant said slowly, as though she needed to pronounce the words carefully to make certain Aesie understood. Then she turned, knocked on the door, and opened it a crack, slipping through into the room beyond and pulling the door closed.

Aesie deflated, letting out a taut breath she had been holding to keep her legs steady. She was trembling. Her hands shook, and her knees wobbled. A wave of vertigo washed over her, and for a terrifying moment she thought she might swoon. She had no doubt that would have completed the servant's day: proof that Aesie's demand to see the king was an utter waste of time. She was not about to give the woman the satisfaction of such a victory. Aesie steadied herself with a hand on the nearby doorframe and took two deep breaths. They didn't calm her, but at least the trembling grew more manageable. No doubt and no second guessing. This was her decision, and she had made it, for better or worse.

When the door opened again, the servant looked no less sour-faced. She ushered Aesie inside, then stepped outside, closing the door behind her. And just like that, Aesie found herself alone with King Emrik Hostain.

It was the fourth time she had met the king—the first time they were alone —and each time Aesie found herself feeling small and insignificant. The man was a titan made flesh. An immortal. A living legend. Before him, Aesie found herself stammering when usually she was so quick-witted. But not this time. This time she would say what she needed to say and no more. Her father's life depended upon it.

The king glanced up at her from behind his desk. He was bent over the polished wood, a length of charcoal in his hands and his fingers smudged with the evidence of its use. Aesie took a quick step forward and could see the paper the king had been scrawling on. Upon that page, Aesie saw a tall figure, feminine by the proportions and dressed in shadowy plate armour. She held a sword in one hand and a kite shield in the other, and all around her were the cheering faces of soldiers with their weapons raised in salute. She had wild hair, thick and unruly, but her face was featureless. Where her eyes and nose and mouth should have been, there was nothing but blank paper.

"I have been trying to capture the likeness of my sister," King Emrik said, his voice weary. "Faces have always been a problem. I remember them all, but have such trouble drawing them." The king sighed and crumpled the paper in one hand, heedless of the art he was destroying. He tossed the paper into the nearby hearth and the flames quickly consumed it.

The king stood and rounded his desk to stand in front of Aesie. "You're the girl from Riverden. The one I sent to New Gurrund."

Aesie nodded, desperately trying to free her tongue. The king towered over her, a truly intimidating figure. He who had shaped the age. Who had seen the God, made war on Heaven and razed it to the ground. He who had slain angels and feasted on divinity. The man who held the key to her father's life.

"You sent me to New Gurrund to forget about me," Aesie said, the words tumbling out of her mouth. "So you wouldn't have to grant me the reward that I was promised for betraying my friend."

The king drew in a deep breath and sat on the edge of his desk, a charcoal smudged hand scratching at his beard. "This is about the reward. Fine. Three thousands orts. Take it and go."

Aesie shook her head, determined to go on. "You promised me more. You promised angel blood."

King Emrik shook his head wearily. There were dark rings around his eyes, and he seemed almost sluggish. "No, I didn't."

Aesie refused to back down. "You insinuated..."

"An insinuation is far from a promise," the king said. "I could insinuate I might hand you the crown for your part in the hunt, but how likely would it be that I would abdicate in favour of a fool from nowhere? That is an important lesson in statecraft. Besides, your information did not lead to the capture of the Herald. Take the reward I offer and go, before I decide to rescind it." He stood from his perch on the desk and started to round it, going back to his chair.

Aesie couldn't let it end like this. Not after she had come so close. The king was before her, her father's salvation in sight. She could not return to him knowing she had come so close and failed. Not to watch her father die a slow, painful death. Not when there was even the slightest chance she could save him.

Aesie took a deep breath and wiped a sleeve across her damp eyes. The King was right, she had been acting foolish. Making the demands of a child rather than the deals of an adult. Her father had taught her better than that. Merchants preferred negotiations to ultimatums, deals to demands. Aesie was a merchant's daughter, and one day she hoped to be the head of the family, all its businesses in hand. It was time she started acting accordingly.

The king sat back down at his desk and pulled out another sheet of paper. It was a dismissal. Her time with him was done. She would change his mind about that.

Aesie turned and took two steps toward the study door, then stopped and pulled out her offerance needle. A delicate thing made of purest silver, with tiny designs of various animals etched along its length. A gift from her father to commemorate her sixteenth birthday, along with a leather pouch similarly decorated to keep it. Aesie held the needle in her right hand and turned back to the king. There she waited until he glanced up her once more, annoyance plain on his face. As soon as their eyes met, Aesie pricked her finger once and squeezed it until a fat drop of blood freed itself and crashed against the wooden floor. The king narrowed his eyes at the ritual. Before he could speak, Aesie stepped forward again, pocketing the needle as she approached his desk.

"Why didn't you tell me my friend was the Herald?" Aesie asked. "You let me believe she was merely caught up in the affairs of angels and that one of them was the Herald. Why hide that from me?"

King Emrik carefully placed the charcoal on the paper and leaned back in his chair. "It was not information you needed to know."

Aesie shook her head and smiled humourlessly. "A better answer would have been to ask a question of your own. How do *I* know Renira is the Herald? If you did not tell me, then who did?"

Silence held the room between them, the only sound the crackling of the fire in the hearth and the wind howling outside.

"They passed through New Gurrund," King Emrik said eventually. "You found them." It was not a question.

"Yes," Aesie said. She glanced sideways to see a chair near the window and considered pulling it across the room to sit in front of the king's desk, to stop the trembling of her knees if nothing else. Yet she knew that might be an act too far. She was aware it was a fine line she was walking, and either side of it lay ruination for her and her father.

"I found Renira and insinuated myself into her group. I believed I could lead Princess Perel to them. It worked. We were chased by your daughter out of New Gurrund and..."

"Is she alive?" the king asked, leaning forward quickly, his voice suddenly urgent. "Is Perel alive?"

"I... I don't know. She ambushed us underground. There was a cave-in and... I don't know if she survived. Maybe. I did. We did, Renira and I." She could have told the king that Renira had died in the cave-in, that he had won and it was over. Why hadn't she? Because, Aesie knew with a damning certainty, it wouldn't get her what she needed.

King Emrik sighed and leaned back. He closed his eyes for a moment and winced at some pain. When he opened them again, his gaze was stone. "You were with the Herald then. And you stand here now alone?"

"You were right before," Aesie said, her voice trembling along with her legs. "You only insinuated that angel blood might be the reward for my information, and I see now you never had any intention of that being the case. So, I will have a contract from you before I tell you anything further." She clenched her teeth to stop them from chattering and gripped her hands together, feeling blood squelching between her fingers.

King Emrik stood, his chair legs scraping across the floor. He rounded the desk slowly, coming to a stop in front of Aesie. He was frowning like a thundercloud as he perched on the edge of his desk again, arms crossed. Aesie's legs gave a treasonous tremble, and she locked her knees. She met his intense stare and refused to buckle beneath its terrible weight.

"What do you know?" the king asked.

Aesie gasped in a breath. "Contract. I want a contract. Angel blood as a reward. This is a deal. A negotiation."

"There are other ways I could secure the information," he said matter-of-factly.

Aesie nodded and quickly wiped tears from her eyes again. "You could. You could torture me," she said, her voice tight. "But you would have no idea if what I said was true, and you don't have the time to suffer lies. Time is of the essence, I assure you. A drop of angel blood means nothing to you, yet to my father it means everything. He's dying. Lung rot. And the only cure is the blood of an angel."

Emrik ran a charcoal-dusted hand through his beard again. "You would betray your friend a second time to save your father?"

"Third time, actually. And yes." Aesie nodded, a new tear escaping and rolling down her cheek before she thought to wipe it away. "He's my father. I would betray Renira a hundred times to save him. And I wouldn't apologise for one of them."

The king nodded at that, his smile a shrewd, measuring thing. He held up a single finger. "One drop of angel blood. If what you say leads to the capture of the Herald. And only if."

Aesie nodded her agreement. She knew the truth though. King Emrik said capture, but he meant something far more final. She was trading Renira's life for her father's. It was unfair.

"And one more thing," she said before she could change her mind. "I want you to promise not to kill her."

"What?" King Emrik growled.

"Renira doesn't deserve to die."

"She is a heretic!"

"She's being led down a path she neither believes in nor understands," Aesie said quickly. She was gambling now, not dealing. Gambling her own life and everything she had come here to demand for the sake of Renira. It was the least she could do. It wasn't enough, not even close, but it was the only apology she could make.

"You don't have to kill her. You could lock her up or exile her or... I don't know. You're the king! And she is just a washer girl from Riverden. You *can* find a way to end this without killing her." She ran out of words and swallowed hard, staring up at the king as he decided whether it would be simpler just to have the information tortured from her. Aesie was under no illusions. She would not hold her tongue in the face of torture.

"If..." the king started and then stopped. He drew in a breath and shook his head. "If I can take the Herald alive, I will."

"Swear it!" Aesie said. She watched the king's jaw writhe and wondered if she had pushed it too far.

"If I can take her alive, I will," he repeated. "Now tell me what you know, Miss Fur!"

Aesie took a steadying breath. She had done it. She had done it! And she had saved Renira in the process. It was more than she had dared hope for. "We entered the city together a day ago."

"This I already suspected. Tell me how to find her."

"I don't know. I don't know where she is now. But I know her plan." The angels' cause meant nothing to her, and she knew they would never willingly give over even a drop of their own blood. This was the only way. "Tomorrow night. The acolytes will cause a distraction in the city. Eleseth will fly in, and she and Renira will climb the Overlook to ring the bell."

King Emrik smiled, victorious. He stepped around Aesie and reached the study door in two easy strides, pulling it open. The disapproving servant waited on the other side.

The king nodded toward Aesie. "Find her some quarters. Somewhere with a door that locks from the outside." And then he was gone, striding down the hall with a swiftness.

Aesie staggered, catching herself on the desk where the king had sat and sucking in deep breaths, trying desperately to stop the world from crowding in around her. A tear fell, breaking apart on the wooden desk, followed by another and more. It was done. For better or worse, Aesie had cast her lot, and there was no turning back now.

CHAPTER 54

If I fall here today do not lose heart, my friends. If every one of our allies is cut down, do not falter. We are the last line of defence against the unbearable. Fight on! Even should the strength or conviction of others fail, believe in yourself and keep fighting. We must turn back this dark tide.

— HELENA HOSTAIN, *BEFORE THE SHATTERING*

A lifetime of distrust saved Sun.

Hawk threw himself at the boy with grasping hands. Sun ducked underneath his reach, kicked the big man as hard as he could in the shin, then ran back to where Gemp was already struggling with the woman, Bear.

Some of the acolytes were arguing, claiming it was madness. Maybe there were some true believers amongst the lot of them, those willing to stand on their conviction, but Sun realised that most of them had no real belief, and certainly no loyalty to the God or his angels. These were not the acolytes from New Gurrund who were willing to sacrifice themselves for the cause. These were men and women who had never even seen an angel. People who claimed belief in something forbidden to make themselves feel important. They would sell Renira out to the Godless King rather than stand up for what was right.

Gemp might have been as shocked by the turn of events as Sun, but he was still a veteran soldier at heart, and whatever Bear might have been, she was not prepared. The struggle was short and ended with Gemp punching the woman twice in the face, then twisting her arm so sharply Sun heard the crack as he rushed past them both towards the door. Bear dropped to the floor, screaming out her pain, and Gemp started backing up, feet wide and apart and ready for a brawl. They were outnumbered, but the acolytes were in disarray. Still, Sun didn't much fancy tangling with Hawk or the fat woman, Frog.

He reached the door and threw it open just as he heard Frog scream for the guards stationed outside. Gemp pushed past Sun, and the first guard went down with a punch to the throat before he knew what was happening. They wore no armour and wielded wooden cudgels. Sun leapt at the remaining guard, colliding and knocking them both to the ground. He rained down blow after blow at the man's face, knocking aside his arms whenever he tried to defend himself.

By the time Sun stopped punching, the man was unconscious, his face bloody. Sun was trembling, his hands shaking and bleeding from cuts on his knuckles. He was panting from the exertion, and the pain of the violence was just now starting to make it through the haze he felt in his head. He looked down at the blood on his hands and felt sick.

Gemp had the door shut and his back braced against it, and there was a solid thumping coming from the other side. "Pull those bodies over here, lad," the old veteran said as another thump hit the door.

Sun moved in a daze as he pushed the first guard in front of the door, and then dragged the second guard on top of the first. He retrieved both wooden cudgels and handed one to Gemp.

"What do we do now?" Sun asked. Nothing was going according to plan. What could they even do without the help of the acolytes?

Gemp frowned in concentration and shook his head at Sun. "As soon as these traitors get out, they'll alert the city guard. Their choice is made, and there's no going back now. None of them were believers. If only Eleseth had come. She'd have changed their hearts."

"What do we do, Gemp?" Sun asked again, panic making his voice brittle.

"The only thing we can, lad," Gemp said. He was sweating into his unruly beard. "We start the distraction ourselves. Now. Burn this shit hole to the ground and set fire to as much of the city as we can before the guard stop us. And hope, lad. Hope Eleseth and Renira are ready tonight."

"It won't be enough, will it?"

"No, lad. It won't."

CHAPTER 55

Before Hunter Hostain brought civilisation to Ashvold, it was known as the Burning Lands and the people there called themselves Ashmen. Unsurprisingly, they worshipped fire, claiming it protected and destroyed and cleansed in equal measure. Those who survived fires were lucky or holy. It is a most primitive form of worship, and yet it has survived. There are those who still worship the flames even after seeing God's holy light.

— KRYSTLE GREYSON, HEAD HISTORIAN OF
STONELORE UNIVERSITY FROM 298-334 OF THE
THIRD AGE. *HISTORICAL RELIGIONS OF PRIMITIVE
HUMANITY*, 2ND EDITION

Emrik stalked down the halls with vigour and a savage smile on his face. He hadn't felt so energised since killing the Rider. They had her, this new Herald. They had her, and he would see her dead regardless of how *innocent* she might be.

Emrik had no doubt the angels had filled her head with lies to convince her to their cause. It was how the angels worked, after all. How the God worked. Lies and deception, indoctrination and the threat of the unknown. But he had them now. The Herald would die, and with her all hope of the God's resurrection. He might have promised the Riverden girl to spare her friend, but there was simply no way. As long as the Herald lived, she presented a threat. Only weak men were bound by promises.

"Honours only value is in keeping weak men in line by making them believe themselves strong." His grandfather's words proved true yet again.

Servants scuttled out of his way, bowing and scraping and murmuring placations. He had no time for any of them. Arik had moved his quarters to the second wing, to be closer to his family. His sons and grandsons, all so short-lived. Emrik understood the desire well.

He had fathered dozens of children over his thousand years of life, and most of them were long dead now. He remembered them all though. Their faces, the sounds of their voices. The way Famil used to ink moustaches on all the statues in the palace when he was a child. Jacinla, who understood even as a child she could get whatever she wanted just by batting her eyelids at her father. She looked so much like her mother. All gone now. Famil and Jacinla and dozens of others. Emrik had gifted them all with immortality, but he couldn't protect them from the wrath of God, and each one of them had been cut down by the bastard's angels during the last thousand years. With Perel gone, only three of his children remained. He missed Perel most of all. Never had he met someone with more passion than his youngest daughter. Even as a young girl, she had been fearless. Emrik wished he could believe, like Borik, that Perel was still alive, but he never hid from the truth.

Emrik's good mood evaporated. One more thing the God and his angels had taken away from him. One more reason to stamp them all from existence.

"Find Borik," Emrik snapped at a servant cowering in a nearby alcove. "Tell him to meet me in his brother's rooms now." He moved on without even breaking stride, trusting his orders would be carried out immediately.

Suddenly the walk to Arik's rooms seemed far too lengthy. He needed his son closer at hand, in case of emergencies. Emrik decided he would order Arik to move back to the main wing, to be closer to Emrik's own quarters. He would still have plenty of time to see his family in between his duties.

Emrik stopped at his son's door and pounded on the wood so hard it rattled the hinges. He hadn't meant to hit it so forcefully, but he was distracted, and it was sometimes difficult to control his strength.

An old woman opened the door. She had a stoop to her shoulders, skin that sagged around her eyes and cheeks, and hair as grey as cold steel. She wore a voluminous royal blue dress with a long shawl wrapped around her neck and shoulders to keep the draft away, and from her ears hung rubies. Emrik never forgot a face, but this was one he did not recognise.

"Father," said the old woman, her mouth crinkling with a smile. "I would bow, but those days are behind me. I might not get back up again."

Recognition hit Emrik. "Sephone. I... It's been a long time."

"A long time," the old woman agreed. "I think, oh, at least twenty winters since I last saw you, Father. You haven't aged a day." Her voice had aged far better than her face, time putting a creak of old leather in the warmth it had always held.

"Time is..."

Sephone took Emrik's arm and led him into the room, pushing the door closed behind them. "I know. Arik has explained it to me, and I see the hurt it causes him. I'm just amazed he still loves me even though I look like this." She cackled. "And he no older than the day we met. Hmmm. Back in my day I'd have thought it a scandal seeing such a young man with an old woman." She cackled again, and there was real mirth in her eyes. "Time makes fools of us all, Father, and none more so than the young. The irony is the more of it we have, the harder it is for us to see that foolishness."

Emrik remembered the day Arik had married Sephone. She had been barely eighteen winters old and truly stunning in her traditional crimson gown. She and Arik had said their vows beneath Emrik's gaze, and both had shed tears and bound their hands with ribbons and blood. The only woman in four hundred years to hold his son's attention, Emrik had demanded Sephone call him father, and she had every time since. Could it really have been twenty winters since he had last seen her?

"How are the children?" Emrik asked as Sephone led him into a seating area and motioned towards a plush couch of brown velvet. He remembered little Aron and Tider running about their mother's legs, hitting each other with sticks and pretending they were fighting angels like their father.

"Having children of their own," Sephone said with a smile. She ushered Emrik to sit down and then sat next to him. "Nothing makes a person feel old quite like the birth of a grandchild. But I don't need to tell you that, now, do I?"

Emrik nodded. But she was wrong. Nothing made a person feel old quite like watching their grandchildren die from old age. Seeing progeny so far removed from him, that he no longer recognised his own line in them. Sephone thought she was wise because she was old, but she was still but a child compared to Emrik. They all were.

"They're a lot like you," Sephone said. "My boys. You should meet them."

"I have met them," Emrik said.

Sephone cackled again. "You met the children, Father. You should meet the men they have become. Maybe you could..." She paused. "Give them the same gift you gave my husband."

Emrik felt his mood sour and his jaw calcify. Sephone knew better than to ask that, but a parent would do almost anything for their child, even risk the wrath of a king. Just as the Riverden girl had so recently risked that same wrath for the sake of her father.

"No," he said slowly. "You know the laws, Sephone." None but he and his own children were allowed to taste divine flesh and blood. He might dangle the lure of divinity to keep the people working for it, striving to achieve, but it was nothing but bait.

The old woman nodded and let out a sigh. "I understand, Father. But I had to ask. Arik never will."

Emrik patted the old woman on the leg and stood. "Where is my son?"

"Through the study, out on the balcony," Sephone said, smiling an old woman's knowing smile.

"Borik will be here soon," Emrik said.

"I'll let him in."

"Thank you." With that, Emrik moved around the couch and made for the study door. If anyone else had asked for angel blood to extend the life of their children, Emrik would have punished them, but he could see in Sephone's eyes she was past fearing it. That was a thing age only did to mortals. Something an immortal could never understand. There came a point in a mortal's life where age made fear redundant.

Emrik opened the door to Arik's study and walked toward the balcony. It was far more richly decorated than his own study, with walls festooned in trophies and accomplishment. Weapons taken from enemies, laws written and passed, and even a board of wood with the name of a wine upon it. Emrik recognised it as a celebrated vintage, and the board was numbered as the first. He realised then that none of the trophies in the study were Arik's. They all belonged to his sons.

Arik was waiting out on his balcony. The winter air had a nasty bite to it, yet Emrik's son weathered it without complaint. He had chosen his quarters with a southern facing balcony, so he could look out over the city he governed. He was dressed in a winter suit of trousers, shirt, and overcoat, all in Hostain black and gold, and held a glass of whisky in one hand. A second glass rested on the table behind him, next to a bottle that was on the emptier side of its life.

"Will you drink with me, Father?" Arik asked without turning away from his vigil over the city. It felt right; he had stood the watch for many years while

Emrik was away hunting angels. Arik always had a better head for governance than his father.

Emrik turned the bottle to look at the label and smiled. "One from your own distillery," he said and scooped up the waiting glass, then joined his son at the railing. Of all the sons Emrik had fathered, Arik was most like him in many ways, but also so much like Ertide, though with a healthy dash of Rikkan as well. He mixed the best of the past three generations of Hostains. Yet one day he would die, and Emrik would watch it and live on. Eternal. Immortal. Exhausted.

"Fifty-year-old," Arik said with a wistful smile. "The casks were sealed the day I met Sephone. Only twenty bottles ever made of this vintage, and this is the first opened. Named after the woman who would become my wife and mother of my children. And opened only when it became apparent her time was soon at an end."

Arik glanced over at his father, and Emrik saw both grief and understanding there. Now his son knew one of Emrik's greatest pains; he had watched seven wives grow old and die, and he had loved every one of them with a fierceness that belied his ancient heart. But the laws were there for a reason, laid down by Emrik himself, and he would never break them. None save the king and his immediate family were allowed to taste immortality. There were exceptions, of course. Sight bonded animals were too precious to allow a normal lifespan, and Ezerel, the Chief Carver, was simply too valuable. But none others, not even the Red Weavers or Seers, were given divinity. They would all grow old and die. Only Emrik and his children were allowed immortality, and only Emrik himself was truly eternal.

"She's dying, Father. Liver rot, the physicians tell me. They're not sure how long we have, but not long." He sniffed, took a gulp of whisky. "My wife is dying."

Emrik swirled the whisky around in the glass, then sniffed at it, breathing deep. He sipped, tasting the fruity, spicy bite that turned to heat as he swallowed. There was a time he had been quite the connoisseur of every type of drink the empire could make, and he had to admit that his son's whisky was indeed the finest. He nodded. "A whisky to make its namesake proud, son."

Arik snorted. "The irony, Father, is that Sephone has never cared for whisky. Always wine and tea, even in her youth."

They were both silent for a time, staring out over their city. Emrik placed a hand on his son's shoulder.

"I see you've started without me," Borik said as he stepped out onto the balcony with them. He pulled his coat a little closer when the chill hit him.

"Well, that's bracing, but I suppose it will keep the, uh..." He reached down and picked up the bottle from the table. "Whisky, is it? Well, it will be nicely chilled then. I see I haven't been provided with a glass."

Arik turned around to lean against the railing, all smiles hiding the pain. "You rarely bother, little brother. Straight from the bottle is more your style."

Emrik turned as well and held out his glass to his youngest son. Borik took it with a grin and poured himself a large portion. "Even I can tell that this is a particularly fine drink and should be consumed with the correct amount of ceremony." He placed the bottle back on the little table, though there was barely a sniff of whisky left inside. "To what are we toasting?" Borik asked, holding up his glass.

"Victory," said Emrik. "I received a visit just now from our little traitor within the Herald's ranks."

"The Riverden girl?" Borik asked.

"She brought me some interesting news. The Herald is indeed here, inside the city walls. And she will be making her move tomorrow. Her allies within the city will cause a distraction, and the Herald will use it to attempt to reach the bell."

"And we'll be there to stop her," Arik finished.

Borik seemed shocked, mouth hanging open and the raised glass forgotten in his hand.

"Something wrong, son?" Emrik asked.

"Uh, I," Borik stumbled over his words and then coughed. "What is that?" He pointed with a finger out toward the city.

Emrik blinked into his hawk's sight. The bird was sleeping atop the shrine at the Overlook, waiting there on Emrik's command. Upon sensing his presence, the bird opened its eyes, and through them Emrik looked down upon his city. There was a fire raging near the eastern edge of the wall, one warehouse already an inferno and others nearby were quickly joining it as the fire spread. A great plume of black smoke rose up into the sky. Another block of buildings just to the south of the first fire were glowing with the beginnings of a blaze, too far away for the fire to have spread to them naturally.

"Fire!" Arik said. "Why have the alarms not sounded yet? Dammit! I'll have the fire chief's hide for this."

Another building to the north of the inferno was starting to glow. Again, too far away to have spread naturally. Emrik blinked back into his normal sight to find both his sons standing at the railing, staring out towards a glowing orange smudge on the horizon, their drinks forgotten.

"She lied," Emrik said, his voice dark with fury, his hands trembling. "The Herald is making her move today, not tomorrow."

For a moment, silence held out on the balcony, all three of them just staring.

"Your armour, Father," Borik said eventually. "Quick, back to your quarters!"

The boy was right. If the Herald was making her move, she would likely have angels supporting her. Emrik would need his God-forged armour.

Arik shook his head. "If that's the distraction, then there's no time. Wear my armour." He pointed into the study to where his own suit of red plate stood on a rack.

Emrik nodded gravely. It was not as sturdy as his own armour, nor a perfect fit, but it would have to do. "Help me into it." He let out a savage smile. "I have a Herald to kill."

CHAPTER 56

Kindness and betrayal are two sides of the same coin, forever traded back and forth, their worth never diminished.

— FROM THE 6TH SCRIPTURE, SALVATION

Sun had lost track of Gemp. After setting the tannery on fire, they had scuffled with a few of the workers and then broke free into the evening air. The sun had already set, and the people on the streets had no idea what the two of them had just done, no idea their neighbourhood would soon be a blazing inferno.

They had turned south, hiding their faces from guards and slipping away from the building owned by the traitorous acolytes. They'd barely made it across the street before Hawk barrelled out of the burning building, yelling about the fire and limping from the bruised shin Sun had given him. Four other acolytes followed and before long Sun and Gemp were running through the streets, hounded by those they had sought as allies.

Gemp had pulled them into a warehouse and knocked the startled guard who had been on duty unconscious before he could raise the alarm. They had kicked over a few barrels, only to find a smell that rivalled that of the tannery, but it was a smell Sun knew well. Bask oil, no doubt imported from Ashvold. The bask were docile creatures during the day, but fire breathing slugs at night. Their legs were stunted and unable to do much more than drag their scaled girth along the ground, and they did nothing but eat rocks and crap out a volatile paste that quickly set into a slurry as hard as the rocks they ate. And more importantly, the oil that could be harvested from their innards was as flammable as tar.

That warehouse had gone up in a torrent of flame that put a wall between them and the acolytes. Unfortunately, it had also created a cloud of noxious black smoke that burned the lungs and clung to everything it touched. Gemp and Sun had staggered out of the back of the warehouse, coughing up a storm and barely able to see. They'd headed north, along a different street, coughing and clinging to each other, until the people panicking in the street had jostled them apart.

Now, what had begun as people fleeing a fire was quickly turning into a riot. The soldiers were trying to impose order, shouting at people to go back to their homes and let the legions deal with the fires, but they were doing such a poor job that the people were pushing back. Insults were thrown, then a few rocks, and Sun watched as a building ahead of him went up in flames from a fire they did not start. He was trapped in amongst people caught in fear and anger, with no release other than to rebel against those in charge.

Sun squeezed through gaps and ducked under arms, searching faces everywhere for Gemp and not finding the old veteran. The noise was deafening, people screaming at each other accompanied by the crackle of a fire on the verge of getting out of control. Some people looked at him as he barged past them, and others just pushed back without thinking. Sun wished he had his spear with him. People always respected someone more when they were armed.

A face he recognised swam into view. Another man pushing through the crowd, but unlike Sun, this man moved and the people parted before him like ash before a plough. Hawk towered over most of those around him, his burly arms battering aside anyone who didn't move in time. Their eyes met, just for a moment. Sun turned and bolted.

He pushed and shoved, no longer thinking about slipping through the gaps, only escaping any way he could. The crowd crushed him in return. Some shouted, and a few even made grabs for him, but Sun slipped away from those grasping hands and pushed even harder. Then he was free of the press and stumbled out into charged air, thick with tension and drifting embers. He collapsed forwards onto his face, tripped by the last of the crowd.

Sun glanced about quickly to find himself in the empty space between the roiling crowd of people on the verge of rioting and a battalion of soldiers, armed and armoured and standing in rigid formation just a short way up the street. Behind them all and in front, buildings burned.

Embers floated through the air, and Sun tasted ash in the back of his throat. It was a taste that brought back foul memories. His homeland was always raining ash from the fires of the Forgemistress' furnaces and living volcanoes.

Sun staggered to his feet to find a lot of eyes on him from both sides of the mounting conflict. A swarm of rats broke the cover of one building, running into the street around Sun's feet, desperate to escape the burning buildings all around. One of the rats stopped for a moment, and Sun was sure he saw golden eyes instead of little black orbs, then it was gone after the rest of its kin.

"That's him!" Hawk shouted, pushing his own way free of the crowd and advancing on Sun like a bull in full charge. "This is the little shit who started the fires!"

Sun dove to the side, but Hawk caught him with one arm, bearing him down onto the cobbled streets with such force Sun smacked his head, and his vision flared white. He went limp, a horrible numbness spreading throughout his body.

Sun felt himself dragged upright. One hand was twisted around his back, and a thick arm wrapped around his shoulders, holding him tight. His vision started to clear as Hawk dragged him towards the tightly packed formation of soldiers.

"We got them both!" Hawk shouted.

Sun glanced to his left to see Bear and two men half carrying, half dragging Gemp along between them. The old veteran was stumbling on feet that wobbled, and he was covered in ash and bleeding from a nasty-looking head wound. His eyes drooped, and if he saw Sun at all, he didn't show it. They'd been caught, and there was no one coming to their rescue. But at least they had done it. As much as they could. Sun had to hope it would be enough.

"These two started the fires!" Hawk shouted again as he dragged Sun closer to the soldiers. "Take them and help us save the neighbourhood before it burns down."

The big man was paying more attention to the soldiers than to his captive. Sun ducked his chin down and bit as hard as he could into the flesh of Hawk's forearm. He tasted blood and sweat and ash and heard a scream at the same time he was thrown forwards, free of Hawk's grasp.

With a bloody roar of triumph, Sun surged back to his feet facing Hawk.

He needed to free Gemp somehow, and then the two of them could escape in the confusion of the fires burning all around them.

Hawk swung something, and Sun caught a glimpse of dark wood just before it connected with his face.

Everything went dark.

CHAPTER 57

I do not think I want to die. But neither would I like to live forever.

— SAINT DIEN HOSTAIN. THE LAST DAY OF THE
FIRST AGE

Eleseth blinked back into her normal sight to find a young man staring up at her with mouth agape. She was standing outside the inn on the road-side, leaning against the wooden wall between the main building and the stables, watching through the eyes of animals inside the city. It was dark, the last rays of sunlight already below the horizon. The Blood Moon was up in the west, high and red and almost full, and the Bone Moon was to the north, barely a sliver of bronze light.

They were a day early. A day too soon.

Gemp and the boy had made a mistake in trusting the acolytes of Celes-garde, but they had done their best to salvage the situation. The fire was young, but growing fast, already blossoming into a raging blaze. Now it was up to Eleseth and Renira. Whether they were ready or not, it was happening tonight. Eleseth would be lying if she claimed she wasn't apprehensive. How could she not be? Everything had been leading to this night. Orphus' grand plan put into motion many decades ago. If they failed now, God would remain dead, and angelkind would soon join their father. They had bet it all on this.

Eleseth drew in a deep, steadying breath. The glowing fires raging in Celesgarde were visible in the night sky now, an orange smudge flickering against the dark. She slipped into the sight of a fat city-dwelling bird that fed on human waste. It was preening its feathers but stopped when it sensed Eleseth's presence. Humans who stole the power to sight bond had no idea what it was truly capable of. They swapped their vision with that of one animal, but angels with the ability could see through the eyes of any animal. Eleseth's own skill was limited in range and scope, but Orphus was more powerful by far. He could watch through the eyes of an animal a hundred days' ride away. But then Orphus had always been the strongest of them.

Renira was right where Eleseth had last seen her. Huddled in a narrow alley just a few streets from the western entrance to the Overlook. She had her coat pulled tight around her and was nestled against an old pile of straw that had been thrown away but not yet collected and removed. She was cold, shivering. And she had no idea that Gemp and the boy were early with their distraction.

Eleseth blinked back to her normal sight again. The young man was still staring at her. She was used to it. The God had made Eleseth to be beautiful as no human could ever hope to be. It was a beauty that went beyond her appearance, her very essence tugging at the hearts of men in a way they didn't understand. Her presence inspired awe in those nearby, even from those who knew her best. She had lived for over two thousand years, and not a day had gone by where someone had not stared at her the way the young man was now. She would give him something worth such rapt attention. Something no one had seen in centuries.

"Are you one of them blood worshipping barbarians?" the man asked.

"No. I am an angel."

Eleseth shook her wings, the glamour that made them appear as a grey cloak falling away. It was finally time she stopped hiding and stopped limiting herself. It was time she revealed her true power and set the world ablaze with worship once more. Her glow returned, her skin and hair and wings radiating holy light like molten gold. Light and warmth suffused her, shone from her, revealing the world and the people around her all in their best luminescence.

The young man dropped to his knees in the grass, his arms hanging limp by his side and his jaw quivering, tears streaming down his face. Eleseth turned her golden gaze upon him and smiled. The man was struck dumb by the sight.

More people approached, some who had been on the road, and others who had been inside the inn, all come to see what the light was, all drawn to Eleseth even without understanding why. As it should be, she was created to inspire awe and hope, to make people desire to be better than they were. To make people look to Heaven and place their belief in God's virtue.

Her glow continued to intensify until it was too bright for the humans to look at without squinting. The heat around her grew until her wings were no longer feathers, but living flames. This was Eleseth's true form, an angel of light and fire. Herald of the Second Age, she may be, but she was created in the First Age. As much warrior as scholar, and almost as strong as Orphus himself. The ground around her started to burn, blades of grass going up in tiny gouts of flame, the earth singed black beneath her feet.

She had an audience now. A dozen men and women all come to gawk at the fiery angel, more gathering all the time. Eleseth smiled. All was as Orphus had planned.

"I am Eleseth," she said. Her voice, like a thousand bells all ringing in unison, washed over those gathered nearby and silenced them all. "The Light Bearer. I have returned in humanity's darkest hour to light the way for a new age.

"You have been beaten, broken, forced into a mould that glorifies sin rather than virtue. It is not your fault. The corruption that has seeped into your hearts stems from one man. His greed has cast a pall over this kingdom. It is insidious. It is darkness. But not all is lost. You can yet be saved. You can cast off the shackles of fear that have held you in his thrall. I know it is difficult, change always meets resistance. But humanity yearns for righteousness, for liberty, for the light.

"I am the Light Bearer and in God's name I will chase away the darkness one more time. I go now to save you all from a tyrant king who would see his own people crushed by the despair he has nurtured. A monster who holds humanity down for his own ambition."

Eleseth unfurled her fiery wings to their full span, and the humans who had ventured closest staggered back with gasps. "The God will soon return. Listen for the bells and know that when they ring, a new age will dawn. An age of retribution."

Eleseth let them all gaze upon her brilliance for a few moments longer, then crouched down and leapt upwards, her wings beating the air, carrying her higher. She rose in lurches. Up and up until the inn below was a small thing, dark shapes with a few specks of light. The city of Celesgarde stretched out before her.

She hung there for a while, the beat of her wings keeping her altitude even. It was all for show. All so humanity could see a new star rising, shining with a brilliance they had never imagined. It was likely no mortal living in Celesgarde had seen an angel, just as likely they believed the divine to be nothing but a rumour spoken of only in hushed voices upon fear of death. She would show them the truth. She would give them proof not even Emrik could stamp out.

Eleseth angled downward and tucked her wings into a dive, beating the air to increase her speed over and over. Faster and faster, until she pulled out of the dive just before hitting the ground, the wind whipping at her clothes and hair. She beat her wings again, still gaining speed along with altitude, her wings trailing fire behind her that set the earth below her ablaze. Her weapon formed in hand, a molten whip hotter than any forge, and she levelled off at the same height as the walls of Celesgarde.

They could see her coming now. Speeding along toward the walls, trailing fire, how could they not? She was meant to be seen. She was flame incarnate.

The first few scorpion bolts shot by Eleseth in a blur, and then she was past the wall, her blazing trail setting soldiers and stone alike on fire. More bolts were loosed her way, and Eleseth dodged them as best she could. Her fiery wings made her an easy target, but they also made her far more manoeuvrable in the air than most angels. One bolt slammed into her arm, and she grunted with pain, her course faltering for a moment. Her immortality shield held, and as soon as she tore the bolt free, the wound closed in mere moments.

Eleseth flew close to the rooftops, her trail setting fire to everything in her wake. She lashed her whip left and right, tearing scorpions in half and rending scorched flesh from bones. She felt each death. Each mortal life she took brought her immortality shield one step closer to shattering. She was in the southern side of the city now, far away from both Gemp's distraction—and from Renira. It was time to cause a distraction of her own. With a pounding beat of her wings, she came to a stop in mid-air and blew fiery embers into the building ahead of her. Its rooftop exploded in a blaze.

She was in the centre of a square with buildings all around. A bolt flew past her and careened into a stone wall behind, splintering with a crack. Eleseth folded her wings around her and drew on her essence, then flung her wings and arms wide. Fire exploded out from her in all directions, setting the nearby buildings ablaze and scorching the ground. She heard screams and felt the deaths of more mortals batter against her immortality shield. It had to hold only long enough to get Renira to the top of the Overlook.

Enough time wasted. But half the city would have seen her by now, and none could deny her existence. The deaths she had caused weighed heavily, but they were far from the first mortal lives she had taken, and God would lay the blame at the feet of Emrik, not her.

Eleseth dodged away from another scorpion bolt, then turned her course west and beat her wings to gain speed. Renira needed her, and it was time to climb the Overlook. Time to ring in the new age.

CHAPTER 58

A thing cannot be broken that has not first been made. Do not let fear of failure stop you from trying, little bug.

— - UNTER HOSTAIN

Plate armour was, in functionality, just a series of metal plates held together by leather straps and metal clasps, and it was just one reason why Borik hated to wear it. Even with angel-forged plate, lighter than normal steel by far, he still found it too heavy and unwieldy. Luckily for him, he was not the one being squeezed into the damned stuff.

He tightened another strap around his father's forearm, and then secured his father's dagger inside the vambrace. It was a short-bladed dirk, barely more than a dinner knife really, but one of the seven Godslayer arms all the same. Arik's armour was not a perfect fit on their father, but it was close enough as to make little difference. Borik cursed that stroke of ill luck. It would have slowed them down significantly if they'd had to run half the palace to fetch father's God-forged plate. That was time the Herald and the angels could use. He'd done all he could to minimise the forces guarding the Overlook, but they would still have to fight their way to the top.

"Hurry!" Father growled. It was clear the delay was weighing heavily upon him. Borik considered fumbling some of the armour or making sure a strap was too loose. It was pointless though. If he took too long, Father would simply run off before he was ready, and that would put his life at risk. Borik wanted the angels to resurrect their God, it was true, but that didn't mean he wanted any harm done to his father. It was a fine line he trod, and a dangerous one should either side realise his true game.

There was another worry on Borik's mind as well. "What about you, Brother?" he asked. "You need armour as well."

Arik shrugged as he fixed a scaled pauldron to their father's shoulder. "I have my shield. It will have to do. Besides, you fight without armour all the time, Borik."

"I'm used to it," Borik said. He glanced up at their father, but Emrik didn't appear to be listening. His gaze was ice, locked on the view of the city beyond the balcony.

"My shield and skill will have to serve," Arik said. "Though I think it far more likely Father will kill them all before we have a chance, eh?" He finished with a gleeful grin.

Emrik growled and stalked forward to the balcony. Arik was still affixing one of the greaves, and Borik plucked the helm and his father's sword from the floor and followed. To the south, on the horizon, it looked as though a new star was rising, far brighter than any other it shared the sky with.

"Eleseth," Emrik said in a low voice, fists clenched so tightly the angel-forged gauntlets groaned.

"Are you sure?" asked Arik.

Emrik nodded. "She has cast off her glamour and revealed her true form. An angel of fire, as equal taking lives as saving them. Burn bright; desire and passion unbound and rampant, the flame of wisdom a wildfire."

"Very poetic, Father," Borik said. "Though a little tart for my ears."

Emrik sneered. "My own words, when I was younger. When I was still trying to flatter my way into her bed."

Borik glanced at Arik who shrugged in return. Their father was often melancholic, but he rarely gave such lurid glimpses into his past.

The burning star fell, plummeting toward the ground, then changed direction again and started racing towards the city, trailing fire.

"We're out of time!" Emrik growled. He grabbed the helm from Borik and placed it over his head. It fit well, leaving only his eyes visible through the two horizontal slits. Borik held out his father's sword and Emrik grabbed that, too, in one big gauntleted fist. Then Emrik leapt up onto the balcony railing and stepped off into the void.

Borik and Arik rushed to the railing and stared down as their father hit the flag stones below. They cracked from the impact, throwing up debris. For a few heartbeats, Emrik was still, staring up at a statue of Saint Dien. Then he started into a sprint, throwing up shards of stone behind him and moving far faster than any mortal man could ever hope.

"Well, shit." Borik watched on in shock. He hadn't expected Father to be so brash.

"Get after him!" Arik hissed, pushing Borik toward the railing. "I'll follow as best I can." Arik turned and ran back into the study. Without his armour, he couldn't make the jump to the ground below. He would have to take the stairs, descending like any mortal man.

Borik sprang up onto the railing just where his father had done the same, then leapt off into the air. For a couple of seconds, it was almost like flying, then gravity took hold, and the wind caught his breath as Borik plummeted to the ground. A moment before he hit the flagstones, Borik used the fate splitting power he had taken from the angel Aranthall. He split into two flickering images of himself. One crashed into the stone, legs snapping on impact, the pain unimaginable. The other image was already sprinting forwards after his father. Borik chose to be the latter. And he was. The first image disappeared, leaving no trace.

A powerful ability, but one he had yet to master even after fifty years. Aranthall had been able to summon a dozen images of herself in such a fashion, but Borik could only manage the two. Still, it had saved his life more times than he cared to count. Yet he felt every death, every injury, everything both images of him experienced. In that moment, he had been two of himself, and the agony of his legs shattering against the stone would haunt him until he managed to drink the memory away.

His father had a head start, but Borik was unarmoured and swifter on his feet. Even so, Emrik had already made it out of the palace grounds and was away into the city. Borik sprinted after him, one hand on the sword sheathed at his hip to stop it from tangling in his legs. People passed by in hazy blurs.

Ahead, in the distance, Borik saw his father crash into a building shoulder-first. The stonework imploded inward at the force, and Emrik disappeared into the yawning hole. Borik followed him in. It was a nobleman's house, richly furnished and now covered in rubble and floating dust. A serving woman crouched in the corner near a smouldering hearth, screaming.

Another crash from up ahead as Emrik shouldered his way through the far wall, back out into the street. Borik followed, all thoughts of slowing his father down gone. He had to find another way to stop Emrik from killing the Herald, or all was lost.

CHAPTER 59

Heinrule was an angel with the ability to work stone, to mould it as easily as clay. He was an artist at his core and loved to create statues with unmatched likenesses. His death was felt most keenly.

— ARMSTAR, THE BUILDER.

B ells rang all over the city. Renira heard only one or two far off in the distance at first, but soon others joined in, adding their own toll to the cacophony. But the most important bell of all remained silent. Only she could ring that one.

A sour feeling worked its way into her gut. So many bells couldn't be a coincidence. Something had gone terribly wrong. She felt alone and lost, huddled in her alleyway, coat pulled close against the chill. Her only company was a black cat that watched her through blue eyes. It licked a paw and wiped its ear but never took its azure gaze from Renira. She wondered if she were intruding on its territory perhaps.

There were people on the streets now, rushing to and fro. Renira could see them from her little alleyway. Some were silent but moving in panic, and others shouted about fire in one of the work districts. Though she wanted nothing more than to curl up and sleep, Renira knew she no longer had the time. They were a day early for some reason, and it was happening now. She hoped Sun and Gemp were safe, that they had escaped whatever distraction they had caused. She hoped, too, that Aesie was at her father's estates and had put the whole adventure behind her, poised to begin her studies at the Arkenhold University, not caught up in the chaos.

It was time. There was no way to delay it any longer, and no amount of procrastinating would make it any easier. It was time for Renira to make her way up the Overlook. Time to ring the Bell of Ages and resurrect the God to save the world from the tyrannical grip of the Godless King. *Easy as drying on a summer's day.*

Renira stood and dusted herself off. Her maid's dress was already stained beyond the ability of any washer, even her mother, and her coat was held together by nothing but hope and the grime it had picked up along the way. She looked like a mess, not a shining Herald.

She emerged onto the street and marvelled at how empty it was. Here and there, people rushed about, but most of those simply entered their homes and slammed the doors shut behind them. There was smoke in the air, the bitter tang of it making her nose itch. Armstar had been right, people would have to die in order for Renira to reach the bell. It was likely people were already dying.

A patrol of soldiers in black armour marched toward Renira. There was an urgency to them, and Renira felt her throat tighten, her stomach fluttering as panic ignited within. They knew. They had to know. They had found her somehow. She froze, unable to move, just watching the patrol draw closer. Renira knew she should back up into the alley behind, turn and run for the next street over, even if it did lead her further from the entrance to the Overlook.

Two of the soldiers split off from the patrol and approached, and still Renira was frozen to the spot.

"Ma'am," said one of the soldiers, a tall man with a narrow nose and hair only on his cheeks. "You need to get inside."

Renira tried to think of something to say, but her mind was blank. If she ran, would they chase her? She doubted she could outrun them, but maybe if she had a head start, she could find somewhere to duck into and hide.

"Ma'am?" The two soldiers reached her, and suddenly Renira found herself surrounded. She couldn't run now, even had her legs not been wobbling from fear. "Are you all right?"

They didn't know who she was. They just assumed she was any other person out on the streets when they shouldn't be. "Is it fire?" Renira asked, trying to seem innocent.

The second soldier shook his head, his mop of blond hair fluttering in the light breeze. "The city is under attack."

"Attack?" She gasped. "By who?"

The two soldiers exchanged a look. "We need you to go home, ma'am," said the bald soldier. "Right away. Inside and lock the doors. Don't come out 'til morning."

"Aye," said the soldier with blond hair, a sly smile on his face. "You go and hide. If you're scared, I could always stay with you. Protect you all night."

The bald soldier gave the other a shove. "Leave it out, Briggs. She's scared."

"And I'd be happy to comfort her is all."

"She doesn't need you fawning over her," the bald soldier said and turned back to Renira. "Where's your home, ma'am?"

Renira needed to get rid of them, not have them escort her to a home that didn't exist. She had a job to do, and she couldn't allow them to delay her. "I don't have one," she said and backed away a step.

The two soldiers shared a glance, then the bald one looked her up and down. Renira pulled her coat a little closer and took the opportunity to squeeze at the amulets nestled against her skin. Just the feel of them there, one from her mother and the other from Armstar, made her feel stronger, braver, able to take anything the world threw at her.

"Damned vagrants," said Briggs, already turning away.

The first soldier stepped closer, taking hold of Renira's elbow. "We need to get you to a shelter, ma'am."

"Just leave her, Galley," said Briggs. "Gutter rats always survive."

Galley ignored his comrade. "You can't be out on the streets, ma'am. There's shelters set up for times like this. Come with us, and we'll take you to the nearest one." His grip on her elbow tightened, and he pulled her away from the alley, out into the middle of the street. Renira thought about resisting; she couldn't afford to be placed in a shelter now. She had just decided to kick the soldier in the shin and make a break for it when something small sailed over a nearby building and hit the cobbles, skittering along the surface between a couple of the other soldiers who jumped aside to give it space.

"Was that a bolt?" Briggs asked.

A fireball crested the buildings ahead of Renira, trailing flames that set the city alight. It dipped suddenly and dropped down in front of them, hitting the ground and only then resolving into the form of a person.

Eleseth stood before them transformed. Her wings were fire, the feathers replaced by gouts of flame. Her hair floated weightlessly around her head and shone with a brilliance that hurt to look at. Her eyes were like burnished gold catching the final light of a setting sun. From one hand trailed a whip of flames, and everywhere around her the cobbles smoked and turned black from the heat.

Renira saw the violence coming a moment too late. Eleseth lurched forward, her whip snaking out and snapping across Briggs' chest, rending flesh and incinerating all at once. Galley never even moved, he stared at the angel in awe even as she closed the distance between them and kicked his legs out from under him. The heat from her wings was intense, and with just a brush of those flames, he was on fire, writhing and screaming on the ground.

Eleseth pushed Renira aside with a slight shove that sent her tumbling to the ground and rushed in to deal with the rest of the patrol. Renira turned away from the slaughter and whisked her coat from her shoulders, beating out the flames that engulfed Galley. He'd stopped screaming by the time she had the flames out, his skin black and red and bubbling, a mewling whine escaping from seared lips. There was nothing she could do for him. From watching her mother, Renira knew how to clean wounds, stem bleeding, and even sew flesh, but burns were a different matter entirely. Nearby, Briggs was still burning, long dead.

The fiery whip cracked again. A burning soldier flew through the air, crashing through a window of a nearby house, prompting new screams to echo from within. The patrol was done, all ten soldiers dead or dying with rent flesh and horrific burns. Eleseth turned her golden eyes on Renira and stalked closer, her fiery wings couched behind her and determination in her step.

"We have to go," Eleseth said. Even her voice sounded transformed, and Renira felt something tug at her from the sound of it, an overwhelming desire to obey, to fall to her knees and worship. "Renira, come with me." The angel held out her hand, and Renira flinched away.

"What happened to you?" Renira asked.

Eleseth frowned, and the disapproval Renira saw there made her want to cower. "Nothing. This is my true form. I am simply no longer suppressing the power my father gave me."

Renira glanced past Eleseth to the ruin she had left of the patrol. Burning bodies scattered about the street, blood shining in the light, terrified faces peering out from nearby windows. She glanced down at the soldier she was crouched by, a man who had wanted to help her, to see her to safety on a night when violence was about. It wasn't right that he would be so injured just because he had tried to help her. Guilt flooded her, threatening to wash away her determination.

"Heal him," Renira said, staring up at Eleseth. "You can heal people. Heal him!"

"We don't have time, Renira," Eleseth said, the full weight of command and authority in her voice hitting Renira like a slap. "The Godless King is coming, and I cannot stand against him. We must leave. Now!"

She was right. Of course she was right. They didn't have time. But it wasn't fair. "He's dying because of me!" Renira said. She just wanted the angel to heal the poor soldier, to ease his suffering. Nobody deserved such pain, least of all someone who was trying to help.

"No. He's dying because of whom he chose to serve. Besides, he's beyond healing, Renira. He's beyond anything but a swift, merciful end."

Renira had seen it before. Her own mother had occasionally been forced to kill animals for mercy's sake. A horse with its leg too badly broken to mend, a calf born malformed, a dog on the roadside its belly sliced open and guts spilled yet clinging to life. Her mother had given them all a quick death.

Galley wheezed. His face was a melted ruin, his skin blackened and bloody and smoking. He was in agony.

"I'm sorry," Renira said through tears. She snatched the dagger from Galley's belt and thrust it into his neck. The soldier jerked once then went still, his blood spilling over the blade and her hands. "I'm sorry." She pulled her mother's coat, now scorched and ruined, up over his head to hide his face.

"Time to go, Renira," Eleseth said, holding out a glowing hand.

Renira stood on her own. Sticky red blood coated her fingers and she felt ill, but she clenched down on the feeling. They didn't have time. She took a deep breath and looked up at the angel. "Let's end this."

A wall ahead of them exploded outward, scattering rock and plaster and an iron stove out into the street. Amidst the settling rubble and dust stood a figure in blood red armour, a sheathed sword held in one hand. The figure's helmet turned toward them. "HERALD!"

They were too late. The Godless King had found her.

CHAPTER 60

Dust and debris drifted out into the street from the wall Emrik had just crashed through. He paid no mind to the destruction. Buildings could be repaired, lives could be replaced, but the bell could not be un-rung if the Herald reached it. Some outcomes were worth even the steepest price.

Eleseth stood in the middle of the street, her true form revealed. Heat scorched the cobbles beneath her, and behind her bodies burned. It had been a long time since Emrik had last seen her and he felt the old tug at his heart still. She was magnificent.

To Emrik's left, a building was on fire, flames licking up out of windows and devouring the home from the inside. The Light Bringer was an awe-inspiring sight. A glorious creature to look upon, but everything she touched burned to ash. Emrik had not seen her like this since the Crusade. Memories of Celesgarde on fire once before threatened to rise up and carry him away. There had been hundreds of angels in the sky that day, raining down death upon the people cowering inside their walls, praying for mercy from a God who knew not what the word meant.

Behind Eleseth, standing above one of Emrik's dead soldiers with his blood still on her hands, was a plain woman. Emrik never forgot a face, even one only glimpsed for a moment. He'd seen her before, a single face amidst a sea of them. Back in Riverden, the day of the parade. He had seen this new Herald then and thought nothing of it. He could have saved them all so much trouble back then if only he had known. But could haves were a fool's game. The past was a seductive trap, snaring minds in idle thoughts and numbing nostalgia.

This new Herald was so human. A young woman with brown eyes, pale skin, and freckles scattered across her nose and cheeks. She was wearing a maid's dress. Her hair was shorter and lighter than he remembered from the parade, and her face more weathered by hardship rather than time. Two amulets hung about her neck, dangling against her chest.

Emrik removed his helm, holding it in one hand, his sheathed sword in the other. He took three paces toward the two Heralds and stopped. Eleseth was strong and not one to attack with reckless abandon. He had no idea what powers the other Herald might possess from her angelic parentage. Time was on his side though, he had but to keep them here until reinforcements arrived.

"Eleseth, you look... I have m..." A thousand years and still his infatuation for the angel had not waned. It was a weakness in him, one that he had never been able to excise. He hated that she made him feel such desire.

"So, this is the new Herald?" Emrik shouted over the bells echoing throughout the city. Behind him, timbers cracked and gave way. The building collapsed in on itself, gutted by Eleseth's flames. Ash and embers plumed upward into the night sky.

Eleseth took a step forward, positioning herself between Emrik and the new Herald. "You can't have her, Emrik," the angel said, shaking her head. She glanced up at the Overlook, looming large above them all.

"And you can't carry her," Emrik shouted. "I know the rules, Light Bearer. The Herald must make the journey to the shrine by herself."

He shifted his gaze to the young woman glaring at him. "What have they told you, Herald? What lies have they fed you? Did they tell you God saved humanity from demons? I suppose the old lies are still the best. There are no demons, Herald. There never were."

Borik climbed out of the hole in the building Emrik had left and dusted himself off as he moved to stand behind his father. There was no sign of Arik yet, but Emrik trusted his eldest son would not be far behind.

Eleseth laughed, yet there was no humour in her sonorous voice. "I see you still cling to your own lies, Emrik. It's not surprising. You have built a kingdom founded upon mistruth and mistrust. You keep your people oppressed by the threat of death for no crime but choosing to believe in something other than you. And still you don't see it. The truth. You do not see that you are everything you are seeking to destroy. You have hated this fiction you have created for so long, you have become it. The God has never wished to oppress humanity nor trap it in an endless cycle of hatred. All he ever wanted is to see humanity rise above its base instincts and claim your true enlightened potential. Asking nothing in return but your faith.

"But you! You seek only to steal *our* potential, the potential of angelkind, and use it to hold humanity back."

Emrik shook his head. "You say worship, but what you mean is servitude. You claim enlightenment, but what you mean is indoctrination." He turned his gaze back to the young woman. "There were no demons, Herald. The First Age was not some glorious redemption, it was a massacre. The God sent his angels to cull humanity, to wipe out the most rebellious of us and make us easier to enslave." The Apostle had told Ertide the truth long ago, and that truth had led to the Crusade.

The new Herald clutched at the heretical amulets about her neck with one hand and a bloody dagger with the other. There was confusion on her face, clear as the light of day. So, it was true, the angels had been filling her head with their lies. Perhaps he could sway her with words rather than violence, take the God's greatest weapon away from him. Not that the outcome would change. Regardless of any promises he might have given, Emrik could not allow this new Herald to live. To do so would be dangerous, inviting destruction. The Herald had to die. God had to stay dead.

"You're lying!" the woman shouted. "There were demons. There still are. I've seen them."

Emrik took another step forward and shook his head. The smoke was thick now, drifting down into the street in thick, grey plumes. "There are monsters. Most of them unleashed upon the world by the God himself. *We* were monsters, maybe. Humanity can be monstrous, but we are still human, always human. We are not demons."

"And I should believe your truth, then?" the woman shouted. She took a few steps forward, standing next to Eleseth despite the flames dripping from the angel's wings. "You who persecute anyone who dares believe in anything but your rule. A corrupt system you put in place that murders innocent people. I have seen the truth you peddle, and the world you have created in your image, and it is broken."

Arik climbed through the hole in the wall Emrik had created, coughing and spluttering. He had no armour, only a padded gambeson, but he carried his shield on his back and his axe at his hip. Emrik now had his two sons by his side, and none could stand in his way.

"The time for debate is done. It's over, Herald. You'll never make it to the shrine." Emrik flicked his sword to the side and the scabbard slipped off the black and red blade. One of the seven Godslayer arms, a blade of great power, and capable of killing an angel even with their immortality shield intact.

Eleseth laughed, a sound like glass shattering. "Do you really think we didn't see you coming, Emrik?"

Thunder rumbled above, an ominous crack echoing through the streets and drowning out the noise of the alarm bells ringing throughout the city. Emrik looked up to see something fall from the sky, like a shooting star careening to the earth. It was a sword, and it struck the cobbles with such force it embedded itself into the stone halfway between Emrik and the Heralds. Lightning crackled around the blade, resolving into the shape of a giant man holding onto the hilt. A blinding flash of light erupted from the sword, and there was Orphus, one knee on the stone cobbles, a gold-gauntleted hand wrapped around his sword's hilt.

Orphus let go of the sword and stood, towering over them all, even Eleseth. His armour shone bronze, reflecting the dancing firelight, and his wings glittered silver. His face was hidden in the darkness of his helm, only two azure eyes blazing from within.

Emrik let out a savage, humourless laugh. "Finally! You have gathered the courage to face me, Archangel."

Orphus glanced back over his shoulder at the Herald and then turned that sapphire stare on Emrik. "It was never fear that stayed my hand, Emrik. It was hope. I heralded the First Age, and I lived through the Second. I have seen humanity at its worst and at its best. You are not yet beyond redemption." The Archangel held out a hand. Another sword fell from the sky like a lightning bolt, and Orphus caught it by the hilt.

"Do not try to convert me, Orphus," Emrik said, rage filling the emptiness he so often felt inside of him. "I have seen through your lies, and I will never again allow humanity to become a slave to the whims of your vainglorious God."

Orphus turned his head just slightly to the Heralds behind him. "Go! I will hold Emrik here."

Emrik knew he should attack now, before the Herald made her escape. Before Orphus could talk them all into submission. But something stayed his hand, something he hadn't felt in a long time. Fear. For all the times he had wished the Archangel would cease his hiding and face him, Emrik was afraid. No one else had ever seen what Orphus was truly capable of. No one else had seen the battlefield littered with swords fallen from the sky. He still remembered his sister's severed head, eyes wide and mouth agape. *Hope*, the Archangel claimed, had stayed his hand for a thousand years, and now it was fear that stayed Emrik's. He hated that the Archangel made him feel it.

Eleseth grabbed the hand of the new Herald and dragged her away. They ran together a short way up the street, then ducked down an alley, the buildings nearby catching fire as Eleseth passed.

"Go after them, both of you," Emrik said, his voice ground out between clenched teeth.

"Father?" said Borik. "What about you..."

"Go!" Emrik shouted.

His sons backed away down the street, then turned onto the next. Finally Emrik was alone with Orphus. His old mentor. His confidant. His friend. His most hated enemy. Emrik griped the hilt of his sword tightly and shook his head, his anger a searing thing that made him tremble and threatened to blot out all reason.

"We don't have to do this, Emrik," Orphus said, unwittingly sealing his fate. He should have kept quiet.

Emrik placed his helm back on his head and settled into a swordsman's crouch. The very one taught to him by Orphus.

"You are not your grandfather, Emrik. Your actions were once guided by reason, not blind hatred."

Behind him, another building gave a final crack and collapsed in on itself. Eleseth's fires were spreading. The bells had stopped, but now Emrik heard screams. His people were dying on the streets of Celesgarde. Dying from fires the angels had brought upon them. They were creatures of immortality and power. They claimed to bring enlightenment and hope to the world. It was all a lie. All the angels had ever brought humanity was death and slavery.

"You're right," Emrik said. "I am not my grandfather. He thought it over once we had slain your God. He believed you when you said you were defeated. Not I! I have always seen the truth, Archangel. The war was not over then. It will never be over until I hold your heart in my hands and sink my teeth into your flesh."

Orphus leapt into the air, crossing the distance between them with a single beat of his wings and brought his sword crashing down upon Emrik.

CHAPTER 61

R enira laboured down the burning street after Eleseth. She rubbed her bloody hands on her dress again and again, staining the cloth crimson, and yet the blood clung to her fingers. She stared at the dagger; the same one she had used to kill the soldier. *Mercy. I gave him mercy.* She felt a deep loathing for the knife, and yet she couldn't seem to unclench her hands to throw it away.

The Godless King had found them. Orphus was battling him even now, and Renira wondered if he could win. Power surrounded the king like a dizzying haze, but Orphus was the Archangel!

Behind them, fire trailed from Eleseth, and though Renira felt the sweltering heat, she didn't burn. She caught sight of faces peering at her from behind windows and through doors opened just a crack. The people of Celesgarde were hiding in their homes, afraid to come out. How many of them would burn to death in those homes, from fires started in order for her to complete her task?

The Godless King had made a wild claim, that demons had never existed, that it was humanity itself God had sent his angels to cull. *It's a lie. It has to be a lie!* Everything she had seen of the angels and their followers told of a God who was driven towards raising humanity up to achieve greatness. And Renira had seen the evidence of the Godless King's rule, a world driven to suspicion and hate, to the murder of friends and family for nothing more than the claims of a corrupt official. It was a madness the king had planted within the people of Helesia. He had planted it, watered it, nurtured it, and made it grow into something evil.

He has to be stopped. I have to stop him! But what if he's right?

The Overlook towered above them. Their destination. The closest entrance was just one street over. It was a heavily guarded gate that turned into a winding path leading up, eventually merging with the other paths and reaching the summit of the Overlook high above. Up there, Renira knew, would be the shrine and the Bell of Ages.

"I..." Renira struggled to find her breath, such was Eleseth's pace. "I still don't know his name."

"You will," Eleseth said in a voice like lilting music.

It was one of the conditions. The Herald needed to know the name of the God, revealed to her by the God himself. She still didn't understand how such a thing was possible given that he was dead. Why couldn't Eleseth just tell her?

They stopped at a crossroads, and Renira doubled over, fighting for breath, her lungs burning. Eleseth peered around the corner. "Whatever you do, stay behind me," the angel said.

"What... are you... going to do?" Renira asked, collapsing to her knees and sucking down hot air.

"I'm going to fight our way to the top."

"More people are going to die." She stared at the bloody dagger still clutched in her hands.

Eleseth nodded.

"Is there any another way?"

Eleseth was silent then, staring at her, an apologetic look in her golden eyes.

Renira passed a bloody hand over the amulets around her neck. *The fourth pillar of faith is sacrifice.* "Do it."

Across the street, two figures were approaching at a run. One was a large man carrying a tower shield and an axe. The other was shorter, slimmer, and holding a sword sheathed at his side. The Godless King's sons. Renira felt a

heavy heart as Eleseth turned to meet the two men. She had thought Borik was
on their side.

"Stop, Herald!" yelled the big man. He slowed to a stop across the street, axe
and shield held ready. "You go no further... urgh!" He stumbled a step and went
down on one knee, clutching at his back with his axe hand.

Borik stepped away from his brother, his hand bloody. He gestured wildly
at Eleseth. "Go!"

"Bloody shit, brother, what..." Arik shouted. He grabbed hold of the dagger
Borik had driven into his back and pulled it out with a grunt of pain. "Did you
just stab me?"

Borik moved around his brother, positioning himself between Arik and the
street leading to the Overlook. He couldn't help the Herald any further. Eleseth
would have to fight her own way to the top.

"I'm afraid so, Brother," Borik said. "Don't fight it. The blade is laced with
venom from a monster. A paralytic. So just relax." He hated wounding his
brother, but there was no other way. Arik was almost as driven as father. He
would not stop.

Arik threw the dagger away, and it bounced along the cobbled streets.
"Why?"

Borik sighed. "Because I don't want to fight you. But I can't let you stop
them."

"You're a traitor..."

Borik held up his hands. "Just shut up for a minute, Arik. Shut up and let
me explain." He had hoped this wouldn't happen, but a part of him had always
known it might. He had no choice now but to reveal his involvement and hope
that his brother would see things his way.

"We're not immortal, Brother. You and I, we will eventually grow old and
die when the divine blood runs out. Likely long before that, when father
decides it's too precious to continue feeding us."

Arik placed the rim of his shield against the ground and used it to push
himself up to his feet. He wobbled there for a moment, then collapsed against
the wall of a nearby house. He was panting, sweating from fighting the venom,
and barely able to move. The paralytic was working its way through his system.
Not even an immortal could fight that. "Father's... choice," he ground out
between a jaw clenching in spasms.

"Yes!" Borik agreed. "Father's choice to let us die. Father's choice to slowly rid the world of the most precious commodity it has ever known. But we can make a different choice." Borik took a step closer and stared down at his paralysed brother. "If the Herald rings in the new age, the God will be reborn. There will be new angels. A new influx of divine blood ripe for those with the strength to take it. Us. No longer would we need to worry about when our immortality might run out."

He started pacing. He had thought this through, every angle, and this was how it had to be. "But there's more to it than that." Borik stopped pacing. He could see the dark outline of the Overlook from here, and the blazing light of Eleseth already moving up the path, leaving burning patches in her wake.

"Father is immortal, Arik. Truly immortal. He earned it. He led a glorious Crusade against Heaven, sacked its halls, and slew God. All of that, glory and whatever. He ate the divine flesh and gained immortality and power beyond anything we will ever be capable of. But we can have it, too!"

Borik pointed a finger toward the Overlook. "The God will be reborn. And Father will not sit by and do nothing. He'll raise his armies and lead a new Crusade against the Heavens. With us at his side. This is our chance to earn the same glory Father did. Our chance to earn the same immortality. We, too, can be Godless Kings. Immortal. Truly immortal. Eternal."

Arik shifted a little against the wall he was propped against. It was hard to tell what he was thinking, but whatever it was, it didn't look agreeable. "Father doesn't want a new Crusade, Brother. He wants an end to it."

"It's selfish!" Borik shouted. "Why should he get to live forever, while the rest of us grow old and die?"

Arik raised a hand and gripped hold of the wall, his fingers gouging holes from the stonework. He hauled himself to unsteady feet.

"It's not about immortality, little brother. Father wants it to end, and you... You have facilitated the opposite. You've given his enemy... our enemy, the enemy of all humanity, a chance to live again." Arik shook his head. "Stand aside."

Borik glanced across the street to where the dagger lay on the cobbles. The paralytic was potent stuff, he'd had it analysed. The alchemist said it would put a giant down for a week, yet Arik was not only standing, he was holding his shield ready to fight.

"Sit down," Borik said, pleading. "You can't fight me like this. I really don't want to hurt you."

"I shouldn't *have* to fight you, little brother," Arik wheezed. He pushed away from the wall and lurched forward, shield held up and ready to repel a strike.

"I don't want to do this, Arik," Borik said, backing away. He felt tears in his eyes, sadness where there should have been anger. And there was fear too. In all their years, he had never come close to besting Arik in sparring. Borik was no slouch with a sword, but Arik was something else.

"Then get out of my bloody way!" Arik roared. He was gaining strength with every step, the paralytic wearing off far too quickly when confronted with his immortal constitution.

Borik glanced once up toward the Overlook and the burning trail advancing up the path, then back to his brother. Arik had made his choice, and now Borik had none. If his brother survived, their Father would know what he had done, that he had sided with the angels. He had been betting everything on Arik seeing sense, and he had lost. Now one of them had to die.

"I'm so sorry, Brother," Borik whispered.

He launched himself at Arik, swinging wild, savage blows. Arik weathered the storm, hunkering down beneath his shield, axe held at the ready. He was weak, struggling to summon his true strength while battling against the venom in his veins. It meant Borik had a chance.

He struck left, spun to the right, slipped around his brother's shield and stabbed for Arik's chest. Arik parried the strike with his axe, then thrust out his elbow. Borik's head snapped back, and pain blossomed out from his nose. Something hot and wet ran into his mouth. He staggered, spitting blood. Arik stepped into the space, crouching behind his huge shield and slamming it against Borik, lifting and pushing all at once.

Through vision dancing with spots of colour, Borik felt himself leave the floor and spin away. He hit solid stone, and the air was knocked from his lungs. He fell two meters to the ground and groaned, desperately trying to get back to his feet. His arms and legs felt boneless, unwilling to hold any weight. He struggled back to his knees and shook his head to clear the dancing lights. How could his brother be so strong despite the poison in his veins?

Arik advanced, his body hidden behind his shield and his axe held ready. Borik lurched to his feet and slipped to the side just as Arik chopped at him with his axe, the blade passing a breath away from Borik's bleeding nose. He struck two quick jabs with his sword, but both strikes rebounded harmlessly off the shield.

For all his plotting and all his bravado, Borik knew then that it had come to nothing. The only evidence his schemes would leave behind would be the scratches left in the crossed swords emblem upon his brother's shield. And even those could be buffed out with time.

"You're holding back," Borik said. He backed up a few steps and kicked a bit of rubble at Arik. The stone clanged harmlessly against the shield and dropped back to the ground. "Do you really think you have time to take it easy on me? They've already reached the shrine."

Arik turned his head to glance up at the Overlook. Borik sprang forwards and pulled on Aranthall's power. His fate split in two, both launching towards Arik, one veering to the left and the other to the right. The Borik darting to the right swung his sword high, and the Borik to the left went low. For just a moment both were real. Arik smiled. He launched himself to the right, and threw his axe to the left.

Borik felt the Godslayer axe lodge in his chest at the same time he felt Arik's shield smash into him, pushing him back and crushing him against a wall. He had no choice but to choose to be pinned to the wall. The other version of him vanished, and Arik's axe dropped to the cobbled street, a strip of leather attached to the butt and leading to his wrist.

Borik tried to stab around his brother's shield, but he was pinned against the building behind him and couldn't find an angle. The shield pressed harder, crushing Borik's chest. Arik tugged on the leather strip attached to his wrist, and his axe leapt into his hand. He raised it high and brought it down on Borik's head.

Borik squeezed his eyes shut against his death. In that darkness he heard the axe bite home. Then there was nothing but his own laboured breathing and a strangled sob shuddering past Arik's teeth. Borik opened his eyes to find his brother's face close to his, the axe embedded in the wall at his back, the blade deep into the brickwork.

"Stop this, little brother," Arik said, his voice breaking. He stepped backwards, pulling his axe from the wall and letting Borik slump to the ground. There were tears in his eyes and on his cheeks.

Borik was trembling, his breathing quick and short, rattling past at least one broken rib. He glanced down at the Godslayer sword still in his hand and then back up at Arik.

Arik shook his head slowly. "It's over. Stop this. Please. Father never has to know."

"What?" The question shuddered past Borik's lips.

Arik turned towards the Overlook. "We both know what Father would do if he found out. I don't think he has any mercy left in him." He wiped his eyes and started walking away. "I go to stop the Herald. Come with me and help or stay here. Either way, know that I will keep your secret."

Borik watched his brother walk away, head held high and back broad and straight. Their father might not know mercy, but Arik was not their father. He was better. Better than both of them.

Suddenly there were two of Borik. Two fates. One slumped against the crumbling stone wall. The Godslayer sword fell from his fingers, clattering against the cobbles, and he buried his head in his hands and sobbed. The other Borik lurched away from the wall and rushed towards his brother, sword raised to strike.

Borik chose to be the latter.

CHAPTER 62

I cannot countenance evil done in the name of good nor accept unaccountability as an excuse for ill deeds.

— SAINT DIEN

Their pace up the Overlook was slow and gruelling, punctuated by spilled blood and scorched bodies. The soldiers that attacked Eleseth had no chance of harming her, but that was not their true purpose. They were only there to slow them down, to give Emrik a chance to stop them. And while they could not harm her, it would take so little to kill Renira.

Eleseth glanced toward the city. It burned. She could feel the deaths of so many mortals now. Between the people dying from her fires, and the lives of the soldiers attacking them snuffed out one after another, her immortality shield was cracking. Those cracks, they felt like creeping doom.

More soldiers fell to the lash of her whip, charred corpses smouldering in her wake. Any that did manage to get close she buffeted with her wings, and their fate was no different. She was the divine fire, and no mortal could hope to harm her. At least not while her shield held.

Between guardhouses there was a lull in the soldiers, and for a few moments at least Eleseth and Renira proceeded up the winding path unimpeded. Renira struggled, full of ragged breaths and quiet tears. Eleseth hated that they had to use the girl like this, but there was no other way. She hoped that in time, Renira might forgive them all for what they were putting her through. Even more, Eleseth hoped Renira would one day forgive herself for her part in it all.

Two more soldiers rushed at Eleseth. The first tasted her whip and was launched burning and screaming over the edge of the path, tumbling down the side of the Overlook. The second managed to duck underneath the lashing and stabbed at Eleseth with his spear. The weapon burst into flames before it hit her, and the man dropped it. Eleseth darted forward and slipped her free hand around his neck. So close to her flames, his clothes and hair went up. It was a mercy to snap his neck. Another crack snaked across her shield. A dam on the verge of bursting.

Renira said something, words whispered into the night. Eleseth strained her ears as she walked onward and soon realised—the girl was praying. Not for herself, nor even for the quest. She was praying for the lives being taken for the cause. Each soldier Eleseth killed, each person lost to the fires and chaos in the city. Enemies and innocents alike, Renira was praying for all of them.

"No soul is lost, nor life so vile, that God may not redeem. The sun has set on your time, and Heaven waits at the end of the light."

Eleseth stared at Renira for a moment and felt her heart break. If only she realised the truth, she would run from this atrocity and never look back. They couldn't allow that.

The next guard post was up ahead, and the soldiers had bows. Eleseth wrapped flaming wings around her like a shield and told Renira to stay back. The arrows loosed and turned to ash before they hit. The heads clattered harmlessly against her wings and fell to the ground, already white hot and smouldering.

Eleseth leapt towards the guard post and beat her wings, sending a wave of flames over the wooden building. Two soldiers careened out of the structure, already ablaze. The other six dropped their bows and charged her with spears and swords. Eleseth's whip cracked against two, rending flesh and killing instantly. She buffeted her wings against the first of the soldiers to reach her and sent the woman flying away, already burning.

More cracks crept along her immortality shield, pain like a fist closing around her heart.

She lashed out with a foot, kicking another soldier out into the air to fall away down the side of the Overlook. The last two soldiers reached her, swords slashing. Eleseth struggled to breathe past the icy needles in her chest. A sword thrust into her stomach, and another into her breast. Eleseth cried out, going down onto one knee. She brought her fiery wings around, embracing the two soldiers in flames. They died, adding their screams to Eleseth's own. Flesh melted from bones, and when she drew back her wings, the charred bodies fell to the ground.

Renira rushed forward, stepped around Eleseth's burning wings. "Are you all right?" she asked. But rather than looking at Eleseth, her eyes were fixed on the bodies.

Eleseth grunted and tried to get back to her feet, but the pain was so great.

"Wait," Renira said. "I'll help." The girl grabbed the smoking hilt of the sword lodged in Eleseth's stomach and wrenched it free. Blood spurted from the wound, hitting Renira in the chest and soaking into her dress. Eleseth quickly clamped a hand over the injury.

Renira held the sword up before her for a few moments, staring at the twisted, melted blade, then threw it to the ground.

Eleseth gingerly pulled her hand away. The wound was not healing. Her shield was failing, and with it went her ability to regenerate. For a human, such a wound would be fatal. Eleseth gripped hold of the sword in her breast, it was sunk deep, and the steel grated against a rib. She screamed out her pain as she slid the sword free. The metal was twisted, warped from the heat she gave off. She threw the blade away and struggled back to her feet, panting, her vision dark. Never had her immortality shield come so close to breaking, and she thought perhaps she understood Armstar's bitterness a little better now. A reaction to the pain he felt each day.

"So close to human," Eleseth muttered to herself, then shook her head.

"What? Eleseth..." Renira said. "What's wrong?"

"Nothing," Eleseth said, her voice hoarse. She looked up the path, they were over halfway to the top now, but it still seemed like so far to go. Eleseth struggled to catch her breath and growled out through gritted teeth. "We have no time to waste. Come!" With that, she leaned forward and willed her feet to motion once more.

By the time they reached the top of the Overlook, Eleseth had lost track of the lives she had taken. Her shield was so close to shattering she could feel her immortality slipping away, and the icy pain clutching at her heart was so intense she could only breathe in short, sharp gasps. Renira had taken to helping Eleseth walk, and she was leaning on the girl far too heavily, yet Renira did not complain. Not about the effort and not about the heat causing her to drip with sweat. The bodies behind them still smoked and burned, and the smell of charred flesh clung to Eleseth. A grim reminder of all that she had done. The cost of getting Renira this far.

A statue of Dien Hostain greeted them. The Saint stood tall and regal, her scarred face written in such painful detail. She stared down upon everyone who made the trek to the Overlook. Something about that made Eleseth angry, and she thrust her shoulder against the statue and screamed as she pushed. Rock grated, then the statue toppled to the stony ground. The Saint's head rolled free of her shoulders.

Renira frowned at Eleseth but said nothing. It didn't matter. They were almost done. The girl just needed to stay with Eleseth a little longer.

They passed through a marble archway and stepped onto a flat expanse of almost featureless white rock save for a squat building at the far side made from the same stone. So high up, the wind gusted, tugging at clothing and swirling embers from Eleseth's wings around them.

Ten final soldiers waited for them up on the Overlook, but there was something about the smell of them that Eleseth knew was wrong. These were no mere mortals. They had fed on the flesh of her brothers and sisters, strengthening them beyond what humanity should have been capable of. And each of them wore a suit of angel-forged armour. Yet another atrocity of the Godless King's creation. These men and women were Emrik's elite soldiers, and they would not die as easily as the others. Eleseth was not sure she had the strength left to fight them.

Past the soldiers, at the far end of the Overlook, stood the shrine. On a lip of stone that hung out over the city below were four massive pillars of rock holding up an ornately carved roof. From the roof hung the Bell of Ages.

It was not as Eleseth remembered it. When she had struck the bell, heralding in the Second Age, it was blood red and the symbols upon it told the story of the First Age. Now, it sat black as coal, and if there were any runes still upon it, Eleseth could not see them.

"Should I make a run for the bell?" Renira asked.

Eleseth shook her head wearily, wondering why the immortal soldiers weren't attacking. "It isn't time yet."

"What do you mean?" Renira said.

Eleseth glanced down at the girl and smiled. "Orphus will give us the signal when it is time." She pushed Renira away and stood unsteadily on her own two feet. Blood leaked from her wounds into her robes, and her heart felt ready to burst. "I will clear the way."

She staggered a step forward, and still the soldiers held in front of her. Some carried shields and swords, others spears, and they were spread out, ready to surround her if she tried to engage them. But none of them carried any of the seven Godslayer arms, and for that Eleseth counted herself lucky. If her shield held, there was little chance of them bringing her down. Of course, if it shattered, it would bring ruin to everything up on the Overlook, Renira included. There was no weapon more destructive in an angel's arsenal than the breaking of an immortality shield.

Eleseth chose the biggest of the immortals, a soldier carrying a spear as long as they were tall, and struck. She cracked her whip, aiming for the soldier's head. The man caught the line of fire in a gauntleted fist. The fires were as hot as a volcano, but the angel-forged plate only smoked. Yet Eleseth was more than just fire. She had the strength of a First Age angel to back up her flames. She gripped hold of her whip in both hands and pulled, dragging the soldier through the air toward her. In a panic, the soldier threw their spear, and it struck Eleseth's thigh, sinking into her flesh. She screamed and lashed out at the careening soldier with a punch that snapped their neck back so fiercely bones cracked and flesh tore open, spilling a torrent of blood on the ground. The other soldiers charged her, but it was too late. The dam was breaking.

Eleseth turned to Renira, panicked. "Run!" she screamed.

Too late. It was too late. Eleseth's immortality shield shattered. The sky lit up as a column of light roared from the heavens and struck the top of the Overlook with earth-shattering force. Her angelic emblem bathed everything in holy fire.

CHAPTER 63

An angel's Immortality Shield is much more than a bulwark against age and injury. It is their link to the divine. To the God. The angelic emblem is proof that the link has been severed and once it is, the angel's strength is severely reduced. That is why my father champions the tactic of forcing them to take the lives of humans. Each life taken weighs upon them, and once the scales tip, their shields break and they are weak and vulnerable.

Such cowardice. I prefer to fight them at their strongest. Only then can I prove to them that despite their power and divinity, I am still their better.

— RIKKAN HOSTAIN. YEAR 43 OF THE FOURTH
AGE. 2 YEARS BEFORE HEAVEN FELL

Emrik raised his sword up and caught Orphus' larger blade on his own Godslayer steel. The force of the strike drove him to one knee with an impact that stirred the dust around him into twirling eddies. The Archangel followed up the strike with a speed that belied his size and pushed forward, driving a knee into Emrik's chest that sent him sprawling in the scorched cobbles. He rolled back to his feet, ready to parry the next strike. Yet Orphus waited. The angel's blue eyes blazed from within the darkness of his helm.

Emrik knew he couldn't win a straight fight with the Archangel. Orphus was stronger than any living creature had cause to be, and he fought with a relentless style, always pressing the attack, overwhelming his opponents with indomitable power and boundless stamina. No. This was a fight that would only be decided with divine power.

Snatching up a chunk of stone rubble from the street, Emrik launched it at Orphus. He closed his fist at the last moment, drawing on the angel Heinrule's stoneworking power. The rock burst apart into a thousand jagged shards. Most of the debris pinged harmlessly off the angel's armour, but Orphus was forced to shield his eyes with an arm. Emrik charged. Orphus leapt into the air, silvery wings beating, creating a gust so powerful it staggered Emrik. He knelt, gauntleted fingers digging into the stone cobbles of the street to anchor him against the buffeting.

Orphus swept down towards Emrik, and they met in a clash of steel, trading blows with such force, the nearby buildings shuddered from the impacts. Each clash drove Emrik back another step; each impact rattled his armour and sapped his strength. The angel's greatsword had the reach on his own smaller blade, and the weight of it only seemed to amplify Orphus' strength.

Emrik ducked away from the next swipe of the Archangel's blade and rolled to the side, then stabbed. He scored a shallow hit that dug a gouge out of Orphus' golden armour. The angel replied with a thunderous back swing that caught Emrik's pauldron and sent him careening into a nearby building. Orphus gave him no time to recover. The angel dropped his sword and leapt at Emrik, one massive gauntlet wrapping around his helm, the other pinning his sword arm out to the side.

Orphus pushed, and the wall at Emrik's back gave way, stone and plaster coming down around them as the angel forced Emrik back through the burning house. The heat was suffocating, and flames roared all around them. Emrik could see nothing but Orphus' hand crushing his helm in a vice-like grip. He struggled to free his sword arm, but the Archangel was stronger than Emrik by far. He punched at Orphus, but the strikes only careened off the angel's living armour. Emrik's helm gave a crunch and a groan as the Archangel's gargantuan strength started buckling the metal inward into his flesh. They crashed through the burning building together and then through the far wall, out onto another street.

Orphus tossed Emrik away to sprawl on the ground amidst the rubble and embers. He struggled back to his feet, panting and wincing from the pain of his helm crushing into his skull. Hot blood ran down his face, dripping from his chin onto the gorget. He struggled to get the helm off. It was bent beyond use now, covering much of his sight and too painful to continue wearing, but it was wedged on. Emrik gripped hold of it in gauntleted hands and wrenched. He screamed with pain as the dented helm ripped his flesh, and when it finally came off, it took an ear with it. Fresh blood ran down the side of his head, dripping onto a pauldron cracked by the Archangel's sword. He tossed the helm away with a growl. Angel-forged plate was tough, but even it was scant protection against a divinity as powerful as Orphus.

The Archangel watched Emrik from the building they had torn through. He was standing before the hole in the wall, lit by the fire raging behind him, golden armour shimmering. He held Emrik's sword in one hand.

"You don't even know what this is, do you?" Orphus asked, holding the sword before him, his blue gaze locked on the blade.

Embers blew across the street. Eleseth's fires were spreading, and many of the nearby buildings were burning now. Nobody was trying to fight the blaze, but a few citizens were busy nearby, collecting what they could from their homes and fleeing into the night. Emrik winced at the pain of his missing ear and wondered how he could turn the situation to his advantage. Orphus' strength made him arrogant, and like all angels, he loved the sound of his own voice, even though everything that came out of his mouth was a putrid lie. Emrik flexed his fingers, accessing Heinrule's stoneworking power again.

"It is one of the weapons we used to kill your father!" Emrik snarled. "I thrust it into his gut myself."

Orphus was silent for a moment, then said, "You did. But you have no idea where it came from. A gift from your grandfather, seven weapons given to the seven of you who were sent to kill God. Weapons made by the Forgemistress herself, designed to steal the power of God." Orphus exhaled sharply, took the blade in both hands and snapped it in two. Something escaped the sword the moment it was broken, a rush of air, a shockwave of power, an ethereal scream. The stench of death.

Orphus threw the two halves of the blade aside. "Free now." He bowed his head in prayer.

Emrik threw up his hands and used Heinrule's power to grip hold of the building above Orphus, then he pulled it down on top of the Archangel's head, stone, fire, and all. Orphus had no time to escape and disappeared under the avalanche. The two buildings either side came down as well, crumbling under the force Emrik had unleashed. He had never been a strategist like his grandfather, nor the perfect warrior like his father, but one thing Emrik had always known was how to use the powers he took from angels. It was almost instinctive to him. He backed away into the street as the burning rubble settled. Above them all, he spied the Overlook. He had no time to waste.

A patrol of soldiers hurried down the street, weapons drawn as if they could do anything but get in the way. Struggles like this were beyond mortal intervention.

"Stay back!" Emrik shouted over the sound of the fires raging and the rubble settling. He glanced around for a weapon. The soldiers had swords, but such steel would be useless against Orphus. His own sword was broken, and he wagered whatever had escaped it had taken the blade's power. He could not hope to best the Archangel without one of the Godslayer arms.

Emrik raised a hand to the sky and a bolt of lightning ripped free of the clouds, striking him and resolving into a fizzing spear clutched in his fist. The Rider's power running through his veins meant he would always have a weapon to hand. The lightning crackled around him, sparking off his armour and sending tingling shocks along his arm.

The ruined building exploded outward. The Archangel erupted out of the debris and leapt into the air. A new sword fell from the heavens, and Orphus caught it and brought it swinging down toward Emrik. Emrik parried the strike away with his spear in a shower of sparks and struck back only to have his blow knocked away. Each blow they traded shook the street and arcs of lightning ripped free from Emrik's spear to scorch the cobbles below.

Orphus leapt backward, disengaging, and threw his sword up into the air with such force it disappeared into the night sky. Not about to let him escape, Emrik launched his lightning spear at Orphus, but the Archangel soared over it with a single beat of his wings and hung there in the air. The spear hit one of the soldiers in the chest, passing through him and cooking him from the inside, then continued until it hit the building at the end of the street. The explosion shook the ground, reducing an entire block to nothing but rubble and ghosts. Dust and embers floated up into the sky in a plume like a giant mushroom.

Another crack of thunder sounded and dazzling white light slammed down on the street from the dark sky. Emrik looked up and staggered from the sight of Orphus' angelic emblem unleashed. A gargantuan glowing sword easily as wide as three city blocks and tall as the Overlook hurtled toward them like a falling star. He threw himself back as the blade struck the ground with such force it drove itself halfway to the hilt through street and earth and rock. Nearby buildings collapsed and the ground shook with tremors. Dust plumed into the air. The sword towered over them, massive beyond reason.

Before Emrik could fully comprehend the power Orphus had put on show, the Archangel dropped to the ground and raced toward him. Emrik shot to his feet, hands raised to block. The Archangel's first punch knocked his arms aside, and the second smashed him in the chest, cracking the metal of his breastplate and staggering him. Emrik didn't see the next punch coming. It caught him in the face, and everything went white for a moment. When Emrik's senses returned, he found himself lifted from the ground and a moment later thrown against a nearby home with such force he crashed through the wall.

A man screamed, and Emrik struggled to his feet, shaking the dizziness from his head, to see a family of four huddled in the corner of a kitchen. The parents stood in front of two children, hopelessly trying to defend them.

Emrik shook his head at the family. "Run!" he shouted and then put the unfortunate mortals from his mind.

He charged out into the street. Many of the buildings were now nothing but burning rubble. Orphus' giant sword, glowing with its own inner light, bisected the street, towering over them. Smoke and ash were thick in the air. Embers drifted like a swarm of fireflies. Orphus was waiting, his golden armour tarnished by the dirt, his wings couched upon his back. He held a hand to the side, and a new sword fell from the heavens. The angel caught it without even looking.

"Is this what you wanted, Emrik?" the Archangel asked. "Does this satisfy your lust for blood?" He gestured to the burning wreckage all around them. "For destruction."

Emrik staggered out into the street. His gorget was bent, pressing into his neck, and he fumbled at the clasp for a moment before tearing it away. He was limping from a twisted leg and bleeding from a host of small wounds on his head and one missing ear.

"You mistake me for my father, Orphus," Emrik growled. "I never cared for blood or combat. I never wanted anything but to see humanity free of you and your God."

The Archangel chuckled, and Emrik imagined a smug look on his face beneath his helm. A face he had never even seen. They had spent years together, training, sparring, drinking, laughing. Almost everything Emrik knew about combat came from Orphus, and he had been the first person to teach the Archangel the joys of painting, of expressing oneself upon canvas without the need for blood. Yet Emrik had never seen the angel's true face inside the darkness of his helm.

Again, that arrogant chuckle from inside the angel's helm. "All you've ever wanted is to stamp your name on the world. You don't care about freeing your people from their thralldom. You care about being remembered as the man who killed God. You have built a kingdom that worships you in place of the true deity. You are the immortal king, ruling forever with an iron fist. You have become everything you claim to hate, Emrik. But worst of all, you don't see it.

ROB J. HAYES

For a man who once boasted such vision, you are blind to the most obvious truth."

Orphus hefted his sword and took a step toward Emrik. "Ertide might have been the tactician, Rikkan the warrior. But you, Emrik, were the visionary. That's why the God wished to send you across the Tvean Sea with Mathanial. Do you remember?

"My father brought you to Heaven. He stood before you, not in his glory, but cloaked in his humility. He placed his trust in you, Emrik. He told you his name, and there is no greater proof of his love than that. He had a task for you, an honour that would have chiselled your name in the history of this world. You were supposed to be Mathanial's partner. To explore the rest of the world. To find what was lost in the Exodus. To found a new kingdom..."

"All he wanted was to spread his lies to a new people!" Emrik shouted.

He glanced left and right, desperately searching for something to help him fight Orphus. He saw his discarded helm, bent and bloody. A shard of his sword, the weapon he had carried for a thousand years, now broken and powerless.

The truth dawned on Emrik like a lantern chasing away the dark. His pauldron was cracked from a sword strike that could have shattered his shoulder if Orphus had put his full strength behind it. His breastplate was dented, pressing against his ribs painfully, from a punch delivered by the Archangel, and he had delivered a similar punch to Emrik's head before tossing him aside. It should have killed him. The giant sword Orphus had summoned from the sky was a new wonder, a chasm gouged deep into the city, but the angel must have known it stood little chance of striking Emrik. It was a power used to bring ruin to an army of enemies, not a single man, and it was the Archangel's angelic emblem. That meant his immortality shield was broken. He was weakened. Emrik started fumbling at his vambrace and staggered back a step away from the advancing angel.

"Lies?" Orphus said, stalking closer, his sword held ready to strike. "You, the Godless King, speak of lies? The Sant Dien Empire was founded on the principles of freeing humanity from itself and raising its people up to be better. Your lies have perverted everything we strove to achieve. But it is not too late for you. We were friends once." He stopped just a few paces away, sword raised. "Please, my friend. Stand aside. Do not try to stop the Herald. Do not make me kill you, Emrik. Please."

Emrik struggled to stand up straight, feeling all his muscles protest, all his injuries and aches making themselves known. He shook his head slowly, blood dripping down his face, and met Orphus blue gaze.

"I will never stop, angel. I will die before I allow your God to enslave humanity again. Humanity will burn before I allow it."

For a long moment Orphus was silent. The cold blue light of his eyes seemed damning in the darkness of his helm. "And you wonder why we called your people demons?"

The Archangel struck, a thrust aimed at Emrik's heart. Emrik didn't move. Orphus' eyes went wide, and at the last moment he pushed the strike aside so the blade scraped against Emrik's chest plate, carving apart the metal and scoring his ribs. Orphus staggered, off balance from adjusting so suddenly.

Emrik leapt forward, pulled the dagger from his vambrace, and stabbed it up into Orphus' neck. The blade pierced the angel's gorget and sank into the flesh behind.

Orphus' sword dropped from his grasp, and he fell backwards, clutching at Emrik. Blood gushed out of the wound, washing across the angel's golden armour. It covered Emrik's hand, splashed across his face. Emrik pushed forward, following Orphus down and twisting the knife, dragging it sideways to open the Archangel's throat. He held Orphus' gaze as he tore open his neck, sawing at the flesh, batting away weak, flailing arms. He owed the Archangel that final contact, for the friendship they had shared. There was no fear or panic or even pain in those eyes. Only hope. That angered Emrik more than he could explain.

"Did you think I wouldn't notice?" Emrik screamed, his voice strangled and tears rolling down his cheeks. "You taught me to look for my opponent's patterns. Did you think I wouldn't notice that you were trying *not* to kill me?"

Orphus choked on his own blood as it gushed out of the wound in his neck. Whatever words he might have said could not find their way past that wound.

"Congratulations," Emrik said. He pulled his knife free, the damage done, and stood to stare down at the dying angel. "You could have beaten me any time, but instead you chose to keep your oath. You can die knowing that you have failed because in the end your conviction was weaker than mine."

The noise Orphus made sounded almost like a laugh. The light in his eyes went out.

Emrik fell to his knees next to the body. He had done it. The Archangel, a creature older than the ages themselves, the most powerful angel to have ever lived. Emrik had killed him. The victory felt hollow and tasted sour. Emrik hated the God, and for good reason, and when he had helped slay that monster, he had felt a sense of rightness. It had needed to be done. The world was better off without the God. But Orphus was different. An enemy, murderer of his sister, but also a friend.

Emrik reached down and pulled the helm from Orphus' head. He was the first person, human or angel, to look upon the features of the Archangel. He trailed a hand over the man's face. His skin was cool to the touch, almost clammy. Emrik shuddered, bent down, touched his forehead to Orphus'. The tears he shed then were not forced, and he let them fall freely.

A shudder in the ground brought Emrik out of his grief. He looked up to see a beam of light shining down from the sky, striking the top of the Overlook and bathing it in fire.

"No!" he hissed. It couldn't all be for nothing. He wouldn't allow it. Orphus' death had to mean something. But that beam of light could only be one thing. The Herald had reached the shrine, and Eleseth's immortality shield was broken. Emrik was out of time.

He stared down at the body lying on the scorched cobbles. "I'm sorry," Emrik whispered, and he truly meant it. Then he snatched his knife from the ground, thrust it into Orphus' chest and began carving out the Archangel's heart.

CHAPTER 64

As the blood cooled on the rocks and the last of the den mothers died, I threw down my hammer. The angels didn't understand, they thought it a grand victory, but I alone realised what we had done. I alone understood that I had just murdered an entire people.

— ENTRY FROM DIEN HOSTAIN'S PERSONAL
JOURNAL

Eleseth knelt on the ground as the light faded. It left irregular patches of fire, and bodies charred to ash, frozen in their final moments. Her angelic emblem, folded wings around a flame, was scorched into the rock. Indelible proof that this was where her immortality shield had finally broken. This was where the Light Bearer made her last stand.

The weight in her chest had lifted, the tightness around her heart gone. Strange that now her shield was broken, she felt free. And also more vulnerable. The pain was gone, but so was much of her strength, and she felt... mortal. The wounds given to her by the soldiers were no longer inconsequential things she could ignore, secure in the knowledge they would heal. They were more urgent now, the pain of them making every movement sharp and uncomfortable. She wondered briefly if she could heal herself like she could others. She had never needed to before.

"Renira!" Eleseth said, looking around for the girl. If her emblem had killed Renira, then all would be lost. Everything they had done, everything they had been through would be for naught. Her sacrifice would be for nothing.

The girl was only a few paces away, collapsed on her arse. Her eyes were wide, her mouth hanging open in shock, but she was alive. Unburnt.

"What happened?" Renira asked. She coughed at the ash and embers in the air.

Eleseth struggled back to her feet. She was so weary, and her limbs felt heavy, as though mortality carried such an unbearable weight. They didn't have time for her to worry over it. Nor to figure out how Renira had survived. The girl needed to be in position before it was too late.

"This is what happens when an angel takes too many mortal lives," Eleseth said. She struggled over to Renira and hauled the girl up by her arm. It was so much effort, as though all Eleseth's strength was gone. She dragged the girl onward toward the shrine.

"Your wings are back to normal," Renira said dumbly.

Eleseth hadn't noticed. Her fires had gone out. Her wings extinguished and her hair settled. She no longer trailed flames, nor could she summon them at will. Whether it was because she was too drained or another symptom of her broken immortality shield, she could not say. She brushed past one of the soldiers as she dragged Renira along, and the armour fell backward, crashing to the ground and spilling out the charred ash that was all that remained of the human who had worn it. Renira gasped, but Eleseth ignored her, pulling her along on leaden feet.

"I can't..." Renira started. They reached the entrance to the shrine, the Bell of Ages just a handful of paces away, the black metal foreboding and dull.

"Eleseth, I can't do it. I still don't know the God's name. He hasn't appeared to me. I can't... How is he supposed to tell me his name if he's dead?"

Eleseth smiled down at Renira as she pulled her to a stop just inside the entrance to the shrine. "It doesn't matter, Renira." The girl looked so scared and so earnest. "Just stand here."

Renira was staring at the bell, her hands clutching at the amulets around her neck. They had blood on them, Eleseth's own blood, and the metal had been stained black by it. The runes etched onto the surface of the amulets were starting to glow a sullen crimson. Blood magic. It was no matter. Eleseth kept a hand around Renira's arm. She couldn't have fear causing the girl to run now. Not when they were so close.

"What do I do?" Renira asked. "Should I, um, hit it?"

"Nothing," Eleseth said, her smile a hollow thing, guilt threatening to reveal the lie they had hidden for so long. "There is nothing for you to do."

"What?"

A thunderclap rumbled high above, echoing around them all. A dagger fell from the sky, streaking like a lightning bolt. It hit the Overlook a dozen paces away, burying itself in the ground up to the hilt.

"Is that Orphus?" Renira asked.

Energy crackled around the dagger, resolving quickly into the shape of a man holding onto the hilt. In a flash of light, Emrik appeared, his hand gripping the dagger. His face was a crimson mask, fresh gore spilling down into his beard, and his eyes shone. Eleseth had known it would happen, had to happen, but even so she felt her heart break knowing her eldest brother was dead.

"HERALD!" Emrik roared and raised a hand to the sky. A lightning bolt ripped free of the clouds and struck him, resolving into a spear of crackling yellow energy.

Renira tugged at her arm, trying to pull herself free of Eleseth's grasp. She held on tightly to the girl and looked down at her. And met her terrified gaze.

"I'm sorry, Renira," Eleseth said.

Emrik took a single step forward and launched the spear at Renira.

CHAPTER 65

There is a power in blood beyond that most realise. It carries in it the strength of all those who have come before and the potential of those who may yet live. It is life and magic. Blood is the secret to rebirth and to eternal life. Even God could not change that. But he tried.

— KARNA, THE FORGEMISTRESS

Agony seared through Renira as the lightning spear pierced her. It burned through her chest and out of her back, impacting against the bell with a muted chime. Both amulets hanging around Renira's neck cracked, half of each falling to the ground with a clatter. Renira followed them, her legs giving way. The pain was so intense she couldn't even scream. Couldn't move. Couldn't think. But she knew with a certainty that she had lost. The Godless King had won. She was dying.

"I'm so sorry," Eleseth said as she knelt beside Renira and gathered her up into her arms. The angel began to glow as her power flowed into Renira's body, knitting the flesh back together and forcing it to heal. Her soft yellow light took much of the pain away, but not all of it. Nothing could ever take away all of it. The pain was seared into Renira's flesh, a permanent reminder of how close she had come and of how utterly she had failed. Behind them, the bell resonated. Renira watched it move, swinging backwards.

"It's over, Herald," said the Godless King, taking a step forward. He seemed a giant, looming over them both, spattered with gore and dressed in battered red armour that matched. Even so, Renira saw the tiredness in him, in the way he limped, the set of his shoulders. "You've lost."

Eleseth poured the last of her healing into Renira and looked up. Her glow faded so she was grey and drab. The pain in Renira's chest was intense, like she'd swallowed a burning coal. She could barely breathe, but it was not so bad she still thought she might die. Eleseth had spent the last of her strength healing Renira, but to what end? She would never reach the bell before the Godless King struck her down. Renira buried her head in Eleseth's bloody robe, hands clutching the rough fabric, and she wept.

The angel shook her head. She gently prized Renira away and propped her against the wall of the shrine, then stood to meet the Godless King. "No, Emrik. You've lost. Renira was never the Herald."

The Bell of Ages let out a sonorous chime, loud as a rockslide, that seemed to echo throughout the city and into the lands beyond.

The Godless King faltered in his advance, frowning. "What is this?"

Eleseth stood between the king and the bell, her flames gone, her hands empty of any weapon. She smiled at him. "There are three rules, laid down by the God himself, to dictate who can and cannot be a Herald. The first is that they must know God's true name, spoken to them by his own lips. There is almost no one left alive who remembers it. But *you* do, Emrik. You know his name. You're the only mortal who does."

It was all a lie!

The bell swung backwards and let loose a second echoing chime that reverberated around the city.

"The Herald must have been born in the current age," Eleseth continued. "There are no angels left from the Fourth Age, Emrik. You have hunted down and killed them all. None of my kind could be the Herald for a new age."

They used me.

The bell chimed again for a third time.

"And the Herald must possess a spark of the divine. It's something all angels possess, but not even human immortals can claim such a thing. None except for those who devoured the God."

I was never the Herald.

The bell chimed a fourth time.

The Godless King appeared frantic, glancing from Eleseth to the bell to Renira. He had been used as well. He was just as big a fool as she was.

Eleseth spread her hands. "By the God's own rules, there was no one else capable of being the Herald but you, Emrik. You were our last hope."

The bell chimed a fifth and final time, for the age it had just rung in. Then it fell silent.

Eleseth took another step forward so she was standing over the Godless King. "You, Emrik Hostain, God Eater, are the Herald of the Fifth Age. And it is begun. He is reborn."

"No! What about her?" Emrik waved a hand at Renira. "She's the daughter of an angel."

Eleseth laughed. "Don't be foolish, Emrik. Angels can't have children. You know that."

But Armstar... Renira shook her head. He had never said it. He had always changed the subject even when she asked directly if he was her father. *It was all a lie.*

The Godless King shook his head. "Then why—"

"You would never have rung the bell willingly," Eleseth said. "And Orphus knew you would figure it out unless we sold the ruse dearly. For his plan to work, you had to believe Renira was the Herald. She had to believe she was the Herald. Everyone had to believe. My brother knew he would have to give his life to sell the lie to you." She smiled sadly. "As did I."

"Why me?" Renira asked. "You dragged me from my home, put me in danger time and again. Why me?"

Eleseth turned a sorry look her way. "Opportunity. You were in the right place at the right time, and your mother provided the link to our cause. It was Armstar's choice, and once it was made, we all had to commit. I truly am sorry, Renira. We used you."

Renira gasped, new tears threatening to tear themselves loose. They had all died for a lie. The people of Los Hold, Dussor, Kerrel, all the soldiers on the Overlook, the people in the burning city even now. They had all died for a lie. The angel's lie. The God's lie! Sun had followed Renira into danger time and time again because she was the Herald. Only she wasn't. He had risked his life for the lie. Aesie had risked her life. Renira had been willing to sacrifice herself... *All for a lie!* She looked down at her hands, bloody from the soldier she had killed. She still held his dagger.

The Godless King's hands clenched into tight fists. His jaw writhed, teeth grinding against each other. He was trembling, his battered red armour rattling. "Where is he?" he spat each word with rage.

Eleseth said nothing. She seemed exhausted, barely able to keep her feet beneath her, and her wings drooped upon her back. She was spent.

The Godless King lurched forward, hands wrapping around Eleseth's throat. She fell onto her knees, stared at him in silence as he squeezed her neck. Renira knew the truth then, that Eleseth had come here knowing she would die, that she was prepared for it. She wasn't even trying to fight back.

"Stop it!" Renira cried. She struggled to her feet and grabbed at the Godless King's arm, trying to pull his hand away. But it was useless. They might as well have been stone statues, locked in an eternal embrace, for all the good she did.

The Godless King ignored her as he squeezed the life from Eleseth. Her eyes boggled, her body spasmed. She was choking, unable to breathe.

Renira screamed and thrust her knife forward, blade kissing Emrik's throat. "Let her go!"

The Godless King turned his terrifying gaze her way. He did not let go. Eleseth gave a final spasm and stopped trembling. Renira witnessed her eyes go distant, the glorious gold turning to a lifeless amber. And still the Godless King squeezed until his fingers dug into her pale flesh and fresh blood dripped down onto her robes.

"Do you have the conviction?" the king snarled at Renira, her knife still at his throat, biting into his skin, blood dripping down the blade.

Did she? Her mother loved that prayer; *no life so vile that God may not redeem*, but what did that mean when faced with an evil like the Godless King? He who had killed God, who had spent a thousand years moulding a kingdom with hatred and persecution. Her mother would council mercy, always mercy, that life was sacred, that people could change. But hadn't the king proven that he wouldn't change? What if Armstar was right and some people needed to die? Who was she to judge, other than the one who was holding the knife. In a world full of immortals and angels and demons, she was just a young washer woman from nowhere. And yet, in this moment, she alone held the power to judge an immortal king.

Renira dug for that same rage she had felt after Greenlake, the fury that had helped firm her resolve. The Godless King had broken the world and she had thought herself powerless to stop him. Well, here she was holding all the power. Her choice, her will, her chance to make a difference. To change things for the better. He was responsible for so much death. Los Hold, Dussor and Kerrel. Hundreds of angels. Thousands of people who had the courage to believe in something other than him, all of their ends could be laid at his feet. And now Eleseth, too. She had been kind and comforting, a bright light of healing and passion. Now dead. Dead because of the man at the end of her knife.

Do I have the conviction to do what needs to be done? To make a change to the world. To sacrifice a part of myself to make the world better.

King Emrik met her gaze and his eyes went wide.

"Yes!" Renira snarled and drove the knife into his neck.

The king dropped Eleseth's lifeless body and shoved Renira away, sending her sprawling against one of the shrine's pillars. Blood sheeted down from the wound, around the edges of the knife still lodged in his throat. He staggered back against the far pillar, hand pressed to the wound, trying to staunch the flow. He sagged and sank down until he sat opposite Renira. His eyes were wide and wild and locked on her.

"W—why?" the king wheezed the word and fresh blood spurted between his fingers.

"Because you won't change. You've had a thousand years of rule and what have you done with it? Your people starve. They work themselves to death in your mines to fuel your war. They accuse each other of false crimes to earn your favour. You could have changed things, made life better for everyone, but instead you have spent a thousand years waging a war against a dying people for the power in their blood." The words of the saint came to her then. "I found purpose in justice. I found conviction in strife. And in victory—"

The Godless King snorted and coughed, spraying blood across the stone ground between them. "Victory?" he wheezed and drew in a wet, ragged breath. "You think... you have won. Have you not... seen it yet... Herald?"

The king drew in threw quick rasping breaths and tried to stand, his limbs failed him and he collapsed back against the pillar, one hand still pressed to his neck, trying to staunch the bleeding around the knife. "Everything... they are is built... upon lies. They said... you were special. They said the same... to me once. None of us are born... special, Herald. We are born nothing. The world gives us... nothing, owes us nothing. We are only... what we can take from it, and are remembered... not by what we do, but by what we leave behind."

He coughed again and blood trickled from his mouth. "I have spent... my life erasing everything he left behind. To rid the world... of his rot." A tear rolled down his blood-stained cheek. "A thousand years... I was so close. You have... no idea of the terror... you have unleashed upon us all.

"No! I will... not... die here." The king drew in two sharp breaths, then grabbed the knife by its hilt and ripped it from his neck. Blood spurted and he clamped his free hand over the wound even as he leaned to the side and threw the knife up into the sky. For a few seconds he lay there on the stone ground, wheezing and coughing blood, pale gaze locked on Renira, then white lightning flashed around him and he vanished, fleeing with the power he had stolen from Orphus.

For a long while, Renira stared at the place the king had been, at his blood pooling on the stone ground, mixing with Eleseth's. She didn't know if he'd survive, the wound she had dealt him was certainly fatal. A part of her hoped he wouldn't, but another part knew that it didn't matter anyway. The new age was rung in and the God was reborn. She had won. But more than that, she had made the choice to kill the king, and she had gone through with it. Renira thought she should feel different, changed. Surely in making such a choice, she had lost a part of herself? And yet, she felt neither guilty nor righteous about it.

Renira got to her feet slowly, using the wall of the shrine to pull herself up, and collected the two halves of the broken amulets. The edges of both were melted where the lightning bolt had struck her, the metal stained black by blood. She wasn't sure why exactly, but the amulets had given her strength for so long, she couldn't bear to be without them.

Eleseth's body lay there, blood leaking out onto the stone ground. Her eyes were open and dull, her wings splayed out beneath her. She looked like a bird hit by a slung stone, crashed to the ground.

I should hate her for the lies and the way she used me.

She edged around the Bell of Ages, noticing that it was already starting to change colour, gold etching beginning to shine through beneath the black, runes drawing themselves onto the metal. She trailed a hand against the bell and found it cold to the touch. She reached the far side of the shrine, where it opened out into empty air, and looked down upon the city of Celesgarde.

Fires raged out of control across whole sections of the city, black smoke pluming up into the night sky. People were out on the streets, lit by the flames. Some were fighting the fires as best they could, but many more were gathered in large groups, staring up toward the Overlook. Toward her. They seemed small things from so high up, like insects in a nest, waiting for something they couldn't comprehend.

Do they see me? Do they believe I am the Herald?

The bell had rung, five chimes to ring in the Fifth Age. It was something no mortal had ever witnessed before. No human, not even the Godless King himself. It was something only the angels remembered, and they were dead now as well. Most of them. A new age had begun. Everyone living now had seen the end of one age, and the beginning of another. Despite that, things seemed little different. Renira supposed that was something that would soon change though.

Eleseth had once asked her what she wanted her age to be. A Herald is as much a representation of their age, as the age is of its Herald. Renira had fooled herself with dreams of reconciliation. A peace born not of fear and an iron fist, but of hope and health and laughter. All three seemed like a distant memory now. Besides, it wasn't Renira's age. It was the Godless King's, and she could well imagine what form it would take under his influence if he survived. It had already started how it would go on.

"Born in fire and blood and founded upon lies."

Renira collapsed onto her knees at the far edge of the shrine, staring down at the city in chaos below.

She wept.

She was still there when the sun rose for the first time on the Fifth Age, revealing a sky not crimson, but for the first time in a thousand years as blue as sapphires.

CHAPTER 66

I wish you to explain something to me, Orphus. I have served him for most of my life. I brought people together, asked them to believe, to pray. My life, I gave to him. My work, I did in his name. Every demon I slew and every thrall I freed. All for him. Why, then, has he never shown himself to me? Where is this God I serve?

— SAINT DIEN. THE FINAL DAY OF THE FIRST AGE

Celesgarde, Helesia
Year 1 of the Fifth Age.

The funeral was held at mid-morning on the first day of the Fifth Age. Borik wanted it over with. He did not handle grief well. He supposed he just wasn't used to it. His family, the Hostains, were supposed to live forever. Immortality, that was what it was all about, after all. They weren't supposed to die. But at the end of the day, they were mortal. Even the immortals were mortal. That was a vile bit of irony.

He wanted to be elsewhere. A tavern or skinhouse or... anywhere really. Anywhere but staring at the lifeless body of a once great titan as it was lowered slowly into the ground. He pulled out a flask of wine from his pocket and swigged at it. He knew people were watching, that he should be stoic and stern, just like his father, but he wasn't. He would never be his father. And he just needed something to take the edge off, to make it all bearable.

The city was in turmoil and rightly so. It had to be after all it had lost. The fires were one thing. They had raged for half the night, consuming whole city blocks, entire districts. The fire marshals had ended up tearing down buildings to act as breaks to stop the spread of the flames, but the loss of life was immense. Then there was the confusion, the bell that rang out in the middle of the night so loud everyone in the city heard it. If the reports he had already received were to be believed, everyone in the kingdom heard that bloody bell ringing. The Fifth Age had begun. And of course the sky was now blue, which had everyone on edge. The sky wasn't supposed to change colour, but then Borik remembered his father had once said it had been blue before Heaven fell.

That was proof then. God was alive once more. Somewhere. Borik had succeeded. Well, the Herald had succeeded, he supposed. He had helped. And the cost had been... too high. Too bloody high. The last thing he had wanted was to see any of his family hurt.

An attendant touched Borik's arm and promptly bowed his bald head.

"Right, yes, of course. I should say a few words." Borik stepped forward and stared down into the grave, felt tears stinging his eyes. So many Hostains were buried in this mausoleum. Uncles, aunts, brothers, sisters, fathers, grand whatevers. Borik sniffed and tried to collect his thoughts, tried to think of what words his father might say. Probably some poetic nonsense. A grand eulogy for the regent of Celesgarde.

"Arik was my brother. Before I knew him as regent of this great city, or as first prince of Helesia, or as anything. He was my brother. He turned a blind eye when I stole pastries, covered for me when I spilled paint on the carpet. He taught me how to shave, how to fight, when not to fight. He was always there for me whenever I needed him. My big brother."

Borik drew in a ragged breath and quickly pulled out his flask and swigged from it again. It probably looked bad, but he didn't bloody care.

"Arik Hostain was a great and generous regent," Borik continued quickly. "He cared for Celesgarde and the kingdom like no other. And, um, for his family, too." Borik waved a hand to the side where old Sephone sat upon a wicker chair, her eyes red and puffy from tears. Arik's sons, big bluff Tider and morose Aron, and all their own children who Borik had never bothered to get to know. They were all looking at him. Judging him like they knew that it was his fault. That he had killed Arik.

Suddenly Borik couldn't take it anymore. The harsh stares, the whispered words. It was all too much attention. He glanced up at the crowd of nobles, merchants, bureaucrats, family, servants. All of them watching him.

"He, uh... He will be missed." Borik drew his knife and pricked his finger then squeezed it over the open grave, shedding three thick drops of blood onto Arik's corpse. Then, as others moved forward to do the same, he turned and fled.

Sephone grabbed his arm as he passed and Borik gasped and almost wrenched his hand away, but she was an old woman, mortal and frail. Her pale gaze speared him and tears streamed down all the crevices of her face.

"He loved you so much, Borik. At times I thought maybe too much, that he should have given that love for you to his sons instead." She let go his arm and wiped at her face. "But that was just jealousy. My Arik had enough love to go around, and I'm glad he gave some of it to you."

Borik backed away from the old woman, his face ashen. She didn't know. It seemed a crime that after all Borik had done, this frail old woman would try to comfort him, as if the pain they were all drowning in wasn't all his fault.

He strode away from the funeral and let all those who wished to pay their respects. He suspected the people of Celesgarde would drown Arik's body with their blood by the time the sun set on the first day.

Attendants rushed after him, all of them wanting something. Orders on how to go about rebuilding the city, decisions to be made on troop placements and supply shortages, locations on temporary shelters for the wounded and homeless. It all fell to him now. A responsibility he never wanted. He chased them all away with a growl and turned towards the catacombs, ordering the soldiers standing guard not to let anyone in behind him.

Borik descended into darkness, his hand trailing across smooth stone to guide him. He knew the catacombs well, had explored them many times as a child. They were first built during the Crusade, before the siege of Celesgarde. A way for Ertide Hostain and his forces to move about the city undetected by the angels. Most of the entrances had since been blocked up, and the passages that delved too deep collapsed. It was dangerous to leave open the ways to the subterranean world. But the palace catacombs still led to the vault, the most valuable prize in all Helesia.

Borik squinted against the light when he saw it. Lanterns that were never allowed to go out blazed around the large chamber, revealing worked stone and a metal door five feet thick. The immortal vault where all the stores of divine blood was kept. Only three men had access to the vault; the king, the chief carver, and the regent. Borik was none of them. Yet.

He moved on, turning away from the vault and down a passageway towards the carvers' surgery. An acrid stink of harsh cleaning soaps filled his nose, making it itch. His footsteps rang loud and echoed eerily. There was something off-putting about this place. Something sinister. The carvers used this surgery to perform their operations and experiments. Seers and Seekers, Sighted and Weavers both red and black, all were made here. Borik thought the place should stink of blood, that screams of agony should echo through the halls. It had seen such horrors. He pulled out his flask and took another swig only to find it empty. Was it three or four times he'd emptied it already today? He couldn't remember and didn't care to.

Borik pulled open the door to the king's convalescing chamber and stepped inside. He ignored the questioning look of the chief carver, and instead turned and pushed the door closed behind him and closed his eyes, resting his head against the hard wood. He spent a while just breathing and all the while he could hear Ezerel busying himself about the king's bed.

When Borik felt steady, he turned and crept towards his father's bed. Emrik Hostain had always been an unassailable titan of a man. Indomitable strength and unfailing purpose, marching ever onwards regardless of obstacles either natural or divine. Now he was hurt, broken, maybe even dying. Half his face was covered in bandages and his neck was heavily padded with gauze and still stained red. His breath wheezed in and out with each shallow breath.

The Herald had done this to him somehow. Borik couldn't understand how. She was human, nothing but a young woman, small and weak. He had met her and she had been unsubstantial. Yet she had felled his father, and gone on to ring the Bell of Ages and begin the new age. It seemed impossible, but she had done it. He'd sent people to the Overlook and they'd found Eleseth's body, choked to death, he assumed by his father. No sign of the Herald though. She had done her job, beaten the king almost to death, then vanished.

The rumours of the Herald had already spread. It was impossible to stop them. Word of the king's failure, of his wounding at her hands had spread throughout the city, and they would soon move even further.

Borik hadn't meant it to happen like this.

"How are his injuries?" Borik asked as the chief carver checked on the king's bandages.

"Severe but healing. The king's divine constitution is remarkable. Anyone else would surely have perished. With regular doses of angel blood, I suspect he will make a mostly full recovery. In time."

Borik leaned on the bed and let out a ragged breath. The Herald had failed to kill him. It was something at least. A laugh burst from his lips.

"When will he wake?"

"He already has," Emrik wheezed. His pale blue eyes fluttered open and he glanced about madly for a few moments.

"Father, you're..."

"Report."

"You should probably rest. I have things under control."

His father pinned him with a glare. "Report."

Borik sat then and went over everything that had happened. He told his father of the new age, the blue sky, the rumours that he had been bested by the Herald. And he told him of Arik's death. Of course he claimed it was at the hands of Eleseth. His father could never know the truth.

Emrik Hostain wept then, silent tears streaming down his face into the pillows beneath his head. When he finally spoke, it was haltingly.

"I am the broken man.

My body whole, my heart torn asunder,

I am the broken man.

My life unended, I walk now alone,

I am the broken man.

You are not gone, your memory yet remains, your soul I carry with me,

Be at peace my son, rest easy in your grave, your burdens now mine to bear.

I am the broken man."

They sat there in silence for a while. Eventually, Borik felt his father's hand patting the bed as he searched blindly for his son. Borik took hold of his hand in his own and gently squeezed.

"He was as stubborn as you are," Borik said.

Emrik wheezed in a breath. The new bandage Ezerel had secured around his neck was growing red already. "Mourning will have to wait. We have no time."

"No time?"

Emrik groaned at some pain and then winced as he shifted. Ezerel tutted, but the king ignored his carver and forced himself up to sitting. He rested there a moment, eyes intense, breath panting. "When Ertide led his Crusade, humanity was united behind him. Armies tens of thousands strong. A host of immortals at his back. Father and I at his side. Aunts, cousins. Seven of us, the strongest of the Hostain line, met in battle with the God, and only three of us survived it.

"Humanity has become weak, divided. I allowed it to happen, thinking the greatest threat was over, and all I had to do was clean up the mess my grandfather left behind. We no longer have the power to assault Heaven nor the knowledge to open Heaven's Gate. We must consolidate.

"It's time to unite humanity against its greatest foe reborn. The God will hide in his halls, biding his time and building his forces. It's how he works. He will not strike unless he is sure to win. I must take that certainty from him. Helesia cannot stand alone. I need Dien and Ashvold behind me. I must unite humanity as the Saint once did."

Borik gaped. "Good luck with that. Uncle Arandon has a tight grip on Dien, Father. And he doesn't like you much. No, not much at all. You have more chance of convincing Karna to join you."

Emrik glanced at his son with a look of fury. "Don't be a fool, Borik. My brother has hidden behind his walls gorging on angel blood for too long. He will be the first casualty of this Second Crusade. I cannot rely on alliances and promises, especially not from a man who has already broken them once. Arandon must die, and Dien will swear fealty to me."

"You're serious?" Borik asked. "Father, Celesgarde is in shambles. Arik is dead. You can't mean to..."

"I can and I do," his father growled. "These wounds will not stop me. This loss will not break me. We march forward. Forward to Dien, to Ashvold. Forward to Heaven's Gate."

His father's drive had always been something of legend, but Borik had never seen it laid so bare. Even confined to a bed with one foot dangling over the grave, his father was preparing for war.

"What do you need me to do, Father?"

"Find your sister. Bring Imren to me. I have tasks only she can perform. Summon my commanders. The legions must be prepared to march. I leave the governing of Celesgarde in your hands, son. I know you will not let me down."

Borik stood then, his mind awhirl. He'd never wanted to rule nor govern and had no idea how. It had always been Arik's passion. The bureaucratic nonsense made Borik's head hurt. But if that was what his father needed, then that was what he'd have. Just so long as he took Borik with him on the Crusade. It would all be worth it as long as Borik had the chance to take the fight to God and secure his own lasting immortality.

Borik paused at the door and turned back. His father sat in his bed, his eyes closed. The king raised a single hand as if to the sky and a grim smile tugged at his lips.

"Are you listening, God? Can you hear me? Run from me. Hide from me. It makes no difference. Your rebirth means nothing. I will kill you a second time. A third. I'll kill you as many times as it takes. You and all your allies will fall. This world is mine, not yours!"

Borik slipped out the door and pulled it closed behind him, then fled.

CHAPTER 67

In justice, find purpose. In strife, find conviction. In victory, find peace.

— SAINT DIEN

Celesgarde was in chaos following what was being called the Herald Fires. Renira had descended the Overlook in a numb daze to find panic in the streets, fire fighters doing their best to extinguish blazes that threatened to devour the city. Whole buildings being torn down to create firebreaks. She was glad Armstar wasn't around to see it, knowing how much pain it would have caused him to see his city so ravaged.

Turmoil and strife were everywhere she looked, and so many injured. Homeless, too. She was just another face in the crowd down on the streets. Not the Herald. Not hunted. No one. Just one more citizen of Celesgarde whose home had been destroyed by angels and a mysterious Herald seeking to reduce humanity to ruin. Only she wasn't just another citizen. Not really. She neither lived in the city nor belonged in it.

It was by sheer accident that Renira had found herself in a makeshift infirmary. It was little more than a tent set up in an old market square. The injured were carted in, and those with any knowledge of healing were put to whatever use they could be. Food was handed out to those in need just outside the tent, with soldiers guarding the stores, and though Renira had feared being recognised, the rumbling in her stomach trumped that fear. No sooner had she wolfed down the stale chunk of bread, she put herself to work. Her knowledge of healing was rudimentary at best, but she knew how to assist those with real skill. And she owed it to the people of Celesgarde to give whatever aid she could. She owed them that and so much more.

For two days Renira worked tirelessly in that infirmary. She changed dressings, fetched supplies, held down people who required surgery. She even sat with those who were beyond help and gave them company as they passed.

Rumours flowed through the tent, changing with everyone who uttered them. The king was dead. No, he was alive and well. He had been beaten in single combat by a young woman. No, it had been the Herald of a new age. No, the God had been reborn and had come down to deliver divine judgement. But no matter the rumours, no one seemed to suspect her. Though she thought that would probably change if they saw the dagger she had strapped to her leg.

Renira wasn't even sure why she took it, but on her way down from the Overlook she had spotted the king's dagger buried in the stone. One of the Godslayer weapons forged by Karna, capable of killing an angel even through their immortality shield. Capable of killing God. She'd chiselled it from the rock and taken it with her. One of the most valuable items in the world, hers now. If nothing else, it was a weapon kept from her enemy's hands.

She found an hour each day to go back to the main gate where she had promised to meet Sun and Gemp when it was all over. She waited there and stared up at the blue sky. She wasn't the only one. Everywhere across the city, people occasionally just stopped and looked up in wonder. Despite the destruction in the city, and the pain, the sapphire sky seemed full of hope. Neither Sun nor Gemp showed up.

By the end of the second day, Renira collapsed from exhaustion, and when she awoke on the third day it was in one of the cots. Another attendant, a young man with a kind face and a mop of blond hair, fed her some cold porridge and sat beside her for a while. His name was Kade, and he was studying medicine at Brighthaven University, and he was easy to talk to about nothing. They swapped some stories about home and their lives before Celesgarde, and Renira enjoyed just being her for a time. She didn't need to lie nor worry about his motives.

By then the infirmary was closing, the worst of the injured had been moved to more permanent facilities, and there was a pressing need to get the market reopened. Celesgarde's most immediate concern shifted from the injured and dying to the swarms of people who had no homes left to go back to.

The streets were packed with newly made beggars and those willing to do anything for a few ekats. They gathered in numbers, looking to each other for comfort and protection, but soldiers soon broke up any groups that got too large. They were not gentle in their methods. These people deserved comfort and sympathy for losses that were beyond their control and anything but their fault; instead they received beatings and insults from those who should have been there to protect.

Renira looked to the azure sky and wondered where God was. He was supposed to be reborn, to come and fix all the wrongs the king had visited. Yet Emrik still ruled, alive despite her best efforts, his fist no less iron than before. God was missing.

On the morning of the third day of the Fifth Age, Renira made her way to the gate that led out of the city. She waited for hours in that plaza, scanning the crowds, hoping to see faces she recognised. Neither Sun nor Gemp appeared, and she hoped they were safe, that they had moved on. But she had no way of knowing.

Renira had also agreed to find Aesie at her father's estates, but she wouldn't. Her best friend had betrayed her. The trust they had once shared so easily was shattered. The Apostle was right, he had told her Aesie was a viper, and she had ignored the warning, choosing to believe in her friend. A part of her wanted to go and confront Aesie and demand she account. But what would be the point? No. Renira turned away and hoped with a bitterness she hated to see within herself that she never saw her friend again.

The soldiers did not stop her at the gate. They were turning people away from outside unless they brought supplies, but they were glad of anyone choosing to leave. It was one less mouth to feed and body to house inside the city walls.

Renira found herself consumed by the need to go home, to see her mother's loving face and feel her arms around her. The adventure was over, and she'd won. Kind of. She might not have been the Herald, but they had rung the bell. The Fifth Age had begun. God reborn. That was victory, everything they had strived towards. Renira had a story to tell. She hoped her mother would be proud of her, even the choice she had made at the end. *I tried to kill the king.* She was terrified of what her mother might say about that.

"Wren?" A woman's voice, accented in the Ashvold way.

Renira looked up from contemplating her path to find six horses keeping pace on the road beside her. Sky looked down at her with a frown that seemed wrong on a face made for smiling. Behind her, Shadow, Rock, and Little Rock rode, two more horses attached to Rock's own by their reins.

Renira frowned back. "I thought..." she started, but it quickly devolved into a cough as the dryness in her throat became a harsh scratching.

Sky plucked a skin from her saddle and handed it down to Renira. She drank deeply, savouring the pleasant bite of spiced wine. After a few mouthfuls she coughed again, and this time her throat felt less dusty. Sky took the skin and handed Renira a shiny red apple. She bit into the crunchy flesh and started chewing, quickly realising she was also famished.

"Thank you!" she said, despite a mouth full of apple. "I didn't realise how hungry I was. Weren't you leaving days ago?"

Sky shrugged and leaned on the pommel of her saddle. She had such an easy way about her, as though life were a simple thing unburdened by consequences. Renira envied that.

"We were," Sky said. "Then someone set the city on fire. We heard it was angels and thought to investigate, but everything is rumour. One man says a host of angels descended from the sky, and the king slew them all. Another says a young woman kicked the king's arse all the way down that big flaming mountain. Then we hear the Archangel came avisting and that bell we all heard was the beginning of a new age. Burn it, we even heard Karna herself ventured out of the Everforge to piss upon the streets of Celesgarde."

Rock and Little Rock both laughed at that, and Sky chuckled along with them. Shadow was silent.

"Aye, that was a good one." Sky shrugged again. "But who knows? We delayed for long enough, and there's only so many times you can tell beggars to shuffle off before it becomes tiresome. What about you? You said you were staying."

Renira glanced back at the city. The Overlook and Orphus' giant sword towered above the walls. "I, uh, did what I came to do. I think."

"Did you now?" Sky said, peering down at her, a thoughtful crease pulling her eyebrows together. "I see. I imagine there's not much work to be found for, what was it you said you were, a maid, was it? In a city where all the homes have burned down? Is that it?"

Renira nodded. She didn't want to lie anymore, but she also knew she couldn't tell the truth.

"Hey, have you seen the, uh..." She pointed up.

"The sky?" Sky asked, grinning. "Aye. It's a little hard to miss."

"It's so blue!" Renira said. "Did you ever imagine something so beautiful?"

"Were you hurt?" Sky asked, she was staring at Renira's bandaged hands. "Shadow has some skill with the old healing arts."

"No. Well, a little hurt, maybe," Renira admitted. "Nothing worth worrying over. But, see, they're not so..." She unwrapped the bandages from her hands where she'd gripped her amulets so hard she'd lacerated the skin. Only there was nothing there. The wounds had been deep, but now they were gone, not even leaving a scar.

"That's strange. I guess... I wasn't hurt after all," Renira said. At least not on the outside. Her chest hurt, burned flesh where the Godless King's lightning had pierced her. It was a constant dull ache just above her right breast. A reminder of what she had done, and what she had never been. She wondered if the king would have scars, too.

"Good," said Shadow. Renira got the distinct feeling the man had no intention of helping even had wounds been serious.

"You seem out of sorts," Sky said. "And your sorts were already a little out."

Renira smiled at that. She was feeling a bit giddy. A nervous energy covering up something she couldn't bring herself to explore.

"It's been a trying few days," she said, recognising the understatement.

Sky raised an eyebrow as if waiting for Renira to say more. After a few moments of silence, she nodded. "Are you returning home now? Back to your mother near Riverden. Ner-on-the-River, wasn't it? I've not forgotten your message."

"Yes," Renira said. "I'm going home. It's been, um, weeks? Months? I don't know really. It feels like forever. But I'm going home."

There were other people on the road now, having to move aside as Sky and her companions took up most of the path. If Sky noticed, she gave no sign, and neither did Shadow. Rock and Little Rock, on the other hand, stared daggers at anyone who grumbled, and then giggled like children.

Sky frowned again, then swung a leg over her horse and hopped down to the ground, pulling the beast to a stop. She placed a hand against Renira's chest and stopped her. Renira almost collapsed. She was so weary, and only the rhythmic plodding of one foot in front of the other had kept her going.

"Shit," Renira said, staggering. "I think I'm a little tired."

"I hope you don't mind me saying this, Wren, but I have seen women like you before," Sky said. "You're suffering. You've pushed it down, sure enough, hiding it, but you can't run from yourself. That pain inside, it'll only grow."

Renira stared at Sky, tears welling in her eyes. "I just..." She wiped her eyes and forced a smile. "I just want to go home."

She wanted her mother, her old lumpy bed, Igor and his presents, her friends. She wanted her life back. Her adventure was over. The Fifth Age was rung in, the God reborn, the sky turned blue. She was done, and she wanted nothing to do with what came next. Yet, she had a feeling a battle was coming.

She touched her leg where the Godless King's dagger was strapped to her thigh. *I should just throw it away.* But she knew she wouldn't.

Sky glanced up at her comrades and then back to Renira. "Come with us, Wren. We have a spare horse, and we are travelling in the same direction. And I would appreciate some female company. Shadow says nothing, and both Rock and Little Rock think a fart counts as good conversation. You've already paid us for the trouble, and if you come with us there is no need for me to deliver your message. I have no doubt your mother would prefer to see you than me."

Renira almost broke then. Such a simple act of generosity from people who were little more than strangers chased away her concerns of a coming war. She nodded. Sky gently took hold of Renira's arm and led her to the horse with a saddle but no rider.

Why do they have a spare horse, already saddled?

"Have you ever ridden before?" Sky asked.

Renira shook her head. She'd ridden in carts many times, but never astride a horse.

"Burn me," Sky said with a laugh. "Your arse is gonna hurt like you've been spanked with a hammer." She helped Renira into the saddle. A few moments later they were moving again. Renira quickly realised Sky had not been lying, and riding a horse was anything but pleasant. But it was only discomfort. She could cope with a little more pain.

Sky kept up a steady stream of conversation as they went, sometimes telling stories about places she had been and the people she had met, other times giving pointers to make riding the horse more bearable. Renira only half listened. She was consumed by the thought of going home.

It's finally over. Her part in the angels' plan, her role in ringing in the new age, the betrayal she felt at discovering it was all a lie. It was done. She was going home. If anyone could make sense of all the things she had been through, it was her mother. And even if she couldn't, there was nothing as comforting as her mother's embrace.

Renira glanced back at the shrinking walls of Celesgarde, and the Overlook and Orphus' sword rising above, the glorious blue sky shining down on everything. Then she turned her eyes south to the road ahead.

I'm coming home, Ma.

EPILOGUE

Bestok, Helesia
The last night of the Fourth Age

F ar to the north-east of Celesgarde, on the edge of a frozen forest in the
depth of night, Armstar waited outside a lonely wooden cabin. The
nearby village had a name, but no one would ever recall it, and its people were
too few to matter. All that mattered was the cabin and the people inside.

A scream tore open the silence of the night, startling a nearby owl into
hooting. It was a woman's scream, of pain and frustration, and of labour born
out of love. Armstar waited for the shrill cry to fade, then settled down to wait
again. It was close, but not yet time.

He dusted the piled snow from a felled log and sat down upon it, pulling his
robe closer to ward off the chill. His wings gave a twitch, and a spasm of pain
passed through him. For too long he'd suffered the indignity of being a fallen
angel, all because his love of a human had led him to save her life, just as she had
saved his. He counted it an unfair reprisal, but the God had never cared about
fairness. He always had more important things on his mind.

The woman inside the cabin screamed again. The nearby forest, frozen in
the heart of winter, icicles hanging from the tree branches and forest floor
coated in snow, whispered in return. Creatures within its frigid depths stirred.
Some were drawn by the noise, hearing someone in pain and needing to investigate the source. But others, far older and stronger, were drawn by the presence.

They sensed the return even before it happened. Armstar wondered if a few of the monsters from the forest, even now rising from their slumber, remembered their old master.

Snow began to fall again. Fat flakes drifting down from a dark sky covered in grey cloud. Up here it rarely stopped snowing, and the snow settled with a grim finality, covering everything in an oppressive white blanket that chilled down to the bone.

The woman screamed again, and Armstar rolled his eyes. Humans were such messy creatures. They were loud and aggressive, always in need of validation, clinging to each other for comfort and security they were not strong enough to give themselves. He wondered if Lusa had screamed, all those years ago, alone as she pushed Renira into the world. He should have been there for her. For both of them.

A bell tolled. A loud, sonorous peal echoed across the sky, reaching to every corner of the continent and beyond. It was done. Armstar stood, a grim smile on his face for the first time in so long. The woman inside the cabin screamed again, but it was drowned out by a second toll of the bell.

He approached the cabin window and looked inside. The woman was laid on her back on the floor, in front of a fire that was almost down to ash and embers. Her teeth were clenched tight, her face screwed up and red and coated in sweat. Her naked belly bulged. A man paced behind her, his hands flexing, concern in his eyes. A second woman sat between the legs of the first, her hands underneath the first woman's skirts. She was talking to the first woman, words Armstar couldn't hear and didn't care to.

A third bell toll, the noise of it shaking the forest and causing piled snow to fall from branches that had long stood still. Armstar approached the door to the cabin. It was not locked and swung open at his touch. The woman giving birth glanced his way, fear plain in her eyes. The midwife spared him no attention other than to bark out an order to close the door. The man shouted and rushed Armstar.

"Peace," Armstar said, holding out a hand towards the man.

He faltered in his charge and sank down to sit upon the floor of the cabin, a beatific smile on his face. He appeared to be a hunter by trade, and furs adorned much of the cabin. The head of a snarling beast hung over the hearth, and next to the door rested a flatbow, a quarrel of bolts, and a sheathed sword. Armstar stepped into the cabin and pushed the door closed behind him just as the bell tolled a fourth time. Even inside the cabin, the noise was as loud as if they had been standing upon the Overlook itself.

The pregnant woman screamed again.

"One more push," said the midwife. "He's almost out."

"He?" asked the pregnant woman between panting breaths. "It's a boy?"

Armstar chuckled. "Of course it is."

The pregnant woman glanced at Armstar again, but she had no time to question his presence. The Bell of Ages tolled a fifth time. A final time. The woman screamed as she pushed out the child.

As the noise of the bell faded away, Armstar moved closer to where the midwife was tending to the babe. She used a knife to cut the cord of flesh that linked woman and child together, then swaddled the babe in a rough, woollen blanket. The woman who had just given birth was collapsed on her back, crying tears of exhaustion and relief.

"Congratulations," Armstar said with a smile. His eyes were locked on the child, and he reached out for it. The midwife drew away, staring at Armstar in fear, her gaze drawn to his ruined wings. They twitched, and Armstar flinched, but he reached out again. "Give me the child."

The midwife stood, clutching the babe to her chest and backed away from Armstar. He sighed and pointed at her. "Trust," he said. The fear fell from the woman's face, and she nodded, holding out the babe for Armstar to take.

"What are you doing?" the woman on the floor asked. "Who are you, and why do you want my child?"

Armstar took the babe in his arms and stared down into a face far darker than that of its parents. He didn't cry. The babe just stared at Armstar with eyes that shone with light and understanding and recognition. Armstar crouched down in front of the woman and turned the child in his arms so that she could look upon his face. Love and fear and confusion all mingled together inside the woman as she tried to comprehend the truth.

Armstar laughed and shook his head. He did not offer her the child.

"The Fifth Age has begun. And you have just given birth to God."

AFTERWORD

Thank you so much for reading HERALD and I do hope you enjoyed the end of the Fourth Age. If you did enjoy the book, please consider leaving a rating or review on Amazon, Goodreads, or any other platform you might frequent. Reviews are the lifeblood of books and you never know who you might inspire to give it a read.

And just a quick reminder that there are 2 companion trilogies being written alongside this one.

The God Eater Saga currently consists of:
    Herald (Age of the God Eater #1)
    Deathless (Annals of the God Eater #1)
    Demon (Archive of the God Eater #1)

While each trilogy can be read on its own, the saga is designed to be consumed together to get the best picture of the world, the story, and the characters.

Courage and Hope!

Rob

BOOKS BY ROB J. HAYES

The God Eater Saga (Heroic Epic Fantasy)

Herald (Age of the God Eater #1)

Deathless (Annals of the God Eater #1)

Demon (Archive of the God Eater #1)

The War Eternal (Dark Epic Fantasy)

Along the Razor's Edge

The Lessons Never Learned

From Cold Ashes Risen

Sins of the Mother

Death's Beating Heart

Titan Hoppers (Coming of Age Sci-Fantasy)

Titan Hoppers

Spire Climbers

Fleet Champions

The Mortal Techniques (Asian Sword & Sorcery)

Never Die

Pawn's Gambit

Spirits of Vengeance

The Century Blade (short story)

The First Earth Saga (Grimdark Fantasy)

The Heresy Within (The Ties that Bind #1)

The Colour of Vengeance (The Ties that Bind #2)

The Price of Faith (The Ties that Bind #3)

Where Loyalties Lie (Best Laid Plans #1)

The Fifth Empire of Man (Best Laid Plans #2)

City of Kings

<u>It Takes a Thief...</u> (Lighthearted Steampunk)

It Takes a Thief to Catch a Sunrise

It Takes a Thief to Start a Fire